THE TALE OF THE HEIKE

Translated by A. L. SADLER

The Tale of the Heike
By Anonymous
Translated by A. L. Sadler

Print ISBN 13: 978-1-4209-7316-7
eBook ISBN 13: 978-1-4209-7382-2

Cover Image: a detail of "Six-Fold Screen depicting scenes from the 'Tale of Heike'", Tosa School, Edo Period (pen & ink with colour and gold on panel) / Tokyo Fuji Art Museum / Bridgeman Images.

Please visit *www.digireads.com*

CONTENTS

VOLUME I.

VOLUME II.

VOLUME III.

VOLUME IV.

VOLUME V.

VOLUME VI.

VOLUME VII

VOLUME VIII.

VOLUME IX.

VOLUME X.

VOLUME XI.

Introduction.

Subject and Structure.—The Heike Monogatari, one of the masterpieces of Japanese literature, and also one of the main sources of the history of the Gempei period, is a poetic narrative of the fall of the Heike from the position of supremacy it had gained under Taira Kiyomori to almost complete destruction. The Heike, like the Genji, was a warrior clan, but had quickly lost its hardy simplicity under the influence of life in the Capital, and identified itself almost entirely with the effeminate Fujiwara Courtiers whose power it had usurped, so that the struggle between it and the Genji was really more one between courtiers and soldiers, between literary officials and military leaders. Historically this period stands between the Heian era of soft elegance and the Kamakura age of undiluted militarism. The Heike were largely a clan of emasculated Bushi, and their leader Kiyomori, though he obtained his supremacy by force of arms, assumed the role of Court Noble and strove to rule the country by the same device of making himself grandfather to the Emperor as the Fujiwara family had previously done. Hence his rule bears more affinity to theirs than to that of Yoritomo, of the Genji, who made his headquarters in the Kwanto, well removed from Kyoto influence and enervation, and relied entirely on a purely military form of government by and for samurai.

In its construction the book may be divided roughly into two parts according to Mr. Utsumi, the first half in which the greatness of the Heike is depicted and in which Kiyomori is the chief figure, and the second which describes their overthrow, in which Yoshitsune holds the centre of the stage. Mr. Yamada, however, thinks it falls naturally into three sections; the first, Bks. 1-5; the prosperity of the Heike with Kiyomori as the central figure. The second, Bks. 6-8; the wandering of the Heike, Kiso Yoshinaka being the principal character. The third section, Bks. 9-12; their destruction, the central figure being Kuro Hangwan Yoshitsune. Whichever division be adopted, the work has a regular dramatic form quite unlike that of the Gempei Seisuiki or Taiheiki which are simply historical chronicles.

Of the Heike the two prominent characters are Kiyomori and his son Shigemori, the former rash and turbulent, yet a man of original ideas and at times sympathetic and sensitive, the latter law-abiding, calm and wise, considerate to his neighbours, and showing respect to religion and the Imperial House. The fall of the Heike is ascribed to the rash and impious folly of Kiyomori, but the writer introduces Shigemori into the narrative most skilfully as a means of exciting the sympathy and admiration of the reader for his conduct as well as his indignation at his father's violence, leading to satisfaction that retribution will at last overtake his clan. Shigemori seems to hold back this retributive destiny as long as he lives, but when he dies the clouds gather over his house. After his death the headship of the family falls to his brother Munemori, a rather timid and hesitating character in a crisis, though insolent and overbearing at other times, and apparently much inferior to his two younger brothers Tomomori and Shigehira.

The first of the Genji to come on the scene is the veteran Yorimasa, whose premature revolt and gallant end after the fight at the Ujigawa form a memorable episode in Japanese history. Then Kiso Yoshinaka appears and for a while carries all before him. A vigorous and brilliant leader, he seems to have lacked wisdom and sagacity and soon fell a victim like Yukiie to the jealousy and guile of Yoritomo. The leadership of the Genji forces then devolves on Yoshitsune and the narrative goes on to relate his victories and final destruction of the Heike. Yoshitsune is the ideal type of attractive character in Japan. Youthful and dashing, cunning graceful and elegant, quite unlike the solid and worthy Shigemori with his placidity and rather narrow-minded piety, Yoshitsune might be put in the same category with Nelson or Coeur-de-Leon, with allowances for period and nationality, while Shigemori mightily suggests Aeneas. The whole drama is represented from a Buddhist standpoint as an example of cause and effect working itself out in action, the evanescence of all prosperity and dominion being strongly insisted on.

Authorship and Date.—The authorship and date of the Heike Monogatari, as well as its relation to the other literature of the Kamakura period, have been the subject of much discussion among Japanese scholars of the present time, and no exact pronouncement can be made. Mr. Utsumi says in the 'Heike Monogatari Hyoshaku:' "As to the various statements that it was the work of Shinano-no-Zenji Yukinaga, or Hamuro Tokinaga, or Minamoto Mitsuyuki, one cannot adopt any one of them with certainty, but the following conclusions have been reached by the Society for the Investigation of the National Literature, in their monograph on this work: (a), that the Heike Monogatari was originally composed in three volumes which were afterwards increased to six, and that these were again altered to twelve; (b), that it was composed sometime before the period Shokyu (1219) and enlarged during the time of the Fujiwara Shoguns (1219-1252); (c) that the Kancho volume was not originally separate from the rest of the work; (d) that there was one original source of the work, but that as it circulated it became altered and added to, and that these additions and alterations are the work of different hands at different periods."

The most explicit statement about the authorship is contained in the Tsurezure Gusa of Yoshida Kenko, (1281-1350) Section 226, which is considered by most scholars likely to be correct. It runs as follows: "In the time of the Retired Emperor Go-Toba, Shinano-no-Zenji Yukinaga was renowned for his knowledge of musical matters, so that he was once summoned to take part in a discussion about them, but forgetting two of the Shichi Toku no Mai, Dances of the Seven Virtues, lie was nicknamed 'Go Toku no Kwanja' or 'The Young Master of Five Virtues,' and this he took so much to heart that he forsook his studies and became a recluse; but the priest Jichin, who would take in anyone, however low his rank, if he had any artistic gift, felt sympathy for him and provided him with what he needed. It was this lay priest Yukinaga who wrote the Heike Monogatari and taught a certain blind man named Jobutsu to recite it. He wrote especially well about the affairs of Hieizan, and his detailed knowledge of Kuro Hangwan (Yoshitsune) enabled him to describe him graphically. Of Kaba-no-Kwanja (Noriyori) he does not seem to have had so much information, for he omits much concerning him. For matters pertaining to the Bushi and their horses and arms, Jobutsu, who was a native of the East Country, was able to tell him what he had learned from asking the warriors themselves. And the Biwa-hoshi of the present time learn to imitate the natural voice of this Jobutsu."

This Yukinaga appears to have been the son of the Yukitaka mentioned in this work (vol. 3. Yukitaka no Sata no Koto) who was steward to the Sessho Kanezane, whose younger brother the priest Jichin may have been. In this case he is to be identified with the Yukinaga, former Governor of Shimozuke, who is mentioned in the Gyokuyo Meigetsuki as having ability in literary affairs. The priest Jichin was the Tendai Zasshu Jien Dai-Sojo, afterwards known as Jichin Daishi Zasshu of Hieizan, which would account for the writer's accurate knowledge of that monastery. With regard to Jobutsu 生佛, of whom nothing is otherwise known, the name is conjectured to be a mistaken reading for Shobutsu 正佛, the religious name of Minamoto Suketoki. This Suketoki was born in the family of Ayakoji, which was noted for its musical traditions, and himself became the best musician of his tune, eventually retiring from the world and taking up his abode with the priest Jichin. This attribution of the authorship to Yukinaga certainly gains much force when we note that the chapter concerning Yukitaka is quite unconnected with the main story and would be very well explained as an incident related by the author about his father which he thought worth preserving as an example of the fickleness of fortune.

Another statement is found in the Daigo Zassho to the effect that Mimbu-no-Shosho Tokinaga wrote the Heike Monogatari in twenty four volumes, and yet another that Suketsune wrote it in twelve volumes. The first may refer to a later redaction of the work of Yukinaga or be merely a mistaken reading of his name, whereas concerning the latter, it is not improbable that he may have been one of the redactors, for there is a chapter in the 12th vol., entitled Yoshida Dainagon no Sata, relating to his grandfather Tsunefusa, which also seems to be inserted without any special reason. Thus it is quite certain that the work as originally composed not long after the events of which it treats took place was not the same as that which is now current. The oldest known manuscript of it is one of the period Enkei, (1308-11), and while its contents are rather less than those of the Gempei Seisuiki, it is about twice as long as the ordinary current editions. By a critical comparison of this with other known MSS, the six books it contains may be divided fairly easily so as to give twelve volumes.

As the Heike Monogatari was intended for recitation to the accompaniment of the *biwa*, it is not surprising that there should be in existence a large number of variant editions as used by the different schools of Biwahoshi, each of which had its own traditions and version, and therefore the work has been peculiarly liable to change and corruption of the text as well as addition to it at various periods. Among these variant versions there are two main sources, one known as the school of Ichikata from its originator Akashi Kenko Kyoichi, and the other as the Yasaka school from its founder Yasaka Kenko Kigen. The characteristic difference between them is that the former combines the incidents of the entry of Kenrei-mon-in into Ohara and the visit of the Emperor to the same place into a separate volume called the Kanjin Maki, whereas the other does not.

One of the best MSS of the Heike Monogatari belongs to the school of Kyoichi and is a National Treasure kept at Koryo Jinja, a shrine in the province of Chikugo. It is dated O-an (1368) and is the oldest MS of the Ichihata school: it is taken as the basis of the edition of Yamada and Takagi. It does not contain the story of Giyo and Ginyo or the Saisho Minage.

Buddhist Tendency of the Heike.—One of the most noticeable characteristics of the Heike Monogatari is its strong religious atmosphere, the continual moralizing on the events described from the standpoint of Buddhist philosophy, with its insistence on the vanity and impermanence of the things of this Shaba world, and the desirability of retiring from its turmoils to prepare for the blessed rebirth in the world to come. So much is the work pervaded by this tendency that many have maintained that it was written for the purposes of propaganda, and that the religious element in it is the main motive.

This view, however, seems to be much too extreme, as there is no reason to suppose that the inclination to quote Buddhist sentiments is any greater than might be expected in an age when Buddhism was so potent an influence everywhere. The Gempei period was essentially the time when the emotional aspect of Buddhism was most marked, and when, under the pressure of affliction and wretchedness, of which a very vivid picture is given in the 'Hojoki' of Kamo Chomei, the former ritual and esoteric cults of Tendai and Shingon gave place to the simple and evangelical sects of Jodo and Shinshu, developed respectively by

Honen and his disciple Shinran. Consequently we find the expressions 'raisei ojo,' 'saiho jodo,' and others used by these sects, of very frequent occurrence in this work and this fact has led some critics to describe it as a Jodo sermon, taking the Heike as its text. When we consider, however, that the writer does not by any means confine himself to such phrases, nor to the adoration of Amida Buddha, the special object of Jodo worship, but shows respect and reverence for many other Buddhas, beside the national Kami, and the deities of the great shrines, there seems no sufficient reason for such a view. It is quite natural that the tragic story of the sudden rise and fall of the Heike house should call forth reflections on the impermanence of worldly affairs, seeing that these ideas formed the background of the thought of the age, and that the author was a recluse in a Buddhist monastery, as were almost all the men of letters of the time. Moreover, no doubt Buddhist phrases were considered to lend dignity and sonority to the narrative, as well as being a mark of the author's learning and taste, just as the continual citation of instances from Chinese history with which the book abounds served to edify those acquainted with it.

These details correspond to the religious phraseology and classical references to be found in an English medieval writer like Chaucer, whose age was not, perhaps, very dissimilar. Thus not the least interesting part of the Heike Monogatari for European readers is the detailed description of Japanese Buddhism at this, its most flourishing period, and not only of Buddhism but of the many other cults that the excessively superstitious Courtiers and Buke feared to leave unobserved. The Heike chiefs seem to have left nothing to chance in these matters, as may be especially noted in the elaborate consultations and ceremonies connected with the birth of the son of Ken-rei-mon-in. So far as can be noted all these things were merely ritual and ceremonial and did not necessarily produce any more effect on ordinary conduct than Christianity did on that of Benvenuto Cellini, but like it they gave occupation to many artists and craftsmen and afforded a solace in times of adversity, which might, in such a period, suddenly befall even those apparently most secure, and were not unknown to the Mikado himself. So the stately opening words of the first chapter seem most appropriate:

> "Gion Shōja no kane no koe,
> Shōgyō mujo no hibiki ari;
> Sharasoju no hana no iro,
> Shosha hissui no kotowari wo arawasu.
> Ogoreru mono hisashikarazu,
> Tada haru no yo no yume no gotoshi;
> Takeki hito mo tsui ni wa horobinu,
> Hitoe ni kaze no mae no chiri ni onaji."

The mighty are indeed put down from their seats, but those who are exalted are neither humble nor meek.

The Heike Monogatari and Other Works of the Period.—There has been much discussion among scholars as to the connexion between the Heike Monogatari and the Gempei Seisuiki, some considering that the former work was composed first and the latter adapted from it, while others adopt the converse view, supposing that the Heike consists of such passages selected from the Seisuiki as are most suitable for recitation. Yamada Toshio in his edition of the Heike thinks however that the two books are simply different recensions of the same original and cannot be said to be really two different works. "The Gempei Seisuiki seems," he says, "to be a work to be contrasted, not with the Heike Monogatari, but with the version of the Yasaka school." Mr. Utsumi in his notes considers this is not quite in accordance with the facts, for the material, construction, and treatment of the subject is quite different in the two works, but agrees that the Gempei Seisuiki was probably taken from the other book and not vice-versa, thus assigning the priority to the Heike, and this view seems the prevalent one among the best modern critics. The late Dr. Fujioka however, in his 'Literature of the Kamakura and Muromachi periods', takes the opposite view and considers that as the Gempei Seisuiki is arranged according to chronological order and is principally concerned with the collection of facts, whereas the Heike represents rather an arrangement according to subject matter, having literary elegance as its main object, it follows that the former cannot be derived from the latter, but that the Heike must be the result of a digestion of the material of the Gempei Seisuiki. This argument is not however acquiesced in by most scholars, seeing that the Gempei Seisuiki is the most ornate and profuse of the two, and seems by no means likely to have been anterior in time. Moreover there appear to be many instances of mistakes in the Seisuiki which could only have arisen from a misunderstanding of words or expressions in the Heike.

Another work of the same period having some relation to the Heike is the Hojoki of Kamo Chomei. In this little book of reflections are related the incidents of the Great Fire, (Heike, Vol. I. Nairi Yakiage no koto. Seisuiki Vol. 4.); The Great Typhoon, (Heike Vol. 3.); The Migration of the Court to Fukuhara; The Great Earthquake, (Heike Vol. 12.); the description being very similar, while that of the cell of Kenrei-mon-in on Oharayama in the Kancho Maki or appendix to the Heike, and also in the Seisuiki, bears a strong resemblance to Chomei's hut on Hinosan. In this case also opinions differ as to which has borrowed from the other, but the Heike Monogatari Ko, published by the Kokugo Chushakai, states that the plagiarism is on the side of the Heike, and the Hojoki is the prior source. Now the Hojoki is dated the second year of

Kenryaku, 1212 A.D., so this, if correct, would give a *terminus a quo* for these parts at least. Dr. Fujioka, however, considers the Hojoki a compilation of later date and not the work of Kamo Chomei at all.

Style of the Heike Monogatari.—A critic has said of the three works that have always been regarded as the finest representatives of the War Chronicle (Senki-bun) literature, namely, the Heike Monogatari, the Gempei Seisuiki, and the Taiheiki, that 'the style of the Heike is elegant and that of the Seisuiki is grand, but as that of the Taiheiki combines both qualities, it must be regarded as the perfect War Chronicle.' Mr. Utsumi, however, does not agree with this pronouncement, and considers that though it may be conceded that the Taiheiki is perhaps the most perfect type of this kind of literature, it certainly does not contain the characteristics of the other two. It may be true to some extent that elegance is a feature of the Heike, but this aspect has been rather over-emphasized by the critics, and he considers that it is more to be admired for the soberness and restraint of the writing combined with the skilful construction of the narrative.

He would consider the Heike as surpassing the other two works, first in its general construction and dramatic plan, secondly in the handling of the material, and again in the skill in word-painting, but especially so in its narrative style, in which the Taiheiki is its closest rival. This difference between them is rather to be explained as follows. The Gempei Seisuiki has many shortcomings in its narrative, but at the same time it occasionally rises to heights of eloquence that are unequalled by the other two. It may be compared to a .landscape composed of a dreary plain through which one plods on till one is suddenly confronted with a lofty mountain soaring up to the heavens or a vast extent of sea stretching out to the horizon, whereas the impression made by the Taiheiki and the Heike is rather that of a well watered and wooded series of hills and valleys, relieved by flowers and foliage of varied hues, from any point of which a pleasing outlook may be obtained, and which diverts the mind by its retrospect as well as by its promise of what is to come. Such fine writing as, for instance, the description of the advance at the Ujigawa or the Hiyodorigoe, is not to be found in the Heike, but on the whole this kind of description in the Seisuiki is of a somewhat theatrical nature, and the writer is apt to make mistakes owing to an inclination to appear learned and knowing in all things. The narrative of the Heike is written lightly and easily and depicts the condition of things both internally and externally with a few touches. Though lively and vivid, it avoids harshness. The Taiheiki, though using much detail and taking great pains to describe a scene with care and the proper sentiments, is a little heavy and lacking in taste by comparison. The special accomplishment of the latter work is its coining and use of Chinese expressions which are worked into the Japanese language with much skill and sonorous effect, though this is at times perhaps slightly overdone. Thus the excellencies of the Taiheiki rather lie open for anyone to see, whereas those of the Heike are not so obvious and require some literary taste for their appreciation.

Again, though the material of these works consists mostly of details of war and strife, yet in the handling of this material the Heike Monogatari differs widely from the other two, in that, though not so pre-eminent in describing the actual clash of arms, 'the thunder of the captains and the shouting,' it emphasises the underlying motives and incidental circumstances, pathetic or humorous or otherwise, in a manner that the others do not attempt. Beside being an age of strife it was, as for that matter all ages are, a period of transition, and thus we see portrayed the clash of ideas accompanying it, and the struggle between the views of the age that was passing away and of that which was taking its place. The writer seizes on the collision of the elegant and effeminate ideals and way of life of the Heian period with the comparatively rough and rude manners of the sterner Bushi who were henceforth to predominate in the administration of the country, as a means of touching the feelings of the reader by a recital of the pathetic stories of its victims. These victims were always young people, and especially young women, and the narrator evidently has much sympathy with their sad fate. Examples of this kind are the narratives entitled: Gio; Twice an Empress; Aoi-no-Mae; Kogo; The Wife of Koremori; Ko-Saisho; Dairi-Nyobo; Senju; Yokobue, etc., and especially delicately drawn is the scene entitled Moon-viewing, in the fifth volume. The same contrast is emphasized in the case of Kiyomori, the founder of the new era, and the younger nobles of his house who rather favour the elegant style of the former age.

The texts used for this translation are those of Utsumi, Heike Monogatari Hyoshaku, and Umezawa, Heike Monogatari Hyoshaku. I wish to express my gratitude to Profs. Hara Sakae, Okano Gisaburo, and Shida Masahide for their kind assistance in archeological and Buddhist matters.

A. L. SADLER.

Okayama.

Genealogy.

GENEALOGY OF THE HEIKE.

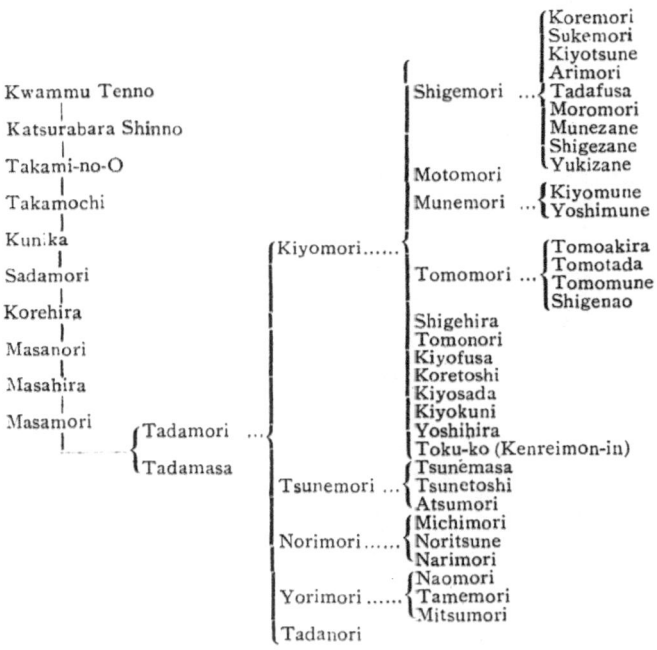

```
Kwammu Tenno
      |
Katsurabara Shinno
      |
Takami-no-O                              Shigemori ...  ┌ Koremori
      |                                                 │ Sukemori
Takamochi                                               │ Kiyotsune
      |                                                 │ Arimori
Kunika                                                  ┤ Tadafusa
      |                                                 │ Moromori
Sadamori                                                │ Munezane
      |                                                 │ Shigezane
Korehira                                                └ Yukizane
      |                          Motomori
Masanori                         Munemori ...  { Kiyomune
      |               ┌ Kiyomori......                   Yoshimune
Masahira             │                                  ┌ Tomoakira
      |              │               Tomomori ...       │ Tomotada
Masamori             │                                  ┤ Tomomune
      |              │                                  └ Shigenao
      └── Tadamori ..│               Shigehira
          Tadamasa   │               Tomonori
                     │               Kiyofusa
                     │               Koretoshi
                     │               Kiyosada
                     │               Kiyokuni
                     │               Yoshihira
                     │               Toku-ko (Kenreimon-in)
                     │                                  ┌ Tsunemasa
                     │  Tsunemori ...  ┤ Tsunetoshi
                     │                  └ Atsumori
                     │                                  ┌ Michimori
                     │  Norimori......  ┤ Noritsune
                     │                  └ Narimori
                     │                                  ┌ Naomori
                     │  Yorimori......  ┤ Tamemori
                     │                  └ Mitsumori
                     └ Tadanori
```

GENEALOGY OF THE SEIWA GENJI.

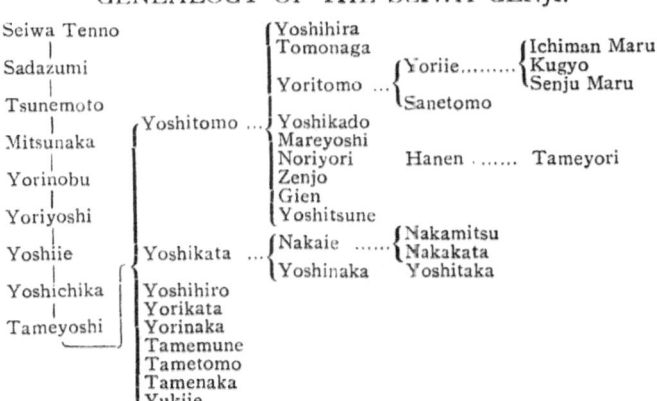

```
Seiwa Tenno          ┌ Yoshihira
      |              │ Tomonaga                            ┌ Ichiman Maru
Sadazumi             │                  ┌ Yoriie.........  ┤ Kugyo
      |              │ Yoritomo ...     ┤                  └ Senju Maru
Tsunemoto            │                  └ Sanetomo
      |   Yoshitomo ...┤ Yoshikado
Mitsunaka            │ Mareyoshi
      |              │ Noriyori        Hanen ....... Tameyori
Yorinobu             │ Zenjo
      |              │ Gien
Yoriyoshi            └ Yoshitsune
      |                                ┌ Nakaie ...... { Nakamitsu
Yoshiie    Yoshikata ...┤                                 Nakakata
      |                                └ Yoshinaka     Yoshitaka
Yoshichika      ┌ Yoshihiro
      |         │ Yorikata
Tameyoshi       │ Yorinaka
      └─────────┤ Tamemune
                │ Tametomo
                │ Tamenaka
                └ Yukiie
```

The Court and Government.

THE COURT AND GOVERNMENT.

The Emperor (Tenno).

The Cloistered Emperor   The Retired Emperor
(Ho-o).   (In or Shin-in).

Sessho   ...   ...   Regent.
Kwampaku   ...   Chief Minister.

THE DAJO-KWAN.

Dajo-daijin   ...   Prime Minister.

Udaijin.   Naidaijin.   Sadaijin.
Minister of the Right.   Minister of the Left.

Sangi $\left\{\begin{array}{l}\text{Dainagon}\\\text{Chunagon}\end{array}\right\}$ Imperial Advisers.

ADMINISTRATIVE.

Udaiben.	Secretaries				Secretaries	Sadaiben.
Uchuben.	of the	}	Shonagon	{	of the	Sachuben.
Ushoben.	Right.				Left.	Sashoben.

OFFICIALS OF THE EIGHT DEPARTMFNTS.

Hyobu.   Nakatsukasa.
Gyobu.   Shikibu.
Okura.   Jibu.
Kunai.   Mimbu.

In each department were

Kyo 卿.   Suke 輔.   Jo 丞.   Sakwan 錄.

MILITARY OFFICIALS.

(Udaisho).   (Sadaisho).
Konoe-fu.   Ukon-e-no-Taisho. Generals   Sakon-e-no-Taisho. Generals
The Imperial   Chusho.   of the   Chusho.   of the
Bodyguard.   Shosho.   Right.   Shosho.   Left.

Emon.   Uemon-no-Taisho.   Saemon-no-Taisho.
The Imperial   Chusho.   Chusho.
Gateguard.   Shosho.   Shosho.

Below whom were Emon or Efu-no-Kami 督.
-Suke 佐.
-Jo 尉.
-Sakwan 志.

Uma-ryo.

    Uma-no-Kami 頭 Right Master of the Horse. Sama-no-kami Left
       -Suke 助.   do.
       -Jo 允.
       -Sakwan 屬.

Dazaifu.   Dazai-no-Sotsu 帥. Gon-no-Sotsu.
                    -Ni 貳.
                    -Jo 監.
                    -Sakwan 典

Chinjufu.   Shogun.
                Fuku-Shogun.
                Gunkan.
                Gunso.

          Provincial Government.
                Kokushi.   Kami 守.
                國   司   Suke 介.
                              Jo 掾.
                              Sakwan 目.

                Shicho.
                使   臔   Betto 別當.
                              Suke 佐.
                              Jo 尉.
                              Sakwan 志.

ECCLESIASTICAL TITLES.

Dai-Sojo 大僧正 Archbishop ⎫
Sojo 僧正 Bishop.   ⎬ Ranks.
Sozu 僧都   ⎪
Risshi 律師   ⎭

Zasshu 座主. Lord Abbot.

Ajari 阿闍梨 (Sk. Ajariya). Instructor of Disciples.

Hoin 法印   ⎫
Hogen 法眼   ⎪
Hokkyo 法橋   ⎬ Titles of Honour.
Kwasho (Tendai) 和尚 ⎪
Washo (Hosso)   ,,   ⎪
Osho (other sects) ,,   ⎭
Hoshi ... ... Priest.
Biku (S. Bikshu)   ... ... Monk.
Bikuni (S. Bikshuni)   ... Nun.
Ubasoku (S. Upasaka) ... Lay Believer.
Ubai (S. Upasika)   ... ... Female Lay Believer.

THE HEIKE MONOGATARI.

Volume I.

Chapter I.

GION SHOJA.

The sound of the bell of Gionshoja[1] echoes the impermanence of all things. The hue of the flowers of the teak[2] tree declares that they who flourish must be brought low. Yea, the proud ones are but for a moment, like an evening dream in springtime. The mighty are destroyed at the last, they are but as the dust before the wind.

If thou ask concerning the rulers of other countries far off; Choko[3] of Shin, Ono[4] of Kan, Shui[5] of Ryo, Rokuzan[6] of To, all these, not following in the paths of the government of all the King and Emperors who went before them, sought pleasure only; not entering into council nor heeding the disorders of their Country, having no knowledge of the affliction of their people, they did not endure, but perished utterly. So also if thou enquire concerning our own country, Masakado[7] in the period Shohei, Sumitomo in Tenkyo, Gishin in Kowa, Shinrai in Heiji, all were arrogant and bold of heart in divers manners, yet if we consider what is told of the former Prime Minister Prince Taira no Ason Kiyomori, the Lay priest of Rokuhara, of a more recent time, neither in their words nor their intentions were they his equal.

As to his ancestry he was the eldest son of Ason Tadamori chief of the department of justice; grandson of Masamori Sanuki no Kami, who was descended in the ninth generation from Katsurabara Shinno, Prince of the first rank and chief of the department of Ceremonies, the fifth son of the Emperor Kwammu. This prince's son Takami no O had died without either office or rank and it was his son Takamimochi-no O who

---

[1] *Gion Shoja.* 祇園精舍 Sk. Djetavana Vihara. The monastery of Djeta, situated in a park, bought and presented to S'akya Muni by Anartha-pindaka, in which many of his sermons were preached.

[2] *Teak tree.* Shorea Robusta, a large tree under which S'akya Mani entered Nirvana. Sk. Sala. Jap. Sharasoju 沙羅雙樹.

[3] *Choko.* 趙高 Prime Minister of Shin during the reigns of the first two Emperors, throw the country into confusion and was put to death while the third was a child.

[4] *Ono.* 王莽 Father of the Empress of Sei Tei 成帝, seized the administration as Regent but was put to death by the nobles shortly afterward.

[5] *Shui.* 周伊 perhaps a mistake for 朱异 Minister of Bu Tei 武帝 who was the cause of his country's ruin.

[6] *Rokuzan*, the famous An-Rokuzan, 安祿山 Minister of Genso 芝宗 who also ruined his country.

[7] *Masakado* etc. famous Japanese rebels.

first received the surname of Taira, and before receiving the office of Kazusa-no-suke he suddenly gave up his royal rank and became a subject. His son Chinjufu Shogun Yoshimochi. afterwards changed his name to Kunika and from this Kunika to Masamori: these six generations, though always receiving government stipends, yet had not such rank as permitted them to appear at Court.

Chapter II.

THE ASSASSINATION AT COURT.

Now Tadamori, while holding the office of Bizen no Kami, by the request of the retired Emperor Toba, had built the temple Toku-cho-juin and the Sa-ju-san-gen-do, or hall 33 ken long, within which were one thousand and one, Buddhas; its first festival being on the thirteenth day of the third month of the first year of Tensho. As a reward he was honoured by receiving the territory of the province of Tamba, which then happened to be unappropriated. Moreover the Emperor of his bounty graciously permitted him to attend the Court; which Tadamori did for the first time at the age of thirty six. But the higher Courtiers were furious with jealousy and plotted to assassinate him on the evening of the festival of Go-Sechi[8] Toyo-no-akari-no-setchie, on the 23rd day of the eleventh month of the same year. Tadamori, who was not a civil official, being born of a line of warriors, on hearing of this was troubled in his heart for himself and his house at this unexpected shame that was come upon him, but finally, as he was in duty bound to serve his August Master under all conditions, he made his preparations beforehand. Before entering the Court he provided himself with a long dirk[9] which he girt on under his long court dress, and turning aside to a dimly lit place, slowly drew the blade, and passed it through the hair of his head so that it gleamed afar off with an icy sheen, causing all to stare open-eyed. Moreover a retainer of Tadamori, by birth of the same family, a grandson of Taira no Mokunosuke Sadamitsu and son of Shinno Saburodaiyu Iefusa, Sahyoe-no-jo Iesada by name, wearing a body armour laced with bright green under a light green "kariginu"[10] or loose overdress, and carrying under his arm a "tachi"[11] with a

---

[8] *Go-Sechi.* 五節 So called became Five Princesses danced at it. The banquet was given on the day after Nii-name-sai or the offering of the new rice harvest to the gods.

[9] *dirk.* 'sayamaki' a short sword without a guard, perhaps so called because the scabbard was bound round like a bow. Cf. illus. in Joy and Inada, Sword and Same, p. 37.

[10] *Kariginu.* For this and other Court dress cf, Sansom, translation of Tsurezure Gusa T.A.S.J. vol. 39. p. 117.

[11] *Tachi.* The slung sword of curved shape always worn by warriors and also by Courtiers up to Ashikaga times after which it was only worn by commanding officers and Courtiers who still wear it when in Japanese dress of ceremony. That of Bushi differed in shape from that of civil officials. Cf, Joly and Inada as above, p. 312.

bowstring bag attached, was waiting in the "koniwa," the small court by the Seiryoden.

Now the Kurando-no-to[12] or Chief of the Record Office and some underlings of his, thinking it strange that one wearing unsuitable costume should be within the balustrade of the steps of the Court near the bell-rope of the library, and wondering if he was not some disorderly fellow, an official of the sixth rank ordered him to depart quickly. But Iesada thus replied: "Because I have heard that to-night they will try to kill my Lord Bizen-no-kami dono have I come hither"; and he remained there and did not depart. And they saw that there was nothing more to be done; and thus the attempt did not take place.

But when Tadamori danced in the August presence of the Mikado at his Imperial wish, the others mocked at him, changing the words of the music and singing "Ise heiji wa sugame nari," ("the winepot of Ise has turned into a vinegar jar.") In thus mentioning the vessels of his province they punned on his title of Ise-heishi;[13] and since Tadamori had a squint in one eye (sugame) they also alluded to this in the lampoon. Tadamori. not being able to do anything, left the Presence before the entertainment had ended, and going behind the Shishinden, a place that could be seen by everyone, deposited the sword that he was carrying at his side in the hands of the Tonomo-no-tsukasa.[14] Iesada, who was waiting for his lord, immediately asked him what had happened, but he, though greatly wishing to tell him, seeing in his face the expression of one who would even do violence in the Palace itself should he tell him the truth, merely answered that nothing out of the common had taken place.

In the Go-setchie festival only such pleasing things as, for instance, white paper,[15] Shuzenji paper, wrapped up writing brushes, or writing brushes having a "tomoe" on the stem, had been accustomed to be mentioned in the songs that accompanied the dance, but there was a certain Dazai Gon-no-sotsu Suenaka no Kyo who was of so dark a complexion that the people of his time called him "kuro-sotsu" (or "black sotsu,") and while he was holding the office of Kurando-no-to, when he danced before the August Presence, they changed the words to: "Oh what a black, black head; someone must have painted him with lacquer." Also the former Prime Minister of Kwanzan-no-In, Prince Tadamasa, who was left an orphan when only ten years old owing to

---

[12] *Kurando.* The office in the Court that had charge of certain state documents and had authority to decide matters of litigation.

[13] *Ise Heishi.* Cf. Sansom. Tsurezure Gusa, p. 66, where another pun on the same name is explained. Heishi 平氏 and Heishi 瓶子 wine bottle, saga-me 素瓶 squint-eyed, and su-game 酢瓶 vinegar-bottle, or 素瓶 unglazed bottle as some MSS read.

[14] *Tonomo.* The department of the Palace that had charge of the Imperial carriages, bath, torches, and cleaning of the Palace courts.

[15] *White paper* etc. intended to suggest metaphorically the dances of women.

the death of his father Chunagon Tadamune no Kyo, was received as
son-in-law by the To-Chunagon Kasei-no-Kyo in the time of Go Naka
no Mikado, when he held the office of Harma no kami, and it was an
exceedingly gorgeous bridal, so that at the Go-sechie of this time they
japed at him with the refrain; "The rice of Harima, the scouring rush
and the "muku" leaves, they polish up people's fine raiment." Though
long ago such things had happened, nothing had been done, and now
people said that what was to be done was doubtful. As he had expected
after the conclusion of the festival, all the courtiers[16] and officials
together appealed against him; for coming to a Court entertainment
wearing a sword and bringing military retainers within the Court
Precincts were things strictly regulated according to rank: for this there
was Imperial Order and ancient precedent, But Ason Tadamori had
stationed a soldier wearing common dress, said to be a retainer of his
family, in the small court of the Palace, and had come to the Go-Sechie
wearing a sword by his side, and both these counts were acts of
disorder such as were seldom met with heretofore. Indeed it was one
crime piled on another, a charge he would find it difficult to escape. All
the Court Nobles together petitioned that his name should be erased
front the list of Courtiers and that he herewith be deprived of rank and
office. His Majesty the Mikado, greatly surprised, ordered Tadamori
into his Presence to make examination into the affair. In his reply he
stated that as to the presence of his retainer in the Palace, he certainly
knew nothing about it: but if his retainers had heard of the designs that
people were plotting against him lately, and in order to help him against
such dishonour had come hither secretly without informing him, then
he had no power to prevent it. "But if there be any blame, do I not yield
my body herewith as for the matter of the sword, I deposited it in the
Tonomotsukasa, and if it be brought out from thence, it may be seen if
it be a real sword or not." As this seemed quite plausible, they hastened
to bring forth the sword and exhibit it. Its outside was that of a dirk in a
black lacquer sheath, but within was only a wooden blade covered with
silver. Although he had displayed the appearance of a sword to avoid
dishonour, his substitution of a wooden blade as a precaution against an
after accusation was exceeding praiseworthy. A plan like this is very
commendable in a warrior. That his retainer should have been in
attendance in the court of the Palace this too is an example for retainers
of the "bushi." So no fault was found in Tadamori, but, on the contrary,
his conduct was greatly admired, and he was pronounced guiltless.

---

[16] *Courtiers.* Kugyo Denjobito. Kugyo were the Sessho Kwampaku and the great
Ministers (Ku), and the Dainagon and Chunagon of above the third Rank. Denjobito were
all who had, the right of attending the Court. Kyo is a title meaning Lord, Court Noble.

Chapter III.

SUZUKI.

Tadamori's children all had the title, of "Ei-no-suke,"[17] and when they attended at Court they were welcomed by everyone. On one occasion when Tadamori went up to the Capital from Bizen and the Retired Emperor Toba augustly deigned to enquire of him about the scenery of Akashi, he answered thus:—

> *"Ariake no tsuki mo,*
> *Akashi no urakaze ni;*
> *Nami bakari koso,*
> *Yoru to mieshi ka.*
> *"When the morning breaks o'er the wind swept sand of Akashi,*
> *Only the moon on high casts its faint beams on the waves.*

The ex-Mikado was pleased to admire this verse and ordered it to be preserved in the collection entitled "Kinyo-shu."[18]

There was a fair lady-in-waiting in the Sendo Palace of the ex-Midado much beloved by Tadamori, whom he was wont to visit every evening. And it chanced that one night, after so doing he left in her room a fan painted with the rising moon; the other ladies seeing it were much amused, saying: "Oh how doubtful is the place where the moon has risen!" to which the lady replied:—

> *Kumoi yori tada mori[19]*
> *Kuru tsuki nareba,*
> *Oboroge nite wa*
> *Iwaji to zo omou.*
> *"If the moon indeed has drifted down from the heavens,*
> *Surely then the sky must be a little obscure.*

Thus showing that her wit was not at all shallow, This was the mother of Satsuma-no-kami Tadanori; as people are drawn to each other by similar dispositions, Tadamori's taste was matched by her elegance. Then Tadamori becoming Gyo-bu-kyo[20] afterwards died at the age of fifty eight on the fifteenth day of the first month of the third year of Ninpei. His eldest son Kiyomori followed in his footsteps. In

---

[17] *Ei-no-Suke.* Officer of one of the Imperial Guards, the Konoe-fu or Saeimon or Ueimon.

[18] *Kinyoshu* A Collection of poems made in the time of Sutoku Tenno.

[19] *Tadamori.* pun on his name read 只 'only,' and 泄 'leak,' for 忠盛.

[20] *Gyobukyo.* Chief of the Department of justice, (Gyobasho)

the first year of Hogen, when the Sadaijin of Uji brought the realm into disorder, he put himself at the head of the Imperial party and was rewarded for his services. At first he had the office of Aki-no-kami, then he was promoted to be Harima-no-kami, and in the third year of the same era he became Dazai-no-dai-ni. In the twelfth month of the first year of Heiji, at the time of the rebellion of Nobuyori and Yoshitomo, he beat down the rebels in the Imperial cause, and the rewards bestowed on him for many meritorious deeds by the August kindness were very great. In the next year he received the Senior Third Rank, and succeeded to the titles of Saisho Eifu-no-kami,[21] and Kebi-ishi-no-Betto[22] one after the other, and passing over the ranks of Chunagon and Dainagon, took rank as a Minister of State. He did not even become Minister of the Left or Right, but rose straight from Naidaijin to be Dajodaijin of the Lower First Rank. Though not a commander of armies, he went armed and surrounded by retainers, and by special permission of the Retired Emperor, entered and departed from the Court riding in state in ox-wagon or palanquin, acting as one who holds alone the whole power of administration. Since it was the function of the Dajodaijin to be a pattern and example of virtue to the whole country, to consider which was the right course in ruling, and to tranquillize the universe by his government, if such an one could not be found, the office was to be declared vacant, for except it were held by such an one, the office would surely be polluted. Now that this lay-monk of a Governor should hold the Heaven and the Four Seas in the hollow of his hand, verily there is no need for further speech.

Now the reason for this great prosperity of the Heike was said to be the favour of Kumano Gongen. And this was the manner of it; when Kiyomori was yet only styled Aki-no-kami, he went to worship at Kumano by ship from Anonotsu in Ise, and a large "Suzuki" fish sprang up into his vessel, as it is related in former times that a white fish leaped into the ship of Bu, king of Shu, and however it may have been he attributed it to the favour of the Gongen. As we have said, he was on religious pilgrimage, so that he was observing the ten prohibitions, abstaining from animal food and making purifications, yet departing from these, he cooked the fish himself and ate of it and gave also to his retainers who were with him. And afterwards nought but good fortune attended him and he at last became Dajodaijin. His posterity too attained high office more quickly than a dragon ascends the clouds, greatly excelling in happiness the nine generations of their ancestors.

---

[21] *Eifu-no-Kami.* Captain of the Imperial Guard.

[22] *Kebiishi-no-Betto.* Chief of the Police. Betto, High Steward, also of Shinto Shrine, e.g. Kumanono-Betto; now fallen to be used only with tic meaning 'groom.' Cf. Eng. Constable, Comes Stabuli (Jap. Samano-kami) formerly Commander of an Army, now only of Police Constable.

Chapter IV.

KAMURO; OR BOY ATTENDANTS.

Now Prince Kiyomori, being overtaken by illness on the eleventh day of the eleventh month of Ninan, at the age of fifty one, retired from the world and took monk's vows to save his life, assuming the religious name of Jokai. As the result of this, his sickness departed and he was cured, fulfilling the decree of destiny. Yet after his retirement from the world he did not put an end to his luxurious living. People obeyed him as grass before the wind, and depended on him as the earth does on the rain that moistens it. If one speaks of the Princes of the house of Rokuhara dono, they were most noble and illustrious, and none might be considered equal to them. Moreover as for the brother of the Nyudo's wife, Taira Dainagon Tokitada Kyo,—all those who did not belong to his house were to be considered people of no position, so that everyone was wishing to make alliance with him. From the manner of wearing the "eboshi" to the style of the crest on clothes, everything must be in the fashion of Rokuhara; so that everyone from one end of the land to the other studied it.

Now however wisely a king or ruler may govern or in the case of the political actions of Regent or Prime Minister, (Sessho Kwampaku) it is a usual thing that certain worthless fellows will gather together to speak ill of him; but against this lay-priest in his prosperity there was not even a casual breath of reviling. And for what reason? Even because, by the device of this monk-regent, about three hundred youths of from fourteen to sixteen years old, having purified themselves and polled their heads, wearing red robes, were everywhere patrolling the streets of the Capital. And if there was anyone who spoke evil against the Taira house, and one of these chanced to hear it, straightway summoning to him his fellows, they would violently enter that man's house, seize his treasures and household goods and bring him bound to Rokuhara. So that none were found to open their mouth about the things they saw or knew. At the very name of the Kamuro of Rokuhara everyone, both pedestrians and those who rode in carriages, made wide room and passed by on the other side. Even when entering or leaving the forbidden gate of the Palace, it was not necessary to declare their name, for the officials of the city looked with averted eyes where they were concerned.

Chapter V.

THE SPLENDOUR OF KIYOMORI.

Not only did Kiyomori himself live in splendour and luxury, but all his house likewise shared his prosperity. His eldest son Shigemori was Naidaijin and Sadaisho, his second son Munemori was Chunagon and Udaisho, his third son Tomomori was Chujo of the third grade, his eldest grandson Koremori Shosho of the fourth grade; sixteen of his house in all held offices of the higher grade (Kugyo), while thirty had right of entry to Court. The whole number of his family who drew revenues from the provinces as military officials were about sixty persons. All others appeared as of no account in the world. Since long ago in the era of Nara no Mikado the office of Nakae-no-Taisho was first instituted in the fifth year of Shingi, and Nakae was changed to Konoe in the fourth year of Daido, only on three or four occasions have brothers occupied the offices of the Right and Left together. In the time of Montoku Tenno, on the Left was Yoshifusa as Sadaijin-no-Sadaisho, on the Right, Yoshisuke as Dainagon no Udaisho; they were the sons of Fuyutsugu, the retired Sadaijin. In the time of Shujo-in, Saneyori Ono no-miya dono[23] was Minister of the Left and Morosuke Kujo dono of the Right; they were sons of Teijin Ko.[24] In the time of Go-Rei-zei-in, Norimichi O-nijo dono was Minister of the Left and Yorimune Horikawa dono of the Right; they were the sons of the Kwampaku Mido. In the time of Nijo-in, Motofusa Matsu dono was Minister of the Left, and Kanezane Tsuki-no-wa dono of the Right; they were the sons of Hoseiji dono.[25] All these were the sons of Regents. Among the sons of ordinary people there is no precedent. As for the grandson, of a man whose presence at Court was barely suffered, wearing the forbidden colours[26] and costume, going clothed in silk gauze and brocade and holding the offices of Daijin and Taisho, his sons being at the same tune Ministers of the Left and Right, it is indeed an extraordinary thing for future generations to hear of. Beside this he had eight daughters, all of whom severally achieved fortunes to be envied. One of them was to have become the wife of Shigemori no Kyo, Chunagon of the Emperor Sakuramachi, and was betrothed to him at the age of eight, but after the revolt of Heiji the matter was altered and she became the wife of the Sadaijin of Kwazan-in, to whom she bore many princes. Now this Shigemori Kyo was called the Chunagon of Sakuramachi for the

---

[23] *Mido dono.* The Kwampaku Fujiwara Michinaga.

[24] *Taijin Ko* Fujiwara Tadahira.

[25] *Hoseiji dono.* Fujiwara Tadamichi.

[26] *Forbidden Colours.* Purple and Vermilion were only allowed by special permission, as were the material damask and brocade.

following reason. Being a man of very delicate taste, he exceedingly loved the scenery of Mount Yoshino; and planting there tiny cherry trees, he built a house in the midst of them and dwelt in it; so that people who went there in the spring of every year to see them gave him the nickname of Sakuramachi (cherry town). Being very grieved that these cherry blossoms should fall within seven days after flowering, he prayed to Ten-sho-daijin and they remained on the tree for a period of three times seven days; the goddess displaying her august kindness owing to the great virtue of the Emperor, and the flowers also requiting his affection by living on for twenty days.

To resume, another of Kiyomori's daughters became Consort of the Emperor, and bore a Prince at the age of twenty two. On this child attaining the rank of Crown Prince, she retired from the world and was known by the name of Ken-rei-coon-in. Concerning this daughter of the Lay-priest Chancellor, since she has risen to the rank of Mother of the Emperor, there is no need of further description. Another daughter became the wife of the Regent Rokujo.[27] She it was who, during the reign of the Retired Emperor Takakura, became Imperial Foster mother, and gained the title of Jun-san-go by Imperial Edict. She went by the name of Shirakawa den, and was a personage of exceeding importance. Yet another daughter had become the wife of Fugenji dono;[28] another of Reizei-no-Dainagon Ryubo-no-Kyo, and another of Shichijo Shuri-no-Taiyu Nobutaka-no-Kyo. One daughter also he had by a lady-in-waiting of the shrine of Itsukushima in Aki, and she had the honour of becoming attendant on the Retired Emperor Go-Shirakawa. Beside her also a Palace-attendant at Kujo-no-in named Tokiwa bore him a daughter who became lady-in-waiting to Kawazan-no-in dono, and was styled Ro-no-on-kata (Unofficial Empress). Now Nippon Akitsushima has but sixty six provinces; and of these the domains of the Heike were thirty; almost half the land. Beside these the manors, rice fields and gardens that they possessed were without number. In the multiplicity of their gorgeous costumes they were resplendent as the flowers of the field; the noble and illustrious crowded before their gates like a throng in the marketplace: the gold of Yoshu, the jewels of Keishu, the damask of Gokun, the brocade of Shiyyokko—of the seven rarities and the myriad treasures not one was lacking. For poetry and music, fishing and riding, perchance even the Mikado's Palaces were not more renowned.

---

[27] *The Regent Rokujo*. Fujiwara Motozane.
[28] *Fugenji Dono*. Fujiwara Motomichi.

Chapter VI.

GIO.

Now not only did this priestly statesman hold the whole country in the hollow of his hand, but, neither ashamed at the censure of the world, nor regarding the derision of the people, he indulged in the most surprising conduct. For example, in the Capital there were two famous "Shirabyoshi" who were sisters, named Gio and Ginyo, both young girls and very skilled in their art. The elder, Gio, was beloved by Kiyomori, and her younger sister also was in high favour with everyone. So they were enabled to build a good house for their mother, who was granted a monthly income of a hundred koku of rice; and a hundred kwan in money by Kiyomori. Their family was consequently rich and honoured, fortunate beyond the lot of most people. Now the origin of Shirabyoshi in our country was in the reign of Toba-in when Shima-no-chisai and Waka-no-mae appeared as dancers. In the beginning the Shirabyoshi wore the "suikan" or silk court robe and "tateboshi" or black court headdress, with a white dirk in their belt, when they danced, and it was like the dancing of a man: but from the middle age the headdress and sword were disused, and they danced only in the white "suikan," hence they were called Shirabyoshi.

But among the Shirabyoshi[29] of the capital, when they heard of the good fortune of Gio, there were some who hated her and some who were envious. Those who envied her said: "Ah! how fortunate is Gio Gozen, if we do even as she does we too may become prosperous in like manner;" so they added the syllable "Gi" to their names to see if they too might not obtain good luck. Some called themselves Giichi, Giji, Gifuku, or Gitoku. Those who hated her said "Surely it is not a matter of the name or character with which it is written, fortune is the result of disposition inherited from a previous existence;" and so few of them took such a name. Now it came to pass that, three years afterwards, another skillful Shirabyoshi appeared; and she was a maiden sixteen years of age, born in the province of Kaga, and her name was Hotoke. And when the people of the capital, both high and low, saw her, they said that although from of old times many

---

[29] *Shirabyoshi*. Cf, Sansom, note on Tsurezuregusa. p. 128. and for illus. of Suikan, p. 127. Yoshida Kenko says here; 'O no Hisasuke says that Michinori no Nyudo selected certain dances that were amusing, and taught a woman named Ise-no Zenji to dance them. She wore a white robe, with a sword, and an eboshi, and thus they were called Otoko-mae, or men's dances. Zenji's daughter, who was called Shizuka, followed her in this profession. This is the origin of Shirabyoshi. They sang the songs of Gods and Buddhas. Later Minamoto-no-Mitsuyuki composed a great number of others, and there are also some that are the work of the Emperor Go Toba, which His Majesty was pleased to teach to Kamegika. Sansom's trans.

Shirabyoshi had been seen there, one so dexterous as she had not been beheld; and she too was in exceeding great favour with all. And in the course of time Hotoke Gozen said: "Though I have made sport for the whole Empire, yet this great Taira minister who now is the source of all fortune and prosperity has not yet deigned to summon me; after the manner of entertainers I will e'en go uninvited." So she forthwith proceeded to the Palace in Nishi-hachijo. On her arrival, a servant entered the presence of the minister and announced: "Hotoke Gozen, now so famous in this city is without." Then the lay-priest grew very angry and replied "How then! do not these players attend only when they arc called? Why is it that she has come unbidden? Whether she be called God or Buddha, (Hotoke) it is not suitable that she come here while Gio is present. Bid her depart at once." Hotoke Gozen was already retiring at these unkind words, when Gio said to the Minister "It is surely the usual custom that players should attend unbidden, and moreover it is because she is still young and innocent that she has thus intruded on you—so it will be most unkind to speak harshly and send her away—how greatly will she be shamed and distressed by it; as I myself have trodden the same path, I cannot but remember these things. If you will not deign to allow her to dance or to sing, yield, I pray you, so far as to call her back and receive her in audience: if you then dismiss her, it will be a favour indeed worthy of her deep gratitude." To this the Priest Minister answered: "Since you wish it to be so, I will see her and then dismiss her:" and he sent a servant to call her. Hotoke Gozen, having been thus harshly treated, was even then entering her carriage to return when she was summoned and turned back again. The Minister met her and granted her an audience. Thus Hotoke, though it seemed unlikely that she would gain an audience, yet through the kindness of Gio, who thus importuned for her, was not only able to enter the Minister's presence, but further it happened that he, wishing to hear her voice, directed that she should sing a song of the kind called "Imayo:"[30] and thus she sang:

"*When I first enjoyed the sight of your bountiful presence,*
   T'was like the evergreen pine, flourishing age after age.
   Like to the pond on whose rocks is basking the turtle thrice
      blessed,
   Numberless storks beside it happily preening their wings."

---

[30] *Imayo.* A verse of eight or twelve lines of seven and five syllables alternating, fashionable from the middle ages.
   'Kimi wo hajimete, miru toki wa,
   Chiyo mo henubeshi hime komatsu,
   Mimae no ike naru kame oka ni
   Tsuru koso mure ite asobu mere.'

And those who heard it were greatly wondering at her skill and her beauty, and pressed her to repeat it even to three times. The Lay-priest also was greatly diverted and said "Since you are so skilful at Imayo you must also be able to dance well; we wish to see one of your dances." Then the drums were ordered to be beaten and she danced forthwith. Now Hotoke Gozen was renounced for the beauty of her hair and features, and her voice was no less exquisite; how then should she fail in the dance? So when she put forth all her skill and charm in dancing, Kiyomori was enraptured and his heart turned wholly toward her. But when Hotoke Gozen said to him: "Did I not present myself uninvited, and when almost rejected was I not only brought back by the entreaty of Gio Gozen? I pray thee grant me leave that I may return quickly;" the lay-monk by no means agreed to the proposal, and thinking that she was only embarrassed because of the presence of Gio, proposed to send Gio away.

But Hotoke Gozen answered "How can this be? If we were to remain here both together, I should be most embarrassed, and if your Excellency send away Gio Gozen and keep me here alone, how ashamed will she not feel in her heart? Indeed it will be most painful to her. If you deign to think of me again in the future, I am always able to come at your call. I beg that to-day I may be allowed to retire."

Kiyomori, seeing how the matter lay, straightway ordered Gio to leave the Palace, and to that end sent a messenger three times. Although Gio had expected this thing from long before, she did not think that it would come to pass to-day or to-morrow. But as the Nyudo continually repeated this unreasonable demand, there was nothing for her but to sweep her room clean and to go. Even those who meet under the shade of the same tree, or who greet each other by the riverside, since it is owing to relations in a previous existence, ever feel pain at parting with each other; how much more grievous a thing it is, when two have been together in affection for the space of three years. So in regret and grief she shed unavailing tears. Thus as it was a thing that must be, Gio went forth, but ere she went she wrote on the shoji this verse, thinking to bring perchance to remembrance the forgotten image of one who was gone.

"The fresh or fading flowers of the same moor,
In autumn meet with the same hapless fate."

Then riding in a carriage to the place where she lived, she cast hers if down within the shoji and wept unceasingly. Her mother and her younger sister, seeing these things, asked many questions, but Gio would by no means give any answer, and only by enquiring of her maid did they come to know what had happened. Moreover the hundred koku and hundred kwan of monthly allowance ceased; it was now the turn of the relations of Hotoke Gozen to taste the enjoyment of this prosperity. Soon all the people of the capital heard of these matters, and wondered if it were true that Gio had been dismissed from the Nishi-hachijo palace. There were some who went to see her, some who sent letters, and some who sent their servants, but Gio, since she had no inclination to amuse anyone now, did not even receive their letters, neither did she treat in any way with the messengers. She became more and more melancholy and only shed unavailing tears. Thus the year ended and the next spring came.

Then the Nyudo sent a messenger to Gio asking after her affairs and her health and saying that as Hotoke Gozen wished for someone to beguile her tedious hours, would she not come up to the palace to dance, or it might be sing Imayo, and thus cheer her, but Gio returned no answer, only she lay down and restrained her tears. Again the Nyudo sent to know why she did not go, and why at least she did not answer; if she would not go, for what reason was it? For Jokai himself wished to confer with her. When her mother heard this, weeping bitterly, she thus admonished her; "Why at least do you not deign to send an answer? and why do you not go when thus rebuked? At which Gio said, restraining her tears: "If I thought I ought to go, I would answer, but since I shall by no means go, I know not what answer I can give. As I do not go when I am thus summoned, he has somewhat to discuss with me, he says; and what may this be but perchance to drive me from the city, or it may be to take my life. Beyond these two things no worse is possible. Even though one go forth from Miyake, the way is not so sorrowful. Again if one is called away from life, would one grudge this body so much? Once having known the bitterness of being disliked, shall I look on his face a second time? "Now when she did not feel it necessary to reply, her mother again admonished her, weeping" Among those who dwell in this land, the commands of the Nyudo ought not to be disobeyed, and moreover the relation of man and woman is from a former existence, it does not begin in this life; even though the pledge be for a thousand or ten thousand years, there are many that soon are parted, and though some think that it will be but for a little while, yet it may endure unto the end of life. The thing that has no certainty in this life of ours is the relation between man and woman. If you do not go now when you are summoned, it is not likely that you will be put to death, but certainly we shall be driven from Miyako. Even if you must leave the capital, you are both still young, and whatever space there may be between the rock and the tree it is easy to pass over; but I am old, and when weak and declining, to go and live in a strange place, is sad even to think of. Oh that I might be allowed to live and die in Miyako!" Thus considering her filial duty both in this life and the next, though Gio had determined that she would not go, not disobedient to her mother she stood ready to set out, bathed in tears;

indeed her feelings were very pitiable. As it would be lonely for her to go alone, her younger sister, Ginyo prepared to accompany her, with two other Shirabyoshi beside, making in all a company of four. In one carriage they rode together and came to the Nishi-hachijo palace.

On entering however, she was not called to take the seat she had formerly occupied, a place much lower down being provided for her. "Alas!" thought she, "how shall this be? Although there is no fault in me, and although I have come hither, how am I distressed in being given a lower seat." And not knowing what to do, she said nothing to anyone, but her tears fell plentifully from beneath the sleeve she pressed to her face. When Hotoke Gozen saw this, she was greatly affected and said to Kiyomori, "It would have been better if you had not sent for her; but now let her be called up hither, or if not, suffer me to be dismissed and go away."

The Nyudo would not at all consider this and would not permit her to go away, but by and by he deigned to receive Gio and to greet her and enquire how she did, explaining that, as Hotoke Gozen was lonely, it would be very pleasant if Gio would comfort her by dancing and singing Imayo. Gio replied, with difficulty suppressing her tears, "Indeed I came wishing not to disobey your august command," and sang the following verse of Imayo:—

"Even Buddha himself was once an ordinary person,
I also at last like unto Buddha shall grow.
Everything on this earth can partake of the nature of Buddha.
Only to be estranged, this is painful indeed."

Twice she sang it, weeping bitterly, and as she sang all the Princes and Courtiers of the Heike and the high officers and samurai shed tears of admiration and sympathy. Kiyomori also acknowledged the justice of her complaint and frankly confessed it before them all.

So when the dance was finished he intimated that, as at present he had to attend to other matters, in future she should come without any especial summons to dance and sing and amuse Hotoke. But Gio, repressing her tears, went forth without returning any answer.

Thus Gio, not having intended to go, but thinking it cruel to disobey her mother, a second time suffered ignominious treatment. How pitiable it was indeed! Then thinking that if she remained in this world, she was always liable to meet with such afflictions, she determined to put an end to her life. Her sister Ginyo, hearing this, also made up her mind to die with her.

Then their mother, being aware of their resolve, again with tears more gravely admonished them. "If you have determined to do this, how greatly do I regret that I persuaded you to go; for in truth your chagrin is the cause of this, and if you indeed take your own life and your sister follow you, you my two daughters thus dying first, what profit is it to me your mother, who am aged and declining, if I still live on? I too with you will cast away my life. Now to cause one's mother, who has not yet attained the limit of her years to cast her life away, is it not even as one of the five great sins?[31] This life is but a temporary abiding place, shame upon shame even, what is it to be accounted? There is only sadness of heart in the long darkness of this world. If in this life we become attached to things, in the next life we must tread an evil way in sadness." Thus melted in tears she persuaded them. Gio, also weeping, admitted that she spoke truth; doubtless it was as one of the five great sins that, because of regret at being put to shame, she should determine to put an end to her life. So it was that she gave up her intention of dying by her own hand: but since if she should stay in Miyako she would still be liable to humiliation Gio, at the age of only one and twenty, deserted the capital and became a nun. In a mountain village in the recesses of Saga, building herself a but of brushwood, she continually murmured her invocations to Buddha. When her sister Ginyo perceived that she did thus, having made compact to die with her, how much more when the world has become so hateful shall she not at least accompany her sister. So at the age of nineteen she changed her condition, and retiring from the world with her elder sister, devoted herself to prayers for their future happiness. Then their mother, seeing that she was left alone, aged, grey haired and feeble, since her two young daughters had forsaken the world, despairing of any future happiness, at the age of forty five shaved her head; earnestly giving herself up to prayer to Buddha, with her two daughters she sought a happier birth in future.

Thus the spring passed by and the summer grew late; the first winds of autumn began to blow. Gazing at the Milky Way where the lover stars[32] meet in the heavens, when verses are accustomed to be traced on the leaves of the "kaji," watching the evening sun hide herself behind the ridge of the western hills, they likened the sun-set to the Pure Land of the West,[33] wondering when they should be reborn in that blessed region and with all desire extinguished abide there for ever. Thus they continued to meditate on their sad condition, their tears alone being inexhaustible. But one evening when twilight was passing into darkness they had shut their latticed door of bamboo and lighted their

---

[31] *Five great sins.* Sk. Pantchanantarya. i.e. five rebellions. Matricide, parricide, killing an Arhat, causing divisions among the priesthood, shedding the blood of a Buddha.

[32] *Lover Stars.* Orihime, or the Star Vega who is supposed to meet her lover Hikoboshi on the Festival of Tanabata, the seventh day of the seventh month. Of Lafcadio Hearn, The Milky Way.

[33] *Pure Land of the West.* Saiho Jodo. The paradise of Amida in the West, from which the Jodo-shu or Pure Land sect derives its name. Sk Sukhavati.

dimly burning lamp, and mother and daughters together were repeating the "Nembutsu" when there came a knocking on the lattice. The three nuns were at once overcome by fear: "Ah! perchance it is some goblin who has come to disturb our prayers and make our Nembutsu of no avail. For what human being will approach such a brushwood but as this by night to which none comes even by day? Such a slight bamboo gate as this, even if we shut it, is easy to break through, therefore let us open it without delay. If indeed it be a pitiless one who will deprive us of life, relying on the True Vow of Amida on whom we now we have called, if we ceaselessly repeat the Nemburou, surely the Buddha and the attendant Bosatsu hearing our voice will comp and meet us, leading us safely to the Paradise of the West." Thus earnestly repeating the Nembutsu, admonishing each others' hearts and holding each the hand of the other, they opened wide the bamboo lattice.

But behold it was no evil spirit but only Hotoke Gozen that stood outside. While Gio was enquiring how Hotoke Gozen had come to visit them, whether in a dream or in her actual person, Hotoke answered amid her tears. "It is a strange thing to speak of what has happened, but if I speak it not, perhaps I may not be remembered. So I will relate all things as they were from the beginning in detail. When first I came to the Court uninvited and was about to go away disappointed after being dismissed, it was at your request that I was called back again; but a woman is a person not to be relied on, so that, not obeying my own conscience, I allowed you to be sent away and even stayed myself in your stead. Now in consequence of this I am overwhelmed with shame and conscience stricken. When I saw you go away I felt it to be through my fault and could not feel at all happy. Moreover when I saw the lines written by your hand on the shoji, "In autumn meet with the same hapless fate," I thought it was indeed true. And then when you were once more summoned and when you recited the Imayo verse, the whole matter came to my mind again. But as I did not know where you were, I enquired and heard that you were together in a certain place absorbed in prayer and meditation. Then indeed I felt envious of you, and having zealously begged my freedom since the Nyudo has no further need of me, when I thought attentively about the matter, the glory of this Shaba-world is a dream of a dream—pleasure and prosperity, of what value are they? Very difficult it is to receive a body and obtain the mercy of the Buddha. If now I go down in sorrow to the underworld even though I escape from the endless circle of births and deaths; yea how difficult will it be to rise up again. In a world of uncertainty for both old and young how can we rely on our youth? The day when the breath enters our body or goes forth we cannot know; our life is more fleeting than gossamer or a flash of lightning; if we boast of the glory that endures for a moment, loss of happiness in the future life must be our portion. So this morning stealing out unperceived, I have come hither as you see, putting away my ordinary dress to become a recluse; thus having changed any condition, I entreat that you will condescend to pardon my former trespass, that together repeating the Nembutsu we may sit on one lotus in Paradise together. But if I can not attain my desire, I will wander away whither I know not, falling down under some tree or on some mossy bank, and ever zealously repeating the Nembutsu, I will strive to attain rebirth in Paradise."

So pressing her sleeve to her face she entreated them. Gio answered her, scarce withholding her tears: "Not even in a dream did I imagine that you would think thus, while I lived according to the custom of this fleeting world; when I thought of the unhappiness of my condition, often I felt resentment at your conduct in spite of myself, thus suffering loss in this life and the next. But as now you have changed your condition, your former faults have passed away like the dew of morning. Now do I feel extreme happiness knowing that you will without doubt attain your desire and be reborn in bliss. If people may say that my having become a nun was a difficult thing, shall I too so consider it? It was because I hated this world and wished to put an end to my life that I did this. But that you, having no resentment or sorrow, and being now but seventeen years old, should thus despise this world and so earnestly set your mind on the Pure Land, thinking only of the Noble Path, what a happy state of virtuous enlightenment is this indeed!

So the four of them retired from the world together, morning and evening offering flowers and incense before Buddha's shrine, and with one mind fervently pouring out their petitions; each one sooner or later obtaining her desire for rebirth in bliss. And in the register of the temple Cho-ko-do built by the Ho-o Go-Shirakawa the Honourable spirits of the four are found enshrined. Indeed it is a very marvellous thing.

Chapter VII.

TWICE AN EMPRESS.

From ancient times to the present day, since the families of Gen and Hei were both called in to assist in the government, if there were any who, making light of the constitution of the land, did not obey the Imperial laws, they were corrected by the other party, and thus any disorder was prevented. But after Tameyoshi was killed in Hogan and Yoshitomo in Heiji, some of the Genji went into exile and others lost their lives, so that now only the Heike were flourishing and no one else dare raise his head; and it seemed as if this state of things would last for ever. But after the death of the Retired Emperor Toba wars ensued, and murders, banishments, vacant offices and suspensions were continually occurring, so that the whole country was disquieted and society was not able to rest in peace, Especially from the period Ei-ryaku and O-ho when some personal retainers of the Retired Emperor were punished by the Imperial Court and conversely some of those of the Imperial Court were chastised by the Retired Emperor; so that high and low were afraid, and no one felt at ease, but all were as though looking into a deep pool or walking on thin ice. And the relations between the Emperor and the Retired Emperor, however estranged they night be, were remarkable for their extraordinary circumstances. According to the way of a degenerate age like this, people tried to anticipate each other in cunning. Though the Emperor was continually contradicting the orders of the Retired Emperor, yet one thing especially there was that caused great astonishment to all, and many found fault with his Majesty: it was as follows:—The Consort cf the late Retired Emperor Konoe, who was entitled to be styled Taiko-tai-kogu or Grandmother of the Emperor, was the daughter of Prince Kinyoshi the Udaijin of Oi-no-mikado. After the former Emperor had pre-deceased her she moved to the detached palace of Konoe, called Kawahara, outside the Court precincts, and about the period Ei-ryaku, having come to the age of about two or three and twenty, she was a little past her prime. But as she still had the reputation of being the first beauty in the land, the Emperor fell deeply in love with her and secretly ordered several of the bravest of his retainers to go to the detached palace, and privately sent love letters to her. She however, did not presume to assent to his August suit. So straightway showing his affection openly, His Majesty deigned to intimate to the Udaijin's family that he wished to bring her into the Palace as official Empress. Now as this was a decree unprecedented in the country, the courtiers took counsel together about it, and all uttered different opinions. There is, it must be regretfully admitted, an example in a foreign country, in that of Soku-ten Kogo of China, the Consort of Taiso of To, and thus step mother of the Emperor Ko-so, who after the death of Taiso became the Consort of Koso. This having happened in a foreign country is a different matter, but in our country from the time of Jimmu Tenno, in all the seventy or more generations of mortal Emperors we have heard of no such thing as becoming Empress for the second time. The courtiers having expressed their decision unanimously, the Retired Emperor[34] declared to the Emperor that this thing must not be but His Majesty answered: "The Emperor has neither father nor mother; we sit on the Jewel Throne by merit of the Ten Virtues.[35] Such a thing as this must be, entrusted to the

---

[34] *Retired Emperor.* Go-Shirakawa Ho-o. The Emperor at this time was Nijo Tenno.

[35] *Ten Virtues.* In Buddhism, not committing the ten wicked deeds, i.e. killing, theft, adultery, lying, exaggeration, abuse, ambiguous talk, covetousness, malice and unbelief. The expression 'Emperor of Ten Virtues' is to be explained by the saying that one who

Imperial Will."

As the date of the official entry of the new Empress was soon communicated by Imperial Edict, .the Retired Emperor could do nothing more. When the lady heard it she was overcome by tears. "If' she said "I had not out-lived my former Lord, but at the beginning of the autumn of the period Kyu-ju I had terminated my dew-like existence with his, or if I had become a nun and retired from the world, I should not have had to hear such unhappy tidings." But the Minister her father spoke as follows: "One who resists the Emperor's will is no more than a madman; already the Imperial. Edict has been published, so there is nothing more to be said; only you must go quickly. If a Prince should be born you will be styled "Kokubo, Mother of the country, and I too shall become the grandfather of an Emperor; truly an auspicious thing. If thus you will help your father it will be indeed an extremely filial act." To these words the Empress Dowager made no answer.

Somehow or other in the course of her writing practise she had written this verse:

> *"Better by far it had been to have died when in my bereavement;*
> *Than to live on and hand down a name unexampled like this."*

How this thing will be published in the world, a pitiful and sad case will people consider it!

Soon the day for the State Entry into the Palace arrived. The Minister her father and the Courtiers attendant on the Emperor hastened on the ceremony of departure from the Palace with all speed, but as she was very reluctant, evening came on and she had not yet started. Thus it was past midnight when she entered her carriage. After making her State Entry into the Palace she was conducted into the Reikei-den, and then straightway assisted in the morning ceremony of government administration. In the Imperial apartments of the Shishin-den[36] were the shoji painted with the figures of the Chinese Sages I-in, Tei-ko-rin, Gu-sei-nan, Tai-ko-bo, Ro-ku-ri Sensei, Riseki and Shi-ba. There were also shoji with paintings of long-armed people, long-legged people, and horses. The Oni-no-ma, or Devil's Room, had shoji painted with a lifelike figure of the Chinese general Ri. There is reason to suppose that the shoji of the seven Sages were painted by Owari-no-kami Ono-no-Tofu. Moreover is it not among the paintings of the shoji of the Sei-ryo-den that there is to be seen one by Kanaoka of the moon at down on the distant hills? When the retired Emperor Konoe was a child, he had

---

accumulated merit by practising the ten virtues may be reborn as an Emperor in his future existence. The Emperor is unique and has not the limitations of ordinary people.

[36] *Shishinden.* The hall in the Palace where ceremonies were performed. On its sliding panels were painted the portraits of thirty two Chinese sages.

in the course of his play made some marks on the paper, and when his former consort looked, they were there all unchanged: and she thought fondly of his memory and made this verse:

"*Ah! to think of the sorrows that note have fallen zip, oil me*
When I look at the moon, lining again I'll the Court."

And during this second intimacy with the Emperor her unspeakable sadness affected her so much that she fell, sick.

Chapter VIII.

THE QUARREL ABOUT THE TABLETS.

Now about the spring of the first year of Ei-man, His Augustness the Mikado fell sick, and in the beginning of the summer of the same year his disease became exceedingly severe. Now the daughter of the Minister of the Treasury, Iki-no-Kanemori had a son by His Majesty who was two years old, and it was expected that he would be made Crown Prince;[37] but on the twenty fifth of June scarcely had a decree been published appointing him Crown Prince than he was immediately that same night placed on the Throne: whereat everyone was much astonished. Those learned in such matters said that if investigation be made into the Imperial Line, Seiwa Tenno inherited the Throne of Montoku Tenno at the age of nine: at this time Chu-jin Ko (Fujiwara Yoshifusa) assisted his young Lord in the government, just as in China Shu-kodan administered all the affairs of state in behalf of Sei-O, and this was the beginning of the office of Sessho (Regent).

Toba-in came to the Throne at five and Konoe-in at three years of age, but even if these be quoted, the present Prince was only two years old: still even if without precedent, it is foolish to be disturbed about it. On the 27th, of July of the same year the Retired Emperor departed this life at the age of twenty two like the untimely falling of a flower in bud, and within the Jewel Curtain and the Brocade Vail all were choked with tears. That same night he was borne to Funa-oka Yama behind Rendai-no to the North East of the Temple of Ko-ryu-ji. After the August Obsequies, many priests from the En-ryaku-ji temple of Hiei-san and the Ko-fuku-ji at Nara came to blows about the question of putting up their tablets.

It was the custom after the death of an Emperor that he should be borne to the place of burial attended by the monks of the South and

---

[37] *Crown Prince*. It was the custom to proclaim the succession of the Crown Prince immediately the Emperor died (Senso), and the proper ceremony of accession (Sokui) was performed some time afterwards. This Child Emperor was Rokujo Tenno.

North Capitals, (Nara and Kyoto,) and as they went in procession round the tomb, they put up the tablets of their repective temples. When there was no temple endowed by Shomu Tenno to dispute it, the tablet of To-dai-ji was put up, and next came that of Ko-fuku-ji founded by[38] Tan-kai-Ko. Of the Northern Capital, opposite to that of Kofuku-ji the tablet of En-ryaku-ji was to be put up, after that the tablet of En-jo-ji, the foundation of Tem-mu Tenno begun by Chisho Daishi. But on this occasion the priests of En-ryaku-ji, respecting what precedent I know not, fixed up the tablet of their temple after that of To-dai-ji and before that of Ko-fuku-ji, and while the priests of the South Capital were taking counsel with one another what they should do, there stood forth two very worthless priests of the Sai-kon-do of Ko-fuku-ji, called Kwannon-bo and Sei-shi-bo; Kwannon-bo was attired in a hara-maki, or body armour, corded with black silk, and held a white hilted naga-maki or short halberd, grasped in both hands; Sei-shi-bo was in armour laced with green thread and carried a huge tachi in a black lacquered scabbard. Both of these ran up, and cutting down the tablet of En-ryaku-ji, broke it in pieces and threw them hither and thither.

Then, shouting out the words of a song, which run thus:

> *"How gaily flows the water*
> *Hark to the sound of the waterfall,*
> *Even as the sun shines,*
> *It pours unceasingly down."*

they disappeared again among the monks of the South Capital.

Chapter IX.

TILE CONFLAGRATION AT KIYOMIZU.

Now the faction of En-ryaku-ji, in the matter of resisting the violence that had been done, very carefully watched for an occasion, but said no word. After the decease of the Mikado everything, even the trees and flowers, was grief stricken and of sorrowful appearance, and after this undignified wrangle, all, high and low, dispersed to the four quarters crestfallen and abashed. On the same 29th, clay, at the hour of the Horse, hearing that a great company of the priests of En-ryaku-ji was going clown to Kyoto, Bushi and Kebi-ishi went out to Nishi Sakamoto to prevent them, but in spite of this they burst through, and a great tumult arose. Then the Retired Emperor Go-Shirakawa, how it happened is not certain, sent orders to the En-ryaku-ji faction, and, thinking that the Heike were to be attacked, sent soldiers to the Palace

---

[38] *Tankai-Ko.* Fujiwara Fuhito.

to strengthen all the guard houses for protection. The Heike all gathered together at Rokuhara, and the Retired Emperor also betook himself thither in haste. Kiyomori was at that time only Dainagon no Udaisho, and was in a very great state of agitation. Komatsu dono, wondering what all the mater was about, tried to pacify them, but there was much tumult and reviling among the soldiers. The monks of Hiei-san did not go to Rokuhara, but casually proceeded to press on to Kiyomizu, where they burned all the temple buildings and monastery. This was to revenge the insult they had received on the night of the Imperial Funeral; since Kiyomizu was a branch temple of Kofuku-ji. The day after their burning Kiyomizu, they wrote the text: "By Kwannon's aid[39] the cave of fire will become a lake," and affixed it to the great gate, but the next day another tablet was substituted bearing the text "Her wondrous power is without equal for all ages." When the crowd returned, the Retired Emperor came back hurriedly from Rokuhara, and Shigemori Kyo alone went to meet him.

The Chancellor his father did not go; this was out of precaution. When Shigemori returned his father the Dainagon spoke thus to him: "I am rather afraid of this visit of the Retired Emperor; he has been thinking of doing something or other, and sometimes he has even expressed it, and for that reason be has come, so I cannot altogether rid my mind of suspicion." You must not show any such suspicion either in word or deed," replied Shigemori, "it is not a good thing to reveal one's thoughts to people. You must submit entirely to the will of the Ho-o: If you show sympathy you may secure the protection of both 'Kami' and 'Hotoke.' If you do thus there will be no need to fear about your person." "Indeed Shigemori is most generous," said his father.

When the Ho-o returned, those retainers who were most intimate with him remarked: "What a strange thing is this that is said! The Ho-o has not the least idea of such a thing." Now a man of influence in the Ho-o's Palace named Saiko Hoshi was there at this time, and he came forward and said: "Heaven alone cannot say anything, man must say it. The Heike have now exceeding great power and I think it is Heaven's will that someone should protest." But the others said one to another: "This is not a good thing to say. Walls have ears. Take care! "whispering in trepidation. Now as this year was a year of mourning, the ceremonies of 'Gokei' (purification of the new Emperor), and 'Daishoei' (presentation of new rice to the Imperial Ancestors) were not performed.

Now Ken-shun-mon-in, while yet she was called Higashi-no-Onkata, had conceived a son by the Ho-o, and this Prince was now five

---

[39] *By Kwannon's aid.* This teat as well as the reply is a quotation from the Hokke-Kyo. By faith in Kwannon even the most difficult things can be accomplished. Here it is cited as an ironical taunt.

years old and there was a rumour that he was to be nominated Crown
Prince. So it was that on the twenty-fourth day of the twelfth month he
was suddenly given the title of Shinno. On the advent of the New Year
the era was changed to Nin-an. On the eighth clay of the tenth month of
the same year the Prince who had been raised to be Shinno the year
before was proclaimed Crown Prince at Higashi Sanjo Palace. Thus the
Crown Prince was an uncle of six years old, and the Emperor was his
nephew three years old, their relation and age being quite abnormal and
improper. Yet in the second year of Kwan-wa Ichijo had become
Emperor at the age of seven and Sanjo Crown Prince at eleven; it was,
therefore not without precedent. The Emperor (Rokujo) had come to
the throne at two years old and was dethroned when barely five,
becoming a priest on the 19th day of the second month and taking the
title of Shin-in before he had attained the age of Genpuku. Both in
China and in our own country this is the first time that such a thing has
happened. On the twentieth day of the third month of the third year of
Nin-an, the new Emperor[40] was enthroned in the Daikyoku-den. When
this Emperor came to the throne the fortunes of the Heike family stood
at their zenith, for his mother Kenshun-mon-in was the younger sister
of Hachijo-no-Ni-i Dono the wife of the Lay-priest Chancellor, while
Taira Dainagon Tokitada was her elder brother and so the Imperial
Uncle, so that he assume] the position of Regent in matters both within
and without the Court, all appointments of officials both in spring and
autumn being in his hands alone. His position was just like that of
Yokoku-chu, while his younger sister Yokihi[41] was the favourite of the
Emperor of China. How very enviable was his prosperity and
popularity. As the Nyudo consulted him about all political matters both
great and small, the people of the time called him Hei-Kwampaku. (i.e.
K responsible to Kiyomori, not, as usual, to the Emperor.)

Chapter X.

A COLLISION OF GRANDEES.

On the sixteenth day of the seventh month of the first year of Ka-o
the Retired Emperor Go-Shirakawa became a priest, but as, even after
this, he continued to direct the administration as before, there was no
difference between the Retired Emperor and the Reigning one: so that
the Courtiers of the Retired Emperor and the Military Guards (Hoku-
men) of both upper and lower ranks received rank and emolument in
abundance Still, as is the way of man's heart, they were not contented,

---

[40] *New Emperor.* Takakura Tenno.
[41] *Yokihi.* The favourite consort of Genso Emperor of To. Proverbial in Chinese and
Japanese literature as the fascination that destroys kings.

but would say to their intimate friends when they met;

"Ah, if that man loses his position then that demesne will be vacant;" or "if that fellow could be done away with, then I should get his office." The Ho-o himself murmured in secret; "From of old there have been many who have subdued the enemies of the country, but never before have they been so rewarded. When Sadamori defeated Masakado and when Yoriyoshi put down Sadato and Muneto, when Yoshihide conquered Takehira Yoshihide and Iehira a reward was given them, but it was nothing more than a demesne; so that this arbitrary conduct in rewarding them is not according to reason. This is because the times are degenerate, and the principle of monarchic government is no longer observed." He could find no opportunity to utter any open reproof however. The Heike, on the other hand, bore no special ill-will to the Imperial House.

The primary cause of all the disturbance that was to follow was that on the sixteenth day of the tenth month of the second year of Ka-o, Shinsammi no Chujo Sukemori, second son of Komatsu dono, a young man of thirteen years old who was then Echizen-no-kami, wishing to see the beauties of the snow scenery at Karino, the snow having fallen in patches here and there, went out with a train of thirty youthful retainers on horseback to Rendaino, Murasakino and Ukon-no-baba, and Hew many hawks at the quails and skylarks from morning till evening, returning to Rokuhara about twilight. Now just at this time the Sessho Motofusa was proceeding from the Palace of the Ho-o at Higashi-no-do to the Imperial Palace, and going to enter at the Yuho gate, he went southward from Higashi-no-do, and turned to the East at Oi-no-Mikado, so that Sukemori met I him face to face between Oi-no-Mikado and I-no-kuma. Immediately the Minister's retainers shouted peremptorily," Who goes there? Dismount! Dismount! It is His Excellency who passes! But Sukemori, being too proud and careless of his behaviour, his retainers too being all youths of under twenty who understood little of courtesy, spite of it being a Minister who passed, did not dismount according to custom, as etiquette demanded: on the contrary they threatened to break through his train. As it was dark perchance the Minister's retainers were not aware that it was Kiyomori's grandson, or if they were they made as if they were not, but anyhow they pulled Sukemori and all his retainers from off their horses and put them to exceeding shame. Sukemori could do nothing but make his way back to Rokuhara and relate all these circumstances to his grandfather the Lay-priest Chancellor. The Nyudo was extremely wrath; "Even a Minister," he said, "must respect my family, and it is a most hateful thing that he should insult such a young man; for a thing like this our house maybe despised. Thus I cannot help letting the Minister know these things and indeed I hope to make him rue it." But Shigemori said; "We are not affected by such a thing; if we be mocked by men like Yorimasa or Matsumoto of the Genji, then we should indeed be put to shame, but it was exceedingly discourteous of my son. not to alight when he met the Minister." Then he called the samurai who had been in attendance during the incident and said; "From henceforth take great care lest you should by mistake insult a Minister." But afterwards the Nyudo, without saying anything to Komatsu dono, collected about sixty men, led by Namba and Seno, all rustic samurai of exceeding bad manners who heeded nothing except the commands of the Nyudo, and bade them go and wait for the Minister when he went out on the twenty first day, and cut off the front hair of his outriders and retainers as a revenge for the insult to Sukemori. The samurai respectfully assented, and went forth. The Minister, never dreaming of such a thing, went out with more state than usual, owing to his having to stay in the apartments of the Sessho to fix the time for the Emperor's coming of age ceremonies, (Gempuku, Assuming the Kammuri,[42] and Reception of Officials) to be held next year. On this occasion he had to enter by the Taikenmon, and as he was going to the west of Naka-no-mikado, at Inokuma near Horikawa, he met about three hundred retainers of Rokuhara all armed to the teeth, who surrounded him on all sides with shouts of exultation: then, chasing his retainers and outriders this way and that, they treated them with contumely and cut off their front hair. Among his sixteen retainers, Takemoto, a retainer of the Udaijin also had his haircut off. When they cutoff the top knot of To Kurando-no-Taiyu Takanori they said; "You must not consider this as your own top knot but as though it were your master's."

Then poking the ends of their bows into the car, they broke the curtains, cut the harness and trappings off the oxen and drove them hither and thither, finally returning to Rokuhara with shouts of glee, whereupon the Nyudo praised them for carrying out his orders so well. But the two retainers who rode next to the Minister's car, Inaba-no-Saizukai and Toba-no-Kunihisa-Maro, though of quite low rank were very shrewd fellows, and putting the car in order again they brought their master to the palace of Naka-no-Mikado. He, wiping away his tears with the sleeves of his dress of ceremony, returned home again in a truly pitiful state. It is not necessary to speak of Kamatari and Fuhito of the Fujiwara house, but since the time of Yoshifusa and Mototsune to this day no such insult as this outrage of the Heike has ever been known to befall a Sessho Kwampaku.

When Komatsu dono heard of it he was greatly disturbed in his mind, and all the samurai who had taken part in it were dismissed from their posts. "However strange a thing the Nyudo ordered you to do, why did you tell me nothing of it," he said, "this is Sukemori's fault:

---

[42] *Kammuri*. Ceremonial head dress worn by Emperor and Nobles.

the Sendan[43] is fragrant even from the time when it has but two leaves; so even a boy of twelve or thirteen years knows what courtesy is and ought to practise it. He is guilty of unfilial conduct in bringing the name of the Nyudo into disrepute by such ill manners and must bear he responsibility." So Shigemori removed him to Ise-no-kuni a discipline. He was indeed a leader to be admired both by lord and vassal.

Chapter XI.

SHISHI-NO-TANI.

Owing to this incident the Emperor's Gempuku was postponed to the twenty fifth day of the same month, and was fixed take place at the Palace of the Retired Emperor, and as the Sessho's presence would be then required, he received an Imperial communication appointing him Dajodaijin on the fourteenth day. Soon after, on the seventeenth day, he paid a visit of thanks to the Retired Emperor, but still the condition of things generally seemed unsettled.

Thus this year ended and the third year of Ka-o began. In the fifth day of the first month the Gempuku of the Emperor took place, and on the thirteenth day he visited the Retired Emperor in state. The Ho-o and his Consort received him. His Majesty looked splendid indeed wearing the Kammuri for the first time. As Imperial Gonsort he received one of the daughters of the Lay priest Chancellor, and at the age of fifteen he was adopted as step son by the Ho-o.

Now Myo-on-in-den, (Fujiwara Moronaga) was still at this time Naidaijin-no-Sadaisho, and on his resigning this office, one Tokudaiji-no-Dainagon Jittei-no-Kyo aspired to it in his stead; Kwazan-in-no-Chunagon Kanemasa-no-Kyo also wished for it; and Shin-Dainagon[44] Narichika-no-Kyo, the third son of the late Naka-no-Mikado To-Chunagon Kasei-no-Kyo also greatly desired it. This Dainagon, being high in favour with the Retired Emperor, began to offer many prayers for it. He stationed a hundred priests before the shrine of Hachiman to read the Dai-Hannya Kyo[45] from beginning to end for seven days, and while this was taking place, three doves flew forth from Otoko-yama to the Tachibana tree which was before Koura Daimyojin and fought one another to the death. Now doves are the well known messengers of Hachiman Dai-Bosatsu,[46] and in a shrine or temple such a thing was an

---

[43] *Sendan.* S. Tchandana. Sandal Wood.

[44] *Shin Dainagon.* Newly created Dainagon, of whom there were many at this time.

[45] *Dai-Hannya Kyo.* Sk. Maha-prajna-paramita Sutra. or the Sutra of Intelligence by which Nirvana may be reached. It is the great text of Mahayana and is in six hundred volumes.

[46] *Hachiman Daibosatsu.* Hachiman, the deified Ojin Tenno, is a Shinto deity, but regarded as an avatar of Buddhism and so worshipped with Buddhist rites.

extraordinary portent. The Kengyo[47] of that time, Kyosei-hoin by
name, reported it to the Imperial Court. This was no ordinary matter, so
the omens must be consulted, and a soothsayer among the Shinto
priests, on being referred to spake thus; "This is a portent of great
weight, but it is not one that concerns the Emperor, but one of his
subjects." Then the Dainagon, not at all perturbed thereat, since in the
daytime people would see him, went out every night from his Palace at
Naka-no-Mikado Karasu-Maru to the shrine of Kamo on foot seven
nights in succession. On the last night of the seven, on his arriving
home again tired out, he fell asleep for a short time and dreamed that he
went to the shrine of Kamo and opened the door of the Holy of Holies,
whereupon a very majestic voice sounded forth with these words; "*O
cherry flowers, do not hate the river breeze of Kamo, for it will not stop
the flowers falling.*" Then the Dainagon, not at all afraid, set up an altar
in a hollow cedar tree behind the sanctuary of the Yashiro of Kamo and
put there a saintly priest and had prayers offered according to the
Dakini[48] rite for a hundred days. Then it happened that suddenly the
sky clouded over and it thundered exceedingly, a thunderbolt striking
the great cedar tree and setting fire to it so that the shrine seemed in
danger. All the priests ran together to put it out, moreover they wished
to drive out the holy priest who was praying there, but he said; "I intend
to stay praying in this shrine for a hundred days, and is now the seventy
fifth day, so I cannot depart now," and he'd not move. This was
reported by the Shrine to the Imperial Palace, but the Emperor bade
them do nothing that was not in accordance with the law. Then the
priests took white rods in their hands and struck the holy priest on the
neck so that at last they drove him out from the street Ichijo to the
southward. The gods do not accept discourtesy, and this Dainagon had
fished to become Taisho, a thing quite unsuitable to his rank, hence this
strange happening. Now at this time the appointment of officials was
not in accordance with the will of the Ho-o, nor, with that of the
Sessho-Kwampaku, but lay solely in the power the Heike. Even
Tokudaiji Kwazan-in did not get this nice, but Komatsu Dono
Shigemori, the eldest son of the Nyudo, who was then Dainagon-no-
Udaisho, changed over to "Sadaisho, while the second son Munemori,
who was Chunagon, passing over the heads of others his superiors,
became Udaisho his stead. It is quite needless to say that Tokudaiji
Dono, who was a Dainagon of high lineage and of distinguished
literary attainments and moreover head of his family, felt great chagrin
at being thus passed over in favour of Munemori, who:, as only second
son of the Heike family.

    Although it was at first rumoured that he would become a priest,

---

[47] *Kengyo.* 検校 the superintendant of a temple.
[48] *Dakini.* A mystic rite of the Shingon sect.

Tokudaiji Dono, wishing to see how affairs would turn it, merely resigned his office of Dainagon and went into retirement. Now the Shin Dainagon Narichika-no-Kyo would naturally come after Tokudaiji Kwazan-in, but how great was his wrath at the elevation of such a person as Munemori, second on of the Heike family. So he went to the length of saying that would attain his long sought goal through the destruction of the Heike. His father had only been Chunagon when he was his age, but his youngest son had become Dainagon of the upper second rank, and had received a great province as his fief, while his sons and retainers also basked in the Imperial favour. What then was lacking to him that he should plan such a thing? It seems like the action of a demon. In the period of Heiji, when he was Echigo-no-Chujo, he had taken the part of Nobuyori and ought properly to have lost his head then, but his neck was saved by the intercession of Komatsu Dono. Now however, forgetting all gratitude for this, even when no one was his enemy, he was spending all his time in preparing weapons and collecting soldiers and practising military activities to the exclusion of all else. Now Shishi-no-tani on Higashi-yama, having Miidera behind it was a very fine strategic position, and there was the mountain seat of Shunkwan Sozu, so he was always repairing thither to plot the overthrow of the Heike. One evening the Ho-o went also and with him went Joken-Hoin the son of the late Shonagon Nyudo Shinsai. During the evening banquet they talked about this matter, and Hoin said; "What a foolish thing; many people may overhear it and it will soon leak out and a crisis will ensue in the country." Then the Dainagon, changing his countenance, stood up suddenly, and knocked over with the sleeve of his 'Kariginu' a jar (heiji) that stood before the Ho-o. His Majesty asked what he meant by it. The Dainagon returning to his seat replied; "The overthrow of the Heishi." The Ho-o thereupon smiled with satisfaction and said, "Let someone advance and dance the Sarugaku." Hei Hangwan Yasuyori came forth and said; "There are too many jars (heiji) here and so we are all intoxicated." Shunkwan Sozu replied, "Then what shall we do with them?" "It is best to take off their necks," interjected Saiko Hoshi, as he took of the necks of the jars.[49] Hoin, considering this all great folly, said little. However we consider it, it was a terrible thing. Now who are those who were in favour of it? Omi-no-Chujo Reiyo, commonly called Narimasa, Hosshoji-no-Shugyo Shunkwan Sozu, Yamashiro-no-kami Motokane, Shikibu-no-taiho Masatsuna, Hei Hangwan Yasuyori, So Hangwan Nobufusa, Shin Hei Hangwan Sukeyuki. Among the retainers Tada-no-Kurando Yukitsuna was the foremost: among the Court Guards (Hokumen) also many were affected.

---

[49] *Jars.* Here main the pan or; Heishi referring to the Heike family is introduced.

Chapter XII.

THE FIGHT AT THE UGAWA.

Now this Hosshoji-no-Shugyo[50] Shunkwan Sozu was the grandson of Kyogoku-no-Gen-Dainagon Gashun-no-Kyo and the son of Kidera Hoin Kwanga. The house of his grandfather the Dainagon was not a military one, but he, being a man of violent nature, did not easily let anyone pass before his house near the Sanjobo Gate in Kyogoku, but usually would stand at the middle gate grinding his teeth in a menacing manner. Being therefore the grandson of such a formidable person, this Shunkwan also, though a priest, had a pugnacious and proud nature so that he was just the person to take part in such an unreasonable rebellion. Shin-Dainagon Narichika-no-Kyo, calling Tada-no-Kurando Yukitsuna, appointed him leader of one of the forces saying; "If you accomplish this affair successfully, you shall have as much as you wish of fief and domain." And he gave him fifty 'tan' of white silk for bow bags as a gratuity.

On the fifth day of the third month of the third year of An-gen Myo-in-den became Dajodaijin, and Komatsu Dono, passing over Gen-Dainagon Sadafusa-no-Kyo, became Naidaijin,, so that soon after there was a great banquet to congratulate him on becoming both Daijin and Taisho. The guest of honour was Oi-no-Mikado Udaijin Tsunemune Ko. The Sadaijin ought to have taken the upper seat, but as his father was Uji-no-Akusafu (Fujiwara Yorinaga), there was some fear about such a precedent.

There were no Hoku-men[51] (Imperial Guards) in ancient rimes, but they were first established from the time of Shirakawa in, and many of the Eifu obtained these posts. Tameyoshi and Morishige, who were in their youth pages called Inumaru and Senshumaru, and many other unimportant people also became Hokumen. During the time of Toba-in, Sueyori and Suenori, father and son, were both serving in the Court, and though sometimes acting as Courier from the Ho-o to the Imperial Court, always behaved in a manner suitable to their rank, but the Hoku-men of this time had too much power and did not respect Kugyo and Denjobito at all. Passing from lower Hoku-men to upper, from that many were allowed to enter the Court, and as they could achieve this they became puffed up and even went so far as to join in this foolish rebellion. Among these were Moromitsu and Narikage, who served the late Shonagon Nyudo Shinsai. Moromitsu was in the government office in Awa and Narikage was a man of the capital: he was born in a very

---

[50] *Shugyo* or Shitsuji, Chief Steward or Administrator of the temple.
[51] *Hoku-men.* Guards at the Court of the Retired Emperor.

low station, being a 'Kondei-warawa,' or foot-soldier or perhaps a kind of table page. As he was sagacious he came to be employed by the Ho-o. Moromitsu became Saemon-no-jo and Narikage Uemon-no-jo, then both of them became Yukie-no-jo. Once when. something happened to Shinsai they both became priests, taking the titles of Saemon-no-Nyodo Saiko and Uemon-no-jo Saikei; but still after this they continued to hold the office of Master of the storehouses to the Ho-o. This Saiko had a son Morotaka, who also became powerful and rose to be Kebi-ish Go-i-no-jo. Furthermore on the nineteenth day of the twelfth month of the first year of An-gen, at the appointment of officials at Tsuina, (year end ceremony) he became Kaga-no-kami.

While he was on duty in his province of Kaga he behaved in a lawless and barbarous manner, seizing the domains of shrines and temples and influential families, and doing always what was disorderly in everything. Now even if there is no virtuous governor, peaceful government may still continue, but among his arbitrary actions, during the summer of the second year of the same era, this Governor Morotaka brought his younger brother Kondo Hangwan Morotsune to act as Mokudai (Deputy). Now there was a certain mountain temple called Ugawa near the official residence of the Governor, and just as the Mokudai arrived from the capital, the priests happened to be bathing, whereupon he broke in among them, drove them off and bathed in their stead, driving away those of lower rank who were bathing near them so that his horse might be washed in their place. Thereupon the priests became very angry and cried out; "From of old this temple has been a sacred place where officials cannot enter, so let us defend our privilege and stop this invasion." Then the Mokudai replied angrily, "The former Mokudai were all fools, so the present one has no reason to follow their example: Obey the law!" But while he was speaking the priests began to drive out his men, and they on their part tried to force their way in, so that one of the legs of the favourite horse of the Mokudai Morotsune got broken in the struggle. Then with their weapons they shot and hacked at each other for several hours.

At length when night began to fall, the Mokudai, seeing that he could not overcome them, discreetly drew off his men. Afterwards the officials of the province, gathering together about a thousand men, came out to Ugawa and burnt down all the buildings of the monastery. Now Ugawa was a branch temple of Hakuzan and thither the chief priests went to appeal for help, namely Chishaku, Gakumyo, Hodaibo, Shochi, Gakuon, and Tosa-no Ajari. Hakuzan consisted of three shrines and eight temples, and all of these came out together, a great multitude about two thousand men. On the ninth day of the seventh month of the same year in the evening they made for the official residence of the Mokudai Morotsune. "Today is already past; tomorrow we will fight," they said and only went thus far that day. The dew-laden wind of autumn blew out the tough sleeves of their bow bands; the lightning flashing in the sky gleamed on the stars of their helmets. The Mokudai, fearing that he could not hold his own, fled by night to Kyoto. At the hour of the Hare (6. a.m.), the enemy rushed to the assault, fiercely shouting their war cry. From within the castle there is no sound. When they send men to explore, they report that all have vanished. Then the multitude, seeing that attack is needless, draw off their forces, and, carrying with them the sacred emblem of the middle shrine of Hakuzan, go off to appeal to Hieizan. At the hour of the Horse (12. noon.), they brought it to Higashi Sakamoto on Hieizan: from the northern provinces the thunder rolled ceaselessly toward the capital; snow fell and covered the land on the mountain and in the city: all was white even to the twigs of the evergreens on the mountains when they brought the sacred emblem to the shrine of Marodo. This shrine was the Myori Gongen of Hakuzan, the relation of the two gods being that of father and child. Though it was uncertain whether there would be any response from the deity, it was a great pleasure to the two gods to meet thus; greater even than that of Urashima[52] when he met his descendant of the seventh generation, or than that of the son of Buddha[53] at meeting his yet unknown father at Ryosen. So this multitude of three thousand priests from seven shrines each following close on the heel of the other, sleeve by sleeve continually chanted the holy Sutras; it was indeed a sight that defied description. Then the priests of Hieizan appealed to the Emperor for the banishment of the Kokushi Kaga-no-kami Morotaka and the imprisonment of the Mokudai Kondo Hangwan Morotsune, but no answer was made to the appeal. Seeing this some of the influential nobles of the Court complained to one another: "Alas! Why does not the Emperor decide the affair quickly? From old times appeals from Hieizan have been different from all others. Okura-no-Kyo Tamefusa and Dazai Gon-no-Sotsu Suenaka-no-Kyo were very important Court Officials but they were banished by appeal of Hieizan, how much more Morotaka who is a man of little account; the thing ought to be done properly." But, as the Chinese saying goes: "The high officials fear for their emoluments and do not advise the Throne, while the lower ones fear to make a mistake and so keep silent." So in this case everyone kept his mouth shut in council.

"The waters of Kamogawa, the dice of Sugoroku[54] and the monks of Hieizan are things quite beyond my control," quoth the Ho-o Go-

---

[52] *Urashima.* The tradition is that Urashima went to the Horai or Palace of the Dragon Sea god in the twenty second year of the Mikado Yuriaku, the twenty first Emperor, and came back to the coast of Tamba in the second year of Tencho, during the age of the Emperor Junwa.

[53] *Son of Buddha.* Rahula, (Jap. Ragora son) son of Siddhartha and Yas'odhara, who only met his father after the latter had become a recluse.

[54] *Sugoroku.* A game played with dice, backgammon.

Shirakawa. In the time of Toba-in too the gift of the monastery of Heizenji in Echizen to Hieizan showed no small confidence in that temple; for when Hieizan had pressed the Emperor to give it to them he had answered that it was doing evil that good might come, whereupon they appealed to the Ho-o, and Go-no-Sotsu[55] Kyobo-no-Kyo enquired, "If the monks of Hieizan bring down the sacred emblem[56] of Hiyoshi and make an appeal, what had better be done?" to which the Ho-o replied: "How difficult it is to resist the appeals of Hieizan," and complied.

Chapter XIII.

THE VOW.

Formerly, on the second day of the third month of the second year of Ka-ho, Mino-no-kami Minamoto Yoshitsune Ason had slain En-o, a veteran priest of Hiei, for depriving him of his newly obtained fief, whereupon the chief priest of Hiyoshi and the heads of Enryakuji, about thirty in all, came down with a crowd of retainers and presented a petition demanding satisfaction. On account of this, the Kwampaku of Go-Nijo (Fujiwara Moromichi) ordered Yamato Genii Nakatsukasa Gon-no-Sho Yoriharu to take measures of defence, with the result that his retainers shot arrows at the monks, killing eight of them on the spot and wounding more than ten, so that the chief priest and the rest fled in all directions. Then the superior priests of Hieizan flocked down in great numbers to report the matter to the Emperor, but were met at Nishi-Sakamoto by samurai and Kebiisni and driven back again: therefore, while the Emperor was hesitating about his decision, they brought the sacred emblem of Hiyoshi to the Komponchudo and chanted through the six hundred volumes of the Dai-Hannya Sutra before it to lay a curse on the Kwampaku of Go-Nijo. And the manner of the petition was this; Chu-in Ho-in, who presided, (at that time he was only Chu-in Gubu),[57] taking the upper seat, rung the bell and with reverence addressed the god thus, praying with a loud voice; "O thou Gongen[58] of Hachioji, who hast nurtured us and cared for us from our youth up, do thou, we beseech thee, shoot a whizzing arrow at the Kwampaku of Go-Nijo." Thereupon ensued a strange portent; someone dreamed that the whirring sound of a Kaburaya[59] was heard to proceed

---

[55] *Go no Sotsu.* Oe Masafusa.

[56] *Sacred Emblem.* The car or Mikoshi in which is the emblem of the deity, the Japanese 'ark of the covenant.'

[57] Gubu. Priest attendant on the Mikoshi.

[58] *Gongen.* a Buddha Incarnate, a Shinto deity who is so regarded.

[59] *Kaburaya.* Turnip headed arrow, having a bulb like a turnip, preforated with holes and making a whizzing sound as it flew.

from the shrine of Hachioji and go over toward Kyoto, and the next day, when they opened the lattices of the mansion of the Kwampaku they saw a branch of 'Shikimi'[60] wet with dew as if it had just come from the mountain, and that night the Kwampaku was stricken with a sore disease because of the anger of the deity and took to his bed. His mother O-Dono-no-Kita-no-Mandokoro[61] in great grief went to the shrine of Hiyoshi, clothed scantily like a very low menial, and prayed for seven days and nights, offering for the success of her petition these gifts to be dedicated to the god; a hundred performances of the dance called Shiba Dengaku, a hundred horse races, a hundred courses of equestrian archery, a hundred bouts of wrestling, a hundred priests to chant the Nio Sutra, the same number to chant the Sutra of Yakushi,[62] a hundred statues of Yakushi half a hand high, one life size figure of the same deity together with similar statues of Shaka and Amida. Beside this she had in her heart three other vows and, though there was no reason for anyone to know what was in the depth of her mind, yet wonderful to relate, at the close of the seventh night at the shrine, it happened that a boy-priest, who had come with many others from the remote province of Mutsu, died suddenly at midnight. When they carried him out from the shrine and offered prayers, to the amazement of the onlookers he stood up and danced, and after dancing for the space of about half an hour, the god entered into him and uttered this awe inspiring oracle: "Give ear O ye people: for seven days of this month the mother of the Kwampaku has prayed in retirement before me: in her heart are three vows. She asks that the life of her son may be spared: if this be granted, first she will serve the shrine among the lowest mendicants for a thousand days. I am moved with compassion that the mother of the Kwampaku, who is so great that she regards all the world as of no account, is so affected by her care for her son that, forgetting the squalor of these people, she deigns to serve the shrine among the lowest menials for a thousand days. Secondly she will build a corridor from the Hashidono of the main shrine to the shrine of Hachioji. How blessed a thing it is that such a corridor should be built, for I feel pity for the three thousand priests who must go across to the shrine whether it rain or shrine. In the third place she will endow a Hokke Mondoko[63] to be held in perpetuity every day. All these vows are by no means foolish, for though the first two might perhaps be foregone, the Hokke Mondoko is most desirable. Now the appeal that the priests made to the Emperor was very proper, but no answer was

---

[60] *Shikimi*. Illicium religiosum. A sacred tree.
[61] *O-Dono*. Fujiwara Morozane. *Kita-no-Mandokoro*. Title of the wife of Kwampaku or of a noble of one of the five families from which this dignitary was chosen, (Go-Sekke).
[62] *Yakushi*. Buddha the Healer. Sk. Bhechadjya.
[63] *Hokke Mondoko*. A Catechism of the Hokke-kyo or Saddharma-pundarika Sutra.

given, only they were shot at and killed; wherefore they came and
called on me with tears so that I was moved to compassion and felt that
it was a thing I could never forget; moreover the arrows that were shot
at them injured my body in its Buddha manifestation. See here whether
I speak truth or falsehood; "and the medium, doffing his clothing,
displayed under his left armpit a hollow like the mouth of a cup. Then
he continued: "indeed this is so grievous to me that however much she
vows I cannot prolong his life to the natural span, but if the Hokke
Mondoko be endowed I will allow him to live for three years longer. If
this be thought too little, I can do no more." With this the god ceased
and withdrew himself.

Now the mother of the Kwampaku had not said anything to anyone
about her vow so that it never entered her mind that it could be known,
and she was deeply impressed that the secret thoughts of her heart
should thus become the subject of an oracle; and especially was she
thankful that the life of her son should be prolonged for a day or even
for half an hour, how much more that three years should be granted
him. Thus, restraining her tears, she departed homeward. Afterwards
she presented her son's domain of Tanaka-no-Sho in the province of
Ki-i to the shrine of Hachioji for ever, and so it is that we hear that to
the present day the Hokke Mondoko is held every day without ceasing
at the shrine of Hachioji.

Thus the sickness of the Kwampaku of Go-Nijo was healed and he
was restored whole as before to the great joy of his family, but alas, the
three years flew by like a dream, and in the twenty-first day of the sixth
month of the second year of Ei-cho a boil broke out at the edge of his
hair, so that he took to his bed, and on the twenty seventh day of the
same month he passed away at the age of thirty-eight. Though he was
brave, strong-minded and valiant in his actions, when his illness
became critical he could not bear to die. Indeed it was a sad case, and
sadder too that he should die before his father before reaching the age
of forty. There is no reason why a father should die before his children,
but even Buddha the perfection of virtue, or the most enlightened
Bosatsu have no power to change the decrees of life and death. A god
who is really just and merciful cannot fail to punish for the good of
mankind.

Chapter XIV.

CARRYING DOWN THE SACRED CARS.

Thus, though the priests of Hieizan had many times petitioned the
Emperor for the banishment of the Kokushi Kaga-no-kami Morotaka
and the imprisonment of the Mokudai Kondo Hangwan Morotsune, yet
no answer was given them, so, without celebrating the festival of

Hiyoshi, on the thirteenth day of the fourth month of the third year of An-gen at the first hour of the Dragon, (8. p.m.) they set out with the Mikoshi or sacred cars of the three shrines of Juzenji, Marodo, and Hachioji at their head, while with them went the priests of the gods and Buddhas from Sagarematsu, Kiretsuzumi, Kamo-no-kawara, Tadasu, Umetada, Yanagihara, Tohoku-in, and others with their monks and followers, an innumerable host. As they entered Ichijo from the western side, people wondered if the sun and moon had not fallen from heaven. Thereupon the Emperor ordered the generals of the houses of Gen and Hei to secure the four quarters of the Palace enclosure and to protect the city against the priestly multitude. Then Komatsu Naidaijin Sadaisho Shigemori with about three thousand horsemen secured the three gates of the Palace called Yomei, Taiken, and Yubo, while his younger brothers Munemori, Tomomori and Shigehira, with his uncles Yorimori and Tsunemori held the south western gates. Of the Genji, Gensammi Minamoto Yorimasa the Warden of the Palace with his retainers the Watanabe father and son, and about three hundred horsemen held the Nuidono Palace at the north gate. This position being an extensive one and the troops few, they presented a very scattered appearance, so that the priests, perceiving this to be the weakest point in the defences, determined to try and bring in their sacred emblem by the north gate. Then Yorimasa quickly leapt from his horse, and taking off his helmet and rinsing his mouth with water, made humble obeisance before the sacred emblem, all his three hundred retainers likewise following his example, after which he sent Watanabe Choshichi Tonau as an envoy to the priests. He was attired that day in a 'hitatare' of light green, and body armour ornamented with cherry blossoms on a yellow ground, and wore a sword with mounts of red copper; in his quiver he carried twenty four arrows feathered with white and under his arm was a bow lacquered in black and bound with red bands. Taking off his helmet he slung it over his shoulder by the thong, and standing reverently before the sacred car, spoke thus: "Be silent a while, I pray you, and hear my message from Gensammi Dono. The appeal of Hieizan to the Throne was certainly justified, and we also regret the slowness of the decision, so that not without reason do you bring hither your sacred car: Yorimasa however has but few men wherewith to hold this gate, and if you decide to force your way in at such an unguarded place you will be a laughing stock to the children of the city and it will be remembered to your shame in days to come. If we open the gate to you we shall be disobedient to the Imperial Order and if we try to defend it, I, who have always revered the god of Iozan, can no longer follow the way of the warrior. Truly either path is beset with difficulty. The eastern side is held in strong force by Komatsu Dono, so it is there that you ought to try and enter."

On hearing this the priests hesitated and were undecided as to what to do, when some youthful and worthless ones among them cried out: "Wherefore do ye thus delay; push on through the gate." As many took up this cry, an aged priest called Setsu-no-Rissha Ko-un, the wisest of all in the three halls, stood forth and said: "This request is very reasonable. If we break through the strongest place with our sacred car it will be greatly to our credit in time to come; and moreover this Yorimasa is of the purest line of the Genji, descended from the sixth Imperial Grandson, having no equal in martial arts, and renowned not only as a warrior but also as a poet; for while Konoe-in was on the Throne, it happened that a verse-party was proposed at which the subject suggested for composition was, "Flowers in the recesses of the mountains;" and this theme embarrassed the verse-makers very much, but Yorimasa won great admiration from the Emperor by his famous improvisation;

> *"Cherry boughs do not show 'mid the trees in the depths of the mountains;*
> *But at the time of bloom, beauteous the flowers appear."*

Do not then let us put to shame one who has merited the Imperial admiration on an occasion like this. Let us carry in the sacred car elsewhere." Moved by this advice, thousands of the monks from front to rear shouted assent, and, forthwith carrying the sacred car round to the eastern side, made to enter the Palace through the Taiken gate. Here a struggle ensued, for the samurai drew their bows and shot at them so that many arrows struck the sacred car of Juzenji and some of the priests were killed, many of their followers being wounded, the noise of the shouts and groans ascending even to the Bonten Paradise,[64] while Kenro-Chijin, the mighty Earth deity, was struck with consternation. Then the priestly bands, leaving their sacred cars behind at the gate, fled back lamenting to their temples.

Chapter XV.

THE BURNING OF THE PALACE.

That night the Retired Emperor gave orders to Kurodo-no-Sashoben Kanemitsu that a council of the Courtiers should be held immediately. At the time that they brought down the sacred cars before in the fourth month of the fourth year of Ho-an, the Emperor had ordered the Zasshu to take it into the shrine of Sekizan: also in the

---

[64] Bonten Paradise. Sk. Brahmaloka. The Heavens of Brahma. Here perhaps means the third of the Three Worlds, (Sankai) which consist of the Worlds of Desire (Yokukai) The Worlds of Form (Shikikai), and the Worlds of No Form (Mushikikai) after which comes Nirvana. Sk. Kamadhatu, Rupadhatu and Arupadhatu.

seventh month of the fourth year of Ho-en, he had ordered the Betto of Gion to bring it into the shrine of Gion; now, according to the precedent of Ho-en, he ordered Gondai Sozu Choken, Betto of Gion, to bring it again to that shrine at nightfall, and this being done the arrows that stuck in it were pulled out by the priests. From of old, reckoning from the period of Ei-kyu, until now the priests of Hieizan have brought down their sacred car six times, but, though every time the samurai were ordered to restrain them, arrows had never been shot until this occasion. The people of the capital were greatly terrified, fearing that the anger of the god would bring calamity on the city.

On the fourteenth day at midnight the monks of Hieizan again flocked down into the city, so the Emperor, ordering his palanquin in the middle of the night, went to the Retired Emperor's Palace at Hojuji-den, while the Imperial Consort and the other Ladies of the Palace went in their cars to some other palace, the Kwampaku and Dajo-daijin and other inferior Courtiers precipitately following them in a panic. The Naidaijin Komatsu Dono attended them wearing ordinary dress with a quiver of arrows on his back, his heir Gon-no-suke Koremori going with him in ceremonial costume carrying a flat quiver. Both in the Palace and in the city, high and low, rich and poor, all were in a state of confusion and tumult.

Now at Hieizan three thousand priests met in council, clamouring that as their sacred car had been shot at and many of their company killed and wounded, they must burn all the temples from Omiya and Ninomiya to Kodo and Chudo as a protest against the indignity, and go forth and take up their abode on the mountain and moor. At this point it appeared that the Ho-o wished to propose something with regard to the matter, and the senior priests of Hieizan in Kyoto went to ascend the mountain to inform the others, but these came down in great numbers as far as Nishi-Sakamoto and drove them back again. Now Taira Dainagon Tokitada-no-Kyo, who at this time held the office of Saemon-no-kami, had been appointed one of the siding ministers (Jokei), and he was sent as an envoy to the monks; these however assembled in the courtyard of the Daikodo and cried out; "let us seize Tokitada, pull off his 'Kammuri' and then bind him and throw him into the lake." On seeing this, Tokitada begged them to listen quietly to what he had to say, and taking a small ink-stone and paper from his bosom, he wrote a few words and gave it to them. What they read was this; "The lawless violence of the priests is the work of a devil: a righteous monarch restrains it by virtue of his enlightened birth." Abashed by this reproof the monks forbore to lay hands on him, but admitting the truth of his statement with one accord, they all dispersed in silence to their cells and valleys. Thus did Tokitada-no-Kyo win the admiration of everyone by calming the wrath of the three thousand priests of the Three Halls by writing a few words on a piece of paper, and thus averting insult from the Emperor and himself. The monks too, who had hitherto been regarded as only wishing to stir up disorder, were now respected for their reasonable conduct.

On the twentieth day an Imperial Mandate was issued through Kwazan-in-Gon Chunagon Tadachika-no-Kyo the Jokei that the Kokushi Kaga-no-kami Morotaka should be dismissed and banished to Idota in Owari and that his Brother Kondo Hangwan Morotsune should be imprisoned: also on the thirteenth day six samurai who had shot at the sacred car were also imprisoned; they were all retainers of Komatsu Dono.

On the evening of the twentieth day at the hour of the Dog (8. p.m.), a fire broke out at Higuchi Tomi-no-koji and a great part of Kyoto was burned. A south-east wind was blowing strongly at the time and the flames swept across the city diagonally like a great wheel and burned through to the south-west, the distance of from three to five cho: a very terrible sight deed. Guhei Shinno's palace at Chigusa, the Kobai palace at Kitano Tenjin, Ritsu Issei's palace at Haematsu, the Oni palace, the Takamatsu palace, the Kamoi palace, the Kanin palace of Higashi Sanjo Fuyutsugu-no-Otodo, the Horikawa palace of Fujiwara Mototsune, beside thirty other palaces famous from ancient days. Sixteen palaces belonging to Court Nobles of the highest rank were burned, beside those of other Courtiers and high officials without number. At last the fire reached the Imperial Palace, and starting from the Shujaku gate, the Oten gate, the Kaisho gate, the Daikoku-den, the Buraku-in, the eight offices[65] of the Palace administration and the Office of Records were all reduced to ashes in a moment; the annals of families and the documents of many generations beside many treasures of great worth were all burnt to cinders. No one could estimate the damage. Several hundred people were burnt to death and cattle without number. Moreover it was no ordinary event that there were some who dreamed of two or three thousand great monkeys coming down from Hieizan with torches to set fire to the city as a punishment from the god of that place.

The Daikyokuden was burned for the first time in the age of Seiwa Tenno in the eighteenth year of Jokan, and on the third day of the first month of the nineteenth year the Coronation Ceremony of the Emperor Yosei took place in the Buraku-in. On the ninth day of the fourth month of the first year of Gwankyo they began to rebuild it, and it was finished on the eighth day of the tenth month of the second year. In the reign of Go-Reizei-in, on the twenty sixth day of the second month of the fifth year of Tenki it was again burned and on the fourteenth day of the eighth month of the fourth year of Jiryaku they again began to

---

[65] *The eight offices.* i.e. Nakatsukasa, Shikibu, Jibusho, Mimbusho, Hyobusho, Gyobushio, Okurasho.

rebuild it, but the Emperor Go-Reizei died before it was finished. In the reign of Go-Sanjo-in on the fifteenth day of the fourth month of the fourth year of Enkyu it was finished, and the Imperial Court removed to it, the literary men dedicating many compositions and the musicians making melody. As the present age was a degenerate one and the strength of the country was exhausted, it has not yet been rebuilt.

Volume II.

Chapter I.

EXILE OF THE ZASSHU.

On the fifth day of the fifth month of the first year of Jisho the Tendai Zasshu Mei-un Dai Sojo was prohibited from attending Court, and the Nyo-i-rin Honzon,[66] the tutelary Buddha of the Court, being brought back by an official of the Kurodo-dokoro, he was also deprived of his office of Chaplain-in-waiting. This was because the Kebiishicho had been ordered to hand over the ringleader of the bands of priests who had lately brought down the sacred car to the Palace. Now the Ho-o had heard a slanderous tale from Saiko-hoshi and his son to the effect that the Zasshu had some fiefs in Kaga and that when the Kokushi Morotaka confiscated them, in his resentment at it he had got the priests to make their petition so that it might trouble the Court, and this made His Majesty exceedingly angry so that he ordered him to be punished severely. So, as the Ho-o was thus ill-disposed to him, Mei-un relinquished his seal of office and resigned his position. On the eleventh day of the same month Kakukai-ho Shinno, the seventh son of Toba-in, was made Tendai Zasshu[67]: he was the pupil of Gyo-ken the Dai-Sojo of Shoren-in. On the twelfth day, in addition to depriving him of office and emoluments, two officers of the Kebiishi-cho were about to apply the examination by fire and water, putting "a cover on the well and throwing water on the fire; whereupon, fearing that the priests would again descend on them, the people of the city made a great outcry.

On the eighteenth day thirteen Courtiers below the Dajodaijin assembled in council to pronounce sentence on the ex-Zasshu. Then Hachijo-no-Chunagon Nagakata-no-Kyo, who was then only Sadaiben-no-Saisho and took the lowest seat, arose and said; "Though according to the advice of the lawyers we ought to abate the death penalty one

---

[66] *Nyoirin Honzon.* Honzon is the principal object of worship. This was a picture or statue of Nyoirin Kwannon, or Kwannon holding the sacred jewel called Nyoi Hoju.

[67] *Tendai Zasshu.* Heizan was the chief seat of the Tendai sect, so called from the mountain Tendaisan in China (T'ien t'ai) and founded by Dengyo Daishi, so the head of it was called the Tendai Zasshu.

degree and pass sentence of exile, yet, seeing that the ex-Zasshu Mei-un Dai-Sojo is not only learned in both the Tendai and Shingon doctrine, but is a man of pure and holy life who has taught the Mahayana Sutras to the Courtiers and instructed the Ho-o in the Buddhist commandments, it is indeed difficult to pass a severe sentence on such a teacher of the Sutras and the Law: it were better if we mitigate the sentence of exile." When he had thus spoken his opinion unreservedly, all the other Courtiers agreed to his suggestion, but as the resentment of the Ho-o was so deep, in the end they passed the sentence of exile. Kiyomori Nyudo also, when he heard of it, proceeded to visit the Ho-o to persuade him to remit the sentence, but the Ho-o being indisposed with a cold and unable to see anyone, he had to return without effecting anything. In the case of a priest committing a crime it is the custom that he should render up his orders and become a layman, and in accordance with this rule the ex-Zasshu took the civil title of Dainagon-no-Taiyu Fujii Matsueda. This Mei-un, we speak it with all reverence, was the son of Kuga-no-Dainagon Akimichi-no-Kyo, a descendant in the sixth generation of Guhei Shinno seventh son of Murakami Tenno, and the most revered and virtuous ecclesiastic in the land, respected by both Emperor and subject: he was also the Betto of Rokushoji, one of temples of Tennoji. Now the chief of the Court Diviners, Onyo-no-kami Abeno-Yasuchika, had said of him; "It is incomprehensible to me that such a wise man as this should take the name of Mei-un,[68] for thought the sun and moon are shining (Mei) above, yet unfortunately clouds (un) are below." He became Zasshu on the twentieth day of the second month of the first year of Ninan, and was deposed on the fifteenth day of the third month of the same year.

It is related that, on opening the treasury of the Chudo as the custom was, among various other treasures there was a box about a foot long wrapped in white linen, and when this faultless Zasshu opened it and looked therein he found a roll of yellow paper on which Dengyo Daishi had written the names of all the Zasshu who should be in time to come, and he read as far as his own name, but after that, reading no more, he rolled up the scroll again and put it back as it was before. It was very sacs that even such a venerable priest as he could not escape the results of the karma of his previous existence. On the twenty first day it was decided that he should be exiled to Izu. Many people said different things about the cause of it, but really it was owing to the slander of Saiko hoshi and his son that this thing was done. As he was to be expelled from the capital immediately, the officials who were entrusted with this duty went to his residence at Shirakawa: the Zasshu left his residence weeping and went to a place where the holy Sutras were kept near Awataguchi. At Hieizan they came to the conclusion

---

[68] *Mei-un*, written 明雲. shining clouds.

that their opponents were none other than Saiko-hoshi and his son, and writing their names on a paper they put it under the left foot of Kompira Taisho,[69] the first of the twelve Shinsho, in the Kompon-chudo and cried aloud with many imprecations on the twelve Shinsho and the seven hundred Yasha to take away the life of Saiko-hoshi and his son without delay. Only to hear them was a terrible thing. On the twenty third day the Zasshu went out from the Hall of the Sutras to his place of exile. How pitiful to behold one of the high rank of Dai Sojo, being expelled by these officials, about to cross the eastern boundary on this his last day in the capital! When he came to the shore of Uchide near Otsu and saw the white eaves of the Monju-ro shining in the sun, without taking a second glance, burying his face in his sleeve, he was choked with tears. There were many aged and virtuous priests at Hieizan but among them Choken-hoin, who was only Sozu at that time, was the most renowned, and he felt so much regret that he went as far as Awazu to see him on his way. On taking leave of him there the Zasshu, out of gratitude taught him the theory of concentration and the three contemplations,[70] a doctrine that he had kept stored up in his mind for many years and that was originally possessed by Shaka himself and handed down through Memyo[71] the Bikkhu of Benares and Ryuju Bosatsu[72] of southern India. It is most praiseworthy that though our country is on the confines of the world, small and scattered like grains of millet, and was at this time most degenerate, yet Choken, on possessing this doctrine, wept for joy as he returned to the capital. Then at Hieizan the priests again assembled and took counsel together saying;" Since the time of Gishin Osho who first held the office of Tendai Zasshu, for fifty five generations until now no Zasshu has ever been sent into exile; and when we consider that, since the period En-ryaku when the Emperor founded the Imperial Capital, and Dengyo Daishi ascended this mountain, where woman who possesses the Five Defects[73] has never set foot and taught us according to the Doctrine of the Four Enlightenments, three thousand holy priests have taken up their abode on this peak, where the Hokke-Kyo is chanted continuously, while at its foot the Spirit of the god is daily revealed to

---

[69] *Kompira Taisho*. The first of the Twelve Shinsho or Divine Commanders who led the Yasha (Sk. Yakcha) or Daring Devils, a kind of Buddhist Jinn. Sk. Khumbhira, explained as 'a crocodile'

[70] *Three contemplations*. i.e. of Illusion, Impermanence, and the Madhyamika (dissolving every proposition into thesis and antithesis, and denying both, e. g. the soul is neither existent nor non existent.)

[71] *Memyo* (lit. horse neighing) the patriarch Asvagosha.

[72] *Ryuju Bosatsu*. The patriarch Nagardjuna or Nagasena, chief representative of the Mahayana School and founder of the Madhyamika School, the greatest Buddhist philosopher.

[73] *Five defects*. or Hindrances. According to the Hokke Kyo women are unable to become either Indra or Brahma or Mara or Tchakravarti or Buddha.

men; and that just as Ryozen[74] the sacred mountain of Gesshi,[75] where is the sacred cave of Shaka, is situated on the north east of the Imperial city, so is this mountain of Hieizan also placed at the north east of Kyoto, as a sacred site to protect the land: seeing that generations of revered sovereigns and wise ministers have elected to worship therein, why, even in a degenerate age like this, do they dare to offer us so great an insult? "So all the priests of the mountain with their followers again came down to Higashi Sakamoto and held a council before Juzenji Gongen saying: "Let us go to Awazu and bring back our chief, but as he is guarded by the officials who have expelled him, it will not be so easy to take him away: thus we have no other refuge but the deities of our mountain. If we are to rescue him without any untoward event let us first obtain a favourable omen." To this end the elder priests betook themselves vigorously to prayer.

Now there was a youth of eighteen named Tsuru-maru, a servant of Yo-en Risshi a priest of Mudoji, who suddenly fell into a trance, both body and mind being in travail, so that the sweat ran from his limbs, for the Juzenji Gongen had entered into him, and he spoke saying: "Even though this is a degenerate age, how do they dare to send my priest into exile to a far country? My heart is cast down, therefore there is no reason why I should stop at the foot of this mountain from henceforth:" and he pressed his sleeves to his eyes and wept. Astonished at this portent the priestly multitude exclaimed. "If this be indeed the oracle of Juzenji Gongen, let this be a sign; restore each of these to its rightful owner: "and four or five hundred of the elder priests threw down the rosaries which they held in their hands on to the verandah of the shrine of Juzenji Gongen. Then the possessed youth, running round and gathering them up, without an error distributed them each to the one who owned it. Then all the priests wrung their hands and wept for joy at this miracle that the deity had manifested anew. "Let us go and take him from them;" they shouted as they rose up and swept on like a great cloud, while on the shore road toward Shiga and Karasaki another multitude came trooping, and yet another took ship on the lake toward Yamada and Yabase.

When they saw this the officers who were charged with the expulsion of the Zasshu scattered and fled in all directions. The multitude them came on to Kokubunji, whereat the ex-Zasshu was greatly astonished and exclaimed: "I have heard that one who is exiled by the Emperor cannot see the shining of the sun and moon, how much less can I, whom the Retired Emperor has ordered to depart immediately, remain in this place: return I beseech you to your

---

[74] *Ryozen.* Ghridhrakuta, the Vulture Peak famous for its caves inhabited by ascetics. At its foot was Radjagriha the city of royal palaces where the Magadha Princes from Bimbisara to A'soka lived.

[75] *Gesshi* India.

temples." Then advancing to the edge of the temple verandah, he addressed them thus "Since I left the princely mansion of my father and entered the school of the Tendai sect, I have studied widely the ordinances thereof, learning the doctrines of both Tendai and Shingon, being only concerned for the prosperity of Hieizan, not neglecting to pray for the welfare of the nation and deeply considering the education of the monks: to this the deities of both Koya and Hieizan will testify. There is no fault on my part, but innocent of any crime I have received this heavy sentence of exile. I have no enmity toward either the world or man or gods or Buddhas; indeed for your good intention in coming thus far to see me my gratitude is past expressing; "and he wrung the sleeves of his garment wet with tears. The priests also wept into the sleeves of their armour, but on their bringing up the palanquin and urging him to enter it, the ex-Zasshu refused and continued; "Formerly I was the chief of three thousand priests, but now I have become a mere exile, how shall I be carried on the shoulders of such noble disciples and deeply learned monks? Even if I come back again I ought to walk shod in straw sandals like any common priest." Now there was a certain disorderly priest of the Saito Hall named Kaijo-bo-no-Ajari Yukei, a huge fellow who stood seven feet high, dressed in armour of black leather and metal loosely laced, with very long thigh pieces; removing his helmet he gave it to one of his fellow priests, and leaning on the white handle of his halberd and pushing aside the crowd on either side, he stood before the ex-Zasshu. Glaring at him with wide open eyes for a while, he said peremptorily: "It is because you are of such a mind that this misfortune has befallen you. Now get in immediately!" Then the Zasshu in fear of him straightway entered the palanquin.

In their joy at recovering him only the noblest of the priests his disciples and none of those of low rank took turns in carrying his chair, but Yukei continued without being relieved, going on in front gripping both the pole of the palanquin and the handle of his halberd with such vigour that it seemed they would break asunder. Thus they traversed the eastern slope of the mountain as though they marching over level ground. Putting down the chair in the court of Daikodo, they once more held a confabulation, debating thus; "Now we have gone even to Awazu and brought back our Zasshu, but how can we appoint as our head one who is under sentence of exile by the Emperor?" Then Kaijobo Ajari Yukei again came forward and said; "This our mountain is a holy place unequalled in Nippon, a place of holy doctrine that protects our nation, the power of whose gods is very mighty. Buddha is equal in authority to the Emperor, so that men do not hold in light esteem the opinion of even the lowest priest; how much more then that of the most noble chief of three thousand priests, the holy and virtuous head of our whole mountain. That he should be punished without fault, does it not call for the wrath both of Hieizan and the capital that we should thus be made a derision to Kofukuji and Onjoji? How sad to lose the greatest master of the law of Tendai and Shingon, and that our students should for long have to neglect their studies. Make me the leader of your hosts and though I be imprisoned or exiled or lose my head, it will be a good memorial in this world and the next." Thus he spoke, weeping vehemently, and the assembled thousands assented to his words. Since this time Yukei was called 'Ika-me-bo' (the wrathful priest) and his pupil Eikei Risshi the people also nicknamed Ko-Ikame-bo, (the lesser wrathful priest).

Chapter II.

Ikko Ajari.

Now the priests brought their ex-Zasshu to Myo-ko-in which is in the southern valley of the To-to or eastern pagoda. Perchance even a Gonge (manifestation of Buddha) cannot avoid a chance misfortune like his.

Of old time in China, Ikko Ajari, Court Chaplain to the Emperor Genso of the To dynasty, was raised to favour and confidence by the Empress Yo-ki-hi, and as both then and now in great and small countries people will babble, he fell under suspicion, and even though it was groundless he was exiled to the land of Kara. To this land there were three roads; that called Rinchi-do, the Imperial Road, that called Yuchi-do by which the common people travelled, and that called Anketsu-do (dark cave way) by which criminals travelled; so this Ikko Ajari, having committed a great crime, had to go by the Anketsu-do, and for seven days and nights without seeing the sun or moon he travelled on it. As it was thus dark and there was no inhabitant, he lost his way, wandering on the shore of a lake and going through a deeply wooded mountain, while only the voice of a bird was heard in a watery ravine. While he was weeping there so that his garments were wet as moss, a god took pity on him, exiled without cause, and delivered him by showing nine luminaries in the sky. Then Ikko, biting a finger of his left hand, drew the nine luminaries on his left sleeve with the blood. So it is that in both China and Japan the mandara[76] of nine luminaries is the chief object of worship of the Shingon-shu.

---

[76] *Mandara.* A circular picture in which is depicted a representation of the various heavens and Buddhas and Bodhisattvas.

Chapter III.

EXECUTION OF SAIKO.

When the Ho-o learned that the priests of Hieizan had prevented the Zasshu from being exiled, he was much perturbed then Saiko-hoshi said; "From of old the monks of Hieizan have been in the habit of making these disorderly uprisings; this is not the first time, but this time they have gone too far, and if you do not punish them in an exemplary manner from henceforth the government will always be unstable." Thus he spoke, unaware of the prayers for his own destruction, or of the appearance of the god of the mountain, and confusing the mind of the Emperor. "A subject who advises the Emperor falsely stirs up confusion in the country." This is a true saying; even though one tries to grow many orchids, the wind of autumn will destroy them, and even when rulers desire to be clear in their minds a lying minister will speak thus to darken their counsel.

Soon it was rumoured that the Ho-o had ordered Shin-Dainagon Narichika-no-Kyo to assemble his retainers and attack Hieizan, and that some of the priests of that mountain thought that as they were subjects of the Emperor, it was not right to resist the Ho-o's command and secretly intended to obey them so the ex-Zasshu, living at Myokobo, hearing that the minds of the priests were thus divided, was much troubled wondering what fresh misfortune would come upon him; but still no decision was made concerning his sentence of exile.

Thus the long cherished plan of the Shin Dainagon for the overthrow of the Heike was delayed owing to the riotous conduct of Hieizan. Some deliberation and preparations had been made, but they were only pretence, and as it seemed that the plot was not likely to succeed, Tada Kurando Yukitsuna, who had been entrusted with the arrangements, thinking apparently that it was no use going further, used the linen which had been presented to him as material for bow cases to make 'hitatare' and 'katabira' for his retainers. Then, on meditating over the affair and seeing the prosperity of the Heike, it seemed a very difficult thing to overthrow them; and if the matter chanced to leak out, he himself would be the first to be executed, so he thought it would be better to betray it before anyone else could do so, and thus save his own life. So on the twenty ninth day about midnight he went to the mansion of the Nyudo at Nishi Hachijo saying that he had important business. As Yukitsuna was not accustomed to visit him, the Nyudo, wondering why he had come, sent Shume-no-Hangwan Morikuni to enquire. Yukitsuna however replied that he could not tell anyone else, whereupon the Nyudo himself came out to the corridor at the middle gate. "As it is now midnight," he said, "what can you have to any to me at such a time?" "In the daytime there are many people about," replied Yukitsuna," so I have come under cover of night; what do you think is the meaning of the warlike preparations now going on at the Palace of the Ho-o?" "I understand that the Ho-o has a plan to attack Hieizan," replied Kiyomori carelessly. Then Yukitsuna drawing nearer whispered to him: "That is not the reason, it is against your house that they make these preparations." "Has the Ho-o any knowledge of it?" asked the Nyudo. "Without doubt he knows about it; it is with his authority that Shitsuji-no-Betto Narichika-no-Kyo is collecting his forces." And he went on to explain what Yasuyori, Shunkwan and Saiko had, done; after which he retired and the Nyudo called out loudly to summon his samurai. Yukitsuna, having said what had better have been left unsaid, fearing that he might be called on to prove his words, girded up his hakama and fled from the precincts though no one pursued him, feeling like one who is afraid of being caught in the fire that he has kindled. Then the Nyudo, calling Chikugo-no-kami Sadayoshi, cried out. "The capital is full of traitors who plot to overthrow our house, make haste and report it to all our clan and assemble the retainers quickly,—let all hear!" Soon Udaisho Munemori, Sammi Chujo Tomomori, To-no-Chujo Shigehira, Sama-no-kami Yukimori and others of their kinsmen came up in full armour with their bows on their backs, together with a multitude of samurai innumerable. That night there assembled at the Nyudo's mansion of Nishi Hachijo about six or seven thousand armed men. The next day was the first day of the sixth month and, while it was yet dark, Kiyomori called Abe-no-Sukenari and ordered him to proceed to the Palace of the Retired Emperor, and calling Taizen-no-Taiyu Nobunari, to say to him as follows; "There is a plot of Shin Dainagon Nari-chika-no-Kyo and other retainers of the Ho-o to overthrow our fan lily and throw the empire into confusion: arrest everyone and make enquiry; the Ho-o is evidently aware of the plot." Sukenari immediately hastened to the Palace and, calling Nobunari gave him the message. He, turning pale, straightway went and told the Ho-o. "Ah, someone has revealed the secret," he remarked, "but even so, how did it come out, I wonder?" And he gave no direct answer.

Sukenari, immediately returning, reported this to his master, at which the Nyudo replied that evidently Yukitsuna had spoken the truth and that if he had not revealed the plot their lives would have been in danger. Then he gave orders to Chikugo-no-kami Sadayoshi and Hida-no-kami Sadaie to arrest all who were implicated; so, taking bands of two or three hundred horsemen, they went hither and thither and seized them all. He also sent foot soldiers to the mansion of the Shin Dainagon at Naka-no-Mikado Karasu Maru with orders that he should come immediately. The Dainagon, thinking that it was not anything concerning himself, but that Kiyomori intended to forbid the Ho-o to attack Hieizan, though as the latter was much enraged it would be of no avail, gracefully donned a costume of delicate material and mounted into an elegant car, accompanied by three of four retainers, his servants and ox-drivers being more ceremonial than usual; only to find out soon after that it was for the last time. When they came near to Nishi Hachijo for four or five cho they saw nothing but armed men and he felt a little anxious, wondering why there were so many, but when they arrived at the front gate and were bidden to enter, they saw that the inside also was filled with dense masses of soldiers. At the middle gate many fierce looking warriors were standing, who, when they saw the Dainagon enter, cried out; "Shall we seize him and bind him?" Whereupon the Nyudo, looking out from behind a curtain, replied; "There is no necessity." So fourteen or fifteen soldiers, surrounding him on all sides and seizing him by the hand, pulled him on to the verandah and shut him into a small apartment. The Dainagon, like one in a dream, did not comprehend what was happening. The samurai who were with him, separated by overwhelming forces, were scattered in different directions, and the servants and ox drivers in consternation abandoned the ox car and took to flight. Then Omi no Chujo Nyudo Renjo, Hos shoji-no-Shugyo Shunkwan Sozu, Yamashiro-no-kami Motokane, Shikibu-no-Taiyu Masatsuna, Hei Hangwan Yasuyori, So Hangwan Nobufusa, and Shin Hei Hangwan Sukeyuki were also arrested and brought in: Saiko-hoshi, on hearing this, fearing that it was a matter concerning him also, rode in haste to the Palace of the Ho-o. On the way, however, meeting some soldiers from Rokuhara they accosted him, saying; "You are required at Rokuhara, haste thither at once;" but he replied that he had business at the Palace of the Ho-o and afterwards would do as they ordered. "What is it that you have to say to him, O most worthless of priests?" they answered as they dragged him from his horse and carried him bound to Rokuhara. As he was the mainstay of the plot from the beginning, they bound him firmly and put him in ward in a certain courtyard. Then Kiyomori. standing on the verandah above, glared at him fiercely for a while and then exclaimed; "This is the way I treat a worthless fellow like you who makes plots against me. Bring him here!" So they brought him to the edge of the verandah and the Nyudo trampled on his face with his footgear, "You, who were at first a Courtier of the lowest rank and were advanced by the favour of the Ho-o to a high office that you did not deserve, you and your son, have behaved outrageously, and procured the exile of the Tendai Zasshu, though he was guilty of no offence, and not only that but you have taken part in a plot against me and my house. Now confess the whole thing at once and tell the truth!" But Saiko, being by nature a bold fellow, showed no fear, and recovering himself and not at all taken aback, replied with a laugh; "As I served as a confidential retainer of the Ho-o's Household I cannot say I took no part in the raising of forces by the Shitsuji-no-Betto Narichika-no-Kyo. Indeed I did have a hand in it. Why do you say things that I cannot overlook? Before other people it does not matter but in my hearing you shall not speak thus. You are the eldest son and heir of the late Gyobu-no-Kyo Tadamori, and you did not enter the Court at all until you were fourteen or fifteen years old, and then you were serving in the train of the late To-Chunagon Kasei-no-Kyo of Naka no Mikado, when even the children of the city called you Takaheita: but in the period Ho-en you arrested three pirate leaders and were rewarded with the fourth rank; and when you were called Hyoe-no-suke of the fourth rank, people said it was too high a rank for you, so it is certainly too much that, being of the line of a men who had not the right of going to Court, you have raised yourself to be Dajo-daijin. From old time there is precedent for military families like mine to obtain fiefs and hold positions in the Kebiishi. That is not promotion beyond one's position." Thus he spoke out boldly without fear, and the Nyudo could neither restrain his anger nor could he utter a word for rage; after a while he managed to ejaculate; "Do not take leis head off now, examine him well aid find out all the plot; then away with him to the river and behead him." There upon Matsuura-no-Taro Shigetoshi applied torture by squeezing his arms and legs. Saiko did not resist at all and the torture was very severe: after they had written his confession on four or five sheets of paper, his mouth was split open by order of Kiyomori and he was executed at Shujaku on the west side of Gojo.

His eldest son Kaga-no-kami Morotaka, who had been dismissed from his office and banished to Idota in Owari, was now ordered to be executed also by Oguma-no-gunshi Koresue of that province. His younger son Kondo Hangwan Morotsune was also taken out of prison and put to death. The third son Saemon-no-jo Morohira together with three of his retainers lost his head also. These men had all been raised up from humble positions and interfered in matters in which they had no right to meddle, procuring the exile of the innocent Tendai Zasshu, and thus they met their fate and were overtaken by retribution as a punishment from the deity of Hieizan.

Chapter IV.

THE LESSER ADMONITION.

The Shin-Dainagon, being thus confined in a small chamber, was in such a state of terror that a cold sweat broke out all over him and he thought to himself; "Ali, this is the result of someone letting out our secret. Who can it be that has turned informer? It must be one of the Ho-o's Palace Guards." While he thus continued turning over everything anxiously in iris mind, he heard a loud footfall approaching from behind and thought it was the soldiers coming to put him to death.

It was however the Nyudo himself who came tramping loudly over the Wooden floor and abruptly opened the shoji of the apartment. Dressed in a somewhat short costume of white silk and striding along in an o-kuchi-hakama,[77] wearing a sword without any decoration loosened in its scabbard, Kiyomori, in wrathful mien, glared fiercely for a space at the Dainagon. "You ought to have been executed at the time of the revolution of Heiji, but Shigemori saved your neck. That kindness you have forgotten. What is your grievance that you wish to overthrow our house? To understand gratitude is the part of a man, but he who forgets it is merely an animal; as however our family is not yet doomed to fall, I have had you brought here so that I may find out what has been going on lately." "You are entirely mistaken," replied the Dainagon," someone must have surely slandered me, so pray make close enquiry into everything." At this Kiyomori interrupting him called, "Ho! there." When Sadayoshi immediately appeared, "Bring the confession that fellow Saiko has made" ordered the Nyudo, and on its being produced read it through loudly several times to the Dainagon, "Now you villain, what have you to say to that?" he shouted, as, flinging the document into his face, he slammed the shoji to and went out. His anger was not yet appeased however, so he called to Tsuneto and Kaneyasu and bade them throw the Dainagon down into the courtyard. At this they demurred saying that Komatsu Dono might not approve of such treatment.

"What?" demanded Kiyomori, "do you regard the orders of Shigemori, and pay no attention to mine? It seems I can do no more." But they, thinking it inadvisable not to obey after all, seized the Dainagon by both his hands and threw him down into the courtyard. Then the Nyudo, exulting in his revenge, ordered them to throw him to the ground and beat him till he cried out, whereupon the two, wishing to spare him, whispered: to the Dainagon's ear that he should cry out quickly, and so threw him down and he cried out several times. It looked just like a scene in the Meido[78] when those who have sinned in this Shaba[79] world are tortured by the devils after being weighed in the balance and their misdeeds examined in the mirror of clear crystal. Thus in China also Sho and Han were thrown into prison, and Kan and Ho were slain with their families to the third generation; Choso also was executed and Shugi was punished. Of these men the first four were all loyal subjects of the Emperor Koso, but through the slanders of

---

[77] *Okuchi-hakama.* Cf, Sansom Tsurezure Gusa p. 117, a variety of hakama or loose trousers.

[78] *Meido.* The dark road, the underworld, Sk. Nirika. Here men were judged by Emma-O or Yama Raja and his attendants, (Ahora Setsu) by means of the balance and the mirror that reflected all things.

[79] *Shaba.* Sk. Sahaloka. perh. world of suffering. Those subject to transmigration. popularly for this world.

worthless fellows they were innocently disgraced.

On this misfortune happening to the Shin-Dainagon his first thought was about the fate of his son Tamba-no-Shosho Naritsune and the other younger children. As it was now the sixth month it was extremely hot, and as he could not loosen his dress of ceremony, his condition became unbearable so that he gasped for breath and sat bathed in tears and sweat. Though he thought that Komatsu Dono would not forsake him, there was none to bring him any tidings.

After some hours had passed, Komatsu Dono, undisturbed as usual either by good or ill, arrived at Rokuhara with his eldest son Gon-no-suke Koremori riding at the back of his car. He had four or five guards in attendance and two or three retainers but no military escort, and his bearing was entirely calm and unmoved. The Nyudo and his family were somewhat surprised to see him come thus, and on his alighting at the middle gate Sadayoshi came forward and said; "Why do you go without an armed escort seeing that the times are so critical?" "Critical is a word that should only be used of the affairs of the nation," replied the Minister, "we cannot use it of our own private quarrels." On hearing this the crowd of samurai who stood by armed to the teeth looked somewhat uncomfortable. Shigemori then proceeded to search through many rooms to find where the Dainagon had been confined, and at last came to a shoji over which was an arrangement of beams and ropes like a spider's web. Ordering these to be removed he discovered the Dainagon within. He, sitting choked with tears did not at first look up, but on being greeted kindly by Shigemori his face lighted up like that of a sinner in Hell who sees the approach of Jizo Bosatsu. "I know not what is the reason," he said, "but this morning I have fallen into this evil plight; as however you Nave deigned to come to me, I am not without hope that you will be able to deliver me. When in the period of Heiji I was about to be executed, it was your compassion that saved my life and since then I have advanced to be Dainagon and obtained the second Court Rank, being scarcely more than forty years old Although I can never repay your kindness, I pray you to save my worthless life once more. If that be granted I will retire from the world, and entering the way of Buddha retire to some hamlet far remote, where I may give my whole mind to attain enlightenment as a Buddha in the future life." "Even so" replied Shigemori, "I think they will not go so far as to put you to death, and should they wish to do so, I myself will go surety for your life, so set your mind at ease." Then seeking out his father Kiyomori, he addressed him thus; "I pray you consider most carefully what you do in putting the Dainagon to death, for since his ancestor Shuri-no-Taiyu Akisue, who was Courtier of the Retired Emperor Shirakawa, he has been the only one of his family to be promoted to Dainagon of the upper second rank: he is, besides, extremely high in favour with his master the Ho o,. wherefore it is not good to put him to death. It will be quite sufficient to expel him from the capital. Kitano Tenjin, owing to the slander of the Minister Tokihira, spent his remaining days in sorrow and exile across the western sea, and the Minister Nishi-no-miya, owing to the traduction of Tada no Manchu, spent his days in bitterness amid the misty mountains of the Sanyo, both being innocent of any crime. All this was luring the righteous era of En-ki, and tradition calls it the injustice of the Mikado of An-wa; so if even in great antiquity such things happened, how much more in an evil age like this? Even a wise ruler makes mistakes; how much more an ordinary person Since you have already arrested him, there is no more cause for anxiety, even if you spare his life.

The Chinese sages have said; "[80]Give the benefit to the accused where guilt is in question, but give him the credit where merit is in question." Moreover, to consider another side of the matter, I have married the younger sister of this Dainagon, while my son Koremori has married his daughter, and being bound by such intimate ties, perhaps you may think that is the reason I speak thus. That however is not the case, but it is for the sake of the Emperor, of our country, and of the time, that I entreat you. Remember what an extreme measure it was considered when the late Shonagon Nyudo Shinsei, when he was regent, revived the death sentence, which had not been imposed since Uhyoe-no-kami Fujiwara Nakanari was condemned to death, in the time of Saga Tenno twenty five generations ago, and had the body of Uji-no-Akusafu (Sadaijin Yorinaga) dug up and the head cut off: and though people may have said in old times if the ringleaders were executed, rebels would cease out of the land, yet, only two years after Hogen there was the rebellion of Heiji, when the body of Shinsei which had been buried was dug up and the head cut off and exposed; truly a salutary example that the deed which he did in Hogen should so soon be paid back on his own head. Now as this man is not a rebel against the. throne, you ought to hesitate to put him to death. I do not think that our family is at the summit of its prosperity yet, but I hope that its present glory will continue for many generations: yet, as the good or evil acts of the sires are visited on their descendants, we see that "the accumulation of good deeds produces happiness whereas misfortune waits at the gate of him who piles up evil ones." So at all events he must not beheaded this evening." So the Nyudo, admitting the reasonableness of this speech, gave up the intention of executing him.

Then Shigemori went out to the middle gate and thus addressed the samurai; "You must by no means put the Dainagon to death even if you are ordered to do so, for when the Nyudo is angry he is apt to do rash things which he afterwards regrets; so do not make mistakes that you will be sorry for afterwards." At these words all the men at arms

---

[80] Give the benefit etc. From then 尙書大禹謨.

trembled with apprehension. Shigemori continued; "this morning Tsuneto and Kaneyasu treated the Dainagon harshly and violently: this was a very ruffianly deed; why did they not fear lest I should hear of it? Rustic samurai are all of this kind." Then Namba and Seno also quaked with fear, while Shigemori, having thus admonished them, returned again to the Komatsu Palace.

The retainers of the Dainagon had hurried back to their lord's mansion at Naka-no-Mikado-no-Karasu-Maru, and related all that had passed, whereupon their mistress and her ladies lifted up their voices and wept. Then the retainers, telling them of the arrest of the heir and other younger members of the family, advised them to hide themselves quickly. "Having come to this," replied the wife of the Dainagon, "even if we live unmolested, what hope have we for the future? All that I wish now is to die with my husband like dewdrops that melt on the same evening. Alas! that I did not know that this morning's meeting would be our last." And casting her clothes about her she threw herself on the ground in despair. After a while however, as there was a rumour that the soldiers of the Heike were approaching, and not wishing them to behold her wretched condition, taking a daughter of ten years old and a boy of eight with her, she got into her carriage and fled away, going she knew not whither. As she could not continue thus without any aim, going up to Omiya and reaching the U-rin-in, a temple on the northern hills, she alighted before one of the buildings, when those who had so far accompanied her, fearing for their lives, took leave of her and returned again to the city. What a sad plight it was for her, left with only these young children, and with no one to help her with sympathy or advice. As she saw the shades of night falling, and reflected that her lord's life might pass away like the dew that very evening, she wished that she might give up the ghost.

At the Dainagon's mansion many retainers and ladies were left, but they were too apprehensive even to take any food and did not so much as shut the gates, and though there were many horses in the stables there was none who gave them any food. Formerly from early dawn there would be rows of carriages at the gate and innumerable guests coming to spend the day in dancing and merriment, as though the cares of life did not exist, while their inferiors who approached them dared not so much as raise their voices in their presence. This haughty state continued until yesterday, but in one short night all was changed. How are the mighty brought low! Now can we appreciate, the saying of Ko-sho-ko,[81] "Pain comes when pleasure is at it height."

---

[81] *Ko-sho Ko.* Oe Tomotsuna. The whole verse runs: Those who live; must die; even Buddha cannot escape the smoke of the sandalwood; when pleasure is at its height comes pain; even the angels have their five failings.

Chapter V.

THE SHOSHO IS PUT IN CHARGE OF THE SAISHO.

Tamba-no-Shosho Naritsune stayed that night in the Hojujiden, the Palace of the Retired Emperor, and did not go out at all. The retainers of the Dainagon hurriedly rode up to this Palace and summoned him forth, and on their relating the arrest of his father to him, he replied: "Why did not the Saisho (Chief Minister) inform me of an affair like this until now?" But hardly had he finished speaking when a messenger arrived from the Saisho. Now this Saisho was the younger brother of Kiyomori, and his mansion was by the outer gate (kado-no-waki) of Rokuhara, so that he was called Kadowaki-no-Saisho; and he was the father in law of Tamba no Shosho. "I know not the reason," said the messenger, "but I have been ordered by Nishi Hachijo to bring you hither at once." On hearing this the Shosho summoned the ladies-in-waiting who always attended him and said: "Last night I heard some uproar outside and thought it might be the priests of the mountain coming down into the city; but it seems to be something connected with my affairs. As the Dainagon is to be put to death this evening, I also shall be included in the same condemnation: I should like to visit the Ho-o once more, but as this misfortune has happened to me, I must refrain." The ladies then went to the Ho-o and reported the matter to him. The Ho-o, understanding from Kiyomori's messenger that morning that the secret plot had been revealed, intimated that he wished The Shosho to visit him, whereupon the latter did so. The Ho-o, weeping said nothing, while the Shosho, also choked by tears, was silent likewise. So, after a short space, he retired from the Presence and the Ho-o saw him off at some distance, saying, "How sad is this degenerate age! This is the last time I shall see him: "and he could not restrain his tears. When the Shosho retired from the presence of the Ho-o, all the Courtiers and Court Ladies were much grieved at parting with him, pulling him by the sleeves and shedding tears, so that no one was dry-eyed.

When he arrived at the house of his father-in-law the Saisho found that his wife was just on the eve of her confinement, and that, as the result of the shock of the morning's upset, it seemed as if she were about to expire. Now since his departure from the Ho-o's Palace he had not ceased to weep, and now, seeing the condition of his wife, he gave way completely to his despondency. Also the milk-nurse of the Shosho, named Rokujo, came to him in tears and said, "Since I came here as nurse I have brought up my lord until now, and since I brought him up I did not grieve at my increasing years but only rejoiced seeing my lord grow up; and though not yet quite full grown, has this year attained the age of twenty-one. Never for even half an hour have I been parted from him; when he went to the Palace of the Ho-o I was always anxious if he came back late, gad now at last what misfortune has he met with?" Then the Shosho tried to comfort her, assuring her that as the Saisho was there he would most probably escape with his life. But she would not be consoled and gave herself up to violent weeping in spite of the presence of other people. Meanwhile several Messengers came from Nishi Hachijo and the Saisho decided that there was nothing to be done but to go, whatever might happen, and started forthwith, the Shosho taking his seat at the back of his car. Since the age of Hogen and Heiji the Heike family had nothing but prosperity, and no misfortune came their way, save only to this Saisho who suffered through his unhappy son-in-law.

When they came to the Nishi Hachijo mansion and enquired what they were to do, they were told that the Shosho must not enter within the gate, so leaving him in the care of some samurai, the Saisho entered by himself. Then Kiyomori's men surrounded the Shosho on all sides and guarded him strictly, and being thus parted from the Saisho on whom he so much r; lied, his heart failed him and he felt very forlorn.

The Saisho went in to the middle gate but the Nyudo did not come out to meet him, so after a while he sent word by Gendaiyu-no-Hangwan Suesada saying. "I much regret that I am related to this troublesome fellow but it cannot be helped; his wife is now ill and this morning misfortune has fallen upon him so that she is now at the point of death. If he is in my hands I will not permit him to do anything improper, so I pray you give him into my charge for the present." When Suesada reported this to the Nyudo, Kiyomori only answered, "This unfortunate Saisho has no discrimination", and gave no decision about the request. Some time afterward however he said to Suesada, "The Shin Dainagon Narichika-no-Kyo and other Imperial retainers intended to destroy our house and disturb the peace of the land, and this Shosho is the eldest son of this man. Whether he is deeply implicated in it or not I cannot overlook it. If this rebellion had been carried out would you have been likely to be unharmed?" When the Saisho heard this he looked entirely crestfallen and replied; "Since Hogen and Heiji I have many times risked my life in battle on your behalf and hereafter also I will ward off from your person the strong wind of adversity. Though I am an old man I have many young children and they too may become a strong protection, yet when I ask you this one thing namely to put the Shosho in my charge, you do not willingly accede. That must be because you think that I too have some treasonable design. If I am thus doubted it is of no use my living any longer in the world, so I will retire and become a monk, dwelling in seclusion in Koya or Kogawa and praying earnestly for a rebirth in a better world. Verily the relationships of this world are of no avail. When one is in the world one has hope, but when the object of hope cannot be attained, spite arises. Nothing is better than, despising this fleeting world, to enter the way of Buddha." Then Suesada repeated to Kiyomori the words of the Saisho, adding that his mind seemed to be made up and begging the Nyudo to grant his request. Truly it would be a foolish thing for him to retire from the world, so I will place the Shosho under his charge," replied Kiyomori, and Suesada returned and informed the Saisho.

"Ah" he exclaimed, "it is not good to take the responsibility for the child of another; if he was not thus related to my daughter I should not be so distressed" and he went out. The Shosho who was waiting for him enquiring how the matter had gone, he replied." The Nyudo was very wrathful and would not receive me, repeating that he would not grant my request, but when I threatened to become a monk, then he consented to put you in my charge; but I fear it is only for a time." "Then I shall at any rate obtain a reprieve for a while by your favour," replied the Shosho, "and, by the way, have you heard aught of the fate of my father the Dainagon?" "Truly" answered the Saisho, "I could only put in a word on your behalf, I could certainly go no further." Thereupon the Shosho, bursting into tears "I fear for my own life, it is true, but how much do I wish to see my father again. This night the Dainagon is to be put to death, so what use for me to live longer? I wish to share my father's lot whatever it may be, so do you please inform the Nyudo of my desire." The Saisho, much troubled at this prospect, replied; "I spoke of your affair indeed, but farther than that I did not go; I have heard however that Shigemori the Naidaijin advised his father this morning not to put him to death, so probably his circumstances will not be so unfavourable." Without waiting to hear any more the Shosho clasped his hands together and wept for joy. Who but a child would be able to forget all anxiety for himself and thus rejoice at his father's safety? Indeed the strongest bond of relationship is that of father and child. How necessary a thing it is to have children. Then the Saisho and the Shosho returned to the mansion of the Saisho in the same carriage just as they had gone forth: and the ladies in waiting and the retainers wept and rejoiced on their arrival as over those who have come back from the dead.

Chapter VI.

THE ADMONITION.

The Lay-priest Chancellor, though he had had so many people arrested, still seemed unsatisfied. Coming forth to the middle gate of his mansion with a menacing aspect, he called in a loud voice for Sadayoshi. He was dressed in a red embroidered 'hitatare' worn over a black suit of armour with the breastplate ornamented with silver, and gripped under his arm the short halberd with silver mounted handle that he had received many years before from the god of Itsukushima when he was favoured with a divine message in a dream, while he was yet only known as Aki-no-kami, and which he always kept by his pillow.

Chikugo-no-kami straightway stood before his lord. He was attired in 'hitatare' of yellowish red hue and his armour was of scarlet. "What do you think, Sadayoshi? In the period of Hogen, Taira Uma-no-suke Tadamasa and more than half our family came to the help of the Newly Retired Emperor (Sutoku Tenno) and Ichi-no-miya (Shigehito Shinno) was the adopted son of the late Gyobu-no-Kyo Tadamori my father, so that it was most difficult for me not to support him; in spite of these things however, following the instructions of the late Emperor (Toba Tenno), I assisted the party of the Emperor (Go-Shirakawa Ho-o). This was one service that I did for the Imperial House. Then at the time of the rebellion of Nobuyori and Yoshitomo in the twelfth month of the first year of Heiji, when the Palace was seized and the Court entered, the country therefore falling into disorder, at the risk of my life I drove out the rebels and arrested Tsunemune and Korekata. Many times therefore have I put my life at the disposal of the Imperial Court, so that whatever people may say against us the Imperial House ought not to forsake our family even to the seventh generation. Still the Ho-o has listened to such a pair of worthless rascals as Narichika and Saiko. This plan of destroying us, which the Ho-o seems inclined to, must by no means be carried out. I suppose that hereafter, if any accuse us falsely, the Emperor is likely to issue a mandate for our destruction, and if we are once proclaimed enemies of the Emperor, however much we regret it, we cannot redeem ourselves again. Formerly for a time until the country was quiet again the Ho-o was removed to the North Palace of Toba; what then do you think about bringing hire here to Rokuhara now? If this be done perhaps some of the Imperial Guard may make armed resistance; so order our retainers to make ready, I will serve the Ho-o no longer. Saddle my horse and bring out my general's armour!"

Then Shume-no-Hangwan Morikuni rode hard to the mansion of Shigemori and hurriedly told him what was happening. Without waiting to hear all the Naidaijin exclaimed, "Ali, now they have taken off the head of Narichika-no-Kyo." "That is not so" replied Morikuni, "but the Nyudo has assumed his general's armour and is going to lead his retainers to the Ho-o's Palace at Hojuji, declaring that until peace be restored he will remove the Ho-o to the North Palace of Toba, or if not will bring him to Rokuhara; but we think his real intention may be to banish him to the western confines of the country. Then the Naidaijin, doubting if this was really so, but judging from his father's demeanour of the morning that he was quite beside himself, hastily got into his car and proceeded to Nishi Hachijo.

When he alighted at the gate and entered, he saw the Nyudo in his body armour with scores of Courtiers and nobles of his family all in armour and 'hitatare' of various descriptions and colours, sitting in two rows along the verandah by the middle gate, besides a crowd of provincial lords and bodyguards and officials of all ranks overflowing into the courtyard beneath: their standards were marshalled and their horse-girths and helmet thongs tightened so that they looked as if immediately about to set forth.

Komatsu dono, clad only in 'raoshi', with his 'hakama' of large pattern girt up, and an 'eboshi' on his head, entered with a peaceful rustle of his silk garments, making a striking contrast to them all. Kiyomori, casting down his eyes in embarrassment, thought in his heart, "Ah, how calmly does this minister deport himself as one detached from the world; it seems I must rebuke him." Still, even though it was his own son, in the presence of one who kept the Five Prohibitions and did not offend in the matter of the Five Virtues, who was charitable, courteous and polite in all his dealings, he felt ashamed to be found in warlike attire, so, slightly closing the shoji, he drew on hastily over his armour a white priestly garment, the bosom of which he continually pulled together to conceal the shining metal of the breastplate.

The Naidaijin then took his seat one above that of his younger brother Munemori, neither he nor the Nyudo saying anything. After some time the silence was broken by his father. "A rebellion of Narichika is a thing of no account, but this affair has been planned by the Ho-o," said he, "so what do you think about bringing him to the North Palace of Toba, or if not, making him proceed hither until matters have quieted down? Not waiting to hear any more the Naidaijin burst into tears." "What is the matter then?" enquired the Nyudo in surprise; whereupon Shigemori, repressing his tears, replied. "If I am to judge by your words I must suppose that the prosperity of our house is drawing to its close, for it is when people are on the downward path that they always commit some crime. Your appearance in this guise seems to me but as an illusion, for though this our land is a remote and narrow realm, yet since under the sovereignty of the descendants of Ama-Terasu-Omi-Kami the stock of Ama-no-Koyane-no-Mikoto have administered it, those who have held the office of Dajo-daijin have never been accustomed thus to appear in warlike attire. Moreover you, a lay priest, putting off the garments sacred to the Buddhas of the three worlds that are the garb of those who are liberated front the passions,[82] do suddenly assume armour and gird on bow and arrows, thus not only transgressing the Five Prohibitions and being guilty of shameless crime, but disregarding entirely the hive Virtues. It is not pleasant to speak thus, but I cannot hold back what is in my mind. In this world

---

[82] *Liberated from the passions.* 解脱 gecatsu. Sk. Vimokcha or Mukti.

there are four obligations, that to Heaven and Earth, that to the Emperor, that to Father and Mother, and that to one's fellow men, and of these the most important is that to the Emperor. All the land is the Emperor's dominion; we know the example of those two sages in China, he who washed his ears in the waters of Ei-sen and he who ate the bracken on the mountains of Shuyo, how they teach the difficulty of opposing the Emperor. How much more must it be so with one who has advanced to the high office of Dajo daijin, from a family in which such an office is without precedent? I too, an ignorant and stupid person, have become minister, and more than half the country is subject to our ordinances. Is not all this the reason for a rare obligation to the Emperor? But you, unmindful of all this great obligation, are about to treat the Ho-o's person in a violent manner, a thing quite contrary to the will of Hachiman and Ama-Terasu. Nippon is the land of the Gods and the Gods will not permit discourtesy. Thus the Emperor's plans cannot be without reason. That our house has for several generations subdued the foes of the Emperor and pacified the angry waves of the four seas may be indeed great patriotism, but to boast of it is only inconsiderate to others. In the seventeen, articles of the constitution of Shotoku Taishi it is written; "Every man has a mind, and every mind has self will; some say one thing is good and some another, so who can decide which is right? There is wisdom and folly in both, it is like a circle having no end; this being so, when one is angry he must first condemn himself." But as the fall of our house is not yet destined this plot has already been revealed: moreover we have already taken Narichika into custody, so there is no need for anxiety about anything the Emperor may do; after suitably punishing these people you must explain the matter to the Ho-o. Thus serving the Emperor and cherishing the people with sympathy you will receive the protection of the gods and not disobey the will of Buddha. If you are favoured by the gods and Buddha, the Emperor will change his opinion of us. If I compare the Emperor and yourself, there is no distinction between the affection I have for both, but when comparing what is right and what is wrong one must of necessity prefer the right. Since then right is on the side of the Emperor, I will protect the Ho-o's Palace to the best of my ability, seeing that my having risen. to my present high position of Daijin-no-Taisho from a low rank is entirely due to the Imperial favour. When I consider the greatness of this favour, it is more than ten thousand times ten thousand clusters of jewels, yea deeper than the double dyed purple. Therefore I must go to the Ho-o's Palace, and my samurai who have vowed to lay down their lives for me at any time will doubtless go with me and if I gather them together and go to protect the Hojuji den, a great crisis will come about. How unhappy am I! For if I remain loyal to the Emperor I must forget the gratitude I owe to my father, which is higher than the peaks of Mt. Meiro.[83] Verily my pith is a hard one; for if I avoid unfilial conduct then I shall be a rebellious subject and undutiful to the Emperor. I know not which way to take, for it is difficult to decide on one or the other. I beseech you then, order me to be beheaded, for then I can neither go with you against the Ho-o, nor can I be on his side to protect him. In China Shoka attained merit beyond ordinary men and became Prime Minister, being permitted to attend at the Court wearing shoes and with his sword girt on, but on one occasion he was disobedient, and the Emperor Koso punished him severely. Considering this precedent, even if a man attain to great wealth, rank and prosperity, Imperial favour and the highest office, it is not so difficult to fall. If a wealthy and noble house like ours accumulate stipend and rank too easily it is like a tree that bears too much fruit and is injured in its roots. Alas! I care to live no longer to see my country in such disorder. Born in a degenerate age to encounter such misfortunes, what an evil destiny indeed! How easy it would be to order one of your samurai to take me out into the courtyard there and strike off my head. Consider these things all of you!" And wiping his tears with the sleeve of his 'naoshi', he wept bitterly, and all the Heike, as they sat row upon row, lifted up their voices and wept also.

The Nyudo, hearing Shigemori, in whom he put all his trust, speak thus, felt his heart fail him, as he answered; "Indeed I have never even contemplated such a thing, but I only fear as to what may happen if the Ho-o adopt the plans of these rascals." "Whatever mistake may be perpetrated," replied the Naidaijin, "how can we lift a hand against the Ho-o? Then, suddenly standing up in the middle gate, he addressed the samurai; "I think you have heard everything that I have said. I was present from this morning and tried to calm this disturbance, but it is beyond my power, so I must return home; do not march against the Ho-o while my head is on my shoulders! Then calling his retainers he returned to the Komatsu den. On arriving there he summoned Shume-no-Hangwan Morikuni and instructed him thus; "I have this morning learned that the country is in a critical condition, so let those who consider themselves dutiful retainers arm themselves and follow." At this all thought that such a summons from one usually so little moved by rumour must be of great import and hasted to obey. The retainers came pouring out from the villages of Yodo, Hatsukashi, Uji, Okanoya, Hino, Kwanjuji, Daigo, Ogurusu, Mamezu, Katsura, Ohara, Shizuhara, and Serifu, some in armour but without helmets, some with arrows and no bow, some with one foot only in the stirrup and some with neither,

---

[83] *Mt. Meiro.* Sk. Sumeru, the wondrous mountain in the centre of the universes that supports the various tiers of the heavens and is the centre round which the heavenly bodies revolve. It is of great height, one side is of gold, the second of silver, the third of; lapis lazuli and the fourth of glass.

so great was their haste and disorder. Now when they heard of the activity at the Komatsuden, the horsemen, who were at Nishi Hachijo to the number of several thousand, hastened thither without the knowledge of the Nyudo, so that not a single warrior was left in the household Chikugo-no-kami who alone remained was summoned by Kiyo-mori: "Why has Shigemori called away everyone thus, can it be that he intends to attack me as he said this morning?" Sadayoshi weeping replied; "Such things depend on a man's character; he is not likely to do it, for he will already regret what he has said here this morning." Kiyomori however thought that it was not advisable to fall out with his son, the Naidaijin, so he modified his violent intentions towards the Retired Emperor. Hurriedly stripping off his armour, he donned the robe and scarf of a priest and betook himself to his prayers, which, however, by no means arose from his heart. Meanwhile at the Komatsu den Morikuni was ordered to make a roll of the retainers who had mustered, and it was found that their number was more than ten thousand horsemen. After inspecting this muster-roll, Shigemori came forth to the middle gate and thus addressed the assembled samurai. "I am greatly moved at your rallying here so quickly without regard for your own affairs. In China there is an example of this kind; Yu-o of the Shu dynasty had a favourite consort named Ho-ji, and she was the greatest beauty in the kingdom, but in one thing she did not please Yu-o; she never laughed, never at all did she even smile. Now it is the custom in China that when a rebellion breaks out in the army they light beacon fires and beat drums to assemble the soldiers, and it happened that a revolt took place at this time so that the beacons were lighted; and when this consort saw them she exclaimed; "Oh! what a lot of them there are," and smiled for the first time. And when she smiled her expression was very winsome, and Yu-o was highly delighted, so that many times after he had beacons lighted without any special reason, and when the generals came and found there was no revolt they had nothing to do but to go away again. This happening many times, at last they did not even come, and then it chanced that an enemy from a neighbouring country made a raid and attacked the capital of Yu-o, but though he had beacons lighted, thinking it was only for the consort's amusement, no soldiers responded, so that the capital fell and Yu-o himself was killed: whereupon the consort changed herself into a fox and ran away. This being so, whenever I summon you, come hither quickly as you have done today, for I called you together because this morning I heard that there was a great crisis, but afterwards when I investigated more fully I was convinced that the report was mistaken: so you may return again to your quarters." On this the retainers retired. Now it seems that Shigemori had not really believed that there was any crisis, but after rebuking his father that morning he wished to find out whether the soldiers would be on his side or not, and that he did not intend to attack Kiyomori, but only used this device to prevent any inclination on his part of interfering with the Emperor. As Confucius has said; "even if the Emperor does not behave as Emperor, the subjects must behave as subjects; and even if a father does not behave as a father, a son must behave as a son: loyalty to the Emperor is like filial piety in a son."

When the Ho o heard of these things, he exclaimed: "It is not the first time that I feel ashamed to face the Naidaijin, for he repays enmity with kindness." His contemporaries also praised him, declaring that it was a most fortunate thing that such a man had become Daijin-no-Taisho who was superior to all in courtesy and etiquette, beside being supreme in intellect and ability: "If there is a minister who dares to advise the Emperor, then the country will be at peace; and in the family if there is a son who advises his father, that house will stand firm. Happy is the country that has such a minister both in ancient and modern times."

Chapter VII.

THE EXILE OF THE SHIN-DAINAGON.

On the second day of the sixth month they brought forth the Shin Dainagon Narichika-no-Kyo into the reception chamber of the mansion and entertained him with a repast, but his heart was too full even for him to touch a morsel. Then his guard Namba-no-jiro Tsuneto ordered his car and bade him enter it, whereupon the Dainagon reluctantly did so. He expressed a wish to see Shigemori once more, but unhappily was not permitted to do so. Looking round on the escort that surrounded him, he could not see one of his own men, "Ah," he exclaimed, "even one exiled for a great crime ought to be allowed at least one of his own retainers." When the guards heard this their tears flowed even on to their sleeves of mail. Thus going along the west side of the Shujaku to the southward, he only saw the buildings of the Court from a distance, who had so long been in attendance there, whereat everyone even to the servants and ox-drivers he knew so well buried their faces in their sleeves and wept. How much more sad must be the state of his wife and children left behind in the cite. On passing by the Toba Palace, he called to mind how he always accompanied the Ho-o when he visited there. Farther on he saw his own country seat, Suhama, in the distance. Passing out through the south gate of Toba den, they hurried to take the ship. He then expressed the wish that he might at least be executed at a place like this that was near the capital. On enquiring the name of the retainer who was to accompany him, the samurai told him it was Namba-no-jiro Kaneyasu. Then the Dainagon asked if any of his own retainers were present, as he had something to say before: he embarked, but when Tsuneto went round and searched, there was not one to be found. Then the Dainagon weeping exclaimed; "Ah, in the time of my prosperity I had two or three thousand retainers, but now there is not one who comes to see the last of me even from afar off;" whereat the rough soldiers were again moved to moisten the sleeves of their armour. A copious flood of tears indeed was all that followed him. Formerly when he went to visit the shrines of Kumano or Tennoji, he used to go in a state barge of great magnificence accompanied by twenty or thirty other ships, but now he had to embark on a rough vessel with nothing but a large tent on it, escorted by strange soldiers, and today as he leaves the capital for the last time, to sail far off across the sea, his wretched feelings can only be imagined. It was only owing to the urgent pleadings of Komatsu Dono that his death sentence was lightened to one of exile. That day they reached the coast of Daimo-tsu in the province of Settsu. The next day, that is the third, a messenger from Kyoto came hurrying to this place, whereupon the Dainagon thought he was to be executed there, but the messenger had only brought news that he was to be exiled to Kojima in Bizen. There was also a letter from Shigemori in which was written; "I bad thought to get you sent to some country place near the capital, but alas, it cannot be; so I have no further use for this world: however I have at least managed to save your life, therefore set your mind at ease." To Namba-no-jiro he also sent a message, adjuring him to pay great respect to his charge and to take care not to oppose his wishes, adding also directions in detail about preparations for the journey. Ah! whither does he go, leaving the Ho-o to whom he owes so much, and parting from his wife and children who have never left his side before even for a moment? Never again will he return and see his family. Once before at the appeal of Hieizan he had been exiled, but the Ho-o, taking compassion on him, recalled him again from Nishi Shichijo: so his present punishment was not by the Imperial will. "Why has this happened?" he gasped, looking up to heaven and down again to earth: however much he wept it was in vain. As soon as, the dawn came the ship put out and as they journeyed he did nought but weep and seemed not to wish to survive any longer: still his fleeting life did not come to an end. As the white waves dropped away in their wake the capital receded farther and farther. As the days went by one after another, the distant goal came nearer and nearer. When they arrived at Kojima in Bizen, they brought him to a rude farmer's house roofed with brushwood; the mountains were behind him and the sea before, for it was an eland; the sounding waves and pine breeze on the shore, everything gave him a sad and lonely feeling.

Chapter VIII.

THE PINE OF AKOYA.

The Shin Dainagon was not the only person who was thus punished, for many of his companions suffered likewise. It was decided that Omi-no-Chujo Nyudo Renjo should be banished to Sado, Yamashiro-no-kami Motokane to Hoki, Shikibu-no-taiho-Masatsuna to Harima, So Hangwan Nobufusa to Awa, and Shinkei-no-Hangwan Sukeyuki to Mimasaka. At this time the Nyudo was staying at his villa at Fukuhara. On the twentieth day his messenger Settsu-no-kami Morizumi reached the Kadowaki mansion, the residence of the Saisho Taira Norimori, and ordered him to bring quickly Tamba-no-Shosho whom he had in charge as he intended to do something in regard to him. To this the Saisho replied; "It is very sad that I should again be grieved about this; it had been better that something had been done before: "but he bade the Shosho hasten to Fukuhara: The Shosho started on his way weeping, and his wife and ladies-in-waiting begged him to ask for the Saisho's good offices once more, since all else was unavailing. "As for me, I have said all I can," replied the Saisho," there is nothing else left for me but to forsake the world. What can I say more? Anyhow to whatever place you may be sent I will come and see you as long as I live." Now the Shosho had a child of three years old, but as he was himself young, he had not paid any special regard to his children; now however when he found himself in this situation they became somewhat dear to him and he thought that he would like to see him once more. The milk nurse therefore brought him, and the Shosho, taking him on his knee, stroked his hair and wept. "Alas, when you were seven years old I wished to bring you into the Imperial Household, but now that is all in vain. If by chance you should live to grow up you must become a priest and pray for my happiness in a future life." The child naturally could not comprehend these words, but when his father finished speaking, he nodded his head, so that the Shosho and the child's mother, beside the milk nurse and others who were in attendance, even the most unfeeling, were fain to burst into tears.

The messenger from Fukuhara bade him start for Toba that evening, but the Shosho asked that, as he had not long to stay, at least he might stop that night in the capital: this was not however permitted and so, abandoning hope, he went to Toba that night. The Saisho was so grieved that he did not accompany him, and on the twenty-second of the same month he arrived at Fukuhara, whereupon the Nyudo gave orders to Seno Taro Kaneyasu who dwelt in Bitchu to take him to that province. Kaneyasu, fearing that the Saisho would hear of it, did not treat him at all harshly but was very kind to him on the way. The Shosho, in spite of this refused to be comforted, but night and day called on the name of Buddha, praying and interceding for his father.

Now the Shin Dainagon Narichika-no-Kyo was yet in Kojima of Bizen, but as this was considered to be an unsuitable place, being near to a port, he was removed to the village of Niwase on the confines of Bizen and Bitchu and lodged in a mountain temple named Ariki-no-Bessho in Kibi-no-Nakayama, so that he was not more than fifty cho distant from Seno in Bitchu where the Shosho was, and the Shosho yearned toward that quarter for tidings of his father. Calling Kaneyasu therefore, he enquired of him how far it was to Ariki-no-Bessho, but Kaneyasu, thinking it was not wise to inform him, told him that it was twelve or thirteen days journey. The Shosho weeping replied; "Of old Nippon had thirty three provinces and now it is divided into sixty six, so that what is now called Bizen, Bingo and Bitchu were formerly all one country: Dewa and Mutsu in the eastern quarter also formed one province consisting of sixty six districts, but now twelve districts of it have been separated and called Dewa. When Sanekata Chujo was banished to Mutsu and wished to see the famous pine of Akoya, he went round the whole province, but was returning again without having found it, when he met on the road an old man whom he addressed as follows; "I see you are an old man, so can you tell me where the pine of Akoya in this province may be?" "It is not in this province" replied the old man, "but in the province of Dewa." "Then you do not know where it is either;" replied the Chujo; "in this evil age people even forget the famous places in their own province;" and he was making to pass on, when the old man caught his sleeve and said; "When you asked for the pine of Akoya in this province, you were thinking of the verse:

"Hid by the Akoya pine that stands in the province of Mutsu;
though the moon would rise, yet its beams cannot appear."

But those lines were written when the two provinces together were known by the one name; when the twelve districts were divided from it they were given the name of Dewa." So Sanekata Chujo went to the province of Dewa and saw the pine of Akoya. "From Dazaifu to Tsukushi," continued the Shosho, "is only a fifteen days' journey for the courier who carries fish to the Emperor, so that fifteen days' journey from here will take one as far as Kyushu, will it not? Even at the farthest the distance between two places in Bizen, Bitchu, and Bingo cannot be more than a three days' journey, and that you thus call near far is only because you will not tell me where my father the Dainagon is lodged." After this, though still longing to see him, he asked about him no more.

Chapter IX.

THE DEATH OF THE SHIN DAINAGON.

Meanwhile Hoshoji-no-Shugyo Shunkwan Sozu, Tamba-no-Shosho Naritsune, and Hei Hangwan Yasuyori were all exiled to the island of Kikai-ga-shima in the bay of Satsuma. This is a place that can only be reached from the capital after many hardships and the crossing of stormy seas. It is a place that even sailors cannot find unless quite certain of the way, and it is an island in which few men live. There are some people there it is true, but as they wear no clothing, they are not like ordinary folk of the mainland; neither can they understand our language. Their bodies are covered with hair and black like oxen, and the men do not wear 'eboshi' neither do the women have long hair. As they have nothing else to eat they must kill animals for food; they do not cultivate the fields and so have neither rice nor corn, nor do they grow mulberry trees, and so are lacking in silk. In this island there is a high mountain that burns with eternal fire and the land is full of sulphur, so that the island is also called Io-ga-shima (Sulphur Island). Thunder rolls continuously up and down the mountain and at its foot rain falls in abundance. It is not possible for anyone to live there for a moment. The Shin Dainagon was feeling more calm in his mind now, but hearing that his son Tamba-no-Shosho Naritsune was exiled to Kikai-ga-shima in Satsuma bay with two others, thinking that there was now nothing more to wait for, he informed Shigemori by messenger of his desire to shave his head and become a priest; and this being reported to the Ho-o, he also gave his assent. Thus putting off the bright-sleeved dress of prosperity, he forsook this fleeting world and came down to wear the black costume of a recluse.

Now the Dainagon's wife, having retired to the vicinity of Un-rinji in the northern hills, not only found such an unaccustomed life grievous to her, but had nothing to occupy her days and so felt extremely miserable. In her former residence she had had many ladies-in-waiting and retainers, but now they were either afraid or ashamed to visit her, all except one retainer named Gensaemon-no-jo Nobutoshi, who took pity on her and came to see her continually. One day she called this Nobutoshi and addressed him thus; "My lord has been so far staying at Kojima in Bizen, but lately I have heard that he has been removed to Ariki-no-Bessho. Ah! how much I should like to send a letter to him and to receive an answer in return." "Since I was a child," replied Nobutoshi, bursting into tears," how many are the benefits I have received from you, and never yet have I been parted from you. Your commands I have always obeyed and I have always heeded your advice. When my lord went down to the western province I would have accompanied him, but Rokuhara would not allow it, and so I could not, but now whatever hardships I may encounter I will surely bear your august message to him." His mistress was overjoyed at these words and forthwith wrote the letter. Her little son and daughter also wrote a message, and Nobutoshi taking them proceeded to go down to Ariki-no-Bessho in the far off province of Bizen. Making enquiries of the guard Namba-no-jiro Tsuneto, that warrior, respecting his dutiful conduct, soon brought him to where his lord was. His master the Dainagon Nyudo, now, as always, occupying himself with sadly musing about his home in the capital, on seeing Nobutoshi arrive from Kyoto, hardly understanding whether it was dream or reality, sprang up and bade him enter immediately. Nobutoshi advanced, but on seeing the condition of his lord, his lowly dwelling and his black priestly garments, his heart sank within him and he could not restrain his tears. Then, controlling himself somewhat, he related all that his lady had said to him, and presented the letter. The Dainagon, on opening it and seeing the writing all blurred with tears, and reading how much his children sorrowed for him, not to speak of his wife's unbearable grief and anxiety, felt that his former longing was as nothing to his present anguish.

Thus four or five days passed and Nobutoshi requested that he might stay with his master till the end; but this the soldier who guarded him could by no means allow, and the Dainagon himself dissuaded him saying; "As you cannot stay any longer please return at once; I feel that my end will not be long in coming and when you hear of my death I beg you pray for my welfare in the world to come." So Nobutoshi received an answer to his letter and took his leave, promising to come again soon. "Ah," replied the Dainagon, "I think there will be no need for that: you will never see me again;" and in his grief and regret at parting, he called Nobutoshi back again and again; but as there was nothing else to be done, the retainer, restraining his grief, returned again to the capital and delivered the letter to his lady. When she opened it she immediately perceived his change of state, for inside the packet there was a lock of his hair that he had shaved off: She could read no farther but exclaiming: "Ah! how grievous is such a memento!" covered her head and threw herself to the ground. Her children also lifted up their voices and wept aloud.

Now on the nineteenth day of the eighth month of the same year the Dainagon was at last put to death at Ariki-no-Bessho in Kibi-no-Nakayama in the village of Niwase in the province of Bizen. And of the manner of it, it is said that first, they put poison in his wine, but as this had no effect, planting tridents in the ground under a cliff about twenty feet high, they pushed him over it and he was pierced through by them so that he died. What a pitiful death it was! When his wife heard of his death she exclaimed; "Until now I have not changed my condition and become a nun because I thought I might see him again, but now it is of no avail;" and retiring to a temple called Bodai-in, she became a nun and devoted herself to a religious life. Now this lady was the daughter of Yamashiro-no-kami Atsukata, and she had been loved by the Ho-o Go-Shirakawa, being of exceeding great beauty; and as this Dainagon was beloved by the Ho-o she had been given to him afterwards. So his young sons and daughters passed their days bringing flowers and drawing water for the offerings to Buddha and praying for the welfare of their father in the world to come. And thus the events of the time went on changing just like the five changes[84] of the angelic beings.

Chapter X.

THE TOKUDAIJI DAINAGON GOES TO ITSUKUSHIMA.

Now as the Tokudaiji Dainagon Sanesada-no-Kyo was passed over by Taira Munemori, the second son of the Nyudo, in the matter of the office of Taisho, he retired from his office of Dainagon and lived in seclusion, watching to see what turn things might take; but when he was inclined to become a priest, all his house grieved and lamented greatly. Among them was one who had the title of Shodaibu, To Kurando-no-Taiyu Shigekane by name, a man capable in all matters. One moonlight night Tokudaiji Dono had his lattice drawn up on the south side and was singing to the moon, when this To-no-Kurando came up to him. "Who is there?" enquired the Dainagon. "Shigekane" was the answer. "It is now moonlight, what is your purpose incoming here?" "Tonight the moon is very clear and so I have come to calm my spirit by contemplating it."

"It is most admirable that you have come," replied the Dainagon, "for tonight I feel melancholy beyond measure and the hours are very tedious." After, a while, when they had spoken of, various things both present and past, the Dainagon said; "Consider the prosperity of the Heike; the eldest son Shigemori and the second son Munemori have become generals, if the right and left; and still there is the third son Tomomori and the grandson Koremori: if both of these take their turn, it does not seem as if anyone of another family will ever become Taisho at all. That is the end of things for me. I will become a recluse." To-no-Kurando weeping replied; "If you become a monk all of your family will be without anyone to guide them. I have lately thought of a novel plan: you know that Itsukushima, in Aki is exceedingly revered by the Heike family. Do you go and visit it. In that shrine there are

---

[84] *Five changes*, or degenerations. These were supposed to be; first withering of the flowers on their head; second, sweating under the armpit; third, extinction of their halo; fourth. becoming blind; fifth becoming dissatisfied with their place in heaven.

many elegant dancing-girls who have the title of 'Naishi'[85] or Imperial ladies-in-waiting, and they will entertain you in a most interesting way." "But what shall I pray for?" enquired the Dainagon. "Tell them the real state of affairs," replied Shigefusa, "and when you leave, bring one or two of the chief of these Naishi back with you to the capital, and then they will certainly go and pay a visit at Nishi-Hachijo, and when the Nyudo asks the reason, they will relate the whole circumstances to him, and as he is easily interested in such things it will be a very suitable occasion to obtain his favour." "I had not thought of such a thing," replied the Dainagon, "but I will certainly act on your advice immediately: "and straightway he purified himself and set out for Itsukushima. On his arrival there he found that there were indeed many beautiful dancing girls there, and they declared that though the Heike lords were accustomed to visit the shrine, other courtiers seldom came, and so his pilgrimage was very interesting to them. So ten of the principal Naishi kept him company continually day and night and entertained him very agreeably. When these Naishi enquired the reason of his coming, he replied that it was because he had been passed over in the appointment to the office of Taisho in favour of another person, and had come to pray about it. So he tarried there seven days, and they performed the sacred music and dance called Kagura as well as many local sacred songs and dances, while the entertainment called Bugaku was given three times. Then, when he started on his return journey, the ten chief Naishi prepared boats and went with him a day's journey to see him off, and Tokudaiji, regretting to part with them, first persuading them to come another day, and then two, at last brought them right to Kyoto, and taking them to his mansion, entertained then splendidly and made them many presents. The Naishi, declaring that as they had come from such a distant place to the capital they must certainly visit their patrons the Heike lords, proceeded to Nishi Hachijo with that purpose. The Nyudo, who came forth and received them, enquired for what reason they had journeyed all the way to Kyoto, whereupon they explained that Tokudaiji Dono had visited their shrine, and that having prepared ships and decided to come with Min one day's journey, to see him off and then to return, he had persuaded them to come farther and farther until at last they had come to the capital with him. Then the Nyudo asked why Tokudaiji had gone to Itsukushima, and they told him that it was to pray about being passed over in the election to Taisho. Hearing this the Nyudo nodded his head and said to himself; "How admirable a thing it is that he has made a pilgrimage to the distant shrine of Itsukushima that I revere above all others, instead of going to the many influential and potent shrines and temples in the

---

[85] *Naishi*. Title of Ladies of the Court, but here also of the attendants of the Shrine or Miko, the sacred Dancing a girls.

capital. If his desire is so earnest, then I will see." So he made Shigemori the Naidaijin retire from the office of Sadaisho and elevated Tokudaiji Dono to it in his place over the head of his second son Munemori the Udaisho. What a clever device this was indeed! How sad that the Shin Dainagon did not adopt such a plan as this instead of making a useless rebellion which led to the destruction of himself and his descendants.

Chapter XI.

THE DESTRUCTION OF HIEIZAN.

Now the Ho-o, having become the disciple of Kogen Sojo of Miidera, was studying the esoteric doctrines of Shingon: and having read the three secret Sutras called Dai-nichi Kyo,[86] Kongo-cho Kyo[87] and So-shitsuji-Kyo,[88] on the fourth day of the ninth month was to undergo the ceremony of Kwancho or Baptism. When they heard this the priests of Hieizan were wrath and said; "From ancient days it has been the custom that the ceremony of Kwancho should be performed by our temple, and it is for the especial purpose of admonishing and baptizing the Emperor that our god manifests himself in this mountain. If therefore the ceremony is to be performed at Miidera there is nothing for it but to burn our useless temple. Therefore the Ho-o, considering his idea unprofitable, gave up his intention of receiving Kwancho, and only requested that the purification ceremony be carried out. But in order to carry out his original intention, he summoned Koken Sojo and went to Tennoji where he built a temple called Gochiko-in, and decided on the well of Kame-i as his sacred water of baptism. Then, finishing his study of the Sutras, he received baptism at the original sacred spot of Buddhism in Japan. But though the Kwancho was not performed at Miidera in order to pacify the wrath of the monks of Hieizan, yet at that temple differences of opinion between the Doshu (lay brothers) and the Gakusho (student priests) led to pitched battles between them in which the Gakusho were defeated; so that the destruction of Hieizan and a great disaster to the Imperial family seemed likely. These Doshu were either youthful attendants on the Gakusho who had become priests, or else priests who did menial work in the temples, and at the time when Kakujin Gon-Sojo, the Zasshu of Kongo-ju-in was the head of Hieizan, they were called Geshu and lodged in the three pagodas, being

---

[86] *Dai-Nichi*. Vairochana, the Buddha of boundless light, first of the three representations of Buddha, identified in Japan with Ama-Terasu the Sun-goddess, the central figure of the Shingon|System.

[87] *Kongo*. Vajrapani, a deity much invoked in the Yogacharya Buddhism practised by the Shingon Sect in Japan.

[88] *So-shitsuij*. The Susiddhikara Sutra, another text of the Tantra School.

employed in offering the flowers before the Buddhas. Of late years however they were called Gyonin, and, setting at nought the higher priests, they got the upper hand by force. So when these Doshu, disobeying the orders of the higher priests, planned a revolt, their superiors appealed to the Court nobles for an order to punish them and asked the samurai to carry the order into execution. Then the Nyudo, at the order of the Ho-o, sent Yuasa-Gon-no-kami Muneshige of the province of Kii with about two thousand men of the Kinai district to attack the Doshu in cooperation with the Taishu or upper priests. Now the Doshu were at this time lodging in the building called Toyobo, but when they heard of this they came down to Sanga-no-shorin Omi and gathered a large force with which they returned to Hieizan, where they built a fortification at Sobisaka and took up their position in it. On the twentieth day of the ninth month and the first part of the hour of the Dragon (8 a.m.), three thousand of the Taishu or upper priests with two thousand men of the Imperial army, five thousand in all, made an attack on Sobisaka, shouting their war cry vigorously. Those in the fort however shot arrows and cast stones upon them so that their united forces were shot down to a man. As the Taishu tried to get before the Imperial forces while the Imperial army strove to outstrip the Taishu, this vying with each other divided their councils and they were not able to fight effectively. Moreover the band of ruffians who composed the Doshu were made up of thieves, brigands, mountain robbers and pirates, all consumed with a lust for booty and fighting each for himself, reckless whether they lived or died; so that on this occasion also the Gakusho had the worst of the battle.

After this Hieizan gradually fell into dilapidation. Except the twelve branches of the Zen sect, few priests were left to live there; the lectures in the valley were gradually abolished, the religious ceremonies were performed no more, the academies of learning were closed, and the floor for Zen meditation became deserted. No longer was the flower of the Tendai fragrant, and the moon of its clear doctrines was clouded. There was none of light the sacred lamps that had never gone out for three hundred years; the smoke of the perpetual incense ceased. No longer do the vast buildings tower aloft, cleaving the blue heavens with their three storied bulk, with their crossbeams of immeasurable height and their rafters that are scarcely discerned amid the white mists. The Buddhas are adored but by the mountain blasts; their golden statues are wetted by the muddy raindrops: the moonbeams streaming through the chinks of the roof are their sacred lamps, and their lotos seats are encrusted with the diamond dew of dawn. In this unhallowed and degenerate age the Buddhist Law that was supreme in the three countries declined. Consider the remains of Buddhism in far off India; the Chiku-rin Shoja[89] and the Gitsu-kodoku-on,[90] where of old the Lax was preached, are they not the haunt of wolves and foxes, their foundations alone remaining? The waters of the lake of Hakuro have dried up and the tall grasses have grown up within it. The Taibon and Gejo[91] pillars are moss-covered and leaning to their fall. In China also Tendaisan, Godaisan, Hakubaji and Gyokusenji are now dilapidated and forsaken, and the sacred volumes of the Mahayana and Hinayana are rotting at the bottom of their boxes. In our country too the seven great temples of Nara are laid waste: the eight sects, yea the nine have left no race. Of old at Atago and Takao the sacred halls and pagodas raised on high their ranging roofs, but in one night they we: utterly ruined and became a place for Tengu to dwell in. So also may it not be that the noble law of Tendai has been abolish d in this era of Jisho? There were none among the men of understanding who did not fail to lament it. Who wrote it we know not, but upon a pillar of one of the monasteries this verse found:

"*See this mount of prayer returns to its former condition*;
 Now becomes once more a lonely and desolate peak."

Was he not thinking of the prayer[92] of Dengyo Daishi when first he established these temples: "O unexcelled[93] perfect intelligence of Buddha, show forth thy Divine help on this mount whereon I build." It was indeed most touching. How admirable was the writer of it.

The eighth day is the feast of Yakushi, but there was no sound of the invocation to be heard. The fourth month is the month of the incarnation of Sakya Muni, but there was none to make the offerings of silk and money. The red fence of the brine is hoary with age, nothing is left but the straw rope of the Gods.

---

[89] *Chiku-rin Shoja*. The Karanda Venuvana or Bamboo park, given S'akya Muni by Bimbisara, king of Magadha, who was converted by him.

[90] *Gitsu-kodoku-on*. The Jetavana Vihara.

[91] *Taibon and Gejo*. Two Stupas or memorial tumuli or pillars, set up by S'akya Muni on the road, when he was staying at Gridhrakuta. cf. Tsurezure Gusa. p. 119. note.

[92] *Prayer*. This refers to a famous prayer of Dengyo Daishi, the words of which are echoed in this verse.

[93] *O unexcelled*. a title of Buddha. Sk. Anuttara Samyak Sambodhi.

Chapter XII.

THE BURNING OF ZENKOJI.

At this time the temple of Zenkoji in Shinano was burned down. Now the Tathagata of this temple are a set of three Mida[94] half an arm long, unequalled in the three countries, cast after profound concentration by Mokuren Choja[95] from the gold of Enbudan[96] which the wisdom of Gekkwai Choja procured from the Palace of the Dragon King, when of old in Shae[97] in mid-India five kinds of disease broke out and priests and people died in great multitudes. After Buddhism was destroyed they stayed in India more than five hundred years. Since Buddhism moved to the eastward they were brought to Kudara, and after a thousand years, Seimei being Emperor of Kudara and Kemmei Tenno of this land, they were brought thence to Japan and lodged at Naniwa-no-ura in the province of Settsu. Since golden rays always shone from them the name of the era was called Konko (golden rays).

In the third month of the third year and during the first ten days Honda Yoshimitsu of Omi in Shinano same up to the capital to meet the statues and took them back with him to his own place: by day Yoshimitsu carried the statues but by night they carried him. Arriving at Shinano he lodged them in the district of Mizunouchi. Since then five hundred years have gone by but this was the first time a fire broke out. It is said that if the monarchical principle is destroyed Buddhism will first be abolished, so that people said that the destruction of this holy mountain and its many temples was a portent of the coming overthrow of the monarchy.

Chapter XIII.

THE PETITION OF YASUYORI.

Now the three who were exiled to Kikaigashima did not particularly value their lives, which trembled in the balance like dew on the tip of a leaf, but food and clothing were provided for Tamba-no-Shosho from the domain of his father-in-law Taira-no-Saisho Norimori at Kase in Hizen, so that Shunkwan and Yasuyori also managed to

---

[94] *Mida*. Amida or Amitabha with Kwannon and Seishi (Mahasthama) form|this trio of statue, They are perhaps the oldest in Japan.

[95] *Mokuren Choja*. Mahamaudgalyayana, the left hand disciple of S'akya Muni. Choja, elder. Sk. S'rechthi.

[96] *Enbudan*. Sk. Djambudvipa. the continent situated south of Mt. Sumeru.

[97] *Shae*. Sk. S'ravasti, or Kosala, a t ancient city, N.W. of Kapilavastu, which S'akya Muni frequented.

support themselves from it. Moreover Yasuyori on being exiled on his way had become a priest at Murozumi in Suwo, and was henceforth known by the religious name of Shōshō. He had originally intended to do this before, so he made this couplet:

> "*Now that the way of the world has gone so entirely against me*;
> *How very foolish I was not to have left it before.*"

As Tamba-no-Shosho and Yasuyori had always been believers in the god of Kumano, they wished to build a temple to supplicate the three Gongen in this island that they might be delivered and return to the capital. Shunkwan, however, being by nature a sceptic, took no part in it at all. So the two, being agreed, went round the island searching for a place like to Kumano.[98] One spot they found with a wooded bank, its cliff covered with creepers like red embroidery; another a wondrous peak hidden in the clouds with variegated scenery below it like green damask outspread, the mountain landscape and splendid groves surpassing all they had so far seen. Looking to the southward the sea spread out far as the eye could reach, its distant waves dissolving into clouds and mist. Northward from the lofty precipice a waterfall leaped out a hundred feet down with an eternal roar of sound. Since the age of the gods the wind had sounded in the pines. It was a spot that greatly resembled Nachi with its waterfall sacred to the Gongen. So they gave it the name of the mountain of Nachi, and the peaks they also named Hongu and Shingu, giving the names of the different gods to various places. Then Yasuyori Nyudo, taking Tamba-no-Shosho with him, went round them every day after the style of the worship of Kumano, praying for their safe return to the capital: "Namu[99] Gongen Kongo Doji, send down thy pity upon us, we beseech thee, that we may once more return to the capital and see again our wives and children." As the days went on, having no change of clothes, they put on hempen ones, end purifying themselves in the water of the marsh they feigned it to be the pure streams of Iwata in Kumano; climbing up a hill there as though it were the Hosshin-mon.[100] Whenever Yasuyori Nyudo made his pilgrimage to the Sansho Gongen and recited the sacred 'norito,' having no paper for 'gohei' he would wave flowers aloft in his hands with these words: "On this the first year of Jisho, the year of the cock, and the second day of the tenth month thereof, being the three hundred and fiftieth day of our sojourn, choosing a favourable day and a propitious hour, we, Urin Fujiwara Naritsune and the priest Shosho, faithful worshippers of the Sansho Gongen of Kumano, roost

---

[98] *Kumano.* The famous Shrine in Kii, where Amida, Yakushi and Kwannon were worshipped. The goddess of the shrine is Izanami-no-mikoto.

[99] *Namu.* Sk. Nama. I humbly adore.

[100] *Hosshin-mon.* The gate of Kumano. Urin, Chinese form of Shosho.

efficacious in all Nippon, and the Holy Law of the great Bosatsu of the waterfall, fervently and truly with whole heart, with body, mind, and speech in full accord, humbly make petition. Oh, Shojo Dai-Bosatsu, Lord of the Law who givest help to those struggling in the painful sea of this world, Wise King and Perfect in the Three Manifestations, and thou Pure Ruby who dwellest in the Eastern Quarter, Divine Physician, Nyorai who healest all sickness, and thou who dwellest in the south, Kwannon the exhorter who art manifested in the Fudaraku,[101] Great Master of Nyuju-gen-mon, Prince who art the Chief Lord of this Benevolent Master,[102] show thy face to us in the world, thou who grantest the petitions of all creatures. Thou to whom the Emperor and all his subjects pour out evening and morning the pure holy water, washing away the filth of this world; that they may have peace in this world and happiness in the world to come, turning every evening toward thy mountain and calling on thy jewel Name, for thy mercy never faileth. Thy goodness is boundless as the lofty mountains and thy pity deep as the valleys; so will we climb to the mists above and stiffer the dews beneath. How should we tread these rough paths unless we relied on them as a place in which is thy spirit, and unless we could look on the goodness of the Gongen how could we go to this remote mountain? Therefore O Shojo Gongen and Hiryu[103] Dai-satta,[104] turn toward us thy lotus eyes of grace and incline thine all-hearing ears to listen; behold our burning zeal and grant all our petitions. Guide when in need those who are enlightened in the Law and save those who are yet in ignorance; leaving thy jewel abode and hiding thy eighty four thousand beams of light, show thyself in the dust of the Six Ways[105] and the Three Regions. Earnestly we lift up our hands together in prayer for the removal of retribution of our sins in a former existence and for the required blessing of long life, waving the 'gohei' without intermission, clad in the garments of purification and offering the flowers that symbolise knowledge of the way, making the sacred floor to vibrate with our zeal, and offering pure water with earnest mind that it may fill the lake from which flow thy benefits. Thus mayest thou receive our petition and fulfil all our desires. Thus looking upward we petition the twelve Gongen, that with salvation in their wings, oaring over the sky of this Sea of Pain, they may restore us to our former rank, and speedily and at a near time grant our petition to return to our

---

[101] *Fudaraku.* Sk. Putchekagiri. A mountain where Kwannon or Avalokitesvara appeared.

[102] *Benevolent Master.* Dai Nichi Nyorai.

[103] *Hiryu.* Spirit of the Waterfall.

[104] *Dai-satta.* Sk. Mahasattva. a perfected Bodhisattva.

[105] *Six ways.* Sk, Gati, Six conditions of sentient existence, viz. devas, men, asuras, beings in Bell, pretas, anima's. *Three regions,* Sk. Trailokya, desire, form and formlessness.

homes.

Chapter XIV.

THE FLOATING SOTOBA.

Thus these two, continually praying before the Three Gongen, at times spent the whole night before them; so that it happened that one night when they had thus stayed until morning singing 'Imayo' and dancing, toward dawn they allowed their eyes to close for a moment with weariness, and in a dream they saw a small ship with white sails rowing in from the offing, and twenty or thirty court ladies in scarlet hakama coming on shore from it, beating drums and chanting in chorus, "Better than prayer to ten thousand Buddhas is the vow to Kwannon of the Thousand Hands; straightway the withered herbage will put forth flowers and fruit." Repeating this chant three times they vanished. Then Yasuyori Nyudo, awaking from his dream, thought it a wondrous sign: indeed it must have been sent by the Dragon God; for seeing that one of the Three Gongen of Kumano called Nishino-Gozen was the Kwannon of the Thousand Hands in India, and the Dragon God of the sea is one of the twenty eight servants of this Kwannon, no doubt they would obtain their desire.

Another night the two spent there also, and in a dream they saw two leaves blown in by a breeze from the offing and wafted into their sleeves, and when they looked at them, lo! they were leaves of the 'Nagi'[106] tree at Kumano. On the leaves of the Nagi these lines had been bitten in by insects:

"Since your prayers to the god have been so long and incessant;
Surely you are allowed soon to return to your home."

So much did Yasuyori desire to return that as one method of consoling himself he made a thousand 'Sotoba' and wrote on them the character A[107] in Sanscrit, with the clay of the month and his name and priestly name, adding these stanzas also:

"That I am here in au isle of the bay of Satsuma dwelling;
Prithee O salt sea breeze, tell to my parents afar." and:
"Dear is his native land to him who is not so far distant;
Feel then more pity for me exiled so lone and so far."

---

[106] *Nagi.* Podocarpus Nageia.
[107] *Letter* 阿 the first letter of the Sanskrit alphabet, much reverenced by Buddhists, especially by the Shingon sect.

Then taking them down to the shore he cast them into the white sea waves one by one with this invocation: "Namu Kimyo chorai, O Shaka Nyorai and Four Great Heavenly Kings and Ye God of Heaven and Earth, and all the deities who protect this Imperial land, especially the Gongen of Kumano and the deity of Itsukushima in Aki. May it please you to grant that one of these may reach the capital." As he went on making them and casting them into the sea thus, as the days passed the number of the sotoba increased with them, and whether the winds assisted him or the gods and Buddhas sent it, one of the thousand sotoba was cast up on the shore before the shrine of Itsukushima Daimyojin. It chanced moreover that a priest who had some connexion with Yasuyori Nyudo had just come to Itsukushima in the course of a pilgrimage to the western part of the country, and this priest had the intention of going to the island if he could find occasion, to enquire the whereabouts of the Nyudo. There a servant came out from the shrine dressed in a kariginu and looking like an ordinary person, and in the course of their talk the priest said: "It is true that the gods appear in the world in divers guises to save mortals, but in what connexion does the god of this place appear as a sea dragon?"[108] "Because the third daughter of the Dragon King of Shakatsura[109] is manifested here as Taizokai (the mandara of wisdom)," replied the shrine servant. (Since the goddess appeared in this place she has continued to help mortals until the present day and many miraculous events have taken place, so that these eight shrines stand raising their lofty roofs by the sea shore, the moon shining on the ebbing and flowing tide: when the tide flows the great torii and the red shrine-fence shine like emerald, and at the ebbing tide even in the summer night the sand before it is covered with frost.)

Then the priest, wondering at these marvels, offered gifts to the shrine with peace of mind, and as the moon rose and the tide came in at dusk he saw the sotoba come floating among the seaweed that drifted in from the offing, and idly picking it up he saw the verse upon it, and as the characters were cut in the wood they were not washed off by the waves but stood out clearly. Thinking this very strange, he stuck it on the side of his pilgrim's box and went back to Kyoto. On arriving there he showed it to the old mother of Yasuyori and his wife and children who were living in retirement at Murasakino north of Ichijo. "Ah!" they said sadly, "why should this have come here, instead of going across to China which lies nearest, to renew our grief by the sight of it?" Then the matter came to the ear of the Ho-o, and when he looked on it he exclaimed, weeping "Ali, how cruel that the wretched man

---

[108] *Dragon King of Shakatsura.* The third of the Eight Dragon Kings. Sk. Sagara.

[109] *The Dragon gods,* Sk. Nags, probably came into Buddhism from China. The daughter of the Dragon King is well-known in Japanese legend in connexion with the stories of Hohodemi and Urashima.

should still be living." It was sent on by him to Komatsu Dono, and he in turn sent it to his father.

Of famous verses there is the stanza that Kaki no moto Hitomaro made about 'the ship disappearing among the islands,' thinking fondly of his native laud, and that of Yamabe-no-Akahito in like case celebrating 'the storks among the reeds.' So the god of Sumiyoshi also spoke of 'the shingled roof of his shrine,' and the Miojin of Miwa of 'the cedar trees of his shrine gate,' when afar from his home. Since Susa-no-o-no-mikoto first made the verse of thirty one syllables, even the gods and Buddhas have thus expressed their feelings in it.

Chapter XV.

SOBU.

Now the Nyudo, being neither wood nor flint, was touched and felt pity, and there was none in Kyoto among high or low, old or young who did not murmur the stanzas of the exiles of Kikaigashima, and even though they had made a thousand sotoba, they were very small things, so that it was very wonderful that the verses should be carried all the way to Kyoto from the far distant shore of the bay of Satsuma.

When one comes to consider the matter, there was also a example of this kind in old time in China. When formerly the king of Han made war on the barbarians, Ri-sho-kei was first made general and led an army of three hundred thousand horsemen, but his forces being the weaker, the barbarian army conquered, and Ri-sho-kei was taken alive by the barbarian king. Then Sobu set out against them with five hundred thousand horsemen, but again his army proved the weaker and the barbarians were victorious, capturing six thousand prisoners and amongst them Sobu himself. Selecting six hundred and thirty of the most important of these, they cut off one of the legs of each and let them go. Of these some died immediately and others some time afterward, and Sobu was the only one who survived. Having only one leg, he managed to keep himself alive by eating the fruit of the trees on the mountains and by plucking the 'nezeri'[110] berries in the fields or by picking up the gleanings of the rice fields in autumn. So long did he do this. that the wild geese that abounded in the rice fields ceased have any fear of him, and looking on them and meditating sadly that they would fly over his beloved native land, at last wrote his thoughts on paper, and having caught one of them he tied the massage to its wing, and, earnestly praying it to be the document to the king, let it go. Faithfully enough, as was its wont, the wild goose flew over from the south to the

---

[110] *Nezeri*. Oenanthe Stolonifera.

capital and as Sho[111] king of Han chanced to be walking in the Imperial garden and feeling somehow rather sad, was gazing at the dusky twilight sky, a line of wild geese came soaring overhead and one of them, flying low, bit off a letter from one of its wings and let it fall, An official immediately picked it up and brought it to the king who opened it and read as follows: "Having spent the first three months of the year in a cave in the rocks, now I am cast forth wandering among the narrow paths between the rice fields, a survivor with one leg among the northern barbarians. Even though I leave my dead body in the barbarian country, yet shall my spirit surely again serve my Emperor." (Now this is the reason why, since that time, a letter is often called 'Gansho' or 'Gansatsu,' 'goose-script' or 'goose-note'!) "Ah! how pitiful,' said the king, "Sobu is still alive; how praiseworthy is this intimation." Then he sent out an army of a million horsemen under the general Ri-ko and this time the forces of Han were victorious and the army of the barbarians was routed. On hearing of the victory, Sobu came crawling along out of the fields and proclaimed his name and title. With his one leg, and aged by the frosts of nineteen winters, he was borne in a litter to his former country. When he had set out against the barbarians at the age of sixteen he had wrapped round his body the banner presented to him at that time by the Emperor, and now taking it off again he presented it once more in the Imperial presence, whereat both Emperor and subjects were filled with admiration beyond measure. As a reward for his great and meritorious conduct Sobu received a grant of large territories from the Emperor, and was raised to the high office of Ten-shoku-koku.

Now Ri-sho-kei stayed in the barbarian country and did not return, and though he did nothing but lament and try to find a way of getting home, the barbarian king would not permit him and so he could do nothing. The king of Han however had no idea of this, and thought that Ri-sho-kei was a disloyal subject, so he had the dead bodies of his parents dug up and beheaded, while his six nearest relations, father, mother, elder and younger brothers, wife and son, were all treated as criminals. When Ri-sho-kei heard of this he was extremely grieved, and writing a letter in which he stated that he was by no means disloyal, but ardently desired to return to his country, he sent it to the king of Han. The king having read it, exclaimed; "Ah! how sad, he is indeed no disloyal subject;" and greatly regretted that he had caused the bodies of his father and mother to be disinterred and desecrated.

Thus just as Sobu of Han fastened a letter to a goose's wing and sent it to his native land, so did Yasuyori in Japan send his verses home with the waves for bearers: one sending a written message, the other a couple of stanzas, one in a remote age and the other in these latter days.

---

[111] *Sho.* 昭帝, Sobu was captured in the reign of Bu 武 and came back in the sixth year of Sho. The story here differs somewhat from Chinese histories.

Though the one was far away in a barbarian land and the other was but in Kikaigashima, and the times were so different, yet the spirit of both was the same. How truly worthy of admiration they were.

Volume III.

Chapter I.

THE LETTER OF RELEASE.

On the first day of the New Year of the period Jisho the ceremony of New Year greeting took place in the Palace of the Retired Emperor, and on the fourth day the Emperor himself proceeded thither in state. These ceremonies did not depart in any way from the usual precedent, but as in the summer of the preceding year the Shin-Dainagon Narichika-no-Kyo and other of his retainers had been banished or executed, the Retired Emperor still felt much resentment and could not give himself to affairs of state with a quiet mind, and was in an unsettled condition about things in general. Kiyomori Nyudo also, since the revelations of Tada Kurando Yukitsuna, felt uneasy about the Ho-o, and though outwardly appearing unaffected, beneath his apparent calmness he took precautions and wore always a cynical smile.

On the seventh day a comet appeared in the eastern quarter that is called in China 'Shiyuki,'[112] of evil omen; it is also called 'Sekiki'. On the eighteenth day its light increased. Kiyomori's daughter Ken-rei-mon-in, who at this time bore the title of Chugu or second consort of the Emperor, falling ill, there was lamentation both at Court and throughout the country. In all the temples the holy Sutras were recited and envoys were sent to all the shrines, divination was performed and the physicians concocted their medicines, using all the resources of their art both exoteric and esoteric, but still the sickness did not pass away. Then she was found to be pregnant.

The Emperor was now eighteen years old and the Chugu twenty two, and so far neither son nor daughter had been born to His Majesty, so that if a son should how be born to the Chugu it would indeed be fortunate. The Heike rejoiced loudly together, declaring that a son would surely be born, and other noble families also, seeing how fortune now favoured the Heike, did not doubt that so it would turn out. When she was decided to be pregnant, the Nyudo, summoning all the priests of high rank and saintly reputation, bade them use all their knowledge both open and secret in bringing his star before the Buddhas and Bodhisats and praying with all fervour that a son might be born.

---

[112] *Shiyu.* said to be the name of a certain band of rebels in the time of the Emperor Ko-Tei.

On the first day of the sixth month was held the ceremony of assuming the belt of pregnancy, and Kaku-ho Shinno the Lord Abbot of Ninnaji hastened to the Palace with the Kujaku Sutra[113] and performed the incantation ceremony of the Shingon sect. The Tendai Zasshu Kakukai-ho Shinno and the Lord Abbot of Miidera, Enkei-ho Shinno also came up and recited the prayers for obtaining a male heir.

Now as the months passed the Chugu suffered more and more severely, just as was the case with the lady Ri[114] in Han, whose one smile contained a hundred charms; whose illness in the Shoyoden was of like nature. Yo-ki-hi in China also was said to have suffered more and more through the three seasons, as the branch of blossoming pear[115] held the spring rain, as the lotus blossom withered, and as the dew fell heavy on the 'Ominaeshi'. Considering the season of this illness it seemed likely that some evil influences might be the cause, and on enquiring by divination by means of a medium from Fudo Myo-o, it was declared to be owing to evil spirits, especially those of Sanuki-no-in Uji-no-Akusafu Yorinaga, the departed spirit of the Shin Dainagon Narichika-no-Kyo, the evil spirit of Saiko Hoshi and the living spirits of the exiles of Kikaigashima. So in order to placate both the living and the departed spirits, first of all Sanuki-no-in was given back his former title of Sutoku Tenno, and Uji-no-Akusafu was raised posthumously in rank and office, being made Dajo-daijin of the upper first rank. Shonaiki Korekata was appointed Imperial Envoy to proclaim these things.

Now the tomb of Uji-no-Akusafu was at Gosan-mai in Hannyano in the village of Kawakami in the district of Sou-no-kami in Yamato, and as in the autumn of Hogen it had been dug up and the body thrown out on the roadside, since then the grass had overgrown it more every year. How joyful must his departed spirit have been when the Imperial Envoy arrived and read his message. Then the deposed Crown Prince Sagara was given the title of Sudo Tenno and thus Princess Igami was restored to the rank of Empress. All this was done to appease their angry spirits, for from ancient times angry spirits have been considered very terrible. The madness of Rei-zei-in and the deposition of the Retired Emperor Kwazan were said to be owing to the angry spirit of Motokata-no-Mimbu-no-Kyo: there was also the matter of the eye disease of the Retired Emperor Sanjo; it was said to have been due to the spirit of Kwanzan the Imperial Chaplain.

Now when the Kadowaki Saisho heard of these things, he sought Komatsu Dono at his residence and said: "I hear that there is to be a

---

[113] *Kujaku Kyo.* Sk. Mayura Raja Sutra. the Sutra of the Peacock King, one of the former incarnations of S'akya Muni.

[114] *Lady Ri,* favourite of Bu-Tei.

[115] *Branch of blossoming pear.* a quotation from the verse of the famous poet Haku-raku-ten. (Po-chu-i).

very great pardon of offences beyond all precedent in connexion with the prayers for the birth of a son to the Chugu, and that such a virtuous and meritorious act as the recall of the exiles of Kikaigashima is contemplated." On hearing this the Naidaijin at once went to his father and said "It is indeed pitiable how Kadowaki-no-Saisho laments for Tamba-no-Shosho, and especially with regard to the sickness of the Chugu it is said that it is due to the angry spirit of Narichika-no-Kyo, and if you intend to placate the departed spirit of the Dainagon you will perhaps also recall the living Shosho: for if you can thus allay peoples' anxiety, if it is thus according to your will to accomodate the wishes of others, you will obtain your own desire in that the delivery of the Chugu will be easy, and she will bear a prince, and so will the glory of our line increase greatly." The Lay-priest Chancellor, chancing to be more soft-hearted than usual replied: "Then what is to be done with Shunkwan and Yasuyori Hoshi?" "Surely they too should be recalled;" replied Shigemori, "for if one of them be left behind it will be an evil deed." "That may be so with Vasuyori, but as for Shunkwan, he is a fellow who rose through my recommendation, and this is the man who, though he had other places besides, held meetings at his villa at Shishi-ga-tani on Higashiyama for his audacious designs against me. Him I will certainly not pardon." So Shigemori returned and calling his uncle the Saisho told him that the Shosho would be pardoned, that he might set his mind at rest. The Saisho, without waiting to hear more, clasped his hands together and wept with joy. "Ah how pitiable it was when he went into exile to see his wistful eyes full of tears whenever he looked at me, wondering how it was I could not obtain his pardon." "Indeed so you must have felt," replied Shigemori, "for a child is dear to anyone. I will see further to the matter." And he went out. Thus it was settled that the exiles of Kikaigashima should be brought back again, and the Nyudo issued the letter of pardon. An envoy was entrusted with this and immediately left Kyoto. The Saisho in his joy sent a messenger of his own to accompany the official envoy. Though they made haste both by night and day, since the sea will yield to none, and they must brave the waves and wind, though they left Kyoto during the last decade of the seventh month, it was not until about the twentieth day of the ninth month that they reached Kikaigashima.

Chapter II.

STAMPING OF THE FEET.

The   envoy   was   Tanzaemon-no-jo   Motoyasu.   Quickly disembarking from the shin he called with a loud voice on "Hei Hangwan Yasuyori Nyudo and Tamba-no-Shosho exiled in this place." Now the two were away as usual praying before their Kumano Shrine;

only Shunkwan was there, and he, hearing them, at first thought it could only be a dream or that he was being deceived by demons or evil spirits. Then wondering if it might possibly be real, he hurried along so flurried that he fell as he ran, and so presented himself before the envoy crying out that he was the exiled Shunkwan. Then the envoy produced from a bag that his servant carried the letter of pardon which the Nyudo had sent, and Shunkwan opened and read thus "The crime for which exile was ordered is pardoned and the persons herein mentioned may return to the capital. In connexion with the prayers for the safe delivery of the Chugu a special pardon has been granted: the exiles of Kikaigashima Shosho Naritsune and Yasuyori Hoshi are pardoned." This only was written and there was no word of Shunkwan. Thinking that perhaps it was written on the envelope, he looked, but there was nothing there also. He read it from the beginning to the end and from the end to the beginning, but two persons only were mentioned, there was nothing said of three. Then the Shosho and Yasuyori appeared, and, each reading it in turn, verily it was only they two whose names stood written and there was nothing of anyone besides. It all seemed indeed a dream, and when they thought it a dream it was a reality, when they thought of it as a reality it was even as a dream. Beside this there were many letters for the two from Kyoto, but for Shunkwan Sozu there was nothing at all. It seemed that all his friends and connexions had disappeared from the capital. "Ah," he cried, "the three of us were exiled for the same offence and to the same place, how then is it that two only are granted a pardon and I only am left out? Is it that I have been forgotten by the Heike, or is it a mistake in the letter, or is there some other reason?" He looked up to heaven and cast himself down to the earth, weeping and lamenting, but all in vain. Catching hold of the sleeve of the Shosho, he cried in tones of agonised entreaty: "That I have fallen into such a plight is because of the worthless plot of the late Dainagon your father, you must not think it was anything else; if I am not pardoned I cannot go to the capital, but at least take me in this ship and bring me along with you as far as Kyushu, for while you were here with me, just as the swallows come in spring and the wild geese of the ricefields in autumn, so I could get tidings occasionally of my home, but now I am left alone from whom shall I hear anything?" "Indeed that is so," replied the Shosho," and when we witness your anguish, all our joy at returning is taken away and we feel as though we wish to stay with you, but as to taking you with us in this ship, though we greatly wish to do so, the envoy will not permit it at all, and if it were found out that without permission three of us had left the island it would be indeed a serious thing. But when I return to the capital I will intercede with various people and entreat the favour of the Nyudo so that he may send someone to bring you back: be patient and stay here awhile as before, and as your life has been so far preserved, though you have been overlooked in this pardon, at last you are certain to go free." But though they spoke many consoling words, yet Shunkwan would not be comforted, and when the ship made to put off again he tried to embark in it, and falling off jumped up again with the madness of despair. The Shosho left him his mattresses as a memento and Yasuyori a part of the Holy Sutras. When they came to cast off the hawser and put the ship off, the Sozu, seizing hold of it, was dragged out up to his loins and then up to his armpits, following after them as long as he could keep his foothold in the water and entreating them: "Comrades, how can you thus abandon me to my fate? Where is your former fellow feeling fled? Since there is no pardon for me I cannot go to Kyoto, but at least take me with you to Kyushu." But the envoy from Kyoto would not give permission, and they pushed away his hands as he clutched the vessel and at last rowed away, while Shunkwan, giving himself up to despair, flung himself down on the beach and stamped his feet on the sand like a little child that has lost its nurse or mother. "Take me with you! Let me go with you!" he shrieked and cried, but it was all of no avail, and soon, as the ship rowed away, nothing was left but the white waves. The ship was not yet so far distant, but his eyes were blinded with tears so that he could not see it. Then, running up to a high place, he kept on calling to mind the pathetic story of how in former days Matsuura-no-Sayohime[116] waved her long sleeves, calling back the Chinese ship that bore away Otomo Sadehiko.

Thus the ship rowed away till it was seen no more, and though the sun set Shunkwan did not return to his poor hut, but spent the night lying where he was wetted by the spray and dew. The Shosho, being a man full of pity, when he returned did everything he could for him and indeed grieved that he had not drowned himself on that shore. Thus we can understand the grief of So-ri and Soku-ri[117] of old when they were abandoned on Kaiganyama.

Chapter III.

THE AUGUST LYING IN.

Thus the two exiles left Kikaigashima and came to Kase in Hizen, And since the messenger whom the Saisho sent urged them not to proceed to Kyoto that year, as the weather was rough and the passage dangerous, but to wait till spring, the Shosho spent the rest of that year in Kase. Now from the hour of the Tiger (4. a.m.) on the twelfth day of

---

[116] *Matsuyama-no-Sayohime.* referring to the famous story of Sayohime, wife of Otomo, who went up to the top of Matsuura-yama to wave her husband back when he was starting for Shinra (Korea) in the thirty seventh year of Kinmei Tenno.

[117] *Sori and Sokuri.* two brothers in ancient India who were hated by their stepmother and exposed on this mountain.

the eleventh month of the same year the Chugu began to be in travail, and Rokuhara and all the capital were in an uproar. The place of lying in was the Ikedono[118] mansion at Rokuhara and the Ho-o himself made an august visit of ceremony: after him all the Courtiers[119] from the Kwampaku[120] and Dajodaijin downwards, everyone who could be considered anyone at all, and everyone without exception who held emolument or office and hoped for place and promotion in future, came and presented themselves at Rokuhara. When we refer to former cases of the lying-in of Consorts and Empresses there was always a great pardon. On the first day of the ninth month of the second year of Daiji, when Tai-ken-mon-in[121] was brought to bed, a great pardon was proclaimed, and on this occasion things were done according to that precedent and a very extensive pardon was issued, so that among those guilty of serious offences Shunkwan Sozu was unhappily the only one who did of share in it. A vow was made that there should be an Imperial progress of the Empress and Crown Prince to the shrines of Hachiman, Hirano and Oharano if the birth was easy and a prince was born. This vow Sengen Hoin respectfully heard: we speak of it with reverence. Prayer was also made at twenty shrines of the Kami beginning with Ise Daimyojin, and the Sutras were read at the temples of Todaiji and Kofukuji beside sixteen others, those who read the Sutras being chosen officials among those who served the shrines. Retainers wearing kariginu of ornamented brocade and girt with swords walked in procession, carrying various sacred vessels and the Imperial sword and The Imperial Vesture, crossing over from the Higashi-no-dai to the southern court and going forth from the middle gate. A most auspicious and beautiful scene. Komatsu Dono, as was natural to his calm and unmoved nature, came long after the others with his eldest son Gon-no-suke Shosho Koremori and many nobles of lesser rank in a procession of cars bringing presents; forty changes of garments of various kinds, seven silver ornamented swords borne upon large trays, and twelve horses. This was according to the precedent of the Kwampaku Fujiwara Michinaga, who sent horses when his daughter Joto-mon-in, Consort of Ichijo Tenno, was brought to bed in the era Kwanko. Shigemori was the elder brother of the Chugu and since his relation was especially paternal there was reason why he should send these horses. Gojo-no-Dainagon Kunitsuna-no-Kyo also sent two horses, and people wondered if this was because of his great desire for a prince to be born or because of his great virtue. Moreover horses were presented to seventy shrines from Ise even to Itsukushima in Aki, and

---

[118] *Ikedono.* The mansion of the Chunagon Yorimcri.
[119] *Courtiers.* Keisho Unkaku. Keisho, all above the third rank; Unkaku, all above the fifth,
[120] *Kwampaku.* Fujiwara Motofusa.
[121] *Taiken-mon-in,* the Empress of Toba Tenno.

very many sets of decorations for the horses in the Imperial Stables. The Lord Abbot of Ninnaji, Kakuho Shinno, read the Kujaku Sutra, while the Tendai Zasshu Kakwaiho Shinno chanted the Sutra of the Seven Buddhas.[122] The Lord Abbot of Miidera, Enkei Shinno, chanted the Sutra of Kongo Doji, beside which Godaikoguzo,[123] the Six Kwannon,[124] the Ichiji Kinrin Godan Sutra,[125] Rokuji Karin,[126] Hachiji Monju,[127] and the Fugen[128] of long life were all invoked and recited from beginning to end. The smoke of incense filled the whole Palace and the sound of bells echoed to heaven, while the sonorous chanting of the Sutras made men's hair stand up. Whatever evil spirits there might be, and in whatever direction they might turn, they were put to flight. Then too a life-size statue of Yakushi Nyorai and the Five Wondrous Kings[129] was begun for the chapel of Buddha.

Now though all these things were done and the pains came continually upon the Chugu, yet she was not quickly delivered, and the Nyudo and the Ni-i-no-dono his consort, pressing their hands to their breasts in perplexity, continually ejaculated: "What is to be done? What shall we do?" And ever when anyone enquired something of them, all they replied was: "Do as you please; Do as you like:" the Nyudo adding, "Ah, if I were with my army in the field I should not feel anxiety like this." All the while the diviners, the two Sojo, Hokaku and Sho-un, Shunkei Hoin, and the two Sozu, Kozen and Jissen, were chanting the Sutras and incessantly telling their rosaries and praying, invoking the Three Treasures of their temples and all their ancient and venerated statues and books and holy pictures. Indeed it was a most blessed sight. And amid all this sanctification, the Ho-o, who was just at this time engaged in purification ceremonies preparatory to making a pilgrimage to Kumano, sat in a chamber near the brocade curtain behind which the Chugu was, and recited the Sutra of Kwannon of the Thousand Hands.

Now at this moment a change came. Though the holy mediums who were wildly dancing went into a trance, for some time they were silent. "Ah," quoth the "Ho-o whatever evil spirit there may be, how can it come near when I am present? Beside which all these hostile

---

[122] *Seven Buddhas.* Sk. Saptatathagata purva pranidhana visecha vistara.

[123] *Godaikoguzo.* Hokaikoguzo, Kongokoguzo, Hokokoguzo, Rengekokuzo Gyoyokoguzo. Koguzo, Sk. Akasagarva Bodhisattva.

[124] *Six Kwannon.* Senju Kwannon, Sei Kwannon, Bato Kwannon. Ju-Ichi-men Kwannon, Juntei Kwannon, Nyoi-yin Kwannon.

[125] *Ichiji Kinrin.* refers to Dai Nichi Nyorai.

[126] *Rokuji Karin* refers to the Six Kwannon.

[127] *Monju.* Sk, Manjusri, the Buddha of Wisdom in Japan.

[128] *Fugen.* Samantabhadra. All these Sutras seem to be of the Dharani or Mantra School, used as magic spells.

[129] *Five Wondrous Kings.* Fudo Myo-o, Kosanse Myo-o, Gunchari Pasha Myo-o, Taiitoku Myo-o, Kongo Yasha Myo-o.

influences have been granted Our Imperial Benevolence and restored to mankind, and even though they are not grateful "yet how can they now hinder us? Let them quickly be put to flight!" (When women have difficult labour and there is some obstacle hindering them, however troublesome and difficult it may be, if a mighty spell be chanted earnestly then the demon will depart and the birth become easy and successful.) So they all applied themselves diligently to their crystal rosaries with the result that not only was the Imperial Consort safely delivered but a Prince was born. Then Hon-Sammi Chujo Shigehira-no-Kyo, who was then acting as Chugu-no-Suke, came forth from behind the curtain and announced in a loud voice: "The august labour is safely ended and a Prince has deigned to be born."

The Ho-o was the first to offer his congratulations; then the Kwampaku Matsu Dono and the Dajo daijin and all the courtiers below him and all the assistants and acolytes, the chief astrologers, chief physicians, and all the diviners high and low, shouted aloud their joy in concert so that the sound reverberated even to without the gates and did not subside for some while. The Nyudo too, in the excess of his joy, lifted up his voice and wept: these were tears of joy indeed.

Komatsu Dono immediately hurried to the Palace of the Chugu bringing ninety nine mon in coin to place beside the pillow of the baby Prince saying: "Heaven is father and Earth is mother. May your life be as long as that of To-ho-saku and Hoshi:[130] may your mind be as that of Ten-sho-ko-daijin." And taking a bow of mulberry and six arrows of 'yomogi,'[131] he shot them toward heaven and earth and the four quarters of the world.

Chapter IV.

THE VISIT OF THE COURTIERS.

The wife of the former Udaisho Munemori had been chosen as the milknurse for the child, but as she had died in labour on the seventh month, the wife of Taira Dainagon Tokitada-no-Kyo was appointed in succession, and she was afterwards known by the title of Sotsu-no-suke. After a while the Ho-o made his August return journey to his Palace, and when his car came to he gate of Rokuhara to receive him, the Nyudo in an excess of joy offered a thousand pieces of gold and two thousand ryo in weight of Fuji cotton as a present. And this was surprising to people and they said it was not fitting.

There were many things too that people thought laughable in the

---

[130] *To-ho-saku and Hoshi.* Two Chinese sages who knew the secret of eternal life and youth.
[131] *Yomogi.* Artemisia vulgaris or mugwort. This was done to ward off evil influences.

lying in of the Chugu. For instance, the Ho-o acting as a soothsayer; and in the second place, as it is the custom at the lying-in of an Imperial Consort that a rice-vessel (koshiki[132]) should be rolled dawn from the ridge of the Palace roof, if a Prince is born it is to be rolled down the south side, and if a Princess down the north side, this was done as usual; but by mistake it was rolled down the north side,[133] whereat there was a great uproar, end it was brought up again and rolled down once more in the roper manner. This was an ill-omened event in the opinion of host people. What appeared ridiculous was the flurry and agitation of the Lay Priest Chancellor, in contrast to the conduct of Shigemori, which was much admired. Much to be regretted was it that the former Udaisho Munemori-no-Kyo, having lost his much-beloved wife, resigned both his offices of Dainagon and Taisho and retired into seclusion: how happy had it been if both elder and younger brothers had been there. Then came seven astrologers to perform a thousand exorcisms and among them was an old man named Kamon-no-kami Tokiharu. He was a man of small property and office, and as so many people came thronging there like the bamboo shoots that stand thick together, yea even like rice sprouts, flax, bamboos and reeds, he cried out: "I am an official. Make way!" and pressing through the midst of the crowd, what a sight he presented! Having trodden off his right shoe, he was resting for a moment when his headdress also got knocked off, and at such a time to see a dignified old man in ceremonial court costume, with his hair in disorder, pacing along was more than the younger courtiers were able to endure, and they burst forth into uncontrollable mirth. For the astrologers say that their peculiar gait must be most punctiliously observed. A strange thing too was that he knew nothing about it: all at the time, though afterwards when he came to think about it he remembered everything. Now at the time of the August lying-in the following notables visited Rokuhara. The Kwampaku Matsu Dono (Fujiwara Motofusa), the Dajodaijin Myo-on-in (Fujiwara Motonaga), the Sadaijin Oi-no-Mikado (Fujiwara Tsunemune), the Udaijin Tsuki-no-wa Dono (Fuji Kanezane), the Naidaijin Komatsu Dono, the Sadaisho Sanesada, the Gen-Dainagon Sadafusa, Sanjo-no-Dainagon Sanefusa, Gojo-no-Dainagon Kunitsuna, To Dainagon Sanekuni, Azechi Sugekata Naka no Mikado Chunaagon

---

[132] *Koshiki.* Cf. Sansom's note on Tsurezure Gusa, p. 46. Explaining the custom the Tsurezure Gusa says. "In the case of a birth, in the Imperial Family the dropping of a 'koshiki is not a fixed custom but is a:harm used when the afterbirth is obstructed. When it is not obstructed it is not done. The custom came from the common people and has no authority. The 'koshiki used are brought from the village of Ohara. In pictures treasured from ancient times one sees the dropping of these rice vessels shown when a birth is taken place among the common people." The charm originates in the assonance of 甑 koshiki, rice box, and 腰氣 koshiki pain in the loins. The name of Ohara (also=great belly) is also significant.

[133] *North Side*, The quarter of the women's apartments. Cf. Kita-no-kata.

Muneie, Kwazan Chunagon Kanemasa, Gen-Chunagon Kanemasa, Gen Chunagon Masayori, Gon-Chunagon Sanetsuna, To Chunagon Sukenaga, Ike-no-Chunagon Yorimori, Saemon-no-kami Tokitada, Betto Tadachika, Hidan-no-Saisho-no-Chusho Saneie, U-no-Saisho-no Shusho Sanemune, Shin Saisho-no-Chusho Michichika, Hei Saisho Norimori, Rokkaku-no-Saisho-Iemichi, Horikawa-no-Saisho Yorisada, Sadaiben-no-Saisho Nagakata, Udaiben-no-Sammi Toshitsune, Sahei-no-kami Shigenori, Uhei-no-kami Mitsuyoshi, Kotaigo-gu-no-taiyu Tomokata, Sakyo-no-taiyu Naganori, Dazai-no-daiji Chikanobu, Shinsammi Sanekiyo and t thirty three others. Except the Udaiben they wore 'naoshi.' Among those that did not come were the former Dajo-daijin Kwazan-in Tadamasa Ko, Omiya-no-Dainagon Takasue-no-Kyo and about ten others of lesser rank. Some time afterwards wearing 'hoi,' these went to visit the Lay priest Chancellor his mansion at Nishi Hachijo.

Chapter V.

BUILDING OF A GREAT PAGODA.

Now as the result of the great efficacy of their prayers, rewards were given to the various temples. The eastern temple of Ninnaji was repaired. Afterwards seven days' prayer was ordered to be made, beside the reading of the Law of Daigen and the ceremony of Kwancho or baptism. Enryo Hogen was raised to be Hoin while the Imperial Zasshu was given the second rank of Princes of the Blood and allowed the privilege of proceeding to Court in an ox-car. As Ninnaji resented this Kakusei Sozu was raised to the rank of Hoin, besides which other rewards were bestowed too numerous to mention.

After some time had elapsed the Chugu returned from Rokuhara to the Palace. Since the daughter of the Lay priest Chancellor had become Imperial Consort, monthly pilgrimages had quickly been begun to Itsukushima the greatly venerated, to pray that a prince might be born to her, and that he should soon ascend the Throne in order that the Nyudo and his wife might become Imperial Grandparents, and the Chugu had soon become pregnant and been safely delivered of a Prince to their great joy.

Now the time that the Heike family began to revere the shrine of Itsukushima in Aki was when Kiyomori only held the office of Aki-no-kami, and with the income he derived from Aki repaired the great pagoda at Koya. This work was finished in six years, having been entrusted to the steward Watanabe-no-Endo Rokuro Yorikata, and when it was finished Kiyomori himself proceeded to Koya and worshipped before the great pagoda after which he visited the Oku-no-in. Whereupon from somewhere or other there suddenly appeared an old priest with white hair and hoary eyebrows, his forehead furrowed with many wrinkles, leaning on a cross handled staff, who addressed him thus: "From ancient days this holy mountain has yielded place to none as a home of the Shingon doctrine; and now our great pagoda has been repaired there is none like it in the land. Now Kebi in Echizen and Itsukushima in Aki are the two shrines where our doctrine of the Two Worlds[134] is revealed. Keki is very prosperous but Itsukushima is in a very dilapidated condition: do you therefore report this to the Throne and repair it in like manner, and if this be done you shall rise to high office so that there shall be none in the whole country to equal you." Having spoken thus, he departed, and where he had been standing a wondrous fragrance of incense arose; and when Kiyomori went to look and see whither he had gone he could see him but for a distance of three cho, and then he disappeared. "This was no mere man; it was the Daishi:"[135] he thought, reverently pondering over the vision, and as a remembrance in this Shaba-world he painted two Mandaras in the Kondo of Koya. The western Mandara he had executed by a painter named Jomyo Hoin, while the eastern one he painted himself. And for what reason I know not he painted the crown of Dai-Nichi Nyorai, the central figure, with blood which he took from his own head.

Afterwards he went up to Kyoto and reported this to the Retired Emperor, whereat, the Emperor and the Court being greatly moved, he was again appointed Aki-no-kami and bidden to restore the shrine of Itsukushima. So he rebuilt it, raising up its torii and renovating its many shrines, constructing also a gallery measuring three hundred and sixty yards in length. When all the work was finished, Kiyomori went to worship at the shrine, and, in a dream which came to him while spending the night in worship, he saw the doors of the Holy of Holies open and a beautiful youth with tightly bound hair come out and say: "I am the messenger of the Daimyojin of this shrine; do thou take this blade and make secure therewith the Throne of this Imperial Realm;" handing him a short halberd ornamented with silver bands. On his awaking and reflecting on the dream lo! it was a reality, for there was the halberd beside his pillow. Moreover he received also this oracle from the Daimyojin: "Whether you remember or forget, I know not, but the words of the sage of Koya will stand; if however your actions be evil, your preeminence will not be transmitted to your descendants.

---

[134] *Two Worlds.* The Kongo kai and the Daizo-kai, The world of Ideas or the Diamond World and the Hidden World, the peculiar doctrines of the Shingon sect. Vairochana, the great deity of Shingon, was identified with Ama-terasu, whose daughter Ichiki-shima-hime was the goddess of Itsukushima.

[135] *Daishi.* Kobo Daishi, the Founder of Koya.

Chapter VI.

RAIGO.

When Shirakawa in was on the throne, the daughter of the Kwampaku Fujiwara Morozane of Kyogoku became Imperial Consort, and being a clever lady, was much beloved by the Emperor, so that His Majesty, wishing to have a son by her, summoned a priest of Miidera named Raigo Ajari, who was renowned for the efficacy of his supplications, and promised him that if he could successfully intercede with the Buddhas to grant him a son by this lady, he should be given whatever he might wish. Raigo respectfully assented and, returning to Miidera, applied himself to his prayers with all his might to such effect that the Chugu soon became with child, and on the sixth day of the twelfth month of the first year of Shoho was safely delivered of a Prince. The Emperor, greatly overjoyed, again summoned Raigo and asked him what reward he wished for, whereupon Raigo replied that he wished that a ceremonial dais should be built at Miidera. Now the Emperor, thinking that he would probably ask to be made Sojo at one step, was greatly astonished at this unexpected request, for this ceremonial dais for the ordination of priests was only allowed at Hieizan. "Now this Prince is born," replied the Emperor, "we hope that lie will succeed to the Throne and that the land will remain in pace and quietness, but if your request be granted Hieizan will be wroth, the Empire will be disturbed, war will break out between your two temples and the Tendai sect may be destroyed." So that his desire was not granted.

Raigo, greatly disappointed, returned to Miidera and determined to die by starvation. The Emperor on hearing of this was greatly amazed, and calling Oe Masafusa, who was then Mimasaka-no-kami, said to him. "Since you have been a pupil of Raigo, go and see what you can do about this affair." Oe hastened to Miidera and found that Raigo Ajari had retired to his cell to ponder over the Imperial decision. Following him thither he discovered the Ajari sitting in a small smoke-blackened oratory from which he shouted in a voice of thunder: "The word of the Emperor is no joke: an Imperial speech[136] is like sweat. If I cannot obtain my request I will carry away the Prince that my prayers have made and take him with me to the Meido:" and without another word he retired to his cell. Mimasaka-no-kami returning reported his experience to the Mikado, whereupon His Majesty was exceedingly grieved. Eventually Raigo died by starvation as he had said, and

---

[136] *An Imperial speech is like sweat.* i.e. can only go forth and cannot return or be revoked,

thereupon the little Prince fell sick and took to his bed, and although many prayers were said for him it seemed of no avail. Always a white haired priest holding a 'shakujo'[137] appeared to stand at the little Prince's pillow, and this not only in peoples' dreams but in the reality of broad daylight, and on the sixth day of the eighth month of the first year of Sho-ryaku the Prince at last expired at the age of four years. He was known as Atsubumi Shinno. The Emperor's grief was extreme, but at that time, hearing that there was a priest at Hieizan, the chief priest of the Saito Hall named Ryoshin Dai-Sojo, who was then only Sozu of Enyubo, who was reputed to be very potent in prayer, he summoned him to the Palace and asked him what he could do. "The Imperial Wish," he answered, "can certainly be accomplished by the power of our sect, for was not a Prince born to the Mikado Rei-zei-in by the effective prayers of Jie Dai-Sojo, when requested by the Udaijin Kujo Morosuke Ko? It is not a difficult thing. So, returning to Hieizan for a hundred days he gave himself up to earnest prayer, and within this time the Chugu conceived, and on the ninth day of the seventh month of the third year of Sho-ryaku she was safely delivered of a Prince who afterwards became the Mikado Horikawa Tenno. So even in ancient times evil spirits were terrible things.

At the time of this most auspicious lying in of Ken-rei-mon-in, it was a pity that, in spite of the amnesty that was granted, Shunkwan Sozu alone should have been omitted. On the eighth day of the twelfth month of the same year the Prince was nominated heir to the Throne, the Naidaijin Shigemori being appointed Instructor and Ike-no-Chunagon Yorimori appointed Daiyu. This year having ended it became the third year of Jisho.

Chapter VII.

THE SHOSHO'S RETURN TO KYOTO.

In the last decade of the first month Tamba-no-Shosho Naritsune and Hei Hangwan Yasuyori Nyudo left Kase in Hizen and started for Kyoto with all speed, but as the cold was still severe and the sea rough, crawling from harbour to harbour and from one island to another, it was the tenth of the second month before they reached Kojima in Bizen. Thence they went to see Ariki-no-Bessho where the Dainagon, the father of the Shosho, had lived. Here they found various writings on the bamboo pillars and on the shoji that the Dainagon had left. "Ah," he said, "there is no better memento than a person's handwriting. If he had not written this here how could we have seen where he was?" And the two of them read and reread it again and again with tears. "On the

---

[137] *Shakujo*. a staff ornamented with metal rings carried by priests.

twentieth day of the seventh month of the third year of Angen, became a priest; on the twenty sixth day of the same month Nobutoshi came from Kyoto." was written. Thus they learned that Gensaemon-no-jo Nobutoshi had been to visit him. On the wall near by was incribed: "If we trust to the Three Holy Buddhas[138] to receive us, surely we shall be reborn in Paradise." Whereat, seeing that he had hoped to be reborn in the Pure Land, they felt somewhat comforted amid their limitless grief.

When they enquired for his tomb, alas, there was no mound raised over it, only a place where the earth was a little higher than usual. Adjusting his sleeves respectfully, the Shosho spoke as to a living person, weeping as he addressed him. "The tidings that you had passed away to the world beyond were indeed brought to me in the island where I was living, but not being free I could not hasten hither. Since I was exiled to the island I was so melancholy that life was unbearable even for a day: but I sustained my frail life and existed for two years, and am exceeding joyful to return thus far, and if I could have found my honoured father alive how blessed it would have been. As it is now, length of days has become but vanity. Thus far I have made great haste hither, but from to day there will be no need for hurry." Thus he spoke weeping, and had his father been living how much would he have found to say in reply; but with those in the grave, there dwells no regret: who is there that can smile when under the moss? The wind in the pines was the only answer. That night the two spent in vigil at the grave, and when day broke they made a new tomb, fencing it about with stakes and building in front a temporary but where they stayed seven nights, repeating the Nembutsu and reading the Sutras. Then erecting a great sotoba they inscribed thereon these words: "The deceased, a pure spirit, delivered from the wheel of birth and death, now surely entered into the great enlightenment;" with the date of the year and month and beneath it, "Naritsune, a filial son." Surely no wood-cutter or lowly peasant, however ignorant, could help weeping at this proof of a child being the supremest treasure on earth. As the years roll on, nothing is more unforgettable than gratitude for a kind bringing up, like a dream it is and like a vision; yea, and difficult to end are the present tears of love. The countless Buddhas of the Three Worlds[139] and Ten Quarters[140] must have deigned to grieve, and the revered spirit of the departed, how must it have rejoiced. Then, though wishing to stay longer to say the Nembutsu, yet knowing the anxiety of those awaiting them in Kyoto, they took their leave of the late Dainagon, promising to return again, and departed weeping. Even from those beneath the shadow of the grass it is hard to part. On the sixteenth day

---

[138] *Three Buddhas.* Amida. Kwannon and Seishi.

[139] *Three Worlds.* Present. Past, and Future.

[140] *Ten Quarters.* N.S. E.W. NW, NF, SIB', SE. and Upper and Lower Quarters.

of the third month at dawn the Shosho reached Toba, where was the country residence of the late Dainagon, called the Suhama mansion. On coming to the mansion they found it all ruinous, the fence without a roof and the doors gone from the gate. In the garden there was no trace of anyone, and the moss had grown thick over everything. Walking round beside the pond, the spring breeze of Aki-no-yama was rippling its surface with white waves, the purple duck and the white sea gull swimming hither and thither. When could they cease weeping and longing for him who had made it all?

The mansion still stood, but the entrance was broken in and the shutters and doors had disappeared. The Shosho could do nothing but fondly linger over everything associated with his father, referring to him in words such as these: "Here it was that the Dainagon did so and so; here is the gate by which he used to enter; that is the tree that he himself planted." It was the sixth day of the third month, and some flowers were still remaining in bloom; the willow, the plum, the peach, and the apricot, recognizing the season by their flowering twig: "Though their former master was gone, yet the flowers forget not the spring." The Shosho, standing beneath the blossom murmured to himself the ancient verses:

> "*Peach and apricot cannot record the seasons that vanish*
> *There is no smoke to be seen; was it lined here of old?*"
> "*Ah, if the flowers could speak that grow in the home childhood;*
> *Would I not ask them to tell all they remembered of you?*"

Yasuyori too, on hearing this was affected by melancholy feelings and could not but moisten his black sleeves with tears. They wished to stay there much longer and, loath to leave, they remained until the evening: as it grew dark the moonbeams, as is their wont in ruined houses, fell through the ancient eaves and flooded the mouldering chambers with light. Even when the dawn began to break on the mountains they did not haste hasten homewards, but as he could not remain there for ever, the Shosho sent for the palanquin, since it had not waited for them, and reluctantly left the Suhama mansion in tears, going on towards Kyoto rejoicing and sorrowing by turns. A palanquin, had also come to meet Yasuyori Nyudo, but being unwilling to part from his companion yet, he did not use it, but getting into the back of the Shosho's vehicle, went with him as far as Shichijo Kawara, where their ways divided, but still they did not wish to part. Those who spend half a day together under the cherry-blossoms, friends who look at the moon together for an evening, travellers who stand under the same tree out of a sudden shower until it is over, all these feel regret at parting; how much more those who have lived a life of misery in the same island, on the same ship and in the same storms; since they have the same Karma must not their relation in the former life have been most deep?

The Shosho's mother, who was living at Ryozen, had come the day before to the house of the Saisho to await her son, and when she but caught sight of him as he entered, in her emotion at seeing him alive, she covered her face and lay prostrate. His wife too, who had been in the flower of her beauty when he left, had become so emaciated with anxiety about him that he hardly thought her the same person, while the black hair of his nurse Rokujo had become snow-white. His child, who was three years old at the time of his exile, had now grown old enough to bind his hair. Seeing another child of three beside him, the Shosho enquired who it might be, but Rokujo could only falter: "Ah, that one indeed...." when she was overcome by tears. Then the Shosho remembered with sorrow that his wife had been about to give birth when he was exiled and that this must be the child that she had brought up safely. The Shosho then visited the Ho-o as he had formerly been accustomed to do, and was promoted to the office of Saisho-no-Chujo. Yasuyori Nyudo retired to a country seat that he had at Sorinji on Higashi-yama and there lived quietly. His sentiments he thus expressed:

"*Thickly the moss has grown on the eaves of the roof of my*
    home place;
Through the opened chinks filter the beams of the moon."

And so, living a secluded life, he pondered on his former unhappy days, and diverted himself by writing a work called 'Hobutsu-shu' or 'Treasury.'

Chapter VIII.

THE VISIT OF ARIO TO THE ISLAND.

Thus two of the exiles of Kikaigashima were recalled and returned to the capital, and now only one was left, a pitiful guardian of the isle. Now Shunkwan Sozu had a servant called Ario whom he had taken pity on and brought up from his childhood. This Ario, hearing that the exiles of Kikaigashima were returning to the capital, had gone as far as Toba to meet his master, and not seeing him had enquired and been told that, as his crime was most heinous, he alone had been left behind on the island. Grief-stricken at the news, he took to frequenting Rokuhara, and as he did not hear that a pardon was likely to be granted, he went to the daughter of the Sozu where she was living in retirement and said: "This time he has been left behind and has not come back; now I must go anyhow to the island and find out how he is faring: so I pray you write me a letter that I may take it." The lady was overjoyed at this and immediately wrote as he had suggested. He would have wished to take leave of his parents openly, but fearing they would not agree, he went off without telling anyone. As the China ships used to sail on the fourth or fifth month, thinking that to set out in the summer would be too late, he started from Kyoto at the end of the third month, and, after suffering a hard sea passage, arrived at last in Satsuma Bay. At the port whence he tried to cross over to the island, however, he was suspected and trapped and search but, nothing daunted, he secreted the letter he was carrying his top knot and in the end managed to get a passage in a merchant ship and reach the island. He had heard some slight account of it in Kyoto, but it was nothing to what he actually found. No ricefields, no gardens, no houses, no village. There were some inhabitants, but he could not understand their speech, and thus when he went to enquire of them: "Where is Shunkwan Sozu, the Shugyo of Hosshoji, who has been exiled to this place?" whether they understood the words 'Hosshoji' or 'Shugyo,' or not, they answered nothing, but only shook their heads. There was however one who knew that there had been three men on the island and that two of them had gone back to the capital, leaving one behind who wandered about hither and thither as though beside himself, but lately he had not been seen. On hearing this Ario plunged deep into the uncertain mountain paths, climbing the peaks and descending into the valleys. Losing the track in the mists, he could not find his way until the golden sunset found him still on the hills and there he lay down and slept, but never once did he see the figure of his master. Then, not finding him on the mountains, he searched along the shore, but there was none who answered his cries but the sea gulls, whose footprints he saw on the sands or the chidori that flocked on the beach. But one morning he saw a figure creeping along by the rocks on the shore, searching for drift wood and thorns, emaciated as a dragon fly, looking like a priest whose hair had grown long and bristling up on his head. Over his skinny wrinkled frame a few rags were hanging, whether of silk or cotton could not be discerned. In one hand he had some 'arame,' and in the other a fish that someone had given him. He was trying to walk, but could scarcely get along and staggered like one drunken. Ario had seen many beggars in Kyoto, but never yet had he seen one like this. "All the Asuras[141] dwell by the ocean; the Asuras and the Three Evil Things[142] dwell in the depths of the mountains and by the ocean;" say the Buddhist Sutras, and he thought for an instant that he had unwittingly entered the Gaki-do (Preta[143]-world). But as he approached he wondered if even such a

---

[141] *Asura.* A kind of demon or titan, the fourth class of sentient beings.

[142] *Three Evil Things.* The beings of the Three Evil Ways, i.e. Hells, Preta and Beast Worlds.

[143] *Preta.* Hungry spirits with huge belly and mouth, but extremely narrow throats.

creature might perchance know something cf his master, and going up
to him repeated the question that he had put to the islanders the day
before: "Can you tell me where I can find Shunkwan Sozu the Shugyo
of Hosshoji?" The servant did not recognise his master, but how could
Shunkwan forget Ario? And crying out "Here! here he is," the things
that he was carrying fell from his grasp and he sank down senseless on
the sand. And thus it was that Ario found his master. Then taking his
dying master on his knees Ario cried: "Alas! after having braved the
rough seas and come so far, it is of no avail. Thus to find my master in
such distress!" As he thus lamented in tears, the Sozu, coming to
himself and sitting up, said: "Indeed you are beyond praise thus to dare
the dangers of the sea and come so far a journey. Day and night I have
never for a moment ceased to think of home, and the faces of my dear
ones were ever before me both in dreams and in illusions. Since I have
become so ill and weak I cannot tell dream from reality. Even now I
wonder if your coming is not a dream. If it be indeed a dream, what
shall I do when I awaken?" "Indeed it is real," replied Ario, "but when
I see your condition, it seems a miracle that you can have lived to see
me." "Not, only so," answered the Sozu, "but last year, when they cam
to fetch the Shosho and the Hangwan Nyudo, I scarcely refrained from
dying by my own hand. Foolishly I relied on the consoling words of the
faithless Shosho that he would send someone hither when he arrived at
Kyoto, but though not willing to live in this island there is no food; so,
while I had the strength, I used to go up into the mountains and collect
the sulphur that is found there. This I would barter for food with the
merchants who come from time to time from Kyushu, but growing
gradually weaker, I became unable to do so, and row when the weather
is fine. I can but mange to creep out to the beach and beg a little fish
from the fishermen, or, when the tide is out, pick up some shell fish or
edible sea weed. Thus holding on to my dew like existence by the moss
of the sea, I have managed to keep alive in wretchedness until now; and
I wonder what reason there is for me to continue longer in this fleeting
world? But let us go to my house, for there are many things I wish to
say." Then Ario, thinking it strange that one in such a state should
possess a house, took him on his back and went towards a place that the
Sozu pointed out. It was in the midst of a pine wood, a hut made with
bamboos for pillars and bundles of reeds for crossbeams, thickly
covered inside and out with pine-needless: too frail it seemed to keep
off rain and wind. How strange a place is this for one who of late was
Bursar of Hosshoji, and had eighty manors in his charge, who had in
his gate houses four or five hundred servants and retainers at his beck
and call! Indeed there are various kinds of Karma that which reacts in
the present life, that which reacts in the next life, and that which will
continue for many lives. This Sozu had all his life been occupied with
nothing but the business of great temples and the affairs of Buddha, but

while thus professing the Way of Buddha, having committed a shameless crime, I in receiving the emoluments of office without teaching the Law, the result of this Karma fell upon him thus quickly in this world.

The Sozu had now perceived that Ario was no apparition and enquired; "Last year when they came for the Shosho and the Hangwan there were no tidings for me; have you also no letters from anyone?" Ario, choked with sobs, pressed his face to the ground and for some time could answer nothing. Then raising himself again, restraining his tears he replied: "After my lord went to Nishi Hachijo the Nyudo's officials came and confiscated all our property, and after arresting all the retainers they examined them with respect to the revolt and then put them all to death. Our lady fled with her youngest daughter and went into retirement on Mount Kurama. I alone went sometimes to see them and found them ever in a sorrowful state. The child, as she missed you so much, would always embarrass me by asking: "Please take me to Kikaigashima." But in the second month, being taken with small pox, she died. Our lady mistress, unable to bear this added blow, then sank into melancholy and took to her bed, and on the second day of the third month she also departed this life. Only the elder daughter is now living safely in retirement with her aunt at Nara, and it is from her that I have brought this letter." The Sozu opened and read it and therein was written all that Ario had said, to which was added: "Ah! why is it that when three were exiled two have returned and one only is left, and so far you have not come back? Alas! high or low there is none so useless as a woman; if I had been a man I would have come to the island whither you have gone. Pray come back again soon with this youth. "Ah," said Shunkwan, "see, Ario, the pathetic simplicity of this girl, writing that I should soon come back with you. If I had been free to please myself should I have stayed three years in such a place? She must now be about twelve years old; how will such a simple child be able to marry? Perchance she may be able to keep herself by serving in some great household," and he burst into tears afresh. How does this remind us of the saying: "Even a wise parent goes astray in considering his own children."

"Since I came to this island," he continued, "as there was no calendar I have had no knowledge of the days and months only by the blossoming and falling of the flowers do I know that three springs and autumns have passed, and the voice of the cicada alone tells me that wheat harvest is over and summer is come. The piling up of the snow tells me that it is winter; by the waxing and waning of the moon I perceive that thirty days have gone by and by counting on my fingers I know that my little boy will be six this year. Has he too preceded me to the other world? When I went out that fateful day to Nishi Hachijo, he wanted me to take him with me, and to console him I said I would soon be back. It seems indeed but yesterday. When I think of all these things the future is nothing to me. The relation of parent and child, husband and wife is not for this world only; now it is only about my daughter that I am anxious, and if she be alive she may continue to live, even though it be in wretchedness. But as for me, if I continue to live thus the sight of my misery must pain you greatly."

So from this time he steadfastly refused all food and earnestly gave himself up to invoking Amida and saying the death-prayers, and on the twenty-third day from the coming of Ario, the Sozu expired in his hut at the age of thirty-seven. Ario, clasping the lifeless body, looked up to heaven and cast himself on the ground, weeping unrestrainedly: "Ah, how gladly would I follow you to the other world, but for my young mistress's sake who is left behind, and because there is no other to pray for my master's happiness in the after life, I must continue to live and pray that he may attain enlightenment. So without changing his resting place, breaking down the hut and heaping up dry pine branches and reeds upon it, he lighted the pyre, and the smoke ascended heavy with brine. Then, the cremation being finished, he gathered up the whitened bones and, hanging them round his neck, awaited the coming of a merchant ship and returned to Kyushu. From thence returning home he sought out the place where the Sozu's daughter was dwelling and related everything in detail from beginning to end. "Very much I had hoped to have brought you a letter," he said "and your father thought much about it, but in that island there was neither inkstone nor paper, so that it was not possible to write one: we live not only in this world but throughout many worlds to come, and in another world in the far future we may hear his voice and see his face, so let us earnestly pray that he may receive enlightenment." Thus he spake, but ere his young mistress had heard him to the end she fell forward on her face and wept bitterly. Though but twelve years old she straightway became a nun and lived a holy life in the Hokkeji at Nara, praying for the happiness of her parents in the hereafter.

Ario, taking with him the bones of Shunkwan Sozu, went up to Mt. Koya and deposited them before the inmost shrine called Oku-no-in where Kobo Daishi sleeps. Then, becoming a priest at Renge-dani, he made a pilgrimage seven times round the whole country, saying prayers for his master in the next world. Now all these miseries accumulated to bring a terrible end on the Heike house.

Chapter IX.

THE WHIRLWIND.

On the twelfth day of the fifth month at noon a mighty whirlwind blew through the midst of the capital and many houses were overturned; the wind started from Naka-no-Mikado Kyogoku and blew across to the south-west, tearing the roofs off the gate-houses of the mansions and carrying them away to a distance of from four or five to ten cho. Rafters and beams and pillars flew about in the air, and the wooden shingles from the roofs blew about everywhere like leaves in the wind. The mighty roaring of it was such that even the wind of Karma[144] that blows people to Hell could not be greater. Not only were houses destroyed but many people lost their lives, and cattle without number were killed. This was no ordinary occurrence, so that divination was necessary and the Official Soothsayers proceeded to make it. "Within a hundred days, a minister in receipt of great emoluments must look at himself, beside which there will be a crisis in the Empire, and the Throne and the Law of Buddha will decline: wars will also follow one on another:" So the Official Soothsayers and Court Diviners both decided unanimously.

Chapter X.

THE ARGUMENT ABOUT PHYSICIANS.

In the summer of the same year Komatsu Dono, feeling melancholy and distressed about these and other matters, made a pilgrimage to Kumano, and spent the whole night before the Shojoden of the main shrine, calmly making his offerings and humbly praying thus: "My father the Lay priest Chancellor, acting in a worthless and immoral fashion, is likely to trouble even the Imperial Throne. Seeing this, even the prosperity of this generation seems endangered. I, being the eldest son, continually tender him advice, but being a stupid fellow, he does not adopt my recommendations, so that it will be difficult to honour our ancestors and exalt the name of our family. At this time I find myself very incompetent, and thus I, unworthy descendant of my line, cannot act as a good minister and wise son to guide the fortunes of my house. Better were it to give up my name, and, forsaking all hopes in this life, to try to attain enlightenment in the future. But an ignorant and ordinary person like myself surely will go astray in making choice;

---

[144] *Wind of Karma.* The force of the Karma of evil deeds that carries people away to hell.

so I cannot do as I would. Namu Gongen Kongo Doji, I beseech thee, let the prosperity of our line continue, that we may still be favoured with the gracious friendship of our Sovereign, and that the evil mind of my father may be softened, and that the Empire may be peaceful in our days. But if our house is to be prosperous in this one generation only, and shame is to fall on our posterity, then I pray thee cut short even now the life of Shigemori and deliver him from the wheel of sorrow[145] in the life to come. I look to thy mystic aid in both these petitions." And as he prayed earnestly thus, a light as of a lamp issued from the body of the minister and then suddenly disappeared as though extinguished, and though there were many who saw it, yet for fear none said anything about it. When the minister returned to Kyoto and while he was crossing the Iwata-gawa his eldest son Gon-no-suke Koremori and some other Courtiers, who were wearing a violet coloured under-dress beneath their white hemp costumes, it being the hottest time of summer, for some reason or other went into the water and were sporting there, so that the violet showed through their wet upper garments and it looked like a single garment of mourning colour. Chikugo-no-kami, seeing this, called out: "A dress that suggests mourning is very ill-omened; I pray you haste and change it quickly." But Shigemori replied: "There is no need to change it; it is a sign that my petition is to be fulfilled." And from Iwata-gawa he sent offerings to Kumano with a thankful heart. The others present thought it strange, but he did not deign to enlighten them at all. (But these Courtiers, strange to say, soon had to put on the colour in real earnest.) After Shigemori returned to Kyoto, a few days passed and he became ill. Thinking that the Gongen had soon accepted his petition, he applied no remedy, neither did he pray for recovery. About that time a famous physician came from the Sung Court of China and was staying in Japan. Now the Nyudo was at this time stopping at his country mansion at Fukuhara, and sent Etchu Zenji Moritoshi as a messenger to Shigemori, saying: "I hear that your ailment is severe: as a very distinguished physician has lately come from the Sung Court, it is a fortunate thing, so pray call him and try his skill." On hearing this, the minister, having himself raised in bed, called Moritoshi into his presence and said: "With regard to this offer of the physician, I am much obliged to you, but as you doubtless know well, that even such a wise ruler as Daigo Tenno, in the era of Enki, should have allowed a foreign physiognomist to be introduced into the capital is to be considered a wise Emperor's mistake and a shame to our country ever after. Far greater disgrace then would it be to our land that a common

---

[145] *Wheel of sorrow.* i.e. sentient existence as a continuous circle of migrations from one state to another, form which deliverance is obtained by the Buddhist Law. Sk. Sansara.

person like Shigemori should bring a foreign physician into the capital. When Koso of Kan, in administering his country, struck down Keifu of Wai-nan with the three foot sword that he carried, and was struck and wounded by a stray arrow, the Empress Dowager Ro called a skilful physician who said: "To heal this wound fifty pounds of gold will be required." Then Koso answered; "As I have been strong in defending myself, I have fought many battles and received many wounds; they have not disabled me for my time has not come. Our lives are in the hands of Heaven, and even if one had such a famous physician as Henjaku,[146] it would be no use." But as he did not wish to appear to grudge the money, he gave fifty pounds of gold to the doctor but did not receive the treatment. This is a precedent with which I am quite satisfied. I, Shigemori, though of no account, rose to be numbered among those of the first three ranks, and further was advanced to be one of the three great ministers.[147] My destiny therefore is in the hands of Heaven why should I question Heaven's will and hanker after physicians? If my illness is destined to be fatal, of what use is a physician? But if it is not so destined, without a physician's help I shall recover. Without availing himself of the skill of Kiba,[148] Shaka Muni declared his entry into Nirvana by the Batsu-dai river.[149] Since this was a disease that was destined to be fatal it was to show that it could not be cured. Only Buddha can heal completely, Kiba can but alleviate sickness. If a fatal disease can be cured by physicians, why then did Shaka die? It is quite clear that medicine is of no value for a fatal disease. But my body is not the body of a Buddha, so that distinguished doctors or even Kiba are not necessary. If we judge by the Four Books,[150] how can even the best of an hundred remedies save this vile mortal body of ours? Is it not also written in the Five Volumes:[151] "Though one can cure ordinary diseases, how can one cure that which is caused by the Karma of a previous existence?" Moreover if I should live as the result of this physician's treatment, it would seem as though there were no skilful doctor in Japan. If his treatment is unavailing, it is not necessary for me to see him; and if one holding the position of one of the first three ministers of Japan comes to ask an interview of a wealthy foreign guest, it is both a disgrace to the country and also a degradation of his morality. So that though I may lose my life, yet I must not for a moment think of disgracing my country." Having heard all these words, Moritoshi weeping returned to Fukuhara and repeated

---

[146] *Henjaku.* A famous Chinese physician in ancient times.

[147] *Three great ministers.* Dajo-daijin, Sadaijin Udaijin.

[148] *Kiba.* Indian physician of great repute.

[149] *Batsudai or Battai river.* Sk. Vati, mod. Gunduck, a river that rises in Nepaul and flows past Kus'inagara, beside which S'akya Muni entered Nirvana.

[150] *Four Books.* Of Medicine, Acupuncture, Massage and Incantations.

[151] *Five Volumes.* Another medical work.

everything to Kiyomori. "From of old time" said the Nyudo, "I have never heard of a minister who would consider the disgrace of his country, and neither did I think there was one in these degenerate days. Shigemori is too good a minister: I fear that he may probably die." So he hastily returned to the capital.

On the twenty-eighth day of the seventh month, Shigemori became a priest, taking the name Jo-ren, and on the first day of the eighth month, having said the death prayers, he passed away at the age of forty three. In such a prosperous time how sad an end indeed. Though the Lay priest Chancellor would try to tear paper across[152] the grain, yet Shigemori was always there t to smooth things over; so that the Empire remained peaceful until this time. But now all classes of society were lamenting and wondering what would happen in times to come. But the, friends of the former Udaisho Munemori were rejoicing greatly, thinking that now the control of everything would fall into leis hands. Parents love for their children is often a cause of sadness to them, but it is doubly sad when they die before their parent. He was the pillar of his house and the wisest man of his age; the loss of his kindness and affection and the decline of his house cannot be too much deplored. The Empire lost a good minister, and his house had to lament the loss of his counsel in the field. Moreover he was a man versed in letters, loyal to the Emperor, talented and accomplished and a man of virtuous conversation.

Chapter XI.

THE UNDECORATED SWORD.

The character of this minister being thus remarkable, may it not be that he could forsee the future? For before his death, on the seventh day of the fourth month, he had a dream. He seemed to be walking a long distance on the shore when he saw a large torii near him; wondering what torii it was, someone said that it was that of Kasuga Daimyojin. Then a crowd of people came thronging to the place and one of them held up the head of a big priest on the pint of a sword. Shigemori asked whose head it was. "It is the head of the Dajo Nyudo Dono of the Heike," was the reply, "for the enormity of his sins the Daimyojin of this shrine has ordered it to be taken." Then he awoke. "Ah," he thought, "our house has subdued the enemies of the Emperor many times since Hogen and Heiji and, being greatly rewarded, has come to, produce a Dajo-daijin who is grandfather to the Emperor. In our clan more than sixty men have received great advancement, and in twenty

---

[152] *Tear paper across*, persist in obstinate and unreasonable conduct Japanese paper will only tear with the grain.

years there is none in all the Empire who can compare with us in rank
and office, and now, through the manifold evil deeds of the Nyudo, the
fall of our family draws nigh;" and he wept bitterly. Just at this time
there was a great knocking at the door of his apartment. On enquiring
who was there, they told him that Seno-no-Taro Kaneyasu, having just
had a very extraordinary dream, in spite of the lateness of the hour,
begged leave to relate it to him, and also requested that everyone
should be sent from the apartment. When all had left him alone,
Shigemori gave him audience, and he related with full detail exactly the
same dream as the Daijin himself had just had. Then, thought
Shigemori, the god has revealed these things to Kaneyasu also.

The next morning, as his eldest son Gon-no-suke-no-Shosho
Koremori was preparing to go to the Palace of the Retired Emperor, his
father called him and said: "For a parent to say such things is perhaps
rather conceited, but you are a very clever son. Ho, there! serve the
Shosho with a cup of sake!" Chikuga-no-kami Sadayoshi poured out a
cup and offered it to the Shosho, but as he would not drink before his
father, the Daijin drank three cups and afterwards the Shosho drank
thrice. Then Shigemori ordered what he intended for the Shosho to be
brought, and they brought a sword in a bag of red brocade. The Shosho,
thinking that it was the sword called 'Kogarasu,'[153] the famous
heirloom of the Heike, looked greatly delighted, but how did his face
fall when he saw that it was only the plain black sword worn at the
funeral of a minister. Then his father said, weeping, "This is no mistake
of Sadayoshi; it is the black sword without decoration to be worn at a
minister's funeral. The Nyudo thought I should wear it to accompany
him to the grave, but now, as I shall certainly die before him, I present
it to you." The Shosho made no answer, but, retiring to his apartment in
tears, he covered his face and lay down and did not go out that day. It
was after this that Shigemori went to Kumano and soon after he
returned was taken ill and died. Truly indeed he must have known.

Chapter XII.

OF LANTERNS.

Now Shigemori was a minister who had a strong desire to destroy
evil and encourage virtue, and therefore, deploring the coming doom of
his house, in imitation of the forty-eight vows of Amida, he built forty-
eight temples at the foot of Higashi-yama, and hung up forty-eight
lanterns, one in each of them. On the fourteenth and fifteenth of every
month they were lighted and prayers were offered, so that they looked

---

[153] *Kogarasu Maru*, The famous sword treasured in the Heike family, said to have
been forged in the third year of Tai-ho by Arnakuni, the first Japanese swordsmith.

like the brilliant effulgence of the polished mirrors that shine in the beauteous palaces of the Paradise of the Pure Land. Moreover two hundred and eighty-eight young and lovely maidens of noble birth were selected, six for each temple, and these were ordained as nuns, that on these two days of every month they might raise their voices in earnest and unceasing supplication. In truth it seemed as if the light of the Nyorai who comes to receive men shone on the earth, as if the rays of the All-Saving Buddha shone on the minister. On the fifteenth day there was a great supplication, and the minister himself walked in the midst of the procession. Turning to the west and joining his hands together he played thus: "Hail Amida Nyorai, Thou who guidest and leadest us to the Paradise of the West, save, we beseech thee, all men of the Three Worlds and Six Ways." When the people saw him thus going round and praying, their hearts were greatly touched, and those who heard of it shed tears of gratitude. Therefore Shigemori became known by the name of 'Toro-daijin' or 'Lantern Minister.'

Chapter XIII.

A DONATION.

Now Shigemori wished to do many virtuous actions in this life and to have prayers said for his benefit in the world to come, but in Japan, however great merit a man may achieve, it is doubtful whether he will have a succession of descendants to pray for him in the future. He thought therefore that he would acquire merit in another country to ensure prayers being said for him after death. So in the spring of Angen he summoned a certain ship captain from Kyushu named Myoden and received him in private audience, giving him the following commands: "You are a man of proved honesty; here are three thousand ryo of gold, and of these I present you with five hundred: do you proceed to the Court of Sung and give a thousand ryo to the priests of Ikuozan,[154] and the remaining two thousand to the Emperor of Sung, that estates may be bought and presented to Ikuozan, and they may say prayers for Shigemori in the life to come."

Myoken, taking charge of the gold, and braving the angry sea for countless miles, at last arrived in the Sung country and met Bussho Zenji Toku-ko, the prior of Ikuozan, to whom he related all his business. The priest, rejoicing greatly, received the thousand ryo and handed it over to the priests of Ikuozan, while he presented another two thousand to the Emperor. When he reported to the Emperor the words of Komatsu Dono, His Majesty was struck with admiration, and

---

[154] *Ikuozan*, short form of Aikuozan, the first of the five famous mountains of China.

ordered five hundred cho of land to be presented to Ikuozan, and it is said that an inscription praying for a happy rebirth in the future existence for the Minister of Japan, Taira-no-Ason Shigemori Ko, is still in existence at that place at the present day. After the death of Komatsu Dono, the Nyudo fell into a state of melancholy, and hastening to Fukuhara, went into retirement there.

Chapter XIV.

THE ARGUMENT OF HOIN.

At the hour of the Dog (8 p.m.) on the seventh day of the eleventh month of the same year, the earth quaked very greatly for a long time, and the chief diviner Abe-no-Yasuchika hurried to the Palace and gave his verdict as follows: "According to the books of divination this earthquake is a very serious portent. Consulting the book called Kongikyo, one of the three books of divination, we find that it is not a matter of years, months or days; it points to a very near and urgent affair," and he lifted up his voice and wept. The Imperial Messenger too was greatly perturbed, and when it was reported to the Emperor, His Majesty was extremely alarmed. But many of the younger nobles and courtiers burst out laughing when they heard of it, saying: "What is this useless Yasuchika weeping about? Is it likely that anything much is going to happen now?" This Yasuchika, however, had received the traditions of five generations, and was deeply learned in astronomy, and as he had always explained the omens accurately up till now without making any mistakes, he was considered a divinely inspired prophet. On one occasion in a thunderstorm the sleeve of his 'kariginu' had been scorched by a flash of lightning, without any injury to his person; in whatever age a sign that he was specially favoured by Heaven.

On the fourteenth day the Lay priest Chancellor, for some reason or other, saw fit to return to the capital with a long train of several thousand horsemen, thereby throwing the city into a tumult, though there was no special reason for it. Someone started the rumour that Kiyomori had come up to Kyoto with hostile intentions against the Imperial Court. The Kwampaku Motofusa also hurried to Court, perhaps in consequence of some secret information. "It seems that the Nyudo has come up to the capital this time to try and overthrow me, and I know not what affliction I may not have to endure;" said the Kwampaku to his Imperial Master. "Whatever may happen to you," replied the Emperor, "I shall feel as though the same misfortune had befallen me:" and the august tears coursed down his Dragon Countenance; we speak it with awe. Though the government of the country was transacted by the Emperor and the Kwampaku, yet none knew what would happen; the matter was as the will of Tensho daijin or Kasuga Daimyojin. On the fifteenth day there was no doubt that Kiyomori intended hostilities against the Court, and the Retired Emperor in great consternation sent Joken Hoin, son of the late Shinsei Dainagon, to Rokuhara with this message: "This year the Imperial Family has been troubled and people are unsettled; the people also are restless and disquieted, all of which causes us much grief. You who have charge of everything, and can entirely pacify the country, do not do so, but come up and make a commotion in the city and menace the Imperial Court; what is the meaning of it?" Hoin proceeded to Nishi Hachijo, but the Nyudo would not receive him, and having waited there from morning till evening, as he could not obtain an audience, thinking it was no use, he transmitted the Imperial Message to Gendaiyu-no-Hangwan Suesada and went to take his leave, when the Nyudo ordered him to be called back, and on his returning, thus addressed him: "Ya-a, priest Hoin. Is what I say untrue? The death of Shigemori is a great blow to our house, and you may guess how deep is my grief. During the disturbances that followed the era of Hogen, when the peace of the Emperor was disturbed, I only administered affairs, while Shigemori also humbly exerted himself to the utmost and pacified the Imperial wrath. Moreover, whether in emergencies or in ordinary matters of administration, a more meritorious minister would have been difficult to find. Then consider the history of former ages, how the Emperor Taiso of China, when his minister Gicho died, was excessively grieved and wrote this inscription on his tomb, so great was his sorrow: "Inso of old dreamed that he had a virtuous minister, but I, when I awake know that I have lost a wise one." In our country also, if I mistake not, when Akiyori-no-Mimbu-no-Kyo died, the late Retired Emperor was excessively grieved, and postponing his visit to Hachiman, refrained from going out. All the Emperors, in fact, when their ministers died, mourned for them, but now, when Shigemori has not yet been dead fifty days, the Emperor goes to the shrine of Hachiman and to other places, not showing the least sign of regret. Even if you forget Shigemori's loyal conduct, why do you not sympathise with my grief? How can you forget Shigemori's loyalty? If both father and son thus lose the favour of the Emperor, both are put to shame. This is one thing: then, though the Emperor promised not to change his demeanour either to my sons or grandsons, as soon as Shigemori is dead, he takes back the domain of Echizen which he had held. For what misconduct was this done? Then again, when the office of Chunagon was vacant and the Nii Chusho Motomichi earnestly desired it, I recommended him for it, but no notice was taken and the office was given to the son of the Kwampaku. However unreasonable I may be, why is it that he was thus favoured? It is much to be regretted that the Emperor should thus pass over one so suitable in rank and birth in so arbitrary a manner. Then again, when the followers and retainers of the Shin-Dainagon Narichika-no-Kyo met together in Shishigatani to foment a rebellion, that was not done on their own initiative; it was in accordance with the wish of the Retired Emperor, and though it is a strange thing to say, though the Emperor ought not to forget the services of my house for seven generations, yet he planned to take away the little remaining life that is left to me in my old age of three score years and ten. It would seem then to be difficult for my descendants to continue to serve the Court in after generations. Thus bereft of my son in my old age, I am like a withered tree that has no branches. What then is the use of my wasting my time in such a case? What will happen you yourself can guess." As he spoke thus vehemently, alternating between anger and tears, Hoin was moved both to pity and fear, and the cold sweat stood out upon him. No one could have made any answer at such a time. Beside which he remembered that one of his own retainers had taken part in the conspiracy of Shishigatani, and was apprehensive lest he might be arrested on that account, feeling rather like one who strokes a dragon's beard or treads on a lion's tail; yet though he felt so terrified he showed nothing in his demeanour, but only replied: "Indeed your services have been very great, and no doubt your anger is not without reason, but surely both as regards rank and emoluments you have no cause for dissatisfaction. Moreover your great merits are always remembered by the Imperial House. But to say that the revolt of the Courtiers was by the design of the Emperor, is it not but a treasonable slander? But to believe the ear and to doubt the eye is always the bad habit of the world at large. To believe the words of people of no account, putting aside the Imperial favour and opposing the Emperor is, whether secret or revealed, a very terrible thing. Heaven is wide and immeasureable in extent and not otherwise is the mind of the Emperor that the inferior should be disobedient to his superior, how can such conduct befit a minister? Pray consider this well. This is the purport of what I have to say." All those who stood by, on hearing this reply, exclaimed: "How bold thus calmly to answer the Nyudo when he is in such a rage." And there was none who did not praise him greatly.

Chapter XV.

BANISHMENT OF THE DAIJIN.

Hoin, returning from Rokuhara, reported the speech of the Nyudo to the Ho-o, and His Majesty, thinking there was much right on his side, said nothing further. On the sixteenth day the Nyudo carried out his intentions by depriving the Kwampaku and forty-three other Courtiers of their offices. The Kwampaku Motofusa, on hearing in addition that he was transferred to the office of Dazai-no-Sotsu and was to depart to Kyushu, remarking that in an evil world like this it did not matter what happened, retired to his house at Furukawa near Toba and became a monk, his age being thirty-five. "He was an unclouded mirror of courtesy," said everyone, and regret at his loss was extreme. As when one sentenced to exile becomes a monk, they do not send him to the province decided on, though it had been decided to send him to Hyuga at first, since he became a monk he was sent to a place called Yuazama near Kofu in Bizen. (Former examples of the exile of ministers are the Sadaijin Soga no Akae, Udaijin Toyonari, tile Sadaijin Uona and the Udaijin Sugawara,[155] I mention him with great respect for he is the present Tenjin of Kitano, besides the Sadaijin Komei Ko and the Naidai-jin Fujiwara-no-Ishu Ko. Six in all, but this was the first example of the exile of a Sessho Kampaku.) The son of the Naka Dono Nii Chujo Motomichi, son-in-law of the Nyudo, then became Daijin and Kwampaku. In the time of the late Enyu-in, on the first of the eleventh month of Tenroku, Ichijo-no-Sessho Kentoku Ko died, and his younger brother Horikawa Kwampaku Chugi Ko was then Juni-i Chunagon and another younger brother Ho-ko-in Dai Nyudo Kaneie Ko was Dainagon-no Udaisho: of these two Chugi Ko had been passed over by his brother in rank and office, but when he in turn stepped over his brother and became Sho-ni-i Naidaijin and obtained a private intimation of this from the Emperor, everyone said it was the most extraordinary promotion they had heard of. But a much more extraordinary case was it when one who was only Ni-i-no-Chujo and not a Councillor of State, passing over the office of Dainagon,[156] became Daijin and Sessho in one leap. Fugenji Dono (Motomichi) was the first one who ever did so. The Councillors (Shokei), the Ministers (Saisho), the Chief Secretary and the officials under them were all dumbfounded. The Dajo-daijin Moronaga was deprived of office and exiled to the eastern provinces. As the reflection of the guilt of his father the evil Sadaijin of Hogen, he with three of his brothers went into exile. His elder brother the Udaisho Kanenaga, the younger brother Hidari-no-Chujo Takanaga, and Hancho Zenji did not live to return to the capital but died at their place of banishment, but Moronaga, after nine years spent in Tosa, was recalled in the eighth month of the second year of Chokwan, restored to his original rank, and the following year raised to Shoni-i (Upper Second Rank). In the tenth month of the first year of Nin-an he rose from being Chunagon to the office of Gon Dainagon: the office of Dainagon not being vacant at this time, he was added as supernumerary. It was the first time there had been six

---

[155] *Sugawara*. Sugawara-no-Michizane, now deified as Temmangu or Tenjin: his great temple is at Kitano in Kyoto.

[156] *Dainagon*. These were originally four in number, but afterwards the office of Gon-Dainagon or Vice-Dainagon was created, and their number was not limited; in the time of Takakura Tenno there were ten.

Dainagons at the same time. Also promotion from former Chunagon to Gon Dainagon, with the exception of Uji-no-Dainagon Takakuni-no-Kyo who afterwards became Yamashina-no-daijin Minori Ko, was never known before. He was skilled in music and very accomplished in other arts, so his progress was rapid until at last he became Dajo-daijin. Then as the result of some fault in a previous existence he was again sent into exile. In former times in Hogen he was sent to Tosa by the southern sea, and now in Jisho he was again, it seemed, to go to Owari beyond the eastern boundary. But being guiltless as before, and as a man of taste, only wishing to gaze at the moon in his place of banishment, the Daijin made light of it. Recollecting how of old Haku-raku-ten, when guest of the Crown Prince of China, used to wander about the bay of Jinyo, in like manner he leisurely passed his days, gazing at the distant sea scenery of the bay of Narumi and viewing the clear moon, whistling to the sea breeze and chanting songs to the accompaniment of his biwa. Once he made a pilgrimage to the shrine of Atsuta Myojin in that province, and in the evening performed a recitation on his biwa to please the deity. It was a place where there were none but unlettered people living, and there were none with any elegant taste; but the village people, young and old, girls, fishermen and farmers, came out with bent head and intent ear to listen, though they knew nothing of time or rhythm. So it is said that, when Koba played the biwa, the fish would dance in the water, and when Kuko sang, the dust on the beams would skip about. When a genius performs, then emotion is invoked spontaneously. So the hair of his audience stood on end at the wonder of his playing, and as it gradually grew later, while he sung a piece called 'Fuko' or 'Fragrance', the flowers poured forth their scent, and when singing of the 'Flowing Water' the moon shed its pure clear white light over the scene; until at last the god unable to contain his feelings any longer, caused the sanctuary to tremble greatly. Whereat the Daijin shed tears of joy saying: "If it had not been for the evil conduct of the Heike, I should not have seen such a blessed sign."

Azetsu-no-Dainagon Sukekata-no-Kyo and his son Ukone-no-Shosho Sanuki-no-kami Minamoto-no-Suketoki were both deprived of their office, as also were the three officials Gondaiyu Uhyoe no kami Fujiwara Mitsuyoshi, Counsellor of the Empress Dowager, Okura-no-Kyo, Ukyo-no-Daiyu, Iyo-no-kami, Takashima-no-Yasutsune, and Kurando-no-Sashoben, Chugu-no-Gondaishin, Fujiwara-no-Motochika, Azetsu-no-Dainagon Sukekata his son Ukonye-no-Shosho and his grandson U-shosho Masakata were moreover expelled the same day from the capital. Thereupon the Dainagon remarked: "The three worlds are wide, but there in no room for my five foot length; though life is short it is difficult to live for a single day. If you go out of the Ninefold Imperial Court by night, you have got to go beyond the Eightfold

Clouds." So, going by Oeyama and the way of Ikuno, first he came to a place called Murakumo in Tamba where he stayed some time, then at last going on from thence he is said to have reached Shinano.

Chapter XVI.

THE CASE OF YUKITAKA.

Now among the retainers of the former Kwanpaku Motofusa was a samurai named Ko-no-Taiyu Hangwan Tonari, who was not favourable to the Heike. Hearing that he was to be arrested by Rokuhara, he took his son Ko Saernon-no-jo Ienari with him and fled to the south country. Ascending Inariyama and dismounting from their horses, father and son took counsel together saying: "We had hoped to flee to the east and find refuge with the former Uhyoe-no-suke Yoritomo, but he has been excommunicated and is himself in jeopardy, and there hardly seems any other place in Nippon that is not a Heike fief. As therefore we cannot escape, and it is a disgrace to let our ancestral home fall into strange hands, let us go back again, and when the Rokuhara retainers come, we will set fire to the house and cut open our bellies and die in the flames." So they went back again to their mansion at Kawarasaka and, just as they had expected, Gendaiyu-no-Hangwan Suesada and Settsu-no-Hangwan Morisumi carne against them with three hundred horsemen, shouting their warcry exultantly. Then Ko-no-Taiyu Hangwan came forth on to the verandah and shouting in a loud voice: "See that you tell this at Rokurara!" set fire to the house, and cutting himself open with his son, both perished in the flaming pile. Now the reason why all these misfortunes fell on so many people was the rivalry for the office of Chunagon between the former Kwampaku's son Sammi-no-Chujo Moroka and Ni-i-no-Chujo Motomichi who became Kwampaku. How ever much the former Kwampaku suffered for it did not so much matter, but how about the justice of the forty three others? And the Nyudo did not stop at these things only, so that people said an evil spirit had entered into him and he had lost all self-control, so that the city was troubled thereat. In spite of the title of Sutoku Tenno being given to Sanuki-no-in, and Fujiwara-no-Yorinaga, the evil Sadaijin, being promoted in rank and office, still there was no tranquillity.

Now there was a certain former Sashoben Yukitaka, the eldest son of Nakayama-no-Chunagon Akitoki-no-Kyo, who had been made Shoben in the time of the Retired Emperor Nijo, and was a very energetic official, but for the last ten years or so had been retired from his office and was living in such straitened circumstances that he had not sufficient food or clothing. To him the Nyudo sent a message to make haste and repair to Rokuhara, as he had some matter to discuss with him. Yukitaka on hearing this was greatly perturbed, thinking that, in spite of his having held no office or appeared in society for some ten years, someone had slandered him to Kiyomori with intent to bring about his complete destruction. His wife and children, also terror stricken, uttered loud lamentations; however, as repeated messages came from Rokuhara, Yukitaka, seeing that he must obey, borrowed a car from someone and set out. Quite contrary to his supposition, the Nyudo immediately came forth and received him cordially; "Your noble father," said he, "did me various services, and I will not be negligent toward his son. I have felt very sorry for your long exclusion from office, but in face of the Ho-o's decisions I had no power to remedy it: but now I bid you resume your duties and will give orders about your new office." On his return home his family received him, weeping for joy, as one that has returned from the dead. Afterwards, by the hand of Gendaiyu-no-Hangwan Suesada, estates and fiefs were granted him as emolument, and as a convenience besides, he was presented with a hundred pieces of silk, a hundred ryo of gold, and abundance of rice. As accessories of his office he was also granted a liberal allowance of servants, ox-carts and drivers. Yukitaka was so overcome with joy that he hardly knew where he was going or what he was doing, it was so like a dream. On the seventeenth day he was made Kurando of the fifth rank and again resumed his former office of Sashoben. He was then fifty-one years of age, but appeared to have suddenly become young again. It was however a transient prosperity.

Chapter XVII.

THE EXILE OF THE HO-O.

On the twentieth day of the same month the forces of the Heike surrounded the Palace of the Ho-o, and all the ladies-in-waiting and male and female servants, thinking that they would burn the Palace and put all in it to death as Nobuyori had done when he attacked the Sanjo Palace in Heiji, forgetting all but their own safety, fled in wild panic without even waiting to garb themselves. Then the former Udaisho, Munemori-no-Kyo, gave orders to bring the Imperial Car and to make all haste, whereat the Ho-o, much perturbed, exclaimed: "Am I to be banished to some far country or distant island like Narichika or Shunkwan? I am not aware of having done anything wrong except perhaps that since the Emperor is so young I have occasionally given advice on affairs of state; if however this is not desirable, I will do so no more in future." Munemori, shedding tears of sympathy, replied: "Far be it from me to do such a thing; it is only my father's wish that while things are in this unsettled state, Your Majesty should go and stay for a while at the North Place at Toba." "Then," replied the Ho-o, "please deign to attend me thither." But Munemori, fearing his father's anger, did not accompany His Majesty, his conduct in this respect being greatly inferior to that of his late brother Shigemori, who the year before in such a case had at his own risk prevented the Ho-o suffering so great a dishonour and secured his safety until now. But now there was none to reprove the Nyudo, and so this affair had come to pass. There seemed little hope for the future, and the Ho-o thinking of these things wept bitterly. Then, entering his Car, unattended by any of his nobles or Courtiers, with only a few guards of low rank and an attendant priest named Kongyo, he set out. At the back of the Imperial Car rode a nun, who had been the Ho-o's milk nurse, called Kino-Ni-i. As the Car passed along Shichijo toward the west and then along Shujaku toward the south, the bystanders exclaimed: "Ah! the Ho-o is going into exile;" and there were none among the common people who did not moisten their sleeves with their tears at the sight.

Everyone said that the earthquake on the seventh day was a portent of this, and that it was because the Earth Deity who responds even to a thousand million depths had raged furiously. When the Ho-o had come to the Toba Palace there was not a single retainer to wait on him; but Daizen-no-Taiyu Nobunari, having somehow managed to escape notice, came and presented himself before His Majesty. "I think it is likely that I shall be put to death soon, so I wish to have the Holy Water prepared. How do you think?" asked the Ho-o. On hearing this Nobunari, who had been extremely anxious all that morning, was dumfounded, but girding up the sleeves of his 'kariginu,' and pouring water into a cauldron, he broke down a small fence for firewood, and splitting up some small beams of the corricor, heated the water in due form.

Then Joken Hoin went to the Nyudo at Nishi Hachijo and urged that, the Ho-o having gone to the Toba Palace the night before, it was too severe treatment that he should have not a single person in attendance, so he himself wished to go and attend on His Majesty. The Nyudo replied that it as he was a trustworthy priest he might go; whereupon Joken was exceedingly delighted and immediately hastened to the Toba Palace. Alighting from his car at the entrance, as soon as he entered within the gate, he heard the voice of the Ho-o chanting the Sutras, and it had indeed a very melancholy sound. When Hoin hastily entered he saw the Ho-o sitting and shedding tears upon the Sutra that he was reading, and in his grief at the sight, he too pressed the sleeve of his white costume to his eyes and thus came into his presence weeping. Only the nun was in attendance. "Ah, Hoin," said the Ho-o," since you had breakfast yesterday morning in the Hojuji den neither last night nor this morning have you taken any food. Neither have you slept at all through the night: indeed I fear some danger to your life." Hoin, controlling his feelings, replied: "Everything in this world has an end; the Heike have held the Empire in their hands for twenty years, but their evil deeds have gone on piling up and verily their end too will come. And surely Tensho-daijin and Sho-Hachimangu will not forget you, while there is also the deity of Hiyoshi on whom you rely, and who will surely vouchsafe his sure protection. The oft read eight books of the Hokke Sutra will guard you, and then once more the rule will return into your Imperial Power and all the offenders will vanish away like foam on the water." The Ho-o, on hearing these words was somewhat comforted.

The Emperor was much grieved at the exile of his Kwampaku and the loss of so many of his high officials, but when he heard of the banishment of the Ho-o to the Toba Palace, he would take no food, and becoming sick, he entered his august sleeping apartment and would not come forth. The ladies in waiting and the Imperial Consorts were at their wits' end to know what to do. After the Ho-o had gone to the Toba Palace special worship was held in the Imperial Palace; a dais of mortar[157] was made in the Seiryoden where the Emperor worshipped Ise-no-Daijingu every night. These prayers were offered for the Ho-o. The Retired Emperor Nijo was a wise ruler, but since in his opinion an Emperor[158] has neither father nor mother, he was always opposing the Ho-o and did not carry on the Imperial Line successfully. Therefore his son the Retired Emperor Rokujo, after having ascended the Throne, unfortunately died on the fourteenth day of the seventh month of the third year of Angen at the age of thirteen.

Chapter XVIII.

THE SEINAN DETACHED PALACE.

In a hundred volumes we find the saying: "Filial piety is the most important thing. A wise monarch governs the Empire by filial piety." Therefore we see that Tokyo revered his old and feeble mother and Gushun respected his obstinate father. It is very blessed when the Imperial Will follows the example of such wise and pious rulers. About this time the Emperor secretly sent this message to the Ho-o at the Tosa Palace: "In such an age even though one live in the Palace what can one do? Perhaps it is best to retire into the mountains and become a recluse as was done by Uda Tenno in the era of Kwampei and by Kwazan Tenno in former times." To this the Ho-o replied "Do not think of such a thing. If you remain as you are, it is one source of reliance for me, but if you depart from the Palace, on what can I rely? At any rate wait and see what my fate will be." The Emperor, on receiving this

---

[157] *Dais of mortar.* It was made under the eaves on the east side of the Seiryoden, one of the halls of the Palace, at the south end; mortar was spread on the boards to obtain the effect of an earth floor.

[158] *Emperor has neither father nor mother.* Cf. "Twice an Empress." p. 23.

letter, pressed it to his face and wept unrestrainedly.

As the sages have said: "The Emperor is the ship;[159] the subjects are the water. The water may make the ship float well, or again the water may overturn the ship. The subjects may protect the Emperor, or again the subjects may overthrow the Emperor." In Hogen and Heiji the Lay-priest Chancellor protected the Emperor, but now in Angen and Jisho he sets him at naught just as the classic says.

The Grand Chancellor Omiya,[160] the Naidaijin Sanjo,[161] the Dainagon Hamuro,[162] and the Chunagon Nakayama[163] were all dead. and Seirai[164] and Shinhan[165] only were left; but these two, thinking it was no use remaining at Court in such an age, even if they became Dainagon, retired from the world and became monks while still young. Mimbu-no-Kyo Nyudo Shinhan having the hoar frosts of Ohara for company, and Saisho Nyudo Seirai living among the mists of Koya, both had no thought for anything but attaining enlightenment in the next existence. In ancient days in China too there were man who hid themselves in the clouds of Shozan[166] and cleansed their hearts under the moon of Eisen,[167] so what wonder was it that these deeply learned and pure minded men should forsake so troublesome a world?

When the Saisho Nyudo among the recesses of Mt. Koya heard that the Emperor also wished to retire from the world, he exclaimed: "Ah, well it was that I have so soon become a recluse; for though to hear of it while here in seclusion is evil enough, how great a grief would it have been to have heard it while in attendance on His Majesty. The revolts of Hogen and Heiji were indeed evil, but now the age has become more degenerate, and such extraordinary things as this have come to pass. What will happen to the Empire in future no one can tell. Would that I could ascend above the clouds or hide myself deep in the farthest mountains." Verily it could not be considered a world in which anyone with any sense would live.

On the twenty first day the Tendai Zasshu Kakukwai Ho Shinno realized his oft expressed wish and retired, the former Zasshu Mei-un Dai Sojo being reinstated in his place. The Lay-priest Chancellor, though he had thus recklessly overturned and scattered everything, seeing that his daughter was the Chugu and his soil in law the

---

[159] *The Emperor is the ship.* A saying of Confucius.

[160] *Omiya.* Fujiwara Koremichi,

[161] *Sanjo.* Fujiwara Kinnori.

[162] *Hamuro.* Hamuro Mitsuyori.

[163] *Nakayama.* Fujiwara Akitoki.

[164] *Seirai*, younger brother of Hamuro.

[165] *Shinhan.* son of Taira Ienori.

[166] *Shozan.* refers to the four illustrious men of Kan, En-Ko, Kaku-ri Sensei, Ki-ri-ri and Ka-chu Ko.

[167] *Eisen.* Kyo-yu washed his ears in this stream to cleanse them from the pollution of having listened to the treasonable suggestion of Gyo.

Kwampaku, now felt quite easy in his mind about everything, and went off to Fukuhara declaring that the administration was entirely according to the wishes of the Emperor. On the twenty third day the former Udaisho Munenori-no-Kyo hastened to the Palace and reported thus to the Emperor; whereupon His Majesty said: "If I had received authority from the Ho-o according to custom I might do something, but as things are, do you take counsel with the Kwampaku and do as you like about the administration:" and he paid no further attention to the matter.

Now the winter was half over and the Ho-o was in the Seinan Detached Palace. The wind of Yazan[168] sounded shrilly, and the moon shone bright on the frozen garden. The snow fell and piled up on the courtyard, but no one's footsteps were seen upon it. The ice thickened on the ponds, but no flocks of birds resorted thither. The boom of the bell of the great temple resounded in his ears like that of Iaiji[169] in China; the white snow on the western hills reminded him of the scene of the peak of Koro. In the cold frosty evening the clink of the fuller's mallet was borne faintly to his pillow; while at dawn he was awakened by the slow wheels creaking on the ice outside the gate. The travellers passing along the highway, the sight of the galloping warhorses, the pomp and movement of this fleeting world, how vain it seems to one who understands. The guards before the Palace gates who kept watch day and night, by what connexion in a former existence was it that they were now brought into this relation with him? What an awe inspiring thought it was. Thus on every side the Ho-o found things that gave him pain. So during his exile here he could not help occupying his thoughts with the memory of the various excursions and pilgrimages and festivals he had enjoyed, and the recollection of them would bring tears to his eyes; And so things went on and the fourth year of Jisho began.

Volume IV.

Chapter I.

IMPERIAL PROGRESS TO ITSUKUSHIMA.

At the beginning of the New Year of Jisho, since Kiyomori would not give his permission and the Ho-o feared to gainsay him, the usual visits of ceremony were not made at the Toba Palace during the first three days, with the exception of Sakuramachi Chunagon Shigenori-no-Kyo, son of the late Shonagon Nyudo Shinsei, and his younger brother Sakyo-no-daiyu Naganori, who were allowed to go.

---

[168] *Yazan.* Short for Hokoya-no-yama, a mountain where Sennin or genii were supposed to dwell; used as a synonym for the Imperial Palace, cf. Sento-Gosho, Palace of the Cave of Genii, another such title.

[169] *Iaiji and Koro*, are expressions taken from the verse of Haku-raku-ten.

On the twentieth day were held the ceremonies of the first investiture of the Crown Prince with the 'hakama' and the first serving of fish to him; it was a very auspicious occasion but the Ho-o only heard about it by rumour in the Toba Palace. On the twenty-first day of the second month the Emperor, spite of his not having any particular illness, was removed from the Throne and the Crown Prince succeeded him. This also showed how the Nyudo did as he pleased in everything, and everyone excitedly chorused: "Now are the palmy days of the Heike." The Imperial Gem and the Sacred Sword were taken to the Naijidokoro and the Court Nobles all assembled at the camp of the Imperial Guard, everything being done according to ancient precedent, while the Sadaijin also went out to the camp. On hearing of the resignation of the Emperor, all those who understood the circumstances could not refrain from weeping. When an Emperor in the Retired Palace meditates on having resigned the Throne to the Heir of his own accord, the future seems dark and wretched, but when as now his wishes are not consulted, but he is forced to resign, his state of mind must be truly pitiable.

The Sacred Treasures were handed over and taken to the Gosho Palace, where the New Emperor was to reside. When the call of the watchman who gave the fire alarm was heard no more in the Kan in Palace of Takakura Tenno, and Palace Guards no longer kept watch and ward, but all was silent and still, melancholy fell upon the older Courtiers even amidst the rejoicings at the Imperial Accession, and they were affected even to tears. The New Emperor was but three years old this year, and people whispered to each other: "Ah, he too will retire sometime;" but as Taira Dainagon Tokitada-no-Kyo was the husband of the Imperial wetnurse, Sotsu no suke, who was there who could depose this one?

In foreign countries we find Sei-o of Shu aged three years, and Boku Tei of Shin aged two. In our country Konoe-in was three years old and Rokujo-in two, all of them in long clothes and none able to adjust his own dress, but carried in the arms of the Kwanpaku or nursed by their mother they went through the Accession Ceremony. Afterwards Kosho, Emperor of Kan, succeeded to the Throne at the age of a hundred days. These are the precedents for ascending the Throne both in China and Japan, but the learned men of the time grumbled together saying: "Ah, how terrible! Say nothing about it; are these precedents good ones, I wonder?" Since the Crown Prince had come to the Throne the Nyudo and his wife were now grandfather and grandfather to the Emperor, and, having obtained an Imperial Decree for the three ranks of Empress, Dowager Empress and Grand Dowager Empress, he distributed rank and emolument, received and directed the ministers in attendance, had ladies-in waiting dressed in flower-embroidered robes, and in fact deported himself exactly like a Retired

Emperor. With the exception of the O-Nyudo of Hokoin, Kaneie Ko, this was the first time that one who had become a priest had received the Decree of the Three Ranks.

During the first decade of the first month, the Emperor Takakura made a pilgrimage to Itsukushima. As it is the custom for an Emperor who has relinquished the Throne first of all to visit Hachiman, Kamo and Kasuga before going elsewhere, people thought it very strange that His Majesty should go to the far distant shrine of Itsukushima. Some say that the Retired Emperor Shirakawa went to Kumano and that Go-Shirakawa went to Hiyoshi, but I know not. The reason that the Emperor went to Itsukushima was because he had an important petition to make there, and moreover as it was the shrine most highly venerated by the Heike, on the one hand he would comply with their wishes, while on the other there was the example of the Ho-o shut up in the Toba Palace before his eyes, so that no doubt he went to pray that the heart of the Nyudo might be softened.

Now this thing caused Hiezan to be angry, for they argued that if the Emperor did not first visit Hachiman, Kamo and Kasuga on his abdication, he certainly ought to come to their temples, and wondered why he should go to such a distant shrine as Itsukushima in Aki. "Let us go down to the capital with our sacred emblem and prevent it;" they clamoured. So the Emperor postponed his visit for a while until Kiyomori managed to pacify the indignation of Hieizan. Then on the seventeenth day His Majesty started out on his pilgrimage to Itsukushima by visiting the Ni-i Dono, the wife of the Nyudo, at her residence at Hachijo Omiya. That night the festival of the Deity of Itsukushima began. The Kwampaku Motomichi presented a car of Chinese style with changes of horses to the Emperor. On the next day, being the eighteenth, His Majesty went to the mansion of the Nyudo and in the evening, summoning the former Udaisho Munenori-no-Kyo, said to him: "On the occasion of my going to Itsukushima I wish to go to the Toba Palace to visit the Ho-o, do you think I ought to inform the Nyudo or not?" Munemori replying that he thought it did not matter, the Emperor asked him to go that night to the Toba Palace and inform the Ho-o of his intention, and Munemori forthwith hastened thither. The Ho-o, on hearing the news was highly delighted, thinking it too good to be true. So on the next day, the nineteenth, Omiya no Dainagon Takasue no Kyo arrived while it was yet dark, and the Imperial Progress to Itsukushima was at last begun from the Nyudo's residence at Nishi Hachijo. The third month was not yet half over, but the moon of the dawning day shone half obscured and beclouded in mist, and the cry of the wild geese flying back from Echizen and Echigo sounded melancholy in their ears. While it was yet dark they approached the Toba Palace, and the Emperor, descending from his car before the gate, entered to find only a deserted mansion in the shade of the thick trees: a dismal scene indeed.

The spring was almost over and the summer foliage was appearing, the cherry blossoms were fading on the boughs and the song of the 'uguisu' was growing old. His Majesty thought how he had visited the Ho-o at his Palace of Hojujiden on the sixth day of the first month of last year, when the musicians had greeted him with sweet refrains, while the nobles were all in waiting, and with the serried ranks of Guards the Ho-o's own Courtiers had opened the curtained gate, and the attendants of the Kamon spread matting on the ground, the whole ceremony going smoothly and without fault: to day it all seemed like a dream.

Sakuramachi Chunagon Shigemori-no-Kyo now advanced and announced the Imperial visit. The Ho-o immediately came forth into the vestibule of his sleeping apartment to await His Majesty. The Emperor was twenty years old this year and his countenance was bright like the moon of dawn. His figure also was very beautiful. He was exceedingly like his mother, the late Kenshun-mon-in, and the Ho-o, being reminded of his departed Consort, could not refrain from tears. Then the two Retired Emperors seated themselves close together and, so that their conversation might be private, the old nun alone remained in the Imperial Presence. So Their Majesties remained long in converse until the sun rose high in the heavens, when the Emperor Takakura took leave of his Imperial Father and embarked in his ship at Kusatsu in Tuba. The Emperor felt deeply grieved to see the silent and lonely condition of the Ho-o's Detached Palace, and the Ho-o on his part felt very uneasy when he thought of the Imperial journey and the perilous voyage over the waves. Indeed His Majesty's putting aside the claims of the shrines of Ise, Hachiman and Kamo and making this pilgrimage to far-off Aki was most praiseworthy; how can it be without acceptance before the gods? Doubtless the August Petition will be granted.

Chapter II.

THE IMPERIAL RETURN JOURNEY.

On the twenty-eighth day of the same month the Emperor arrived at Itsukushima and was lodged in the mansion of the Naiji most beloved by the Lay-priest Chancellor, spending the days there while the Sutras were chanted and Bugaku dances were performed. At the consummation of the vow the hierophant Kogen Sojo, ascending the high seat, beat on a gong and cried out the words of introduction in a loud voice thus: "How awe-inspiring is the will of our Lord, leaving the Nine Gated Palace to brave the eightfold sea-road to this distant shore!" And both the Emperor and all his subjects shed tears of joy. Then they went round worshipping at all the shrines in succession, beginning with the great shrine of Amida, Fugen and Miroku[170] and the lesser one of Tamonten;[171] going round the mountain five-cho from the great shrine they went to the water-fall shrine of Nyo-i-rin Kwannon. Then Koken Sojo fastened to the pillar of the Haiden the following verse:

> "*As with the snow-white cord of the cascade that falleth
>   from heaven.*
> *So does His Majesty here bind his appeal to the God.*"

The shrine official Saiki-no-Kagehiro was promoted to the Lower Fifth Rank, and the Kokushi Fujiwara-no-Aritsuna to the Lower Fourth, and at the same time permitted to attend the Court of the Retired Emperor. The Zasshu Sonei was made Hogen. Thus it was hoped that by the favour of the god the anger of the Nyudo would be calmed.

On the twenty-ninth day the ship was again made ready and His Majesty started on his homeward journey, but as the wind and the waves rose somewhat, they rowed the ship back again and stopped that day at a place called Gi-no-ura in Itsukushima. Then the Emperor ordered someone to make a poem expressing his regret at parting from the Daimyojin, the god of the island, and Takafusa-no-Shosho composed the following:

> "*Full of regret at parting, again we return to this haven;*
> *Surely these white waves are as a blessing divine.*"

About midnight the wind dropped and the sea became calm, so they rowed away again. That day they reached the harbour of Shikina in Bingo.

Here there was a mansion built in the period Oho by the Kokushi Fujiwara Tamenari to accommodate the Ho-o when he had journeyed that way, and Kiyomori he had it repaired for the Emperor's use, but His Majesty did not go there. This being the first of the month of the Hare (the fourth month) it was the day of the ceremony of Changing Clothes at the Court, and remembering this they all spoke of the affairs of the Capital, and as they were singing snatches of song they caught sight of a deep purple wistaria abloom on a pine branch on the cliff, and the Emperor, noticing it, ordered someone to go and bring it to him. Thereupon Omiya-no-Dainagon Takasue-no-Kyo, respectfully receiving the command, bade Sashisho Nakahara-no-Yasusada, who was rowing in a small boat in front of His Majesty, break it off and bring it. When the Emperor looked at the wistaria as it grew on the pine branch, he was much affected by emotion and asked for a poem to be

---

[170] *Miroku.* Sk. Maitreya, a Bodhisattva, the Messiah of Buddhism. cf. p. 212.
[171] *Tamonten.* or Bishamon, Sk. Vais'ramana, one of the Four Deva Kings.

composed on it, when Takasue-no-Kyo made the following verse:

"Full ten centuries long may the life of our Lord be extended;
Ev'n as the Fuji flower clings to the evergreen pine."

On the second day they reached Kojima in Bizen. On the fifth day the weather became clear and the sea calm, so they put forth again, the Imperial vessel going first and the accompanying ships rowing after. Breasting the head seas that burst in foam like clouds and smoke, the same day they reached the port of Yamada in Harima, and from thence His Majesty entered his palanquin and proceeded to Fukuhara. The sixth day was spent there in visiting various sights, and His Majesty went and inspected the country seat of Ike-no-Chunagon Yorimori at Arata. On the next day the Emperor conferred promotions in rank on Kiyomori's family, to wit, the Nyudo's adopted son Tamba-no-kami Kiyokuni was given the Upper Fourth Rank, Lower Grade, and his grandson Echizen-no-Shosho the Lower Fourth Rank, Upper Grade. The same day they came to Terai. On the eighth day all the Courtiers and Nobles came to Toba to meet the Emperor. On the return journey His Majesty did not go to visit the Ho-c at the Toba Palace, but proceeded straight to the Nyudo's mansion at Nishi Hachijo. On the twenty-third day of the same month, the Accession Ceremony of the New Emperor took place. It should have been held in the Daikyoku-den, but as it had been destroyed by fire a year ago it was not yet rebuilt. Therefore a Council of Courtiers was held, and it was suggested that it might be held in the Dajokwan, but Kujo Dono said that the Dajokwan was only a place that might be called a record office in the case of an ordinary person's house, and that it ought to be held in the Shishin-den. It was held therefore in the Shishin-den. Formerly on the eleventh month of the fourth year of Koho, the Accession Ceremony of Reizei-in was held in the Shishin-den because the Emperor caught cold and could not go the Daikyoku-den. As in the case of Go Sanjo-in in Enkyu, people said that this Accession Ceremony ought to have been held in the Dajokwan, but no one could do anything in the face of the opinion of Kujo Dono. It was called the Accession of the Crown Prince, it is true, but it was the Empress Ken-rei-mon-in who went from the Koki-den to the Ninju-den and sat on the Throne. All the Heike family were present; only the retainers of the late Komatsu Dono, who were in retirement owing to the death of their lord the year before, did not appear.

Chapter III.

GATHERING OF THE GENJI.

Now Kurando-no-Saemon-no-Gonnosuke Sadanaga wrote his congratulations on the Accession Ceremony having been completed without any untoward circumstance, on ten sheets of paper, and sent it to Hachijo Ni-i Dono, the wife of the Nyudo, who rejoiced greatly with her face wreathed in smiles. Still, though it was a very brilliant and auspicious occasion, most people were far from being pleased.

Now the second son of the Ho-o, Prince Mochihito, whose mother was the daughter of Kaga Dainagon Suenari-no-Kyo, was living at the Takakura Palace in Sanjo and so came to be known as Prince Takakura. His 'Gempuku' ceremony had been held secretly when he was fifteen years old, on the fifteenth day of the eleventh month of the first year of Ei-man, at the Omiya Palace at Konoe Kawara. He was known for the elegance of his calligraphy and his brilliant intellect, and might have been Crown Prince and ascended the Throne, but owing to the enmity of the late Ken-shun-mnn-in he had to live thus secluded. In spring time he would divert himself by writing poems as he strolled out under the cherry trees, and in autumn by making exquisite melodies on his flute at the moon viewing banquets. While he thus spending his days, having then reached the age of thirty, in the fourth year of Jisho, Gensammi Nyudo Yorimasa, who was then living at Konoe Kawara, came secretly to his Palace one evening and spoke his mind to him boldly, thus: "Does your Highness not think it a very miserable thing that you, who are of direct descent in the forty-eighth age from Tensho Daijin, and the seventy-eighth generation from Jimmu Tenno, and might become Crown Prince and ascend the throne, should thus live till the age of thirty in obscurity in this Palace? Quickly raise a revolt and overthrow the Heike! Will it not be a most worthy and filial act to relieve the anxiety of the Retired Emperor, repining at his perpetual confinement in the Toba Palace, and to ascend the Throne yourself as Emperor? If your Highness should deign to consider this plan, and issue a Royal Order for its execution, all the many members of the Genji family who are living in the various provinces will gladly flock to your side. In Kyoto, "he continued," are the son of Dewa-no-Zenji Mitsunobu, Iga-no-kami Mitsumoto, Dewa-no-Hangwan Mitsunaga, Dewa-no-Kurando Mitsushige, and Dewa-no-Kwanja Mitsuyoshi. In Kumano, Juro Yoshimori, youngest son of the late Rokujo Hangwan Tameyoshi is in hiding. In Settsu there is Tada-no-Kurando Yukitsuna, but as he betrayed his allegiance after having taken part in the plot of the Shin Dainagon Narichika-no-Kyo, he is not to be relied on, but his younger brother Tada-no-Jiro Tomozane, together with Teshima-no-Kwanja

Takayori, and Ota-no-Taro Yorimoto will certainly come. In Kawachi are Musashi-no-Goro-no-Kami Nyudo Ycshimoto, governor of the district of Ishikawa, and his son Ishikawa-no-Hangwan Dai Yoshikane. In Yamato, the sons of Uno-no-Shichiro Chikaharu, Taro Ariharu, Jiro Kiyoharu, Saburo Nariharu, and Shiro Yoshiharu. In Omi, Yamamoto, Kashiwagi and Nishigori, in Mino and Owari, Yamada-no-jiro Shigehiro, Kawabe-no-Taro Shigenao, Izumi-no-Taro Shigemitsu, Urano-no-Shiro Shigeto, Ajiki-no-Jiro Shigeyori and his son Taro Shigesuke, Kido-no-Saburo Shigenaga, Kaiden-no-Hangwan Dai Shigekuni, Yashima-no-Senjo Shigetaka, and his son Taro Shigeyuki. In Kai, Hemmi-no-Kwanja Yoshikiyo, and his son Taro Kiyomitsu, Takeda-no-Taro Nobuyoshi, Kagami-no-Jiro Tomitsu, and Kojiro Nagamitsu of the same house; Ichijo-no-Jiro Tadayori, Itagaki-no-Saburo Kanenobu, Hemmi-no-Hyoye Ariyoshi, Takeda-no-Goro Nobumitsu, and Yasuda-no-Saburo Yoshisada. In Shinano, Ouchi-no-Taro Koreyoshi, Okada-no-Kwanja Chikayoshi, Hiraga-no-Kwanja Moriyoshi and his son Jiro Yoshinobu, Kiso-no Kanja Yoshinaka, second son of the late Tatewaki-no-Senjo Yoshikata. In Izu, the former Uhyoye-no-Suke Yoritomo, in exile. In Hitachi, Shida-no-Saburo Senjo Yoshinori, Satake-no-Kwanja Masayoshi, and his sons Taro Tadayoshi, Saburo Yoshimune, Shiro Takayoshi, and Goro Yoshisue. In Mutsu, Kuro Hangwan Yoshitsune, youngest son of the late Sama-no-Kami Yoshitomo. All these are descendants of the Sixth Imperial Grandson, and the posterity of Tada-no-Shimpachi Mitsunaka. The two warrior families of Gen and Hei, whose only duty is to quell the enemies of the Throne, have till now been equal in power, but at the present time they are wide asunder as Heaven and Earth; indeed it is not too much to say that their relations are those of servant and master. The provinces are oppressed by the Governors and the fiefs are abused by the commissioners; people are harried in all matters and there is no peace. Consider carefully the state of things at present. Outwardly all submit, but inwardly there are none who do not dislike the Heike rule. If therefore Your Highness will agree to issue an Order, the Genji from every province will pour in night and day, and the destruction of the Heike will soon be completed. In that case, though I myself am an old man, I have many young sons and will bring them to fight against the Heike." The Prince was greatly perplexed to know what to do, so that for some time he did not consent. There was, however, a certain Shonagon Korenaga, grandson of Ako Maru Dainagon Munemichi-no-Kyo, and son of Bingo-no-Zenji Suemichi, who was famous for his skill in physiognomy, so that people called him 'Physiognomy Shonagon', and he came and visited the Prince and told him that by his features he was predestined to ascend the Throne, and that therefore he ought not to abandon the attempt to attain his object. Gensammi Nyudo also kept on urging him, and suggesting that the plan was an inspiration of Tensho Daijin herself, so that at last he made up his mind to act Calling Shingu-no-Juro Yoshimori, he appointed him Kurando, and changing his name to Yukiie, sent him as bearer of his Royal Order to the Eastern Country.

On the twenty-eighth day of the fourth month he left Kyoto and went first to Omi, and then to Mino and Owari to rouse the Genji residing there. On the eighteenth day of the fifth month, arriving at Hokujo Hiru-ga-Kojima, he communicated his message to the former Uhyoye-no-Suke Dono who was in exile there; after which he went to the island of Shinda to his brother Shinda-no-Saburo Yoshimori, and then crossed over to the highlands of Kiso to warn his nephew Kiso-no-Kwanja Yoshinaka. Now Tanso the Betto of Kumano somehow or other had got to know of the matter, and he was an official under great obligations to the Heike. "So Shingu-no-Jiro Yoshimori is out with a Royal Order from Prince Takakura to raise a revolt," said he, "then Nachi and Shingu are sure to take the side of the Genji: how can I, who have received such great benefits from the Heike, forsake them at such a time? I must surely draw bow in their defence before hastening to Kyoto to give all information." Whereupon he marched against Shingu with a thousand men fully armed. At Shingu were Torii-no-Hogen, Takabo-no-Hogen, and their samurai Ui, Suzuki, Mizuya and Kamenoko, and at Nachi Shugyo Hogen and his men, their whole force together numbering about fifteen hundred men. Shouting their warcry, both Genji and Heike drew their bows and the battle began. For three days it raged furiously, the arrows whizzing without cessation, and the humming arrows continuing their whirring, until at last Tanso, when most of his own retainers had been killed and himself wounded, barely escaped with his life and fled back lamenting to his shrine.

Chapter IV.

THE ORACLE OF THE WEASELS.

Now the Ho-o was apprehensive lest he should share the fate of Narichika and Shunkwan and be banished to some distant province or remote island, but this did not come to pass, and the fourth year of Jisho found him still confined in the Toba Palace. Thus it happened that on the twelfth day of the fifth month of that year, at the hour of the Horse (12 noon) many weasels made a great noise by running about the Palace, and the Ho-o, wishing to consult a diviner about it, called Omi-no-kami Nakakane, who was then entitled Tsuru-no-Kurando, and ordered him to go to Abe-no-Yasuchika and ask him, after due consideration of the portent, to send a pronouncement on it. Nakakane, respectfully assenting, went to the residence of Yasuchika, but it happened that he was away at that time, and being informed that he was at Shirakawa, he proceeded thither, and gave him the message of the Ho-o, whereupon Yasuchika after a short time handed him the pronouncement he desired. Nakakane immediately hastened with it to the Toba Palace, but when he came to enter the gate, the guards on duty there would not admit him. As he knew the buildings very well however, he climbed over the wall and then creeping under the floor of the Palace, managed to insert Yasuchika's prognostication through a loose board in the Ho-o's room. When the Ho-o opened and read it, he found this oracle; "Within three days you will have cause both for rejoicing and lamentation." "In this condition," quoth His Majesty, "I may indeed rejoice, but what further misfortune can befall me, I wonder?"

On the thirteenth day, owing to the continued petitions that the former Udaisho Munemori-no-Kyo made on behalf of the Ho-o, the Nyudo at last relented and ordered that His Majesty should be brought back to Kyoto from the Toba Palace and lodged in the Palace of Bifuku-mon-in at Hachijo Karasu Maru the cause of rejoicing that Yasuchika predicted within three days. Now just at this time Tanso, the Betto of Kumano, sent a courier to Kyoto with the report, of the rebellion of Prince Takakura, and Munemori was thrown into great consternation thereat. The Nyudo was at his residence at Fukuhara and when the news was sent to him, he flew into a great rage and ordered Prince Takakura to be immediately arrested and banished to Tosa. The carrying out of this order was entrusted to Nijo-no-Dainagon Sanefusa, with To-no-Ben Mitsumasa under him, the samurai under them being Gendaiyu-no-Hangwan Kanetsuna and Dewa-no-Hangwan Mitsunaga with three hundred fully armed men, and these proceeded at once to the Takakura Palace. This Gendaiyu Hangwan was the second son of Gensammi Nyudo, and the fact that he was included proved that the Heike did not yet know that his father was implicated in the plot.

Chapter V.

THE FIGHT OF NOBUTSURA.

Now on the fifteenth evening of the fifth month, as Prince Takakura was gazing at the beauties of the moon in a cloudy sky, with-no-thought of anything that might happen, a messenger came post-haste from Gensammi Nyudo with a letter, which his foster brother Rokujo-no-Suke-no-Daiyu Munenobu at once brought to him. It ran thus: "The plot is already revealed, and you are to be banished to Tosa: the officials of the Kebiishi have orders to take you, so leave the Palace quickly and go to Miidera. I myself am shortly coming to the Capital." The Prince was dumbfounded at this news, and at a loss how to act, when one of his samurai who was always in attendance on him,

Chohyoye-no-Jō Hasebe Nobutsura by name, spoke out saying: "There is nothing difficult in that; it is easy to escape in woman's attire." This counsel seemed good, so the Prince let his hair loose, donned a female costume, and put on his head a wide straw hat such as the townswomen wear, while Rokujo-no-Suke-no-Daiyu Munenobu went with him to carry his umbrella, and a youth named Tsuru Maru accompanied them, carrying some articles in a bag on his head. Thus imitating the appearance of a young retainer escorting his mistress, they slipped out of the Palace toward the north. Coming to a rather wide ditch, the Prince leaped across it so lightly that some passers by remarked to one another: "How strange to see a woman jump a ditch like that." This made the fugitives quicken their pace and hurry on quickly, fearing to attract more notice. They left Chohyoye-no-Jo Hasebe Nobutsura behind as warden of the Palace, and he at once proceeded to hide the few women of the establishment who remained, and to put away everything unseemly that there might be, when he happened to notice his master's much prized flute called 'Koeda,' that the Prince had forgotten in his hurry and left it by his pillow in his own apartment, a treasure that he would wish to recover even if he had to come back for it. "Ah," exclaimed Nobutsura, "what a pity! It is my master's favourite flute." And running after them, he came up with them within five cho. The Prince, overjoyed at having it again, exclaimed: "When I die, see that you put this flute in my coffin." And then added: "Pray come along with us now." But Nobutsura replied: "When the officials come to the Palace they must not find it abandoned. Moreover everyone knows that I am in the Palace, and if they did not find me there to-night they would know that you had just now escaped, and that must not be. A samurai must live up to his reputation even in the smallest matters. So I will go back and deceive the officials; then I will eat my way out through them and rejoin my master." So he returned alone. That night be girded on under a light blue 'kariginu' a body armour, or 'Haramaki' of bright green colour that grew fainter towards the bottom, and an 'Efu tachi,' and then, opening the great gate of the Palace that fronted on Sanjo and the smaller one that fronted on Takakura, he awaited the Heike officers. As he expected, about the hour of the Rat (12 p.m.). Gendaiyu-no-Hangwan Kanetsuna and Dewa-no-Hangwan Mitsunaga, with about three hundred men, came riding up to the gate. Gendaiyu-no-Hangwan, knowing the circumstances, stayed outside the gate, but Dewa-no-Hangwan rode through the gate and stopped in the courtyard, crying out with aloud voice: "The Prince's plot is already known; by order of the Betto of the Kebiishi we have now come to send him into exile to Tosa. I pray you come forth!" Then Nobutsura, standing above on the floor of the Palace, replied: "His Highness is not here: he has gone to visit some shrine. What is all this? Pray give a fuller explanation." "Why is he not here?" replied Dewa-no-Hangwan, "and where has he gone? Here, men, enter and search the Palace!" "Ho!" returned Nobutsuna, "what rudeness is this of an insolent official? To enter the gate on horseback is strange conduct indeed, but to order your men to search the Palace as well—what do you call such behaviour? I am Chohyoye-no-jo Hasebe Nobutsura. Come on at your peril!" Then a strong and brave man named Kanetake, unsheathing his sword, glared at Nobutsuna and sprang up on to the floor of the Palace, seeing which fourteen or fifteen of his companions followed him. Then Nobutsura, stripping off his 'kariginu,' drew his sword, which, though but a light Eifu-tachi,[172] was a blade of fine make and temper, and flourished it. His opponent carried a huge blade and a great halberd, but Nobutsura at once cut him down with his slender weapon so that he fell suddenly back into the courtyard as a leaf is blown down by a puff of wind. It was the fifteenth evening of the fifth month, and the moon shone out brightly in the rifts of the clouds. The Palace buildings were quite unknown to the Heike soldiers, whereas Nobutsura knew every inch of them, so he struck them down at his pleasure, now springing out on to the verandah to cleave one through, now driving another into a recess to cut him down, punctuating his blows with the fierce shouts of the swordsman. "How dare you treat thus the bearers of an official order?" exclaimed one of the intruders. "Who talks of official orders," returned Nobutsura springing back and setting his bent sword under his foot to straighten it, after which he again slew some fifteen or sixteen stout men at arms in the courtyard. But three inches had now been broken off his sword, so throwing it away, he felt for his dirk to cut open his belly. His dirk, however, had fallen from his belt in the fight, so opening the front gate he made to flee from the postern fronting on Takakura. One of the Heike warriors, however, sprang forward to intercept him with a huge halberd. Nobutsura attempted to jump over it, but missing his leap, the halberd caught between his legs so that he fell to the ground, when, bold as he was, he was overpowered by the weight of numbers and secured alive. Then bursting in, they searched the Palace, but finding that the Prince had escaped, they bound Nobutsura and took him away to Rokuhara. There Munemorino Kyo, standing on the verandah, had him brought into the courtyard beneath, and passed sentence; "Because you have attacked the officials of the Kebiishi, and paid-no-heed to a government order, and moreover have killed and wounded many of our men, you shall be tortured until you give full information, and then taken away to the river bed and beheaded." Then that bold and fearless warrior Nobutsura stood erect and laughed in Munemori's face. "So far I have paid-no-heed," said he, "to people who came spying round the Palace every night, thinking they were of

---

[172] *Eifu-tachi.* A light ornamental weapon carried by the officials of the Eifu or Imperial Guard as a badge of office.

no importance, but when at midnight two or three hundred armed men appeared, and on my enquiring what they wanted, replied that they had an official order, I remembered that I had constantly heard that bands of robbers and thieves and pirates of all kinds are accustomed to say that they are the train of a Courtier or that they have an official order, so I asked what official order it was, and attacked them at once: and if I had been in full armour and had a good heavy sword, not one of these precious officials should have come back here alive. Moreover when the Prince my master will return I do not know, and if I knew, a samurai does not reveal what he has once determined to conceal, whatever torture he may be made to suffer." When he had finished speaking, all the Heike men at arms who were ranged round him exclaimed, "Ah! a stout fellow indeed. Truly he is a match for a thousand." And as they were discussing him one said: "This is not the first famous combat he has fought: last year at a certain place he pursued six robbers single-handed, whom the Palace guard could not arrest, and slew four of them at Nijo Horikawa, taking the other two alive, and it was for this bold deed that he was made Chohyoye-no-Jo. What a pity to put such a man to death. As therefore they were loath to do him to death, whatever the Nyudo might think, they spared his life and he was banished to Hino in the land of Hoki. Afterwards, when the Heike had been overthrown and the Genji had come to their own, he went down to the Eastern Country, and on his relating the whole affair to Kajiwara Heizo Kagetoki, Yoritomo praised him highly and rewarded him with a fief in Noto.

Chapter VI.

Takakura-no Miya Goes to Onjoji.

Thus Prince Takakura, leaving Takakura on the north and Konoe on the east, crossed the river Kamo and proceeded to enter Nyoiyama. Formerly the Tenno of Kiyomihara,[173] when attacked by Prince Otomo, went to Yoshinoyama in the guise of a woman, and this Prince was now in just such a plight, fleeing far away through the trackless and unknown hills the whole night through; his feet, torn and bleeding through the unaccustomed toil, stained the sand like the dark maple leaves, and it must have seemed that the dew of the moist verdure was overwhelmed by his tears. Thus they reached Miidera at morning light, and when the priests heard His Highness had come to seek refuge with them, to save, it might be, his fleeting life, they were exceeding respectfully overjoyed, and appointing the Horin-in as his lodging, gave him food and clothing with due ceremony.

---

[173] *Tenno of Kiyomihara.* Temmu Tenno, so called from his place of residence.

Chapter VII.

KIOU.

On the next day, the sixteenth, when it was known that since Takakura had plotted a rebellion and had fled to Miidera, there was-no-small commotion in the Capital.

Now perchance it may be wondered why this Gensammi Nyudo, who had been living quietly for a long time past, should suddenly start this revolt. The reason was the extraordinary things done by Munemori-no-Kyo. Therefore in this world people should very carefully consider how they inconsiderately say things that ought not to be said, or do things that ought not be done. For example; Izu-no-kami Nakatsuna, the eldest of Gensammi Nyudo, had a famous horse called Konoshita that was renowned in the Palace, and was the most peerless of chestnut steeds, and of its speed and gentle disposition none was ignorant. And Munemori-no-Kyo sent a messenger saying that he wished this horse to be sent to him, for he had a mind to inspect it: to which Izu-no-kami answered that he had the horse indeed, but as he had ridden it much lately it was weary and he sent it to the country to rest. This being the case, nothing could be done, but afterwards many of the Heike retainers spoke saying: "Oh, that horse was there the day before yesterday; "I saw it yesterday:" or "it was being ridden in the courtyard this morning." On hearing this, Munemori exclaimed; "Oh, he grudges it. Indeed? What hateful conduct! Here!" And he sent his retainers with letters to demand it five or six, or seven or eight times in one hour. When Gensammi Nyudo heard this, he said to his son: "Even if it were a golden horse, if anyone desire it so much, one must not grudge him, so send it without delay to Rokuhara. Then Izu-no-kami, seeing that there was-no-other way, sent the horse to Rokuhara with this stanza:

"How can one bear to part with a creature so dearly beloved?
If it attracted you so, could you not visit one here?"

Munemori did not answer this, but exclaimed: "Ah, it is indeed a fine horse; but as he was so loath to part with it, brand its master's name on it." So they made a branding iron with 'Nakatsuna' on it and branded the horse therewith. Then, when anyone came to visit him and asked to see the famous horse, he would call out: "Ho there! Put the saddle on Nakatsuna. Bring him out! Mount him! Whip him up!" and so forth. When Izu-no-kami heard of this, he was very angry and said: "His using his authority to take away a horse I valued as my life is-no-small thing, but how can one remain quiet when one is made a laughing stock in addition?" Gensammi Nyudo also exclaimed: "What is this that the Heike think to treat everyone with contumely and to do such folly? In that case we must risk everything and watch for a suitable opportunity." He himself did not make the plot, but persuaded Prince Takakura to carry it out. This was learned afterwards.

In this connexion people discreetly quoted a story of Komatsu Dono. Once when he had been to Court he went to visit the Empress, when a snake of some eight feet in length got inside the left leg of his hakama. Shigemori, thinking that if he made any fuss the Court ladies would be terrified and the Empress too would be perturbed, gripping its tail with his left hand and its head with his right, put it into the sleeve of his 'naoshi' without making the least sign of confusion; then, turning round, he called for an attendant of the sixth rank. Then Izu-no-kami Nakatsuna who was then only Eifu-no-Kurando, being called by name, came forward and was ordered to take the snake. Taking it he passed though the Yubaden and went forth into a small courtyard of the Palace, where he beckoned to one of the younger attendants of the Imperial Storehouses to take it away; but the man, shaking his head, ran away. Then Izu-no-kami, calling one of his own retainers, Kiou by name, gave it to him to throw away. The next day he received a fine horse and trappings from Shigemori with the message: "In recognition of your exceeding courteous behaviour yesterday I offer you this excellent horse; please make use of him when you hurry off to meet Keisei[174] after your official duties are over." Izu-no-kami, on receiving it, made reply as follows: "In answer to the gracious gift of your excellency, I am delighted to accept it respectfully: allow me to congratulate you on your feat of yesterday, which was indeed just like the Kenjo[175] dance." Inasmuch as the demeanour of Komatsu Dono was so considerate and courteous, Munemori appeared the more lacking, and moreover his coveting another's favourite horse and seizing it thus brought great calamity on the country.

So, on the evening of the sixteenth day of the same month Gensammi Nyudo Yorimasa, with his eldest son Izu-no-kami Nakatsuna, his second son Gendaiyu-no-Hangwan Kanetsuna, Rokujo-no-Kurando Nakaie, his son Kurando Taro Nakamitsu and three hundred armed men, after firing their mansion, proceeded to Miidera. Now there was a samurai of about the same age as Gensammi Nyudo named Watanabe-no-Gensan Kiou, a Takiguchi or Palace Guard, who, happening to come late. He was left behind and summoned to Rokuhara in consequence. "Why is it," they enquired, "that you have not followed your ancestral lord Gensammi Nyudo, but have stayed behind here?" Kiou respectfully made reply: "If it had been an ordinary

---

[174] *Keisei*. Name of some favourite courtesan. Lit. 'Ruiner of castles' significant of their character and habits.

[175] *Kenjo*. Name of a dance in which the dancer held a snake in a bamboo curtain (sudare) in his hand while he danced and afterwards slipped it into his sleeve.

affair I would have been the first to ride forth and risk my life, but I do not know how this affair will turn out and so I have hesitated to go! "You have some connexion with us too," said Munemori, "so consider, in view of the past and future supremacy of our house whether you will follow Yorimasa, the enemy of the Throne, or take service with us." Kiou, bursting into tears, replied: "Spite of my relation to my lord, how can one agree with an enemy of the Throne? I will then take service with you." "Do so then," replied Munemori, "and your recompense shall be-no-less than with Yorimasa." And he re-entered the mansion. But that day from morning till night, Munemori, not quite reassured, kept on asking where Kiou was, and was always told that he was still in the mansion.

When the evening came Munemori once again appeared and Kiou respectfully addressed him thus: "Since Gensammi Nyudo has gone to Miidera, I think he will certainly try to attack us by night; he will have with him my clan, the Watanabe, and also the priests of Miidera, and they are not enemies to be despised, so I pray you let me go and find him and slay him. If I had a good horse I could easily get in by stealth, as I know them all." Munemori, thinking the plan a good one, straightway presented him with a valuable grey horse called Nanryo and a splendid saddle and trappings. Having received it, he immediately went to his own mansion and cried loudly: "Ho! the night comes on: I go to Miidera to die fighting before my lord Gensammi Nyudo." It was almost sunset when, having hidden his wife and children and set fire to his mansion, he set out for Miidera. His heart was heavy as he rode off, but he made a gallant and glittering spectacle, clad in a brocaded kariginu profusely embroidered with chrysanthemums, and wearing a general's armour of scarlet; its name was Kisenaga, and it had been a treasured heirloom for many generations. On his head was a helmet shining with silver stars, and a splendid sword hung at his side. In his quiver were twenty four arrows barred with black on their white feathers, not to speak of the special arrow, feathered with a hawk's wing, always carried by the Imperial Guard of the Takiguchi. His bow was a 'shigeto' of black lacquer with red binding. He rode on Nanryo, while one of his retainers followed with a remount and another bore his shield under his arm.

Now as soon as Rokuhara saw the flames go up from his mansion they were greatly excited. "Ha!" exclaimed Munemori, "that fellow has deceived us. After him and shoot him down before he gets farther!" But Kiou was a warrior surpassed by few in strength and valour, and of great skill in archery; and he shouted to the pursuing samurai to come on at their peril, for with each of his twenty four arrow he would account for one of them, whereat there was none found to engage him and he proceeded on his way unharmed. Now at Miidera where the Watanabe clan was assembled, they were discussing him and saying to one other: "Verily it is greatly to be hoped that Kiou will not forsake us:" when Gensammi Nyudo, who knew the mind of Kiou very intimately, replied: "Certainly he will not be taken alive or fail us, his feeling for me is exceeding deep. See he will soon be with us." And even as he spoke Kiou appeared. "Lo! it is even as I have said:" exclaimed Yorimasa. Then Kiou, making his obeisance, handed over the horse he was riding: "See," he said, "I have brought Izu-no-kami Dono the famous Nanryo from Rokuhara in the Place of Konoshita that he lost." Izu-no-kami, greatly rejoicing, immediately cut short its tail, and, branding it also, sent it back to Rokuhara. At about midnight it came back and entering the stable began to eat with the other horses. Then the grooms of the stable exclaimed in astonishment: "See! Nanryo has come back again; "whereupon Munemori, hurrying out to see; perceived on its back the branded words: "Formerly Nanryo, now called Munemori Nyudo." "Ah," he exclaimed in wrath," If only I had cut off his head before he had time to fool me thus. When we attack Miidera, see that this rascal Kiou is taken alive, and then I will have his head sawn off." But though he continued to dance with rage, Nanryo's tail grew no longer, neither did the branded sentence grow less conspicuous.

Chapter VIII.

THE LETTER TO HIEIZAN.

Now at Miidera they rang the bell and blew the conch to summon the priests to council. "Of late, when we consider the tendency of the time, the decline of the Buddhist Law and the languishing of the Monarchy are especially evident. If we do not now chastise the Nyudo for his evil doings, when will another opportunity occur? Is it not through the protection of Hachiman and the help of Shinra Daimyojin[176] that Prince Takakura has come hither Shall it not be then that the Hosts of Heaven and Earth will pour down their favour, and the power and might of the Gods and Buddhas bend him to our will? Heizan is a place where also the Tendai-shu is devoutly studied, while at Nara, the South Capital, are many who are zealous in meditation and holy attainments: if then we send an appeal to them, surely they will join us in a league together." Thus they decided with one accord and sent an appeal to Hieizan and Nara. That to Hieizan ran as follows:

"Appeal of Onjoji to Enryakuji for co-operation to save us from destruction. Since the Nyudo Jokai wishes to destroy Buddhism and overthrow the monarchy at his will, to our great grief the second son of

---

[176] *Shinra Daimyojin.* A god that was revealed to So-en-chin on his way back from China and introduced by him to Miidera.

the Ho-o fled secretly to our monastery on the fifteenth day of this month to escape persecution. And though we have been repeatedly bidden by a so-called Imperial Order to yield him up, yet we cannot consent. So we are threatened with the despatch of an official army against us. Therefore the overthrow of our monastery is now imminent and all our brethren are in great trouble. Now Enryakuji and Onjoji, though their buildings are separate, yet both revere the one Law of Tendaishu, even as the two wings of a bird or as the two wheels of a cart they are to each other. So that if one be wanting, will not the other feel the loss? If therefore you will unite your strength with us, and save us from destruction, our former animosity will be forgotten and we shall again dwell in good fellowship together. Given by us, the chief priests, at council held on the eighth day of the fifth month of the fourth year of Jisho.

Chapter IX.

THE LETTER TO THE SOUTH CAPITAL.

When the priests of Hieizan read the letter of Miidera they were astonished and said: "How is this? A temple that is tributary to us writes that we are as tho two wings of a bird or the two wheels of a cart! This is strange indeed." And the made no reply. Moreover the Lay priest Chancellor asked the Tendai Zasshu Mei-un Dai-Sojo to calm the priests of Hieizan, and he hastened to the monastery and succeeded in keeping them quiet. Thus he also intimated to the Prince that his fate was yet uncertain. Beside this, by the order of the Nyudo, twenty thousand koku of Omi rice and three thousand bolts of silk of extra length from the North Country were given to Hieizan for the right of passing over its highways. This was distributed among the monks of the various peaks and valleys, but as it was done hastily, there were some priests who received too much, while others went empty-handed. Whose doing it was I know not, but someone scrawled up this lampoon:

> *"The Yamahoshi's gown is short,*
> *He cannot cover what he ought;*
> *The shame he feels his friends to bilk*
> *For Nyudo Jokai's scanty silk."*

While some who had got none at all wrote,

> *"The shame on us may lightly sit,*
> *For we have not received a bit."*

The letter that Miidera sent to Nara ran as follows:

"A petition from Onjoji to Kofukuji to beg assistance that this monastery may not be destroyed. Know that the supreme excellence of Buddhism is to uphold the Monarchy; and the duration of the Throne therefore depends on the Law of Buddha. Now the Nyudo, the former Dajo Daijin, Taira-no-Ason Kiyomori Ko, whose priestly name is Jokai, does his will with the authority of the country and turns the government upside down, so that there is everywhere resentment and lamentation. And on the evening of the fifteenth day of this month the second son of the Ho-o hurriedly fled to our monastery to escape persecution, and though they have demanded repeatedly that we give him up, our priests unanimously refuse to do so, Therefore this Lay priest is collecting an army to enter our monastery, wishing to destroy at one time both Buddhism and the Monarchy. In ancient times in China, when the Emperor Bu-so in the era of Eisho attempted to destroy Buddhism by force of arms, the monks of Joryusen joined battle and repulsed him; if they thus upheld their rights against the monarch, how much more shall we not chastise this great rebel, this transgressor of the first of the Eight Disobediences.[177] Nara was the place where in unprecedented fashion the guiltless Kwampaku was banished. If we do not act now, at what time shall we able to remove this reproach? Thus we pray you to lend us aid lest Buddhism be destroyed, and also that this evil revolt against the Monarchy may be put away. If we are of one mind we shall attain our object. Given at a council of the Chief Priests; eighteenth day of the fifth month of the fourth year of Jisho.

Chapter X.

THE REPLY FROM NARA.

The monks of Nara, when they read this letter, also held a council and after a while made answer as follows:

"From Kofukuji to Onjoji, greeting. According to your communication, the Nyudo Jokai wishes to overthrow your temple and its Holy Law. Now though divided into two branches, both our temples are derived from one Pure source, the golden discourses of the Sutras of Tendai-shu. Thus, both North and South Capitals being equally disciples of the same Buddha, our temples together can surely overthrow even a mighty enemy of the Faith, be he even as malign as Devadatta[178] himself. Now Kiyomori is of the very dregs of the Heike,

---

[177] *Eight Disobediences.* Rebellion, Great Disobedience, Irreligion, Unfilial conduct, Great unfilial conduct, Undutifulness, Wicked disobedience, Faithlessness.

[178] *Devadatta.* (Jap. Chodatsu.) the rival and enemy of S'akya Muni.

and but the off-scourings of the warrior caste: His grandfather Masamori was a retainer of a Kurando of the fifth rank and was at the service of the provincial governors of any fief. Long ago, when Okura-no-Kyo Tanefusa was governor of Kaga, he was employed by the Kebiishi, and when Shuri-no-Daiyu Akisue was lord of Harima, he held the office of Groom of the Stables. When his son Tadamori, father of the Nyudo, was granted the privilege of attending Court, he was universally regarded as an outsider of low birth, and though he thus became a Courtier, people still despised him as an upstart. No Courtier who valued his reputation would have cared to enter such a family. However, in the twelfth month of the first year of Heiji, since the Emperor, in gratitude for his services in one battle, bestowed on him an unparalleled reward, his family have gone on rising until Kiyomori has made himself Chancellor, at the same time wielding all the military power of the country, his sons becoming Ministers and Commanders of the Imperial Guard and his daughters Imperial Consorts or Empresses, while his relatives and even the children of his concubines have been made Courtiers, and his grandson and nephews raised to high office. In addition to this he has appropriated all the fiefs that he desired, and appoints and dismisses governors at his pleasure, making them no better than his slaves and vassals. If anyone provokes his anger in the least, be he Prince or noble, he is immediately arrested, and if anyone speaks anything against him, be he Courtier of the highest rank, he is put in bonds at once; so that in order to escape death or disgrace even the Sacred Emperor is forced to flatter him, while those of the noblest lineage must make low obeisance. Even if his family property held for many generations is taken from him, none dare open his mouth for fear of worse happening, and if even the privileged estates of a Prince are confiscated, for fear of the tyrant's power he holds his pace. Presumptuous in his overweening strength, in the eleventh month of last year, in the winter, he dared to attack the Palace of the Ho-o and send the Kwampaku into exile. Verily such a heinous crime has never been heard of from ancient days. At that time we certainly should have set out against this rebel, but in accordance with the will of our Deity and as the result of consideration we repressed our anger for a season. But now that, again raising an army, he has compassed about the Palace of the second Imperial son of the Ho-o, the Divine aid of Hachiman and Kasuga Daimyojin, overshadowing him with their bright radiance, has protected him and guided him to the protection of the Shinra Gongen, thus clearly demonstrating that the Monarchy can never be overthrown. Therefore what men of discrimination are there who will not rejoice to hear that you are risking your lives to protect him? We, on our part, though dwelling so far away, feeling great pity at the news you secretly convey that Kiyomori is raising forces to attack you, assure you of our readiness to come to your assistance. On the eighteenth day at the hour of the Dragon, after we had roused our monks and informed all the other temples, and called on the tributary temples to send their men, just as we had assembled our forces, you sent by a swift messenger an invitation to join you and in one hour dispelled the doubts of many days. If the monks of the monastery of Shoryo in China could drive off the soldiers of Bu-so, how much more can the monks of the North and South Capitals of Yamato do away with the villainies of this Minister? Do you therefore guard well the residence of the Prince and we will await your sign to advance. Consider our letter and do not doubt us. Given on the twenty-first day of the fifth month of the fourth year of Jisho."

Chapter XI.

ASSEMBLING OF THE MONKS.

The monks of Miidera, after receiving the Prince within their temple, proceeded to fortify themselves by constructing walls round it and then held another council, saying: "Hieizan will not act with us and Nara has not yet come up. It will not do to continue thus. Let us go down and attack Rokuhara tonight: in that case, dividing our force into two parts, the veterans and the younger men, the elder must go down from Nyoi-ga-mine against the back gate of Rokuhara, while they detach some swift runners to fire the dwelling houses of Shirakawa, so that the people of the capital and the soldiers of Rokuhara will run out in surprise to see what has happened. Then, when their attention is thus distracted, we must act on the defensive from the direction of Iwasaka and Sakuramoto, while the main force under the leadership of Izu-no-kami, comprising the younger men and the fiercest fighting monks, must attack the front gate of Rokuhara from Matsusaka and set fire to the buildings from the windward side. Then in the melee and confusion of the onset it ought not to be difficult to burn out the Dajo Nyudo and take his head." At this point a certain monk called Ichi-nyo-bo no Ajari Shinkai, who did priest's services for the Heike, bringing about ten others who lived with him, came forward into the courtyard where they were holding consultation and gave his opinion as follows: "If you think of acting thus, one must think you are partisans of the Heike. A plan like that will not do at all. Surely we must consider the reputation of our temple as well as the interests of the priests. In former days the families of Gen and Hei vied with each other in upholding the Imperial Family by their might, but of late the fortunes of the Genji have declined and the Heike have become supreme in the land, having now stood firm for twenty years like a tree that no gale can bend. How then can you hope to succeed in attacking their mansions with so trifling a force? Consider the matter very carefully. Is it not better to assemble a large force and proceed with the attack at a later time?" And he continued to argue thus with them for a long tine in order to delay the expedition. Then Joen-bo no Ajari Kyoshu, wearing under his robes a body-armour of light green colour, and a great sword thrust through his girdle in front, and brandishing a white handled halberd in his hand, burst into the council. "There is no need of further argument," he exclaimed, "the founder of our temple, Temmu Tenno, while he was yet Crown Prince, being attacked by Prince Otomo, issuing from the mountains of Yoshino, passed over the district of Uda, and making his way across Iga and Ise, with a band of only seventeen men, being joined by the forces of Mino and Owari, overthrew Prince Otomo and eventually ascended the Throne. There is a saying that a man will have pity on a distressed bird that takes refuge in his bosom. I don't know about the rest, but as for me and my followers we go down to attack Rokuhara tonight and die there!" Enman-in no Taiyu Genkaku too broke in exclaiming: "Enough of this discussion; the hour grows late, haste and advance!" So Gensammi Nyudo Yorimasa took command of the elder monks who were to attack the back gate of Rokuhara and with him Joen-bo no Ajari Kyoshu, Rissho-bo no Ajari Nichiin, Sotsu-no-Hoin Zenji and his disciples Giho and Zenyo, with about a thousand men, holding torches in their hands, started off towards Nyoi-ga-mine. The leader of those attacking the front gate was Izu-no-kami Nakatsuna, eldest son of Gensammi Nyudo, and with him was the second son Gendaiyu-no-Hangwan Kanetsuna, Rokujo-no-Kurando Nakaie, his son Kurando-no-Taro Nakamitsu and the soldier monks Enman in-no-Taiyu Genkaku, Rissei-bo-no-Iga-no-Kimi, Horin in-no-Oni Sado, and Joki-in no Aratosa, all arms carrying bow and arrows, swords and halberds, everyone of them worth a thousand ordinary men, caring not whether they met god or devil. From Byodo-in came Inaba-no-Risshi Kodaiyu, Sumi-no-Rokuro Bo. Shima-no-Ajari, Tsutsui Hoshi, Kyo-no-Ajari and Aku Shonagon. From Kita-no-in were Kongo-in no Roku Tengu, Shikibu Daiyu, Noto, Kaga, Sado and Bingo, Natsui, Higo, Chonan-in no Chikugo, Kaya no Chikuzen, Oya no Toshinaga, Gochi-in no Tajima, and among the sixty disciples of Kyoshu, Kaga Kojo, Gyobu Shunsha, Ichiran Hoshi, Tsutsui Jomyo, Myoshu, Okura-no-Songetsu, Sonei, Jikei, Rakuju, Kanako-bushi no Genei, and among the samurai, Watanabe-no-Habuku, Harima-no-Jiro Sazuku, Satsuma-no-Hyoye, Choshichi Tonau, Kiou Takiguchi, Atae-no-Umanojo, Tsuzuku-no-Genda, Kiyoshi and Susumu with about fifteen hundred men-at-arms. These all set out from Miidera, but as, after the Prince had entered, they had made a rampart and moat and set up fences and palisades, and thrown obstacles of trees across the road, the moat had to be bridged and the obstacles removed, so that the night had passed and the cock crow of approaching dawn was heard before all was finished and the way was clear. "If it be now cock-crow,"

exclaimed Izu-no-kami, "it will be morning light when we reach
Rokuhara. What then is to be done?" Then Enman-in no Taiyu
Genkaku, coming forward as before, said: "Of old King Sho of Shin
put Mosho Kun into bonds, but he managed to escape with three
thousand soldiers by the help of one of the consorts of Sho. Coming to
the barrier at Kan, however, he found that, as is the custom in foreign
countries the gate was not accustomed to be opened until cock-crow.
Now among the three thousand soldiers of Mosho was one Denko, who
was so skilled in imitating the crowing of cocks it he was nicknamed
'Keimei' (cock-crow), and he, running to a high place, imitated the
cock crow so well that all the cocks at the barrier hearing it at once
crowed in concert. Then barrier guards, deceived by the sound, at once
opened the gate and they passed through. So perhaps this cock-crow is
only a ruse of the enemy: let us then advance." But as he finished
speaking the dawn began to break mistily, for it was the time of the
short days of the fifth month. Then Izu-no-kami replied: "A night
attack cannot be made now, and we dare not provoke a battle with them
in broad day, so give the order to retire." So the attackers of the front
gate retired from Matsusaka and those of the back gate from Nyoi-ga-
mine. The young and turbulent priests, declaring that it was the fault of
Ichi-nyo-bo who had prolonged their consultations till daybreak,
clamoured for him to be put to death at once, and attacked and
wounded him, and his disciples and followers who strove to defend him
were all wounded also. He, wounded as he was, managed to crawl
away and get to Rokuhara, though when they heard his tale there, since
there were many tens of thousands of armed men assembled, they were
by no means perturbed.

    Then the Prince, seeing that Hieizan had turned against them, and
Nara had not yet sent their men, since Miidera alone could do nothing,
on the twenty-third day of the same month left that temple and started
for the Southern Capital. The Prince had with him two flutes of Chinese
bamboo called 'Semiori' and 'Koeda.' Of these 'Semiori' was made of
a bamboo with joints like a living Cicada (semi), which had been sent
from China as a return gift when in the reign of Toba-in much gold dust
had been sent as a present to the Emperor of the Sung dynasty.
Wondering how such a rare treasure could be well-carved, it had been
sent to Daisei-in-no-Sojo Kakuso of Miidera and placed on the altar
while prayer was offered for seven days, after which it was carved. On
one occasion Takamatsu-no-Chunagon Sanehira-no-Kyo came to the
temple and played on it, but forgetting it was no ordinary flute, he
dropped it to the ground from his knees, and the flute, feeling the
reproach, broke at the joint like a Semi; so that ever after it was called
'Semiori.' As the Prince excelled so greatly at flute playing he had
inherited it. But now, thinking that his end was nigh, he deposited it in
the Kondo Hall before Miroku Bosatsu. How sad the thought that it

was because he wished to seek the way of Miroku Bosatsu and forsake the world. The Prince gave all the elder priests leave to stay behind, but the young and high-spirited monks went with him. The following of Gensammi Nyudo, the clan Watanabe and the monks of Miidera made up in all a force of about fifteen hundred men. Then Joen-bo-no Ajari Kyoshu, leaning on an old man's staff, came into the presence of the Prince with tears streaming from his eyes: "I had wished to accompany you always," he said "but my years are now four-score and so it is very difficult for me to march, but I am sending my disciple Gyobu Bo Shunshu; he is the son of Yamanouchi Sado Gyobu-no-jo Toshimichi of the province of Soshu, who at the time of the fighting in Heiji served the late Sama-no-kami Yoshitomo and was slain at Rokujo Kawara. Having some slight connexion with him I brought him up so that nothing that is in his heart is hidden from me. Take him therefore and let him serve you always." Then the Prince overcome by his feelings, could not refrain from tears and exclaimed: "What have I done that he should show me such great kindness?"

Chapter XII.

THE FIGHT AT THE BRIDGE.

Now the Prince fell from his horse six times between Uji and Mildera because he had no sleep the previous night, so they tore up about six yards of the planking of the bridge at Uji and he entered the temple of Byodo-in and rested there awhile. The men of Rokuhara, learning that he was fleeing to Nara, at once started off in pursuit to take him and put him to death. The leaders of their force were Sahyoye-no-kami Tomomori, To-no-Chujo Shigehira and Satsuma-no-kami Tadamori, while as commanders of the samurai there were Kazusa-no-kami Tadakiyo, his son Kazusa-no-Taro Hangwan Tadatsune, Hida no-kami Kageie, his son Hida-no-Taro Hangwan Kagetaka, Takahashi-no-Hangwan Nakatsuna, Kawachi-no-Hangwan Hidekuni, Musahi-no-Saburo Saemon Arikuni, Etchu-no-Jirohyoye Moritsugu, Kazusa-no-Gorohyoye Tadamitsu, and Akushichi-hyoye Kagekiyo with about twenty-eight thousand men in all. Crossing over Kobatayama they pressed on to the bridge head of Uji. Perceiving that the enemy were at Byodo-in, they raised their warcry three times, when they were answered by that of the Prince's men. The vanguard, seeing the danger, raised a cry of alarm: "Take care! they have torn up the bridge!" But the rearguard paid-no-heed and pushed them on with cries of "Advance! Advance!" so that some two hundred horsemen of the leading company fell through into the river and perished in the stream. Then the warriors of both sides, taking their stand at each end of the bridge, began a duel of archery, and on the side of the Prince, Oya-no-

Shuncho, Gochiin-no-Tajima, Watanabe-no-Habuku, Sazuku, and Tsuzuku-no-Genda shot so powerfully that their shafts pierced the enemy through both shield and armour. Gensammi Nyudo Yorimasa, knowing in his heart that this fight would be his last, went forth in a suit of amour of blue and white spots worn over his long-sleeved Court hitatare, purposely wearing no helmet on his head, while his son Izu-no-kami Nakatsuna wore a suit of black armour over a hitatare of red brocade, he also leaving his head bare for greater ease in drawing the bow. Then Gochiin-no-Tajima, throwing away the sheath of his long halberd, strode forth alone on to the bridge, whereupon the Heike straightway shot at him fast and furious. Tajima, not at all perturbed, ducking to avoid the higher ones and leaping up over those that flew low, cut through those that flew straight with his whirring halberd, so that even the enemy looked on in admiration. Thus it was that he was dubbed "Tajima the arrow cutter." Another of the soldier priests, Tsutsui-no-Jomyo Meishu, wearing armour laced with black leather over a hitatare of dyed cloth, and a helmet of five plates, a sword in a black lacquered sheath at his side and a quiver of twenty-four black feathered arrows on his back, his bow being also of black lacquer, gripping his favourite white handled halberd in his hand, also sprang forward alone on to the bridge and shouted in a mighty voice: "Let those at a distance listen, those that are near can see; I am Tsutsui Jomyo Meishu, the priest; who is there in Miidera who does not know me, a warrior worth a thousand men? Come on anyone who thinks himself someone, and we will see!" And loosing off his twenty-four arrows like lightning flashes he slew twelve of the Heike soldiers and wounded eleven more. One arrow yet remained in his quiver, but, flinging away his bow, he stripped off his quiver and threw that after it, cast off his foot gear, and springing barefoot onto the beams of the bridge, he strode across. All were afraid to cross over, but he walked the broken bridge as one who walks along the street Ichijo or Nijo of the Capital. With his naginata he mows down five of the enemy, but with the sixth the halberd snaps asunder in the midst and flinging it away he draws his tachi, wielding it in the zig-zag style, the interlacing, cross, reversed dragonfly, waterwheel, and eight-sides-at-once styles of fencing, and cutting down eight men; but as he brought down the ninth with an exceeding mighty blow on the helmet. the blade snapped at the hilt and fell splash into the water beneath. Then seizing his dirk which was the only weapon he had left, he plied it as one in the death fury. Now a retainer of Joen-bo-no-Ajari Kyoshu, Ichirai Hoshi by name, a man of great strength and courage, was fighting behind Jomyo, but as the beams were so narrow he could not come alongside him, so placing a hand on the neckpiece of his helmet, he shouted: "Pardon me Jomyo, this is no good," and springing over his shoulder to the front fought mightily until he fell. Ichirai Hoshi being killed, Jomyo-bo crawled back again and retired to the Byodo-in, where he sat down on the grass before the gate, and stripping off his armour, counted the dints of the mows that had struck him. There were sixty-three in all, but of these only five had pierced through, and none of the wounds being very severe, he treated them with cautery; then, covering his head and changing his clothes, using his broken bow as a staff he went down on foot to Nara. Following the example of Jomyo-bo, the soldier monks of Miidera with the Watanabe clan of Gensammi Nyudo's men vied with each other in pressing forward over the beams of the bridge, and fought till sundown some returning with spoil, and some, after being wounded, cutting themselves open and jumping into the river.

Then the commander of the samurai, Kazusa-no-kami Tada-kiyo came to the commander-in-chief of the Heike forces: "See here," he said "the battle on the bridge is very fierce; we ought to ford the river, but after the rains of the fifth month neither man nor horse can live in the stream; shall we go round by Yodoi, Moarai or Kawachiji? What is to be done?" Then Ashikaga-no-Matataro Tadatsuna, a young man in his eighteenth year, spoke saying: "Why not leave the samurai of India or China to go to Yodo, Moarai or Kawachiji, for that is not our way. If we don't rout the enemy that confront us here, the Prince will get away to Nara, and then you will have all the forces of Yoshino and Totsugawa to deal with and that will be no light affair. On the boundary of Musashi and Kozuke there is a great river called the Tonegawa and there the Ashikaga and the Chichibu are always fighting each other, and on one occasion, when the front were attacking at Nagai ford and the rear at Kogasugi ford, a certain Nitta Nyudo of Kozuke, who was coming to the help of the Ashikaga from the Sugi ford, being told by them that the Chichibu had destroyed all the boats that had been provided to cross, exclaimed: "If we do not ford the river here it will be a disgrace to our reputation as samurai; to be drowned is but to die; Forward then!" and using their horses as a raft they forded the river. As the samurai of the East Country say: "Keep your face to the enemy, and when separated by a river, shun the swift rapids by the bank. This river is neither more nor less swift and deep than the Tonegawa, so come along sirs," and he plunged into the stream. Ogo, Omuro, Fukasu, Yamakami, Nawa-no-Taro, Sanuki, Hirotsuna, Shirodaiyu, Onodera-no-Zenji Taro, Heyako-no-Shiro, and among the younger men Ubukata-no-jiro, Kirifu-no-Rokuro, and Tanaka-no-Sota immediately bed in after him with some three hundred men behind them, shouting the Ashikaga warcry. "Put the heads of the weaker horses downstream, those of the stronger upstream!" he shouted "if the horses keep their feet give them the rein and let them walk, but if they get off their feet let them have their heads and swim them; if you are washed downstream stick the butt of your bow down into the bottom; join hands and go across in line if your horse's head gets down, pull it up, but don't pull it too far or you will fall off backwards; sit tight in the saddle and keep your feet firm in the stirrups; where the water is slow and deep get up over the horse's tail; don't shoot while in the water; if the enemy shoots don't draw bow in return; keep your head down and your neck-piece well sloped upwards, but not too far or you will be shot in the crown of the helmet; be light on the horse and firm against the stream; don't go straight across you will be washed away, keep obliquely to the stream." Thus advising and encouraging them he brought the whole three hundred rapidly across without losing a man.

Chapter XIII.

THE FATE OF THE PRINCE.

Then Ashikaga Matataro, wearing armour with red leather lacing over a hitatare of russet gold brocade, with a helmet ornamented with lofty horns, a gold-mounted tachi by his side, a twenty-four black and white spotted arrows on his back, carrying a black lacquered bow lashed with red bands, and riding a light brown horse with a gold-mounted saddle on which is the crest of an owl on an oak bough, stood up in his stirrups and shouted loudly: "I am Ashikaga Matataro Takatsuna, aged seventeen, son of Ashikaga-no-Taro Toshitsuna of Shimotsuke, descended in the tenth generation from Tawara Toda Hidesato, the renowned warrior who gained great fame and reward for destroying Masakado the enemy of the Emperor, and though it may be at the risk of divine anger that one without rank or office should draw bow against a Prince of the Royal House, yet as I owe deep gratitude to the Heike for many favours, here I stand to meet any on the side of Gensammi Nyudo who dares to face me." And he made an onset and fought his way within the gate of the Byodo-in. Then the commander Sahyoye-no-kami Tomomori, seeing this, ordered his forces to cross over, and about twenty-eight thousand horsemen plunged into the river, so that the rapids of the Ujigawa were dammed and stayed by the mass of men and horses, and the foot-soldiers crossing below the horsemen were hardly wetted above their knees. But everything is carried away, by the natural force of water, so the men of Ise and Iga, to the number of six hundred horsemen, were washed away through their ranks being broken by the force of the current, and their armour of various hues, green, scarlet and red, rising and sinking as they were washed hither and thither in the stream, looked like the maple leaves on Kannabiyama, when in late autumn they are blown by the mountain blasts into the Tatsuta river and collect in masses where the flood is dammed. Among them three gallants, clad in the scarlet armour of a leader of armies, stuck helplessly in a fish decoy, and Izu-no-kami, watching them as they struggled in the rapids, composed this stanza:

"Lo! the bright scarlet hue of the mail of the warriors of Ise;
Now they are stuck like fish, struggling in Uji's decoys."

They were Kuroda-no-Gohei Shiro, Hino-no-Jiro and Otobe-no-Yashichi, all men of Ise, and Hino-no-Juro, a veteran soldier, wedging the butt of his bow into a cleft of the rock, scrambled out by its aid and then pulled out his two companions, thus saving their lives.

Now when the whole force had reached the other side they advanced and fought their way in through the gate of the Byodo-in and in the confusion the Prince attempted to escape town; Nara, while Gensammi's men the Watanabe and the warrior priests of Miidera strove to hold back the foe with their bows and arrows. The veteran warrior Gensammi, now more than three score years and ten, was soon wounded in the right elbow by an arrow and was about to retire within the temple to die calmly by his own hand, when a band of the enemy threw themselves in his way, whereupon his second son Gendaiyu-no-Hangwan Kanetsuna turned to counter them and let his father escape. His armour laced with Chinese silk was worn over hitatare of dark blue brocade, and he rode a cream colour horse with a saddle mounted in gold. Then Kazusa-no-Taro Hangwan shot an arrow that struck him beneath the helm, and as he staggered at the blow, Kazusa-no-kami's son Jiro Maru, a strong and valiant fighter, clad in green armour with a helmet of three plates on his head, unsheathed his sword and sprang upon him. They both grappled immediately and fell together, when Gendaiyu Hangwan, who was a powerful man, gripped Jiro Maru, pressed him down and cut off his head, but just then fourteen or fifteen of the Heike horsemen came up and Kanetsune was overpowered at last by numbers and slain. Izu-no-kami Nakatsuna too, after fighting with reckless bravery, covered with wounds, retired to the Tsuridono of the Byodo and there put an end to himself, his head being taken up by Shimokawabe-no-Tosaburo Kiyochika and thrown under the verandah. Rokujo-no-Kurando Nakaie and his son Nakamitsu also fought valiantly until they were slain. This Nakaie was the eldest son of the late Tatewaki Senjo Yoshikata, and when father was killed, being an orphan, he was adopted by Gensammi Nyudo out of pity, and now, faithful to their long compact, they both died together. Gensammi Nyudo, calling Watanabe Choshichi Tanau, bade him strike off his head, but he refused, overcome by the thought of cutting off his master's head while alive, but offered to do so after he had committed suicide. Then Gensammi Nyudo, turning to the West, put his hands together and repeated the Nembutsu ten times in a loud voice, after which he composed this sad stanza;

"Like a fossil tree from which we gather-no-flowers
Sad has been my life, fated-no-fruit to produce."

And with these last words he thrust the point of his sword into his belly, and bowing his face to the ground pierced himself through and died. It was not a time when people usually make poems, but as he' had been extremely fond of this pastime from his youth up, so even at the hour of death he did not forget it. Choshichi Tonau took his head, and fastening stones to it sunk it in a deep part of the Ujigawa. Now though the Heike samurai had been strictly ordered to take the Takiguchi Kiou alive, yet he, after fighting with great bravery, being very severely wounded, at last cut himself open and died. Enman-in-no-Taiyu Genkaku, thinking that the Prince had by this time got far away, gripping his sword in one hand and his halberd in the other, cleft his way through the midst of the foe and leaping into the river, without relinquishing any of his arms, dived beneath the water and emerged safely on the other side. Then ascending to a high place he shouted with a loud voice: "Ho! how now, my lords of the Heike, see I have got thus far!" after which he returned to Miidera. Now Hida-no-kami Kageie, a veteran soldier, suspecting that the Prince would certainly attempt to flee to Nara under cover of the fighting, rode hard on his track with four or five hundred men in full armour, and as he expected, overtook him in front of the torii of Komyozan with his escort of about thirty horsemen. As the arrows flew like rain-no-one could tell whose it was, but one of the arrows of the Heike struck the Prince in the side so that he fell from his horse, whereupon they killed him and cut off his head. Oni Sado, Aratosa, Kodaiyu, and Gyobu-no-Shunshu who accompanied him, not wishing to live after their master, threw themselves upon the enemy and died fighting together. Among them his foster brother, Rokujo-no-suke-no-Taiyu Munenobu, jumped into the pond at Niino, and hiding his face among the waterweed, lay there trembling. Soon after the Heike came riding back again to the number of four or five hundred horsemen, laughing and shouting as they rode, and peeping out he could see in the midst of them a headless corpse in white clothing born on a shutter. It was the Prince without doubt, for in his girdle was the flute 'Koeda' which he had bidden them bury with him in the coffin if he died. He earnestly wished to rush out and throw himself on the body, but fear restrained him, and after the enemy had half passed by he came out of the pond, and wringing out his wet garments returned weeping to the capital, where there was none who did not hold him in aversion.

Now about seven thousand soldier priests of Nara in full armour had gone forth to meet the Prince, and while the vanguard reached as far as Kozu and the rearguard was still surging out of the southern gate of the Kofukuji, they heard that the Prince had been slain before the torii of Komyozan, alas! but fifty cho distant from Kozu. So, unable to do any more, they halted, lamenting that they had not come up in time.

Chapter XIV.

THE YOUNG PRINCE BECOMES A MONK.

The Heike soldiers, sticking the heads of the followers of Prince Mochihito and Gensammi Nyudo, the Watanabe and the monks of Miidera, about five hundred in all, on the points of their swords and halberds, returned to Rokuhara towards evening, flourishing them in the air and shouting exultantly. The head of Gensammi himself could not be found, for it had been sunk in the waters of the Ujigawa by Choshichi Tonau, but after searching hither and thither all those of his sons were recovered. As to that of the Prince, it could not be identified, since there was no one there sufficiently familiar with him to recognize it. The Chief Court Physician Tenyaku-no-kami Sadanari, having been called to attend the Prince when he was sick the year before, could have identified him, but illness prevented him from answering the summons. Then one of the Prince's favourite consorts was sent for to Rokuhara, and as she had borne him several children and they were much attached to each other, she could not well make a mistake. Thus it was that, after only one glance, she buried her face in her sleeve and burst into tears, so that they knew that it was indeed the Prince.

Now this Prince had many children by different consorts and among them he had a son of seven years old and a daughter of five by a lady called Sammi-no-Tsubone, daughter of Iyo-no-kami Morinori, who was living with her children at the Palace of the Princess Hachijo-no-Nyoin, and Kiyomori ordered his brother Ike-no-Chunagon Yorimori to tell her to send the little Prince to him at once, though the daughter might remain. To this Hachijo-no-Nyoin replied that the child's nurse had fled away with him in a panic that very morning and he was nowhere to be found. On this being reported to Kiyomori he ordered soldiers to be sent to the Palace to search. Now the wife of Yorimori was a lady called Saisho Dono, the foster sister of this Hachijo-no-Nyoin, and they had been very friendly with each other, but it happened that shortly before this they had become somewhat estranged. Then the little Prince said to the Nyoin: "It seems that great trouble may befall you on my account, so pray send me back quickly." "Ah!" exclaimed the Nyoin weeping, "how very sad it is that a child of seven or eight year who knows nothing of the world should be so affected by this calamity as to say such a thing. Alas, in vain have I brought him up this six or seven years that this fate should now befall him," and she wept unrestrainedly; but as Norimori-no-Kyo kept on repeating his demand, at last, as nothing else could be done, she delivered him up. His mother Sammi-no-Tsubone too was greatly grieved to think that she was parting from him for ever, but, as it was inevitable, weeping bitterly she put on his clothes and parted and arranged his hair before sending him away, feeling the while like one in a dream, while all the household from the Nyoin to the ladies in waiting and the maidservants buried their faces in their sleeves and wept in concert. Yorimori-no-Kyo, taking the child with him in a car, brought him to Rokuhara: then the former Udaisho Munemori-no-Kyo when he saw him spoke thus to his father the Nyudo: "Surely this is the retribution from a previous existence; just to look on the young Prince makes one feel how pathetic is his case; if there be no objection, grant him his life and hand him over to my keeping." "In that case," replied the Nyudo, "he must be put away in a monastery." Then Munemori-no-Kyo sent a report of this sentence to Hachijo-no-Nyoin, and she made-no-objection but bade them do so: without delay. So the little Prince retired from the world and entered the way of Buddha, becoming a disciple of the Abbot of Ninnaji.[179] In after days he was known as Yasui-no-Miya-no-Daisojo Toson, chief priest of the temple of Toji[180] in Kyoto. Prince Takakura had also another son in Nara, and he also was made monk by his guardian Sanuki-no-kami Shigehide, who accompanied him to the North Country. But Kiso Yoshinaka, when he came down to the capital, had his priestly vows revoked and brought him with him to make him Emperor, so that he was called 'the Kiso Prince' or 'the Prince of the revoked vows', and also, because he lived at Yorino in the vicinity of Saga, he was known as the Prince of Yorino.

In old times, there was a physiognomist named Tojo who prophecied that both Fujiwara Yorimichi and his younger brother Norimichi who were Kampaku under three Emperors would live to the age of eighty, and so it happened. Also that Sotsu-no-Uchi no Otodo (Fujiwara Korechika) had the face of one who would be exiled, and so it turned out. Moreover Shotoku Taishi declared that the physiognomy of Shushun Tenno was that of one who would die a violent death, and he was killed by the minister Umako. Though what the physiognomists predicted did not always come to pass, yet it seems that those in former ages were the more accurate. (This because people said: "Has not the Physiognomy Shonagon made a mistake?")

At a later period too, though Kenmei Shinno and Guhei Shinno were both the sons of wise and pious Emperors, yet they did not succeed to the Throne, but still they made no rebellion. Also in the case

---

[179] *Ninnaji.* A temple to the N.W. of Kyoto, whither Uda Tenno retired; had a special connexion with the Court, as its abbot was a Royal Prince.

[180] *Toji.* or the Eastern Temple. So called because it lay east of the Shujaku Gate of the Palace.

of Sukehito Shinno, the third son of the Retired Emperor Go-Sanjo, an exceedingly clever and distinguished Prince, who was nominated by his father in his will to succeed him on the Throne when the Retired Emperor Shirakawa was only Crown Prince, and yet, on account of some decision of Shirakawa he did not succeed; and the son of this Sukehito Shinno, taking the surname of Genji, rose from having no rank at all to the third rank and became Chujo, being known as Sammi Chujo. Except in the case of Yosei-in-Dainagon Sadamu-no-Kyo, son of Saga Tenno, this is the first time that a member of the Genji family has thus risen from nothing to the third rank. This was Hanazono Sadaijin Arihito Ko.

Now the priests who had made special prayer for the crushing of this rebellion of Prince Takakura were well rewarded for their pains, the Chamberlain Kiyomine, son of the former Udaisho Munemori-no-Kyo, being raised to the third rank at the age of twelve years. At the same age his father Munemori had been only Hyoye-no-Suke, and with the exception of the son of the Kampaku there was-no-precedent for a boy of twelve holding such high rank. And the record of it ran: "These are rewards for the putting to death of Minamoto-no-Mochihito and Gensammi Nyudo Yorimasa and his sons." Not only were they impious enough to shoot a real son of the Senior Retired Emperor, but they had the effrontery to describe him by the name of an ordinary subject. For this 'Minamoto no Mochihito' meant Prince Takakura.

Chapter XV.

NUE.

Now this Gensammi Nyudo Yorimasa was the fifth generation from Settsu-no-kami Raiko, the grandson of Mikawa-no-kami Yoritsuna and son of Hyogo-no-kami Nakamasa. At the time of the fight of Hogen he was on the side of the Imperial Army, but received-no-reward: also in the rebellion of Heiji he forsook all his kinsmen and fought on the same side, but his recompense was small. For long he only held the title of Daida Shugo or Guard of the Palace, and had not the privilege of entry to Court, but after he was old, he obtained the privilege by composing the following verse:

> "*Standing far off outside as guard to the Holy of Holies*
> *How can I see the moon, hid in the shade of the trees?*"

For this he was granted the lower grade of the Upper Fourth rank, and so he remained for some time until, wishing to proceed to the Third Rank, he made another stanza, thus:

"So I go through the world as one who is picking up acorns,[181]
Under the boughs of the oak, doomed not to rise any higher."

Some time afterwards he retired from the world and was known as
Gensammi Nyudo Yorimasa, (Minamoto Third Rank), being seventy-
five the same year. Among the many deeds of renown that Yorimasa
performed in the course of his life the most remarkable was in the
Ninpei period when the Emperor Konoe-in was on the Throne. Every
night the Emperor was frightened by something, and though he
summoned the most celebrated of the priests and had them chant those
Sutras most potent for exorcism it was all of no effect. The time that the
Emperor was thus troubled was about the hour of the Ox (2 a.m.), when
a black cloudy mass used to come up from the direction of the wood of
Higashi Sanjo and hover over the Palace, and it always affrighted him.
So a Council of Courtiers was held about it. Now in former days in the
period of Kwanji, when Horikawa in was on the Throne, this Emperor
was terrified in the very same way, and Yoshiie Ason, who was
Commander of the Guards at that time, took up his position on the
verandah of the Shishinden, and at the usual time of the apparition
twanged his bowstring three times and declaimed in a loud and terrible
voice: "I am Minamoto Yoshiie formerly Mutsu-no-kami," so that the
hair of those that heard it stood on end, whereat the distress of His
Majesty was relieved. So according to this precedent Yorimasa was
chosen from among the warriors of the Taira and Minamoto families.
He was at this time only Hyoye-no-kami, and on being informed of it
he said: "From former times samurai have been stationed at the Palace
to drive away rebels and to smite those who disobey the Imperial
Commands, but it is the first time that I have ever heard of their having
apparitions to deal with." But as it was an Imperial Order he went. He
took with him his most trusted retainer I-no-Hayata of Totomi, who
carried an arrow feathered with the underfeathers of an eagle's wing,
while he himself, wearing a double kariginu, carried his lacquered bow
and two barbed arrows and proceeded to the verandah of the
Shishinden. The reason for his taking two arrows was that one
Masayori-no-Kyo, who was at that time Sashoben, had suggested that
he be chosen to deal with the monster, and so Yorimasa had determined
that if he failed to kill the creature with the one arrow he would shoot
the other straight at Masayori's neck. After awhile, as has been
described, at the time when the Emperor was always wont to be
alarmed, a mass of black cloud came from the direction of the wood by

---

[181] *Picking up acorns.* (shii) there is a word play on the double meaning of 'shii'
oak, here referring to its fruit, and Shi-i Fourth Rank, so that it would then mean "as one
who has only picked up the Fourth Rank."

Higashi Sanjo and floated over the top of the Palace. Yorimasa, looking up, saw a strange shape in the midst of the cloud and determining not to live if he missed, took an arrow, and earnestly, repeating, invocation to the god of war 'Namu Hachiman Dai-Bosatsu!' drew the bow mightily and let fly. The arrow flew straight to the mark and Yorimasa gave a loud shout of triumph as I-no-Hayata came running up, seized the thing as it fell and, pressing it down with might and main, pierced it through nine tunes with his sword. Then many others ran up with torches, and when they came to inspect it they found it was a most horrible monster with a monkey's head, the body of a badger, the tail of a snake and feet like a tiger, its voice being like a Nue bird. The Emperor, out of his great gratitude to Yorimasa, presented him with a famous sword called 'Shishio' or Lion King. This was handed to the Sadaijin Yorinaga to give to Yorimasa, and as His Excellency proceeded to come half-way down the steps of the Palace, it being then the tenth day of the fourth month, the voice of a cuckoo that chanced to fly overhead echoed twice or thrice, whereupon the Sadaijin exclaimed:

> *"How does the cuckoo too wish to make your name known in the heavens."*

But Yorimasa, sticking out his right knee and spreading out his left sleeve, looked up at the crescent moon in the sky and replied:

> *"Only I drew the bow, leaving the arrow to fly."*

Then he received the sword and retired.

This Yorimasa-no-Kyo, beside being a peerless warrior, was also a distinguished poet and much admired by his contemporaries. The bird they put into a boat and set it adrift. In the period Oho also, in the reign of Nijo-in a monstrous bird called Nue was heard to cry in the Palace, so that the heart of the Emperor was troubled, and so as had been done before he summoned Yorimasa. It was the evening of the twentieth day of the fifth month. The Nue only flew once over the Palace and its voice was not heard a second time. It was so dark that nothing could be seen and therefore there was nowhere to aim, so Yorimasa took a great whirring arrow and shot it over the roof of the Palace at the place where the cry had been heard. The Nue, alarmed at the sound of the arrow, sprang up into the sky, when Yorimasa, quickly seizing a smaller whirring arrow, let it fly. It struck and brought down the creature, whereupon all those in the Palace came rushing out shouting confusedly. On this occasion Yorimasa received a robe of honour from the Emperor. This time it was Oi-no-Mikado no Udaijin Kinyoshi who received it to present to Yorimasa. "In ancient China," said he in admiration, "You shot a wild goose beyond the clouds, but now

Yorimasa has shot a Nue in the rain:

"Famous the deed site the dark in the rainy season of springtime."
"Nay at the time it seemed twilight had scarcely gone by,"

replied Yorimasa as he received the robe and retired. Then, having
received the fief of Izu, he appointed his eldest son Nakatsuna as its
Governor, and having attained the Third Rank was living at ease on his
estates in Tamba and Wakasa, when he started this vain revolt and
perished with the Prince and his sons and grandsons.

Chapter XVI.

THE BURNING OF MIIDERA.

The priests of Hieizan who had formerly behaved in a disorderly
manner were now peaceful and quiet, whereas Nara and Miidera, since
they had received and lent their support to the Prince, had put
themselves in the position of enemies of the Throne. Therefore it was
resolved to proceed against both monasteries, but, with the intention of
attacking Miidera first, Sahyoye-no-kami Tomomori with Satsuma-no-
kami as his Lieutenant marched against the Onjoji with about ten
thousand men. At the monastery about a thousand soldier-monks,
arming themselves, made a shield barrier, threw up a barricade of felled
trees and awaited them. At the hour of the Hare (6. a.m.) they began to
draw their bows, and the battle continued the whole day, until when
evening came on three hundred of the monks and their men had fallen.
Then the fight went on in the darkness, and the Imperial forces forced
their way into the monastery buildings and set them on fire.

The main temples of Honkaku-in, Joki-in, Shinnyo-in, Keon-in,
Daiho-in, Joryu-in, Fugendo and the Hall of the Kyodai-kwasho with
the Honzon-do, the sixteen yard Great Hall, the Bell Tower, the
Baptismal Hall, the Shrine of the Tutelary Deity, the new Shrine of the
Deity of Kumano, the Halls, Residences, Pagodas and Shrines to the
number of six hundred and thirty seven, together with one thousand
eight hundred and fifty three houses of Otsu, not to speak of seven
thousand volumes of the Holy Sutras, called the Issai Kyo,[182] which
Jito had brought from China, and two thousand Buddhist statues, were
suddenly reduced to ashes. It seemed as if the Five Pleasures[183] of
Heaven had departed from the world and the Three Hot Torments[184] of

---

[182] *Issai Kyo* also called the Daizo Kyo, the Tripitaka with commentaries.
[183] *Five Pleasures*. The five melodious sounds of the Palace, Trade, Horns, Levies
and Wings.
[184] *Three Hot Torments*. The Dragon is said to plunge into boiling water three times
a day.

the Dragon were at their height.

Now Miidera had originally belonged to the Governor of Omi, but afterwards became the chantry temple of Temmu Tenno. The principal Buddha of this temple was that which this Emperor himself specially worshipped, and which the Kyodai Kwasho,[185] said to be the living Miroku, who for a hundred and sixty years worshipped it, had given over to Jito Daishi. This image is said to have come down to earth from the jewel Palace of the Toshita Heaven, the fourth of the Six Heavens of Desire, and to here await the far off time of the revelation of Miroku under the sacred Dragon Flower. Indeed a most extraordinary matter! As the Daishi here established the three symbols of a well, flowers, and water, as holy memorials that it was a place efficacious in teaching and baptism, it was called Miidera (Temple of the Three Wells). Such a holy place it was and now it has come to nothing. In an instant, the Law of Tendai and Shingon was destroyed, no trace is left of its stately buildings, the Halls of the Law are done away, the sound of the bell is heard no longer, the flowers of the summer preaching have vanished and the splashing of the holy water sounds no more. The aged and virtuous teachers preach the Law no longer, and the multitudes of disciples have forsaken their studies. The Lord Abbot Enkei Shinno is dismissed from his office of Betto of Tennoji and thirteen other chief priests must vacate their posts, and all are committed to the Custody of the Kebiishi, while thirty priests, including Tsutsui Jomyo Hoshi, are sent into exile. Such an upheaval and disorder in the Empire was no ordinary matter and all considered it a portent of the fall of the Heike supremacy.

Volume V.

Chapter I.

THE CHANGE OF CAPITAL.

It was decided that the Emperor should proceed to Fukuhara on the third day of the sixth month of the fourth year of Jisho. People thought that the change of capital was likely to take place about this time, but as they had not expected that it would be fixed so soon, there was a great uproar in Kyoto among all classes. Then, after having been arranged for

---

[185] *Kyodai Kwasho.* Apparently a famous priest of this temple. (Kwasho is the Sk. Upadhyaya, a Buddhist priest, as dist. from other priests; sometimes it signifies the head of a monastery.) This priest was perhaps considered to be an incarnation of Miroku, or it may be revered as much as Miroku Bosatsu or Maitreya. This Bodhisattva is to come as successor of S'akya Muni after a lapse of fifty thousand years, to usher in the golden age. Kobo Daishi, the patron saint of Mt. Koya is said to be asleep there awaiting his advent. He will come and preach under the Dragon Flower Tree.

the day, it was anticipated by one day and finally settled for the second. At the hour of the Hare (6 a.m.) on the second day the Imperial Palanquin was in readiness; the Emperor was now three years old and owing to his tender years could not but acquiesce in anything. When the Emperor was a child it was the custom that the Dowager Empress should go with him in the Palanquin, but this time the precedent was not followed and the Imperial Nurse Sotsu-no-Suke alone went with him. The Empress press Dowager, the Retired Emperor and the former Emperor Takakura also went in the procession. They were accompanied by the Sessho, the Dajo-daijin and all the Court Nobles, and all the Heike house headed by the Dajo Nyudo himself went with them. On the following day they arrived at Fukuhara, and the Emperor proceeded to the country seat of Ike-no-Chunagon Yorimori, the younger brother of the Nyudo, and took up his abode there. On the fourth day the Upper Second Rank was conferred on Yorimori as a reward for the services of his house, so that he was promoted over the head of the Udaisho Yoshi-michi-no-Kyo the son of the Udaijin Kanezane, this being the first time that the second son of an ordinary subject was, advanced over the son of the house of a Sessho Kwampaku. Now the Lay-priest Chancellor, though he had changed his mind and brought back the Ho-o to the Capital from the Toba Palace, enraged by the rebellion of Prince Takakura, had His Majesty again moved to Fukuhara, and, building a wooden chamber eighteen square feet, surrounded by a foursquare wooden fence having only one opening in it, he confined him there, and appointed Harada-no-Taiyu Tanenao to keep guard over him. As it was by no means easy for anyone to gain access to it the young men nicknamed it "Ro-no-Gosho," or "The Prison Palace." An abominable and pathetic thing even to hear of. "As for me," quoth the Ho-o, "I have not the least desire to take any part in the government; all I wish is that I may be allowed to wander at will from temple to temple for consolation." But there seemed altogether no end to the evil deeds of the Heike; ever since the period Angen they had gone on sending Courtiers and Ministers into exile or putting them to death: they had banished the Kwampaku and put the Nyudo's son in law in his place, and shut up the Ho-o in the Seinan Detached Palace, and then they had even dared to put to death Prince Takakura, so that people said that changing the Capital was the only thing left for them to do. But to change the Capital was by no means without precedent. Jimmu Tenno, who was the fourth son of Hiko-nagisa-take-ugaya-fuki-aezu-no-mikoto[186] the fifth Earthly Deity, and whose mother was Tama-yori-hime the daughter of the Sea

---

[186] *Hiko-nagisa.* The fifth generation from Ama-Terasu, who was considered the first of the Earthly Deities.

God, being the descendant of twelve generations[187] of Gods and the ancestor of a hundred earthly sovereigns, in the year of the cock in the cycle Kanoto[188] succeeded to the Imperial Throne in the district of Miyasaki of the province of Hyuga, and in the tenth month of the fifty ninth year, the year of the ram of the cycle Tsuchinoto, subduing the East, he took up his abode in Toyo-ashi-hara-no-naka-tsu-kuni,[189] giving it the name of Yamato. Then, having viewed the mountain of Unebi, he made there his Imperial Capital, and clearing and subduing the land of Kashihara, he built therein his Royal Palace, calling it the Kashihara Palace. Since this age generation after generation of Sovereigns have removed their Capitals to many sites in various provinces to the number of more than thirty times, yea even unto forty. From Jimmu Tenno to Keiko Tenno twelve generations of Sovereigns made their Capitals in the provinces of Yamato and did not remove to another province, but in the first year of Seimu Tenno[190] the Capital was changed to the province of Omi and set up in the district of Shiga. In the second year of Chuai Tenno it was changed to the district of Toyoura in the province of Nagato, and while the Capital was in this province the Emperor died and his Consort the Empress Jingo succeeded to the Throne and reigned as Empress, subduing the lands of Kikai, Korai and Keitan[191] and receiving the submission of the foreign armies. Then, returning to her country she gave birth to a Prince in the district of Mikasa in the province of Chikuzen, wherefore that place was called Umi-no-Miya, and this Prince, we speak it with reverence, is the god Hachiman, and when he succeeded to the Throne he was known as Ojin Tenno. Afterwards the Empress Jingo removed to the province of Yamato and abode in the Palace of Iware-nowaka-zakura, while Ojin Tenno resided at the Palace of Akari in Karushima in the same province. In the second year of Nintoku Tenno it was again removed to Namba in the province of Settsu and the Emperor abode in the Palace of Takatsu. In the second year of Richu Tenno the Capital was again changed to the province of Yamato, and established in the district of Tochi. In the first year of Hansei Tenno it was removed to the province of Kawachi and the Palace was built at Shibagaki. In the forty second year of Ingyo Tenno the Capital was once more changed

---

[187] *Twelve generations.* I.e. seven generations of Heavenly Deities and five of Earthly.

[188] *Kanoto.* cf. also Tsuchinoto, two of the ten expressions used for naming days and years in the ancient Japanese calendar, taken from the five elements, ki, wood; hi, fire; tsuchi, earth; kane, metal; mizu water; kinoe kinoto, hino hinoto, tsuchinoe tsuchinoto, kanoe kanoto, mizunoe mizunoto.

[189] *Toyo-ashi hara*, The Middle Country of fertile Reed Plains, appar. Mid-Japan.

[190] *Seimu Tenno.* This happened in the reign of Keiko Tenno, and seems to be a mistake of the author.

[191] *Keitan.* The northern part of Korea. This is somewhat exaggerated, for Jingo Kogo did not reach so far.

to Yamato and the Palace was established at Asuka in Tobutori. In the twenty first year of Yuryaku Tenno it was again moved to Asakura in Hase of the same province. In the fifth year of Keitei Tenno it was changed to Tsutsuki in the province of Yamashiro, and twelve years afterwards the Palace was built in Otokuni. In the first year of Senkwa Tenno it was removed again to Yamato and the Palace was established at Iruno of Hinokuma. In the first year of the Great Reform of Kotoku Tenno it was changed to Nagara in the province of Settsu and the Emperor dwelt in the Palace of Toyosaki. In the second year of Saimei Tenno it was again removed to Yamato and the Palace set up at Okamoto. In the sixth year of Tenchi Tenno the Capital was made again in t Omi and the Palace built at Otsu. In the first year of Temmu Tenno it was brought back to Yamato and the Emperor dwelt at the South Palace of Okamoto and it was called Kiyomihara-no-Mikado. The two Emperors Jito and Mommu dwelt in the Palace of Fujiwara. From Gemmyo to Kwonin Tenno seven generations had their abode at Nara, but in the time of Kwammu Tenno, on the third day of the tenth month of the third year of Enryaku, the Nara Capital was removed from the village of Kasuga to Nagaoka in Yamashiro, and on the first month of the tenth year the Dainagon Fujiwara-no-Oguromaro, and the Sangi Sadaiben Ki-no-Kosami, sent the Dai-Sozo Genkei and others to inspect the village of Uda in the district of Kadono in the same province. Then they both made the following report to the Emperor: "Having inspected the condition of the locality, we find that it is a most convenient site for the Capital, for it has on the four quarters suitable place. for the four deities, Shoryu[192] on the left, Byakko on the right, Shujaku in front and Gembu behind." Therefore, having reported this to the deity Kamo Daimyojin who dwelt in the district of Otagi, on the twenty first day of the eleventh month of the thirteenth year of Enryaku the Capital was removed from Nagaoka to this site. And from this time to the present day there have been thirty-two generations of Sovereigns during a period of three hundred and eighty years. Since that time many Sovereigns have changed the Capital to many places, but no other spot is so excellent as this, and Kwammu Tenno, deeply convinced of this fact, ordered his Ministers and all the able men of the country to have an image of clay 8 feet high made to stand perpetually, and to attire it in helmet and armour of iron and put a bow and arrows of iron in its hand, adjuring it to protect the capital if in ages to come any one should try to change it to any other province. It was buried, the top of Higashiyama in a standing position looking toward west, and this

---

[192] *Shoryo* etc.Tthe Four Quadrants or Divisions of the Twenty eight Constellations. The Azure Dragon, The Sombre Warrior, The Vermilion Bird, The White Tiger. A Chinese idea quoted from Goshi. 青龍 Shoryo means a great river, the Kamogawa, 白虎 Byakko, a great road, the Shujaku road, 朱雀 Shujaku a marsh land, the fields near Toba, 玄武 Gembu a high mountain, Hieizan.

mound, whenever any great event was to happen, would stir and give forth sounds. It is called Shogun-zuka and is there to this day. And this Capital he gave the name of Heianjo, that is the city of peace and security. It ought to have been greatly revered by the Heike, for Kwammu Tenno was the sovereign from whom their house had its origin, and it was very foolish of them, without any good reason, to remove to another province the Capital that their Imperial Ancestor so much respected. Once in the time of Saga Tenno, his predecessor on the Throne, the Emperor Heijo, persuaded by the Naishi-no-kami, Fujiwara Kusuri, attempted to change it, but as the Ministers and Courtiers and all the people were opposed to it he did not carry out his plan, so how impious was it of this Lay-priest Chancellor, a mere subject, to dare to remove the Capital that the Sacred Sovereign would not change. Most splendid and auspicious was the Ancient Capital; above it rose Hieizan its tutelary deity making soft the sunlight; on all sides the great temples ranged their roofs, protecting it with their holy influence while around a the farmers and townsfolk lived in peaceful security on the Imperial Domains. But now few wagons plough their way over the deserted roads, and but an occasional passer-by is to be seen in some lowly equipage. The houses of the city that formerly jostled each other for room are now daily becoming fewer and more ruinous; broken up and made into rafts they float down the Kamo and Katsuragawa, and the furniture and possessions of their owners are piled up on boats and brought down to Fukuhara. Ah! how sad to see the Flower Capital thus turn into an expanse of rice fields. Who wrote them I know not, but these two stanzas were found affixed to a pillar of the deserted Palace.

> *"Here for four hundred years has stood our loved city unchanging,*
> *When we regard it now— Ah! what a desolate waste."*
> *"Leaving Miyako behind, the city where flowers ever blossom,*
> *Now, on this wind swept shore,[193] what are the perils we face?"*

Chapter II.

THE NEW CAPITAL.

On the ninth day of the sixth month the new capital was begun. Tokudaiji-no-Sadaisho Sanesada-no-Kyo and Tsuchi Mikado-no-Saisho-no-Chujo Michichika-no-Kyo with the former Sadaiben Yukitaka, taking many officials with them, went to Wada-no-No to plan the nine avenues of the new city, but on so doing they found that,

---

[193] *Wind-swept-shore.* Kaze fuku hara, a word-play on the name Fukuhara 福原 Luck-field.

though there was sufficient space for five avenues, there was none left
for any beyond. On their returning and reporting this to the Throne, a
Council of Courtiers was held to consider the matter, and though some
suggested Innamino in the province of Harima as a better site, and
others Koyano in the province of Settsu, yet in the end nothing was
decided. As the thoughts of all still lingered about the old capital, and
the new one was not yet fixed, everyone felt unsettled and distracted.
The old inhabitants of the district were distressed at losing their land,
while those who migrated to it were troubled by the difficulties of
building; indeed it all seemed like an evil dream. Then the Saisho-no-
Chujo Michichika said: "In China there appears to have been a capital
built with three wide avenues and twelve gates, so why can we not
build the Palace in a city of five avenues? At any rate let us build a
temporary Palace." Thereupon the Nyudo, after a Council of Courtiers
had been held, ordered Gojo-no-Dainagon Kunitsuna to use the income
of the province of Suwo and build the Palace. Now this Kunitsuna was
a noble of exceeding great wealth, so that he would not be at all
embarrassed by having to build the Palace, but in using the income of
the province it seemed hardly likely that the people would escape
hardship.

On account of all these critical happenings the Ceremony of the
Accession of the Emperor was put off; indeed when the land was thus
in confusion owing to the change of capital and the building of a new
Palace, the time was highly unsuitable. In ancient times, in the days of
a certain most revered Sovereign,[194] the Palace was built with a
thatched roof without even any eaves, and, noticing that little smoke
went up from the houses of the people,[195] the Emperor remitted the
taxes, thus showing mercy to his subjects and succouring the land. So
also we find an example of the same kind in China where in So the
flowery terraces of the Shokwa Palace devastated the people, and in
Shin the building of the splendid halls of A-ho[196] threw the country into
disorder, while how different was the case of Tai-so of To, who built
his palace of Rinsan of undressed logs and roofed it with a thatch of
untrimmed reeds, who used no decorated boats or chariots, and spent
no wealth on gorgeous dresses, fearing there by to impoverish his
subjects, so that he made no royal processions, and the pine-shoots
grew on the tiles of his roof and the ivy clustered thickly on the walls of
his palace.

---

[194] *A certain most revered Sovereign*. Nintoku Tenno is referred to.

[195] *The people*. 黎民 lit, the black or black headed people.

[196] *A-ho*. the famous palace built by the first Emperor of Shin.

Chapter III.

Moon-Viewing.

The ninth day of the sixth month was fixed for the commencement of the new Palace, the tenth day of the eighth month for the celebration of the raising of the roof-beams and the thirteenth day of the eleventh month for the Imperial Entry. The Ancient Capital was now falling into ruin, but the new one was full of life and bustle. Thus sadly did the summer pass and the autumn had already come on. When the autumn was almost half over, those who were in the new capital of Fukuhara went out to the places famous for moon-viewing. Some went along the shore from Suma to Akashi, recalling the ancient memories of the romance of Prince Genji, and some crossed over the strait to the Isle of Awaji to gaze at the moon at Ejima-ga-iso. Others made their way to Shiraura, Fukiage, Waka-no-Ura, Sumiyoshi, Naniwa, Takasago, or Onoue and stayed to view the moon at dawn before returning. Those who had stayed behind in the Ancient Capital went to Hirosawa at Fushimi for moon-viewing.

Now Tokudaiji-no-Sadaisho Sanesada-no-Kyo, being greatly devoted to the moonlight scenery of the Ancient Capital, after the tenth day of the eighth month went up thither from Fukuhara. Ah! how changed did he find everything. Before the front gate of the few remaining houses the grass had grown thickly, and in the dew-laden courts was a tall undergrowth of mugwort and rushes, while the chirp of the insects shrilled everywhere, and the chrysanthemum and purple orchid grew wild as in the plains. Only the Omiya Palace at Konoe Kawara still recalled the grandeur of former days. The Sadaisho proceeded to this Palace with his retainers and knocked. at the outer gate. From within the voice of a woman called reproachfully. "Who is it that brushes the dew from the weeds of such a neglected place?" "It is the Sadaisho who has come up from Fukuhara," was the reply. "Ah, in that case, since the great gate is locked, I pray you enter by the postern on the eastern side," she answered. So the Taisho entered by the eastern postern. Now the occupant of the Palace, the Senior Dowager Empress, Consort of Konoe Tenno, finding time hang heavy on her hands, had opened the lattice on the south side of her apartment and was solacing herself by playing on the biwa, reviving the while her memories of former days, when unexpectedly the Sadaisho entered. His appearance greatly surprised the Empress, who laid aside her biwa and exclaimed: "Ah! is it indeed reality or am I in a dream? But pray enter." In the volume of the Genji Monogatari called 'Uji'[197] it is written how

---

[197] *Uji.* This passage occurs in the volume entitled 'Agemaki!' It is thus referred to

the daughter of the Lay-devotee Prince,[198] oppressed with melancholy at the passing of autumn, spent the night playing the biwa to calm her troubled spirit, and becoming impatient at last for the moon of dawn to appear, her feelings overcame her and she beckoned to it with the plectrum of her biwa. By this we can understand something of the Empress' feelings.

Now in this Palace was a waiting damsel who went by the name of 'Eve awaiting Maid,' and the reason of this nickname was that once the Empress had asked which was the most affecting, the awaiting a lover in the evening or the parting from him in the morning, and the girl had replied with the verse:

> "*Sadder the bell at eve when we wait in vain for his coming;*
> *Nought is the cry of the bird, hast'ning the parting at dawn.*"

Calling this lady, Sanesada-no-Kyo conversed with her about many things past and present, and then he made the following song in the Imayo style about the ruined state of the former capital;

> "*When we now view the capital of yore,*
> *How is it wasted like a reed-grown plain;*
> *Through all its chambers pours the moon's pale light,*
> *The blasts of autumn pierce me to the bone.*"

This strain he sang three times clearly, and the Empress and all her lady attendants were so moved that they buried their faces their sleeves and wept.

Meanwhile the dawn broke and the Sadaisho took leave of them and returned to Fukuhara. On the way he called a certain Kurando of his company and said to him: "I think that lady-in-waiting seemed very much pained at parting, I pray you go and say something suitable to the occasion." So the Kurando hurried back again at his bidding and improvising this stanza recited it to her as though from his lord:

> "*Though you said it is nought, the cry of the bird at the dawning;*
> *Now at this very dawn, why is your countenance sad?*"

Without hesitation the lady replied:

---

because the section of which it forms a part is called 'Uji jitcho'.

[198] *Lay-devotee Prince.* Ubasoku-no-Miya. Ubasoku is the Sansk Upasaka, a layman who promises to keep the principal commandments, but without becoming a monk.

*"Though we are pained at the bell when at eve we grow weary
of waiting;
Yet when at dawn he returns, hateful the cry of the bird."*

Then the Kurando hastened back again and related the whole affair to his lord, whereat the Sadaisho praised him saying that vas well said indeed; and ever after this Kurando was known Mono-ka-wa-no-kurando, after the first words of his poem.[199]

Chapter IV.

EVIL SPIRITS.

Since the Heike removed the capital to Fukuhara, people were much troubled by evil dreams, and many strange occurrences took place. One night, when the Nyudo had retired to his bed, suddenly the whole room was filled with faces innumerable, peering at him. Kiyomori was not at all perturbed but looked up and glared at them in return, whereupon they all faded away and vanished. And in the Oka Palace which was then being built, though there were no especially great timbers, yet one night there was heard a crashing sound as of great timbers falling, and then a great shout of laughter up in the air as though two or three thousand people were all laughing at once. Verily, it was considered, this must be the work of the Tengu,[200] so a guard was stationed, fifty men by day and a hundred by night, called the guard of the whizzing arrows. For when they shot these whizzing arrows toward the direction where a Tengu was, there was no sound, but if it was shot at a place where there was none, then there was a burst of laughter. Also one morning when Kiyomori went out of his chamber and passed through the wicket gate to view the garden, at once the garden was filled with a heap of skulls of dead men without number that rolled and writhed one over another, up and down and in and out, rattling and clattering as they moved. The Nyudo called to his

---

[199] The three couplets of the lady and the Kurando run thus:

Matsuyoi no fukeyuku kane no koe kikeba,
Kaeru ashita no tori was mono ka wa.

Mono ka wa to kiki ga iikemu tori no ne no,
Kesa shimo nado ka kanashikarurammu.

Mataba koso fuke yuku kane no tsurakaramme
Kaeru ashita no tori no ne zo uki.

[200] *Tengu.* A flying demon, half man, half bird; the Japanese Harpy.

attendants, but it chanced that there was no one to answer. Then all the
skulls came together and united into one huge skull like a mountain in
size, that seemed to fill the whole garden, perhaps a hundred and forty
or fifty feet high, and in this great skull appeared millions of great eyes
like the eyes of a man, that glared at the Nyudo with an unwinking
stare. The Nyudo on his part was quite unmoved, and stood his ground
glaring at them in return for some time, when as the dew or hoar-frost
that melts in the sun, they vanished away leaving not a trace behind.
Also it happened that this Lay-priest Chancellor had in his stables a
horse that he was especially fond of, so that he appointed many
attendants to look after it night and day, and one night a rat made a nest
in its tail and produced young ones therein. As this was a very strange
phenomenon, the Imperial diviners were consulted about it, and they
declared it to be portent of grave significance. Now this horse had been
presented to the Nyudo by Oba Saburo Kagechika of Sagami, and
renowned as the finest horse in all the eight eastern province. It was
black with a small patch of white on its forehead and was named
Mochizuki. It was afterward given to Abeno-Yasuchika chika, Chief of
the Diviners. Now in former times, in the days of Tenchi Tenno, a rat
made its nest and brought forth young in the tail of a horse of the
Imperial Stables, and thereupon there followed an insurrection of
bandits in Korea. It recorded in the 'Nihon Shoki'. It happened also that
a young retainer of Gen Chunagon Masayori-no-Kyo had a very
ominous dream. He dreamed that he was in the Imperial Department
Rites in the Palace and that a number of Lady Officials of the Court,
clad in the stately robes of ancient ceremony, had assembled there as
for a council. She who sat in the lowest seat, and who seemed to be a
supporter of the Heike, was driven out the assembly, while an old man
of dignified bearing, who sat in the highest place, declared that the
Sword of Commission[201] that was deposited with the Heike should be
returned and given to Yoritomo the former Uhyoye-no-suke, now in
exile in the province of Izu; upon which another elder who sat by his
side demanded that afterwards it should be given to his grandson. On
the young samurai asking in his dream what was the meaning; this, yet
another old man told him that the Lady Official who sat in the lowest
place and was a partizan of the Heike was Itsukushima Daimyojin,
while he who said that the Sword should be given to Yoritomo was
Hachiman Daibosatsu, and the other who wished it given to his
grandson was Kasuga Daimyojin, at the same time informing him that
he himself was Takeuchi Myojin. When he awoke, the young man told
this dream to someone, so that it came to pass that the Nyudo heard of

---

[201] *Sword of Commission.* Setto 節刀 The sword presented by the Emperor to a
general with which to subdue the enemies of the Throne, and thus the sign of the supreme
military authority in the Realm.

it, whereupon he immediately sent a messenger to Masayori-no-Kyo bidding him send the young samurai who had had this dream that he might question him further about it. The young samurai, fearing some evil consequences, ran away, and Masayori himself went to the mansion of the Nyudo and denied the whole story; after which no more was heard about it. It was a remarkable thing too that the silver-mounted halberd that had been given to the Nyudo in a divine dream by Itsukushima Daimyojin after he had worshipped at her shrine when he was Aki-no-kami, suddenly disappeared one night in a strange manner. How sad it was that though the Heike had guarded the Imperial House and protected the Empire up till now, they should disobey the Imperial Order and be deprived of their Sword of Commission.

Chapter V.

OBA RIDES HARD TO FUKUHARA.

Now when the Saisho Nyudo Seirai heard these things in his retirement at Koya, he exclaimed: "Truly the end of the supremacy of the Heike draws nigh. That Itsukushima Daimyojin should favour the Heike is quite natural, and as that deity is the third daughter of the Dragon King Shakatsura, she will be a female deity; moreover it is also not without reason that Hachiman Daibosatsu[202] should speak of giving the Sword of Commission to Yoritomo, but I do not at all understand why Kasuga Daimyojin should ask for it to be given to his grandson afterwards. Can it be that after the Heike have been destroyed and the Genji have succeeded to their power the Courtier Ministers of the line of Kamatari will become rulers of the country?" Then a certain priest who was with him answered: "Verily the Glorious Deities deign to put away their effulgence and descend to earth to become incarnate in divers manners, at times appearing as female deities and sometimes again as ordinary mortals, and seeing that this Itsukushima Daimyojin indeed possesses the Three Enlightenments[203] and the Six Supernatural Powers,[204] it is not difficult for her to appear as a mortal. Thus though a

---

[202] *Hachiman Daibosatsu.* Tutelary deity of the Minamoto family, as Kasuga Daimyojin was of the Fujiwara. After the line of Yoritomo became extinct a prince of the Fujiwara family was made Shogun, and as this passage is doubtless a 'vaticinium post eventu,' it gives a terminus a quo for the date of this part of the work.

[203] *Three enlightenments.* 三明 Sk. Trividya, or Three clear conceptions i.e. as to (a) the impermanence of all existence, (b) the wretchedness of all beings, (c) the unreality of bodily existence.

[204] *Six supernatural powers.* 六道 Sk. Abhijina. Acquired by S'akya Muni on the night before he became Buddha, and which all Arhats possess. They are (a) The power to see instantaneously any object in the Universe, (b) Power of understanding every sound of the Universe. (c) Power to assume any shape or form and to be exempt from the laws of gravitation and space. (d) Knowledge of all forms of preexistence of oneself and

man may weary of this fleeting world and enter the True Path, and devote himself with a single mind to the Future Enlightenment so that all else is nothing to him, yet when he hears of good government he will rejoice, and when he learns of trouble he will be moved. This is indeed the way of all men.

Now on the second day of the ninth month it came to pass that Oba Kagechika of Sagami rode hard to Fukuhara with these tidings: "On the seventeenth day of the eighth month the former Uhyoye-no-nuke Yoritomo who was exiled to Izu, in league with his father in law Hojo-no-Jito Tokimasa, attacked the residence of the deputy governor of Izu, Izumi-no-Hangwan Kanetaka, by night and slew him, after which with some three hundred horsemen under Doi, Tsuchiya, Okazaki and others, he retired on the defensive to Ishibashiyama. I then, having got together about a thousand horsemen of our partizans, at once pressed on and attacked them and drove them headlong, so that Yoritomo after making a desperate stand with seven or eight horsemen who were left, fled to Sugiyama of Doi for refuge. Then Hatakeyama on our side gathered together some five hundred horsemen and attacked Miura Osuke of the Genji who mustered about three hundred. The fight took place on the shore of Kotsubo at Yui, and Hatakeyama was defeated and retired to the province of Musashi. After this Hatakeyama gathered his whole clan with Kowagoe, Inake, Koyamada, Edo and Kasai, seven parties of soldiers in all, and numbering about two thousand, and besieged Miura in his castle of Kinugasa. After attacking it was taken and Osuke was slain, the survivors of his force taking boats at Kuri-ga-hama and fleeing to Awa and Kazusa."

Chapter VI.

ENEMIES OF THE MIKADO.

Thus were the Heike soon rudely awakened from their pleasant diversion of removing the capital. The younger among the Nobles and Courtiers exclaimed with apprehension: "Ah it seems that some crisis is at hand, let us then prepare to fight at once." Now at this time Hatakeyama Shoji Shigeyoshi, Koyamada-no-Betto Arishige and Utsu-no-miya-no-Saemon Tomotsuna were in the capital taking their turn as Imperial Guard, and Hatakeyama said: "We all know that Hojo is friendly with Yoritomo and likely to plot with him, but it is difficult to think that the others have thus opposed the Throne." Whereat many others agreed with him, though there were others who dissented, murmuring: "No, no, a great crisis is upon us." The Lay priest

---

others. (e) Intuitive knowledge of the mind of all other beings. (f) Supernatural knowledge of the finality of the stream of life.

Chancellor on his part flew into a great rage: "This Yoritomo," he exclaimed, "ought to have been executed when his father Yoshitomo rebelled in the twelfth month of the first year of Heiji, but the urgent entreaties of the late Ike-no-prevailed and he was sent into exile. Now he is so far wanting in any gratitude as to draw his bow against our house. How can the gods and the Three Sacred Things pardon such iniquity? Surely he will suffer the punishment of heaven."

Now the first example of an opponent of the Throne was in the fourth year of the reign of Iware-Hiko-no-Mikoto (Jimmu Tenno), when in Takao village in the district of Nagusa in the province of Kishu there was a certain spider, long of legs and short of body, whose strength was greater than that of the a strongest man, that wrought great damage to the people. The Imperial Army went forth to meet it, and when they had read the Imperial Decree, made a net of wild vines with which they caught it and killed it. Since that time the following persons have attempted treacherously to overthrow the Imperial Authority. Oishi-no-Yamamaru, Prince Oyama, Yamada-no-Ishikawa, the Minister Moriya, Soga-no-Iruka, Otomo-no-Matori, Bunya-no-Miyada, Tachibana-no-Hayanari, Hikami-no-Kawatsugi, the Imperial Prince Iyo, Dazai-no-Shoni, Fujiwara-no-Hirotsugu, Emi-no-Oshikatsu, Prince Sahara, Igami-no-Hirokimi, Fujiwara-no-Nakanari, Taira-no-Masakado, Fujiwara-no-Sumitomo, Abe-no-Sadato, Muneto, the former Tsushima-no-kami Minamoto-no-Yoshichika, Akusafu, and Akuemon-no-kami, more than twenty in all, and of all these there was not one that attained his desire, but all of them left their carcasses on the mountain or plain, while their heads were exposed on the public scaffold. In the present generation the Throne is held in light esteem, but in former days when the Imperial Decree was read withered herbs and trees would straightway put forth flowers and fruit, and the birds of the air would obey. Not so very long ago, when the Mikado of the Engi era (Daigo Tenno), was proceeding to Shinzen-en, a heron was seen by the brink of a pond, and the Emperor ordered an attendant of the sixth rank to catch it. The Courtier wondered how he was to do so, but as it was the Imperial Mandate, he went towards it, when the heron at once prepared to fly away. "The Mikado Commands," cried the Courtier, whereupon the bird crouched down and did not move, so that he caught it and brought it to the Emperor. "How admirable indeed," said His Majesty, "that this heron should thus obey the Imperial Behest; let the fifth rank be hereby conferred upon it." Moreover the Emperor with his own hand bound round its neck a tablet declaring that from that day it should be promoted to be the King of the herons, after which it was set free. This heron was not; intended to be taken to make sport for His Majesty, but to show the power of the Imperial Authority.

Chapter VII.

THE PALACE OF KAN-YO.

To quote a foreign precedent. Tan, Crown Prince of En, was taken captive by the Emperor of Shin and kept imprisoned for twelve years. Then, weeping, he petitioned the Emperor saying: "I have an old mother in my native land and I long to see her once more; grant me I pray you permission to return." But the Emperor only derided him saying: "If horns grow on a horse and a crow be found with a white head, then I will allow you to return." Then Tan, prostrating himself on the ground and looking up to heaven, prayed earnestly that these things might be caused to happen, that he might return to his country and see his mother once again. Now Myo-on Bosatsu[205] went to Ryosen[206] in India to punish the unfilial, and Koshi and Genkai[207] in China first taught the people filial piety. So the Three Treasures of the Hidden and Revealed felt compassion for his filial desire, and there came a horse with horns to the Palace, and a crow with a white head appeared sitting on a tree in the Imperial Garden. The Emperor was greatly astonished at such an extraordinary thing and, out of respect for his Royal Word, he remitted the imprisonment of Tan[208] and sent him back to his native country.

But afterwards he repented of his generosity. Now between the countries of En and Shin there was another country called So, and on its boundary ran a great river over which there was a bridge called the bridge of So; and The Emperor sent his troops to this bridge to cause him to fall into the river when he should have crossed to the middle of it. But though he fell into the midst of the river, he was so fortunate as not to drown, but going as though on dry land he safely reached the farther bank. Wondering how this could be, he looked back and perceived that innumerable turtles were floating on the water, and that they had ranged themselves in a line on the surface so that he had been able to cross over on their backs. Tan, filled with resentment, would not submit to the Emperor so he sent his army to destroy him. Tan, greatly alarmed, sent for a certain warrior named Kei-ka[209] and made him Prime Minister, whereupon Kei-ka in turn summoned another soldier

---

[205] *Myo-on Bosatsu.* Sk. Gadgadasvara. A fictitious Bodhisat who resides in the fabulous universe called Vairotchana Ras'mi Pratimandita, and appeared in thirty eight different transformations to save mankind.

[206] *Ryosen.* v. sup.

[207] *Koshi, Genkai.* Confucius and Yen-hui.

[208] *Tan.* 丹 En. 燕 Emperor of Shin 秦の始皇帝.

[209] *Keika* 荊軻 Denko. 田光. In the original Chinese history it is Denko who is first summoned and who recommends Keika.

called Den-ko to his aid. Then Denko said: "Did you send for me to assist you thinking I was young and strong? A Kirin may spring a thousand miles it is said, but when he is old he is worse than a bad horse; so how can I, now that I am old, be of any use to you? It will be better to find a more vigorous soldier than I am." "Ah," replied Kei-ka, "do not tell anyone of this affair." "If this thing becomes known," answered Denko, "I shall lose my reputation in the future, and there is no shame worse than that one lose his good name." So saying he dashed his head against the plum tree that stood by the gate and died.

Now there was another warrior named Han-yo-ki, and he was a subject of Shin, but as his parents and relations had been put to death by the Emperor, he fled to En. Then the Emperor of Shin sent a proclamation through the four seas saying: Whoever shall bring me a map of En and the head of Han-yo-ki shall receive five hundred pounds weight of gold." Then Kei-ka went to Han-yo-ki and said: "I hear that anyone who takes your head to the Emperor of Shin will receive five hundred pounds of gold; if then you will give me your head that I may take it to him, he will certainly divert himself by looking at it. At that time it will not be difficult for me to draw a sword and stab him to death." When Han-yo-ki heard this proposal he was greatly amazed and then drew a sigh of gladness. "The Emperor has slain my parents, my uncles and my brethren," he exclaimed, "and I brood over it day and night, for an unbearable resentment has pierced me to the bone; if therefore you will kill him indeed, most willingly I give you my head." And he cut off his head and died.

Now there was another soldier named Shin-bu-yo who had fled to the land of En when he was but a boy of thirteen, after having taken revenge on his enemy; he was a matchless warrior whom little children would embrace when he smiled, while grown men would faint at his angry frown. This man Kei-ka took with him as a guide to the capital of Shin and they both set out. One night as they were stopping at a certain mountain village they heard the sound of music coming from another hamlet near by, and made divination from the tune that was being played in order to determine whether their enterprise would be successful. "The enemy is water and we are fire. The rainbow cannot pierce the sun. Our aim will be difficult to carry out," was the oracle. However, as it was not convenient to return now, they went on and in due time arrived at Kan-yo-kyu the capital of Shin, and announced that they had brought to the Emperor the map of En and the head of Han-yo-ki. The Emperor sent an envoy to receive their presents, but, as they refused to deliver them up except to the Emperor himself, he bade that they should be summoned to be received in audience by the Court. Now the circumference of the city of Kan-yo-kyu was eighteen thousand three hundred and eighty miles, and the Palace was built up three miles above the level plain. Here was the Hall of Longevity and the Gate of Eternal Youth: a sun wrought of pure gold adorned it, and a moon of silver, and it was strewn with sand of pearls, rubies, and gold. It was enclosed on all sides by a wall of iron four hundred feet high, and over the Palace was stretched a net of iron to keep away all evil demons from the under world; and as this wall obstructed the wild geese in their flight in spring and autumn, an iron gate called the Wild Goose Gate was made in it for them to pass through. Within it was the Palace called the Aho-den where the Emperor was wont to proceed to give audience for the affairs of state: it was nine cho in length from east to west and five cho from south to north, its height being three hundred and sixty feet, while banners fifty feet in height could easily stand under its floor. It was roofed with tiles of emerald and shone with gold and silver below. When the two, Kei-ka carrying the map of En and Shin-bu-yo the head of Han-yoki, had half ascended the jewelled staircase, Shin-bu-yo, overcome by the immensity and splendour of the Palace, was seized with a fit of trembling. The retainers, seeing this, said: "Common people must not approach our Lord; the superior man does not approach the common herd, if he does so he risks his life." Then Kei-ka turned and replied: "Bu-yo has no treacherous intent, but he is a rustic only accustomed to the ways of the country, and has no experience of a Court like this, so he is naturally embarrassed." Thus the retainers were pacified, and they were permitted to enter the Emperor's presence and exhibit to him the map and the head. Now as the Emperor was looking at the head, he caught sight of a gleaming knife at the bottom of the box in which it was presented, and immediately started back, but as he did so Kei-ka seized his sleeve and struck at his breast with the knife. At this time, though the Palace was crowded with scores of thousands of armed retainers, not one of them dared to lift a hand to help their master; they only deplored the crime of such a treacherous subject. But the Emperor entreated Kei-ka saying; "I pray you allow me a short respite, for I desire greatly to hear the Empress play on the Koto once more;" to which request Kei-ka assented. Now the Emperor had three thousand consorts, among whom the lady Kwa-yo was an unrivalled player on the Koto, so that the wrath of the fiercest warrior was calmed when he heard her, and the birds would descend from the air, and the trees and flowers move in harmony with her music, and now that in tears she played to her Lord for the last time none could resist the spell of her melody. Kei-ka bowed his head and listened, and for a while his fierce and revengeful mood relaxed. Then the lady Kwa-yo began a second piece and the words that she sung were these:

> *"Though a seven-foot screen may be high,*
> *Is it not possible to leap over it?*
> *Though a length of silk gauze may be strong,*
> *If you jerk it will it not tear?"*

These words passed unnoticed by Kei-ka, but the Emperor heard and understood, and suddenly tearing his sleeve, he leaped over the seven foot screen that stood near and ran and took refuge behind a copper pillar. Then Kei-ka sprang up fiercely and hurled the dagger at him, but the Emperor's Physician in Waiting immediately threw his medicine bag so that it caught the dagger, which struck and pierced half through the six foot copper pillar. Kei-ka had no other weapon, so he could do no more, and the Emperor returning to his place took his own sword and cut him to pieces, Shin-bu-yo being put to death also. Then the Emperor gathered his army and marched against Tan of En. Thus if the blue sky does not permit, the rainbow cannot pierce through the sun; the Emperor escaped and Tan was destroyed at the last. Yoritomo will also come to an end in like manner, said those who wished to flatter the Heike.

Chapter VIII.

THE AUSTERITIES OF MONGAKU.

Now this Yoritomo had been spared and banished to Hiru-ga-kojima in Izu in the domain of Hojo on the twentieth day of the third month of the first year of Eiryaku only through the urgent pleading of the late Ike-no-zenni, when his father Sama-no-kami Yoshitomo was executed in the twelfth month of the first year of Heiji for the rebellion that he made. He was at that time fourteen years of age, and having spent some twenty autumns in exile was now of mature years; and if one should wonder why he stirred up a revolt in this year, it was because of the exhortation of Mongaku Shonin of Takao.

This Mongaku was formerly known as Endo Musha Morito and was the son of Watanabe-no-Endo Sakon-ro-Shogen Mochito, having been a retainer of Josei-mon-in, a consort of Toba-in, but at the age of nineteen, possessed by a desire to enter the Way of Buddha, he shaved his head and started to practise mortification of the flesh. With the intention of proving how much he could endure, he stripped himself naked and lay dawn on his back in a bamboo thicket in the depth of the mountains under the scorching sun during the hottest days of the sixth month, when there was no breath of wind, and the horse flies and mosquitoes and wild bees and ants and every kind of poisonous insect came and settled on his body and bit and stung him; but in spite of this he did not move a muscle. Thus he remained for the space of seven days, but on the eighth day he arose and asked whether religious asceticism demanded as much as this or not. "If it was so severe" was the reply, "how could people, survive it?" Thus reassured, he began his austere life by going to Kumano, intending to live in retirement at Nachi. Now at Nachi is a famous water fall, and Mongaku determined to bathe in it as a religious exercise. It was past the tenth day of the twelfth month when he arrived there and the snow had fallen thickly; the river that ran through the valley was silent in its icy shroud; the freezing blasts blew fiercely from the mountain-tops and the water-fall was a mass of crystal icicles, while the twigs were everywhere hidden under their heavy coat of snow. Mongaku, invoking the magic power[210] of Fudo Myo-o,[211] immersed himself up to the neck in the pool of the water-fall and remained thus two, three, then four days, but on the fifth, unable to endure any longer, losing his senses he was washed away by the mighty volume of the falling water, and carried some six or seven hundred yards down stream, his body dashing against the sharp-edged rocks as it rose and fell in the swirling current. Then suddenly there appeared a beautiful boy who seized his hand and drew him safely up on to the bank. The bystanders, seeing his dangerous plight, soon kindled a fire and warmed him so that he recovered consciousness, for it was not his fate to perish, but as soon as he again drew his breath and opened his eyes, he glared about him in great anger, crying out with a loud voice: "I am under a vow to stand under the water-fall for thrice seven days and repeat the magic invocation of Fudo three hundred thousand times, and to day being only the fifth day, who has dared to pull me out?" On hearing these words the hair of their heads stood up and they could say nothing. Then he plunged again into the water fall and stood as before for two days, and on the second day eight boys appeared and grasped both his hands to draw him from the water, but he resisted them strongly and would not move. On the third day he again became as one dead, whereupon, that the water fall should not be polluted, two heavenly youths, with their hair bound up tightly, descended from above the fall, and rubbed the whole body of Mongaku from head to foot with their warm and perfumed hands, so that he breathed again as one in a dream, and asked who it might be that thus had compassion on him. "We are Kongara and Seitaka,[212] the messengers of Fudo Myo-o," replied the two youths, "and we have come in obedience to the command of the Myo-o. Mongaku has made a

---

[210] *Invoking the magic power.* Lit. the Mantras or magic words of the Dharani practised by the Shingon Sect.

[211] *Fudo Myo-o.* One of the Five Mystic Kings, represented with a ferocious expression, and surrounded with a halo of flame; he holds a sword in one hand and a rope in the other with which to subdue evil influences.

[212] *Kongara* Doji and *Seitaka Doji* stand at the left and right hand of Fudo Myo-o.

sublime vow and is now undergoing unparalleled austerities; go ye and succour him." Then Mongaku cried with a loud voice; "Where is the abode of the Myo-o?" "His abode is in the Tosotten,[213] the fourth Heaven of Desire," they replied as they ascended far aloft above the clouds. Mongaku clasped his hands and exclaimed fervently: "Now am I full of hope, for even Fudo Myo-o knows of my austerities;" and he again took up his position in the water fall. But from henceforth he was favoured by most gracious signs of divine assistance; the bitter wind no longer pierced his body, and the falling water felt warm and soothing, and so he completed the three weeks of his vow and afterwards spent a thousand days in retirement at Nachi. Then he started to travel round the whole country as a pilgrim, ascending Omine three times, Katsuragi twice, and then proceeding to Koya, Kogawa, Kinbusen, Hakusan, Tateyama, the peak of Fuji, Izu, Hakone, Togakushi in Shinano, and Haguro in Dewa, until at last, feeling a longing for his native province, he returned to the Capital, hardened like a well-tempered blade by his privation, and wise enough to pray down a flying bird from the sky.

Chapter IX.

KWANJINCHO.

Thereafter Mongaku retired to the mountain recesses of Takao to meditate. In this mountain was a temple called Shin-goji, which Wake-no-Kiyomaro had built in the time of Shotoku Tenno, and which had not been repaired for a long time. In spring the mists filled it, and in autumn the fog was its only occupant; the doors had been blown down by the winds and lay rotting under the fallen leaves. The rain and dew had despoiled it of tiles, and the altar of Buddha stood bare to the sky. No priest abode there to read the Sutras, only the sun and moon shone betimes into it. Mongaku, having made a vow to rebuild this temple, drew up a roll for donations and went round in all quarters to seek supporters, and in the course of his wanderings he came to the Hojuji-den where the Ho-o was residing, and requested His Majesty to make a contribution. But it chanced that the Ho-o was at the time engaged in some amusement and paid no attention, so Mongaku, who was naturally a bold and uncompromising character, knowing nothing of the Ho-o's disinclination, but only thinking that the attendants had not told him, forced his way through into the Imperial Garden and shouted out loudly: "Oh most merciful Lord, how can it be that you pay no heed to such a matter as this? And forthwith he spread out the roll of

---

[213] *Tosotten.* Sk. Tuchita, the fourth Devaloka, where all Bodhisattvas are reborn, there to promote the Way until they are reborn as Buddha.

Kwanjincho[214] and lifting it up high before him began to read;

"Contribution roll of the novice Mongaku, who, desiring to obtain the great blessedness of happiness in this world and in the world to come, respectfully begs the assistance of all, high and low, priest and layman, in building a temple on the holy site of Mount Takao. When we consider it, all-embracing is the Eternal Mind.[215] Though we use the appellations of Buddha and Mankind, albeit there is no distinction between these things, yet, since the clouds of Illusion accompanying the Buddha nature spread thick over the mountain of the Twelve Causes of Existence,[216] the Moon of the Pure Lotos of the mind is obscured and does not appear in the Great Abyss of the Three Poisons[217] and Four Prides.[218] Alas! how pitiable! The sun of Buddha quickly set, and dark and gloomy is the way of the revolving wheel of births and deaths. So men give themselves up to passion and wine. Who will be grateful for the delusion of the raging elephant and the capering monkey?[219] How can they who hate mankind and the Law hope to escape the torments of Emma and his jailers? I, Mongaku, though I have put away the dust of this world and donned the robe of the recluse, find evil Karma still mighty in my heart; day and night it arises, and the virtue that sprouts up within me becomes unpleasing to my ear and is cast away. Alas! how painful! Returning again to the fire pits of the Three Ways,[220] I must revolve through the grievous wheel of the Four Births,[221] so that, through the ten thousand times ten thousand volumes of the Sakya Sage, revealing in every volume the affinity of the Buddha seed, even the most true Law of Cause and Effect, it may not be impossible to attain to the Farther Shore of Perfect Enlightenment.[222] Thus I, Mongaku, weeping at the gate of this life of impermanence, to encourage priests and laymen, high and low, to make connection with the Paradise of the highest Lotus Throne, am intending to build a holy place for the Buddhas and Bodhisats. Takao-zan is a mount of high peaks, thick wooded like the Vulture Peak of

---

[214] *Kwanjincho.* A book in which contributions for religious purposes were recorded.

[215] *Eternal Mind.* Shinnyo, the Eternal Reality that underlies the Universe. As this is the only reality, it follows that the difference between phenomena is only apparent, and the enlightened person knows that it does not exist.

[216] *Twelve Causes of existence.* Ju-ni-Innen. Sk. Nidana.

[217] *Three Poisons.* Lust, Anger, and Folly.

[218] *Four Prides.* Usually Seven are mentioned, perhaps four of these are meant; another reading here gives, the Three Mysteries and the Four Mandaras.

[219] *Elephant and Monkey,* Prob. Anger and Folly.

[220] *Three Ways.* Hell, Pretas and Animals.

[221] *Four Births.* Sk. Tchaturyoni, i.e. (a) Placental birth, as man or animal, (b) from an egg, as birds, (c) from moisture, as fish or insects, (d) by transformation, as Bodhisattvas.

[222] *Farther Shore.* i.e. Nirvana, which is reached across the 'great ocean of births and deaths'

Ghridrakuta, and of quiet valleys and mossy retreats like those of Shosando in China. The mountain streams gurgle and fall in foamy cascades, the apes scream in the crags and sport in the branches. Remote from the haunts of man, free from the dust and noise of the world, there is nothing to disturb our devotions: it is a very excellent site, most suitable for worshipping Buddha. The contributions are small; who is there who will not assist? Whoever gathers a little sand for a pagoda acquires merit in his Karma relation, how much more he who contributes even a small amount of money or property? So shall all both in city and country, far and near, rustics, priests, and laymen, sing of the Sovereign and this age and its contentment as the golden age of the rule of Gyo and Shun[223] in China, and smile as those who meet after a long parting. And if these sacred rites and mysteries are performed in their entirety, all shall attain to the Terrace of the True Gate of the One Buddha, and enjoy the immeasurable and innumerable blessings of the Three Buddha persons.[224] The above composed by me Mongaku with the purpose of obtaining subscriptions as stated. The third month of the third year of Jisho.

Chapter X.

THE EXILE OF MONGAKU.

Now it happened that at this time the Dajo-daijin Myo-on-in was playing the Biwa and reciting, while Azechi-no-Dainagon Sukekata-no-Kyo was playing the six-stringed Koto, and his son Uma-no-kami Suketoki was singing and dancing the Saibara, Morisada, an attendant of the Fourth Rank, keeping time meanwhile and singing various Imayo measures, so that the Palace resounded with musical strains and they were all very merry. The Ho-o himself had deigned to join in the singing also, when suddenly the loud and strident voice of Mongaku broke in on their melody, spoiling the harmony and entirely upsetting the rhythm. "What is this?" exclaimed the Ho-o in great wrath, "who is this boor who dares to interrupt Our Imperial Pleasure? Strike him down, someone!" At this the young and impetuous among the samurai in attendance rushed forward, each trying to be foremost, headed by one, Sukeyuki Hangwan by name, who shouted out, "Down with this villain who dares to disturb His Majesty's Amusement." "I don't move from here until I receive the grant of a manor towards the cost of my temple on Mount Takao," replied Mongaku calmly, and then as he saw that they meant to attack him, shifting the Kanjincho to his other hand,

---

[223] *Gyo and Shun.* The golden age in China.

[224] *Three persons*, Sk. Trikaya. i.e. Nirmanakaya, Buddha in human form, Sambhogakaya, Buddha as a personification of some virtue; Dharmakaya, Buddha as the Eternal Reality.

he gave Sukeyuki Hangwan a blow on the head that knocked off his eboshi, and then doubling his fist struck him another in the chest that sent him flying backwards, so that he took to his heels and fled into the interior of the Palace. He then drew from his bosom a dirk with the hilt wound with the hair of a horse's tail, and baring the blade stood waiting, ready to strike down any who approached. As he sprang round in all directions with the Kanjincho in his left hand and the blade gleaming like ice in his right, it looked as if he had a sword in each hand. Nobles and Courtiers, terrified at such an amazing scene, ran about in all directions, so that the party of the Ho was quite broken up and the whole Palace was in an uproar. Then one of the Palace Guard, Ando Musha Migimune by name, drew his sword and rushed upon Mongaku, who also sprang forward to meet him. Ando Musha, not wishing to shed blood, turned the edge of his weapon and struck him a heavy blow with the back of his sword-arm, and then, as he staggered back a little, dropping his sword sprang on him with a shout to grapple with him. Mongaku, falling undermost, gripped his opponent's right arm as he did so and held on tight, but in spite of this Ando managed to seize him by the throat, and so, being about equal in strength, they rolled about in their struggles, now one being uppermost and now the other, until the others, who had held back so far, summoned up courage to rush in and overpower Mongaku and bind him, after which he was dragged out and handed over to the underlings of the Kebiishi-cho. As they were taking him away, he drew himself up and glared at the Palace, crying out in a loud voice, the while he pranced up and down with anger: "So! not only do I get nothing, but I am treated in this outrageous manner. Know that the Three Worlds are to be consumed by fire, and how shall even the Palace of the Sovereign escape this fate? Even if one is an Emperor who boasts of the Ten Virtues, will he not descend to the Yellow Springs of Death and be tormented by the Ox-headed and Horse-headed Jailers of Hell?" Then the order was given to put this insolent priest into prison and he was led off to be confined. Sukeyuki Hangwan, covered with shame at the ignominy of having his eboshi knocked off, did not appear at Court for a longtime. Ando Musha, however, was rewarded for boldly seizing Mongaku by being at once promoted to the position of Uma-no-jo over the heads of others senior to him.

About this time it happened that Bifuku-mon in died and there was a general amnesty so that Mongaku was set free, but as soon as he was let out he set forth again with his Kanjincho to collect contributions everywhere; and not only so, but wherever he went he proclaimed that the age was corrupt and that both the Emperor and his subjects would be destroyed, with the result that, as such disrespectful words could not be permitted, he was not allowed to remain in the Capital but banished to Izu. Now Izu-no-Kami Nakatsuna, the eldest son of Gensammi

Nyudo, was at this time Governor of Izu, and when this sentence was pronounced he gave orders that Mongaku should be brought to Izu by ship from the Tokaido, or Eastern Coast, and sent two or three inferior officials of the Kebiishi to take charge of him. These officers then said to him: "It is the custom for minor officials like ourselves to profit somewhat on these occasions; no doubt your reverence has many friends in various places, so when you are sent into exile to a far province, they will certainly wish to give you some presents, and food and necessaries for the journey; will you not then communicate with them?" "I have few friends of that sort," replied Mongaku with a laugh, "but there is someone who lives on Higashi-yama who might perhaps do something for me; I will write a letter." Then they produced some very cheap paper, whereat Mongaku became very angry, exclaiming: "How do you expect me to write on paper like this" and he threw it back at them. Then they got some good thick paper and handed it to him, but Mongakut laughed and said: "Unfortunately I cannot write, so please write the letter for me." So one of them wrote at his dictation as follows: "I, Mongaku, having the intention of building a temple on Mount Takao, have been traveling about the country to raise money by subscription, but the age being such an one as it is, it has pleased the Emperor not only to refuse me any assistance, but even to banish me to the distant province of Izu. This being so I am much in need of supplies and comforts for the long journey, and beg that you will assist me in the matter." When he had written it, he asked to whom he should address it. "To Kwannon at Kiyomizu," replied Mongaku. "Do you then make fools of minor officials like us?" they asked indignantly. "By no means," replied Mongaku, "I always rely on Kwannon of Kiyomizu in need, and indeed now I have no one else on whom to rely."

Then they took ship from the port of Ano in Ise, and when they came to Tenryu-nada in the province of Totomi a great tempest rose, and the ship seemed likely to be overturned by the mountainous waves. The helmsman and the sailors gave up all hope, and thinking their last hour had come, fell to praying, some calling on Kwannon and others repeating the Nembutsu of the dying. Mongaku, however, was all this time lying asleep in the bottom of the ship, snoring loudly, until aroused by the confusion he suddenly sprang up, went to the side of the ship, and glaring angrily at the waves, shouted; "Ho! Thou Dragon King of the Waters! What meanest thou by endangering the ship in which is so holy a sage bound to accomplish such a great vow. Knowest thou not, O most worthless of Dragon Gods, that such conduct will receive the punishment of Heaven?" Then the wind and the waves were suddenly stilled and they arrived safely at the shores of Izu. Since leaving Kyoto Mongaku had always kept vividly in his mind the hope of returning to build his temple on Mount Takao, and prayed fervently that he might not die until he had carried out this vow, but if it was impossible that it should be fulfilled, then he would die on the way to exile. With this intention he fasted all the way to Izu, a period of thirty-one days, for as the wind was not always favourable they had to touch at many havens and islands, but yet in spite of this, his natural vigour did not fail as he continued his meditations at the bottom of the ship. Verily there were many reasons for thinking he was no ordinary person.

Chapter XI.

EDICT OF THE HO-O AT IZU.

After this Mongaku was ordered to live in the inner recesses of Nagoya under the care of Kondo Shiro Kunitaka, a native of that part, and as Hiru-ga-kojima, the place where Hyoye-no-suke Yoritomo was exiled, was not far off, he led often to go there and talk over many things. On one of these occasions he said: "Among the Heike Komatsu Daijin is a man of strong mind and sagacious in counsel, but the downfall of that family seems to be approaching, for he was buried in the eighth month of last year. Now among the Genji and Heike there is no leader as distinguished as yourself, so now quickly raise a revolt and subjugate the country!" But Yoritomo answered: "That is not my wish; as you know, I was succoured by the late Ike-no-Zenni, and to show my gratitude I read through one part of the Hokke-Kyo every day on her behalf. That is all I can do." "He who will not accept the gifts of Heaven," continued Mongaku, "will be considered blameworthy, and he who does not act when the time arrives, will be overtaken by misfortune, as it is written. That you may think I speak thus only to tempt you, see by this how deep has been my regard for your house." And he drew from his bosom a bundle wrapped in white linen from which he took a skull. "This is the skull of your honoured father, the late Sama-no-kami Yoshitomo. After Heiji it was buried in front of his prison house and there was no one to say the prayers for him, so I begged his head from the warders, and hanging it round my neck, went round from temple to temple praying for his happy rebirth, and no doubt he is long since delivered from all evil. Thus you see that I have been a most loyal servant of your father." Yoritomo was not quite assured of the truth of all this, but anyhow, when he was told that it was his father's skull, he was moved to tears. After a while he restrained his tears and said; "How can I raise a revolt unless I receive the Imperial Pardon?" "That is easy to arrange," said Mongaku, "for I will go up and get it for you." Yoritomo smiled sarcastically. "Why you yourself are under the Imperial displeasure; how then do you talk of helping others? Even for such a wise priest it will not be easy." At this Mongaku flew into a rage and answered: "If it were my own pardon it might be so, but as it is for you, where is the difficulty? From here to the new capital of Fukuhara is not more than three days journey, and I shall have to spend a day there to get the Imperial Edict, so that the whole matter will not take me more than seven or eight days." So saying he took his departure.

Returning to Nagoya he told his disciples that he was going on a week's pilgrimage in the mountains of Izu, and set out. Sure enough in three days he arrived at Fukuhara, and as he had some connexion with Uhyoye-no-kami Mitsuyoshi, he went to him at once and said: "If I can obtain an Imperial Edict for the pardon of the former Uhyoye-no-suke Yoritomo, who is now in exile in Izu, we can gather together the men of eight provinces, and so overthrow the Heike and give peace to the land." "Indeed," replied Mitsuyoshi, "I am now in an awkward condition, for I have been deprived of my three offices, and as for the Ho-o, he is closely confined, so it may be difficult to do anything, but I will go and see." And he went and acquainted the Ho-o with the affair secretly. His Majesty was exceedingly pleased to hear it and granted the Edict forthwith. Then Mongaku, greatly rejoiced, hung it round his neck, and after three more days again arrived at Izu. Now Yoritomo was very anxious about it all, and was wondering what would happen to the reckless priest as the result of his rashness, when at the hour of the Horse on the eighth day he presented himself with the laconic remark; "Here is the Edict." Then Yoritomo with great respect put on a new eboshi and a white robe, and washing his hands and his mouth, took the Edict and raised it three times to his forehead, after which he opened it and read as follows:

"For several years the Heike have set at nought Our Imperial Influence, and have not scrupled to govern the country according to their will. This Realm is the Land of the Gods, and their Virtue has descended to its Sovereigns from generation to generation. So that, since the establishment of the Imperial Line, for a thousand years and more, those who have dared to oppose Our rule and endanger the Empire have all perished without exception. Therefore with the ghostly aid of the High Gods, and relying on this Our Imperial Edict, do thou quickly destroy the Heike line, and subdue the enemies of Our House. Thus shalt thou continue the traditions of a warrior family and surpass the loyal service of thy ancestors, exalting thyself and all thy house. The fourteenth day of the seventh month of the fourth year of Jisho. Given through the former Uhyoye-no-kami Mitsuyoshi. To the former Uhyoye-no-suke Dono."

This Edict Yoritomo put into a bag of brocade and hung it round his neck, and kept it on his person even at the battle of Ishibashiyama.

Chapter XII.

FUJIKAWA.

Now when it was rumoured that Yoritomo had raised the standard of revolt, a council of Courtiers was held at Fukuhara, and it was decided to attack him immediately, before he could gather more of his adherents. The Commander in chief was Komatsu-no-Gon-no-suke Shosho Koremori, and the second in Command Satsuma-no-kami Tadanori, while Kazusa-no-kami Tadakiyo was Chief of the Samurai, the force numbering some thirty thousand horsemen in all. On the eighteenth day of the ninth month they set out from Fukuhara, and on the day after they arrived at Kyoto, from whence they started out on the twentieth day to go down to the eastern provinces.

The Commander Gon-no-suke Koremori was at this time twenty-three years old, and his costume and bearing were beautiful beyond the power of brush to depict. His general's armour, an ancestral treasure laced with Chinese leather, was carried in an armour box before him, and on the road he wore a hitatare of red brocade with a light green body armour. He rode a dappled grey horse and his saddle was mounted in gold. Satsuma-no-kami Tadamori wore a hitatare of blue brocade and armour laced with black, and rode a large and powerful black horse with a saddle ornamented with powdered gold lacquer. With their horse trappings and armour and helmets, and even their swords and bows flashing and glittering as they rode, they were a splendid and martial spectacle.

This Satsuma-no-kami Tadanori was accustomed to pay visits to a certain lady, the daughter of a princess, and it happened one night when he went to see her that a guest, a distinguished lady of the Court, had chanced to come also and did not go away until late. Tadanori, standing waiting under the eaves of the roof, fanned himself vigorously. Hearing this the lady in the room hummed softly to herself the line; "Ah, how loudly sounds in the field, the voice of the insects;" whereat he ceased his fanning and returned home again. Afterwards, when he happened to go again, she asked him why it was he had ceased fanning himself, and he answered: "Oh, it was because I thought that you meant to imply that the noise was troublesome to you." When this lady heard that Satsuma-no-kami was departing for the eastern provinces she sent him a suit of silk clothes and the following stanza, to show her grief at parting:

> "*Tis not the garment that brushes the dew from the grass*
>   *of the Eastland,*
> *But my stay-at-home sleeve, that is the wettest of all.*"

To which Satsuma-no-kami replied:

> "*Surely it is not meet to show such regret at our parting,*
> *Is not the road that I take that which my ancestor trod?*"

Thus referring no doubt to the expedition of his ancestor Taira Sadamori, who went down with Tawara Toda Hidesato to subdue the rebel Masakado. Formerly, when a General went forth to subdue an enemy of the Throne, he was received in audience and received a Sword of Commission. The Emperor used to proceed to the Shishinden, the Bodyguards taking up their position at the foot of the Throne, while the Courtiers of the Inner and Outer Council ranged themself in order as for a Festival of the second grade. Then the Commander-in-Chief and the Second in Command, according to the prescribed ceremony, would approach and receive the Sword. But as it was now difficult to follow the precedents of Shohei and Tenkyo by reason of their antiquity, in this case they followed the procedure of the time when Sanuki-no-kami Taira Masamori set out for the land of Izumo against the former Tsushima-no-kami Minamoto Yoshichika, and a Courtier's Bell only was given. This was put in a leather bag and carried after the General, hung round the neck of a retainer. In ancient times when a General went forth from the Capital to subdue the enemies of the Emperor, there were three things he had to forget: his family on the day when he received the Sword of Commission; his wife and children when he departed from the Capital; and himself when he engaged the enemy on the field of battle. So now doubtless the two Generals Koremori and Tadanori must have borne these three things in mind, ill-fated as they were.

Thus leaving the Imperial Capital behind, they set forth by the highway that goes by the eastern sea. Even returning in peace by this road is not without danger, for the traveller must be soaked by the dew of the open plain, and make his bed on the mossy mountain peaks, crossing the passes and fording the rivers by way. So after many days, on the sixteenth day of the tenth month they arrived at Kiyomi-ga-saki in the province of Suruga. When they left the Capital their forces consisted of thirty thousand horsemen, but as other troops had joined them on the way they now had an army of seventy thousand, of which the vanguard reached as far as Fujikawa and Kambara while the rearguard was yet at Tegoshi and Utsunoya.

Then the Commander Gonnosuke-no-Shosho Koremori summoned

the Chief of the Samusai Kazusa-no-kami Tadakiyo and said: "It is my opinion that we had better cross over Ashigara and there give battle; what do you think?" "When we left Fukuhara," replied Kazusa-no-Kami, "His Excellency the Lay-priest Chancellor bade that all military matters should be entrusted to me, and though the forces of Izu and Tsuruga ought to have joined us by now, so far none of them have come up, and although we have an army of seventy thousand horses yet all our forces, both horses and men, are tired out; moreover as all the eastern provinces have taken the side of the Genji the last man, it is impossible to say how many tens of thousand they may muster. I think it wisest therefore to draw up an army on this side of the Fujikawa with the river in front of us and wait to see how matters turn out." And so, as there was nothing else to be done, he consented.

Now Hyoye-no-suke Yoritomo pushed on, and, after crossing Mt. Ashigara, came to the Kisegawa, where the Genji of Kai and Shinano came hurrying up to join him. At Ukishima-gahara in the province of Suruga he drew up his forces in battle array, numbering in all some two hundred thousand horsemen. At this time Satake Taro of the Hitachi Genji sent a letter to one of his retainers to Kyoto, but the messenger was intercept by Satsuma-no-kami's men and the letter taken from him, but when they came to read it, it was only a letter to his wife, so there was no harm in it, they restored it to him. Then Tadakiyo asked him how many men the Genji had, whereupon he replied: "I have knowledge of only from four or five hundred to a thousand of them, but for these last seven or eight days they have been coming in, so that everywhere on plain, mountain, sea and river there is nothing to be seen but armed men, and yesterday at the Kisegawa they said that the whole force of the Genji amounted to some two hundred thousand men." "Ah," exclaimed Kazusa-no-kami, "if only I had not advised the Commander in Chief to delay! That is indeed regrettable; even if I had attacked a day sooner. But why do not the Oba brothers and Hatakeyama come up? If they join us all the forces of Izu and Tsuruga will come with them." But his regret now availed him nothing.

Then Gon-no-suke Shosho Koremori summoned to him Nagai-no-Saito Betto Sanemori, who was their guide to the eastern provinces, and asked him: "Are there many samurai in the eight eastern provinces who are as mighty archers and as bold as you are?" "Do you then consider me a mighty archer?" answered Sanemori with a scornful smile, "I only draw an arrow of thirteen handbreadths, and in the eastern provinces there are any number of Bushi who can do that. One who is really a famous archer never draws a shaft of less than fifteen, and his bow is so strong that it needs four or five ordinary men to bend it. When these shoot they can easily pierce two or three suits of armour at once. Those who have the title of Daimyo never ride with less than five hundred horsemen, and they are bold riders who know not how to fall, neither do their horses stumble even on the roughest ground. Moreover when they fight they do not heed even if their own parents or children are killed, but ride on over their bodies and continue the battle. The samurai of the western provinces are quite different. If their parents are killed they retire and perform Buddhist rites for the repose of their souls, and make the customary mourning; if their children are slain they are overcome with grief and can fight no more. When they grow the rice for the soldiers' rations they plant the fields in the spring and reap them in the autumn and then go out to fight; they dislike the summer because it is hot and grumble at the cold of winter. This is not the way of the warriors of the eastern provinces.

Moreover the Genji of Kai and Shinano, as they know the ground well, will most likely come round the plains at the foot of Mt. Fuji to take us in the rear. Perhaps you may think that I speak thus with the intention of causing apprehension in the mind of the General, but that is not so, for an army does not depend on the number of its men, but on the strategy of the Commander."

Now the hour of Hare (6 a.m.) on the twenty-fourth day was the time fixed for the beginning of the fight between the two armies, so on the preceding evening the outposts of the Heike went forth to observe the disposition of the enemy. But the farmers and inhabitants of Izu and Suruga, in terror at the movements of the armies, had fled away, some to the moorland, some to the hills, and some in boats on the sea and river, and had kindled their cooking fires everywhere, so that the Heike, seeing them on all sides, were struck with consternation, exclaiming "Ah, see! the camp fires of the Genji are without number! Truly the mountains and sea and river and plain are all full of warriors. What is to be done? "Also about the middle of the same night the water fowl of the marshes of Mt. Fuji were startled by something or other, and rose suddenly all together with a whirring of wings like the sound of thunder or a mighty wind, and the Heike soldiers hearing it shouted out: "It is the army of the Genji coming on to attack us! Saito Betto warned us yesterday that the men of Kai and Shinano would come round the foot of Fuji to take us in the rear. There are hundreds of thousands of them. We must fall back to the Owari river at Sunomata or we shall be cut off." So, panic-stricken, they abandoned their positions and fled precipitately without even taking their belongings with them, for so great was their haste that some snatched up their bows without any arrows, or arrows without any bow, springing on to each other's horses, and even mounting tethered animals and whipping them up so that they galloped round and round the post to which they were tied. There were some too who had procured some singing girls and courtesans, and were banqueting and making merry with them when the alarm took place, and these women were hustled and thrown down and trampled on in the confusion, so that they were injured in the head or body and added their cries to the uproar.

Then on the twenty-fourth day at the hour of the Hare, the Genji, numbering two hundred thousand horsemen, advanced to the Fujikawa and shouted their war cry three times so that the heavens reverberated and the earth shook, but on the side of the Heike there was nought but silence. When the vanguard approached their camp there was not a man to be seen, whereupon they raised a shout that the enemy had fled, while some went and gathered up the armour they had left behind, and others bore away in triumph the curtains of the camp that had been left standing. "There is not so much as a fly stirring in the Heike camp," they reported to their Commander.

Then Hyoe-no-suke Yoritomo alighted from his horse, and, taking off his helmet, washed his hands and rinsed his mouth. Turning toward the Imperial Palace he reverently made obeisance and said: "It is not through any merit on my part that this victory has been gained, it is owing to the favour of Hachi man Dai-bosatsu and none other."

Then the provinces that were captured were assigned, Suruga to Ichijo-no-Jiro Tadayori, and Totomi to Yasuda-no-Saburo Yoshisada, and as it was not advisable to extend the attack further, owing to the uncertainty of the situation in his rear, the leader of the Genji withdrew his forces again to Kamakura. At this time the singing girls and courtesans who dwelt by the sea shore mocked the Heike saying: "Ah, what a disgusting General to run away and avoid a battle; how mean spirited are these Heike, not only do they but look at the enemy and run away, they listen to our songs and run away without paying!" Besides this several lampoons were written on the Heike leaders, Munemori the Commander in the Capital, and Gon-no-suke who lead their armies in the field, Heike[225] being read 'Hiraya':

> "*Hiraya naru Munemori ika ni sawagurammu*
>   *Hashira to tanomu suke wo otoshite.*"
> "*How will Munemori, the roof of the structure, be shaken,*
>   *Now Gon-no-suke falls, pillar on whom he relied.*"

and also:

---

[225] Note the wordplays on the different meanings of Heike 平家 read 平屋 one-storied house, and Munemori 宗盛, reading 棟 roof. Suke means assistant or help, hence as a title, adjutant, Gon-no-suke = Assistant adjutant. In the third stanza Tadakiyo 忠清 suggests 只 tada only and kiyo 著し 'only wearing.' The reference is to the black robe of a priest, for Tadakiyo will have no more use for the garments of this world in future. Nige in the fourth stanza may be read 逃 flee, or 鼠毛 mouse-coloured; there is also a play on shirigai 韋秋 crupper, i.e. presenting the back of his horse to the enemy, and 甲斐 advantage. The commander, carried away on his flying horse, is of no use to his men.

"Swift flowing over the rocks runs the foaming flood of the Fuji;
Swifter the Ise Heishi scamper away in their flight."

These two also deride Kazusa-no-kami Tadakiyo for leaving his armour behind him at the Fujikawa:

"Fujikawa ni yoroi wa sutetsu sumisome no
Koromo tada kiyo nochi no yo no tame."
"Leaving his armour behind by the banks of the river of Fuji,
Only remains the black gown meet for a happier re-birth."
"Tadakiyo wa nige no uma ni zo norite keru,
Kazusa no shirigai kakete kai nashi.
"Tadakiyo's grey steed has fled like the wind with his master,
Nought in the hour of need Kazusa's crupper avails.

Chapter XIII.

THE DECISION ABOUT THE GOSETSU FESTIVAL.

On the eighth day; of the eleventh month the Commander in Chief Gon-no-Shosho Koremori returned to Fukuhara. The Lay-priest Chancellor was exceedingly angry, and immediately ordered him to be exiled to Kikai-ga-shima and Tadakiyo to be put to death. On the next day the Heike retainers to the number of many hundred of all ages assembled to discuss whether the death sentence ought to be carried out, and Shume-no-Hangwan Morikuni stood up before the assembly and said: "I certainly do not consider Tadakiyo to be a man wanting in courage; for when he was only eighteen years old, and the two most desperate bandits of the whole Kinai took refuge in the treasury of the Toba Palace and no one dared to go in and seize them, alone he climbed over the wall in broad daylight, and after killing one brought the other out alive, an exploit that is celebrated to this day. So I think there was something mysterious about this disaster. We must at any rate consider this disorder among the army with great care." On the tenth day there was an investiture of officials and Gon-no-suke Shosho Koremori was promoted to be Ukonye-no-Chujo, whereat everyone wondered what the reason might be; since his expedition to the eastern provinces had not been exactly meritorious.

Long ago, when Taira Sadamori and Tawara Toda Hidesato started for the east country to subdue Masakado, and did not find the task at all easy, after a council of Courtiers it was decided to send another expedition under Uji-no-Mimbu Kyo Tadabun and Kiyohara-no-Shigefuji, and they, having been granted the rank of Gunken or Director of Operations, at once set out for the east. When they arrived at Kiyomi-ga-seki in the province of Suruga, Shigefuji, looking out over the surging billows of the sea at night, softly hummed to himself the Chinese poem of Hakurakuten:

> *"The flares of the fishing boats throw a warm glow on the billows;*
> *The jingling of the Courtier's bell sounds over the hills at eve."*

so that Tadabun was moved to tears by the feelings it evoked. Then the first two leaders, having in the meanwhile at last overcome Masakado, met the other two Generals there as they were returning with his head, and all went up to the Capital together. Sadamori and Hidesato were rewarded, and many thought that Tadabun and Shigefuji should also receive rewards, so the Courtiers held a council, at which Kujo Ujo-no-Sho Morosuke Ko spoke as follows: "As the expedition of last year was not able to overcome the enemy, Tadabun and Shigefuji were appointed to do so, but just as they had arrived at the eastern boundary he was at last taken, why then should they not be rewarded also?"

But his elder brother Ono-no-Miya Saneyori, who presided, opposed it saying: "If there is any doubt, let the matter rest; everything must be according to the written precedent." And so nothing was done, whereupon Tadabun, greatly disappointed, swore that the descendants of Ono-no-miya should become servants but that he would protect the family of Kujo Dono for ever; after which he starved himself so that he died. And to this day the family of Kujo Dono has enjoyed great prosperity, while none of the descendants of his elder brother are now to be found among the higher nobles, for they are wholly extinct.

On the eleventh day of the same month the fourth son of the Nyudo, To-no-Chujo Shigehira was promoted to be Sakonye-no-Gon Chujo. On the thirteenth day the palace at Fukuhara was finished and the Emperor moved into it. The ceremony of Daijoe or Accession to the Throne should now have been held, but it was fixed for the end of the tenth month, and His Majesty proceeded to the eastern river for the Ceremony of Purification. The place for the Daijoe was a plain to the north of the Palace where the Imperial Vestures and other objects to be used in the ceremony were arranged. In front of the Daikyokuden at the foot of the dais in the enclosed path called Ryubi-do, or the Way of the Dragon's Tail, the Kairitsuden, in which the Emperor bathed and robed, was set up. By the side of the same dais was erected the Daijogu in which His Majesty made the offerings to the Imperial Ancestors, where the Deities were feasted and entertained. In the Daikyokuden also a great ceremony was held, not to speak of the Kagura, the Sacred Dance in the Seishodo, and the Imperial Banquet in the Burakuin. But in this new capital of Fukuhara there was no Daikyokuden, so that the ceremony could not be performed; there was no Seishodo, so that the Kagura could not take place, and there was no Burakuin for the

Banquet, so it was decided to celebrate only the Shinjosai, or Offering of the New Rice, and the Gosetsu this year, but after a council of Courtiers it was decreed that this also should be performed by the Shrine officials in the old Capital. Now the origin of the Gosetsu dance is that in the time of Temmu Tenno, one night, when there was a keen breeze and a clear moon, they were playing the Biwa in the Palace of Yoshino to calm the mind of the Emperor, when a Celestial Maiden came down from Heaven and waved her sleeves five times.

Chapter XIV.

THE RETURN TO THE CAPITAL.

The removal of the capital to Fukuhara had displeased everyone from the Emperor downwards, and all the Courtiers had made great lamentation and complaint, appealing to all the shrines and temples of Hieizan and Nara and every other place against this arbitrary outrage, so at length even the Nyudo, who would try to tear paper crossways, had to give way, which he did by issuing a Court Order to return to Kyoto immediately.

So on the second day of the eleventh month the capital was suddenly changed again. The new capital was situated in a place where the mountains towered up steeply above it on the north, while the sea washed close up on the south, and the incessant roar of the waves and the salt spray made it unendurable, so that Takakura Shinin was always ailing and was delighted to leave as soon as possible, so he quickly departed with the Empress and the Ho-o, while the Sessho, the Dajo-daijin and the rest of the Courtiers eagerly accompanied them. Then the Dajo Nyudo and all the Heike followed, and as no one wished to remain there even for a short time, so great was their desire to return to the old Capital, it was soon quite deserted. Ever since the sixth month the buildings had been falling into ruins, since they were but frames only, and now, when the order to return to Kyoto was issued, everyone was so anxious to go away quickly that they left everything standing as it was and hurried off. On returning both the Retired Emperors proceeded to the Ikedono at Rokuhara, while the Reigning Emperor took up his abode at the Gojo Palace. The Courtiers, as they had nowhere to lodge, took refuge in the temples and shrines of Hachiman, Kamo, Saga, Uzumasa, and all the others that were scattered about over Nishiyama and Higashiyama, and even the greatest of them did not scorn to take up their quarters in the corridors of the temple or the storehouses of the shrines.

Now as to the reason for changing the capital to Fukuhara, it was because Kyoto was so near to Hieizan, and the slightest thing was sufficient to make the monks bring the sacred car of Hiyoshi or the sacred tree of Kasuga into the city and cause a tumult, so no doubt the Nyudo thought that the site of the new capital would not be so easy for them to threaten, since it was some distance away with mountains and rivers between.

On the twenty-third day an expedition was begun against the Genji of Omi, and Sahyoe-no-kami Tomomori and Satsuma-no-kami Tadanori started for that province with an army of thirty thousand horsemen, and after having defeated Yamamoto, Kashiwagi, Nishigori and other rebel bands, they crossed over to Mino and Owari.

Chapter XV.

THE BURNING OF NARA.

Now Nara was regarded as a rebel against the Throne because it had sided with Miidera and received Prince Takakura when he led the revolt, and when the priests of the Kofukuji heard that an attack on them was being considered, they rose like a swarm of angry bees, and when the Kwampaku sent them a message by Ukwan-no-Betto Tadanari to the effect that he would report to the Emperor anything that they had to say, they tore the messenger from his palanquin, threw him down, and cut off his hair, so that he fled back to the Capital pale and terrified. Then Saemon-no-kami Chikamasa was sent a second time, whereupon they treated him in the same way, while two retainers of the University of the Kwangaku-in had their queues cut off at the same time.

Beside this the priests of Nara made a great wooden head which they struck and kicked about, calling it the head of the Nyudo. Now the rapid spreading of rumour is a thing that invites misfortune, and want of caution in speech is the way that leads to destruction, and this Lay-priest Chancellor, we speak it with the deepest reverence, was the maternal grandfather of the Reigning Emperor, so that these things that the priests of Nara did seemed to everyone like the acts of devils. Now the Nyudo had attached Seno-no-Taro Kaneyasu to the Kebiishi of the province of Yamato with the intent to calm the turbulence of the priests, and Kaneyasu rode off thither with five hundred horsemen. Kiyomori charged him, however, on no account to display any force, and not to use arms even if they offered violence, but the monks, unaware of this, seized some sixty of his men, cut off their heads and stuck them up all round the Pool of Sarusawa. On hearing this the Nyudo declared in great anger: "Now I will certainly attack the South Capital," and forthwith ordered To-no-Chujo Shigehira and Chugu-no-suke Michimori to set out thither with an army of about forty thousand horsemen. At Nara about seven thousand monks, young and old, without distinction, put on their armour and took up their position at

Narasaka and Hannyaji, digging ditches across the road and making breast works and palisades. The Heike, dividing their forces into two, raised their warcry and attacked both these places. The monks fought on foot while the Imperial Army fought on horseback, and as they kept on riding up continuously to the attack, the ranks of Nara were thinned and they began to give ground, so that by nightfall, after fighting from early morning, both of their positions were broken through. Now among the retiring priests was a warrior-monk named Saka-no-shiro Yogaku, who for strength and valour was equal to all the temples of Nara put together: he wore two suits of armour one over the other, a black body-armour over another suit with lacings of light-green silk, and two helmets likewise, one of five plates over a steel cap, while he brandished a white-handled halberd, curved like a reed, in one hand and a huge tachi with black mounts in the other. Gathering some ten of his comrade of the same temple round him, he held the enemy at the Tengai gate for some time and slew very many, but as fast as they fell others came on, so at last when his comrades had all fallen though his heart was still undaunted, being in danger of being surrounded, he escaped by flight to the south country.

Then the Commander To-no-Chujo Shigehira, standing in front of the gate of Hannaji, as it had now become dark, ordered fires to be lit, when a certain lower provincial official of Harima named Jirodaiyu Tomokata split up his wooden shield into torches and set fire to the houses near by. It was the hour of the Dog (5 p.m.) of the twenty-eighth day of the twelfth month and the wind was blowing strongly, so that although only one place was set on fire, owing to the wind veering about in all directions, the flames spread hither and thither and most of the temple buildings were soon in a blaze. By this time all the warrior monks who scorned to surrender for fear of dishonour had fallen fighting at Narasaka and Hannyaji, and those who remained fled towards Yoshino and Totsugawa. Those who were too old to flee, and the unattached laymen, children and girls, thinking to save themselves, went up into the upper story of the Daibutsu-den or fled into the interior of Yamashinadera in their panic. About a thousand of them crowded into the Daibutsu-den and pulled up the ladders behind them so that the enemy could not follow, but the flames reached them first, and such a great crying arose as could not be surpassed even by the sinners amid the flames of Tapana, Pratapana and Avitchi, the fiercest of the Eight Hot Hells.

The Kofukuji, alas! the ancient tutelary temple of the Fujiwara house, founded by Prince Fuhito, was burned; the Tokondo with its famous statue of S'akya Muni the Founder of the Buddhist Doctrine, the Saikondo with its Kwannon of the Bubbling Springs, the Emerald Gallery, the Vermilion Hall of Two Stories, the two Pagodas that lifted their shining spires to heaven, all were consumed to ashes in a moment.

The Todaiji, which was built by Shomu Tenno himself, who was considered as one who on this earth had entered into the domains of the third and fourth Buddha-fields, was destroyed also, and the colossal statue of Vairochana Buddha of copper and gold, whose domed-head towered up into the clouds, from which gleamed the jewel of his lofty forehead, fused with the heat, so that its full-moon features fell to the pavement below, while its body melted into a shapeless mass. The myriad beauties of his Buddha Presence were hidden in the smoke like the autumn moon among the clouds, and the jewelled ornaments of the Bodhisat shone fitfully like the drifting stars on a stormy night. The whole sky was filled with smoke, and the flames roared upward continually. Those who stood looking on averted their gaze, and even those who heard it related felt faint with awe. Of the Holy Sutras of the Hosso and Sanron sects not one volume survived; surely never before had there been such a destruction of Holy Writ, not only in our country but even in India or China. Even the statue of Buddha that Udayana Raja made of fine gold, and that which Vis'varkarman carved from red sandal wood, were scarcely life-size, much less likely did it seem then that this, the greatest Buddha in all the Djambudvipa, would thus fall to ruin. Now, mingled with dust and smoke, it lies low, an abiding sorrow to all. How must the Four Deva Kings, the Eight Dragon Sea-gods, and the Judges and Custodians of the Underworld have been struck with amazement, and what must have been the concern of Kasuga Daimyojin, the Tutelary Deity of the Fujiwara house? Even the dew of Mt. Kasuga changed its hue and the wind howled mournfully on Mt. Mikasa. Of those that perished in the flames there were seventeen hundred in the Daibutsu den and eight hundred in the Yamashinadera; in another temple there were five hundred and in yet another three hundred; in all some three thousand five hundred souls. A thousand monks fell in the fight, some of whose heads were stuck up on the gate of the Hannyaji, while some were carried back to Kyoto. The Nyudo alone was greatly rejoiced at the news, for the Empress, the Ho-o and the Retired Emperor all sorrowed exceedingly at the destruction of so many temples, though willing that the turbulent monks should be exterminated. The Courtiers had decided in council that the heads of the monks should be carried through the streets and exposed on the public gibbet, but concerning this deplorable destruction of the Todaiji and Kofukuji nothing was determined. The ruins lay as they were scattered everywhere in the moats and ditches. Now in the Imperial writing of Shomu Tenno is this sentence: "When my temple of Kofukuji is prosperous the whole Empire shall be prosperous, and when my temple falls to ruin the Empire will decline also." And now it seems that we are indeed to behold the fall of the Empire. Thus this ill-omened year came to an end and the fourth year of Jisho began.

Volume VI.

Chapter I.

DEATH OF THE RETIRED EMPEROR TAKAKURA.

On account of the rebellion in the eastern provinces and the burning of the temples of the South Capital, the customary ceremonies of the first day of the New Year were not performed in this fifth year of Jisho, so that the Emperor did not hold any reception, there was no music or Bugaku, the envoys from Yoshino did not come, and not one of the Courtiers of the Fujiwara family appeared. This was because of the burning of their tutelary temple. On the second day no banquet was given at the Court and no one either of the Courtiers or Ladies-in-waiting was to be seen; the whole Palace was deserted and forlorn. It was most grievous to see that both the Law of Buddha and the Throne had quite lost their influence. "There are four generations of Emperors now living at the same time," complained the Ho-o bitterly, "and since they are all deprived of any hand in the administration, there is nothing else for them but to pass their lives uselessly."

On the fifth day the high ecclesiastics of Nara were all relieved of their official rank and prohibited from entering the Palace, both their place and office being sequestrated. Now as it was necessary that some of these priests should take part in one of the Services held at this time of year, and all those of Nara had been degraded, it was proposed that the priests of Kyoto should act instead, but after the Courtiers had discussed it they discovered a certain priest of the Sanron Sect experienced in the required procedure, who had escaped and concealed himself in Kwanshuji, and him they summoned to go through the bare form of the ceremony. Now there was not a single priest to be found in Nara, for the very few that had escaped being killed with arrow or sword or burnt to death or suffocated in the smoke had fled to the mountains and woods. Among these was the Betto of Kofukuji, Gerin-in-no-Sojo Yoen, who was so overcome at seeing all the precious statues and holy books go up in smoke that he fell ill and eventually died. This Yoen was a person of very delicate taste, and once, on hearing the cuckoo, he made this verse:

"Charming always it is to hear the voice of the cuckoo,
Every time it is heard, always it seems like the first."

Therefore he was ever after called' 'Hatsune-no-Sojo' (first note Sojo).[226]

Now the trouble of the last few years, that is, the confinement of the Ho-o in the Toba Palace the year before last, the execution of Prince Takakura the year after, and the troubled and critical state of the Empire generally, not to speak of the changing of the Capital, so wrought on the health of the Retired Emperor Takakura that he sickened and become very ill, and now, when he heard of the destruction of Todaiji and Kofukuji, his condition grew serious, and at length on the fourteenth day of the same month he passed away at the Ikedono of Rokuhara, to the intense grief of the Ho-o, after a reign of twelve years. His virtuous rule raised up the ways of benevolence and justice that had been abandoned, and continued the way of equity and happiness that had been interrupted, and although in this world of vicissitudes and impermanence death is a thing that cannot be avoided, even by an Arhat who possesses the Three Clear Conceptions and the Six Supernatural Talents, or by an Incarnate Deity who can assume all forms, yet in his case it seemed indeed contrary to reason. Yet that night he was borne to the temple of Seiganji at the foot of Higashiyama, and was wafted upwards like the smoke of evening or the mist of springtime. Now Choken Hein was hastening down from Hieizan to attend the funeral ceremony, but while still on the way he saw the smoke ascending, and immediately bursting into tears he made this stanza:

"*If today we enquire of the journey our Sovereign travels,*
 Mournful will be the reply; whence he shall never return."

This verse too was composed about the Emperor's death by one of his ladies.

"*Like to the moon that passes above the clouds from our vision;*
 What is our grief to see darkened the light of our life.

During the twenty-one years of his life His Majesty had always observed the Ten Precepts, and had been especially compassionate; never had he transgressed the Five Virtues and his courtesy was unfailing. A wise Monarch in this degenerate age, the regret of his subjects was extreme, even as though the sun and moon had ceased to give their light. Thus the people's wish was not granted, and this ill-fortune came upon his subjects, so that sadness brooded over the whole Empire.

---

[226] *Hatsune*. Kiku tabi ni mezurashikereba hototogisu
 Itsumo *hatsune* no kokochi koso tsure.

Chapter II.

AUTUMN LEAVES.

While Takakura Tenno was on the Throne everybody declared that his consideration for others surpassed even that of the Mikados of the periods Enki and Tenryaku, and though generally speaking it was after he had attained to years of discrimination that he obtained his reputation for wisdom and benevolence, yet his disposition was kind and gentle from his earliest childhood.

During the period Shoan, when His Majesty was only about ten years old, being extremely fond of the tinted leaves of autumn, he had a little hill-garden made in the north enclosure of the Palace, and planted it with maple and 'haze' trees that redden beautifully in that season, calling it 'The Hill of Autumn Tints' and from morning till evening he never seemed to tire of looking at it. But one night a late autumn gale blew violently and scattered the leaves everywhere in confusion, so the next morning, when the Palace servants went round early as usual to clean the grounds, they swept up all the fallen leaves and the broken branches as well, and as it was a bleak and cheerless morning they made a fire with them in the court of the Nuidono, and heated some sake to warm themselves. Soon afterwards the Kurando in waiting, hastening to inspect the garden before the Emperor should see it, and finding nothing there, enquired the reason and the servants told him. "What?" he exclaimed, "how could you dare to treat the garden that the Emperor is so fond of in such a way? You deserve to be imprisoned or banished at least, and I too may very likely incur the Imperial displeasure." Just then the Emperor, coming out to see his favourite trees as soon as he had left his bed chamber, was surprised to find they had all disappeared, and the Kurando told him what had happened. To his surprise His Majesty was not at all angry, but only laughed and quoted a Chinese poem by Haku-raku-ten about warming sake in the woods by burning maple leaves. "I wonder" he said, "who can have taught it them. Really they are quite esthetes."

Again in the period Angen, one night when the Emperor was sleeping in a strange part of the Palace according to the advice of the diviners, being naturally wakeful, he could not get to sleep. Perchance it may be that, as the poem says, the voice of the Palace watchman makes a Monarch wakeful, or as the night was very cold he may have been thinking of the occasion when Saga Tenno, on just such a frosty night, feeling compassion for the suffering of his people, stripped off his own bed clothes and exposed himself to the cold, and regretting that he himself could not emulate the virtue of such an Emperor. Thus being more wakeful than usual, he heard late at night the sound of someone crying out some distance away, and immediately summoned an attendant and ordered him to go and find out what it was. When the Courtier on guard went out and searched, he discovered a poor girl in one of the lanes near carrying the lid of a clothes-chest and weeping bitterly. On his enquiring the cause, she told him that she was carrying home some clothes which her mistress, who was a lady-in-waiting at the Palace of the Ho-o, could barely afford to have made, when two or three ruffians suddenly robbed her of them, and that her mistress could not continue to serve unless she had the proper clothes, and she did not know anyone who could help her, and so she was crying. On hearing this the Courtier brought the girl back; with him and reported the whole affair to the Emperor, who was moved to tears at the story. "Alas! how cruel" he exclaimed," who could do such a thing? In the days of the Emperor Gyo in China the people reflected the goodness of their Ruler and were good too, but now in this age the people have only me to imitate and so they are very wicked. When wrong is done in the Empire, ought I not to be ashamed?" Then he asked what kind of garment it was, and on being told, he bade the Imperial Consort Kenreimon-in give her one of same kind, whereupon they brought a dress far more beautiful than the former one and gave it to the girl. Then the Emperor, fearful lest she might again be molested, as the hour was so late, ordered several of the Imperial Guards to escort her as far as the house of her mistress. It was not strange then that everyone, even the poorest and meanest of his subjects, should pray for the long life of this virtuous Sovereign.

Chapter III.

AOI-NO-MAE.

Another story that has a certain pathetic interest is this. There was a certain little maiden who served one of the Empress's ladies in waiting, who was much beloved by the Emperor, and it was no ordinary passing fancy but a true and deep affection, so that her mistress no longer allowed her to wait on her, but rather treated her as her superior and paid her great deference and attention. An ancient poem says; "Do not rejoice when a son is born, and do not despair when you have a daughter, for a son does not always become a Prince, while a daughter may become Imperial Consort and Empress." What a happy future might be before this little maid. She might become Nyogo and Imperial Consort, then Mother of the Emperor and at last Retired Empress. Her name was Aoi-no-mae, but the ladies of the Court already spoke of her confidentially among themselves as Aoi-no-Nyogo.

But when the Emperor heard of this he ceased to summon her to his presence: this was not because he had become tired of her, but because he feared the censure of the world, and being naturally of a brooding disposition he lost all taste for food, and falling sick became unable to leave the Imperial Bedchamber. Then the Kwampaku Matsudono, hearing that His Majesty was thus depressed, hastened to the Palace to comfort him. "Why does Your Majesty thus fret about this affair?" he said, "for there is nothing to worry about. Let the maid be summoned again; her low rank need be no obstacle, for I will make her my adopted daughter and then she need fear no comparisons." "Ah no," replied the Emperor, "that cannot be; after I have retired from the Throne such a thing might be done, but the actions of a Reigning Emperor must be above the criticism of posterity." So, as his Master would not at all entertain the idea, the Kwampaku could do no more, but with tears in his eyes retired from the Palace. Afterwards the Emperor wrote this verse on a sheet of paper tinted in light green:

"Plain indeed is my love, for though I try to conceal it,
All my friends enquire what I am brooding about."

This was an old poem written by Taira Kanemori, but as it expressed his feelings the Emperor gave it to Reizei-no-Shonagon Takafusa to convey to Aoi-no-Mae, who, when she had received it and read it, blushing deeply put it away in her bosom and then, overcome by the violence of her feelings, immediately left the Court and returned to her home, where she took to her bed and died after about a week. Very applicable to a case like this are the lines of Haku-raku-ten; "The hand-maid will rue one day of her lord's favour for a hundred years," and everyone said that the Emperor's feeling was just like that of the Emperor Taiso of To who wished to introduce the daughter of Tei-jin-ki into the Genkwanden, but when Gicho reproved him, and told him that she was already betrothed to Rikushi, he gave up his intention.

Chapter IV.

KOGO.

As the Emperor was so much grieved by this unhappy love episode the Empress sent one of her own ladies to him to console him. Her name was Kogo and she was the daughter of Sakura-machi-no-Chunagon Shigenori Kyo, and not only was she the greatest beauty in the Palace but she was also without equal for her skill in playing the Koto. She had been beloved by Reizei-no-Dainagon Takafusa Kyo, and while he was only Shosho he sent her many poems and letters, but for some time they only accumulated without producing any effect, until at last she was moved to take pity on him and yielded. But now she was summoned to the side of the Emperor they could not but part, and for long her sleeves were moistened with tears of regret. The Shosho too was always going to the Palace to try if by any means he could see her once again, and used to loiter about in the neighbourhood of her apartment, but as she was now in the Emperor's household she would not exchange a word with him, or show, however indirectly, that she still had any tender feelings for him. Then the Shosho wrote a stanza and threw it so that it fell within the curtain of the room where she was. The lines ran as follows:

> "*Near though I am to my love she is far removed as the Northland:*
> *Were she in Mutsu indeed, how would it differ from this?*"

Though in her heart Kogo would have liked to answer it, yet for the Emperor's sake and to avoid causing him any pain she did not even touch it, but bade one of her maids pick it up and throw it out into the courtyard. Takafusa could hardly contain his anger and disappointment at this treatment, but, remembering that if he were seen the results would be serious, he hastily picked up the paper, and, putting it in his bosom, returned to his house and gave vent to his feelings in these lines:

> "*Cruel! she designs not even to take my poor verse in her fingers,*
> *Yet however she feels, never my heart can forget.*"

And he prayed that he might die rather than continue to live on in the world when he could no longer see her.

But when these things came to the ears of the Lay-priest Chancellor he burst forth: "What a condition of things is this! The Empress is my daughter and the wife of Reizei Shosho is my daughter also, and how does this Kogo dare to take the husband of both? Let her be put out of the way forthwith! "Then Kogo, caring nothing about her own fate, but, anxious lest the Emperor should in any way be troubled, fled away one night from the Palace so that no one knew whither she had gone. This grieved the Emperor exceedingly, and he would not leave his bed chamber, but spent his days moping and in tears. When the Nyudo heard of this he remarked: "Ah, His Majesty is distressed about Kogo I see, then something must be done," and he gave orders that none of the Ladies-in-waiting were to be allowed to attend the Emperor, and as he even frowned on other people who paid visits, no one went to Court at all, since they did not care to risk offending him, and all the Palace was gloomy and deserted. Now on the tenth day of the eighth month there was a most beautiful moon without a trace of clouds in the sky, and His Majesty was gazing at it, but as his eyes were full of tears even the moon looked misty, and as the hour grew late he

called for one of his attendants, but for some time no one answered, so
deserted was the Palace. But a certain officer of the Palace Guard
named Nanjo-no-Daihitsu Nakakuni, who happened to be on duty that
night, though in a remote part of the Palace, heard his master's voice
through the silent halls and made reply. Then the Emperor bade him
come near, for he had something to ask, whereupon Nakakuni,
wondering what it could be, entered the Imperial Chamber, and His
Majesty enquired of him if he knew where Kogo had hidden herself.
"How should I know such a thing?" replied the retainer. "I have heard
that she is living in a cottage with a single folding door somewhere near
Saga," said the Emperor, "but I do not know the name of the person
with whom she is staying. Do you think you could find her?" "If I do
not know the name of the master of the house, how can I find her?"
replied Nakakuni in perplexity, whereat the Emperor in despair wept
bitterly.

After some further thought Nakakuni remembered Kogo's skill on
the Koto and said to himself: "Ah, on a moonlight night like this she
will surely be thinking of His Majesty here in the lonely Palace, and no
doubt she will play on the Koto; now when she played in the Palace I
used to be the one to accompany her on the flute, so none knows her
playing as well as I, and if I go round about all the houses in the
neighbourhood of Saga, why should I not find out where she is?"
"Then" he said at last, "though I do not know in whose house she is
lodging, I will go and search for her in that part, but if I find her and
have no letter, perhaps I shall not be believed, so let Your Majesty
write one that I may take it with me." Then the Emperor gave him the
letter and ordered him to take a horse from the Palace Stables, and he
started off at a gallop, whipping up his horse under the clear light of the
moon and singing as he rode the verse that begins: "The mountain
village where the wild stag cries," feeling, no doubt, the pathos of the
autumn scenery of Saga. So he rode on, stopping his horse to listen
whenever he came to a cottage with a single folding door, and
wondering if the lady he sought was within, but no sound of a Koto
broke the silence. Then, wondering whether she had perhaps retired to
some temple, he went to all the temples in that part, but still could find
no trace of her. Thinking it better not to return at all than to return
without any tidings, he wondered if there was anywhere he could flee
to, but as every place near was the Imperial Domain, there was
nowhere that he could go to hide himself. Thus perplexed and knowing
not what to do, he recollected that the temple of Horinji was not far
away, and thinking that perhaps Kogo might have gone thither to gaze
at the moonlight, he turned his horse in that direction. Then in a hamlet
among the pines near Kameyama faintly he heard the sound of a Koto;
straining his ears he was uncertain whether it was not the blasts from
the mountain tops, or the soughing of the wind in the pine trees. Urging

on his horse he rode on further and became aware that the sounds were indeed those of a Koto, and that they proceeded from a cottage with a single folding door, and stopping to listen awhile he perceived that without doubt the player was Kogo, and that the piece she was playing was one called 'Sōfūren,' which expresses the longing felt by a wife for her absent husband. Nakakuni was touched at her tender feeling for His Majesty that prompted her to select this piece from the many that she played, and drawing his flute from his girdle joined in the tune for a few bars, and then knocked softly at the door. The, music immediately ceased, whereupon Nakakuni called out: "It is Nakakuni who has come from the Palace with a message from the Emperor;" but though he knocked several times no one answered from within. After some time there was a sound as if someone coming to the gate, and as he stood there in joyful anticipation, the lock was unfastened, and the gate opened a very little and disclosed only the face of a beautiful young girl. "Have you not mistaken the house?" she asked, "for a Palace Messenger can have no errand here," whereat Nakakuni, since he feared that if he made answer the gate would be shut and locked again, pushed it open by force and entered. Standing on the verandah of the house he told his story: "Why has she come to live in a place like this? The Emperor is grieving for her absence and his melancholy may endanger his life, and that it may not be thought that I speak falsely, see, I have brought you a letter written by His Majesty's own hand;" and he took out the letter and handed it to her. The girl took it to Kogo, who opened and read it, and found that it was indeed His Majesty's writing. In a short while she had written an answer and sent it to Nakakuni with a lady's suit of Court dress as a present. On receiving the answer he said: "Although perhaps I ought not to ask for more than this letter, yet as I was specially sent hither by my Lord, and am not unknown to your mistress, how can I return without a message from her own lips?" Then Kogo, consenting to his wish, came forth and excused herself saying "As you know, in fear of the threatening and angry words of the Nyudo, I fled away secretly one night from the Palace, and as I have been staying in a place like this I have not played the Koto at all, but as I am going away tomorrow into the recesses of Ohara, and this night is my last, the mistress of this house persuaded me to play, saying that it was late and there would be none to hear, and so I yielded, for the remembrance of former days stirred within me and my fingers yearned for my beloved instrument," and as she spoke her tears flowed freely, while Nakakuni too hid his face in his sleeve. After a while Nakakuni calmed his emotion and said: "Doubtless your intention in going into the recesses of Ohara is to become a nun; this, I think, is not a proper thing to do, for how will the Emperor feel about it? Nay, I can by no means allow it?" and turning to his attendant he added; "See that this girl does not leave this place;" and leaving him there to guard the house, he sprung upon his horse and rode back again, reaching the Palace just as the dawn was beginning to break.

Tying up his horse and throwing the lady's dress over the Palace doors, he went toward the Shishinden, thinking that the Emperor would surely be sleeping by this time, and wondering who to send to him, but as it happened His Majesty was still sitting as he had left him the night before in melancholy abstraction, as the Chinese poet says:

> "*Soaring up to the southward and wheeling round to the northward,*
> *Vainly in autumn the goose seeks for the heat or the cold;*
> *Flying forth to the eastward and sweeping round to the westward,*
> *Ever its lonely eye stares at the moon of the dawn.*"

So Nakakuni came and gave him the letter of Kogo and reported all he had done. The Emperor's joy was extreme, and; he ordered him to go again that night and bring her back with him. Nakakuni, though he feared the wrath of the Nyudo if he should hear of it, yet as it was the Emperor's order, borrowed an ox car from somebody and went down that night to Saga, and although Kogo at first refused to accompany him, at last he prevailed on her and brought her back to the Palace. There she lived secretly in a remote chamber, and used to visit His Majesty every night, so that in the course of time a Princess was born to her, and this is the Princess who is known as Bomon-no-Nyoin. Then the matter came to the ears of the Nyudo and he was very angry, exclaiming: "Then it was all a lie that I was told that Kogo had been got rid of; but at all events she shall be removed now," and somehow or other they decoyed her from the Palace and forced her to shave her head and become a nun. She was then only twenty-three years old, and though she had wished to retire from the world before, how sad a fate was it to be compelled to do so in this peremptory manner, and to put on black robes and go and live in the wilds of Saga. It was these painful events that aggravated the illness of the Emperor so that he died. The Ho-o had nothing but troubles, one coming fast after the other. In the period Ei-man his eldest son Nijo Tenno died, and then in the seventh month of the second year of Angen his grandson Kujo Tenno passed away. In the sky the Hiyoku, and on earth the two branches that grow together are proverbial for connubial affection, neither must we forget the Lover stars by the River of Heaven. Not less deep was the affection that existed between the Ho-o and his consort Kenshun-mon-in, and one evening in autumn she fell sick and passed away with the dew of the next mornings; and though months and years had gone by since then, it seemed to him like a parting of yesterday and his tears were not dry even now. Then in the fifth month of the fourth year of Jisho his second son Prince Takakura was killed, and now that the Emperor Takakura, on whom only he could rely for help in this world and prayers in the next, had died before him, he had no one left to turn to in his affliction, but could only shed lonely tears. "The greatest grief to which no other can compare is that of a father left behind by his son in his old age, and the greatest regret above all others is that of a child deprived of his parent in his youth," wrote the Prime Minister Tomotsuna when his son Sumiakira pre-deceased him. So, when the Empire and the Imperial Family suffered such a bereavement, not only the Ho-o, who had acquired great merit by his study of the Hokke Sutra as well as by his admirable knowledge of the mysteries of the Shingon, but all those who dwelt in the Palace, veiled their brocaded robes.

Chapter V.

THE SENDING ROUND OF LETTERS.

But this Lay-priest Chancellor, seeing the Ho-o thus overwhelmed by his troubles and wishing to comfort him, sent him a daughter that he had had by a certain Naiji of the shrine of Itsukushima in Aki, a beautiful girl of eighteen, that he might console himself with her; and as all the Heike as well as the other Courtiers brought her to the Palace in state it was quite as festive as the procession of an Emperor's Consort; but as this took place twenty-seven days after the death of the Emperor everyone thought it most unseemly.

Now there was in Shinano a certain Minamoto called Kiso Jiro Yoshinaka. He was the second son of the late Tatewaki Senjo Yoshikata, and when his father was killed at Kamakura on the twelfth day of the eighth month of the second year of Kyuju by Akugenda Yoshihira, he was but a child of two years old. His mother, in her grief, fled with him to the province of Shinano to Kiso Chuzo Kaneto, and begged him to take the child and bring him up. So Kaneto granted her request and took him and reared him, and now he had grown up to be a young man, distinguished among all for his beauty and noble bearing as well as for his matchless boldness and mighty strength. So powerful and skilled in the use of all weapons of war was he that people ranked him with the great warriors of old, with Tamura Maru, Fujiwara Toshihito, Taira Koreshige, Taira Muneyori, Fujiwara Yasumasa, and his own ancestors Minamoto Yorimitsu and Yoshiie. At the age of thirteen when his Genpuku took place he went to the shrine of Hachiman and spent the night there as the custom was, and offering his queue of hair before the god he prayed: "As my ancestor in the fourth generation, Yoshiie Ason, became the son of this Deity and was called Hachimantaro Yoshiie, so may I also follow in his footsteps;" and he took the name of Kiso Jiro Yoshinaka.

As he often used to go up to the Capital with his foster-father he observed the proud behaviour of the Heike and meditated over it. So it happened that one day he said to Kaneto: "I hear that Hyoe-no-suke Yoritomo has gone up from the Tokaido with eight of the eastern provinces to smite the Heike; now let me haste and join him with the men of the Tosando and Hokurikudo, and when they are destroyed we two will be the greatest leaders in all the land of Nippon." When he heard this Kaneto was overjoyed: "It was for this" he said "that I have brought you up these twenty years, and when I hear you speak thus I know you will be a worthy scion of Hachimantaro." Thus Yoshinaka started to stir up a rebellion, and sent round letters instigating his neighbours to rise, and, as in the province of Shinano Nei-no-Koyata and Shigeno-no-Yukichika were persuaded to support him, all the rest of the warriors of that province came in on his side. The samurai of the district of Tago in Kozuke also, because of their good will to his father Yoshikata, hastened to offer themselves. Thus it seemed that the hour of the doom of the Heike had come, and the Genji were about to accomplish their long cherished desire.

Chapter VI.

THE COURIERS.

Now Kiso was in the extreme south of Shinano on the boundary of Mino and so was very near to the Capital, and great fear came upon the Heike, for they wondered what they should do now that the North had rebelled as well as the East.

But Kiyomori was not perturbed: "Even if all the men of Shinano do follow Kiso," said he, "in Echigo there are the two brothers Jo-no-Taro Sakenaga and Shiro Sukeshige, the descendants of Taira Koreshige, who can muster no small force between them, and if I give the order they will soon fall on Kiso and destroy him." Some of his family were satisfied at this, but others still maintained that the situation was critical.

On the first day of the second month an investiture of officials was held and Jo-no-Taro Sukenaga was appointed Echigo-no-kami. This was done with a view to his attacking Kiso Yoshinaka. On the seventh day all the families of the Ministers and Courtiers assembled and wrote out and offered the Sonjo Darani and the Fudo Darani, most potent litanies to overcome evil, by which they trusted to subdue the revolt. On the ninth day news was brought that Musashi-no-Gon-no-kami Nyudo Yoshimoto, of the district of Ishikawa in Kawachi, with, his son Ishikawa-no-Hangwan-dai Yoshikane had renounced their allegiance to the Heike and were going down to the east to join the Genji. The Heike Generals Gendaiyu-no-Hangwan Suesada and Setsu-no-Hangwan

Morizumi immediately set out against them with a force of three thousand horses, and caught them in their stronghold with only about a hundred retainers, and in the fight which ensued, lasting from early morning to late at night, Yoshimoto was killed and his son wounded and captured. On the eleventh day the head of Yoshimoto was paraded through the streets of the Capital. The precedent for exposing the head of a rebel during a time of National Mourning was taken from the time when, after the death of Horikawa Tenno, the head of the former Tsushima-no-kami Minamoto Yoshichika was thus treated.

On the twelfth day a courier came from Usa-no-Daiguji Kinmichi of Kyushu with the news that all that country; from Ogata Saburo Koreyoshi to the men of Usuki, Hetsuki and Matsuura, had revolted and thrown in their lot with the Genji. These tidings caused the greatest surprise and consternation among the Heike, for now that the West Country had forsaken them, as well as, the south and North, they were at a loss how to act, and smote their palms with rage and perplexity. On the sixteenth day another courier arrived from Iyo in Shikoku, telling how that, since during the last winter Kono-no-Shiro Michikiyo of that province had renounced his allegiance and made common cause with the Genji, Nuka-no-Nyudo Saijaku of Bingo, a strong adherent of the Heike, had crossed over to Iyo and attacked him in his stronghold at Takanao on the boundary of Dogo and Dozen. In the fight, Kono Michikiyo had been killed, and his son Kono-no-Jiro of Aki, who was his uncle on the mother's side, and stayed there awaiting an opportunity to kill Saijaku and thus avenge his father's death.

After putting down this outbreak in Shikoku, Saijaku crossed over to Tomo in the province of Bingo on the fifteenth day of the first month of the new year, where he called together a number of singing girls and strumpets, and proceeded to make merry and carouse with them. Then Kono-no-Shiro Michinobu too with him a hundred men-at-arms, and suddenly burst in on him as he was drinking and revelling, and though Saijaku had some three hundred retainers, they were so surprised at this unexpected attack that they lost their heads and were quickly shot or cut down. Saijaku was thus taken alive and Michinobu brought him back to Takanao in Iyo, where his father had been slain, and there put him to death. And some said that his head was sawn off and others that he was crucified. After this the men of Shikoku submitted to Michinobu and followed him. Then too Tanso, Betto of Kumano in the province of Kii, forgot his great obligations to the Heike and suddenly changed his front and went over to the Genji. Thus did the South and East Sea districts follow the example of the East and the North Country, and men's ears were assailed continually with reports of fresh defections, and as these hordes of savage rebels swarmed out on all sides like angry bees, and the dominion of the Heike began to totter, all serious people, even those outside the ruling family, lamented at the gloomy prospect.

Chapter VII.

DEATH OF THE NYUNO.

On the twenty third day a Council of Courtiers was suddenly called at the Palace of the Ho-o, the Sento Gosho, and the former Udaisho Munemori addressed them thus: "The expedition we made into the East Country did not effect anything very much, so now I myself should like to take command and lead an army to chastize these rebels in the East and North." This bold speech was received with applause by all the rest, and they praised Munemori for his decisive action; the Ho-o too seemed quite delighted, and everyone who had the least experience of martial exercises, even though he might be a Courtier or Noble, declared himself ready to follow Munemori. On the twenty-seventh day they intended to set out, but as Kiyomori had been taken ill during the night they did not move. On the twenty-eighth day it was reported that his condition was grave, and all Rokuhara and the Capital was in an uproar, every one running about and whispering together. From the day that the Nyudo was taken ill, he could not drink even hot water, and the heat of his body was like a burning fire, so that if any one came within eight or ten yards of him the heat was unbearable. All he could do was to mutter 'Ata! Ata!' (Hot! Hot!): it was a most extraordinary sickness. To relieve him somewhat they brought water from the well of Senshuin of Hieizan and filled a stone tank with it, into which they lowered him, but the water began to bubble and boil and immediately became like a hot bath. When water was pour on him a pipe, it flew off again hissing in clouds of steam and spray as though it had struck red hot iron or stone, and the water that did strike him burst into flames so that the whole chamber was filled with whirling fires and thick black smoke. It must have been just such a sight that Hogyo Sozu saw formerly when he entreated Emma, the King of Hades, to show him the place where his mother was; for Emma moved by his prayers, sent his jailers to guide him to the Shonetsu Hell, and when he had passed through the iron gate he saw the flames shooting up like meteors, thousands of miles high.

Moreover the wife of the Nyudo, Hachijo-no-Nii-dono, had a terribly dream. She dreamed that a flaming chariot entered the gate of her mansion without any driver, and in front and behind it stood two creatures, one with the head of an ox and the other with that of a horse, while on the front of the chariot appeared an iron tablet inscribed with the single character MU,[227] signifying Not. The Nii-dono, in her dream,

---

[227] *Mu.* First syllable of 無 間, mugen, without intermission.

asked whither it had com, and the answer was: "Because the evil Karma of the Priestly Chancellor of the Heike is so great, this chariot has come to fetch him front the Palace of Emma-O the Dread King." "Then," said she, "what is the meaning of that tablet?" "Because of the crime of the burning of the great bronze image Vairochana a hundred and sixty feet high, it has been decreed at the tribunal of Emma-O that he shall go down to the Avichi Hell, the hottest of the hot hells where rebirth is unceasing, and so it is that the character Not has been written: but the character signifying 'Cease' has not yet been written." Then the Nii-dono awoke, bathed in a cold sweat; and when she told what she had seen the hair of all that heard it stood up with affright. Then they hastened to offer gold and silver and all manner of precious things to the shrines and temples of the gods and Buddhas, and fetched thither their horses and saddles and armour and swords and bows and arrows, and prayed with might and main, but no sign vouchsafed them; and the Courtiers and their wives assembled around the bed of the Nyudo and mourned and lamented bitterly.

On the second day of the second month, this year being leap-year, the Nii-dono came to the bedside of the Nyudo, in spite of the intensity of the heat, and said; "Though my visits enquire about you every day may seem few, yet perchance, while still you are able, you may tell me of something that you desire." Then, Kiyomori, though his sufferings were so great, summoned up his fast-failing strength and said in a weak voice: "Since the time of Hogen and Heiji my unworthy house subdued the enemies of the Emperor many times and thereby gained great rewards, for which we are most grateful, and I, having been permitted to become the maternal relation of the Heavenly Sovereign and to reach the office of Dajodaijin, am about to hand down my glory to my descendants, wherefore in this world I have nothing else left to desire. The only thing I have to regret is that I cannot see the head of Hyoye-no-suke Yoritomo. When I am dead do not perform any Buddhist services or make offerings for me, or build temples or pagodas; only make haste and slay Yoritomo and cut off his head and lay it before my tomb. That will be the best offering you can make me either in this world or the next." So deep indeed was his guilt. Then they put water on a board and rolled him on it to ease him, but it did no good, and on the fourth day of the same month he at last expired in great anguish. When it was known the commotion and galloping to and fro of horses and carriages was such as to make the sky echo and the earth tremble. Even if he had been the Heavenly Sovereign, the Lord of ten thousand chariots, it could hardly have been greater.

He was sixty-four years old this year. He cannot be said to have died of old age, for when the result of man's Karma comes upon him the most potent Sutras have no efficacy, nor can the power of the gods and Buddhas avail anything; yea, all the deities of heaven cannot protect him, so what can ordinary men do? Even if tens of thousands of loyal warriors, all willing to lay down their lives for him, were ranged around both above and below, they could not fight with the unseen and invulnerable powers of the underworld. And so alone and without a companion he must go down to the Yellow Springs of Death, across the Sanzu-no-kawa, the river of Hades, and ascend the Mountain of Shide whence no traveller returns. And the evil Karma that he has made will take shape as the jailers that come to meet him.

And so, as it must be, on the seventh day his funeral pyre was lighted at Otaki, and Enjitsu Hogen took his bones and brought them down to the province of Settsu, where they were deposited at Kyogashima. Thus though he wielded such great authority that his name was feared through the whole Empire, his body rose up in smoke to the sky of Kyoto, and his bones mingled with the sand of the shore.

Chapter VIII.

KYONOSHIMA.

After the funeral of Kiyomori a strange thing happened. His Palace of Nishi-Hachijō with all its splendid adornment of precious stones and fretted work of gold and silver suddenly went up in flames the same night; and though it was no uncommon thing for houses to catch fire, it was rumoured that it was the work of incendiaries. Also on the south side of Rokuhara there was heard the sound as of some twenty or thirty men, if they were men, dancing and singing the refrain: "Hurrah! the water! Hark to the sound of the waterfall!" mingled with bursts of uncanny laughter. As the Retired Emperor had passed away in the first month of this year and the Empire had been plunged into mourning, and now within scarcely a month or so the Nyūdō had died also, even the common people without understanding were overcome with apprehension and gloom. Some of the bold spirits among the Heike retainers, declaring these strange occurrences to be the work of Tengu, set out in a band of about a hundred to investigate this weird laughter, and found that it proceeded from the Hōjujiden, the Palace of the Hō-ō. As the Hō-ō had not been in residence there for some three years, a certain Motomune, former Governor of Bizen, had been sent there to look after it, and some of his friends had repaired thither that night, bringing liquor with them to carouse on the sly, and although they started their banquet with the intention of making no noise, seeing the nature of the occasion, yet before long they all became drunken; so that their discretion forsook them, and they began to sing and dance without restraint. When the Heike samurai perceived this they rushed in on them and seized and bound the whole twenty or thirty of them, inebriated as they were, and brought them into the courtyard of

Rokuhara. Then the former Udaisho Munemori came out on to the verandah, and they related the whole matter in detail, but he only said: "There seems no need to execute a lot of drunkards like this," and dismissed them.

It was the custom for all, high and low, to have the bell rung after a death, and the proper prayers and offerings Made at stated hours, but after this Lay-priest died no one made the least offering either to priests or Buddhas, but all were occupied day and night with nothing but preparations for war. The painful manner of his death too was repulsive, but this also inclined many to thin' that he was not as other men. When his family went to the Shrine of Hiyoshi accompanied by all the other families of Court Nobles, people used to say how much grander was the procession than that of the Kwampaku when he went to worship at his family shrine of Kasuga.

Concerning the making of the island called Kyonoshima at Fukuhara; it was, a very successful undertaking, for even unto this day all kinds of vessels are able to enter the harbour without mishap. The work was begun in the early days of the second month of the first year of the period Oho, but on the second day of the eighth month a great tempest suddenly rose and the mighty waves swept it all away, Then toward the end of the third month of the third year Awa-no-Mimbu-no-Kyo was entrusted with the work of rebuilding it, and a Council of Courtiers was held to consider the question of following the ancient custom of exposing someone in the sea as a sacrifice to the sea-gods, but they decided that such a wicked thing should not be done, and so texts from the Holy Sutras were cut on the face of the stones instead, and this is why it is called Kyonoshima (Sutra Island).

Chapter IX.

THE ADVENTURE OF THE PRIEST JISHIN.

It was said, as has been related, that Kiyomori was not an ordinary man at all, and it was rumoured that he was an incarnation of Jie Sōjō.[228] The reason for this was the following story. In the temple of Seichoji in the province of Settsu there lived a certain saintly monk named Jishin Bo Sonei. He had formerly been attached to Hieizan, where for many years he had meditated on the Hokke Sutra, but at last his religious zeal drove him to leave that mountain and come and live in this temple, so that all believed on him and were converted.

On the twenty second day of the twelfth month of the period Shoan, Sonei went as usual to the altar of Buddha to perform the

---

[228] *Jie Sojo.* A famous priest who became Tendai Zasshu. Died in the third year of Ei-kwan (985). Also called Ryogen.

evening service, and was sitting supported by his arm-rest reading the Hokke Sutra, when, it seemed neither in a dream or reality, there entered two men clad in white Kariginu and Eboshi and wearing leggings and straw sandals, carrying an open letter. When Sonei, as in a dream, asked them from whom they had brought it, they replied: "From the Court of Emma-O," whereupon he received it from their hands and opening it read as follows: "To the Priest Jishin Bo Sonei, residing in the temple of Seichoji, in the province of Settsu, in the Country of Dai-Nihon which is in the Djambudvipa. On the twenty sixth day at the Palace of Emma Raja there will be held a recitation of the ten myriad portions of the Hokke Sutra, and ten myriad priests from ten myriad countries will be entertained. As you have been included in the number do you proceed hither as appointed. The above given at his Court, at the command of Emma-O. Twenty second day of the twelfth month of the second year of Shoan."

As Sonei could by no means refuse the dread command, he wrote an acknowledgement, after which he awoke, and when he related the vision to Ko-ei, the chief priest of the temple, the hair of all that heard it stood up with affright. Thinking that his end was near he gave himself up to prayer, repeating the Nembutsu continually, and trusting that Buddha would have compassion on him and receive him into his Paradise. On the twenty fifth day he went as usual to the altar of Buddha and recited the Sutras, and at the hour of the Rat (12. p.m.), feeling sleepy, he returned to his room and lay down to rest., At the hour of the Ox, (2 a.m.) the two men came again and urged him to start with them, but when Sonei was preparing to go, he found that he had no proper garments or begging-bowl. While he was wondering what was to be done, for it would be a dreadful thing to disobey the mandate of Emma-O, a priest's robe suddenly wrapped itself round his body, while a begging-bowl of gold descended from heaven into his hand; at the same time two attendant priests, two acolytes and ten lower priests appeared before his apartment with a chariot adorned with the seven precious things. Sonei joyfully mounted the chariot, which soared away through the sky toward the north west and soon reached the Palace of Emma. Around it spread on all sides an immense courtyard, and the vastness of its spaces within was indescribable. The Palace buildings were all of gold and jewels, and shone with a brightness scarcely to be borne by mortal eyes. The service of that day had already been finished and the priests had all departed, so Sonei stood waiting in the middle gate on the south side of the Palace, viewing the buildings from far off. While he stood thus, all the officials and attendants of Emma's realm came to make their obeisance to the Dread King in a procession of extraordinary magnificence, and Sonei, wishing to enquire about his sins and his future life, proceeded in the same direction. As he did so the ten attendants formed into line and the two priests carried boxes, while the acolytes held up an umbrella over him, and in this way they approached the presence of Emma; whereupon the King and all his officials and Courtiers rose up to greet them, for the two priests now appeared in their real form as Yakuo Bosatsu and Yusei Bosatsu, and the two acolytes as Tamonten and Jikokuten, the ten attendants being metamorphosed into ten female demons who ministered to him. "Why have you come thus when all the other priests have departed?" asked Emma "From my childhood," replied Sonei, "I have never neglected daily to recite the Hokke Sutra, but even so I am not sure of my fate in the after life, so it is of that that I wish to enquire. "Rebirth in Paradise," answered Emma, "is granted according to faith, but the Hokke Sutra is the straight way for man to attain Buddhahood, for which purpose all the Buddhas of the Three Worlds appeared on this earth. The merit of earnest faith and understanding of it is greater than that of practise of the Five Paramitas, while the virtue of preaching it five times is more potent than eighty years charity. According to your abounding merit you will be reborn into the highest circle of the Tuchita heaven." Then, turning to an attendant, the Dread King said; "The deeds of this man's life are in the casket of good works; go and fetch them, and show him what is written." Then the ministering demon went to the store-house on the south side and brought the casket, and when he opened it and read what was written therein, every act and every thought that he had done or meditated in his whole life was revealed; not one was lacking. "One request only I have to make," said Sonei, bursting into tears, "show me, I beseech thee, the way by which I may escape from the endless circle of births and deaths, and attain to the highest state of Enlightenment." So, as he ceased not from his tears, Emma, moved by compassion, instructed him in these sacred words of doctrine:

> "Wife and child and kindred, rank and wealth,
> Accompany no mortal after death,
> But devils formed from the ill deeds he did,
> Torment him that he scream for evermore."

Sonei was exceedingly rejoiced and said: "In the country of Dai-Nihon in the Djambudvipa, at Wadamisaki in the province of Settsu, the Lord High Chancellor of the Heike has built cells extending over a distance of ten cho square, and invited many priests to come and recite the Sutras and pray earnestly, even as it might be at the meeting of today." On hearing this, Emma in great admiration and gladness exclaimed: "That Nyūdō is no ordinary person; he is the reincarnation of Jie Sōjō, and it was because he kept the law of Tendai Buddhism that for a while he was born again in Japan. Three times a day we pray for him here in these words which you will remember to repeat to the

Nyūdō.

> "Jie Dai-Sōjō greatly we revere,
> Protector of the Tendai Buddhist Law.
> Revealed on earth as the Great Chancellor,
> His evil Karma even will help mankind."

So, being entrusted with these holy words, Sonei went out from the presence of the King of the Underworld, weeping tears of joy, and when he came to the middle gate of the south side, his ten priestly attendants again brought the chariot and soared away with him toward the south-west, so that he seemed to have returned in the twinkling of an eye, whereupon he awoke as from a dream. Afterwards, going up to Kyoto, he went to the mansion of the Nyūdō at Nishi-Hachijō and told him all that he had seen. Kiyomori was greatly rejoiced, and after entertaining him royally, sent him away with many presents, beside raising him to the rank of Risshi. And this is how it came to pass that all knew that the Nyūdō was the reincarnation of Jie Sōjō. Jikyo Shōnin was also the reincarnation of Kōbō Daishi, while the Retired Emperor Shirakawa was the reincarnation of Jikyo Shōnin. This Emperor accumulated many meritorious actions and piled up many virtuous deeds, and in this degenerate age also Kiyomori, as the reincarnation of Jie Sōjō, both by his evil deeds and his virtuous actions acquired great merit, and thus conferred much benefit on himself and mankind. Not otherwise was it that S'akya Muni and Devadatta both greatly helped the world of men.

Chapter X.

THE IMPERIAL CONSORT OF GION.

But the old men who remembered the former days said that Kiyomori was not as other men because he was really the son of the Emperor Shirakawa. And the reason was this. In the period Eikyu there was a lady, who was much beloved by the Emperor, who lived near Gion at the foot of Higashiyama, so that she was known as Gion-no-Nyogo; and the Emperor used to visit her there continually.

One evening, it was the twentieth day of the fifth month, His Majesty went to see her privately, attended only by one or two Courtiers and a few Palace Guards. As it was the season of heavy rain the night was dark and gloomy, and no moon shone through the clouds. Now there was a temple near the house where the lady was living, and as they approached it they saw something that shone strangely come forth from the side of the buildings. Its head seemed to be covered with needles of burnished silver that glittered as they stood erect, while in one hand it carried what looked like a hammer, and in the other a shining object. The Emperor and Courtiers were panic-stricken; "See," they cried, "it is without doubt a demon! They always carry a hammer in their hand! What is to be done?" At this time Tadamori, the father of Kiyomori, was there as one of the lower Palace Guards, and the Emperor called him and said; "You are the boldest of all my attendants; go shoot that thing to death or cut it down before it falls upon us." Tadamori immediately advanced towards the creature in obedience to the Imperial Command, but when he considered it closely it did not seem such a terrible object. "If it is nothing but a fox or a badger I should look rather a stupid fellow if I shot at it or cut it down," he thought, so he determined to take it alive if possible. As he crept nearer he noticed that the light flashed and then went out intermittently, and after watching this two or three times he sprang upon it and grappled with it. Immediately a voice cried out in alarm, and he found that it was no monster but a man.

Then they all kindled lights and looked, and found that it was a priest about sixty years old, whose business it was to look after the temple, and he was going to light the lamps before the Buddhas, so he carried in one hand a vessel of oil and in the other an earthenware lamp, and as the rain was falling heavily he had thrown a kind of cape made of wheat straw over his head, and it was this that glittered in the light and had the appearance as of steel needles.

Thus when they discovered this, they perceived how foolish it would have been to have shot or drawn sword on him, and the conduct of Tadamori was proved to have been most reasonable and prudent. "How gentle can a samurai be on occasion;" said His Majesty, and as a reward he bestowed on him the lady of Gion whom he so greatly loved. Now the lady was at this time pregnant, and the Emperor said; "If it be a girl that is born, I myself will take it, but if it be a boy, then it shall be given to Tadamori and be educated as a samurai." In due time the lady gave birth to a son, and though nothing was said about it in public they treasured him with the greatest care. Tadamori greatly wished to report the matter to the Emperor, but could not find a suitable opportunity. After a while, however, when His Majesty was on his way to the Shrine of Kumano, it chanced that the Imperial Palanquin was set down at a place called Itogasaka in the province of Kii that the Emperor might rest, when Tadamori gathered some shoots of 'Nukago'[229] that was growing profusely in the bamboo thicket, put them into his sleeve and showed them to the Emperor with an obeisance, at the same time reciting this line:

---

[229] *Nukago.* Or Mukago; a kind of yama-imo or yam. Aceras angustifolia. (Brinkley) There is a word-play here on another meaning of imo, sister or lover. Cf. the words of the verse 'Imo ga ko wa hau hodo ni koso nari ni keri.'

"*See this plant that creeps and crawls like a child in the woodland;*"

Immediately His Majesty, understanding the reference, added the second line of the couplet, thus:

"*Then let Tadamori cherish and nurture it so.*"

So he brought him up as his own child. The Emperor happening to hear that the baby cried very much at night made another stanza, and sent it to Tadamori.

"*If he cries at night you have only to get up and nurse him,
In the future age, pure and successful he'll shine.*"

Whereupon they gave him the name Kiyomori or Pure Success.

When he was twelve years old he came of age, and was appointed Hyoye-no-suke, and at the age of eighteen he was promoted to the third rank, so that people who did not know these things said; "Indeed! he is treated like the son of a great noble," whereat the Emperor Toba, who was aware of origin replied: "He is inferior to none of the noble families."

In former ages too, Tenchi Tennō presented one of his consorts who was in the same condition to the Taishokkwan Kamatari, telling him that he would adopt the child if it were a girl, but that if a boy were born the Minister should bring it up; and a boy was born who eventually became Joei Kwasho the founder of the temple of Tabu-no-Mine. Considering this precedent in ancient days, so in these latter days also it was not strange that Kiyomori, being really the son of the Emperor Shirakawa, should plan such great political changes as the change of capital.

Chapter XI.

THE BATTLE OF SUNOMATA.

On the twentieth day of the same month Gojo-no-Dainagon Kunitsuna Kyo departed this life, He had been on particularly intimate terms of friendship with the Nyūdō, so that it was strange that he should have been taken ill on the same day, and have died in the same month. On the twenty second day Munemcri paid a visit to the Hō-ō and informed him that his Palace was to be moved back to the Hōjujiden. This Palace had been built on the fifteenth day of the fourth month of the first year of Oho, and His Majesty had personally directed the laying out of the gardens with landscapes of trees and hills and ornamental water according to his taste, as well as having new shrines constructed near it to the deities of Hiyoshi and Kumano. In consequence of the ill-treatment of the Heike, however, he had not lived there for the last few years, and so it had fallen into disrepair, so now they proposed to have it put into order before he returned there to reside. But the Hō-ō was so pleased at the thought of going there again that he did not wish to wait for this, and insisted on moving immediately. He at once went to see the apartments of his late consort Kenshun-mon-in, and found that in this short time the pine-tree by the bank and the willow that grew by the edge of the lake had both become quite big trees; and when he looked at the mallow tree by the pond, and the willow at the palace eaves, that stood opposite to them, the remembrance of old times overcame him so that he was affected to tears.

On the first day of the third month all the priests of Nara were pardoned and restored to their offices, and a proclamation was made that they should be confirmed in the possession of their tributary temples and manors as before. On the third day was held the ceremony of inauguration of the rebuilding of the Dai-Butsuden, and the former Sashoben Yukitaka was appointed to direct it. This Yukitaka had made a pilgrimage to Yahata the year before and spent the night praying in the shrine, where he had a dream in which he saw the doors of the inner sanctuary open and an angelic messenger with hair tightly bound up come forth and announce: "I am the messenger of Hachiman Dai-Bosatsu; when you go to direct the inauguration of the rebuilding of the Dai-Butsuden take this with you;" and he handed him a Courtier's baton. Afterwards when he awoke he found the baton by his pillow, whereat he was greatly astonished, wondering what was likely to happen that he should have to undertake such an office, but as it was a supernatural dream he put the baton in his bosom and took it home with him, where he put it away most carefully. Soon after it came to pass that the temples of Nara were burnt through the wickedness of the Heike, and Yukitaka had the good fortune to be chosen from many officials of the same rank to preside at the inauguration of their rebuilding: a most auspicious connexion for him.

On the tenth day the governor of the province of Mino rode hard to Kyoto with the news that the Genji had pressed their attack as far as the province of Owari, where they had blocked the roads so that none could pass, and the Heike chiefs determined to set out against them. The Commander-in-chief on this occasion was Sahyoye-no-kami Tomomori, and with him were Sachujo Kiyotsune, Shosho Arimori and Tango-no-Jiju Tadafusa, while in command of the samurai were Etchū-no Jirōhyōye Moritsugu, Kazusa-no-Gorōhyōye Tadamitsu and Akushichihyōye Kagekiyo, and these marched against Owari with a force of some thirty thousand horsemen. As it was only about fifty days since Kiyomori died, everything was in a sad state of confusion. On the side of the Genji Jūrō-no-Kurando Yukiie with Yoritomo's younger brother Gien and about six thousand horsemen pitched camp by the Owari river, so that both armies faced each other on opposite sides of the stream. Then, during the night of the sixteenth day the Genji force crossed over and made a sudden assault with the intention of taking the Heike by surprise, but the latter, quite undismayed, allowed them to penetrate deeply with their small force, and then closed in and surrounded them, and as they were all dripping with water after fording the river this served to distinguish friend from foe. The fight began at the hour of the Tiger (4. a.m.) and continued till day broke, when Jūrō-no-Kurando Yukiie, finding that Gien had met his death among the foe, and that most of his retainers too had fallen, after fighting bravely gave way and fled back eastward of the river. Then the Genji, crossing the river in their turn, took the remnant of the enemy in the rear and shot them down from behind, so that, though a few here and there stood on the defensive and made some resistance, in a short time the whole force was destroyed. All condemned this attack of the Genji as foolish, and contravening the well-known maxim, "Never fight with water or swamp behind you." Yukiie fled to the province of Mikawa where he destroyed the bridge over the Yahagigawa, and threw up a breastwork of shields on the further side in an effort to hold the enemy, but the Heike pursued him vigorously and dislodged him. Thus keeping up the pursuit, the men of Mikawa and Totomi would certainly have come in on the side of the victors, when at this juncture the Commander Sahyoye-no-kami Tomomori fell sick and retired with his army to the Capital. As he had only driven the enemy out of one position and had not been able to complete the destruction of the remainder, he could not be said to have done great things.

Now since Komatsu Shigemori had died the year before last, and the Nyūdō Kiyomori this year, it appeared to all that the doom of the Heike house was drawing on apace, and so there were few who would support them except those whose fortunes had been linked with theirs for many years, while in the eastern provinces even the grass and trees inclined to the will of the Genji.

Chapter XII.

THE HOARSE VOICE.

Now Jo-no-Tarō Sukenaga of the province of Echigo had been appointed Echigo-no-kami, and out of gratitude for the Imperial Favour he set out with an army of thirty thousand to the province of Shinano to attack Kiso Yoshinaka. On the fifteenth day of the sixth month he was

to start, but about the middle of the night before, the sky suddenly
clouded over, and there was a mighty clap of thunder and a great
downpour of rain, and then, when the heavens had cleared, a hoarse
voice shouted in terrific accents from mid-air: "Here is a supporter of
the Heike who burned the copper-gilt image of Vairochana Buddha a
hundred and fifty feet high, that was in the Djambudvipa; go ye and
seize him!" At this fearful portent the hair of Jo-no-Tarō and his men
stood on end with terror, and some of the retainers exclaimed; "How
can we go on against this sign from Heaven?" But as it was not the way
of samurai to heed such things, they set forth, and had only gone about
the distance of twenty cho when a mass of black clouds appeared, and
hung over the head of Sukenaga and covered him, and immediately his
limbs were cramped and his brain was palsied, so that he fell from his
horse. His men took him up and carried him in a palanquin to his
mansion, where he lay prostrate for about three hours and then expired.
When a messenger was sent with the news to the Capital the Heike
were struck with consternation.

On the fourteenth day of the seventh month the name of the era
was changed to Yo-wa. On this day also an investiture of officials was
held, and Chikugo-no-kami Sadayoshi was appointed Higo-no-kami,
receiving jurisdiction over both the provinces of Chikuzen and Higo,
and being ordered to quell the insurrection in Kyūshū, he set out thither
with a force of three thousand. A great amnesty was also proclaimed on
the same day, and all those who had been exiled in the third year of
Jisho were recalled to Kyoto. The former Kwampaku Matsu-dono came
back from Bizen, the Dajo-daijin Myo on-in from Owari, while Azechi-
no-Dainagon Sukekata-no-Kyo hurried back from Shinano.

On the twenty eighth day Myo-on-in Dono had an audience with
the Hō-ō. When he was recalled in the era of Chokwan he took his biwa
and played in the Imperial verandah the pieces called Gao-on and
Kenjo-raku, and now when he returned again in the period Yo-wa he
played that called Shufu-raku in the Sento Palace, for he had always
that happy and tactful delicacy of feeling that prompted him to do an
elegant thing at the proper time. On the same day Azechi-no-Dainagon
Sukekata-no-Kyo also went to the Palace of the Hō-ō, and His Majesty
asked him to sing, saying that, as he had been living for some time in
an uncongenial and remote country place, he had no doubt forgotten all
his popular ditties, so perhaps he would sing an Imayo. Then the
Dainagon sang the Imayo verse beginning: "*There's a river in Shinano
called Kisojigawa, 'tis said*," and this apposite song gained him a great
reputation for wit, seeing that he must have seen and heard of this river
so often.

Chapter XIII.

THE BATTLE OF YOKOTAGAWARA.

On the seventh day of the eighth month a recitation of the Nio Sutra was held in the Hall of the Dajokwan in memory of the subduing of Taira Masakado, and on the first day of the ninth month a suit of armour and a helmet was presented to the Daijingu Shrine at Ise in memory of the quelling of the insurrection of Fujiwara Sumitomo. The Imperial Envoy to the Shrine Saishu-no-Jingi-no-Gondai-fuku Onakatomi Sadataka, fell ill at Koga in the province of Ōmi soon after leaving Kyoto, and on the third day he passed away in the Detached Palace at Ise. Moreover they held a recitation of the Sutras before the Five Great Buddhist Deities to pray for victory over their enemies, and one of the priests called Dai-Ajari, who was officiating before the image of Gosanze, became unconscious and died before the altar. It was a manifest sign that neither the gods nor Buddhas would accept their supplications. Again, a service was held before the image of Daigen Myo-o, and Jikken Ajari of the Anjoji came and brought many volumes of the Holy Sutras and opened and read them, but all he could prophesy was the downfall of the Heike. When they asked him the reason he replied: "The enemies of the Emperor must be subdued, and when we consider the present condition of affairs, it appears that the Heike are the enemies of the Emperor, therefore they must be overthrown." On account of this ominous prediction they proposed to put the Ajari to death or banish him, but as everyone was so busy with things both great and small, it happened that he escaped. After the Heike had fallen and the Genji had taken their place, this priest went down to Kamakura and told his story there, whereupon Yoritomo was pleased to raise him to the rank of Sōjō as a reward for his boldness.

On the twenty fourth day of the twelfth month the Consort of the late Emperor became a nun and took the title of Kenrei-mon-in, and as the Emperor was quite an infant at the time, this was the only name by which he ever knew her. And so this year came to an end and the second year of Yo-wa began. The Court Festivals of the New Year were held as usual. On the twenty first day of the second month the planet Mars invaded the territory of the Pleiades; and it is written in the astronomical books that if this happens the barbarians will rise, and also that a General will receive the Imperial Commission to march beyond the frontier. On the tenth day of the third month an investiture of officials was held, and most of the Heike received promotion. On the fifteenth day of the fourth month the former Gon-sho-Sozu Genshin held a service at the shrine of Hiyoshi, when the Hokke Sutra was recited ten thousand times according to the rule, and the Hō-ō attended it to acquire merit.

Who it was that began it I know not, but a rumour went forth that the Hō-ō had bidden the monks of Hieizan attack the Heike, and in consequence of this bands of soldiers marched on the Palace and camped about it on all sides. The Heike hastily assembled at Rokuhara, and Hon-sammi-no-Chūjō Shigehira with a force of three thousand horse set out for the shrine of Hiyoshi. When it was reported at Hieizan that their temples were in danger of being attacked, the monks went down to Higashi Sakamo-o and held a council to find out the reason. The Hō-ō meanwhile was in a state of consternation at these things, and the Courtiers and Nobles turned pale with agitation, while most of the Ho o's Guards could not contain themselves in their flurry. Both in the Capital and in the temples the trepidation was extreme. Then Shigehira Kyo met the Hō-ō near Anabu and accompanied him back to Kyoto, and it was found that the stories of His Majesty's inciting the monks to attack the Heike, and the Heike being about to march against the temples, were both groundless falsehoods, upon which there were not wanting those who put them down to supernatural malevolence. "I suppose I mint not go on any more pilgrimages at my pleasure in future;" quoth the Hō-ō.

On the twentieth day an Imperial Envoy was sent to the twenty-two shrines round the Capital; this was on account of the famine and pestilence. On the twenty-fourth day of the fifth month the era was changed to Ju-ei, and on the same, day an investiture of officials was held, at which Jō-no-Shirō Sukemochi of Echigo was made Echigo-no-kami. After the death of his elder brother Sukenaga he rather wished to avoid the ill-omened honour, but as it was the Imperial Order there as nothing to be done. He then changed his name to Nagamochi.

So on the second day of the ninth month Jō-no-Shirō Nagaimochi assembled the men of Echigo, Dewa and Aizu, about forty thousand horsemen, and went forth to the province of Shinano to attack Kiso. On the ninth day he pitched his camp at Yokotagawara in that Province, and Kiso, who had been lying in the fortress of Yoda, issued out with three thousand horse and rode to meet him. Now the Genji of Shinano, by the stratagem of Inoue-no-Kurō Mitsumori, divided two thousand of their men into seven parties, each bearing a red flag, the colour of the Heike, and when the warriors of Echigo saw these emerging over the rocks and winding out of the defiles they set up a shout of joy, thinking that many were for their side in this province also. But as the different bands approached, at a given signal the whole seven drew together into one, and, throwing away their red banners, suddenly replaced them with white ones and advanced to the onset. When the men of Echigo saw this manoeuvre panic seized them and they cried out; "Ah! we have been deceived! The enemy swarms everywhere! We shall be surrounded!" And thus thrown into confusion they were driven into the river and stampeded into deep gorges, so that most of them perished, and but few survived. Jō-no-Shirō, when his most redoubtable champions Yama-no-Tarō of Echigo and Jotanbo of Aizu, on whom he especially relied, had been slain, and himself badly wounded, escaped with his bare life and fled back to his province by way of the river. When he reached Echigo he at once sent messengers to Kyoto to inform the Heike of his mishap, but they carelessly paid no heed. On the sixteenth day Munemori-no-Kyo was again appointed Dai-nagon, and on the third day of the tenth month he became Nai-daijin. On the seventh day of the same month he proceeded to the Palace to offer thanks attended by a brilliant train, including twelve Court Nobles headed by Kwazan-in Chūnagon, and sixteen of lesser rank led by Kurando-no-To Chikamune. Among them there were four of the rank of Chūnagon and three of that of Sammi Chūjō. So, though the Genji of the north and west countries were swarming forth everywhere like bees, and were reported to be even now about to burst in upon the Capital, the Heike, heedless of the impending storm that was to break upon them, continued to spend their days in luxury and extravagance. Thus this year also came to an end and the second year of Ju-ei began. The New Year Festival was as usual. On the fifth day of the New Year the Emperor went on a Visit of Ceremony to the Palaces of His Imperial Relations. There was a precedent for this, for the Emperor Toba made a like visit at the age of six years. On the twenty first day of the second month Munemori-no-Kyo was raised to the Lower First Rank, and on the same day he resigned the office of Naidaijin: this he was said to have done on account of the revolt. Then the monks of Nara and Hieizan and the priests of Kumano and Kinbusen, as well as the chief of the Daijingu Shrine at Ise and all his officials rebelled against the Heike and transferred their allegiance to the Genji, and though an Imperial Decree was issued to all the four quarters of the Empire, and the Hō-ō also published an Order to the whole country, yet as all concluded that this was but a device of the Heike, there were none who paid any attention.

Volume VII.

Chapter I.

THE EXPEDITION TO THE NORTHERN PROVINCES.

At the beginning of the third month of the second year of Ju-ei there arose some ill feeling between Kiso-no Kwanja Yoshinaka and Hyoye-no-suke Yoritomo, so that Yoritomo despatched a force of a hundred thousand horse to the province of Shinano to attack Kiso. Yoshinaka was at this time at his stronghold of Yoda, but when he heard the news he went forth with some three thousand men and camped at Kumasaka-yama on the borders of Shinano and Echigo. Then, as soon as Yoritomo had come as far as Zenkoji in Shinano, he sent a message to him by the hand of his foster-brother Imai-no-Shirō Kanehira, saying:

"As you have now subdued the Eight Eastern Provinces you can now attack the Heike from the East Sea Road and drive them out of the Capital. I also, after occupying the Eastern and Northern Hill Provinces, can fall on them from the Northern Highway, so now, when we both ought to haste and make an end of them as soon as possible, why do you give them occasion to mock by allowing some estrangement to arise between us? It is true that our uncle Jūrō Kurando Yoshiie, who has no love for Your Excellency, has thought fit to come here, but his presence is exceedingly troublesome to me; yet what can I do? Though he is here I myself have no feeling of animosity toward you at all." To which communication Yoritomo replied thus: "Though you speak thus now, I have received information that there is a plot to raise a rebellion and attack me, and that is not all I rely on." So when Kiso heard that an army of many tens of thousands of horsemen under Doi and Kajiwara was advancing against him, to show the sincerity of his intentions, he sent his heir, Shimizu-no Kwanja Yoshi-shige, a boy of eleven, escorted by Umeno, Mochizuke, Suwa, Fujisawa and others, who were reckoned among the most doughty of his warriors, as a hostage to Yoritomo.

Then Yoritomo, acknowledging that his suspicions were false, and that Yoshinaka was quite loyal to him, as he had no grown up son of his own, adopted Shimizu-no-Kwanja as his son, and taking him with him, went back again to Kamakura.

Now when Yoshinaka had coerced the districts of the east and north, he was ready to make an attack on Kyoto, and as the Heike had announced during the winter of the previous year that they would probably move in the spring, the levies from the Sanin, Sanyo, Nankai and Saikai districts came pouring in like mist and clouds. As for the Tosan or Eastern Hill district, the men of Ōmi, Mino and Hida came in, but on the Tōkaidō none joined them from eastward of Ōmi. All the western districts sent their men, but from the Hokurikudo not one arrived from north of Wakasa. After a Council of Courtiers had been held, the Heike leaders decided to proceed against Kiso Yoshinaka first, and then to attack Yoritomo, and with this purpose their army set out for the north. The Commanders in Chief were Komatsu no Sammi Chūjō Koremori and Echizen-no-Sammi Michimori, while the Vice-Commanders were Satsuma-no-kami Tadanori, Kogo-gu no-suke Tsunemasa, Awaji-no-kami Kiyofusa and Mikawa-no-kami Tomonori. Six generals were appointed to lead the samurai, Etchū-no-Jirōhyōye Moritsugu, Kazusa-no-taiyu Hangwan Tadatsuna, Hida-no-taiyu

Hangwan Kagetaka, Kawachi-no-Hangwan Hidekuni, Takahashi-no Hangwan Nagatsuna and Musashi-no Saburosaemon Arikuni, beside whom there were three hundred and forty other valiant warriors apt to command. The forces under them were about a hundred thousand horsemen, and at the hour of the Dragon (8. a.m.) on the seventeenth day of the fourth month they left Kyoto for the north country. As their supplies were insufficient, as soon as they had crossed the pass of Ausaka outside the Capital, they began to seize and appropriate anything they wanted from the estates and houses that lay by the way, not sparing even the government property. As they went along by Shiga, Karasaki, Mikawajiri, Mano, Takashima, Shiozu and Kaizu, the inhabitants of these places could not endure it and fled to the mountains.

Chapter II.

CHIKUBUSHIMA.

Now the Generals Koremori and Michimori pressed on their way, but Tadanori, Tsunemasa, Kiyofusa and Tomonori tarried a while at Shiozu and Kaizu in Ōmi. Of these Kogo-gu-no suke Tsunemasa had excelled in poetry and music from his youth up, and it happened that one morning, wishing to calm his mind in the midst of these alarms and disorder, he went out to the edge of the lake to enjoy the scenery. As he looked out into the offing he saw an island in the distance, and calling to Tohyoye-no-Jo Arinori who had accompanied him, he asked what island it was. "That is the famous island called Chikubushima;" replied Arinori, whereupon Tsunemasa expressed a wish to go out to it, so they got a small boat and escorted by Arinori and Anemon-no-Jo Morinori with six retainers, he crossed over to Chikubushima. It was the eighteenth day of the fourth month, but still the song of the 'Uguisu' of the vale lingered among the green twigs and recalled the favours of spring, and the ever charming early notes of the hototogisu answered it, while the clusters of wistaria hung heavy on the pines. The scene filled Tsunemasa with ecstasy, and he quickly alighted from the boat and climbed up on to the island, gazing at the beauty of the landscape with a heart too full for words. Not fairer it seemed was that magic island of Horai, whither Shiko of Shin sent many fair youths and maidens, and Butei of Kan despatched a magician, if happily they might find it and bring back from thence the water of youth and immortality, but not finding it, and fearing to return to China, age overtook them in their ships while they were still vainly searching the boundless ocean. And in one of the Sutras it is written: "In the Djambudvipa is a certain lake; and in the midst of it, proceeding from the bottom of the world, there is an isle, formed all of crystal, where fairy maidens dwell." And this, they say, is the island.

Then Tsunemasa, respectfully approaching the Myojin, the deity of the place, prayed thus; "O thou goddess Benzaiten, who wert known of old under the title of Nyorai, and dost deign to manifest thyself here in a spiritual body as a saviour; for though we may address thee by the names of Myo-on-ten and Benzai-ten, yet in this place thou art united in one body to save mankind; grant, we beseech thee, the petitions and desires that we offer before thee." And as he was still kneeling before the shrine the dusk fell over the lake, and the waiting moon rose over the water so that it turned into silver, and the white beams bathed the steps of the shrine with light. Then the priest who lived there, knowing Tsunemasa's skill in music, brought him a biwa, and he played and sang the melodies called Jogen and Sekijo, so that the liquid notes rang clear through the silent shrine. So exquisite it was that the Myojin could not restrain her emotion, but appeared over the shoulder of Tsunemasa as he played, in the form of a white dragon. Tsunemasa, overcome by reverential awe, laid aside his biwa and composed the stanza;

> "*Lo! a manifest sign that my humble prayer will be answered,*
> *Since from tire depth of the waves, awful the goddess appears.*"

And so, not doubting that the enemies of the Throne would soon be subdued and the insurgents put to flight, he embarked in the boat and returned to the mainland in great joy.

Chapter III.

THE BATTLE AT HIUCHI.

Now, though Kiso Yoshinaka himself remained in Shinano, he built a stronghold at Hiuchi in Echizen and stationed there Heizenji-no-Chori Saimei-i-gishi, Togashi-no-Nyūdō Bussei, Inazu-no-Shinsuke, Saitoda, Hayashi-no Rokurō Mitsuakira, Ishiguro, Miyazaki, Tsuchida, Takebe, Nyuzen, and Sami with some six thousand men. The situation was naturally strong, surrounded by towering crags, and with mountain peaks on all sides. A mountain rose before it and another behind, while in front of it flowed the Nomigawa and the Shindogawa. At the confluence of these two rivers they piled up rocks and drove in stakes and made a large dam, so that the water came right up to the hills on the north and south and spread out like a lake. As the Chinese poet says; "Shadows steep the southern hills; wide and blue and vast are the waters; the waves melt into the western sun; the waters redden and look like damask." The bottom of this cool lake is of sand pure as gold or silver, and by its brink there float most graceful ships. But the lake of

Hiuchi in our country was dammed up so that its waters were dark and deceive the eye.

As they had no boats the Heike force could not easily cross over it, and so they encamped on the mountain in front and spent some days idly doing nothing. But Heizenji-no-Chori Saimei, who was within the fortress, was a partizan of the Heike, and he went round the foot of the mountain, and, writing a letter, stuck it to the head of an arrow, which he shot into their camp. The soldiers found it and took it to their Commander, who opened it and read thus: "The river was not formerly as you see it now; it is a mountain stream that has been dammed up so that it may look muddy and deceive the eye. If you send men under cover of darkness and cut the dams, the water will quickly run off, and then you can cross over at once; thus you can take the place at a disadvantage. Given by me, Heizenji-no-Chori Saimei-i-gishi." The Heike were overjoyed at this, and when night came they sent men who cut the dykes, whereupon it turned out that the water was indeed only a mountain stream and quickly drained away. Without losing any time they at once crossed over, and although the six thousand men of the garrison made a stout resistance, it was of no avail. Thus Heizenji-no-Chori Saimei showed his loyalty to the Heike; but Togashi-no Nyūdō Bussei, Inazu-no-Shinsuke, Saitoda and Hayashi-no-Rokurō Mitsuaki, seeing that nothing more could be done, retired to Kaga and took up positions at Shirayama and Kawachi. The Heike, however, immediately pursued them into the province of Kaga, and burned the two strongholds of Togashi and Hayashi, then, as there seemed no force anywhere to oppose them, they sent messengers from the several provinces and stopping-places to convey the news to Kyoto. These tidings, when they reached the Capital, greatly encouraged and rejoiced the Naidaijin and all his house. On the eighth clay of the fifth month the Heike reached Shinohara in the province of Kaga, where they divided their army into two parts. a main body and a .smaller force. The main body consisted of some seventy thousand men under the command of Komatsu Sammi-no-Chūjō Koremori, and Echizen-no-Sammi Michimori, with Etchū-no-Jirōhyōye Mori tsugu as Commander of the Samurai, and they set out towards Tonamiyama, at the boundary of Kaga and Etchū. The lesser force consisted of about thirty thousand commanded by Satsuma-no-hami Tadanori, Kogo-gu-no-suke Tsunemasa, Awaji-no kami Kiyofusa and Mikawa-no-kami Tomonori, with Musashi-no-Saburosaemon Arikuni in command of the Samurai. They were to march on Shiboyama, which bounded the provinces of Noto and Etchū. At this time Kiso Yoshinaka was at Kofu in Echigo,[230] but when he heard of this he marched on Tonamiyama with fifty

---

[230] *Kofu in Echigo.* Kofu means the seat of the local government; the provincial capital.

thousand men. After a stratagem that had succeeded before, he divided his force into seven parts, of which one, consisting of ten thousand horsemen, marched against Shiboyama under the command of his uncle Jūrō Kurando Yukiie, while two others, under Higuchi no-Jiro Kanemitsu and Ochiai-no-Gorō Kaneyuki, of about seven thousand each, were sent out to Kitakurosaka. Three other companies of seven thousand horse, under Nishina, Takahashi and Yamada-no-Jiro rode towards Minami Kurosaka while about ten thousand were concealed in ambush round the slopes of Tonamiyama at Matsunaga-no Yanagihara and Gumi-no-Kibayashi. Imai-no-Shirō Kanehira with six thousand horse crossed over the Washinose and took up his position at Hino-Miyabayashi. Kiso Yoshinaka himself crossed over the Oyabe and marched to Hannyu a little to the north of Tonamiyama.

Chapter IV.

THE PRAYER OF KISO YOSHINAKA.

"As the Heike have such a large army they will try to fight a decisive battle," said Yoshinaka, "and a decisive victory or defeat depends on the number of men; but if a large force is menaced by a larger one it will feel in danger of being surrounded. So, if we deceive them by carrying thirty white flags and showing them on the top of Kurosaka, as soon as the Heike see them they will think we have a larger force than we really have, and so, fearing to be surrounded if they move forward, as their present position is high and rocky, they will consider it the safest plan to stop there for a while and rest their horses on Tonamiyama. Then I will manage to keep them there till dusk comes on, and under cover of darkness I will drive their whole army over into Kurikara valley below." So they set up the thirty flags on the top of the hill of Kurosaka, and the Heike, as they expected, imagining themselves to be confronted by superior force, and fearing they would be out flanked, cried out: "Here is plenty of grass and water for the horses, let us dismount and let them rest a while." And the place where they rested was Saru-no-baba among the mountains of Tonami.

Now Yoshinaka was in Hannyu, and as he earnestly scanned the country on all sides, he saw, far off amidst the green trees of Natsuyama, what appeared to be a red shrine-fence with the bevelled cross-beams of the shrine above, and a torii standing before it, and, on asking his guide what shrine it was, and what deity was worshipped there, the guide replied that it was the shrine of Hachiman, and that that place belonged to the god. On hearing this Yoshinaka was glad beyond measure and calling Taiyu-bo Kakumei, who was a capable writer, said to him "By great good fortune I now find myself before the august shrine of Hachiman, even as I am about to go into battle: do you not think it well, both for the sake of future generations, and as a prayer for my present need, that I offer up a petition before him?" Kakumei, replying that it would be most suitable, alighted from his horse to write it. Now Kakumei was this day wearing a hitatare of 'kachi' and armour with black lacing; his sword was of black lacquer, his twenty four arrows were feathered with black feathers taken from the underside of a birds' wing, and he carried a bow bound with rattan and lacquered. Taking off his helmet and slinging it to a thong on his shoulder, he produced a small ink-stone and a paper-case from the bottom of his quiver, sat down respectfully before Yoshinaka, and began to write the petition. This Kakumei had been born of a family of Confucian scholars, and was formerly known as Kurando Michihiro, when he had been an official of the Kwangakuin, or College of Literature, but later he became a monk under the name of Saijobo Shinkyu and dwelt at Nara. The year before, when Takakura-no-Miya had entered the Onjoji at Miidera and Hieizan had sent a letter to Nara, it was this Shinkyu who composed the answer; whatever the priests of Nara may have thought of it I know not, but it contained the words:" Now Kiyomori is of the very dregs of the Heike, and but the off-scourings of the warrior caste." And Kiyomori, when he heard of it, was exceedingly enraged and burst forth: "How does a wretched fellow like this Shinkyu dare to speak of me, Jokai, in such an insulting manner? Go and seize him quickly and put him to death. But Shinkyu got wind of it and fled in haste from Nara and went to the north country, where he became scribe to Kiso Yoshinaka and changed his name to Taiyu-bo Kakumei. And the words of the petition ran thus:

"Kimyo chorai! Obedient to thy commands and with the deepest reverence, O Hachiman Dai-Bosatsu! O Lord who guardeth our Sun-descended Realm. Mighty Ancestor of our Heaven-shining Imperial Line, reveal thyself in thy Three Buddha Persons to protect the Throne and help the people, bursting open the mighty gates in thy three divine personalities. For many years now has this Taira Minister held dominion over the whole Empire and oppressed the people, acting impiously toward the Law of Buddha and opposing the Throne. I, Yoshinaka, born of a warrior line, do unworthily follow my ancestors' calling, and can no longer bear to think over these evils, so, trusting my fate to heaven, I do now offer my body to my country, raising up a loyal army to subdue the rebels. Nevertheless, though the two hosts of the Gen and Hei now stand face to face for battle, while the valour of our soldiers is as yet unconfirmed, and the heart of thy servant is still touched with dread, even as we unfurl our banners before the foe, at once we prostrate ourselves before the altar of thy Three-fold Divine Beneficence. If thy gracious favour be purely manifested to us, without doubt the rebels will be put to the sword; and thus do we eagerly anticipate thy help with tears of joy. Furthermore, especially since my great-grandfather the former Mutsu-no-kami Yoshiie Ason dedicated himself to thee by adoption and took the name of Hachimantaro, his family have ever faithfully served thee, and I Yoshinaka his humble scion, have for many years bowed my head before thee. If I mention his great merit, it is as a child who measures the great ocean with a shell, or as a mantis that lifts up its claws against a war-chariot. Yet, as it is not for my own glory or that of my house, but for the sake of my Sovereign and of my Country, I would commend it. Very urgent is my desire, but the purpose of the gods is dark: verily on thee do I rely that thou wilt make me to rejoice. Humbly prostrating myself before thee, I pray that thou wilt put forth thy power both in the light and in the darkness, and that thou wilt reveal the might of thy divinity to overthrow our enemies and give us the victory. If thou deignest to hearken to my supplication and grantest us thy mighty protection, vouchsafe, we beseech thee, that we may see an auspicious and manifest omen. The eleventh day of the fifth month of the second year of Ju-ei. Reverently offered by me Minamoto Yoshinaka."

Then he himself and thirteen horsemen of his train took each two large turnip-head arrows from their quivers, and these together with the petition they deposited before the sanctuary of the god. Neither was this prayer of such rare earnestness without an answer from the merciful Bosatsu, for he deigned to look upon it from his dwelling afar, and immediately from the midst of a cloud three wild doves came flying, fluttering and circling round the white banners of the Genji. So, in old time, when Jingo Kogo went forth to battle with Shinra, and for a while the foreign foe prevailed against her armies, the Empress lifted up her voice in prayer to heaven, when suddenly three sacred doves came forth from a cloud and fluttered over the shields of her men, after which they again attacked and the enemy were defeated. So it was too when his own ancestor Yoriyoshi Ason, fighting against the outlaws Sadato and Muneto of Mutsu, found the enemy too strong for him, for he cast fire in the face of the rebels, crying out that it was of no earthly kindling, but divine fire from heaven. Then there arose a wind and blew straight in the direction of the foe, so that their stronghold of Kuriyagawa was burned, whereupon their armies were routed and Sadato and Muneto were overthrown. Now, on this occasion Kiso Yoshinaka, remembering these former precedents, alighted from his horse, and taking off his helmet, washed his hands and rinsed his mouth, after which he made obeisance to the holy doves, his heart full of faith in the god.

Chapter V.

KURIKARA.

Now the two armies of the Genji and Heike faced each other in battle array, the distance between them being scarcely three cho, but for a while neither side advanced. Then, after a while fifteen picked horsemen came forth from the host of the Genji, and taking up a position between the two forces, each man loosed a turnip-headed arrow at the Heike. At this fifteen picked men of the Heike also advanced and shot their arrows at the Genji in turn: then the Genji sent forth thirty more horsemen, and the Heike replied with a like number. Fifty again rode forth from the Genji and shot their arrows, and another fifty of the Heike appeared to meet them. When both had sent forth a hundred men, and the two bands engaged each other between the two armies to try a decisive contest, the Genji sent no more men to join them and purposely avoided a decision. While they were thus engaged in holding them in check until the sun should set and the night approach, so that they could drive their whole army into the valley of Kurikara beneath, the Heike, never dreaming of such a piece of strategy, continued to fight on until nightfall. Then the flanking force consisting of some ten thousand men, who had gone round by the way of the Fudo shrine of Kurikara, suddenly beat vigorously on their quivers and shouted their war cry. The Heike, turning to look behind them at the sound, immediately perceived the white flags of the Genji like a cloud in their rear, and, as they had thought themselves safe against any flanking attack owing to the precipitous cliffs on all sides of the position, the sight threw them into a panic and they knew not how to act. At this moment Kiso Yoshinaka himself, with his force of ten thousand men, shouted his war cry, and immediately the other bands who were concealed on the slopes of Tonami, at Yanagihara and Kinbayashi, about ten thousand in all, together with the six thousand under Imai Shirō who lay hid at Miyabayashi, also shouted in unison, so that with the roar of their forty thousand voices it seemed as if the mountain and the river would be shaken from their seats. Then, as it grew darker, the Genji rushed to the attack on both front and rear, and though many adjured their fellows to come back and not to disgrace themselves by flight, when once panic seizes a great army it is not of easy to stop it, so the Heike stampeded in a pell-mell flight into the valley of Kurikara. As those behind could not see those in front, they thought there must be a road at the bottom of the valley, and so the whole army went down one after another, son after father, brother after brother and retainer after lord, horses and men falling on top of one another and piling up in heaps upon heaps. Thus did some seventy thousand horsemen of the Heike perish, buried in this one deep valley: the mountain streams ran with their blood and the mound of corpses was like a small hill; and in this valley, it is said, there can be seen the marks of arrows and swords even to this day. Kazusa-na-taiyu Hangwan Tadatsuna, Hida-no taiyu Hangwan Kagetaka and Kawachi-no-Hangwan Hidekuni, who were in command of the samurai, perished with their men at the bottom of this valley, while Seo-no-Tarō Kaneyasu of Bitchu, a warrior of great renown, deserted by fortune on this occasion, was taken alive by Kuramitsu-no-Jiro Narizumi of Kaga. Heizenji-no-Chori Saimei-i-Gishi, who had been so loyal to the Heike at the fortress of Hiuchi in Echizen, was also taken, which when Yoshinaka heard he exclaimed: "Let that most worthless priest be put to death immediately;" whereupon they fell on him and beheaded him. The Commanders-in Chief, Koremori and Michimori, strange to relate, escaped with their lives and fled to the province of Kaga, but out of the whole army of seventy thousand men, barely two thousand horsemen survived.

On the twelfth day of the same month Yoshinaka received a present of two splendid horses from Fujiwara Hidehira of Mutsu: one was cream-coloured and the other was grey with black spots. These he caparisoned with richly decorated saddles and dedicated to the shrine of Shirayama as sacred steeds. Yoshinaka now felt no anxiety about his position, but was in some doubt how his uncle Jūrō Kurando Yukiie had fared in the battle at Shiho, so, choosing twenty thousand picked horsemen from his army of forty thousand, he rode off thither. On the way they came to the inlet of Himi which must be crossed, but as the tide was high at the time, they did not know whether the water was shallow enough to ford, so Yoshinaka took ten saddled horses and drove them into the waves, and as they reached the further bank without more than wetting the saddles, they all rode in after them and crossed without difficulty. When they got to the other side, as they had expected, they found that Yukiie had retired after being hard pressed by the enemy, and was resting his men and horses. Immediately the fresh twenty thousand men of the Genji rode forward and dashed into the thirty thousand of the Heike with such a shock as caused fire to fly forth as the two opposing hosts crashed together in the melee. Mikawa-no-Kami Tomonori, the Commander of the Heike was killed: he was the youngest son of the Lay priest Chancellor. Beside him many other warriors fell, and the rest sought safety in flight and retired to the province of Kaga. Yoshinaka then crossed the mountain of Shiho with ten thousand men, and pitched his camp before the barrow of Shino at Odanaka in the province of Noto.

Chapter VI.

THE BATTLE AT SHINOHARA.

After these victories Kiso Yoshinaka presented lands to all the shrines in that district; to Yahata at Tada he presented the manor of Choya, to the shrine of Sugabu the manor of Nomi, to the shrine of Kebi the manor of Hanbara, and to that of Shirayama the two manors of Yokoe and Miyamaru, while to the temple of Heizenji he gave the seven parishes of Fujishima.

Now those samurai who had fought against Hyoye-no-suke Yoritomo at Ishibashiyama in the eighth month of the fourth year of Jishō had all fled to Kyoto and joined the Heike, chief among whom were Nagai-no-Saitō Bettō Sanemori, Ukisu-no-Saburō Kagechika, Matano-no-Gorō Kagehisa, Itō-no-Kurō Sukeuji and Mashimo-no-Shirō Shigenao. As they wished to rest for a while before fighting again, they were amusing themselves by going round to each other's quarters in turn every day and having a drinking-bout. When it was the turn of Saitō Bettō Sanemori to be host, and the others had assembled at his house, he remarked: "Judging by the way things are happening just now, it appears that the Genji are the stronger party and the Heike will get the worst of it; what do you think about going to join Kiso Yoshinaka?" The rest seemed to have no particular objection, so the next day, when it was their turn to meet at the house of Ukisu no-Saburō Kagechika, Sanemori began again: "Well, what do you say about carrying out my suggestion of yesterday?" Then Matano Gorō Kagehisa spore out and said: "We are all warriors of reputation, and well known in the Eastern Provinces; it is a disgraceful thing for samurai to change from one side to the other according to the way fortune inclines; as for you others I do not know what you intend to do, but for myself I have made up my mind to die on the side of the Heike." Then Saitō Bettō laughed scornfully and replied "What I said yesterday was only to try you all; I also have determined to go and die in the North Country, and I have already declared my intention to Munemori, and to others as well." On hearing this the remainder all stated their resolution to do likewise, and, pitiful to relate, faithful to their promise, all these twenty samurai afterwards fell in battle in the Northern Provinces.

Now the Heike had retreated to Shinohara in the province of Kaga to gain time to rest their men and horses, but Kiso Yoshinaka pursued after them with fifty thousand horsemen, and on the twentieth day of the fifth month he again confronted them. Imai Shirō Kanehira immediately rode forward with five hundred men, and against him from the Heike ranks came Hatakeyama Shōji Shigeyoshi, Oyamada-no-

Bettō Arishige and Utsunomiya-no-Saemon Tomotsuha with three hundred. These knights were often in Kyōto on guard duty, and as they were veteran warriors Munemori had sent them to the North Provinces to assist in the campaign with their advice. So Hatakeyama and Imai detached first five, and then ten of their samurai to begin the contest end see who would prove the better, after which the two forces attacked each other in mingled combat. It was at high noon on the twenty first day that they joined battle, and both sides fought fiercely and stubbornly, while the sun shone hot over their heads and there was no breeze even to move a blade of grass, so that the sweat poured down over their bodies as if they had been plunged in water. At last, when most of his retainers had fallen, Hatakeyama was compelled to retire, though on Imai's side also very many men were slain. Then Takahashi-no-Hangwan Nagatsuna with five hundred men came forth from the Heike, and Higuchi-no-Jirō Kanemitsu and Ochiai no-Gorō Kaneyuki with three hundred rode out from Kiso's force to meet them, and for some time both parties fought on the defensive; Takahashi's men, however, being samurai from various provinces, did not stand the onset, but broke and fled, each for himself heedless of the orders of their leader. Takahashi himself, though a most valiant fighter, was forced to retreat for lack of support, and rode away alone to the southward. Then Nyūzen-no-Kotarō Yukishige of Etchū, burning to overcome so stout an adversary, urged on his horse with whip and stirrup and overtook him. Coming up beside him he closed and grappled with him, but Takahashi gripped him hard, and pinned him against the front of his saddle so that he could not move, crying at the some time: "Who are you, sir! Declare your name and titles!" "I am Nyūzen-no-Kotarō Yukishige of the Province of Etchū, and my age is eighteen!" replied his assailant. On hearing this the tears ran down Takahashi's face as he exclaimed: "Ah, how pitiful! If my lad, who fell last year, had lived till now, he would be just eighteen; I ought to twist your neck and cut off your head, but as it is I will let you go;" and he released him.

Then Takahashi got off his horse to recover his breath and wait to see if any of his retainers would come up, and Nyūzen also dismounted, but, still thinking what a feat it would be to kill such a famous leader, even though he had just spared his life, he cast about to see how he could take him unaware. Takahashi, never dreaming of such treachery, was talking to him quite without reserve, when Nyūzen, who was famed for the rapidity of his movements, catching him off his guard, suddenly drew his sword and aimed a lightning thrust under his helmet. Just then, as he staggered back from the blow, three of Nyūzen's retainers came up, and Takahashi, stout warrior though he was, was borne down by superior numbers and slain.

Then Musashi-no-Saburōemon Arikuni of the Heike bore down on his foes with three hundred horse, and Nishina, Takanashi and Yamada-no-Jirō opposed him with five hurdred, and for a while both parties fought warily, but by-and by Arikuni, having penetrated very deeply into the ranks of the foe, had his horse shot under him, and then, while he was fighting on foot, his helmet was struck from his head, so that he looked like a youth fighting with his long hair streaming in all directions. By this time all his arrows were exhausted, so he drew his sword and laid about him mightily until, pierced by seven or eight shafts, he met his death still on his feet and glaring fiercely at his enemies. After their leader had thus fallen his retainers gave up the fight and fled.

Chapter VII.

THE DEATH OF SANEMORI.

Now among the retreating Heike retainers was Nagai-no Saitō Bettō Sanemori of Musashi, and he had a certain intention in his mind. He was clad in a red brocaded hitatare over armour with green lacing, and on his head was a helmet surmounted by lofty horns. He wore a gold mounted sword and a quiver of twenty four arrows with black and white feathers, and his bow was of black lacquer bound with red rattan. He rode a grey horse with black spots and his saddle was richly ornamented with gold. Though his companions kept on retiring, he alone continued to turn back and engage the enemy to protect their rear. Then one of Kiso's men named Tezuka-no-Tarō rode forward and shouted to him; "How splendid! Though all your side are in flight, you only, one single knight, dare to face us alone in such gallant fashion; I pray you declare your name." "Who then are you that ask?" replied Sanemori. "I am Tezuka-no Tarō Kanesashi-no-Mitsumori of Shinano," answered the other. "Then," replied Sanemori, "you will suit me well; and I too shall not disgrace your arms, though for a certain reason I cannot declare my name. Come on Tezuka! A grapple!" But as he rushed upon him, one of Tezuka's retainers, fearful that his master might be slain, thrust himself in between and received the onslaught. "Ho! who are you that wishes for the honour of being sped by the greatest warrior in Nippon?" cried Sanemori, as he caught him in his arms and pressed him tight against the front of his saddle so that he could not move, the while he twisted his neck round and cut off his head. Tezuka himself, seeing his retainer thus fall, slipped round to the left side of his opponent, and lifting the skirts of his armour, stabbed him twice and then pulled him from his horse, weakened as he was from the wounds. Thus, spite of his great strength and valour, fell Saitō Sanemori, for he was wearied with his long struggle, besides being well advanced in years.

Then Tezuka, giving the head to one of his men who ran up, came into the presence of Kiso Yoshinaka and bowed low. "I have brought your lordship," said he, "the head of a strange fellow whom I have fought with and slain. He might be a great leader, but he had no following; he might be a simple samurai, but he wears a hitatare of brocade. When I bade him declare his rank, he demanded mine but would not give his own. His speech is that of one of the warriors of the Kwantō." "Ah," exclaimed Yoshinaka, "this must be Saitō Bettō. Indeed? I remember seeing him once when I went over to Kōzuke; I was only a small boy then but I think his hair was nearly white, so he must be over seventy now, and ought to be quite white haired; but this hair and beard is black. Ho, there! summon Higuchi-no-Jirō Kanemitsu; he is about the same age as Sanemori and knew him well." Higuchi, answering the summons, entered, and after a single glance at the head, burst into tears: "Alas!" he exclaimed, "it is indeed Saitō Bettō." "Then," said Yoshinaka, "how is it that his hair is still black, for he must be more than seventy?" Higuchi, repressing his tears, replied: "Ah, that the pitifulness of his fate should have moved me to these weak tears; still, we warriors are apt to be touched by the recollection of even these trifling things. I remember when we were talking together, as we were often went to do, that he said to me; "I am over sixty now, but if I go to fight again I shall dye my hair black and become young once more, for I will not be pitied as a decrepit old knight, or look foolish if I strive for place among the youthful blades." Verily his hair is only dyed, and if you have it washed my words may be proved." So Kiso ordered the head to be washed forthwith, and the hair turned white even as Higuchi had said.

With regard to Sanemori's wearing a hitatare of brocade the reason was this. When he went to take leave of the Daijin Munemori he said to him: "There is one request that I wish to make, and it concerns me alone. Last year, when I went down with our men to the Eastern Provinces, I was startled by the noise of the water-fowl and fled in panic from Kambara in Suruga without so much as shooting one arrow, and that was a disgrace to my old age. Now I am going on the campaign in the North and there I intend to die. It was in that land that I was born, in Echizen, and it is only of late years that I have lived in Nagai of Musashi, the domain that your bounty has bestowed upon me. According to the proverb; "Wear brocade when you return to your birth place," I beg your lordship, if it is not too much to ask, to allow me the favour of wearing a hitatare of brocade." Munemori, touched by the gallantry of his address, gave him permission forthwith. As in China Shu-bai-shin flaunted his brocaded sleeves at Kwai-kei-san, so Saitō Bettō Sanemori would make a name in the North Country. Imperishable, though vain, is the reputation he made, while his corpse mingles with the dust of the Northland. Thus of the ten thousand men of the Heike who set out from the Capital on the seventeenth day of the fourth month, ready to confront any foe, barely twenty thousand returned at the end of the fifth. "If you fish out all the rivers, you will get a lot a fish, but next year there will be none; if you burn the cover to hunt you will catch a lot of beasts, but next year there will be none;" it would have been wiser to have taken thought for the fixture and kept some behind," was the opinion of most people

Chapter VIII.

GENBO.

Now Kazusa-no-kami Tadakiyo and Hida-no-kami Kageie had both become recluses the year before last, when the Nyūdō departed this life, and when they heard that all their sons had been killed in the Northern Provinces, their grief was so sore that at length it terminated their lives and they died. And beside them the multitude of parents who mourned the loss of their children, and wives who bewailed their slain husbands, was without number. In the Capital every door was shut, and night and day could be heard the sound of the ringing of bells and the chanting of the Nembutsu, and weeping and lamentations. And in all the provinces round about, both near and far, it was no different.

On the first day of the sixth month Saishu-Jingi-no-Gonno-Taiyū Ōnakatomi Chikatoshi was summoned to the lower gate of the Palace and informed that the Emperor would proceed in state to the Great Shrines of Ise to pray that the rebellion might be pacified. This was the Shrine of the Sun-Goddess who descended in ancient times from the Plains of High Heaven, and in the third month of the twenty fifth year of the reign of the Mikado Suijin Tennō removed from Kasanui in the province of Yamato, and deigned to be worshipped by the banks of the Iusugawa in the district of Watarai in the province of Ise, "making stout the shrine pillars to the nethermost rock-bottom;" incomparable and preeminent among the three thousand seven hundred and fifty greater and lesser shrines of the sixty provinces of Nippon. But from this time until the reign of Shōmu Tennō, the Mikado of Nara, no Emperor had gone there to worship. Then in the tenth month of the fifteenth year of Tempyō, when Sakonye-no-Shōshō Dazai-no Shōni Fujiwara Hirotsugu, son of Sangi Shikibu-no-Kyō Umagai and grandson of the Sadaijin Fuhito, raised an army of many myriads of men in the district of Matsuura in the province of Hizen, and menaced the peace of the Empire, the Mikado proceeded in state to Ise for the first time to pray for his downfall. Now this Hirotsugu possessed a horse of wondrous swiftness, that could complete the journey from Matsuura in Hizen to the Capital in one single day; and it is said that, when his army was defeated and fled, he mounted this horse and rode into the sea, and that afterwards his wraith appeared in that province and did many terrible things.

And there was a certain Genbo Sōjō who was priest of the temple of Kwannonji in the Dazaifu in the district of Mikasa of the province of Chikuzen, and it happened that on the eighteenth day of the sixth month of the eighteenth year of the era of Tempyō, as he was sitting on his high seat and striking the bell in the service, that the sky suddenly clouded over and there was a heavy thunderstorm, and a bolt struck him and took off his head, carrying it away into the clouds. And this was because he had invoked a curse on Hirotsugu when they marched to overthrow him. This Sōjō went to China with the Daijin of Kibi and brought back with him the Sutras of the Hossō Sect, and the men of China laughed at the name Genbo, saying that it sounded like the word for 'Destruction', and indeed, when he came back to his own country it was prophesied that some misfortune would happen to him. Afterwards, on the eighteenth day of the sixth month of the nineteenth year of Tempyō, a skull, inscribed with the name Genbo, fell into the courtyard of the Kōfukuji, while at the same time there was a sound as of the loud laughter of some two or three hundred men from the sky. It was no doubt because Kōfukuji was a temple of the Hossō Sect. Then his disciples took the skull and made a mound over it, and it is known as the Skull Mound and can be seen there to this day. On the place where the spirit of Hirotsugu is worshipped is the Shrine called 'Kagami-no-miya' at Matsuura in Hizen. And in the time of Saga Tennō, when the retired Emperor Heijō, at the instigation of his consort, tried to seize the Throne and trouble the Empire, the Emperor sent the third princess to Kamo as Sai-in or Imperial Priestess to offer supplication. And this was the first appointment of a Sai-in. Again, in the reign of Shujaku Tennō, a special festival was held in honour of Hachiman to pray for the subjection of the rebel Sumitomo. So now, on account of these precedents, many prayers were offered by the Imperial House.

Chapter IX.

KISO SENDS A LETTER TO HIEIZAN.

Now Kiso Yoshinaka was at Kōfu in Echizen, and he summoned all his relations and retainers and held a consulation saying: "If I march on Kyōto by way of Ōmi, those priests of Hieizan are sure to try to stop me. It will not perchance be difficult to break through them, but because the Heike have paid no respect to the Law of Buddha, but have destroyed temples and killed priests and done all manner of evil things, if I, who am going up to the Capital to protect it, have to begin by fighting with these priests, my conduct will appear not a whit different from theirs, but merely another dance to the same tune. This is no easy matter; what is to be done?" Then Taiyū-bō Kakumei, who had written the former letter, stood forth and said: "There are some two thousand priests on Hieizan, and it is certain that they will not be of the same opinion; some will be on the side of the Heike and others will favour the Genji: if you send a letter to them you will see, for their answer will show their disagreement." "That is well said," replied Yoshinaka; "write them a letter forthwith." So Kakumei indited a letter to the priests, and the words of it were as follows:

"I, Yoshinaka, have well considered the evil deeds of the Heike house. Ever since the time of Hogen and Heiji they have forgotten their duty as subjects and have set up and pulled down Emperors as they please, while high and low could do nothing, and priest and layman were treated with contempt. They have seized provinces at their will, and without right or reason have imprisoned men of standing and authority; putting to death prince, minister, vassal or subject, though their guilt or innocence was yet unproven. They have taken away their goods and given them to their retainers; they have confiscated their manors and improperly curtailed their descendant's possessions. Moreover in the eleventh month of the third year of Jisho they removed the Hō-ō to the Seinan Detached Palace, and exiled the Kwampaku to a lonely and far off coast. The roads have eyes, though all the people kept silent. Again in the fourth year of the same era they laid siege to the Palace of the second son of the Hō-ō, so that the very dust of the Palace Courts was astonished at such an outrage; and when, in order to escape such undeserved injury, he fled in secret to Onjōji, I, who had received intimation beforehand, was exceeding eager to ride at once to his rescue, but the highroads were full of the enemy everywhere, and I was unable to arrive in time.

As the Genji who were near at hand did not go, how much less could those who were far off. Then, as Onjōji could not protect him, he sought to gain the South Capital, and in the fight that ensued on the bridge at Uji, Sammi Nyūdō Yorimasa and his sons, counting their lives as nought in their loyalty, after one last glorious battle, unable to prevail against numberless foes, left their bones to bleach on the moss of the shore. Their names were washed away like the waves of the river, but their Lord's commands were engraved on their hearts, and with sorrow at their loss his life was extinguished. Therefore the Genji of the North and East Country have assembled together to overthrow the Heike, and in the autumn of last year, when I took sword in hand and raised my banner with that purpose, on the day that I went forth from Shinano, Jō-no-Shirō Nagamochi opposed me with many tens of thousands of horsemen and a battle was fought at Yokotagawa. There with but three thousand men behind me I routed and destroyed that mighty host, and the fame of my victory spread everywhere in the land.

At this the Heike sent a great army of a hundred thousand horsemen into the North Country, and in Echizen and Kaga, at Tonami, Kurosaka, Shiozaka and Shinohara many battles were fought. "Wrapping up my plans in a curtain I won my victories in a stone's throw" as it is said. Whenever I struck the foe gave way, and whenever I attacked he was always defeated. As the blasts of autumn level the reeds, and as the winter hoar-frosts wither the grasses, so they gave way before my onset. Such victories were not gained by my power, but were due to the aid of the gods and Buddhas. Now that the Heike armies have been thus defeated, I intend to advance upon the Capital, and in order to enter into its streets I must pass beneath the foot of your Holy Mountain; but as yet I am in doubt which side you favour, whether you incline to the Heike or will help the Genji. If you are in league with that evil faction then surely I must do battle with your temples, and in that case the destruction of Hieizan will follow without delay. Ah, the pity of it! Because the Heike leave caused great grief to the heart of the Emperor, and have made the Law of Buddha of no account, I have raised up a loyal army to subdue their evil ways, and now how painful will it be if I must fight an unlooked for battle with the three thousand priests of Hieizan. If, from respect to Yakushi Nyorai and to the god of Hiyoshi I should hesitate to advance, I shall be culpable as a negligent subject of the Emperor and a disgrace to the warrior caste. Thus in this state of uncertainty I await your esteemed communication, O most reverend brethren of the Tendai sect; and I beseech you, for the sake of the gods and Buddhas, of the Throne and of the Country, that you make cause with the Genji and punish these rebels, that we may all rejoice in the beneficent rule of our Sovereign, and the abundance of his gracious favour.

I thus address you in all respect. The tenth day of the sixth month of the second year of Ju-ei. Minamoto Yoshinaka, to the Venerable Elkōbō Risshi.

Chapter X.

THE REPLY OF HIEIZAN.

When the priests of Hieizan read this letter, as Kakumei had said, some were in favour of the Heike and some of the Genji. All of them expressed different opinions. Then the senior priests held a council and argued thus: "These temples have ever devotedly prayed for the long life and prosperity of our Heaven-descended Sovereign, and the Heike are the maternal relations of our present Ruler, so that it is our duty to pay them especial respect. Nevertheless, as they have grown lawless beyond measure, the people have rebelled against them, so that they have sent armies to put down the rebels, but these have been destroyed by the insurgents. Of late the Genji have been many times victorious and their prospects are ever growing brighter; why then should we alone espouse the waning fortunes of the Heike and resist the rising tide of the Genji? Let us therefore turn away from our connexion with the Heike and ally our forces with the Genji." Thus the three thousand priests decided, and they wrote their answer and sent it. When he received it, Yoshinaka again summoned his family and his retainers, and bade Kakumei read the letter. It ran thus:

"Your letter of the tenth day of the sixth month, being received by us on the sixteenth day, we respectfully perused, and for many days were possessed by great perplexity, which has in one hour been resolved. The evil deeds of the Heike have for many years caused trouble to the Imperial House as the proverb says, "Actions remain in people's mouths; they cannot be lost." Our mountain of Hieizan, whose shrines stand on the north east of the Imperial Capital, is especially bound to pray for the peace and quietness of the Empire, but since the Throne has been menaced by this calamity, the whole Realm has been disquieted. It has been as though the protecting power of the Nyorai had ceased to encircle us, and the might of the tutelary deities had been taken away. You, born of a family of generations of warriors, have been providentially chosen at this crisis. By brilliant tactics you have raised up a trusty and loyal army, and in the face of a thousand dangers have won a glorious victory. Moreover, as this is but the second year of your conquering career, ere long your fame will be known through all the land. Very greatly do we rejoice at these tidings. With all our hearts do we admire your valour and martial exploits on behalf of our country and people and we hear with gladness that your petitions to the high gods have not been in vain, for that they tarried not in coming to the aid of the Empire. And especially do we rejoice that the Buddhist doctrine of these and all other temples, and the bright deities of our shrines both small and great, shall again return to their former prosperity, and once more be revered as in former days. Moreover may the Twelve Warrior Gods, who attend on our Lord Yakushi Nyorai, go with your brave armies to smite the rebels, while we, the three thousand priests of these temples, leaving for a while our sacred studies, will lend our aid to punish the malefactors. May the pure blasts of the Tendai doctrine sweep away the wicked from this peaceful Realm, and the might of the Three Mystic Doctrines of our Holy Law pour down as rain moistens a thirsty land. Given by us in council: second day of the seventh month of the second year of Ju-ei.

Chapter XI.

Combined Petition of Tae Heike.

Now the Heike Lords never even dreamed of such a thing as this. Kōfukuji of Nara and Onjōji of Miidera no doubt harboured resentment against them, so that, if they addressed them it was unlikely that they would respond, but with Hieizan they had had no quarrel, neither had its priests ever up to the present been disloyal to them. So ten of the Courtiers of that family bethought themselves to write a petition and send it to the mountain, to solicit the help of the priests and invoke the divine aid of their gods and Buddhas. And these were the words of it:

"Regarding Enryakuji as our family temple and the god of Hiyoshi as our tutelary deity, reverently worshipping the Buddhist Law of the Tendai Sect. we, members of our one family, do here respectfully offer a petition. And the reason is this. Ever since in the reign of Kwammu Tennō Dengyō Daishi went to China and again returned to this land, and in this temple preached the original Law of Tendai and expounded the Sutras of the Mahayana, it has flourished greatly as a sacred dwelling-place of religion and a source of peace and protection to our Empire. Now Minamoto-no-Yoritomo, who was in exile in Izu, showing no repentance of his fault, on the contrary has set at nought the laws of the country and hatched evil plots, with which Yoshinaka, Yukiie and many other of the Genji are associated, and has seized many provinces both near and far, appropriating all their property and collecting their revenues. Therefore, relying on the meritorious deeds of our ancestors and the skill and prowess of our soldiers, and bearing moreover the Imperial Commands, we have taken in hand the punishment of these rebels and the subduing of the traitors. Up to this time, however, the far-flung hosts of the Imperial Army have not prevailed, but victory has, in some sort, rested with the impetuous and thronging forces of the rebels. Without the aid of the gods and Buddhas how can we overcome the traitors? Moreover, when we speak of the ancestors of our house, it was they who first founded your venerable fanes, and from age to age have their descendants added their tribute of worship and adoration. Now and henceforth will all our house rejoice in the joy of your temples, while the enemies of your shrines shall be counted as our own. Thus will we do and thus will we instruct our descendants, that the memory of it may never perish. The house of Fujiwara hold the god of Kasuga as their tutelary deity and Kofukuji as their family temple, revering the Mahayana doctrine of the Hossō Sect; and so also are the fortunes of the Heike house bound up with the shrine of Hiyoshi and the temple of Enryakuji, and the perfect teachings of its Holy Law. It has been our legacy from old time to consider the glory of our house, but now it is for the sake of our Sovereign that we pray for the punishment of the rebels. We beseech ye, O deities of the Seven Great Shrines, and Ye gods of the far-ranging shrines of the whole mountain, and thy twelve sacred promises, O Yakushi Nyorai; pour upon us the beneficent light of thy kindly truth, and come to meet us with thy gracious aid. That the hands of these evil plotters may be bound at the gate of our camp, and that we may bring their heads in triumph to the Capital. This is the united petition of our whole house. Jū-sammi Echizen-no-kami Taira-no-Ason Michimori, Ju-sammi Ukonye-no-Chūjō Taira-no Ason Sukemori, Shō-sammi Ukonye-no-Chūjō Iyo-no-kami Taira-no-Ason Koremori, Shō-sammi Sakonye-no-Chūjō Harima-no-kami Taira-no Ason Shigehira, Sho-sammi Uemon-no-kami Ōmi Tōtōmi-no-kami Taira-no-Ason Kiyomune, Sangi Shō-sammi Kōtaigō-gū-ro-Gon-no-taiyū Shūri-no-taiyū Kaga Etchū-no-kami Taira-no-Ason Tsunemori, Jū-nii Chūnagon Sei-i-taishōgun Sahyōye-no-kami Taira-no-Ason Tomomori, Jū-nii Gon-Chūnagon Hizen-no-kami Taira-no-Ason Norimori, Shō-nii Gon-Dainagon Mutsu Dewa-no-Azechi Taira no-Ason Yorimori, Jū-ichii Zen-no-Naidaijin Taira-no Ason Munemori. Fifth day of the seventh month of the second year of Ju-ei.

When the Zasshu of Hieizan received this latter he was deeply grieved, and did not show it to the other priests at once, but retired and spent three days in prayer before the Juzenji Gongen, after which he showed it to them. On his opening the petition, this verse, which he had not noticed before, fell out of it:

> *Tairaka ni hana saku yado mo toshi fureba,*
> *Nishi ye katamuku tsuki to koso mire.*
> "*Peaceful the years we have passed in this spot where tire flowers ever blossom,*
> "*Now is the moon, like our fate, waning to sink in the west.*"

The Chief Priest of Hiyoshi was also very sad, and bade the three thousand monks lend their aid, but, as for long the deeds of the Heike had been contrary to the will of the gods as well as unpopular among the people, prayers were of no avail and no one would pay any heed. The priests were indeed sorry that things had come to such a pass, but, as they had already sent the letter promising help to the Genji, as to their lightly changing their mind, there were none ready to consent to it.

Chapter XII.

DEPARTURE OF THE EMPEROR FROM THE CAPITAL.

On the fourteenth day of the seventh month Higo-no-kami Sadayoshi with three thousand men under Kikuchi, Harada and Matsuura, returned to Kyōto after having put down the rebellion in Kyūshū. But though the revolt in Kyūshū had been quelled, that in the North and Fast Country was by no means subdued. On the twenty second day at midnight a very great tumult arose at Rokuhara. Horses were saddled, girths were tightened, and people were running in all directions carrying goods to hide them, while cries of: "The enemy are upon us! They are entering the city!" arose on every side. When the dawn broke the reason was found to be as follows. There was a certain warrior of the Genji of Mino named Sado-no-Emon-no-jō Shigesada, who in the war of Hogen had captured Chinzei Hachirō Tametomo when he fled after the fight at the Palace of the Retired Emperor, and had as a reward been raised from his office of Hyōye-no-jō to that of Uemon-no-jō. As the result of this he was disliked by the rest of his family, and lately had been making, advances to the Heike, and now he came riding to Rokuhara with the news that Kiso Yoshinaka was advancing on the Capital at the head of fifty thousand horsemen, and Tate-no-Rokurō Chikatada, one of his captains, with Taiyū-bō Kakumei, the ready writer, had ridden hotfoot to Hieizan, where the three thousand monks had made common cause with them, and that the whole force was now pressing on the Capital itself. When they heard this the Heike were thrown into state of great confusion and sent out bodies of men in all directions. A force of three thousand horsemen under the command of Shin-Chūnagon Tomomori-no-Kyō and Hon-sammi-no-Chūjō Shigehira-no-Kyō at once rode out to take up a position at Yamashina, while Echizen-no-sammi Michimori and Noto-no-kami Noritsune went to hold the bridge at Uji with two thousand, and Sama-no-kami Yukimori and Satsuma-no-kami Tadanori guarded the highroad at Yodo with about a thousand. Meanwhile it was rumoured that Jūrō Kurando Yukiie with several thousand men had crossed the bridge at Uji and entered the city; that Yada-no-Hangwan Yoshikiyo, son of Mutsu-no-Shin Hangwan Yoshiyasu had crossed over Ōyeyama; and that the Genji of the provinces of Settsu and Kawachi had also risen in revolt and were marching on the Capital from that direction. Then the Heike, abandoning all hope of saving the city, recalled the forces that they had sent out and all crowded together in one place, quite at a loss to know what do no next.

As the Chinese saying goes; "The Imperial Capital[231] is a place ever busy with fame and gain; after cockcrow it has no rest." If this is so when it is quietly governed, what must it when all is confusion. Doubtless they would have liked to flee, to the innermost recesses of Mount Yoshino, but their enemies were in possession of all the highroads and all the provinces were hostile, so that they could only find refuge by the sea. As we read in the golden words of the Hokke Sutra; "In the Three Worlds there is no rest; it is even as a house that had taken fire." Not otherwise was the state of the Capital at his time. On the twenty fourth day at dusk the former Naidaijin Munemori-no-Kyō went to the Ikedono at Kokuhara where Kenrei-mon in was staying and said: "Kiso Yoshimaka is coming up to attack the Capital with fifty thousand horsemen, and has already arrived at Higashi-Sakamoto in Ōmi where the monks of Hieizan have joined him; we must stay here at all events, but as it would be most unfortunate if either yourself or your august mother the Nii-dono came to any harm, we think it best that you, with the Emperor and the Hō-ō, should for a while retire to the Western Provinces." "As affairs now are," replied the Empress "that will be perhaps the best plan;" and as she spoke her feelings overcame her and she sobbed unrestrainedly into the sleeve: of her Imperial Robe. The Naidaijin also moistened the sleeve of his Naoshi with his tears.

Now when the Hō-ō heard privately of this design of the Heike to take him away to the Western Provinces, he departed secretly from his Palace at midnight, attended only by Uma-no-kami Suketoki, the son of Azechi-no-Dainagon Suketaka-no-Kyō, and made an Imperial Progress by himself to some place the whereabouts of which remained augustly unknown. And one was aware of it.

But among the Heike samurai was a certain shrewd fellow named Kitsunai Saemon-no-jō Sueyasu, who was accustomed to serve at the Hō-ō's Palace, and on this night Also he was on guard there, and although he was at some distance from the private apartments, he became aware, from the sound of subdued weeping of the Ladies-in-waiting, and other signs of agitation, that some extraordinary and distressing event had occurred. On his enquiring what it was, they told him that the Hō-ō had disappeared suddenly, and must have taken his august departure somewhere or other, whereupon he went off in great haste to Rokuhara and reported the matter to Munemori-no-Kyō. The Minister at first thought he must be mistaken, but on himself going to the Palace he learnt that the Hō-ō was indeed not to be found. The Ladies in attendance on His Majesty, the Nii-dono, Tango dono and others, were all aghast and helpless with consternation, and there was not a single one of them who knew whether he had gone, so Munemori

---

[231] The Imperial Capital is a place, etc. A quotation from Haku-raku-ten (Po-Chu-i).

could do nothing but return weeping to Rokuhara.

When it was known that the Hō-ō was no longer in the city the excitement was extraordinary, and the flurry and confusion of the Heike was such that it seemed that it could have hardly been greater if the enemy had actually been entering the houses of the Capital. As they had thus made preparations to send the Emperor and the Hō-ō the Western Provinces and then found that their plan was already upset, they felt like one who takes refuge, under a tree that does not keep off the rain. However they determined to carry out their design in the case of the Emperor at least, so at the hour of the Hare (6 a.m.) the Imperial Palanquin was made ready, His Majesty being at this time a child of six years old, and knowing nothing of what was taking place. His Imperial Mother Kenrei-mon in rode also in the same Palanquin. Hei-Dainagon Tokitada-no-Ky ō had given orders that all the Treasures of the imperial House should be taken with them, the Sacred Jewel, the Sword, the Mirror, the Imperial Seal and Key, the Tablet[232] for marking the hours, and the Imperial Biwa and Koto, but such was the flurry and excitement that many of them were left behind. His Majesty's own sword was also, forgotten in the hurry. Tokitada-no-Kyō and his two sons Kura-no-kami Nobumoto and Sanuki-no-Chūjō Tokisane accompanied the procession in full court robes, while the Imperial Guard of the Konoe-tsukasa and the Mitsuna-no-suke escorted them in armour, carrying their bows and quivers. So they proceeded along the Shichijo to the west and the Shujaku to the south.

Thus the dawn began to break on the twenty fifth day of the seventh month; the light of the stars faded out, and the clouds spread shelving over the eastern hills as the cocks crowed clamorously. Of such a departure from the Capital as this they had never even dreamed, though, when they thought of it, the rash and hasty change of the capital the year before seemed like a precedent. The Sesshō also followed the Imperial train, and when they came to Shichijō Ōmiya a beautiful youth with bound up hair was seen to speed along in front of the Imperial Car. On the left sleeve of his dress were the characters 'Haru-no-hi' or 'Spring day'; and as these two characters are also read 'Kasuga', it seemed to them that Kasuga Daimyōjin, the Divine Guardian of the Hossō Sect, had come to protect the descendant of Fujiwara Kamatari the great founder of his shrine. As they were giving thanks for this supernatural aid, it seemed that the divine youth spoke the following verse:

---

[232] Tablet for marking the hours. Used for announcing to the Emperor the time of day, which was calculated by a water-clock.

> "*Ika ni sen Fuji no Uraha no kare yuku wo,*
> *Tada haru no hi ni makasetara nan,*"
> "*Though we cannot prevent the leaves of the Fuji from fading,*
> *Let then fade at any will, in the bright sunshine of spring*"[233]

Then the Sesshō Motomichi called Shin-dozaemon-no-jō Takanao who was in attendance on him, and said in a low tone: "This may be called an Imperial Progress, but when we consider the state of affairs it is no Imperial Progress but a pitiful Imperial Parting, and what hope is there for the future?" At this Takanao made a sign to the ox drivers, and they, understanding, whipped up their animals so that their car dashed along the Ōmiya highroad at a great speed, and at length they entered the temple of Chisoku-in at the foot of the northern hills.

Chapter XIII.

FLIGHT OF KOREMORI FROM THE CAPITAL.

Etchū Jirō-hyōye, seizing his sword, tried to stop the Sasshō from running away in this manner, but he was held back by the others and so was able to do nothing. Among them Komatsu-no-sammi Chūjō Koremori had long made up his mind that something of this sort was likely to come to pass, but now that it had actually happened he was none the less grieved. His wife was the daughter of the late Naka-no-Mikado Shin-Dainagon Narichika-no-Kyō and as her father and mother had both died, as has been already related, she was an orphan. She was a lady of peerless beauty; her complexion was like a peach blossom wet with dew, her large dark eyes were soft and blandishing, and her long black hair swayed about her like willow shoots in the wind. She had two children, a son of ten years old named Rokudai and a little daughter of eight, and they all clung about Koremori and begged with tears to be allowed to accompany him. "But" explained he, "I must go down with the rest of the men to the Western Provinces, and the foe are besetting the roads so it is not likely we shall get through without danger. If I am killed, however, there is no need for you to become a nun; it would be better to look out for another husband and so bring up the two children. In this world kind hearted people are not lacking." But though he tried to comfort her thus, she would not heed, and when the Chūjō was just about to start she clung to his sleeve crying out; "Alas! I have now no father or mother in this city, and although you give me permission to marry again after you have left me, it does not

---

[233] The meaning of this verse would seem to be that the deity was warning them not to follow the Heike into exile.

seem kind but hateful. From connexion in the former life it is that people are kind or that they receive compassion. You often said that we would never part, but that we should both melt into the dew of the same moor, or sink to the bottom of the same water. Ah! it was not true, it was but the babbling of a lover in the night time. If I am left behind here what am I to do? Can you bear to desert me when you know how I shall suffer? And who is to look after these little children? Though we may vex you, I pray you, do not leave us thus." "In truth" replied the Chūjō, in accents of mingled affection and impatience, "ever since you were thirteen and I fifteen we have looked forward to being together until death should separate us, until the same fire or water should enfold our bodies; but now, since we have fallen on these evil days, I must put on my armour and go forth to battle, and how could I bear that you should accompany me to face the unknown perils and hardships of a doubtful campaign? But, though there is no place for you with me now, I will send and fetch you as soon as we gain the security of some favourable coast." Speaking thus decisively he went out into the verandah by the middle gate and put on his armour, and calling for his horse was just about to mount and ride away, when his little son and laughter ran out and caught hold of the sleeves and skirts of his armour, crying: "Father! where are you going? Please take us too! Let us go with you!" As they thus wept and clung round him, he could not for the moment tear himself away, and while he was meditating over the hampering ties of this world, his five younger brothers, Sammi-no-Chūjō Sukemori, Sa-Chūjō Kiyotsune, Shōshō Arimori, Tango-no-Jijū Tadafusa, and Bitchū-no-kami Moromori, rode into the courtyard, reined in their horses, and called out loudly: "The Imperial Train has gone on a long way; why are you so long in coming?" Then the Chūjō tore himself away and sprang on to his horse to follow them, but again they called to him, so he drew his horse to the edge of the verandah and with the tip of his bow pushed up the bamboo curtain that hung before it, disclosing his children to his brothers outside. "You see how these little ones twine round me; it is this that has delayed me until now;" and as he spoke his feelings overcame him and the tears ran down his face, so that those in the courtyard were moved to weep in sympathy till the sleeves of their armour were wet with tears.

Now there were two samurai in the train of the Chūjō named Saitō Go and Saitō Roku, two brothers. the eider of who, was nineteen years old and the younger seventeen, and they tools hold of the bit of the horse on each side and said: "Wherever you may go we will follow you;" "Ah," replied the Chūjō, "I remember when your father Nagai-no-Saitō Bettō Sanemori went to the North Country you wanted to go with him, but he prevented you and went to his death there alone. It seems as if he knew beforehand that you would be needed here. Now I have to leave Rokudai behind, and I have no one but you two with whom to entrust him. So, though it may seem unreasonable, I must bid you stay behind." The two brothers, therefore, repressing their tears of disappointment, could do nothing but comply with the orders of their lord. As Koremori rode away his lady cried out: "Never till now did I think: that his heart would be so hard;" and she covered her face and fell prone on the ground. The children and the ladies of the household, reaching out beyond the curtain, lifted up their voices and welt aloud, and the sound echoed in the ears of the Chūjō until it was drowned by the roar of the wind and waves of the Western Sea.

When the Heike fled from the Capital they set fire to all their mansions, and Rokuhara, Ikedono, Komatsudono, Hachijō, Nishi Hachijō and others, in all twenty mansions, beside some forty or fifty thousand houses of their retainers in the cite and in Shirakawa, went up in flames.

Chapter XIV.

The Imperial Haunts.

Thus the places that the Emperor used to frequent were reduced to ashes, and nought but the foundation stones was left of his residences; the Imperial Car was his only refuge, of the gardens of the Princesses but the site remains, and on the place of their elegant chambers the dew falls like tears and the blasts whine mournfully. The splendid apartments where the ladies tired themselves behind the long curtains, the hunting lodges and fishing pavilions, the residence of the Sesshō, the mansions of the Courtiers, the labour of many years made vain in an hour, what now remains of them but charred logs? How much more the lodging of their retainers and the houses of the common people? In all the area that the fire devoured was a score of cho and more. Not otherwise, when the power of Go was overthrown, the terraces of Kōso were suddenly abandoned to the thistles and dew, and when the might of Shin was at last laid low, the smoke of the palace of Kanyō obscured the land. Though the slopes of the pass of Kwan-koku were made strong, the northern barbarians broke through, and though they relied on the deep waters of the Yellow river the eastern marauders took possession of it. What then are we to think of it? Thus driven out of their elegant Capital and forced to seek refuge in an unknown shore; it is as if the Dragon God, who yesterday rode in triumph on the clouds, commanding the rain, should to-day lie like a fish out of water beside the storehouses. So can all see that adversity and prosperity take the same road, and rise and fall are as a turn of the band; and who is there who does not grieve? Though in the former days of Hogen they flourished like the flowers in spring time, in this era of Ju-ei they have fallen like the leaves of autumn.

At this time Hatakeyama Shōji Shigeyoshi, Oyamada Bettō Arishige and Utsunomiya Saemon Tomotsuna, who had been in the service of the Heike from Jishō to Ju-ei, were lying under sentence of death in the Capital, but Shin Chūnagon Tomomori-no-Kyō gave his opinion as follows: "It will hardly make any difference to the fate of our house if the heads of a hundred or a thousand men are cut off, so why cause bereavement to the, wives and children of these men who are waiting for them at home? It may be against reason to say so, but if our fortunes should again revive, they may come up to Kyoto and enter our service again to show us some gratitude for our clemency." "Then let it be as you say;" said the Daijin Munemori, and he set them free. Overjoyed at their unexpected release, they raised their heads and put their hands together, crying: "Let us share the fortunes of your house to the end;" but Munemori replied: "Your hearts are in the East Country with your families; why should you go with us to the West, empty handed as we are? Return, then, to your homes." And they went out, finding it hard to restrain their tears when they thought of those whom they had served for twenty years.

Chapter XV.

DEPARTURE OF TADANORI FROM KYOTO.

Satsuma-no-kami Tadanori, who had already left the Capital, wishing to see Gojō-no-sammi Shunsei-no-Kyō once again, rode back again to the city with a small train of five retainers and a page, all, like himself, in full armour. When he came to the gate of the mansion, however, he found it shut fast, and even when he called his name, it was not opened, though there was a sound of people running about within crying out that one of the fugitives had returned. Then Satsuma-no-kami hastily dismounted from his horse and himself cried out with aloud voice: "It is I, Tadanori, who have come; I have something to say to Sammi dono; if you will not open the gate, at least beg him to come forth here that I may speak with him." "If it is indeed Tadanori," relied Shunsei-no-Kyō, "you need have no fear, but admit him." Then they opened the gate and he entered, and the meeting between the two was most moving and pathetic. "Ever since I became your pupil in the art of poetry years ago," said Tadanori, "I have never forgotten you, but for the last few years the disorder of the Capital and the risings in the provinces have prevented me from coming to see you. Now the final scene in the fall of our house hurries on apace, and the Emperor has already departed from the Capital. But there is one thing that I very greatly desire. Some time ago I heard that an Anthology of Poems was to be made by the Imperial Command, and I wished to ask if you would condescend to submit one of my poor verses for consideration, that my name may be remembered in time to come; and I felt great regret when the Collection was postponed owing to the unsettled state of the country. If, however, at some time in the future, when peace is restored to the Empire, this Anthology should be made, I would beg your favour for one of the stanzas in this scroll, that my spirit may rejoice under the shade of the long grass, and from that far off world may come and aid you." And with these words he drew out from beneath the sleeve of his armour a scroll containing a hundred verses that he considered to be the best he had so far composed and handed them to Shunsei-no-Kyō. "Truly does this memento show that you have not forgotten me," replied Shunsei as he opened and perused it. "and I find it hard to keep back my tears when I think of the manner of your coming. Verily the sadness of it is unutterable and your affection to me most deep." "Whether my bones will bleach on the hills or my name be echoed by the billows of the Western Sea, I care not," answered Tadanori, "for I feel no regret for this fleeting world; and so, as it must be, farewell; "and he sprang up in his horse, and, replacing his helmet on his head, rode away to the westward. Sammi-dono stood looking after him a long while until lie was out of sight, and as he looked the words of the following Chinese verse were borne back to his ears in the voice, as it seemed, of Tadanori:

> "*Far is the road I must travel; so do I gallop into the evening mists of Ganzan.*"

Overcome by his melancholy thoughts, Shunsei controlled his feelings with difficulty as he slowly returned to his mansion.

In after days, when the Empire was once more at peace, an Imperial Order was issued to make an Anthology called the Senzai-shū and Shunsei remembered the request of Tadanori and his conversation, but though there were many verses worthy of immortality in the scroll that he had written, as at that time he and all the Heike had been declared to be rebels against the Throne, all that he could do for the memory of his unhappy disciple was to include one of them under the title of "A flower of my native land," by "An unknown author." The stanza runs thus:

> "*Though desolation has stricken the City of rippling wavelets,*
> *Still does the cherry tree put forth its blossoms of yore.*"

Chapter XVI.

DEPARTURE OF TSUNEMASA FROM KYOTO.

Kōgō-gū-no-suke Tsunemasa, the eldest son of Shūri-no-taiyū Tsunemori, had, as a child, served as page to the Imperial Abbot of the temple of Omuro Ninnaji, and still felt so deeply attached to him that he determined to pay him a farewell visit, even in spite of their great haste; so he took five or six retainers with him, and, riding off thither at great speed, hurriedly alighted from his horse and knocked at the gate. "Our Sovereign has already departed from the Capital," he said, "and the doom of our house is at hand, but all I regret in this fleeting world is that I must part from my lord. Since I first entered this Palace cloister at the age of eight until my Gempuku at the age of thirteen, except for a slight interval of sickness, never did I leave my lord's side; but to day, alas, I must go forth to the wild waves of the Western Sea, not knowing when, if ever, I shall return. So I have come, wishing to see his face more, though I feel ashamed to enter his presence in this sough soldier's garb." When he heard this, the Imperial Abbot, moved with compassion, replied: "Bid him enter as he is, without changing his dress." Tsunemasa was that day attired in a hitatare of purple brocade and body armour laced with green silk. A gold mounted sword hung at his side and a quiver of twenty four arrows with black and white feathers at his back, and under his arm he carried his bow of black lacquer with red binding. Taking off leis helmet and hanging it from his shoulder, he reverently entered the little garden before the apartment of the Abbot. His Reverence immediately appeared and bade them raise the curtain before the verandah, on which he invited Tsunemasa to be seated. When Tsunemasa had seated himself he beckoned to Tōhyōye-no-jō Arimori who attended on him, and he brought a bag of red brocade containing his master's Biwa, which Tsunemasa laid before the Abbot. "I have brought back this famous Biwa 'Seizan,' which Your Reverence presented to me last year, with deep regret, for it is not proper that I should take such a thing, one of the most precious treasures of our land, into the rude wilds of the country. May I then deposit it with Your Reverence, that if a happier day should perchance dawn again for our family, and we should return to the Capital I may receive it from your land once more?" At this the Abbot was much moved and replied with the following stanza:

> "*So will I keep it unopened, this much regretted memento,*
> *Just as though the bag held the affection you feel.*"

Tsunemasa, borrowing his master's inkstone, then wrote the following:

"*Though the water way cease to flow from this spout in your garden,*
Never will cease my desire her c to remain by your side."

When he had said farewell and retired from the presence of the Imperial Abbot, all those who were living in the monastery, acolytes, monks, and priests of all ranks, flocked round trim, clinging to his sleeves and bedewing them with their tears, so sad were they at parting with him. Among them was a certain young priest named Dainagon-no-Hoshi Gyōkei, a son of Hamuro-no-Dainagon Mitsuyori-no-Kyō, who had been much attached to him ever since his boyhood; and he was so loath to part with him that he went to see him off as far as the banks of the Katsuragawa, where he bade him farewell and returned to the monastery. As he parted with him, weeping he composed the following verse:

"*Ah, how sad is this life, both the gnarled old tree and the cherry,*
All must fade and pass; never a flower is left."

To which Tsunemasa made reply:

"*In this passing world, each night that we lie down to slumber*
Is as a traveller goes farther and farther away."

Then his samurai, who had been waiting in groups here and there, unfurled their red banners and formed into a company of about a hundred horsemen in all, and as he took his place at their head they all whipped up their horses and galloped on after the Imperial Procession.

Chapter XVII.

CONCERNING 'SEIZAN.'

It was when he was seventeen years old that Tsunemasa was presented with the Biwa 'Seizan,' and about the same time he was sent as Imperial Envoy to the shrine of Hachiman at Usa. When he arrived there he played certain secret pieces of great beauty on it before the abode of the deity, and all the assembled priests were so touched that the sleeves of their ritual garments were wet with their tears. Even those without any discrimination, who had never had any opportunity of hearing good music, were delighted, thinking it sounded like showers of rain. And the story of this Biwa is that, when in the time of Nimmyō Tennō, in the third month of the third year of the period of Ka-shō, Kamon-no-kami Sadatoshi went to China, he learned three styles of playing from Renshō-bu, a very renowned master of the Biwa, and before he came back to Japan he was presented with three Biwas called 'Genshō,' 'Shishi-maru,' and 'Seizan.' But while he was returning over the sea, the Dragon god "of the waters was moved by envy to raise a great storm, so they cast 'Shishi maru' into the waves to appease him, and brought back only two to this country, which were presented to the Emperor.

Many years after, in the period Ō-wa, the Emperor Murakami Tennō was sitting in the Seiryō-den one autumn at midnight, when the moon was shining brightly and a cool breeze was blowing, arid was playing on the Biwa called 'Genshō', when suddenly a shadowy form appeared before him and began to sing in a loud and sonorous voice. On the Emperor asking him who he was and whence he had come, he answered thus. "I am Renshō-bu, that master of the Biwa who in China taught the three secret styles of playing to Fujiwara Sadatoshi; but in my teaching there was one tune that I concealed and did not transmit to him, and for this fault I have been cast into the place of devils. Having this night heard the wondrous beauty of your playing, I have come to ask Your Majesty if I may transmit the one remaining tune to you, and thus be permitted to enter the perfect enlightenment of Buddha." Then, taking 'Seizan' which was standing before His Majesty also, he tuned the strings and taught the melody to the Emperor. And this is that which is called 'Jogen' and 'Sekijo.'

After this apparition the Emperor and his Ministers feared to play on this Biwa, and it was presented to the Imperial Temple of Ninnaji, and Tsunemasa received it because he was so much beloved by the Imperial Abbot. The front of it was made of a rare wood called Shito, and on it was a picture of the moon of dawn coming forth from among the green foliage of summer mountains, hence its name 'Seizan' (Green Mountain). It was a most precious treasure not at all inferior to 'Gensho.'

Chapter XVIII.

THE HEIKE ABANDON KYOTO.

Now Ike-no-Dainagon Yorimori-no-Kyō set fire to the Ikedono Palace and set out from the city, but when he came to the south Toba gate with his following of some three hundred horsemen, they tore the red badges off their armour and returned to the city on the pretext that they had forgotten something. When Etchū-no-Jirō-hyōye Moritsugu perceived this, he galloped off to Munemori with his bow in his hand and said: "See there! A party of samurai, following the example of Yorimori, has returned to the city, and their designs look suspicious. I would respect the person of Yorimori, but let me draw bow against these fellows." "Under present conditions," replied Munemori, "I think it would perhaps be as well to pay no heed to such a pack of runagate knaves; but have you seen or heard aught of the men of Komatsu dono?" "So far" answered Yorimori, "none of them has yet come up." "It is no good omen if people begin to desert us when we have but left the Capital a single day;" reflected Munemori. "I said it would be better to stay in the Capital, when every other place is so uncertain;" said Shin Chūnagon Tomomori-no-Kyō, casting a resentful glance at Munemori.

Now the reason why Yorimori stayed behind in Kyoto was because Yoritomo had sent him many letters, swearing by Hachiman that he would always regard him with the same feeling as he had his late mother Ike-no-Zenni, and had given special orders to his army not to attack the samurai of Ikedono; and so, though all the Heike family were fleeing its despair from the Capital, he alone remained behind, trusting the good will of Yoritomo. As Saisho dono, the wife of this Yorimori, was the foster mother of the Princess Hachijō-no-Nyoin who had taken refuge in the Tokiwa mansion of the temple of Ninnaji on account of the uproar in the Capital, Yorimori also fled there for safety; for though he trusted to Yoritomo to help him, the Nyoin was not entirely assured, saying that in a world like the present no one knew what might happen; for even if Yoritomo was friendly the attitude of the other Genji was uncertain, and as they had thus rashly separated from the rest of their family they were in a perilous position, neither in the waves nor on shore.

So when the Courtiers of Komatsu-dono, the six sons of Shigemori and their retainers, about a thousand men in all, came up with the Imperial Procession by Matsuda-kawara at Yodo, the Daijin Munemori was greatly rejoiced, and enquired of them why they were so long in coming. "It is because I was so long delayed by the affectionate pleadings of my little ones," replied Koremori. "Then why did you not bring Rokudai with you? You are a hard hearted father to be able leave him behind;" said Munemori. "But when our future is all uncertain like this——" said Koremori, while the tears ran down his face at such an unfeeling cling question.

Those of the Heike who fled from the Capital were; The former Udaijin Munemori, Hei Dainagon Tokitada, Hei Chūnagon Norimori, Shin-Chūnagon Tomomori, Shūri-no-taiyū Tsunemori Uemon-no-kami Kiyomune, Hon-sammi Chūjō Shigehira, Komatsu-sammi Chūjō Koremori, Shin-sammi Chūjō Sukemori, Echizen-no-sammi Michimori; and among the Courtiers; Kura-no-kami Nobumoto, Sanuki-no-Chūjō Tokizane, Sa-Chūjō Kiyotsune, Sa-Shōshō Arimori, Tango-no-jijū Tadafusa, Kōgō-gū-no-suke Tsunemasa, Sama-no-kami Yukimori, Satsuma-no-kami Tadanori, Musashi-no-kami Tomoaki, Noto-no-kami Noritsune, Bitchū-no-kami Moromori. Owari-no-kami Kiyosada, Awaji-no-kami Kiyofusa, Wakasa-no-kami Tsunetoshi,

Kurando-no-taiyū Narimori, Tsunemori-no-Otogo-taiyū Atsumori, Hyōbu-no-shōyu Masaaki; and of the priests; Nii-no-Sozu Senshin, Hoshōji-no-Shikkō Noen, Chūnagon-no-Risshi Chūkai, Kyōjū-bō-no-Ajari Yuen, while of the Bushi, of Lords of manors, Kebiishi, Efu, and those in various offices in the government, there were a hundred and sixty. The total number amounted to some seven thousand men, this being all that was left after the wars of the last few years in the various provinces of the North and East. Hei Dainagon Tokitada-no-kyō, stopping the Imperial Car at Yamasaki Sekito-no-in, prostrated himself in the direction of Otokoyama and prayed thus: "Namu Kimyō-chōrai Hachiman Dai-Bosatsu, we beseech thee that thou wilt grant that Our Lord the Emperor and all our family may again return to the Capital;" a most pathetic prayer indeed! And now, as they looked back toward the city, nothing was to be seen but the clouds of smoke from the burning buildings rising into the sky like mist; in truth a melancholy sight. Hei Chūnagon Norimori and Shūri-no-taiyū Tsunemori each composed a stanza on this occasion, which run thus:

> "*Ah! this fleeting life! Our Sovereign far from his Palace,*
>   *sees it go up in smoke, rising aloft to the sky.*"
> "*When we look sadly back at the blackened plains of our*
>   *homeland,*
>   '*tis as if we rode over an ocean of smoke.*"

Indeed we can imagine the sadness they felt when at the same time they saw their homes reduced to ashes and smoke and contemplated the long road they must travel. Higo-no kami Sadayoshi, hearing that some of the Genji were at Kawajiri, rode off with five hundred men to drive them away, but, finding that the report was false, he was returning again to the city when he fell in with the Imperial Procession near Udono. Hastily alighting from his horse he sought the presence of Munemori. After the customary obeisance he burst forth: "What wretched plan is this? Whither are you intending to go? If you are proceeding to the Western Provinces, everyone will reproach you for taking to flight, and it will be a disgrace to our family. It would be far better to remain and await events in the Capital." "Perhaps you are not yet aware," replied Munemori, "that Kiso Yoshinaka is now advancing on the Capital with My thousand men, and that the priests of Hieizan have occupied Higashi Sakamoto, and that moreover the Hō-ō has disappeared during the night: we were all ready to fight to the end in the Capital, but, wishing to avoid all risk of danger to the Imperial Mother and the Nii dono, we thought it well to escort them into retirement for a while in the Western Provinces until the danger is past." "In that case," answered Sadayoshi, "I will ask your leave to return to the city and see what can be done;" and, ordering his force of five hundred men to join the retainers of Koremori, he rode back to Kyoto with only a small band of thirty horsemen. Somehow or other the rumour spread that Sadayoshi was returning to take vengeance on the Heike who had stayed behind in the city, and when Ike-no-Dainagon Yorimori heard it, he was greatly terrified for his own safety.

So Sadayoshi went and encamped on the burnt ruins of Nishi Hachijō, and spent the night there, but not one of the Heike Courtiers returned to bear him company. As solitude and desolation reigned everywhere and the future seemed ominous, he went to the grave of his master Shigemori and dug out the bones that they might not be trodden under foot by the horse hoofs of the Genji. Taking his place before the bones as if they had been a living person, in a voice choked with tears he addressed them thus: "Alas! how pitiable! Behold the fate of your august house! Though it has been said from of old time that the living must surely die, and that at the height of pleasure comes pain, yet hard it is to behold this doom with our own eyes. How happy that my lord, knowing before what was about to take place, prayed to the gods and Buddhas to shorten his life; and would that I, Sadayoshi, had then accompanied him to the other world; for now I have vainly lived thus long only that this affliction might come upon me. I beseech you that, when I come to die, you, my master, will come to meet me and guide me to the same Buddha land." Thus weeping he communed with his master in the far off land, and then, sending the bones to Kōya-san, he threw the earth of the tomb into the river Kamo, after which he took his way in the opposite direction toward the Eastern Provinces, thinking he could rely on Utsunomiya to assist him in return for the kindness shown him by the Heike in former years. Now all the Heike lords of high rank from Munemori downwards, with the exception of Koremori, had taken their wives and children with them, but as this was not possible with those of lower rank, they had had to leave them behind in the city, not knowing when they would see them again. Whenever people leave their family, even when the day and the hour of their return are fixed exactly, the parting is always sad; how much more on an occasion like this, when they took leave of each other for perhaps the last time, were the sleeves of both those who went and those who stayed moistened with their tears. So old and young were fain to set forth, looking backwards always with longing eyes, for how could they forget the intimate ties of their ancestors or the benefits themselves had enjoyed in later days? Some made the journey by sea, braving the dangers of the troubled waves, while others went by land; some on horseback and some rowing in boats, each than leaving his Home in the way he thought best.

Chapter XIX.

THE HEIKE AT FUKUHARA.

When the Heike arrived at their former capital of Fukuhara Munemori called together the most trusty retainers, old and young, to the number of several hundred, and addressed them thus: "Since the results of the good deeds of our house are now exhausted and those of its evil actions predominate, we have thus been abandoned by the gods and compelled to flee the Capital, to wander like homeless vagrants, deserted even by the Hō-ō. On whom then can we rely? Even when people take shelter under the same tree, it is from some connexion in a former life. and when they stoop to drink from the same stream their Karma relation is not slight, so you are not mere casual dependants, but hereditary retainers of our house; some bound by the ties of close relationship, some by gratitude for the bounty of many generations. Let each of you consider how many were the benefits he received in the days gone by, in the time of the prosperity of our house, and will you not now repay this favour? Moreover, seeing that we are escorting the Sovereign possessing the Ten Virtues, and carrying with him the Three Sacred Treasures, must we not stand by His Majesty to the last, to the most inaccessible mountain or the remotest plain?" Then his hearers, controlling their emotion, replied with one voice: "When birds and animals know how to repay kindness, how should we rational men forget it? It is the part of the warrior to be ashamed of double dealing, and it is but by the favour of the Taira house that for the last twenty years we have supported our families. Therefore will we follow our August Lord the Emperor even beyond the confines of this Realm of Nippon, yea, even to Kikai, Kōrai, or Keitan, to the farthest boundaries of sky and sea." At these words Munemori and all the Heike felt some confidence return to them.

That night the exiles spent at Fukuhara. The sky was clear and calm, and the bow shaped new moon of autumn shone brightly. As they lay on their grassy couches, in doubt whether they should ever again behold this scene, their pillows were damp with both dew and tears. When they looked round upon the many buildings of the new capital that the Lay priest Chancellor had erected, the pavilion on the hill for flower viewing in springtime, the mansion by the sea for the moon viewing of autumn, the mansion of the bubbling spring, the pavilion of the pine tree shade, the resort for horse racing, the lofty palace of two stories, the snow viewing palace, the houses of the various retainers, the newly built Imperial Palace which had been designed by Gōjō-Dainagon Kunitsuna-no-Kyō with its glistening tiles and mosaic pavements, in the short space of three years the roads were all thickly mossed and the gates closed by the autumn grasses, while on the tiles the pines were sprouting and ivy clustered thickly on the walls. Over the mossy terraces only the pine breeze blew; the curtains were gone and the bed chambers lay open to view, but only the moon beams cared to enter. The next day, after setting fire to the Palace of Fukuhara, they escorted His Majesty to his ship and all set sail. Though not as painful as when they left the Capital behind, this parting also wrung their hearts with grief. The smoky torches that were kindled by the fisherman; the calling of the deer at dawn at Once; the sound of the waves beating on the shore; the shadows of the moon on their long sleeves; the shrilling crickets among the grasses; every sound and sight that fell on their eye and ear was melancholy, and there was nothing that did not deepen their sorrow. Yesterday they stood at the eastern frontier with ten myriads of horsemen; to-day they weigh anchor on the western sea with but seven thousand followers. Calmly the clouds float over the waves, and the blue sky slowly darkens; the evening mist drifts over the lonely islets and the moon comes up over the waters, and so the ships plough their way over the boundless ocean toward their far distant haven. As the days pass the Capital recedes farther and farther from their vision and has become as it were beyond the clouds. Even thoughts of their far off home did but cause fresh tears, the one thing that seemed to have no end. When they saw a flock of white seabirds swooping over the waves, they remembered the question of Arihara-no-Narihira that he asked at the Sumida river, and the beloved name Miyako-dori, or Bird of Miyako, held a melancholy interest for them. It was on the twenty fifth day of the seventh month of the second year of Ju-ei that the Heike fled from the Capital.

Volume VIII.

Chapter I.

On the twenty fourth day of the seventh month of the second year of Ju-ei at midnight, the Hō-ō, accompanied only by Uma no kami Suketoki, the son of Azechi no Dainagon Sukekata-no-Kyō, fled secretly from the Palace and escaped to Kurama; but as the priests of the temple thought it was rather too near to the Capital to be safe, he again removed, and, after braving the hard and dangerous path over the mountains by Shino no mine and Yakuō-saka, he arrived at the small temple of Jakujō-bō at Gedatsu-dani at Yokogawa. When the priests of Hieizan heard of this, they pressed him to proceed to the Hall of the Eastern Pagoda of Enryakuji, so His Majesty took up his abode at Minami-dani Enyū-bō, which was forthwith designated the Imperial Palace, and strictly guarded by their monks and samurai. Thus the Hō-ō fled from his Palace and went to Hieizan, and the Emperor left the

Palace of the Phoenix Gate for the Western Ocean, while the Sesshō took refuge in the recesses of Yoshino, and the Imperial Ladies concealed themselves at Hachiman, Kamo, Saga, and Uzumasa, and other remote places in the hills to the east and west of the city. As the Heike had fled and the Genji had not yet entered, the Capital was thus without a Lord, a thing that had never been known from the beginning of time. In the book of the Prophecies of Shotoku Taishi, wonderful to relate, these things are written.

As soon as it was known that the Hō-ō was holding his Court on Hieizan, all the former Courtiers and officials came flocking round him: the former Kwampaku Motofusa, the Sesshō Motomichi, the Dajō-daijin Moronaga, the Sadaijin and Udaijin and Naidaijin, the Dainagon and Saishō, all the Courtiers of the Third, Fourth, and Fifth Ranks; everyone who was anyone, and who desired place, office, or promotion, presented himself; none were wanting. So great was the number of those who crowded to the Enyū-bō that neither in the upper or lower chambers, nor within or without the gate was any vacant space at all to be found. Great was the prosperity of Hieizan through the presence of this Imperial Abbot.

On the twenty eighth day of the same month the Hō-ō deigned to return to the Capital. He was escorted by Kiso Yoshinaka with fifty thousand horsemen, and Yamamoto no Kwanja Yoshitaka of the Ōmi Genji rode at the head of the procession bearing the white banner of the Minamoto. It was indeed a strange sight for the people of Miyako to see again the white banner in their streets, where for more than twenty years it had not waved. Jurō Kurando Yukiie with many thousand horsemen crossed the Uji bridge and entered the Capital, while Yada-no-Hangwan dai Yosihikiyo, son of Mutsu-no-Shin Hangwan Yoshiyasu, entered it from Ōyeyama. Besides these the Genji of Settsu and Kawachi came in also from that direction, so that the Capital was filled to overflowing with the Genji warriors.

Then Kade-no-koji Chūnagon Tsunefusa-on-Kyō and Kebiishi-no-Bettō Saemon-no-kami Saneie called Yoshinaka and Yukiie to the verandah of the Hō-ō's Palace. Kiso was wearing a suit of armour laced with Chinese brocade over a hitatare of red silk, and a sword exquisitely ornamented with gold and silver. His quiver held twenty four arrows with black and white spotted feathers, and he carried a bow of black lacquer with red binding, and he took off his helmet and hung it from his shoulder cord as he knelt down and made low obeisance. Jurō Kurando Yukiie wore a hitatare of dark blue brocade and his armour was laced with black, while his sword was decorated in lacquer of the same colour. He carried a quiver of twenty four arrows with white feathers having a black bar across them, and his bow was lacquered black over the binding. He too doffed his helmet and hung it from his shoulder as he made his obeisance. Having been bidden to subdue the former Naidaijin Munemori and all the Heike family, they both again made obeisance and retired. As they both intimated to the Court that they had no place to lodge, Kiso was given the Nishi-no-dōin in Rokujō, the residence of Daizen-nc-taiyū Naritada, while the Southern Hall of the Hojijiden called the Kaya Palace was appointed for Yukiie. The Hō-ō was exceedingly grieved that the Emperor should have been thus rapt away by his maternal relations the Taira Nobles, and that he should be tossed about on the waves of the Western sea, and therefore sent his Imperial Command to the West that they should immediately send him back with the Three Sacred Treasures safe to the Capital. But the Heike paid no heed.

Now there were three Princes, sons of the late Emperor Takakura, beside the Emperor, but as the Heike had also taken the middle one with them in order to make him Crown Prince, there were only two remaining in the Capital. So on the fifth day of the eighth month the Hō-ō proceeded to the Palace where they were being brought up. On his calling to him the third Prince, aged five, the child began to cry in a fretful manner so that the Ho o bade them take him away again, but when the fourth son, who was then four years old, was brought into the Imperial Presence, he immediately got upon the knees of the Hō-ō and nestled up to him affectionately. The eyes of the Hō-ō became filled with tears as he said: "See how he comes affectionately to an old monk like me that he does not know! He is my grandson indeed; he is just like the late Emperor when he was a child; I have never had such a charming remembrance of him till now." Then Jōdōji-noNii-dono, who was then known as Tango-dono, being in attendance on His Majesty asked: "Is it then decided that this Prince shall be appointed to succeed to the Throne?" To which the Hō-ō replied that it should certainly be so. The oracles were then consulted privately and the response was given that if the Fourth Prince should succeed to the Throne his descendants would rule Nippon for a hundred generations. The mother of this Prince was the daughter of Shichijiō Shūri-no-taiyū Nobutaka-no-Kyō, who was one of the Ladies in waiting of the Empress, and had been much favoured by the late Emperor, so that she had borne him many children. This Nobutaka no Kyo had many daughters and greatly wished that one of them might become an Imperial Consort, and having heard that if anyone kept a thousand white fowls he would certainly have a daughter who would become Imperial Consort, lie provided himself with a thousand white birds forthwith, and perhaps this was the reason that his daughter bore so many Princes. Nobutaka was extremely pleased in his heart, but as he feared the Heike and was anxious about the Empress he did nothing about them, bu: Hachijō-no-Nii-dono, the wife of Kiyomori, reassured him, saying that there was nothing to fear, and that she would herself see to their bringing up and would make one of them Crown Prince. So she provided many milk nurses for them and had them under her care. So it happened that this Fourth Prince was adopted by the elder brother of the Niidono, Hōshōji-no-Shugyo Nōen Hōin, and this Hōin went down with the Heike to the Western Provinces, leaving his wife and the child in the Capital.

Soon afterwards, however, he sent a messenger from thence asking her to bring the little Prince to him, and his wife, much rejoiced, started out with him and had gone as far as West Shichijō, when her elder brother, Kii-no-kami Norimitsu, stopped her, saying that it was a foolish thing to do, for now fortune was likely to favour the little Prince; and it was on the next day the Hō-ō came to see him. On this account Norimitsu expected that he would be appointed to some office, but time went on and his wishes were not realized, so at last in his disappointment he wrote these two verses and sent them to the Court:

"*Does not the cuckoo sing at least one note of remembrance, of the midnight glade where he was nurtured of old?*"
"*Pity the poor tomtit, for lonely if free in the mountains, much he envies the day when he was still in his cage.*"

The Emperor, who had not till then thought of the condition of Norimitsu, was touched by his case and promoted him to the Upper Third Rank.

Chapter II.

NATORA.

On the tenth day Kiso Yoshinaka was appointed Sama-on-kami, and was presented with the fief of the province of Echizen, beside having the title of Asahi Shōgun, or Rising Sun General, bestowed on him by Imperial Edict. Jūro Kurando Yukiie was presented with the province of Bingo and entitled Bingo-no-kami at the same time. As Yoshinaka, however, disliked the province of Echizen he was given that of Iyo instead, and Yukiie also, being dissatisfied with Bingo, received Bizen in its place. Moreover some ten more of the Genji were appointed captains of the Kebiishi and Imperial Guard of the Efu and Emon. On the sixteenth day the former Naidaijin Munemori and all his family, a hundred and sixty in all, were deprived of their offices and' their names erased from the Court List. Among them, however, the names of Hei Dainagon Tokitada-no-Kyō and his two sons, Kura-no-kami Nobumoto and Sanuki-no-Chūjō Tokizane were not erased, and this was because orders were being frequently sent to these three officials to bring back the Emperor and the Three Sacred Treasures to the Capital.

On the seventeenth day the Heike reached Dazaifu in the district of

Mikasa of the province of Chikuzen. Kikuchi-no-Jirō Takanao, who had gone down with them from the Capital, now, under the pretext of going on in front to open the barrier at Otsuyama, crossed over the province of Higo and retired into his own stronghold, from which he did not come forth in space of repeated injunctions. Beside this, of all the men of the two. islands of Kyūshū who were bidden to join the Heike, not one appeared with the exception of Okura Tanenao of Iwado. On the eighteenth day the Heike arrived at Anrakuji, where the Courtiers spent the whole night in composing poems and Renga. On this occasion Hon-sammi Chūjō Shigehira made a verse that brought tears to the eyes of all:

"One of the gods[234] once knew the longing we feel for Miyako,
Parted like us from the land where for so long he had dwelt."

On the twentieth day, by an Imperial Edict of the Hō-ō, the Fourth Prince was proclaimed Emperor in the Kan-in Palace. The Sesshō remained as before, for Motomichi continued in office, and the Chiefs of Departments and Kurando also returned to their posts. The milk nurse of the Third Prince shed tears of regret, but it was of no avail.

"In heaven[235] there are not two suns, and in a country there are not two sovereigns;" is an ancient saying, but now, through the evil deeds of the Heike, there were two Emperors one in the Capital and one in the country. In ancient times Montoku Tennō, who died in twenty third day of the eighth month of the second year of Ten-an, had many sons who wished to succeed to the Throne, and who offered up prayers in secret to that effect. The eldest, Prince Koretaka, who was also called Prince Kinohara, was an exceedingly wise prince, learned in all matters of importance to one who would govern a country, and therefore seemed to all worthy of succeeding to the Throne, but the second, Prince Korehito, was the son of the Lady Some dono, the daughter of the Kwampaku Fujiwara. Yoshifusa, and so had the support of the whole of the Fujiwara family. It was thus a very difficult question to decide. On the one side was a wise and learned Crown Prince; on the other a Minister most potent in all the affairs of state. Both were much to be pitied, and everybody was greatly perplexed The priest who prayed for Prince Koretaka was Kaki-no-moto Ki-Sōjō Shinzei, the greatest man in the temple of Tōji, and a disciple of Kōbō Daishi, while on the side of Prince Korehito was Eiryō Kwashō of Hieizan, the chaplain of the Kwampaku Yoshifusa, a priest by no means inferior to him in any way. Everyone said it would be difficult to settle the matter, and when the

---

[234] One of the gods. i.e. Tenjin, the deified Sugawara-no-Michizane, who was exiled to Kyushu and died there.
[235] *In heaven*, etc. From the Li Chi. 禮記.

Emperor died and a Council of Courtiers was held to say who should succeed him, as all the Ministers maintained each his own opinion and refused to listen to anyone else, the deliberation became a mere wordy warfare, and at last it was decided to settle it according to the result of a horse race and a wrestling match; the Throne to go to the side that was successful. So on the second day of the ninth month both the Princes proceeded in state to the race course of Ukon-no-baba, and all the Courtiers gathered there apparelled in their gayest costumes, making a scene of unimaginable brilliance and splendour. In two long lines on either side of the course the supporters of each Prince were drawn up, with beating hearts and hands clasped tightly together, anxiously awaiting the result of this most unparalleled contest.' Nor must the priests and their prayers be passed over. Shinsei Sōjō set up his altar at Toji, while Eiryō Kwashō set up his at the temple of Shingon in within the Palace, and thinking that if it was reported that he had died, Shinsei would relax his zeal somewhat, Eiryō put it about that he was dead, while he applied himself to his orisons with redoubled vigour. Then the horse races began, and out of ten races the first four were won by the elder Prince Koretaka, but the next six fell to the party of Prince Korehito. After this the wrestling match was held, and a certain Natora Uemon-no-kami, a doughty champion who possessed the strength of sixty men, stood forth on behalf of Prince Koretaka. On the side of the younger Prince appeared Yoshio Shōshō, a small and delicate looking man, who looked as if the other might throw him with one hand. He was chosen, however, because the Prince had had a supernatural dream in which he was bidden to select him. So Natora and Yoshio faced each other, and after feinting a little retired. Then they engaged again and Natora, gripping Yoshio, lifted him off his feet and flung him a distance of twenty feet away. But he came down on his feet and did not fall to the ground. Then Yoshio in his turn sprang at Natora and tried to throw him, but owing to the great size of his opponent he was in danger of being borne down from above, and seemed about to be overcome. On seeing this, a crowd of the retainers of Some dono, the mother of the second Prince, rushed to the Palace in a throng thick as the teeth of a comb, and cried out: "Our side is like to lose; what shall we do?" Then Eiryo Kwasho, who was repeating mystic prayers and incantations of mighty efficacy, frenzied at their failure, seized his Tokko,[236] and, dashing his head open with it, took some of his brains, pounded them and mixed them with milk, and putting them in the sacred 'Goma' fire, raised a thick black smoke, wrestling so mightily in prayer that at last Yoshio won the contest. Thus did the second Prince Korehito succeed to the Throne, to be known thenceforth as Seiwa

---

[236] Tokko. The Vadjra or mace of Indra. Emblem of the power to destroy evil, used by Shingon priests in their ritual.

Tennō, and afterwards also as Mizu-o-no-Tennō. And so thereafter the priests of Hieizan would often say; "When Eiryō dashed out his brains the second son was made Emperor, and when Son-i[237] wielded the sword of wisdom the curse of Tenjin was overcome." Thus we may understand the power of the Law of Buddha, but beside that everyone considered that it was according to the will cf Tensho-daijin.

Chapter III.

THE EMPEROR PROCEEDS TO USA.

When the Heike in Tsukushi heard of this, they all exclaimed: "Ah, if we had only brought the third and fourth Princes with us also!" "Even if we had done so," said Hei Dainagon Tokitada-no-Kyō, "there is the son of Prince Takakura whom his guardian Sanuki-no-kami Shigehide made a monk and brought to the North Country; for Kiso Koshinaka has had his vows revoked and brought him with him to the Capital with the intention of placing him on the Throne." But the others objected, saying: "How is it possible for a Prince whose vows have been revoked to succeed to the Throne?" "Of a surety it is possible," replied Tokitada, "for in other countries there are precedents for it, and in this country also, when Temmu Tennō was Crown Prince, he was attacked by Prince Ōtomo and cut off his hair and retired to Mount Yoshino; but after Prince Ōtomo had been overthrown lie came back again and ascended the Throne. Kōken Tennō also was moved by the Buddha-mind to lay aside his dignity and become a recluse, changing his name to Hokini, but afterwards he resumed the Throne as Shōtoku Tennō. Therefore there is no reason why Kiso should not make this Prince Emperor in spite of his revoked vows."

On the third day of the ninth month an envoy was sent to Ise from the Court. He was the Sangi Naganori. There have been three examples of Retired Emperors sending envoys to Ise, namely the Emperors Shujaku, Shirakawa and Toba; but in their case it was done before they became recluses; so that this is the first example of sending one after retirement.

The Heike thought to establish a capital in Tsukushi, and a Council of Courtiers was held, but they could not decide the matter. The Emperor was then residing at the house of Okura-no-Tanenao of Iwado, while the others lodged among the fields and farms: though they did not wear garments of hemp, as the poet says, yet they certainly lived in a rustic way. As the Palace was thus in the wilds, it was but a Log-Palace, but even so there was something about it that was most

---

[237] Son-i. Zasshu of Hieizan who appeared the wrath of the god Tenjin, which tie manifesto striking the Palace with lightning in the eighth year of En-cho.

dignified. So the Emperor again proceeded to the shrine of Usa. Here the apartments of the Dai guji served as the Imperial Lodging, while the Courtiers lived in the main building of the shrine, and the officials of the fifth and sixth ranks in the side galleries. Around them in the courtyard were encamped the samurai of Shikoku and Kyūshū in serried ranks of mail-clad warriors. The ancient vermilion of the shrine fence seemed to renew its youthful brilliance at the unwonted honour. After sleeping seven nights in the shrine the Daijin Munemori had a dream. The doors of the Inner Shrine opened and in a mighty voice these words boomed forth

> *"Are not these painful misfortunes a sign of the anger of heaven?*
> *Why then do you thus earnestly pray to the gods?"*

Munemori, confounded and cast into the depths of gloom and anxiety, murmured to himself the words of the ancient verse:

> *Thinking of this my heart, in tune with the voice of the insects,*
> *Feebler and feebler grows; autumn is waning indeed.*

So they returned to Dazaifu. It was now about the tenth day of the ninth month. The evening blasts howled over the Hagi leaves, and as they slept in their day garments their sleeves were wet with tears, so hard to endure was this rough journey in the dreary days of fading autumn. The moon of the thirteenth day of the ninth month was the famous moon of autumn, but as they thought of their present state, and remembered the moon as it shone on the Court in their Ancient Capital in the days of their grandeur, their eyes grew blurred so that they could only behold it through a mist. On this occasion Satsuma-no-kami Tadanori, Shūri-no-taiyū Tsunemori, and Kōgō-gū-no-suke Tsunemasa made these three stanzas:

> *"Those with whom last year we viewed the moon at Miyako*
> *On this self-same night, fondly are thinking of us,"*
> *"This is the moon that last year we gazed at together, beloved*
> *Recollections of you hover about me to-night."*
> *"Here the dew never dries on these sad fields of our exile.*
> *On what undreamed of shore come we to gaze on the moon."*

Chapter IV.

THE BALL OF THREAD.

The province of Bungo was the fief of Gyōbu-kyō Sammi Yorisuke, and he had installed his son Yoritsune Ason in it as Deputy, but he sent messengers from the Capital to Yoritsune informing him that the Heike had been forsaken by the powers of heaven and abandoned by the Emperor, so that they had fled the city and were now exiles tossed hither and thither by the waves of the sea. It was best therefore that the people of Kyūshū should neither receive them, nor have any dealings with them, and the province of Bungo should cast off its allegiance and join the Genji of the East and North, driving them away from the islands of Kyūshū. This order Yoritsune made known to Ogata[238] Saburō Koreyoshi; now of this Koreyoshi's ancestry a fearsome story was told. In a certain mountain village of the province of Bungo, there lived in ancient days a man who had an only daughter, and though she was not yet married, someone used to visit her every night, so that in the course of time she became pregnant Her mother, thinking this strange, asked her what kind of a person it was that came to her. "I only see him come," said the maiden, but I never know when he returns." "In that case" replied the mother, "fasten something to him, and tie a thread to it that we tray know." So the damsel, in obedience to her mother's behest, stuck a needle into the collar of the light bloc Kariginu that her lover wore, to which was affixed the end of a ball of thread. Following this to see where it led, the girl and some companions crossed right over the province of Bungo until they camp to the borders of Hyūga. There they found that it went into the mouth of a great cave at the foot of a peal; called Uba-ga-take. Then the girl, standing at the mouth of the cave, cried out with a loud voice to the inmate: "It is I, who have come thus far that I might look on your face." At this, from the cave came forth the response: "My form is no human shape, and if you saw it your senses would depart with amazement The child you will bear will be a son, and in the two islands of Kyūshū there shall be none to equal him; with sword or bow." The girl, however, was, not convinced, and again addressed him: "Whatever form you mad have," she pleaded, "if you have not forgotten our long attachment, I pray you let me see you this once at least." Then from out of the cave in an answer to her request there crawled forth a monstrous snake, fourteen or fifteen feet long, swaying and quivering as it carne.

---

[238] There is a variant of the story of this Japanese Cupid and Psyche in the Kojiki, where it is told of the deity of Miwa, Ōkuni-nushi-no-mikoto, from whom it is said the family of Ogata derived their descent. Takachiho is the mountain in Hyūga upon which Ninigi-no-mikoto alighted when he came down to Japan from the Takama-ga-hara.

The damsel swooned with horror and surprise on seeing it, and the companions who had accompanied her shrieked with fear and fled in all directions, The needle that she had stuck in the collar of her lover was seen to stick out from the windpipe of the snake.

The girl returned to her home and not long after was delivered of a son, who was given to her grandfather to bring up, and who grew so fast that before he was yet ten years old he was huge of body and long of face. At the age of seven he made his Genpuku, and was called Daida on account of his grandfather whose name was Daidayū. As during both winter and summer his hands and feet were covered with chaps, he was nicknamed Chapped Daida. And this Daida was the ancestor of Koreyoshi in the fifth generation; and since Koreyoshi was the descendant of such a formidable hero, when he sent round the order of the Governor, saying that it was an Edict of the Retired Emperor, all the chief men in Kyūshū obeyed him. And the monstrous serpent is said to be the manifestation of the deity of Takachiho who is worshipped in the province of Hyūga.

Chapter V.

THE FLIGHT FROM DAZAIFU.

Thus though the Heike proposed to establish a capital in Tsukushi and build there an Imperial Palace, and a Council of Courtiers was held to consider it, yet, on account of the hostile attitude of Ogata Koreyoshi, the plan could not be carried out. Then the Chūnagon Tomomori gave his opinion thus: "Seeing that this Ogata Koreyoshi was a retainer of the house of Shigemori, if one of that family were to go and see him something might be arranged." In accordance with this advice, which, they considered reasonable, Shin sammi Chūjō Sukemori set forth with five hundred horsemen, and, crossing the Province of Bungo, entered into negotiations with Koreyoshi; but, in spite of all his persuasions Ogata paid no heed, but on the other hand drove them away again, saying: "I ought to seize you all and make you prisoners, but in great matters small things are nothing, so you had better go back to Dazaifu and do what you please." A short time afterwards he sent his second son Nojiri Jirō Koremura to Dazaifu with a message, saying: "If the Heike were on the side of the Emperor, we would certainly doff our helmets and loose our bowstrings in submission, but the Hō-ō has ordered that you are to be expelled from Kyūshū at once." Then Hei Dainagon Tokitada-no-Kyō, clad in a hakama laced with scarlet thread and a hitatare of grass-cloth, and wearing a lofty eboshi on his head, advanced to meet Koremura and spake thus: "Our Emperor is descended in the direct line from forty nine generations of heavenly posterity, being the eighty first Earthly

Sovereign since Jimmu Tennō, therefore will Tensho-daijin and Hachiman Bosatsu protect our Lord from all his enemies. Moreover our house has from Hogen and Heiji to this day put down many rebellions, keeping the peace of the Realm, and by our favour were all the officials of Kyūshū appointed to their authority: but now, forgetting all the gratitude they owe us, they have believed the promises of the rebels of the East and North, Yoritomo and Yoshinaka, that, if they drive us out, they will receive many provinces and manors as a reward, and so have meanly acted according to the instructions of that big nose Bungo'.[239] (Now it was because Gyōbu-Kyō-Sammi Yorisuke, who held the fief of Bungo, had such a large nose, that he was thus spoken of). Koremura then returned and reported their answer to his father, who replied: "It may be so, but old times are old times and the present is the present, so now we must drive them out of Kyūshū." Then, hearing that Koreyoshi was gathering his forces, Gendaiyu Hangwan Suesada and Settsu Hangwan Morisumi, exclaiming; "Now we are hindered even by our friends; let us go and smite them;" took with them three thousand horsemen and, crossing over the province of Chikugo, met the enemy at Honjō of Takano and fought with them for a day and a night, but at last, owing to the great number of Koreyoshi's men, were forced to retire.

Then the Heike, hearing that Koreyoshi was advancing to attack them with thirty thousand men, fled in a panic from Dazaifu, without stopping to take anything with them. Bidding a reluctant farewell to the hospitable shrine of Tenjin, they hurried away, and as there were no proper bearers for the Imperial Phoenix Car, the Emperor was borne in an ordinary palanquin which was dignified with the name only. His Imperial Mother and all the noble ladies of her train had perforce to gather up the long skirts of their hakamas and wall: barefoot, as did also the Daijin Munemori and all the Courtiers and Nobles, lifting high their loose silk costumes.

And so they set out once more and made for the port of Hakozaki, while the rain fell in torrents and the gusts of wind blew the sand in all directions, and the rain-drops mingled with and simulated their tears. Praying to the deities of the shrines of Sumiyoshi, Hakozaki, Kashii and Munakata, they made supplication that the Emperor might again return to his own Capital. After enduring the steep and dangerous climb over the cliffs and rough rocks of Tarumiyama and Uzurahama, they emerged on to the wide sandy plain, and the blood that flowed from their feet, so unaccustomed to any toil, dyed the sand, deepening the colour of the scarlet hakamas of some, while it reddened to a scarlet hue the white skirts of others. Even the trials of Genzo,[240] when he travelled over lofty mountains and shifting sands from China to India to

---

[239] big-nose. Bungo. Jap. Hana-Bungo.
[240] Genzo. Chin. Hiuen Tsiang.

seek the Holy Pitakas, were not more severe, but as he was in quest of the Sacred Sutras he endured them for his own benefit and that of mankind; this was but the way to the trials of battle that they trod, the melancholy road to the other word.

Now Harada-no-taiyū Tanenao had accompanied, them from Miyako with a force of two thousand men, but when Hyōtōji Hidetō came forth from his hold of Yamaga to meet them with a large force, since there was bitter enmity between the two, Tanenao left them and turned back again. As they were proceeding on their way they passed through a village that went by the name of Ashiya, and as this was the name of a place between Miyako and Fukuhara that they all knew well, it pleased them more than other places, though it made them the more homesick. So, though they had declared themselves ready to go to Shinra, Keitan, Kōrai, and other distant regions beyond the sea, yet meeting this wild weather they were glad to take refuge in Yamaga, the stronghold of Hyōtōji Hidetō. Hearing again, however, that the enemy was advancing on them there also, they fled once mere, and, embarking in small boats, voyaged all night till they came to the port of Yanagi-ga-ura in Buzen. Here again they meditated on fixing their new capital, and a Council of Courtiers was held about it, but as their mans would not permit of building a Palace, and also because they heard tidings that the Genji were threatening them from Nagato, they again put to sea in fishing boats to be tossed hither and thither on the ocean. Now the third son of Shigemori, Sa-Chūjō Kiyotsune, was of a meditative nature and much given to deep thought; and as he stood by the gunwale of the ship one moonlight night of the tenth month, playing the flute and reciting verses, he reflected how the Capital was in the hands of the Genji, and now they had fled to Kyūshū they had been driven away by Koreyoshi, so that they were like fish caught in a net. If they were thus to be shunned wherever they went, of what profit to live any longer? So, calmly he chanted the solemn words of the Sutras and repeated the Nembutsu, after which he dropped from the ship and sank in the waves. Deep though unavailing was the lamentation among the Courtiers, both men and women alike.

As Nagato was the fief of Shin-Chūnagon Tomomori, the Mokudai Kii-no-Gyōbu-no-taiyū Michisuke, hearing that the Heike had nothing but small fishing boats, presented them with a hundred large vessels in which they re-embarked and sailed to Shikoku. There by the invitation of Awa-no-Mimbu Taiyū Shigeyoshi, on the seashore of Yashima in Sanuki, they built in rough timbers a representation of the Imperial Court and Palace; but, as they shrank from permitting His Majesty to inhabit such a common structure, it was decided that the real Palace should be a ship. Munemori and the Courtiers had to spend their days in the thatched huts of the fishermen, while they passed the nights on shipboard. Thus the Imperial Vessel floated like a dragon on the waves, a moving Palace that knew no rest. Plunged in sorrow deep as the tide, their lives were frail as the frosted grasses. At dawn the clamour of the sea birds on the spits increased their anguish, and at night the grating of the ships on the beach tormented them. When they saw the flocks of herons in the distant pines, their hearts sank, wondering if they were the white flags of the Genji; and when the cry of the wild geese were wafted from the offing, they trembled lest it might be the oar beats of the foe by night. The keen breeze lashed their blackened eyebrows and painted faces, and the salt spray penetrated their delicate eyes, which home sick longing filled so oft with tears. For their green-curtained chambers of scarlet they had exchanged the earthen walls of the reed-hung cottage, and instead of the scented smoke of their braziers rose the briny fumes of the fisherman's driftwood. The features of the Court Ladies, bereft of cosmetics and swollen with continual weeping, were so altered as hardly to be recognised.

Chapter VI.

YORITOMO PROCLAIMED OUTLAW QUELLING SHOGUN.

To continue; since the martial reputation of Hyōye-no-suke Yoritomo of Kamakura seas now supreme, the title of Sei-i Shōgun was conferred upon him by Imperial Edict, and Sa-shisho Nakahara Yasusada was appointed as Envoy to convey it. On the fourth day of the tenth month Yasusada arrived at Kamakura. "Since it is in acknowledgement of my reputation for military prowess that I receive this title," declared Yoritomo, "it is well that I receive it at the shrine of the god of battles, Hachiman Dai-Bosatsu. Now the shrine of Hachiman at Tsuru-ga-oka is, as to its site, exactly as that of Iwashimizu in the Capital, and is built with long galleries and a two-storied gate, while the paved avenue that leads up to its lofty seat is more than ten chō in length. As to who should receive the Imperial Edict, it was decided, after a consultation, that the privilege should be given to Miura-no-suke Yoshizumi. He was of the stock of Miura-no-heita Tametsugu, famed as a mighty warrior in all the Kwantō, and as his father Ōsuke had fallen in battle for Yoritomo, this honour would shed lustre on his spirit in the gloom of the Yellow Springs of death. With Yasusada came two of his house and ten retainers, and Miura took also the same number of followers. Those of Miura's household were Hiki-no-Toshirō Yoshikazu and Wada-no-Saburō Munezane, while his retainers were all great lords, each fully equipped for the occasion. He himself was arrayed in a hitatare of dark blue and armour laced with black silk. His sword was mounted in black lacquer, and in his quiver were twenty four black and white feathered arrows; he carried his Shigetō bow under his arm, and hung his helmet over his shoulder and bowed low as he received the Imperial Edict. To the formal enquiry of the Envoy: "Who is it who is present to receive this Edict? Let him declare his name and titles;" Miura, seemingly abashed to proclaim his master's name, gave his own: "Miura-no-Arajirō Yoshizumi." He then received the Edict in a casket and presented it to Yoritomo, who returned it again after a short interval. Yasusada thinking it rather heavy, opened it, and found that it contained gold dust to the value of a hundred ryō. Yasusada was then entertained at a banquet in the Haiden of the shrine, and waited upon by officials of high rank. He was also presented with three horses, one of which, fully apparelled, was led forward by Kudō Ichirō Suketsune. A special lodging, built in ancient style, thatched with rushes, was provided for him, with a clothes chest containing two suits of bedding of thick cotton and ten sets of lined garments. He received, moreover, a thousand rolls of white linen with patterns of indigo. The cups and dishes that he used were also of the most rich and beautiful description.

The next day he paid a visit to Yoritomo in his own mansion, which was guarded within and without by samurai. Outside were ranged his own household retainers on bended knee, while within, on the upper dais, sat all the Genji lords, succeeded by all the lords of the Kwantō, great and small, in the lower seats. Yasusada was seated among the lords of the Genji, and, after a while, was introduced into an inner chamber lard with fine mats with borders of Korai brocade of black and white, the adjoining verandah being also laid with similar mats with an edging of purple. When the Envoy had taken his seat there, a curtain was raised, disclosing Yoritomo himself. He was attired in a plain Court robe and a high eboshi. His stature was small, though his face was large; his features were handsome and his speech clear and distinct. "The Heike," he began, "in fear of my might have fled from Miyako, and now, strangely enough, Kiso Yoshinaka and Jūro Kurando Yukiie have forced their way into the city receiving Court Rank and choosing provinces for themselves in virtue of my exploits. Moreover Hidehira of Mutsu has been appointed Mutsu no-kami, and Satake-no-Kwanja leas been made Hitachi-no-kami, by no means according to my will. I wish therefore that an Imperial Edict be issued giving me authority to subdue them." "For that I will go surety," replied the Envoy, "and though now I am only carrying out the Imperial Command, when I return to the Capital I will see that it is done. My younger brother, Shi-no-Taiyū Shigeyoshi will also assist me." "In the position I now am," replied Yoritomo, with a contemptuous smile, "sureties are hardly needed, but I shall know if you do as you say." Yasusada had declared that he wished to start back again for the Capital on that very day, but he was persuaded to remain until the morrow. The next day he again repaired to the mansion of Yoritomo. He was then presented with a body armour laced with green silk, a sword mounted in silver, a Shigetō bow of red and black lacquer with a set of arrow, and thirteen horses, three of them saddled. His twelve followers also received a complete equipment each, comprising, hitatare, kosode, okuchi hakama, horsy and weapons. The number of the horses that he received amounted in all to three hundred. Moreover from the time that they left Kamakura until they reached the boundary of Omi, at each stopping-place they were provided with ten koku of rice, an amount that was not only more than sufficient for their own use, but enabled them to give generously in charity.

Chapter VI.

CONCERNING NEKOMA.

As soon as Yasusada returned to the Capital lie presented himself at the Palace of the Hō-ō, and, sitting down humbly in the courtyard, reported all that had taken place in the East. The Hō-ō was struck with admiration at all he heard, and the faces of all the Cōurtiers and Nobles were wreathed in smiles, for this s gallant behaviour of Yoritomo was very different from that of Kiso Yoshinaka who was now protector of the Capital. He was of fair complexion and handsome appearance, it is true, but his manners and way of speaking were rough and unpolished in the extreme. For this indeed there was good reason; for how could anyone be other who had been brought up from the age of two until over thirty in the wild mountain country of Kiso? The following incident may show his rudeness. There was a certain Courtier called Nekoma-no-Chūnagon Mitsutaka-no-Kyō, who had something to say to Yoshinaka, so he sought him at his mansion. On his entering a retainer announced: "Nekoma-dono has deigned tc arrive." On hearing this Yoshinaka burst into a loud laugh; "Do cats (neko) call on people here?" he asked. "It is a Courtier named Nekoma-no-Chūnagon-dono, Your Excellency," replied the retainer "Oh, then admit him," returned Yoshinaka, and after a while, not using his proper name Nekoma, he called out in his rough dialect: "It is now the feeding time for Neko-dono, bring in the meal!" And although the Chūnagon politely declined, Kiso pressed him, saying: "Oh, but I have some 'unsalted' mushrooms; come along;" thinking, in his ignorance that the epithet 'unsalted' meant 'fresh' when used of anything, though it can only be properly applied to fish. Nenoi-no-Koyata served them at the meal, and large deep bowls piled high with food, such as are used in the country, were set before them; and beside the three side dishes eaten with the rice there were mushrooms boiled in broth. Kiso seized his chop sticks and began to eat heartily, but the Chūnagon, whose palate revolted at this coarse rustic food, could not eat anything. "Perhaps you think my bowls are not clean," said Yoshinaka, "but these are the ones I use for

ceremonially pure meals, so pray don't be afraid to eat." Being thus
pressed, and fearing it would give offence if he touched nothing, the
Chūnagon took up his chop-sticks and pretended to eat, merely toying
with the food. Kiso, noticing this, laughed boisterously "Neko-dono has
a very small appetite; don't stand on ceremony, have a good 'cat's
surfeit.' The Chūnagon, however, was quite upset by this treatment and
left again without even saying what he had intended.

On another occasion, when Yoshinaka went to the Palace of the
Hō-ō, thinking it not necessary to wear the official hitatare of a Courtier
of high rank, he hurriedly put on a ho-i and went in that, and the set of
his headdress, the way he managed his long sleeves and the hang of his
hakama were so awkward and clumsy that his whole appearance was
boorish and ridiculous in the extreme. How extraordinary was the
contrast to his imposing figure when on his horse and clad in complete
armour with his bow and arrows at his back. But this time he must
needs ride in an ox car, and he used one that belonged to Munemori,
with his ox-drivers and a very fine yoke of oxen. The oxen had not
been driven for a long time, and so were exceedingly spirited, and as
soon as they got out of the gate the ox drivers whipped them up so that
they started off at a gallop. The sudden jerk threw Yoshinaka off his
balance and he fell on his back inside the car, and as he lay there with
his wide sleeves spread out on each side of him, he looked like some
huge butterfly. He struggled to get up again, but somehow he could not
manage it, and though he shouted to the drivers to stop the car, they
misunderstood his rustic dialect, and thinking he was telling them to
hurry on, kept the animals at a gallop for five or six chō. Then Imai-no-
Shirō spurred on his horse and overtook them, shouting out: "What do
you mean by driving on in that way?" "The noses of the honourable
oxen are too strong to stop them," replied the ox drivers, and then,
wishing to help Kiso to right himself, they told him to hold on to the
handrail with which the car was furnished. "Ah, that's a good idea,"
exclaimed Yoshinaka as he did so, "I wonder whether the drivers
thought of it, or whether that is the way their master used to do." In this
way he reached the gate of the Palace, and when he came to alight he
made to do so from the back of the car, as he had got in. Seeing this the
servants corrected him, saying: "When your Excellency gets into on ox
car it is proper to get in at the back, but when alighting, it is proper to
do so from the front." "It is my car," replied Yoshinaka, "so I shall do
as I please;" and he got out at the back. Many other ridiculous things
Yoshinaka did also, but I hesitate to speak of them. The ox-drivers
were afterwards put to death.

Chapter VIII.

THE FIGHT AT MIZUSHIMA.

Meanwhile the Heike abode at Yashima in Sanuki, and from that place fought with and subdued the eight provinces of the Sanyōdō and the six of the Nankaidō districts, fourteen in all. Kiso therefore, feeling uneasy, despatched a force of seven thousand men to the Sanyodo under the command of Yada-no-Hangwan-dai Yoshikiyo, the son of Mutsu-no-Shin-Hangwan Yoshiyasu; Umeno-no-Yaheijirō Yukihiro of Shinano being the leader of the samurai. It was the first day of the tenth month when they arrived at Mizushima in Bitchu and set about launching their ships to cross over to Yashima, and as they were thus engaged a small boat came insight, rowing across from the other side. At first they thought it was only a fishing boat, but as they looked they saw that it was one of the enemy ships coming to spy out their position, or perhaps to negotiate. Immediately the Genji rushed their five hundred ships into the water with great haste and sailed to the attack. The Heike were then coming on to meet them with a fleet of a thousand vessels. Their commander was Shin-Chūnagon Tomomori-no-Kyō, with Noto-no-kami Noritsune as captain under him. The Heike ships were made fast alongside each other by hawsers from the stem and stern, and between these hawsers other rope were fastened, on which planks were stretched for walking, so that the whole fleet became like a level surface for the fighting men. As they were about to begin the onset, Noto-no-kami Noritsune cried out in a mighty voice: "Ho! men of Shikoku! how can you bear the shame of being taken alive by these boors of the North? Upon them ad grapple!" And so, shouting their warcry, they began the fight, drawing their bows and pouring in a hail of arrows until they came to close quarters, when they drew their swords and engaged each other hand to hand. Some also plied long iron rakes with which they pulled their opponents into the water, and some, locked in the death-grip, stabbed each other and fell into the waves. Thus the battle went on and there was no gap made in the Heike ships, but after a while Umeno-no-Yahei Yukihiro, who led the Genji samurai, was smitten to death. Then Yada-no-Hangwan Yoshikiyo, desperate at his fate, sprang into a small boat with six of his retainers and led a fierce attack on the very forefront of the battle, but all in vain, for his boat was capsized by the enemy and all in it were drowned. Now the Heike had brought their horses with them in the ships, and as they approached the shore they pushed them off into the water to swim to the beach. Since they were ready accoutred, as soon as they found a foothold the riders clambered into their saddles and rode them with a mighty splashing through the shallows to the shore, and five hundred horsemen, led by Noto-no-kami Noritsune, precipitated themselves on the Genji, who, discomfited by the death of both their leaders, fled headlong in confused panic. Thus by this victory of Mizushima the Heike wiped away the shame of their former defeat.

Chapter IX.

THE DEATH OF SENŌ.

When Kiso heard of this defeat he was filled with anxiety and at once rode off to the province of Bitchu with ten thousand horsemen. Now Senō-no-Tarō Kaneyasu of Bitchu, a partizan of the Heike and a famous warrior, had by ill luck been taken prisoner by Kuramitsu-no-Jirō Narizumi of Kaga in the fighting of the fifth month in the North Country, and would have been put to death but for the intervention of Yoshinaka, who told hill) that it was a pity to slay such a brave fellow. Narizumi accordingly put him in charge of his younger brother Saburō Nariuji, and as Senō was a man of fine character and easy manners he was very well treated. Still, as we read that even the men of old fretted their hearts when in exile in a far country, so his grief was not unlike that of So-shi-kei when he was imprisoned in the land of Ko, or of Ri-sho-kei when he was unable to return to the Court of Kan. Even as these Chinese warriors passed their days among the barbarians, "satisfying their hunger and thirst with sour milk and raw flesh," so Kaneyasu, abstaining even from sleep, spent his nights and days in continual planning how he might take his enemies by surprise and slay them and return to his former lord. At last he said to Kuramitsu-no-Saburō: "Since you have spared my worthless life and treated me thus, for whom beside should I have any thought? In the next battle it is on the side of Kiso that I will risk my life. Moreover, on my estate at Senō in Bitchu there grows fine fodder for horses in great abundance, and if you wish I can guide you there to take it." On this being told to Kiso he exclaimed: "Ah, I am sorry for that fellow; but go down and get the fodder at once." So Kuramitsu-no-Saburō taking thirty men with him went down to Bitchū accompanied by Senō. But Senō's eldest son Kotarō Muneyasu, also a supporter of the Heike, hearing that his father had been set free by Kiso, gathered about a hundred horsemen from among his younger retainers and set out to welcome him, meeting the party at Kōfu in the province of Harima. From thence the two bands went on together until they came to Mitsuishi in Bizen where they stopped for the night, and as the friends of Senō had brought a quantity of sake with them, they all sat down to a drinking bout in which the thirty retainers of Kuramitsu soon became heavily intoxicated, so that they could by no means stand upright whereupon Senō's men fell upon them and put them all to death. After this they set off to Kōfu, the

residence of the Deputy Governor of Bizen, who had been appointed by
Jūrō Kurando Yukiie, to whom Bizen had been given in fief, and
attacked and slew him. Then said Senō: "I have obtained my freedom
from Kiso Yoshinaka and come back home again; now let all who are
on the side of the Heike prepare to give battle to Yoshinaka when he
comes down here against us." So all the men-at-arms of the Provinces
of Bizen, Bitchū and Bingo armed themselves and came with their
horses and men to the support of the Heike, and even the old men who
had retired from active life put on again their faded yellow hitatare and
shortened their linen kosode, girding on their worn out and damaged
body armour and providing themselves with homemade quivers of
bamboo that held but few arrows. So there gathered to Senō's mansion
a force of some two thousand men, and these made a fort amid the
bamboo thickets and narrow field-paths at Fukuryūji in Bizen, digging
a moat twenty feet wide and the same number of feet deep, fortifying it
with barricades and defences of felled trees and building a high tower
within.

Now when the Deputy Governor of Bizen was slain, his men fled
toward the Capital, but at Funasakayama on the boundary of Bizen and
Harima they met Kiso and his army and told him what had occurred.
"Ah," exclaimed Yoshinaka in great wrath, "it was after all a pity that I
did not put him to death." "Indeed," replied Imai Shirō-Kanehira, "you
can see by his face he is no ordinary man, how many times did I not
urge you to put such a daring and formidable foe out of the way; at any
rate let me go after him and see what he is about to do now?" So Imai
galloped off to Bizen with three thousand men. Now the path that led to
Senō's stronghold at Fukuryūji was only about seven feet wide, while
its length was one ri as computed in the Western Provinces. On each
side of it were deep rice-fields where horses could get no foothold, so
that, although Imai's force pressed on hotly, their pace was hindered by
the crowding of their mounts.

Senō-no-Tarō, seeing Imai himself push forward at their head,
hasted to the top of the tower and cried out in a loud voice: "Pray
receive this as some slight return for your care of me while I was with
you!" and he emptied his whole quiver of twenty four arrows at them.
Paying no heed to this, however, Imai-no-Shirō, Miyazaki Saburō,
Umeno, Mochizuki, Suwa, Fujisawa and other valiant warriors, each
worth a thousand ordinary men, spurred forward to the onset and held
grimly on though many fell pierced by arrows, both men and horses.
One taking the place of another who fell, they bent low over their
horses heads, shielding themselves with the neck-pieces of their
helmets, and plunging recklessly through, the rice-fields till they sank
to the bellies of their steeds, heaving them up by the breast-strap of
their harness, and caring, nothing for the deepest morasses. So they
pressed on, shouting their war-cry and fearing nothing, till of the

followers of Senō, few in number as they were and unsupported, very many received mortal wounds.

When night came, as the fortress on which he relied had been broken through, Senō, unable to make further resistance, retired to the river Itakura in the extremity of Bitchū and threw up a barricade to await the enemy. Imai soon followed and renewed the attack, and the Heike retainers s fought as long as their supply of arrows lasted, but when these had been all used and they could hold off their foes no longer, they scattered and fled in all directions. Senō himself, with the only two of his retainers who were left, retired to the hills that skirted the Itakuragawa.

Now Kuramitsu-no-Jirō Narizumi, who had captured Senō on the former occasion, bitter at the thought of his younger brother who had been killed, and wishing to avenge him, pressed hard on his heels to take him again. Coming up alone to within one chō of his enemy, for he had outdistanced all the others, he called out in a loud voice: "Ho there! Senō! Turn back! it is not for a Samurai to show his back to a foe." Senō was just at this moment crossing the river, but when he heard this he drew back again and faced his enemy.

Kuramitsu in great joy spurred his horse and charged upon him, grappling him with such force that they both rolled over; and as they where both men of great strength neither would give way, but they rolled over and over, first one on top and then the other, until, coming nearer in their struggles to the brink of the river, they rolled over the edge and fell in. Kuramitsu was not able to swim while Senō was exceedingly expert, so, pressing his foe against the bottom, he drew the dagger from his side, and pulling up the skirts of his armour, stabbed him so deeply with it three times that the hilt and his hand sank in also. This done, as his own horse was overridden, he mounted that of Kuramitsu and rode off to the west with his enemy's head.

Senō's eldest son Kotarō Muneyasu was only twenty years old, but as he was very fat he had only managed to get to the distance of one chō, while his father had ridden on more than twenty. His father noticing this said to one of his retainers." Many times before have I faced a host of foes and fought with a light heart, but to day, as I have left my son behind, my mind is oppressed with gloom. Even if I escape alive and once more join, my friends, I am over sixty years old and know not how much longer I have to live, and what will my companions say of a samurai who leaves his only son behind to save his life?" "Then," said the retainer, "it were best to return; I will go back also and see what, has befallen your son." So they rode back and found Muneyasu fallen by the roadside, for his feet were so swollen that he could go no further.

Then Senō alighted from his horse and said to his son: "See, I have come back again to stay by you whatever may happen." "As I can do no more;" answered Kotarō weeping bitterly, "I shall now put an end to my life, for it would be as one of the Five Iniquities if you were to risk your life on my account: I pray you hurry on." To This request his father would not listen, and moreover, just at that moment about fifty fresh soldiers of the Genji came riding up to where he was resting. Then Senō-on-Tarō drew from his quiver the eight arrows that he had left, and fitting them to his bow, brought down eight men from their saddles, though whether they lived or died I know not. Then, drawing his sword, he swept off the head of his son first, after which he dashed into the midst of the Genji and fought desperately, swinging his blade downwards, sideways, crosswise and in a circle, until at last he fell, overcome by weight of numbers. His two retainers also fought around him with equal courage till they were badly wounded and taken prisoner, dying eventually the day after. The heads of all three were then taken and exposed at Sagi-ga-mori in the province of Bizen. "He was a valiant warrior indeed," said Kiso, when they told him; "how I wish he were still alive."

Chapter X.

THE FIGHT AT MUROYAMA.

Meanwhile Kiso was collecting his forces at Manju-on-Shō in the province of Bitchū, with the intent of moving against Yashima, when Higuchi-on-Jirō-Kanemitsu, whom he had left behind to represent him in the Capital, sent him a letter stating that, while his master was away, Jūrō Kurando had obtained great influence with the Hō-ō and was telling many slanderous tales about him; so that it would be well that he should leave the campaign in the west for a time and come back immediately to Miyako. Yoshinaka immediately started off for the Capital without a moment's delay, and Yukiie wishing to avoid an open quarrel with his nephew, started off by way of Tamba for the povince of Harima with fifty thousand men. Kiso travelled to the Capital through the province of Settsu.

The Heike, on the other hand, now entered the province of Harima with an army of twenty thousand to attack Kiso. It was commanded by Shin-Chūnagon-Tomomori and Hon-sammi Chūjō Shigehira, and in command of the samurai were Etchū-on-Jirōhyōye Moritsugu, Kazusa-no-Gorōhyōye Tadamitsu, Akushichi-hyōye Kagekiyo, and Iga-no-Heinaizaemon Ienaga. Jūrō Kurando Yukiie, thinking to regain favour With Kiso by attacking the Heike, advanced to Muroyama where they were encamped with a force of five hundred horsemen. Now the Heike had arranged their men in five separate camps. Iga-no-Heinaizaemon Ienaga with two thousand men occupied one; Etchū-on-Jirōhyōye Moritsugu with two thousand another; Kazusa-no-Gorōhyōye

Tadamitsu, and Akushichi-hyōye Kagekiyo held the third with another three thousand; Hon-sammi Chūjō Shigehira with three thousand held the fourth; while Tomomori-no-Kyō with ten thousand commanded the fifth. They had, moreover taken counsel together and settled that each of these four smaller forces, beginning with that of Ienaga, should engage the enemy in turn and break through his centre, after which they would move round his rear and flanks to surround him and smite him on all sides at once; and so, in accordance with this plan, they advanced vigorously on Yukiie's small army. Jurō Kurando. finding himself thus outdone and surrounded, yet did not blench or fly, but fought where he was to the last without taking any account of his life. Kishichiemon, Kihachiemon, and Akushichiemon, three of the most trusty and brave of Tomomori's guards fell by his single hand; and then, when his five hundred men had been reduced to but thirty, breaking forth through the Genji, who rolled about them like clouds of mist, himself unhurt, though most of his retainers were wounded, they took ship from Takasago in Harima and crossed over to Fukei in Izumi, from whence they fled for refuge to the stronghold of Nagano in Kawachi. As the Heike had now triumphed in the two battles of Muroyama and Mizushima, their forces grew continually greater.

Chapter XI.

Tsuzumi Hangwan.

The soldiers of the Genji swarmed everywhere in the Capital, and entered any place at their will to plunder. Not excepting even the sacred precincts of Kamo and Yahata, they reaped the crops for their use and broke into people's storehouses to take what they wanted; "they even waylaid the citizens in the street and robbed them. In fact they were a much worse plague than the Heike had been before them, for, as the people of the city said; the men of Rokuhara did not steal the clothes from off your back. Therefore the Hō-ō sent a message to Kiso Sama-no-kami to put an end to this violence, and Iki-no-Hangwan Tomoyasu was appointed to bear it. As he was an exceedingly good player on the drum (Tsuzumi) he was commonly called Tsuzumi Hangwan. When Kiso met him, without giving any reply to the Hō-ō's communication, he enquired: "Why is it that you are called Tsuzumi Hangwan? Is it because you are accustomed to be beaten or drummed on by everybody?" Tomoyasu immediately left in disgust without giving any answer, and returning to the Hō-ō's Palace, declared: "Yoshinaka is a presumptuous fool and must be put down at once. He is certainly disobedient to the Throne." To this the Hō-ō agreed, but those whom he entrusted with his order to attack Kiso were not warriors of repute, but the chiefs of Miidera and Hieizan, who accordingly assembled their bands of unruly monks, and the Nobles and Courtiers, who could not muster anyone better than a motley crowd of begging priests and prowling streetloafers to their standard. On the other hand Murakami-no-Saburō Hangwandai of the Shinano Genii forsook the side of Kiso and adhered to the Hō-ō. As soon as the men of the five provinces of the Imperial Domains saw that Kiso was out of favour with the Hō-ō, they too abandoned the allegiance they had previously proffered him and adhered to the side of the Throne. Then Imai-on-Shirō gave his advice to Kiso as follows: "Seeing that matters have now assumed a very serious aspect, how can you put yourself in opposition to our Sacred and Blameless Emperor? There is nothing to be done but humbly doff your helmet and lay aside your weapons in submission." At this speech Kiso flew into a great rage: "Ever since I came forth from Shinano," he exclaimed, from my first battles at Ōmi and Aida I have never once turned my back to the foe: at Tonami, Kurosaka and Shinohara in the North, and at the strongholds of Fukuryuji arid Itakura in the West everywhere I have conquered; why then should I lay down my arms and surrender, even to an Emperor of the Ten Virtues?"

Chapter XII.

THE FIGHT AT THE HŌJŪJIDEN.

"If I have been appointed to protect the Capital," continued Yoshinaka, "my men must at least have a horse to ride, so why should the Hō-ō object in this unreasonable way to their getting a little fodder from the fields? If the young men go into the country districts of the eastern and western hills round the city and take some rice for their rations, what is the harm in that? They don't go to the Palaces or the mansions of the Courtiers for it. But I know the cause of it: it is that Tsuzumi Hangwan who has been slandering me to his Majesty. Go and beat that 'Tsuzumi' until you break it! This may be the last fight of Yoshinaka, and without doubt it will come to the ears of Yoritomo; so quit yourselves well, men!"

Now the Northern forces had formerly numbered fifty thousand horse, but so many had deserted that only some six or seven thousand were left.

According to Yoshinaka's usual strategy these were divided into seven companies, of which one of some two thousand men was put under the command of Higuchi-no-Jirō Kanemitsu to lead the attach from the direction of Imakumano, while the rest were ordered to be ready, each in the avenue or street where they were quartered, so as to be able to unite in Rokujō-kawara. As a sign of recognition they all wore a badge of pine leaves.

It was the morning of the nineteenth day of the eleventh month that the fight began. Hearing that twenty thousand men were posted in the Hō-ō's Palace of the Hōjujiden, Kiso rode round by the western gate to see what was doing, and there he perceived Tsuzumi Hangwan Tomoyasu, who appeared to be in command there, standing on top of the west wall of the Palace, wearing nothing else but a hitatare. of red brocade and a helmet on his head, on which were written the names of the Four Deva Kings. In one hand he carried a short halberd and in the other a kind of sistrum such as is used by Yamabushi, and this he kept on shaking, posturing and capering as he did so. This caused much amusement among the Nobles and Courtiers, who thought his behaviour not quite dignified, and remarked: "Tomoyasu seems possessed by a Tengu." When he perceived Kiso, he called out in a loud voice: "In the good times of old, when the Imperial Edict was read, even the withered plants and trees immediately burst into flower and bore fruit, while the birds of .the air fell from the sky and all evil spirits and demons trembled and obeyed; and, even in this present worthless time he who dares to draw bow and shoot an arrow against His Sacred Majesty shall find his arrow fly back against his own body, and the sword that he draws turn back on himself." "Such talk needs no reply," said Kiso laconically as he shouted his warcry for the onset.

At the same time Higuchi-no-Jirō and his two thousand men rushed to the attack with loud shouts from the direction of Imakumano, and Imai himself, putting fire into the head of a turnip headed arrow, shot it so that it stuck in the roof of the Hōjujiden Palace, and as the wind was blowing strongly, the flames immediately shot up high into the air and the sky was filled with sparks. When he saw the Palace suddenly enveloped in black smoke, the commander Tomoyasu was the first to take to his heels, and when his army of twenty thousand men perceived the flight of their leader, panic seized them and they turned and fled with one accord. Such indeed was their haste that some took their bows without any arrows, and some their arrows without any bow; while others; dropping their halberds upside down in their flurry pierced their own legs with the sharp blades; some too there were who, catching the tips of their bows in some obstacle, left them as they were that they might flee the faster. When they came to the end of Shichijō in their flight, however, another misfortune awaited them, for this quarter was strongly guarded by another band of Settsu Genji who had joined the Hō-ō's party, and who had been ordered to fall upon any of Kiso's men who might flee from the Hōjujiden, so that they had taken up positions on the house tops and put up their shields there, providing themselves with heavy stones and missiles to throw down on the heads of the enemy. When therefore their own men came along in headlong flight, they immediately began to hurl their stones at them, whereupon the fugitives cried out that it was a mistake, for they were of the party of the Hō-ō. "That cry won't do;" replied the other Genji." we have the

Imperial Order; "kill them! kill them!" and they continued to pelt them with their missiles until many were killed, and others, with their heads or backs crushed, fell from their horses and managed to crawl away to some place of refuge.

The end of Hachijō was held by the warrior monks of Hieizan, but when the bolder among them were killed, the more cowardly who were left also took to flight. Here Mondo-no-kami Chikanari, attired in. a light blue kariginu worn over a body armour laced with green silk and mounted on a moon white steed, was ascending the river bank to make his escape, whom when Imai-no-Shirō Kanehira perceived he drew his bow with great strength and let fly an arrow at him. Whirring it flew straight at his skull, piercing it through so that he fell backwards from his horse. He was the son of Seidai-geki, Yorinari, and was a learned doctor of the Academy it was first time that he had ever put on armour. Ōmi-no-Chūjō Tamekiyo, Echizen no Shōshō Nobuyuki, Hōki-no-kami Mitsutsuna and his son. Hōki-no-Hangwan Mitsutsune were also shot through and their heads taken. Murakami-no-Saburō Hangwan dai of Shinano, who had deserted Kiso's camp and gone over to the Hō-ō, was killed also, and the grandson of Azechi-no-Dainagon Sukekata no Kyō, U-Shōshō Masakata, who went forth to the battle in armour and a high eboshi, was taken alive by Higuchi-no-Jirō Kanemitsu. Both the Tendai Zasshu Mei-un Dai-Sōjō, and Enkei-no-Shinnō the Abbot of Miidera had gone to the Hōjujiden, but when it began to go up in smoke they mounted their horses and hastened away, only to fall victims to the fury of Kiso's samurai, who shot them down from their horses and cut off their venerable heads.

The Hō-ō himself, at this disaster, entered his Car to make an Imperial Progress to some safer Palace, but the northern samurai, not knowing who he was, continued to shoot their arrows at it. Then Bungo-no-Shōshō Munenaga, who, clad in a yellowish-red hitatare with a high eboshi on his head, was accompanying the Imperial Car, cried out to them: "Make no mistake! It is His Majesty!" whereon all the samurai sprang from their horses and did obeisance. On His Majesty's enquiring who they were, one of them stood forth and gave his name and title as Yashima-no-Shirō Yukishige of the province of Shinano, after which they escorted the Imperial Car to the Palace in Gojō, keeping strict guard over it.

Gyōbu-kyō Sammi Yorisuke no Kyō, the before mentioned Governor of Bungo, had also been in the Hōjujiden, and when it took fire he escaped and fled toward the river, but on the way he was stripped of all his rich garments by some of the lesser samurai, so that he had to go on stark naked, and as it was the morning of the nineteenth day of the eleventh month the cold wind from the river cut him to the bone. His elder brother Echizen-no-Hōkyō Shō-i who had gone out to see the battle, noticing his brother in this plight, and feeling sorry for him, straightway ran, to his assistance. As he was wearing two white 'kosode' under his koromo or priestly garment, he took off one of them and gave it to his brother, after which he parted with his koromo also; so that he was left with one kosode only. His appearance in this guises without any sash, seen from behind was truly ridiculous and as the two hurried along the streets; accompanied by some lower priests in white robes, enquiring at his house and that where they could find a lodging, the passers-by clapped their hands in glee and laughed inordinately. The baby Emperor was put in a boat and launched on the waters of the lake in the grounds of the Hōjujiden, and as the opposing samurai shot arrows at this also, Shichijō-no-jijū Nobukiyo arid Kii-no-kami Norimitsu, who were with His Majesty, called out to them to stop lest the Emperor be harmed. On learning who it was they dismounted and did obeisance. Soon after His Majesty was accompanied to the Kanin Palace in Nijo, but, sad to relate, the Imperial Procession was of a pitiably attenuated kind.

Now Gen-no-Kurando Nakakane was holding the western, gate of the Hōjujiden with fifty horsemen, when Yamamoto-no-Kwanja Yoshitaka of the Ōmi Genji spurred up to him and shouted: "Who is it you are guarding here? The Hō-ō and the Emperor have both proceeded elsewhere." On hearing this Nakakane rode off and precipitated himself into the battle and fought hard until his force was reduced to eight in all. Among these was a certain warrior priest of the party of Kūsaka named Kaga-bō, who was riding a cream coloured horse with a very hard mouth. "My horse's mouth is so hard that I can hardly manage him;" he cried, whereon Nakakane replied: "Take mine and give him to me instead; and mounted him on his own horse, a chestnut with a white tail, Then they charged at full speed into a party of two hundred hostile samurai who were waiting at Kawarasaka under the command of Nenoi-no-Koyata and fought until but five of the eight were left alive. Kaga-bō, although he was mounted on his master's horse, met his fate here and fell fighting at last.

Now one of the retainers of Nakakane named Jirō Kurando Nakayori, seeing the chestnut horse with the white tail galloping wildly along riderless, asked his servant whether that was not the horse of his master, and on his answering that it was, he further enquired from what direction it had come. "As our master rode into the enemy at Kawarasaka," replied the man, "it is from that fight that his horse has come." Then Jirō Kurando, bursting into tears, exclaimed; "Ah! how wretched that he has fallen thus; ever since we played together as children we have pledged ourselves to die together, and now, unhappy, we must die separate." Taking farewell of his wife and children he rode off alone and dashed into the fight at Kawarasaka. Rising high in his stirrups, he shouted loudly: "I am Jirō Kurando Nakayori of Shinano, twenty seven years old, the second son of Shinano-no-kami Nakashige, and a descendant in the ninth generation cf Atuzane Shinno; come! anyone who thinks himself somebody and let us see!" And he swung his sword about him, cutting and slashing in all directions until at last he fell, borne down by the weight of numbers.

His master Gen-no-Kurando, quite unaware of all this, had escaped and ridden off toward the south with his brother Kawachi-no-kami Nakanobu and another retainer. And it chanced that, as the Sessho Motomichi, taking fright at the war in the Capital, was on his way to take refuge at Uji, the two overtook him at Kobatayama. Dismounting from their horses they saluted him, and on his enquiring who they might be, they declared themselves as Nakanobu and Nakamichi. The Sessho was greatly rejoiced to hear this, for he had feared that they might be some of the Kiso samurai, and requested them to accompany him, which they did, and escorted him as far as the Fuke mansion at Uji. Thence they parted and the two fled to the province of Kawachi.

On the next day, the twentieth, Kiso Sama-no-kami Yoshinaka proceeded to the Rokujō-kawara to count and identify the heads of those who had been killed the day before, and which were there exposed to view, and behold, their number was six hundred and thirty; and among them were the heads of the Tendai Zasshu Meiun Dai-Sōjō and Enkei-hō Shinno the Abbot of Miidera; and of those who looked on these there were none who did not shed tears. Then Kiss Sama-no-kami, ordering his seven thousand men to turn their horse's heads toward the east, bade them shout their war cry three times, whereat the heaven echoed and the earth trembled. At this there was a great uproar in the city, but it was only a shout of joy.

Now the Saishō Naganori, son of the late Shōnagon Nyūdō Shinsai, went to visit the Hō-ō at the Gojo Palace, but was refused admission by the soldiers on guard at the gate. Stepping aside into a small house near by that he knew, he cut off his hair and put on a black koromo and hakama, after which he demanded admission, again, pleading that in such a habit there could be on objection, upon which the samurai gave way and admitted him. Weeping bitterly he entered the Imperial presence, and when he told the Hō-ō of all those who had been done to death in the fighting, His Majesty burst into tears also, saying: "Ah that Mei-un should have been thus innocently put to death; it seems as though he had sacrificed his life for mine."

On the twenty third day Sanjo-no-Chūnagon Tomokata-no-Kyō and forty nine other Courtiers beneath him were removed from their offices and put in prison. Under the rule of the Heike forty three had been dismissed at once, but this present treatment was worse than their's for the number was greater. Having also taken the daughter of the Kwampaku Motofusa and made her his wife, he assembled his retainers and gave his opinion thus: "I, Yoshinaka, have confronted the Sovereign Lord of this Empire in battle and have conquered. If I would,

I might become Emperor or I might become Hō-ō: but I don't want to become Hō-ō, for I must become a shaven priest; and how can I become Emperor, for I should have to be a child. Very well then, I will become Kwampaku." At this his official scribe, Taiyū-bō Kakumei, stood up and said: "A Kwampaku must be of the princely house of Fujiwara, of the stock and lineage of the great Kamatari; Your Excellency is of the Genji line, and therefore cannot hold such office." So it ended by Kiso consoling himself with the title of Groom of the Stables to the Retired Emperor, and appropriating the province of Tanba as his fief. That a Retired Emperor was called Hō-ō if he became a monk, and that the Emperor looked like a child because he had not yet performed Gempuku, were things that unfortunately Yoshinaka did not know.

Now the former Uhyōye-no-suke Yoritomo of Kamakura had ordered his brothers Nori-yori and Yoshitsune with an army of sixty thousand men to march against Kiso and subdue him, and they had already started, but when they heard that war had broken out in the Capital, and that the Palaces of the Emperor and the Retired Emperor had been burnt, and the whole country was plunged in gloom, they thought it inadvisable to begin more fighting at present, and halted their men near Atsuta in the province of Owari. Then Kunai Hangwan Kintomo and Tonai Hangwan Tokinari, members of the bodyguard of the Retired Emperor, came down to Owari to report all that had happened in the Capital, and when Noriyori and Yoshitsune heard their tidings, they advised them thus: "It were better that Kintomo should go down to Kamakura to report the matter direct to Yoritomo, for with a messenger, who does not know all the details of the matter, trouble is likely to arise."

As all his retainers had been killed in the recent fighting and he had none else left, Kintomo hastened down to Kamakura accompanied by his young heir Kunaidokoro Kinnari, a boy of fifteen. "This is all owing to the folly of Tsuzumi Hangwan;" pronounced Yoritomo, "and it is through him that the Emperor has been thus grieved, and so many venerable priests have been put to death. If such worthless fellows as this are employed as messengers, disturbances will never cease in the Empire." When this was reported to Tomoyasu, he hurried to Kamakura with the utmost speed, and argued his case most persistently with Kajiwara Heizō Kagetoki, begging him to intercede with Yoritomo; but Yoritomo refused to see him, however often he begged an audience, so that at last he returned in disgrace to Miyako, where, somewhat in danger of his life, he lived in obscurity somewhere near Inari. Kiso Yoshinaka, thus at open war with Yoritomo, immediately sent messengers to the Western Provinces inviting the Heike to return again to the Capital, that both together might make common cause against Kamakura. On hearing this both Munemori and all the Heike were much rejoiced, but Shin-Chūnagon Tomomori gave his opinion to the contrary: "Even when things have come to such a pass," he said, "how are we to join with Kiso Yoshinaka? If we should return to the Capital with our Emperor and the Three Sacred Treasures, should we not have to lay down our arms and make humble surrender?" So Munemori rejected the advances of Yoshinaka, but Kiso, on his part, did not believe it final.

One day the Kwampaku Motofusa called Yoshinaka and said to him: "Kiyomori Nyudō was a man of evil conduct, it is true, but in him there was at the same time some extraordinary virtue, through which he was enabled to govern the Empire peaceably for twenty years. Bad conduct alone cannot rule the Empire, so it would be well if you were to pardon those Courtiers whom you have put in prison." Yoshinaka, even though he was savage Eastern Barbarian, saw the wisdom of this and acted accordingly.

Motofusa's son Moroie, who was at that time only Chūnagon of the lower third rank, was, by the plan of Yoshinaka, made Daijin and Sesshō, but, as at that time there was no office of Daijin vacant, he borrowed the rank from Tokudaiji-dono, who was Naidaijin and Sadaishō, in consequence of which people called the new Sesshō, 'Kari-no-Daijin' or 'the Minister of Borrowed Rank.' On the tenth day of the twelfth month the Hō-ō left the Gojō Palace and proceeded to the residence of Daizen-no-taiyū Naritada in Rokujō. On the thirteenth day a recital of the Shingon Sutras was held in the Palace, and on that day also an appointment of officials was held, the nominations being made entirely at the will of Kiso. So the Heike held the Western Provinces and the Genji the Eastern, while Kiso lorded it in the Capital; just as Ōmō seized the supremacy and ruled the country for eighteen years between the former and latter dynasties of Kan in China.

As all the barriers were closed no taxes could be paid, and as their yearly revenues were cut off, everyone in Miyako was as uncomfortable as a fish in shallow water. And so the year ended in anxiety, and the third year of Ju-ei began.

Volume IX.

Chapter I.

On the first day of the New Year of the third year of Ju-ei the customary reception of the Retired Emperor and Audience of the Emperor were not held, for the mansion of Daizen-no-taiyū Naritada, which the Hō-ō was using as his temporary Palace, was not considered suitable. The Heike also welcomed the New Year by the shore of Yashima in Sanuki, but though the Emperor was present, the Festival of the Setchie was not held, nor the Imperial Worship of Heaven and

Earth. No envoys brought the tribute of fish from Tsukushi, nor did the time honoured messengers arrive from Yoshino. All the Courtiers lamented the disorder of the times, declaring that in the Capital, however, things could not be so bad. Spring had now come, and though the sea breezes blew softly and the sunshine was warm and genial, the Heike Nobles still shivered like tropical birds amid the ice. Thus they spent the long drawn tedious hours in talk and reminiscence of their pleasant life in Miyako; of the times of the blossoming and fading of the various trees and flowers, of the cherry blooms and the moonlight nights, of their verses and music and games of foot-ball and archery, the competitions of painting and writing stanzes on fans, and all their elegant diversions with insects and grasses; and as they lingered over the recollections of all these lost delights their hearts were filled with sadness.

Chapter II.

THE CROSSING OF THE UJIKAWA.

On the eleventh day of the first month Kiso Sama-no-kami Yoshinaka proceeded to the Palace of the Hō-ō and announced that he was about to start for the Western Provinces to subdue the Heiki, and on the thirteenth day he was just setting forth from the Capital when word was brought to him that Uhyōhe-no-suke Yoritomo had despatched a large force of many myriads of horsemen under the command of Noriyori and Yoshitsune to chastize him for h s outrageous conduct, and that they had already reached the provinces of Mino and Ise. Much astonished at this news, Kiso at once ordered the bridges at Seta and Uji to be destroyed and his forces to be divided to meet the foe. Since he had not many men left by this time, he sent eight hundred horsemen under Imai-no-Shirō Kanehira to the bridge at Seta as his main army, while a smaller force of five hundred under Nishina, Takanashi, and Yamada-no-Jirō was ordered to march to that at Uji. His uncle Shida-no-Saburō Yoshinori also rode off to Imoarai with three hundred men.

Now the main body of the Eastern forces was under the command of Kaba-no-Onzōshi Noriyori, while the lesser army was led by Kurō Onzōshi Yoshitsune, while ranking after these were thirty six great Nobles, the whole army numbering some sixty thousand horsemen. Yoritomo had at this time two famous horses named Ikezuki and Surusumi, and Kajiwara Genda Kagesue greatly coveted Ikezuki and asked that it might be given him for this campaign, but Yoritomo answered that he was keeping it in case he might wish to ride it himself, and presented him with Surusumi instead. A little while afterwards Sasaki Shirō Takatsuna of the province of Ōmi came to bid him farewell, acid Yoshitomo gave Ikezuki to him, saying: "Remember that there are many who desire this horse, so look well to him." Sasaki bowed low in obeisance and replied: "On this horse I will be the first to cross the Ujikawa; if you hear that I am dead, you will know that someone else has crossed before me, but if you learn that I still live, then rest certain that Takatsuna has crossed before all the rest." "These are strong words," muttered all the Nobles, both great and small, who were in attendance, as Sasaki retired.

So, leaving Kamakura behind, this great host started for the West, some crossing over Ashigara and some over Hakone, according to the will of their leaders, and Kajiwara Genda Kagesue, drawing aside a little, ascended to a high place at Ukishima-ga-hara in the province of Suruga, and viewed all their horses as they passed by, each with its varying saddle and trappings, both in profile and head-on. As he thus scrutinized' the seemingly endless procession of steeds Kajiwara was greatly pleased that he saw none that could compare with his own mount Surusumi, when his eye fell on a splendid horse that he recognised at once as Ikezuki. His saddle was inlaid with gold and his crupper gaily decorated with many tassels, and he foamed at the mouth as he champed the bright polished bit. He had many grooms to lead him, but even so his mettle could not be entirely curbed, for he reared and caracolled as he advanced. Kajiwara came forward and asked the attendants whose horse he was. "It is the horse of Sasaki dono;" they replied "Which Sasaki does it belong to," he continued; "Saburō or Shirō?" "It is the steed of Shirō Dono;" answered the attendants as they passed on. At this Kagesue felt bitter resentment, for it was most mortifying to be thus passed over in favour of his fellow retainer Sasaki. First he thought he would rush on to the Capital and engage in mortal combat with Kiso's Four Deva Kings, Imai, Higuchi, Tate and Nenoi, or else die fighting with one of the famous champions of the Heike in the Western Provinces, but this seemed, on second thoughts, a vain revenge, and so, he stood muttering and raging and waiting for Sasaki, pondering the while what a loss it would be to Yoritomo should two of his stoutest retainers thus fall on each other and do each other to death. Meanwhile Sasaki himself came along quite unsuspecting, and Kajiwara, uncertain whether to ride at him headlong or to come up alongside and grapple, thus addressed him: "How is it, Sasaki Dono, that our lord has come to present you with Ikezuki?" Whereupon Sasaki, perceiving that Kagesue too had coveted the horse, replied thus: "When I set out on this campaign I felt quite sure that the enemy would destroy the bridges at Seta and Uji, and that I should want a good horse to swim the river; but as I had not such an one, I greatly desired Ikezuki. Hearing, however, that you had asked for him and been refused, I knew that a fellow like myself would have no chance, and so, in spite of the risk of our lord's anger afterwards, I won over the grooms and stole his precious steed. What do you think of that, Kajiwara Dono?" Disarmed by this retort, Kajiwara burst into a laugh and replied: "Ah, I See, I too ought to have stolen him." Now this horse that Takatsuna had received was of large and powerful build, four shaku eight sun in height, and its colour was a dark chestnut, and as it was fierce and would bite anyone, man or horse, who came near it, it had been named Ikezuki (Quick-biter). Kajiwara's horse was also large and strong, no whit inferior to the other, and on account of its very black colour had been named Surusumi (Ink-black).

From the province of Owari the army was divided into its two parts, and the larger body, consisting of some thirty five thousand horsemen under Noriyori, pitched their camp at Noji-Shinohara in Ōmi. With Noriyori were also Takeda-no-Tarō, Kagami-no-Jirō, Ichijō-no-Jirō, Itagaki-no-Saburō Inamo-no-Saburō, Hangai-no-Jirō, Kumagai-no-Jirō, and Inomata-no-Koheiroku. The smaller force of twenty five thousand men under Yoshitsune, with whom were also Yasuda-no-Saburō, Ōuchi-no-Tarō, Hatakeyama-no-Shōji Jirō, Kajiwara Genda, Sasaki Shirō, Kasuya-no-Tōda, Shibuya-no-Uma-no-suke and Hirayama-no-Mushadokoro, passed through the province of Iga and pressed upon the bridge at Uji. Now after destroying the bridges at Seta and Uji, the enemy had planted sharp stakes in the riverbed and made fast a great hawser in the stream together with a floating boom of tree trunks to obstruct the crossing. It was now the twentieth day of the first month and the snow had melted on the slopes of Mount Hira and Shiga, while the ice of the valleys below mingled with it and rushed down in torrents of water. The Ujikawa rose high in spate, and its white capped waves surged tumultuously as the boiling flood rushed down between its banks with a roar like a waterfall. As the chilly dawn broke the river mist hung heavy over the water, so that tone could clearly discern the colour either of the horses or the armour of their riders. Then the commander Yoshitsune rode up to the bank of the river, and wishing to try the courage of his men, with a glance at the foaming torrent, called out: "Shall we turn off to Yodo or Imoarai, or shall we go round by Kawachiji? Or what do you think of waiting till the flood abates?" Then Hatakeyama Shōji Shigetada of the province of Musashi, who was then but twenty-one years old, stood forth and said: "This river is one that we have often spoken of at Kamakura, and is no unknown stream to baffle us; and moreover, as it flows out directly from the lake of Ōmi, its waters will not quickly subside, however long you may wait, and as for building a bridge, who is there who can do such a thing? In the battle that was fought here in the era of Jishō, Ashikaga Matataro Tadatsuna crossed over, and he was but a youth of seventeen years, so here is no matter for god or devil. I, Shigetada will be the first in the flood. And as lie and his band of five hundred followers were pushing together into the waves, two warriors were seen to gallop forth from the point of Tachibana-no-kojima at the north-east of the Byōdō-in: they were Kajiwara Genda Kagesue and Sasaki Shirō Takatsuna. Each had made up his mind to be the first across, though no sign of their determination was visible to the onlookers: Kajiwara was about three yards in front of Sasaki. "Kajiwara Dono! Your saddle girth seems to be loose; this is the greatest river in the Western Provinces, so you had better tighten it up." Thus warned, Kajiwara dropped the reins on to his horse's mane, kicked his feet from the stirrups, and, leaning forward in the saddle, loosened the girth arid tightened it afresh. While he was thus engaged, however, Sasaki rode on past him and leapt his horse into the river. Kajiwara, thinking he had been tricked, immediately sprang in after him. "Ho! Sasaki Dono," shouted Kajiwara, "take care if you want to be famous; there is a great hawser at the bottom of the river. Look out!" At this Sasaki drew his sword and cut through the rope as it caught his horse's feet, and in spite of the strength of the current, as he was mounted on the finest horse in the land, he rode straight through the river and leapt up on to the farther bank. Kajiwara's horse, Surusumi, however, was swept aside by the rush of the water and his rider reached land some distance farther down stream. Then Sasaki, rising high in his stirrups, shouted with a loud voice: "Sasaki Shirō Takatsuna, fourth son of Sasaki Saburō Yoshihide of Ōmi, descended in the ninth generation from Uda Tennō, is the first over the Ujikawa!" Hatakeyama, who was leading his five hundred men across, had not gone far when his horse was struck deep in the head by an arrow shot by Yamada-no-Jirō from the other bank, and reared violently, upon which, using his bow as a staff, he slid off into the stream only to find the rushing waters sweep right over his head. Nothing daunted by this he vigorously breasted the current, and diving through the waves swam across; but just as he was about to scramble up the bank he felt someone drag at hint from behind. "Who is that?" he called. "Shigechika!" was the answer. "Ōgushi?" "The same." Now Hatakeyama had been sponsor at the Gempuku of Ōgushi Jirō Shigechika. "The current is so strong that my horse has been washed away and I have no strength to go any farther." "Ah, I always have to help you fellows;" replied Hatakeyama, as he gripped Ōgushi and flung him by main force it on to the bank. The young man, immediately recovering himself, sprang erect, and drawing his sword, laid it to his forehead, shouting loudly: "Ōgushi-no-Jirō Shigechika of Musashi is the first to cross the Ujikawa on foot!" Whereat all who heard it, both friends and foes, burst out into a roar of laughter. Hatakeyama, mounting another horse, shouted his war cry and spurred fiercely against the ranks of the foe, when to meet him there came a single horseman clad in an embroidered hitatare and a suit of armour laced with scarlet, ling a dappled horse with a gold mounted saddle. In answer to Hatakeyama's challenge he gave his name title as "Nagaseno-Hangwan-dai Shigetsuna, a retainer of Kiso Yoshinaka." "Thinking to make him the first sacrifice to the god battles that day, Hatakeyama rode up alongside him and grappled, pulling him from his horse and squeezing him against pommel of his saddle, where he twisted his head and cut it off without more ado, passing it over to Honda-no Jirō, who fastened it to the left side of his saddle. After this Kiso's men who were guarding the bridge kept up a defensive fight for a while, but when all the Eastern army had crossed over and advanced to the attack, they gave way and fled toward Kobatayama and Fushimi. At Seta also, by the strategy of Inamo-no-Saburo Shigenari, the other army passed over the river at the ford of Gugo at Tagami.

Chapter III.

THE FIGHT AT THE RIVER KAMO.

After he had gained this victory, Yoshitsune at once sent messengers to Kamakura with an account of the battle, and as soon as they arrived in his presence Yoritomo put the question "How is it with Sasaki?" "He was the first across the Uji river;" was the answer: then unrolling his despatch the messenger read forth: "First across the Uji river, Sasaki Shirō Takatsuna; second, Kajiwara Genda Kagesue."

When he saw that both these positions at Uji and Seta were lost, Kiso Yoshinaka rode off to the Hō-ō's Palace at Rokujō to say farewell for the last time; but having arrived at the gate, he found that he had nothing particular to say, so he turned back again, and as a lady, with whom he had lately fallen in love, happened to live at Takakura in Rokujō, he went in to see her, and as he was very loath to part from her, he did not emerge at all quickly. Seeing this, a new retainer of his, named Echigo-no-Chūta Iemitsu, called out to his master: "Why does your Excellency thus deign to waste time in this dalliance when the august enemy is even now pressing on the river hard by? That way lies a dog's death; so hasten, I pray you." As his master still paid on heed to his warnings, however, Chūta at length made up his mind to put an end to his life, and cut open his belly there and died, with these words on his lips: "Since it must be, I, Iemitsu, will go on before, and on the Mountain of Shide will I await my master."

Then Kiso, at last noticing that his faithful retainer had laid down his life to enforce his warning, tore himself away from his lady and left the house. At this time the whole force that he could muster consisted of not more than a hundred men under Naba-no-Tarō Hirozumi, and as they rode out to the river by Rokujō to reconnoitire, they saw about thirty horsemen of the enemy coming to meet them, with two warriors spurring forth in front. These two were Shioya-no-Gorō Korehiro and Teshikawara-no-Gosaburō Arinao. Seeing them Shioya at once shouted: "Let us wait until the main body come up!" "By no means," said Teshikawara, "when the front is broken the rest will soon give way; forward!" and so both parties rode at each other and the fight began, for the soldiers of Yoritomo aimed at enveloping Kiso in the midst of their ample forces, if he would stay and fight to the last.

Yoshitsune himself, leaving the conduct of the battle to his subordinates, rode off with five or six retainers to the Palace of the Hō-ō in Rokujō, to guard it against any further perils. Here Daizen-no-Taiyū Naritada had mounted up on to the eastern wall and was surveying the turmoil outside, his whole body shaking in the extremity of his terror, when he saw the small band approaching with their helmets hanging loose from the fight, their bow hand sleeves flying loose in the wind, and the white colours of the Genji displayed. "Alas! how terrible!" he shrieked, "it is Kiso who has come again!" Whereat all the Courtiers and Nobles and Ladies in waiting within, thinking that now at last their hour had come, ran about wringing their hands and making vows to every god and Buddha they could think of, when the voice of Naritada was heard again: "It may be the warriors of the East who are just entering the town, for the insignia they wear are different." Then the Eastern Commander Kurō Onzōshi Yoshitsune, rode up to the gate and knocked, shouting loudly: Kurō Yoshitsune, younger brother of the former Uhyōye-no-suke Yoritomo, who has broken through the enemy at Uji, has arrived to protect the Palace! "When he heard this, Naritada was so overcome with excitement that, as he hastily scrambled down from the wall he slipt and hurt his back, but so great was his joy that he did not trouble about the pain, but went on limping into the Palace and reported the facts to the Hō-ō, who was also overjoyed to hear it, and immediately ordered the gates to be opened.

Yoshitsune was clad that day in a hitatare of red brocade, and armour of shot purple, while his helmet was surmounted by upstanding horns. By his side hung a gold mounted sword, and twenty four black and white arrows were stuck in his. quiver: the upper half of his bow was wound leftwise with a strip of paper about an inch wide, which was at this time the sign of a General Commanding. Then the Ho o went out to the middle gate, and viewed them through a lattice window, exclaiming: "Ah, what a brave show they make! Let us hear their names and titles."

Then the six captains declared themselves; Tai-Shōgun Kurō Yoshitsune, Yasuda Saburō Yoshisada, Hatakeyama Shōji Jirō Shigetada, Kajiwara Genda Kagesue, Sasaki Shirō Takatsuna, Shibuya Umanosuke; and through they may have differed in their armour and trappings, in bearing and courage none was inferior to the others.

Then, after a low obeisance Yoshitsune spoke as follows: "In order to punish the lawless conduct of Kiso, the former Uhyōye-no-suke Yoritomo of Kamakura has sent out an army of sixty thousand men under the command of Noriyori and myself, but as Noriyori is advancing by way of Seta, as yet none of his men have entered the Capital. I, having overcome the forces of the enemy at Uji, have straitway hastened to protect this Palace, while my men are even now engaged with Kiso to cut him off as he is trying to flee up the river, and I doubt not have already seized him." At these straightforward and informal words the Hō-ō was much gratified and relieved "See that you guard this Palace well," he directed, "lest Kiso return again and commit more violence." Yoshitsune bent low in assent, and ere long his men had come up to the number of ten thousand horsemen, who were drawn up to keep watch on all four sides of the Palace.

Meanwhile Kiso with twenty of his stoutest followers was waiting for an opportunity to seize the Hō-ō and flee with him to the West to join the Heike, but when he saw that his designs had been anticipated by the strict guard that Yoshitsune had placed round the Palace, he started off up the river Kamo to escape, and between Rokujō and Sanjō he was many times almost surrounded and slain. Then the tears ran down his cheeks as he exclaimed: "Ah, if I had only known this, I would never have sent Imai to Seta, for from our earliest days when we played together as children we swore that when we came to die it should be together; and now, alas! it seems we are to fall separated from one another." So riding up the river to see if he could hear any tidings of Imai, the enemy rolled down on them like the evening mists, and five or six times did Kiso and his little band fling them back between Rokujō and Sanjō until at last he cut through them and reached Matsusaka at Awataguchi. Last year he rode forth from Shinano with fifty thousand horsemen, now he flees along the river bed with but six retainers, already half lost in the melancholy twilight where lies the nether world.

Chapter IV.

THE DEATH OF KISO.

Now Kiso had brought with him from Shinano two beautiful girls named Tomoe and Yamabuki, but Yamabuki had fallen sick and stayed behind in the Capital. Tomoe had long black hair and a fair complexion, and her face was very lovely; moreover she was a fearless rider whom neither the fiercest horse nor the roughest ground could dismay, and so dexterously did she handle sword and bow that she was a match for a thousand warriors, and fit to meet either god or devil. Many times had she taken the field, armed at all points, and won matchless renown in encounters with the bravest captains, and so in this last fight, when all the others had been slain or had fled, among the last seven there rode Tomoe. At first it was reported that Kiso had escaped to the North either through Nagasaka by the road to Tamba, or by the Ryūge pass, but actually he had turned back again and ridden off toward Seta, to see if he could hear aught of the fate of Imai Kanehira. Imai had long valiantly held his position at Seta till the continued assaults of the enemy reduced his eight hundred men to but fifty, when he rolled up his banner and rode back to Miyako to ascertain the fate of his lord; and thus it happened that the two fell in with each other by the shore at Otsu. Recognizing each other when they were yet more than a hundred yards away, they spurred their horses and came together joyfully.

Seizing Imai by the hand, Kiso burst forth: "I was so anxious about you that I did not stop to fight to the death in the Rokujō Kawara, but turned my back on a host of foes and hastened off here to find you." "How can I express my gratitude for my lord's consideration?" replied Imai; "I too would have died in the defence of Seta, but I feared for my lord's uncertain fate, and thus it was that I fled hither." "Then our ancient pledge will not be broken and we shall die together," said Kiso, "and now unfurl your banner, for a sign to our men who have scattered among these hills." So Imai unfurled the banner, and many of their men who had fled from the Capital and from Seta saw it and rallied again, so that they soon had a following of three hundred horse. "With this band our last fight will be a great one," shouted Kiso joyfully, "who leads yon great array?" "Kai-no-Ichijō Jirō, my lord." "And how many has he, do you think?" "About six thousand, it seems." "Well matched!" replied Yoshinaka, "if we must die, what death could be better than to fall outnumbered by valiant enemies? Forward then!"

That day Kiso was arrayed in a hitatare of red brocade and a suit of armour laced with Chinese silk; by his side hung a magnificent sword mounted in silver and gold, and his helmet was surmounted by long golden horns. Of his twenty four eagle feathered arrows, most had been shot away in the previous fighting, and only a few were left, drawn out high from the quiver, and he grasped his rattan bound bow by the middle as he sat his famous grey charger, fierce as a devil, on a saddle mounted in gold. Rising high in his stirrups he cried with a loud voice: "Kiso-no-Kwanja you have often heard of; now you see him before your eyes! Sama-no-kami and Iyo-no-kami, Asahi Shōgun, Minamoto Yoshinaka am I! Come! Kai-no-Ichijō Jirō Take my head and show it to Hyōye-no-suke Yoritomo!" "Hear, men!" shouted Ichijō-no-Jirō in response; "On to the attack! This is their great Captain! See that he does not escape you now! "And the whole force charged against Kiso to take him. Then Kiso and his three hundred fell upon their six thousand opponents in the death fury, cutting and slashing and swinging their blades in every direction until at last they broke through on the farther side, but with their little band depleted to only fifty horsemen, when Doi-no-Jirō Sanehira came up to support their foes with another force of two thousand. Flinging themselves on these they burst through them also, after which they successively penetrated several other smaller bands of a hundred or two who were following in reserve. But now they were reduced to but five survivors, and among these Tomoe still held her place. Calling her to him Kiso said: "As you are a woman, it were better that you now make your escape. I have made up my mind to die, either by the hand of the enemy or by mine own, and how would Yoshinaka be shamed if in his last fight he died with a woman?" Even at these strong words, however, Tomoe would not forsake him, but still feeling full of fight, she replied: "Ah, for some bold warrior to match with, that Kiso might see how fine a death I can die." And she drew aside her horse and waited. Presently Onda-no-Hachirō Moroshige of Musashi, a strong and valiant samurai, came riding up with thirty followers, and Tomoe, immediately dashing into them, flung herself upon Onda and grappling with him dragged him from his horse, pressed him calmly against the pommel of her saddle and cut off his head. Then stripping off her armour she fled away to the Eastern Provinces. Tezuka-no-Tarō was killed and Tezuka-no-Bettō took to flight, leaving Kiso alone with Imai-no-Shirō. "Ah," exclaimed Yoshinaka, "my armour that I am never wont to feel at all seems heavy on me today." "But you are not yet tired, my lord, and your horse is still fresh, so why should your armour feel heavy? If it is because you are discouraged at having none of your retainers left, remember that I, Kanehira, am equal to a thousand horse-men, and I have yet seven or eight arrows left in my quiver; so let me hold back the foe while my lord escapes to that pine wood of Awazu that we see yonder, that there under the trees he may put an end to his life in peace." "Was it for this that I turned my back on my enemies in Rokujō-kawara and did not die then?" returned Yoshinaka; "by no means will we part now, but meet our fate together." And he reined his horse up beside that of Imai towards the foe, when Kanehira, alighting from his horse, seized his master's bridle and burst into tears: "However great renown a warrior may have gained," he pleaded, "an unworthy death is a lasting shame. My lord is weary and his charger also, and if, as may be, he meet his death at the hands of some low retainer, how disgraceful that it should be said that Kiso Dono, known through all Nippon as the 'Demon Warrior' had been slain by some nameless fellow, so listen to reason, I pray you, and get away to the pines over there." So Kiso, thus persuaded, rode off toward the pine wood of Awazu. Then Ima-no-Shirō, turning back, charged into a party of fifty horsemen, shouting: "I am Imai-Shirō Kanehira, foster-brother of Kiso Dono, aged thirty-three. Even Yoritomo at Kamakura knows my name so take my head and show it to him, anyone who can! "And he quickly fitted the eight shafts he had left to his bow and sent them whirring into the enemy, bringing down eight of them from their horses, either dead or wounded. Then, drawing his sword, he set on at the rest, but none would face him in combat hand-to-hand: "Shoot him down! Shoot him down!" they cried as they let fly a hail of arrows at him, but so good was his armour that none could pierce it, and once more he escaped unwounded.

Meanwhile Yoshinaka rode off alone toward Awazu, and it was the twenty third day of the first month. It was now nearly dark and all the land was coated with thin ice, so that none could distinguish the deep ricefields, and he had not gone far before his horse plunged heavily into the muddy ooze beneath. Right up to the neck it floundered, and though Kiso plied whip and spur with might and main, it was all to no purpose, for he could not stir it. Even in this plight he still thought of his retainer, and was turning to see how it fared with Imai, when Miura-no-Ishida Jirō Tamehisa of Sagami rode up and shot an arrow that struck him in the face under his helmet. Then as the stricken warrior fell forward in his saddle that his crest bowed over his horse's head, two of Ishida's retainers fell upon him and struck off his head. Holding it high on the point of a sword Ishida shouted loudly: "Kiso Yoshinaka, known through the length and breadth of Nippon as the 'Demon Warrior', has been killed by Miura-no-Ishida Jirō Tamehisa." Imai was still fighting when these words fell on his ears, but when he saw that his master was indeed slain cried out: "Alas, for whom now have I to fight? See, you fellows of the East Country, I will show you how the mightiest champion in Nippon can end his life!" And he thrust the point of his sword in his mouth and flung himself headlong from his horse, so that he was pierced through and died.

Chapter V.

HIGUCHI IS PUT TO DEATH.

Imai's elder brother, Higuchi Jirō Kanemitsu, had gone to the stronghold of Nagano in Kawachi with five hundred horsemen to take Jūrō Kurando Yukiie and put him to death, but not finding him there, and hearing that he was at Nagusa in the province of Kii, he was following him to that province, when he learned of the fighting in the Capital and immediately retraced This steps thither. When he came to the bridge of Owatari at Yodo there met him one of the retainers of his brother Imai, who greeted him thus: "Whither then is it that your Excellency is going? There is war in the Capital and our lord has been slain. Imai also has fallen by his own hand." When Higuchi thus heard that all was lost, he burst into tears, and then turned and addressed his men: "Hearken to me, sirs! All of you who have a mind to repay the gratitude you owe our lord, make your escape to whatever place you may, and as begging pilgrims pray that he may obtain enlightenment in the world to come, As for me, I go to die in Miyako, and once more to attend our lord on the Dark Road, for it is my wish to be with Imai in that world." And with that he rode on again, and as his followers withdrew hither and thither by the way, his force of five hundred men melted away so that when he passed the south Toba gate, scarcely twenty were left. Now when the enemy heard that Higuchi Jirō Kanemitsu was just about to enter the city, all their great captains of noble lineage rode out with their men to Shichijō, Shujaku, Tsukurimichi and Yotsuzuka to meet him. Then one of Higuchi's men, Chigo-no-Tarō Mitsuhiro, spurring his charger against a great mass of foemen who were waiting at Yotsuzuka, rose in his stirrups and shouted; "Are there any of the retainers of Ichijō Jirō Dono of Kai present among you?" At this a great laugh rose from the other side. "Will you fight with none but the followers of Ichijō Jirō then?" they returned; "take all comers! don't pick your men!" "It was not that I might choose my opponents that I spoke," replied Mitsuhiro, declaring his titles in answer to their laughter; "I am Chino-no-Tarō Mitsuhiro, son of Chino-no-taiyū Mitsuie of Kaminomiya in Suwo of the province of Shinano, and I have left my two children behind me at home; and that they might be taught what a death their father died, whether good or ill, I wished to meet my fate before the eyes of my younger brother Shichiro who serves in the train of my lord Ichijō-Jirō of Kai. There is none that I fear!" And riding at one after another he cut down three men, and grappling with a fourth, both fell together and stabbed each other to death.

Now Higuchi had many friends among the party of Kodama, and some of them came to him and persuaded him thus: "It is but natural that the friendships that we warriors bear to each other should at times result in our sparing one another's lives, and so now for the sake of our former intimacy we would save you from death. Though among Kiso's captains there are none to equal his Four Deval Kings Imai, Higuchi, Tate and Nenoi, yet take it not to heart that Kiso has been slain and Imai has taken his life, for if you will now give yourself up, as a reward for our recent prowess we can plead for your life." So, tempted by this promise, bold veteran as Higuchi was, in accordance with the decree of destiny and unmindful of the dictates of chivalry, he shamelessly surrendered to the Kodama clan. When this came to the ears of the Commanders Noriyori and Yoshitsune they forthwith sent a petition to the Hō-ō on his behalf, but all the Courtiers and Nobles and Ladies in waiting even to the maidens of tender years opposed it with one accord, crying out that when Kiso had stormed the Hōjujiden and burnt it, thereby causing the death of many venerable priests of high rank, Imai and Higuchi were the names that they had heard shouted everywhere, and that it was a great mistake to spare the life of such a fellow. And as in face of this nothing more could be done. Higuchi was at last condemned to die.

On the twenty second day the new Sesshō was removed from office and the former one restored to his place: that he should have held the office for the transient period of but sixty days must have seemed like a dream from which he had not yet awakened; though in former days there was the case of the Kwampaku Michikane who was in office for but seven days before he died. Still, as during even this short period of sixty days both the Setchie Festival and also an Appointment of Officials had been held, he had something to think about in after years.

On the twenty fourth day the heads of Kiso Sama-no-kami and four others were brought into the Capital and carried through the streets. Though Higuchi had yielded himself as a prisoner, yet as he begged to be allowed to accompany them, permission was given, and he escorted the heads of his companions clad in a dark blue hitatare and high eboshi. He was put to death on the next day, the twenty fifth; for though Noriyori and Yoshitsune many times interceded for his life, all felt that to spare one of Kiso's Four Deva Kings was as dangerous as keeping a tiger at large. We have heard how in China, when the power of Shin declined and all the Princes rose in rebellion like a swarm of bees, Haikō though he entered the Palace of Kanyō, did not waste his time in dalliance with the fair Court Ladies, or stop to seize gold or treasure, but calmly secured the pass of Kwankoku, after which he was able to destroy his enemies at leisure and thus become supreme in the Empire. So this Kiso Sama-no-kami, if he had obeyed the orders of Yoritomo after he entered the Capital, might have become no less powerful than Heike.

Now the Heike had departed from the coast of Yashima in Sanuki the winter of the year before, and crossed over to the bay of Naniwa in Settsu and took up a position between Ichi-no-tani on the west, where they built a strong fortification, and the wood of Ikuta on the east, where the entrance to the fort was made. Between these points, at Fukuhara, Hyogo, Itayado and Suma were encamped all the forces of the eight provinces of the Sanyōdō and the six provinces of the Nankaidō, a total of a hundred thousand men in all. The position at Ichi-no-tani had a narrow entrance with cliffs on the north and the sea on the south, while within it was very spacious. The cliffs rose high and steep, perpendicular as a standing screen, and from them to the shallows of the beach a strong breastwork was erected of wood and stone, well protected by palisades, while beyond it, in the deep water rode their great galleys like a floating shield. In the towers of the breastwork were stationed the stout soldiery of Shikoku and Kyūshū in full armour with bows and arrows in their hands, dense as the evening mists, while in front of the towers, ten or twelve deep, stood their horses, fully accoutred with saddle and trappings. Ceaseless was the roll of their war drums; the might of their bows was like the crescent moon, and the gleam of their blades was as the shimmer of the hoar frost in autumn, while their myriad red banners that flew aloft in the spring breezes rose to heaven like the flames of a conflagration.

Chapter VI.

SIX BATTLES.

But after the Heike crossed over to Ichi-no-tani the men of Shikoku became disaffected, and especially the subordinate officials in charge of Awa and Sanuki broke into open rebellion and wished to go over to the Genji, but as they had been on the side of the Heike right up to this time, they doubted whether the Genji would believe in their sudden change of face, and decided to prove their hostility to their former allies by a deliberate act of war. Learning therefore that Kadowaki-no-Hei Chūnagon Norimori and his two sons Echizen-no-Sammi Michimori and Noto-no-kami Noritsune were at Shimotsue in the province of Bizen, they set sail thither with ten ships of war to attack them. Noritsune's wrath was great. "These are the fellows," he exclaimed, "who have been living on our pasture right up till yesterday, and now they have turned traitor! Kill them all, let none escape! "And he put to sea with his men in a number of small boats, and attacked them fiercely. Now the Shikoku men had only intended to shoot a few arrows at them, as a proof of their rebellion, and then retire, so when they found themselves attacked thus vigorously they at once gave way and beat a hasty retreat to the port of Fukura in Awaji. In this island of Awaji were two Genji chiefs; they were the youngest sons of the late Rokujō-no-Hangwan Tameyoshi, Kamo-no Kwanja Yoshitsugu and Awaji-no-Kwanja Yoshihisa, and under their leadership the rebels threw up a stronghold and awaited the foe. This availed nothing under the impetuous onslaught of Noritsune, and Kamo no Kwanja was killed and Awaji-no-Kwanja wounded and captured, while the remaining two hundred and thirty men who still resisted were taken and beheaded, their heads being labelled with the names of their captors and sent to Fukuhara, whither Kadowaki Norimori also proceeded. His two sons then crossed over to Shikoku to deal with one Kawano-no-Shirō of Iyo, who had not obeyed the Heike summons, the elder brother Michimori soon after arriving before the stronghold of Hanazono in Awa.

Now when Kawano-no-Shirō Michinobu of Iyo heard that Noto-no-kami Noritsune had arrived at Yashima in Sanuki, he went over to the province of Aki to join his maternal uncle Nuta-no-Jirō who lived there, and as soon as Noritsune heard it he started from Yashima without delay, and reaching Mino-shima in Bingo the same day, on the next he was already before the fortress of Nuta. He immediately delivered a violent assault on the two rebels, with the result that Nuta laid down his arms and surrendered. Kawano, however, resisted stubbornly, and when his five hundred men had been reduced to fifty, he sallied forth from the walls to make his escape. Being surrounded by a band of two hundred men under Heihachi-hyōye Tamehisa, one of Noritsune's samurai, he fought until but six of his men were left, and as they were retreating along a narrow path to gain the shore and evade their foes by boat, Sanuki-no-Shichirō Yoshinori, son of Heihachi-hyōye, a very fine archer, shot down another five so that only himself and one retainer remained. Then Yoshinori, taking the retainer for his lord, sprang upon him and grappled, with him and would have slain him, when his master turned, swept off his head as he bent over his retainer, and flung it into a ricefield. Then he shouted loudly: "I am Kwano-no-Shirō Ochi-no-Michinobu of Iyo, aged twenty one, and this is the way I fight. Stop me now, any of you who thinks himself someone!" And thus eluding them, he escaped with his retainer to Iyo. Noto-no-kami, though he had been unable to capture Kawano, then returned to Ichi-no-tani with his prisoner Nuta-no-Jirō.

Ama-no-Rokurō Tadahisa of the province of Awa also rebelled and went over to the Genji, setting sail for the Capital with two large warships fully loaded with men and provisions. As soon as this came to the ears of Noto-no-kami in Fukuhara he set off in pursuit with many small and swift ships, and overtook Tadahisa off Nishinomiya. Ordering his men to let none escape, he attacked them fiercely, but Tadahisa, fearing destruction, fled to Fukehi in Izumi. Then Sonobe-no-Hyōye Tadayasu, who was not well disposed to the Heike, when he heard that Ama-no-Rokurō had been thus roughly handled by Noritsune and was in Fukehi, went thither and joined him with a hundred horsemen, and the two allies built a fortress there to resist attacks. Noritsune soon assaulted it, however, so seeing no chance of stemming his vehement onset, they made their escape to Miyako, leaving a hundred and thirty of their followers behind, whose heads were duly taken and sent to Fukuhara.

Soon after, Usuki-no-Jirō Koretaka and Ogata-no-Saburō Koreyoshi of the province of Bungo joined themselves with Kawano-no-Shirō Michinobu, and assembling two thousand fighting men, crossed over to Bizen and established themselves in the fortress of Imaki in that Province. News of this soon reached Noritsune at Fukuhara and filled him with wrath and apprehension, so that he was soon on the march to Bizen with three thousand horsemen. "The rascals are in some force there, so we must send a larger army," quoth he at Fukuhara, and when this speech was reported to the rebels, they thought that many tens of thousands of horsemen were being sent against them, and the soldiers in the fortress declared that, as they had already had their fill of fighting and won much fame and booty, it would be a shame if they were surrounded and annihilated by overwhelming numbers, so that it would be better to retire to some safer place and rest themselves awhile. Usuki-no-Jirō and Ogata-no-Saburō accordingly hastened back to Bungo, while Kawano recrossed the sea to Iyo, and Noto-no-kami, seeing that there was no longer any enemy to fight, made his way back to Fukuhara, to be greatly praised by Munemori and all the Heike Courtiers for his many successful expeditions.

Chapter VII.

THE MUSTER AT MIKUSA.

On the twenty ninth day of the first month Noriyori and Yoshitsune proceeded to the Palace of the Hō-ō to announce their intention of marching into the Western Provinces against the Heike; and after receiving the Imperial exhortation to restore to the Capital the Three Sacred Treasures, the Jewel, the Sword, and the Mirror, which have been handed down in the Imperial Family since the Age of the Gods, they made low obeisance and withdrew.

On the fourth day of the second month, being the anniversary of the death of the Lay-priest Chancellor Kiyomori, the customary Buddhist services were performed at Fukuhara. Thus the days and months had passed in incessant fighting, and ere they were aware of it the preceding year had glided away and the ill-omened season of spring had begun. Under more happy circumstances there would have been a great erecting of Sotoba and lavish offerings to the priests and Budhas, but as it was the Courtiers and Ladies could only assemble for mourning and lamentation. Soon afterwards an Appointment of Officials was held at Fukuhara and both priests and laymen received promotion. Among them Kadowaki-no-Hei Chūnagon Norimori-no-Kyō was to be raised to Dainagon of the Upper Second Rank, but on receiving the intimation of his advancement from the Daijin Munemori he made this stanza:

*"Wondering still how it is I am spared from one day to another,
    This new honour seems as but a dream of a dream;"*

in consequence of which his appointment was cancelled.

Suwō-no-suke Morozumi, the son of the Secretary of State Nakahara-no-Moronao was made Secretary of State, and Hyōbu-no-Shō Masaakira became Kurando of the Fifth Rank, being therefore known as Kurando-no-Shō. In ancient days when Masakado conquered the eight provinces of the East and established his capital in the district of Soma in Shimosa, he gave himself the title of Hei-Shinnō, and created many officials, but among them a Master of the Records was not found. The present occasion, however, was by no means, the same;

for though the Emperor had gone forth from the Ancient Capital, he yet held the Imperial Authority and the Three Sacred Treasures, and so there was nothing irregular in these appointments to rank and office.

When they heard that the Heike had succeeded in fighting their way back to Fukuhara, their relatives who had been left behind in Miyako were filled with joy and encouragement, and Kajii-no-Miya, the Tendai Zasshu, often exchanged letters with his old friend Nii-no-Sōzu Senshin, who was in the Heike camp, in which he declared his sympathy with his friend in exile, but informed him that things were not yet quiet in the Capital and so forth, and in one of these letters he sent this verse:

"*All unknown to the world nay heart ever yearns for your friendship*
How I long to roam where the moon wanes in the west."

When the Sōzu read this lie pressed it to his face and burst into tears.

Meanwhile, as the days and years passed, the thoughts of Komatsu-no-Sammi Chūjō Koremori dwelt ever on his wife and children whom he had left behind in the Capital and he was very sad. They could at tines send letters to each other by the hands of merchants, and when he heard of her lonely life in Miyako he felt much inclined to try to bring her to Fukuhara that they might be together, but when he reflected on the hard life they led there he could only refrain and abandon himself to his gloomy thoughts.

The Genji had intended to begin their attack on Fukuhara on the fourth day of the second month, but when they heard that Buddhist rites were being performed on behalf of the departed Nyūdō they desisted, and as the fifth and sixth days were unlucky, it was not till the seventh day at six o'clock in the morning that the battle began on both the eastern and western entrances of Ichi-no-tani.

On the fourth day, as it was a lucky cne, they had divided their army into two parts, the main body being commanded by Kaba-no-Onzōshi Noriyori with whom rode the following captains: Takeda-no-Tarō Nobuyoshi, Kagami-no-Jirō Tomitsu, Kagami-no-Kojirō Nagakiyo, Yamana-no-Jirō Noriyoshi, and Yamana-no-Saburō Yoshiyuki, while in command of the samurai were Kajiwara Heizō Kagetoki, his eldest son Genda Kagesue, his second son Heiji Kagetaka, Kajiwara Saburō Kageie, Inage-no-Saburō Shigenari, Hangai-no-Gorō Shigeyuki, Oyama-no-Koshirō Tomomasa, Naganuma-no-Gorō Munemasa, Yuki-no-Shichirō Tomomitsu, Sanuki-no-Shirōdaiyū Hirotsuna, Onodera-no-Zenji Tarō Michitsuna, Soga-no-Tarō Sukenobu, Nakamura Tarō Tokitsune, Edo-no-Shirō Shigeharu, Ōkawazu-no-Tarō Hiroyuki, Tamai-no-Shirō Sukekage, Shō-no-Saburō

Takaie, Shō-no-Shirō Takaie, Shodai-no-Hachiro Yukihira, Kuge-Jirō Shigemitsu, Kawara-no-Tarō Takanao, Kawara-no-Jirō Morinao, and Fujita-no-Saburōdaiyū Yukiyasu with a force of some fifty thousand horsemen under them.

On the fourth day of the second month at eight o'clock in the morning they departed from the Capital, and about evening of the same day they arrived at Koyano in the province of Settsu and pitched their camp.

The smaller body was under the command of Kurō Onzōshi Yoshitsune and with him were Yasuda-no-Saburō Yoshisada, Ōuchi-no-Tarō Koreyoshi, Murakami-no-Hangwandai Yasukuni, and Tajiro-no-Kwanja Nobutsuna. The samurai of this army were commanded by Doi-no-Jirō Sanehira, his son Yatarō Tōhira, Miura-no-suke Yoshizumi, his son Heiroku Yoshimura, Hatakeyama-no-Shōji Jirō Shigetada, Hatakeyama-no-Nagano Saburō Shigekiyo, Sawara-no-Jurō Yoshitsura, Wada-no-Kotarō Yoshimori, Wada-no-Jirō Yoshimochi, Saburō Munezane, Sasaki Shirō Takatsuna, Gorō Yoshikiyo, Kumagai-no-Jirō Naozane, his son Kojirō Naoie, Hirayama-no-Mushadokoro Toshishige, Amano-no-Jirō Naotsune, Ogawa-no-Jirō Sukeyoshi, Hara-no-Saburō Kiyomasu, Tatara-no-Gorō Yoshiharu, his son Tarō Mitsuyoshi, Watariyanagi Yagorō Kiyotada, Beppu Kotarō Kiyoshige, Kaneko-no-Jūrō Ietada, Kaneko-no-Yoichi Chikanori, Gempachi Hirotsuna, Kataoka-no-Tarō Tsuneharu, Ise-no-Saburō Yoshimori, Mutsu-no-Sato Saburō Tsuginobu, Sato Shirō Tadanobu, Eda-no-Genzō, Kumai-no-Tarō and Musashi-bō Benkei, in all about ten thousand men. These also started from the Capital at the same time as the others, and taking the Tamba road, made a two days match in one, taking up their position at a place called Onohara on the eastern slope of Mikusayama, which is on the boundary of Tamba and Harima.

Chapter VIII.

THE FIGHT AT MIKUSA.

The commanders on the Heike side were Komatsu-no-Shin-sammi Chūjō Sukemori, Komatsu-no-Shōshō Arimori, Tango-no-Jijū Tadafusa, and Bitchū-no-kami Moromori, while in command of the samurai were Iga-no-Heinaihyōye Kiyoie and Emi-no-Jirō Masakata with about three thousand horsemen, who took up their position on the western slope of Mikusayama. That night at about eight o'clock Yoshitsune summoned to him Doi-no-Jirō Sanehira, and said to him: "The Heike are only about three ri distant from us: they are encamped on the western slope of Mikusayama with a large force; shall we attack them by night or to-morrow?" The Tajiro-no-Kanja stood forth and said: "We have a great advantage, for our force numbers ten thousand men, whereas the Heike have only about three thousand. If we wait to fight to morrow their numbers will most likely have increased, so let us attack then; at once to night." "Excellently spoken, Tajiro Dono," said Doi-no-Jirō, "that is what we all think; so let us make a night attack on them." When this order was given to the soldiers, however, they said each to his neighbour: "How dark it is what are we to do in this darkness?" "How about torches then?" suggested Voshitsune. "So it must be;" replied Doi, and they set fire to all the houses of Onohara and then to all the trees and brushwood on the plain and on the mountain slopes, so that it became as bright as day, and so they crossed the hills for the distance of three ri without any hindrance. Now this Tajiro no Kwanja was the youngest son of the Chūnagon Tametsuna, the former Governor of Izu, and was the issue of an amour that he had with the daughter of Kanō-no-suke Shigemitsu, being brought up to the profession of arms by his maternal grandfather, so that he was a skilful warrior as well as of high lineage, being descended in the fifth generation from Sukehito Shinnō, the third son of the Emperor Go-Sanjō.

As the Heike never dreamed that they would be attacked that night, their leaders bade them sleep well till morning, for as they would have to fight on the morrow, they must by no means be drowsy, so, though the vanguard kept the usual watch, those in the rear lay stretched out in careless plumber with their heads pillowed on their helmets or quivers, or the sleeves of their armour, entirely heedless of any danger. Then suddenly, at about midnight, the ten thousand horsemen of the Genji came sweeping down with ringing shouts on the western slope of Mount Mikusa, and the Heike, taken completely by surprise, rose and fled in wild confusion, leaving their weapons behind them in their hurry and excitement, and scattering everywhere in their fear of being trampled under the horse-hoofs of the enemy. Then the Genji rode right through their ranks and pursued them and cut them down at their will, so that at the first onset five hundred men were slain outright, beside a large number who were wounded. The three commanders, Shin-sammi Chūjō Sukemori, Komatsu Shōshō Arimori, and Tango-no-Jijū Tadafusa, overcome with shame at the rout of Mikusa, took ship from Takasago in Harima and crossed over to Yashima in Sanuki. Bitchū-no kami alone, accompanied by Heinaihyōye and Emi-no-Jirō, somehow contrived to make his way back again to Ichi-no-tani.

Chapter IX.

THE OLD HORSE.

Forthwith the Daijin Munemori dispatched Aki-no-Uma-no-suke Yoshiyuki with this message to all the chiefs of his house. "We hear that Kurō Yoshitsune has attacked and broken through our outpost at Mikusayama so that the hillside on our flank is threatened: can you come to our assistance?" But they all declined. Then the Daijin called once more on Noto-no-kami Noritsune, saying: "Many times before have you aided us; may we reply on your help once more?" "War" replied Noritsune, "is just like fishing or any other sport; he who always chooses the comfortable positions and refuses the unfavourable ones will never win a victory. As for me, have no fear, for I am ever ready to hasten where the greatest danger threatens. Trust me to deal with the forces of Yoshitsune." When this was reported to Munemori, he was exceedingly glad, and at once put an army of ten thousand men, led by Etchū Zenji Moritoshi, at the disposal of Noritsune.

Then Noritsune, taking with him his elder brother Echizen-no-sammi Michimori, set out for the hills. And these were the hills that lay at the foot of the pass called Hiyodori-goe, behind Ichi-no-tani. Michimori, however, called his wife to the camp of Noritsune in order that he might take a tender farewell of tier before the expedition, and when this came to the ears of Noto-no-kami he was greatly enraged and rebuked him: "The position 'we are to hold in one of great peril," said he, "and matters are now most critical, for if the enemy should succeed in descending on us over these hills, disaster stares us in the face. To take a bow and not lay an arrow on the string is bad enough, but to lay an arrow on the string and not to draw it is worse still; so what is the use of wasting time in this soft talk? "Then Michimori, feeling the truth of his words, dismissed his wife and put on his armour.

About dusk on the fifth day the Genii started from Koyano and pressed on to attack the wood at Ikuta, and as the Heike looked out over Suzume-no-matsubara, Mikage-no-matsu and Koyano, they could see them pitching their camps everywhere, while the glow of their thousand watch fires reddened the sky like the moon rising over the mountains. The fires that the Heike kindled also showed up the dark outline of the wood of Ikuta, and twinkled as they flared up like stars in the brightening sky; reminding them too of the glimmering fire-flies on the river bank, so often the subject of their verse in the happy days gone by. So, as they beheld the Genii thus deliberately pitching their camps here and there, and feeding and resting their horses, they watched and wondered when they would be attacked, their hearts filled with disquiet.

At dawn on the sixth day Kurō Onzōshi Yoshitsune, dividing his ten thousand men into two companies, ordered Doi-no-Jirō Sanehira to make an attack on the western outlet of Ichi-no-tani with seven thousand, while he himself with the remaining three thousand horsemen went round by the Tango road to descend the pass of Hiyodori-goe to take them in the rear. At this his men began to murmur to each other: "Everyone knows the dangers of that place; if we must die, it were better to die facing the foe than to fall over a cliff and be killed. Does anyone know the way among these mountains?" "I know these mountains very well;" exclaimed Hirayama-no-Mushadokoro of Musashi, in answer to these muttering. "But you were brought up in the Eastern Provinces, and this is the first time you have seen the mountains of the West," objected Yoshitsune, "so how can you guide us?" "That may be even as your Excellency says," replied Hirayama, "but just as a poet knows the cherry-blossoms of Yoshino and Hatsuse without seeing them, so does a proper warrior know the way to the rear of an enemy's castle!" After this most audacious speech, a young samurai of eighteen years old named Beppu-no-Kotarō Kiyoshige of Musashi spoke up and said: "I have often been told by my father Yoshishige Hōshi, that whether you are hunting on the mountains or fighting an enemy, if you lose your way you must take an old horse, tie the reins and throw them on his neck, and then drive him on in front, and he will always find a path." "Well spoken," said Yoshitsune, "they say an old horse will find the road even when it is buried in snow!" So they took an old, grey horse, trapped him with a silver plated saddle and a well-polished bit, and tying the reins and throwing them on his neck, drove him on in front of them, and so plunged into the unknown mountains.

As it was the beginning of the second month, the snow had melted here and there on the peaks and at times they thought they saw flowers, while at times they heard the notes of the Uguisu of the valleys, and were hidden from sight in the mist. As they ascended, the snow-clad peaks towered white and glistening on either side of them, and as they descended again into the valleys, the cliffs rose green on either hand. The pines hung down under their load of snow, and scarcely could they trace the narrow and mossy path: When a sudden gust blew down a cloud of snow flakes, they almost took them for the falling plum-blossom. Whipping up their steeds to their best pace they rode on some distance, until the falling dusk compelled them to bivouac for the night in the depth of the mountains.

As they were thus halted, Musashi-bō Benkei suddenly appeared with an old man he had intercepted. In answer to the to the questions of Yoshitsune lie declared that he was a hunter who lived in these mountains, and that he knew all that country very well. "Then," said Yoshitsune, "what do you think of my plan of riding down into Ichi-no-tani, the stronghold of the Heike?" "Ah," replied the old man, "that can hardly be done. The valley is a hundred yards deep, and of that about half is steep cliff where no one can go. Besides, the Heike will have dug pitfalls and spread caltrops inside the stronghold to make it impossible for your horses." "Indeed?" returned Yoshitsune, "but is it possible for a stag to pass there?" "That stags pass there is certain," replied the hunter, "for in the warm days of spring they come from Harima to seek the thick pasture of Tamba, and when the winter grows cold they go back towards Inamino in Harima where the snow lies lighter." "Forsooth!" ejaculated Yoshitsune, "then a horse can do it, for where a stag may pass, there a horse can go also. Will you then be our guide?" "I am an old man now; how can I go so far?" replied the hunter. "But you have a son?" "I have." And Kumaō Maru, a youth of eighteen soon appeared before the Genji leader. Then Yoshitsune performed the ceremony of Gempuku for the young man, giving him the name of Washio Saburō Yoshihisa, the name of his father being Washio Shōji Takehisa, and he accompanied them, going on in front to guide them down into Ichi-no-tani. And after the Heike had been overthrown and the Genji obtained the supremacy, and his lord Yoshitsune fell into disfavour with his brother and fled to Mutsu and fell there, Washio Saburō Yoshihisa was one of those who followed him to the death.

Chapter X.

THE FIRST AND SECOND ASSAULTS.

Until midnight of the sixth day Kumagai and Hirayama had ridden with the party of Yoshitsune, when Kumagai called his son Kojirō and said: "This party of ours is to attack on difficult ground, so there will be little chance of being the first in the onset. Let us join the army of Doi and see if we can be first in the assault on Ichi-no-tani. "That is a good plan," replied Kojirō, "and I think there are others of the same opinion, so let us make haste." "That is true" answered Naozane, "there is Hirayama; he does not care to be one of the crowd; keep your eye on him;" he added to one of his men. As he had expected Hirayama soon showed signs of leaving the camp and was heard to mutter to himself: "I must get away unseen; it won't do for me to appear to run away." "This beast is a long time over its feed," exclaimed his groom, as he gave it a crack with the whip. "Let it alone;" said Hirayama, "for this night may be its last." Kumagai's retainer, hearing all this, hastened to tell it to his master, and he too left the camp with all speed. Kumagai was clad in a hitatare of dyed cloth and armour laced with red leather, with a red Horo, or arrow guard, on his back, and bestrode a splendid horse called Gondakurige. His son Kojirō Naoie wore a hitatare

ornamented with a design of water plantains and armour laced with
blue and white leather, and rode a cream coloured horse called Seiro.
His standard-bearer wore a hitatare of light green with yellow designs,
and armour laced with yellow and green leather; he bestrode a grey
horse with dark yellow spots. Thus the three retraced their steps, and
leaving the valley they were to descend to the left, they turned off to the
right and rode along an old path, that had long been untrodden, called
Tai-no-hata, which brought them out hard by the beach at Ichi-no-tani.

Now Doi-no-Jirō Sanehira had withdrawn to a place called Shioya
near Ichi-no-tani to spend the night with his forces, and Kumagai,
making a circuit round them, passed them by in the darkness and
approached the western entrance of the Heike stronghold. It was yet
dark and there was no sound from within the place. "This is a hard
place to attack," said Kumagai to his son, "and you may be sure that
there will be many who will strive to be first in the assault. Doubtless
some are already here waiting for the dawn, so we must not suppose we
are alone. I will challenge them with our name and titles": and riding
close up to the enemy's breastwork, he shouted out with a loud voice:
"Kumagai-no-Jirō Naozane of the province of Musashi, and his son
Kojirō Naoie! First in the assault on Ichi-no-tani!" In answer to this the
enemy were heard to shout within the barricade: "Pay no heed, let them
tire out their horses and shoot away their arrows!" And so none came
forth from the stronghold to meet them. After a while, hearing two
horsemen come up behind them, Kumagai hailed them, enquiring who
they were. "Hirayama Sueshige;" was the reply; "and who is it that
calls?" "Naozane." All. Kumagai Dono, how long have you been
here?" "All night." "I also should have been here before," said
Hirayama, "but I was tricked by that fellow Narita Gorō, for he got me
to take him with me on the plea that he had sworn to die with me, but
on the way he persuaded me not to ride on so fast, saying that if we left
all our own men a long way behind, and rode into the enemy alone to
be killed, nothing much would be gained thereby, and I listened to his
words and halted my horse on a little knoll from which I could see our
men coming up, thinking that Narita was following me, but instead of
that he rode on past me. When I saw I had been tricked, I whipped up
my horse and rode on after him, and as he had only gone on about
twenty yards, and his mount was rather tired, I soon caught him up, and
after reproaching him for thus deceiving me, I rode on and left him
behind so that he is not yet in sight."

The dawn was now growing grey, and Kumagai and Hirayama
with their retainers were still alone before the Heike Stronghold, and
though Kumagai had already challenged the enemy once, as this was
before Hirayama had come up, he bethought him to do so once more,
so rising again in his stirrups he repeated his name and titles. At this
there was a stir within the barricade, and thinking to take Kumagai and

his son alive, Etchū-no-Jirōhyōye Moritsugu, Kazusa-no-Gorōhyōye
Tadamitsu, Akushichihyōye Kagekiyo and Gotōnai Sadatsune with
twenty retainers issued forth from the entrance to give them battle.
Then Hirayama also lifted up his voice find declared himself:
"Hirayama-no-Mushadokoro Sueshige of Musashi, who has won great
renown by his prowess in the fighting of Hogen and Heiji!" He was
attired in a hitatare of patterned brocade and armour laced with scarlet,
having at his back a Horo with two wide stripes, and rode a splendid
horse that was dappled about the eyes. His standard-bearer was in
armour laced with black leather, and rode a cream-coloured horse: his
helmet was thrown back so as to expose his face. Thus the fight began,
and Kumagai and Hirayama both bore themselves most valiantly, one
charging forward when the other gave back, and neither yielding to the
other in strength and boldness, hewing at the foe with loud shouts while
the sparks flew from their weapons, till at last the Heike retainers,
wounded and battered by the fierce onslaughts of the two champions,
retreated within their barricade and shut the enemy outside.

Kumagai's horse had been shot in the belly, so he Dismounted and
stood leaning on his bow, while his son Naoie, who was only eighteen
years old, and had been ever foremost in the fighting, had received an
arrow in the left forearm, and alighting also, stood beside him. "How is
that, Kojirō, are you wounded?" he asked. "Ah, you should shift your
armour about well so that the arrows don't go through it. Keep your
neck guard well sloped, and don't get shot in the face." Naozane then
pulled out the arrows that were sticking in his own mail, and turned and
glared fiercely at the Heike behind the wall. "When Naozane left
Kamakura last winter," he shouted, "he pledged his life to his lord
Yoritomo, and swore that his bones should whiten on the sands of Ichi-
no-tani. So much for Etchū-no-Jirōhyōye, Kazusa-no-Gorōhyōye, and
Akushichihyōye, the famous victors of Muroyama and Mizushima! Is
not Noto Dono within there? Here we stand, father and son! Come forth
and meet us, any who dare! "At this defiance Etchū-no-Jirōhyōye,
Moritsugu glared at the pair and advanced towards them. He was clad
in a hitatare of purple and a suit of armour with red lacing, and wore a
helmet adorned with lofty horns. His sword was mounted in gold, and
his saddle inlaid with the same metal, while on his back he carried a
quiver of arrows with black and white feathers. His black lacquered
bow was bound with rattan, and he rode a horse of dappled gray. Side
by side, without yielding a pace, the two Kumagai met him, and
drawing their blades pressed on him without shifting either to the right
or left. At this bold front Etchū-Jirō felt his courage fail him, and
straightway retreated whence he had come. "What," shouted Naozane,
"does Etchū-no-Jirōhyōye refuse our challenge? In what do we fail
him? On to the attack!" But Jirōhyōye refused to be enticed and
continued his progress toward the stronghold. "How cowardly is the

conduct of you fellows," cried Akushichihyōye when he perceived this, retreat, "there is none who dares to close with them or come to grips!" And he was riding out to attack them himself, when Jirōhyōye seized the sleeve of his armour and held him back saying: "Your life is too precious to risk it here; forbear! forbear!" And being thus restrained he did not venture.

Then Kumagai, mounting a fresh horse, again rode to the assault, and Hirayama, who had rested his charger while Kumagai was fighting, now came on to his support. Seeing this the Heike drew their bows with might and main and rained their arrows on the little band, but so crowded were they and so small was their mark that none of their shafts took effect, and when they tried to charge them, as the Heike steeds were badly fed. and over-ridden, and had been long cooped up on shipboard, they would by no means obey the hand of their masters; whereas the horses of Kumagai and Hirayama were stout and well fed animals that in the shock of battle would overthrow and trample down both horse and rider, so that one of the Heike were found willing to face them. Just then it happened that Hirayama's standard-bearer, for whom he would have given his life, was slain, and his master, driven to desperation at his loss, made a rush into the stronghold and cut off the head of the enemy who had killed him, emerging again safely once more Kumagai. had taken much spoil and had been the first to arrive before the entrance, but as the gate was shut he was unable to enter, whereas Hirayama, who had come up later, charged within the gate when it was opened, so that it was difficult to decide which had the honour of being the foremost.

Chapter XI.

THE SECOND ASSAULT.

Meanwhile Narita Gorō had come up also, and the seven thousand men of Doi no-Jirō Sanehira, shouting their warcries, came on to the attack under the banners of their different leaders. Now among the fifty thousand horsemen of the main force of the Genji; who were besetting the other entrance at Ikuta, were two brothers, Kawara Tarō and Kawara Jirō, of Musashi; and the elder of these, Kawara Tarō, called to the younger and said to him: "Though a Daimyo may win renown without fighting himself, through the deeds of his retainers, that reputation is not one that I covet, for I cannot bear to take no part in the battle. To wait here with the enemy before our eyes without drawing bow on him makes the courage fail, so I have determined to get within the defenses and let fly at them there. As I am not likely to come forth alive, do you stay here to bear witness to my posterity." Bursting into tears the younger brother replied: "For two brothers like ourselves how inglorious is it that one should die thus and the other still survive? Let us not then die separately but fall together in one place": and calling their retainers and bidding them bear the tidings of their end to their wives and children, they dismounted and put on straw sandals, and then carrying their bows only, they climbed over the barricade under cover of darkness. Standing within the stronghold, though the colour of their armour could not be distinguished in the star light, they shouted loudly: "Kawara Tarō Kisaichi Takanao, and his brother Jirō Masanao, first in the attack on Ikuta-no-mori!" "Hearing this the Heike within were astonished and said to one another": How terrible are these warriors of the East! See how these two brothers have ventured alone into the midst of our great host! "Tis a pity to touch them." And for a while none lifted a hand against them. But the two brothers were both exceedingly skilful archers, and now they drew their bows and let fly their shafts with the greatest rapidity, so that the Heike cried out to spare them no longer but to cut them down. Now among the Western samurai there were two brothers also who were archers of renown, men of Bitchū, Manabe-no-Shirō and Manabe-no-Gorō by name, and the elder brother Shirō was with the force at Ichi-no-tani, while Gorō the younger was posted at Ikuta. Coming forward he drew his bow to the arrowhead, and taking careful aim, let fly his shaft at Kawara-no-Tarō, who staggered forward pierced through the breastplate. As he tried to support his failing strength on his bow, his brother Jirō ran up, and taking him on his back, made to climb the barricade once more, when Manabe, fitting a second arrow to the string, shot him under the skirts of his armour, so that both brothers fell dead together. His retainers then ran up and cut off both their heads, which they brought and showed to the commander Shin-Chūnagon Tomomori." Ah, the pity of it, "said he, that two such valiant men at arms should die. Would that their lives could have been spared, for they were each worth a thousand men."

Then the retainers of Kawara hasted and told Kajiwara Heizō that the two brothers had scaled the walls of the strong hold and had died within it. "That the two brothers Kawara have fallen is indeed a dire loss for the Kisaichi clan," said Kajiwara, "but the time is now ripe for the attack, so let us advance," So the five hundred men under Kajiwara swept forward to the defences to fight their way into the stronghold. Then Kajiwara Heizō, seeing that his second son Heiji had already far outstripped his men, sent a retainer after him saying: "Those who ride on so that their men cannot follow will be held culpable. It is the order of the Commander." When this was communicated to Heiji he drew in his horse a space while he made the following verse:

> "*If the warrior's bow be once well bent for the arrow,*
> *Who is the foolish wight who will unbend it again?*"

After which he rode on again, shouting loudly. "See that Heiji is not killed! After him, all of you!" cried his father, as, with his eldest son Genda and his third son Saburō, he led his force in a charge into the Heike ranks, where, cutting and slashing in all directions they bowed a way for themselves, and then turned and as quickly withdrew. His son Genda, however, did not emerge with the rest, and in answer to his father's question the retainers declared that they had not seen him for some time, and imagined him to have penetrated too deeply, so that he had been surrounded and slain. "Ah!" exclaimed Heizō, bursting into tears, "it was to save my son that I made this charge, and now to think that Genda is dead and I, his father, am still alive! Back again! At them once more!" And he rose in his stirrups and shouted loudly: "Ho! I am Kajiwara Heizō Kagetoki, descended in the fifth generation from Gongorō Kagemasa of Kamakura, renowned warrior of the East Country, a match for any thousand men! At the age of sixteen I rode in the van of the array of Hachimantarō Yoshiie at the siege of the fortress of Sembuku Kanazawa in Dewa, and receiving an arrow in my left eye through the helmet, I plucked it forth and with it shot down the marksman who sent it, thereby gaining honours and leaving a name to posterity! Come on now, all you who think yourselves somebody, and we will see! "At this proud defiance the defenders shouted: "This is one of the greatest warriors of the East! Strike him down! Don't let him escape!" and they rushed upon him from all sides to cut him down. Heizō, caring nothing for his life, dashed through their midst looking everywhere for signs of his son Genda, and soon found him, as he expected, dismounted and fighting on foot, for his horse had been shot under him, with his helmet struck off from his head and his long hair flying in the wind, his back against a rock twenty feet high, and two of his retainers on his left and right, fighting desperately with five soldiers of the Heike. As Genda was thus fighting, as he thought, his last fight, his father, overjoyed at finding him still alive, sprang from his horse and shouted: "Ho! Genda! Kagetoki is here! Let us die together and not show our backs to the foe!" Then, after they had killed three of the enemy and wounded the other two, Heizō exclaimed: "Warriors advance or retreat according to circumstances. Come Genda!" And they made good their escape. Thus was the second assault made by Kajiwara.

Chapter XII.

THE DESCENT OF THE HILL.

Thereafter the battle became general and the various clans of the Gen and Hei surged over each other in mixed and furious combat. The men of the Miura, Kamakura, Chichibu, Ashikaga, Noiyo, Yokoyama, Inomata, Kodama, Nishi, Tsuzuki and Kisaichi clans charged against each other with a roar like thunder, while the hills re-echoed to the sound of their war-cries, and the shafts they shot at each other fell like rain. Some were wounded slightly and fought on, some grappled and stabbed each other to death, while others bore down their adversaries and cut off their heads: everywhere the fight rolled forward and backward, so that none could tell who were victors or vanquished.

Thus it did not appear that the main body of the Genji lead been successful in their attack, when at dawn on the seventh day Kurō Onzōshi Yoshitsune with his force of three thousand horsemen, having climbed to the top of the Hiyodori-goe was resting his horses before the descent. Just then, startled by the movements of his men, two stags and a doe rushed out and fled over the cliff straight into the camp of the Heike. "That is strange," exclaimed the Heike men-at-arms, for the deer of this part ought to be frightened at our noise and run away to the mountains. Aha! it must be the enemy who is preparing to drop on us from above!" And they began to run about in confusion, when forth strode Takechi-no-Mushadokoro of the province of Iyo, and drawing his bow transfixed the two stags, though letting the doe escape. "Thus," he cried, "will we deal with any who try that road and none are likely to pass it alive!" "What useless shooting of stags is this?" said Etchū Zenji Moritoshi when he saw it; "one of those arrows might have stopped ten of the enemy, so why waste them in that fashion?"

Then Yoshitsune, looking down on the Heike position from the top of the cliff, ordered some horses to be driven down the declivity, and of these, though some missed their footing half-way, and breaking their legs, fell to the bottom and were killed, three saddled horses scrambled down safely and stood, trembling in every limb, before the residence of Etchū Zenji. "If they have riders to guide them," said Yoshitsune, "the horses will get down without damage, so let us descend, and I will show you the way;" and he rode over the cliff at the head of his thirty retainers, seeing which the whole force of three thousand followed on after him. For more than a hundred yards the slope was sandy with small pebbles, so that they slid straight down it and landed on a level place, from which they could survey the rest of the descent. From thence downwards it was all great mossy boulders, but steep as a well, and some fifty yards to the bottom. It seemed impossible to go on any further, neither could they now retrace their steps, and the soldiers were recoiling in horror, thinking that their end had come, when Miura-no-Sahara Jūrō Yoshitsura sprang forward and shouted: "In my part we ride down places like this any day to catch a bird; the Miura would make a race-course of this;" and down he went, followed by all the rest. So steep was the descent that the stirrups of the hinder man struck against the helmet or armour of the one in front of him, and so dangerous did it look that they averted their eyes as they went down. "Ei! Ei!" they ejaculated under their breath as they steadied their horses, and their daring seemed rather that of demons than of men. So they reached the bottom, and as soon as they found themselves safely down they burst forth with a mighty shout, which echoed along the cliffs so that it sounded rather like the battle-cry of ten thousand men than of three.

Then Murakami-no-Hangwan-dai Yasukuni seized a torch and fired the houses and huts of the Heike so that they went up in smoke in a few moments, and when their men saw the clouds of black smoke rising they at once made a rush toward the sea, if hopefully they might find a way of escape. There was no lack of ships drawn up by the beach, but in their panic four or five hundred men in full armour and even a thousand all crowded into one ship, so that when they had rowed out not more than fifty or sixty yards from the shore, three large ships turned over and sank before their eyes. Moreover those in the ships would only take on board those warriors who were of high rank, and thrust away the common soldiers, slashing at them with their swords and halberds, but even though they saw this, rather than stay and be cut down by the enemy, they clung to the ships and strove to drag themselves on board, so that their hands and arms were cut off and they fell back into the sea, which quickly reddened with their blood. Thus, both on the main front and on the sea shore did the young warriors of Musashi and Sagami strain every nerve in the fight, caring nothing for their lives as they rushed desperately to the attack. What must have been the feelings of Noto-no-kami Noritsune, who in all his many battles has never been vanquished until now? Mounting his charger Usuzumi, he galloped away toward the West, and taking ship from Takasago in Harima, crossed over to Yashima in Sanuki.

Chapter XIII.

THE DEATH OF MORITOSHI.

Now Shin-Chūnagon Tomomori-no-Kyō was in command of the Heike at Ikuta-no-mori, and as all his mind was bent on the eastward, a messenger from the Kodama clan came riding up to him. "Your lordship was Governor of Musashi last year," said he, "and because of that connexion the Kodama clan has sent me to warn you. Look to your rear!" Then the retainers of Tomomori turned and saw the clouds of black smoke ascending behind them, and crying out that all was lost and the western army had given way, they were stricken with panic and broke and fled in wild confusion.

Etchū Zenji Moritoshi was the leader of the samurai on the cliff side, and when he saw all the others take to flight, disdaining to follow them, he reined in his charger to await the foe, when Inomata-no-Koheiroku Noritsuna, rejoicing to meet so redoutable an antagonist, urged on his horse and bore down upon him. Rushing upon each other, they grappled fiercely so that both fell from their horses, and though Inomata was famous for his great strength in all the eight provinces of the East, and was said to have torn off the upper branches of a stag horn with ease, Etchū Zenji had the strength of twenty or thirty ordinary men, and indeed so powerful were his limbs that he could haul up or down a heavy ship that it took sixty or seventy men to move, and so he gripped his adversary and pinned him down so that he could not rise. Thus prostrate beneath his foe, try how he would to shift him or draw his sword, he could not so much as stir a finger to the hilt, and even when he strove to speak, so great was the pressure that no word would come forth. Spite of all this, however, he was yet undaunted, and after a short breathing space he managed to ejaculate: "When a samurai takes the head of an enemy it is the custom that he first enquire his name and also declare his own. It is great merit to take a head, but of what value is one without a name?" Thinking this most reasonable, Moritoshi then declared himself: "I am Etchū Zenji Moritoshi, formerly a Courtier of the Heike house, but now only worthy to be an ordinary samurai. I pray you tell me your name also." "I am Inomata-no-Koheiroku Noritsuna," replied the other faintly, "and if you will spare my life I will obtain yours as a reward for my share in the victory, and so you may escape the doom of your house." "What disgraceful speech is this?" cried Moritoshi in great wrath. "Unworthy though I may be, I am yet a Taira, and never will I stoop to ask or grant favours to any of Genji blood!" And he was just about to cut off his head when Inomata pleaded again: "Who is so unchivalrous as to cut off the head of a surrendered foe?" Whereupon Moritoshi relented and spared his life.

Now the place where they had fought was solid ground in front, but behind them lay deep and swampy ricefields, and on a narrow path between these the two sat down to rest and recover their breath, when a single horseman rode up, clad in scarlet armour and mounted on a cream coloured horse with saddle decorated with gold. Moritoshi glared at him suspiciously. "That is Hitomi Shirō, a friend of Inomata; he has come to see what has happened, but I will deal with him too;" and he sprang up and prepared to grapple with him as soon as he came near enough. Now Etchū Zenji kept an eye on both his foes at first, but as the other drew nearer, his attention became more fixed on him, which Inomata perceiving, he suddenly sprang up from the ground and dealt Moritoshi a heavy blow on the breast plate with his closed fist. Losing his balance at this unexpected attack, Moritoshi fell over backwards, when Inomata immediately leapt upon him, snatched his dagger from his side, and pulling up the skirt of his armour, stabbed him so deeply thrice that the hilt and fist went in after the blade. Having thus dispatched him he cut off his head, and as Hitomi Shirō had come up by then, and at such times disputes about heads were apt to arise, he stuck it on the point of his sword and held it aloft, at the same time shouting loudly: "The head of Etchū Zenji Moritoshi, the famous demon-warrior of the Heike, slain by Inomata-no-Koheiroku Noritsuna of the province of Musashi!" And on the roll of those who died valiantly that day the name of Inomata stood first.

Chapter XIV.

THE DEATH OF TADANORI.

Satsuma-no-kami Tadanori the Commander of the western army, clad in a dark-blue hitatare and a suit of armour with black silk lacing, and mounted on a great black horse with a saddle enriched with lacquer of powdered gold, was calmly withdrawing with his following of a hundred horsemen, when Okabe-on-Rokuyata Tadazumi of Musashi espied him and pursued at full gallop, eager to bring down so noble a prize. "This must be some great leader!" he cried. "Shameful! to turn your back to the foe!" Tadanori turned in the saddle; "We are friends! We are friends!" he replied, as he continued on his way. As he had turned, however, Tadazumi had caught a glimpse of his face and noticed that his teeth were blackened." There are none of our side who have blackened teeth," he said, "this must be one of the Heike Courtiers." And overtaking him, he ranged up to him to grapple. When his hundred followers saw this, since they were hired retainers drawn from various provinces, they scattered and fled in all directions, leaving their leader to his fate. But Satsuma-no-kami, who had been brought up at Kumano, was famous for his strength, and was extremely active and agile besides, so clutching Tadazumi he pulled him from his horse, dealing him two stabs with his dirk while he was yet in the saddle, and following them with another as he was falling. The first two blows fell on his armour and failed to pierce it, while the third wounded him in the face but was not mortal, and as Tadanori sprang down upon him to cut off his head, Tadazumi's page, who had been riding behind him, slipped from his horse and with a blow of his sword cut off Tadanori's arm above the elbow, Satsuma-no-kami, seeing that all was over and wishing to have a short space to say the death-prayer, flung Tadazumi away from him so that he fell about a bow's length away. Then turning toward the west he repeated: "Kōmyō Henjō Jippō Sekai, Nembutsu Shujō Sesshu Fusha; O Amida Nyorai, who sheddest the light of Thy Presence through the ten quarters of the world, gather into Thy Radiant Heaven all who call upon Thy Name!" And just as his prayer was finished, Tadazumi from behind swept off his head.

Not doubting that he had taken the head of a noble foe, but quite unaware who he might be, he was searching his armour when he came across a piece of paper fastened to his quiver, on which was written a verse with this title; "The Traveller's Host, a Flower."

> "*Seeking where I may lodge a on my weary way, in the evening
> Under a tree I lie; now is any host but a flower.*"

Wherefore he knew that it could be none but Satsuma-no-kami.

Then he lifted up the head on his sword's point and shouted with a loud voice: "Satsuma-no-kami Dono, the demon-warrior of Nippon, slain by Okabe-no-Rokuyata Tadazumi of Musashi!" And when they heard it, all, friends and foes alike, moistened the sleeves of their armour with their tears, exclaiming: "Alas! what a great captain has passed away! Warrior and artist and poet; in all things he was preeminent."

Chapter XV.

SHIGEHIRA IS TAKEN ALIVE.

Hon-sammi Chūjō Shigehira was second in command at Ikuta-no-mori, and he was attired that day in a hitatare of dark-blue cloth on which a pattern of rocks and seabirds was embroidered in light yellow silk, and armour with purple lacing deepening in its hue toward the skirts. On his head was a helmet with tall golden horns, and his sword also was mounted in gold. His arrows were feathered with black and White falcon plumes, and in his hand he carried a 'Shigetō' bow. He was mounted on a renowned war horse called Dōji-kage, whose trappings were resplendent with ornaments of gold. With him was his foster-brother Gotō Hyōye Masanaga in a hitatare of dyed brocade and a suit of armour with scarlet lacing, and he too was mounted on a splendid cream-coloured charger named Yome-nashi As they were riding along the shore to take ship and escape, Shō-no-Shirō Takaie and Kajiwara Genda Kagesue, thinking they looked a fine prize, spurred on their horses and bore down upon them. Now there were many ships ranged along the shore, but the enemy pressed on them so hard from behind that there was no Opportunity to embark, so the two, crossing the Minatogawa and the Karumogawa, and leaving Hasu-no-ike on the

right and Koma-no-hayashi on the left, rode hard through Itayado and
Suma and endeavoured to make their escape to the west. As Sammi
Chūjō was mounted on such a famous charger as Doji-kage it seemed
unlikely that any ordinary horse would overhaul him, and the pursuers
mounts were already weakening, when Kajiwara drew his bow to the
head sent an arrow whizzing after then. Though a long venture the shaft
flew true to its mark, and buried itself deeply in the hind-leg of the
Chūjō's steed, just above the root of the tail. Seeing its pace slacken his
foster-brother Morinaga, thinking that the Chūjō might demand his
mount, whipped it up and made good his escape. "Ah!" exclaimed the
Chūjō, "why do you desert me thus? Have you forgotten all your
promises? "But he paid no heed, and tearing off the red badge from his
armour, thought of nothing but saving himself by flight. Then the
Chūjō, seeing that his horse could go no farther, plunged headlong into
the sea to die by drowning, but the water was so shallow that there was
no time, and as he started to cut himself open, Shō-no-Shirō Takaie
rode up, and springing from his horse, called out to him: "Desist I pray
you; allow me to take you with me." And placing him on his own
horse, he bound him to the pommel of his saddle and escorted him back
to the Genii camp.

The Chūjō's foster-brother Morinaga, who had ridden away and
deserted him, fled to seek refuge with Onaka Hōkyō, one of the priests
of Kumano, but after his death returned again to the Capital with his
widow, when she came up on account of a lawsuit that she had. There
he was recognised by many of his associates who had known him in
past times, and they pointed the finger of scorn at him saying: "How
disgraceful! There is Gotō Hyōye Morinaga, who deserted the Chūjō in
his need and refused to aid him. He has come back again with the
widow of the Hōkyō." And Morinaga, when he heard it was so
ashamed that he hid his face with his fan.

Chapter XVI.

THE DEATH OF ATSUMORI.

Now when the Heike were routed at Ichi-no-tani, and their Nobles
and Courtiers were fleeing to the shore to escape in their ships,
Kumagai Jirō Naozane came riding along a narrow path on to the
beach, with the intention of intercepting one of their great captain's.
Just then his eye fell on a single horseman who was attempting to reach
one of the ships in the offing, and had swum his horse out some twenty
yards from the water's edge. He was richly attired in a silk hitatare
embroidered with storks, and the lacing of his armour was shaded
green; his helmet was surmounted by lofty horns, and the sword he
wore was gay with gold. His twenty four arrows had black and white

feathers, and he carried a black-lacquered bow bound with rattan. The horse he rode was dappled grey, and its saddle glittered with gold mounting, Not doubting that he was one of the chief captains, Kumagai beckoned to him with his war-fan, crying out: "Shameful! to show an enemy your back. Return! Return!" Then the warrior turned his horse and rode him back to the beach, where Kumagai at once engaged him in mortal combat. Quickly hurling him to the ground, he sprang upon him and tore off his helmet to cut off his head, when he beheld the face of a youth of sixteen or seventeen, delicately powdered and with blackened teeth, just about the age of his own son, and with features of great beauty. "Who are you?" he enquired; "Tell me your name, for I would spare your life." "Nay, first say who you are;" replied the young man. "I am Kumagai Jirō Naozane of Musashi, a person of no particular importance." "Then you have made a good capture;" said the youth. "Take my head and show it to some of my side and they will tell you who I am." "Though he is one of their leaders," mused Kumagai, "if I slay him it will not turn defeat into victory, and if I spare him, it will not turn victory into defeat. When my son Kojirō was but slightly wounded at Ichi-no-tani, did it not make my heart bleed? How pitiful then to put this youth to death." And so he was about to set him free, when, looking behind him, he saw Doi and Kajiwara coming up with fifty horsemen. "Alas! look there," he exclaimed, "the tears running down his face," though I would spare your life, the whole country side swarms with our men, and you cannot escape them. If you must die, let it be by my hand, and I will see that prayers are said for your re-birth in bliss." "Indeed it must be so," said the young warrior, "so take off my head at once." Then Kumagai, weeping bitterly, and so overcome by his compassion for the fair youth that his eyes swam and his hand trembled so that he could scarcely wield his blade, hardly knowing what he did, at last cut off his head. "Alas!" he cried, "what life is so hard as that of a soldier? Only because I was born of a warrior family must I suffer this affliction! How lamentable it is to do such cruel deeds!" And he pressed his face to the sleeve of his armour and wept bitterly. Then, wrapping up the head, he was stripping off the young man's armour, when he discovered a flute in a brocade bag that he was carrying in his girdle. "Ah," he exclaimed, "it was this youth and his friends who were amusing themselves with music within the walls this morning. Among all our men of the Eastern Provinces I doubt if there is any who has brought a flute with him. What esthetes are these Courtiers of the Heike!" And when he brought them and showed them to the Commander, all who saw them were moved to tears; and he then discovered that the youth was Taiyū Atsumori, the youngest son of Shūri-no-taiyū Tsunemori, aged seventeen years. From this time the mind of Kumagai was turned toward the religious life and he eventually became a recluse.

The flute of Atsumori was one which his grandfather Tadamori, who was a famous player, had received as a present from the Emperor Toba, and had handed down to his father Tsunemori, who has given it to Atsumori because of his skill on the instrument. It was called 'Saeda.'[241] Concerning this story of Kumagai we may quote the saying that "even in the most droll and flippant farce there is the germ of a Buddhist Psalm."[242]

Chapter XVII.

THE FIGHT ON THE SHORE.

Kurando-no-taiyū Narimori, the youngest son of Kadowaki Dono was slain by Tsuchiya-no-Gorō Shigeyuki of Hitachi, and Kōgō-gū-no-suke Tsunemasa also fell by the hand of Kawagoe-no-Kotarō Shigefusa of Musashi, while Owari-no-kami Kiyosada, Awaji-no-kami Kiyofusa, and Wakasa-no-kami Tsunetoshi charged headlong into the midst of the foe, and after fighting valiantly for a while, at last fell gloriously together.

Shin-Chūnagon Tomomori-no-Kyō, who was in command at Ikuta no mori, after all his men had either fled or been slain, rode off toward the beach with his son Musashi-no-kami Tomoakira and a faithful retainer named Kenmotsu Tarō Yorikata, when ten horsemen of the Kodama clan, carrying a fan as their standard, put their steeds to a gallop and gave chase. Kenmotsu Tarō, a famous archer, turned and let fly an arrow at the standard-bearer who rode in front, and pierced him through neck and backbone so that he fell dead from his horse. Then the leader of the band bore down on Tomomori to come to close quarters, but his son Tomoakira, anxious to save his father, sprang in between them and grappled with the enemy, throwing him to the ground and then springing down on him and cutting off his head. No sooner had he done this, however, than his opponent's page sprang down also, and taking him at a disadvantage, succeeded in despatching him. Then Kenmotsu Tarō, falling in his turn on the retainer who had slain Musashi-no-kami, killed him also, after which, having shot away all his arrows, he drew his sword to continue the conflict, but, after being severely wounded in the left knee' by an arrow, unable to stand up any longer, he was overcome and killed.

Shin-Chūnagon Tomomori, taking advantage of the confusion of the fighting, spurred on his horse and escaped, and, plunging into the sea, after swimming his horse, which was renowned for its long wind,

---

[241] *Saeda*. 'Little Branch'.

[242] *even in*, etc. i.e. how much more does a serious incident like this turn the mind to religion.

more than a mile, he managed to reach the ship of the Daijin Munemori. As the ship was crowded with men, there was no room to bring the horse on board, and so they drove it off back to the shore. Then Awa-no-Mimbu Shigeyoshi took an arrow in his hand, saying; "Let me shoot it so that it may not fall into the enemy's hands;" But Tomomori forbade him. "That must not be," he said, "for it has just saved my life." So Shigeyoshi did not shoot. The horse was very loath to leave its master, and kept close to the ship for a while, swimming right out into the offing, and it was not until it was at some distance from the shore that it reluctantly turned round and swam back to the beach, and even then, as soon as its feet touched the ground, it turned again and looked after the ship, neighing loudly three times.

Afterwards, as it was resting on the shore, Kawagoe-no-Kotarō Shigefusa caught it and brought it to the Hō-ō. It had originally been the most prized animal in the Hō-ō's stables, and had been presented to Munemori the year before on the occasion of his becoming Naidaijin, and he had given it to Tomomori, and so much did he prize it that he had prayers offered to Taisanfukun, the god of longevity, on its behalf on the first day of every month. And that is why it was so long winded, and was enabled to save its master on this occasion. It was reared in the province of Shinano at a place called Inoue, and so was called Inoueguro, but now, as Kawagoe had caught it, its name was changed to Kawagoeguro.

Then Tomomori entered the presence of the Daijin Munemori, and with tears running down his face, spoke thus: "How sad am I to be alive when my son Musashi-no-kami is gone, and my retainer Kenmotsu is slain also. What is to be thought of a father like me, who cannot help his son when he turns the attack of the enemy on to himself to rescue his father, but leaves him to his fate and saves himself thus? In the case of another I should think that he grudged his life, and now in my own what shame must I feel to merit a like reproach?" And he hid his face in the sleeve of his armour and sobbed aloud. "Indeed it was a splendid thing that Musashi-no-kami thus gave his life for his father; skilled in fight and valiant of heart, how great a captain he was! He was even now the same age as Kiyomune here; just sixteen this year." And looking at his own, son Uemon-no-kami Kiyomune, he too burst into tears. And none of those present, even the most hard-hearted, could refrain from moistening the sleeves of their armour.

Chapter XVIII.

THE FLIGHT.

Bitchū-no-kami Moromori, the youngest son of Komatsu Shigemori, had just embarked in a small boat with six of his retainers, when one of the samurai of Tomomori, Seieimon Kinnaga by name, galloped down to the water's edge and begged them to take him on board, so they backed a little way to take him in. Hastily he jumped in from his horse's back, and as he was a heavy man and in full armour, and the boat was small, it rolled over with the shock and capsized. Bitchū-no-kami was thrown into the water, and as he was struggling in the waves, Honda-no-Jirō Chikatsune, one of the retainers of Hatakeyama, rode up with thirteen of his men, and quickly dismounting, dragged him from the water with an iron rake and decapitated him on the spot. He was then fourteen years of age.

Echizen-no-sammi Michimori-no-Kyō was also in command by the hillside, and when all his men had either fallen or fled, and he was cut off from the main body, since his younger brother Noto no kami Noritsune had already escaped and left him behind, he determined to put an end to himself in peace. As he was turning to retire to the eastward for this purpose, however, he was suddenly surrounded by Sasaki-no-Kimura Saburō Naritsuna of Ōmi and Tamii-no-Shirō Sukekage of Musashi with five others, who quickly slew him and cut off his head. He had with him one retainer only, but when the end came he too deserted him and escaped.

Thus as the day wore on both Genji and Heike fell in great numbers at the eastern and western barriers, and before the towers and beneath the barricades the bodies of men and horses lay in heaps, while the green grass of Ichi-no-tani and Osasahara was turned to crimson. Countless were those who fell by arrow and sword at Ichi-no-tani and Ikuta-no-mori, by the hillside and by the strand of the sea. Two thousand heads did the Genji take in this battle, and of the Courtiers of the Heike, Echizen-no-Sammi Michimori, his younger brother Kurando-no-taiyū Narimori, Satsuma-no-kami Tadanori, Musashi-no-kami Tomoakira, Bitchū-no-kami Moromori, Owari-no-kami-Kiyosada, Awaji-no-kami Kiyofusa, Kōgō-gū-no-suke Tsunemasa the eldest son of Tsunetoshi, his younger brother Wakasa-no-kami Tsunetoshi, and his younger brother Taiyū Atsumori, beside ten others, all fell at Ichi-no-tani.

When their stronghold was thus captured, the Heike were compelled to put to sea once more, taking the child Emperor with them. Some of their vessels were driven by wind and tide toward the province of Kii, while others rowed out and tossed about, buffeted by the waves, in the offing of Ashiya. Some rocked on the billows off Suma and Akashi, steering aimlessly hither and thither, their crews weary and dispirited as they turned on their hard plank couches, and viewed the moon of spring mistily through their tear-dimmed eyes. Some crossed the straits of Awaji and drifted along by Ejima-ga-Iso, likening their lot to the sad sea birds that fly there seeking by twilight the mate they have lost, while others still lay off Ichi-no-tani uncertain where to steer. Yesterday, with a host of a hundred thousand, feared and obeyed by fourteen provinces, they lay with high hopes but one day's journey from the Capital, and now, after the defeat of Ichi-no-tani they were scattered and, dispersed along the coast, each unaware of the fate of his friend.

Chapter XIX.

KOZAISHŌ.

Now Kenda Takiguchi Tokikazu, a retainer of Echizen-on-Sammi Michimori, fled in haste to the ship in which was then wife of Michmori, and said to her: "This morning my lord was surrounded by seven horsemen at the Minatogawa and fell fighting, and among them were Sasaki-no Kimura Saburō Naritsuna of Ōmi, and Tamai-no-Shirō Sukekage of Musashi. I too would have stayed with him to the end and died, but he had strictly charged me before, saying that if anything should happen to him I must at all costs escape to look after my mistress; and so it is that I have saved my worthless life and come to you." On hearing these tidings his mistress uttered no word, but covered her face and fell prostrate. Though she had already heard that he was dead, she had not at first believed it, but for two or three days had waited as for one who had gone out for a short time and would soon come back, but when four or five days had passed, her confidence was shaken and she fell into deep melancholy. Her feelings were shared by her foster-mother who alone accompanied her and shared the same pillow.

From the seventh day, on which the news was brought to her, until the evening of the thirteenth she did not rise from her bed. At dawn on the fourteenth day the Heike were starting to cross again to Yashima, and until the evening before she still lay on her couch. Then as night drew on and all was quiet in the ship, she turned to her foster-mother and said: "Though I had been told it, until this morning I did not realize that my husband was dead, but now; this evening, I know it is true. Everyone says he was killed at the Minatogawa, and after that there is none who says he has seen him alive. And what grieves me most is that when I saw him for a short while on the night before the battle he was sad and said to me: "I am certain to be slain in tomorrow's battle, and I wonder what will become of you after I am gone." As there have been so many battles I did not pay any special heed to it, but if I had thought that it was the last time indeed, I would have promised to follow him to the after world. Then, fearing that he might think me too reserved, I told him what I had up till that time concealed, that I was 'not-alone.' He was extremely pleased to hear it and said: "Ah, I have reached thirty years of age without having any children; I hope you will make it a boy if you can, for that will be a good memento of myself to leave behind in this fleeting world." Then he went on to ask me how many months it was, and how I felt, and bade me keep as quiet as was possible in this ever-rolling ship that the birth might be easy. Ah, how sad it all is! If women die at that time it is a most shameful and melancholy end that they suffer, and yet, if I bear this child and bring it up so that it may recall to me the features of him who is gone, every time I look on it will bring back the memory of my former love, and that will cause me grief without end. Death is the road that none may avoid. Even if I should by good luck pass scatheless through these dangerous times, can I trust myself to escape the common fate of being entangled in some other passion? That too is a melancholy prospect. To behold him in my dreams when I sleep, and to awake only to look on his features! Better to drown in the depths of the sea than to live on thus bereft of my love. My heart is full of sorrow at leaving you thus alone, but I pray you send to Miyako this letter which I have written, and take my robes to some priest, that his prayers may hasten the Enlightenment of my husband, and may assist me too in the after world." When she had made an end of speaking, the older woman, repressing her tears, replied: "How can you thus resolve to forsake your little one and leave your mother, alone in her old age? Is your loss any greater than that of the other wives of the nobles of our house who have fallen at Ichi-no-tani? Though you may think you will sit on the same lotus as your husband, yet after rebirth you must both pass though the Six Ways and the Four Births, and in which of these can you be sure of meeting? And if you fail to meet, of what use is it to cast away your life? So be brave and calm your mind until your child is born, and strive to bring it up, whatever hardships may threaten. Then you may become a nun and spend your days in prayer for the happy rebirth of your departed husband. Moreover, as for Miyako, who is there who can carry such a letter?" Then the lady, wishing to comfort and reassure her weeping parent, replied: "If I seem strange, you must remember that under the stress of misfortune or the pain of parting to think of ending one's life is a natural thing, though really to nerve oneself to do so is not so easy; and if I should indeed resolve to carry out this intention I will be sure to let you know. But now it is late and I would sleep." Now her foster-mother, seeing that the lady had not even taken a bath for the last four or five days, concluded that her mind was indeed made up, and had herself determined that if she did so she would follow her even to the bottom of the sea, for she did not wish to live a day longer if her daughter was dead, so for some time she remained awake watching by her side, but at last she fell asleep, whereupon the lady, who had been awaiting this opportunity, slipped out quietly and ran to the bulwarks of the ship. Gazing out over the wide expanse of waters, she was uncertain in which direction lay the western quarter, but turning toward the setting moon as it was sinking behind the mountains, calmly she repeated the Nembutsu. The melancholy cry of the sea-birds on the distant sand-spits and the harsh creaking of the rudder mingled with her voice as she repeated it a hundred times. "Namu Amida Nyorai, Saviour who leadest us to the Western Paradise, according to Thy True Vow unite on the same lotus flower an in, separable husband and wife!" And with the last invocation still on her lips she cast herself into the waves. It was about midnight of the day on which they were to start for Yashima, and all aboard the ship were sleeping soundly, so no one perceived her. But as she plunged into the waves she attracted the attention of the helmsman, who alone of the crew was not asleep, and he cried out loudly that a woman had gone overboard from the ship, whereon the foster-mother, suddenly awaking, felt by her side, and finding nothing, was overcome by sorrow and amazement. Then, though all did their utmost to get her out of the water and save her life, as usual in spring, the sky was cloudy and the moon obscured so that they could not see where she was, and when at last they did discover her and pull her out of the water, her life was already departing. Thus they laid her on the deck with the salt water streaming from her white hakama and the thick double layers of her Court costume, and dripping from her long black hair, arid her foster-mother, taking her hands in hers and pressing her face to her cold features, exclaimed; "Why did you not let me know your resolve, and let me follow you to the bottom of the sea? Woe is me, now I am left here all alone! At least will you not speak to me once more?" But though she thus addressed her daughter in tones of agonized entreaty, she was already destined for that other world, and her breath, which until now had just barely fluttered in her body, at last departed for ever.

Then, as the moon of the spring night was sinking in the sky, and the glimmer of dawn was just beginning to break through the clouds, grieved to the heart at her loss, as it must be, they bound a suit of her husband's armour to her body that it might not rise again, and committed it again to the waves. Her mother, unwilling to be left behind, tried to leap in after her, but being prevented by the others, she shaved her head and was afterwards received as a nun by Chūnagon-no-Risshi Chūkai, the younger brother of the late Michimori, observing the ordinances of Buddha and pray for the happiness of the deceased. From ancient times it he been a common custom for women to forsake the world on the death of their husband, but those who have put an end to their lives have been few indeed. Still, as there is the injunction, "A loyal retainer[243] does not serve two masters, nor a chaste woman have two husbands," such things did sometimes happen:

This lady was the daughter of Tō-no-Gyōbu Kyō Norikata, and was the greatest beauty of the Court, where she was formerly known by the name of Kozaishō, being in attendance on Joseimon-in. In the spring of the period Angen, when she was about sixteen years old, she accompanied her mistress to Hōsshōji to view the cherry-blossoms, and Michimori-no-Kyō, who was also in attendance as Chūgū-no-suke, then first saw her and fell in love with her. From this time he continued to send her poems and letters, but she only put them by without taking any notice.

After this had gone on for three years Michimori wrote her a letter which he determined should be the last, and sent it to her by a messenger. It happened on this occasion that the lady was not to be found, and the servant was returning again with the letter, when he met Kozaishō proceeding from her residence to the Court. As he did not wish to go back to his master without delivering the letter, he made as though to pass close by her carriage and threw it in through the curtain. Being asked by her companion who was riding with her who had sent it, she said that she did not know, but on opening it she found that it was from Michimori. As she could not leave it in the car, and it was not a thing that could be thrown out on to the road, she thrust it into the band of her hakama and so entered the Court. Thereafter it chanced that, while engaged in her duties of lady-in-waiting, though the Palace was exceedingly wide, she happened to drop it right in front of her mistress. The Princess at once picked it up and put it into the sleeve of her dress, after which she called her ladies and said to them: "Here is a strange thing that I have found; to whom does it belong?" All the other ladies swore by the gods and Buddhas that they knew nothing about it, and only Kozaishō blushed furiously and said nothing. Then the Princess; perceiving that the letter was from Michimori, opened it to scan the contents. It was heavily scented with incense and the writing was extremely elegant. "Although you are very hard-hearted, I am very delighted......." it began, and when she had read it through to the end, she found appended the following verse:

> "*Like is my love to a bridge that is built of the slippery pine-logs,*
> *If you trample it down, surely my sleeves will be wet.*"

---

[243] *A loyal retainer*, etc. from the 史記、回單傳。

"This is a very strong letter," said the Princess, "and I fear, if, you are too hard-hearted, this love may turn into hate. Ono-no-Komachi was famous for her beauty, but she did not know what pity was, and so in time everyone came to hate her. So, though loved by many, her stony heart in the end brought her to such a sorry plight that she had not even the wherewithal to keep off the wind and rain, and was driven to live like a vagrant in the open fields with nothing but the moon and stars to gaze at through her tear-dimmed eyes. At any rate an answer must be sent to this letter." And the Princess called for her ink-stone and wrote a reply with her own august hand.

> *"If the bridge of logs on which he relies be down-trodden,*
> *Will nod size who breaks it certainly fall in the stream?"*

Love smoulders in the bosom like the smoke of Fuji, and the tears that moisten the sleeve are like the waves of Kiyomigaseki; so in the end Michimori obtained this lovely lady, and their affection for each other was most profound. So she followed him even to the wind-tossed waves of the Western Sea, and in death their path was not divided. Kadowaki-no-Chūnagon, thus bereaved both of his eldest son Echizen-no-Sammi Michimori and his youngest son Narimori, had now none to rely on save Noto-no-kami Noritsune and the priest Chūnagon-no-Risshi Chūkai, so the death of this lady, who was the only legacy of his late son, could only add still more to his grief.

Volume X.

Chapter I.

CARRYING ROUND OF THE HEADS.

On the twelfth day of the second month of Ju-ei the heads of the Heike that had been cut off on the seventh day at Ichi-no-tani in Settsu were brought into the Capital, and all those who were related to them were cast into deep dejection and mourned together, wondering what evil tidings they might hear, or what fresh misfortune they might suffer. And among them the wife of Komatsu-no-Sammi Chūjō Koremori-no-Kyō, who had hidden herself in the temple of Daikakuji, hearing that most of the Heike had perished at Ichi-no-tani, but that one of them who went by the title of Sammi Chūjō had been taken alive, was in extreme anxiety to know whether it was indeed her husband. But soon a woman came to the Daikakuji and said that this was not so, but that it was Hon-Sammi Chūjō Shigehira who had been taken; whereat her fears were only increased, lest his head should have been taken with the other.

On the thirteenth day the officials of the Kebiishi under Taiyū-no-Hangwan Nakayori proceeded to Rokujō-kawara to receive the heads, and passed on by Higashi-no-Dō-in to the northward, while Noriyori and Yoshitsune sent word to His Majesty that they would be exposed on the public gibbet. At this news the Hō-ō was much perturbed, and sent for the Dajō-daijin, the Sadaijin, Udaijin, Naidaijin and Horikawa-no-Dainagon Tadachika-no-Kyō to consult with them about it. The five Ministers then said: "From ancient times there is no precedent for carrying the heads of Ministers and Courtiers through the streets of the Capital: and moreover these are near relations of the Late Emperor who have for long served at Court. Therefore it is by no means advisable to listen to the demands .of Noriyori and Yoshitsune."

The Hō-ō accordingly decided that the heads were not to be exposed, but when this was reported to the two Commanders they again insisted, saying: "When we consider the insurrection of Hogen they were the enemies of our grandfather Tameyoshi, and in the former days of Heiji they were the foes of our father Yoshitomo. Therefore did we jeopardy our lives to appease the wrath of the Emperor and to cleanse the stain on our father's memory, by destroying the enemies of the Throne. If the heads of these Heike be not exposed, how shall we be bold to subdue rebellion in the future?" And so, as they thus persisted in their demand, the Hō-ō could not but give way, and the exposure took place at last. Among the innumerable multitudes that thronged to see them were many who had feared and dreaded them in the days of their prosperity, but even these were moved to lamentation when they saw their heads thus paraded in the public street. Then Saitō Go and Saitō Roku, the two brothers who were in attendance on Rokudai Gozen, the young heir of a Sammi Chūjō Koremori, who was concealed in the Daikakuji, no longer able to restain their anxiety, disguised themselves as menials and mingled with the crowd, looking carefully at all the heads, but to their joy did not find that of the Chūjō among them. Unable, however, to control their feelings at the sad sight, they feared the eyes of the crowd, and hastened to return to the Daikakuji. Immediately the wife of the Chūjō asked them how they had fared, whereupon they replied: "Though we looked carefully at all the heads we did not see that of the Chūjō among them. Among the brothers of our lord, Bitchū-no-Kami Moromori's head alone was there; and beside his there were the heads of so-and-so and so-and-so." But his mistress could bear no more, and covered her face with her garment and bowed herself to the ground. After a while Saitō Go controlled his feelings and continued: "For these two years we have-been here in hiding, and thus have seen no one, but now I have been able to look round as I wished, and moreover I have found out from one who has an exact knowledge of everything that the lords of the house of Komatsu Dono took no part in this battle. And the reason was that they were stationed at Mikusa-yama on the borders of Harima and Tamba, and when this line was broken by Kurō Yoshitsune, Shin-Sammi Chūjō Sukemori, Shōshō Arimori and Tango-no-Jijū Tadafusa took ship from Takasago in Harima and crossed over to Yashima in Sanuki. Why it was that lie came to be separated from his brothers I know not, but Bitchū-no-Kami alone fought and fell at Ichi-no-tani." Then, as they questioned him further about the matter of the Chūjō Koremori he went on: "They say that it was because he was taken with a grievous sickness that he was not present at this engagement, but went over to Yashima before the battle." "Ah" exclaimed his mistress, "it is because of his anxiety about us, his anguish of mind when day and night he thinks of our lot, that he has fallen sick; when the winds are contrary how must his heart sink to be at sea, and before the battle how dread the suspense lest it be his last! And on his sick-bed who is there to soothe his uneasy pillow? Oh, that we could know these things!" And the young lord and his sister added their complaint also, saying: "Why did you not find out what sickness it was?"

Sammi-no-Chūjō too was equally tormented by anxious' thoughts: "Alas" he mused, "in Miyako they will be wondering what has happened to me; for though my head is not there with the others, they cannot be sure that I have not been drowned or killed by a chance arrow, and so perchance they think I am no longer of this world." So to let them know that he was still living he sent a messenger with three letters, and in that to his wife he wrote: "How sad I am to think of you living in the Capital surrounded by so many enemies, and with no proper place to go to: and to have the children to look after must be a greater trial still. How much would I wish to have you all here together with me, but, though I can endure it, it would be a cruel place for you." in this wise he wrote, and among many other things was this verse:

"These sad thoughts I indite—like sea-weed gathered together,
As a memento of me, should we meet never again."

"I fear you must find your days very tedious at present," he wrote to his children, "but I intend soon to come and fetch you."

When the messenger arrived at Miyako with these letters, and delivered them to his wife, and she opened them and saw his writing, she was so overcome by her feelings that she could do nothing but hide her face in her garments and weep.

After four or five days had passed the messenger came and asked her to write an answer that he might start back again with it, and she did so, bedewing the paper with her tears. The two children too took up their pens to write and asked her: "What shall we say in our letters to our father?" "It is best that you write whatever you think," the lady answered, and so the two both wrote the same reply: "Why leave you not come to fetch us before this? We are both so longing to see you again. We hope you will come very soon." When the messenger returned to Yashima with these letters and presented them to the Chūjō, and he read those of his children, he was so affected that he could do nothing: "Even for the Paradise of the West I have little care," he declared, weeping; "for so strong are the bonds of affection that bind me to this world that Heaven itself has no attraction. If only I could get across the mountains to the Capital and there see my children once again I should be quite content to die by my own hand."

Chapter II.

OF A COURT LADY.

On the fourteenth day of the same month Hon-Sammi Chūjō Shigemori-no-Kyō who had been taken prisoner was brought into the Capital and paraded through the streets. The front and back curtains of the car in which he rode were lifted and the windows on each side were opened, while Doi-no-Jirō Sanehira, clad in a hitatare of yellowish-red hue and half armour, rode in command of thirty men-at-arms who surrounded the car on all sides. "How sad!" cried all the people of the Capital on beholding the spectacle, "that of all the Heike Courtiers such a fate should befall this one. He who was the especial favourite of the Nyūdō and his Consort, the most respected of all their house, and even when he went to the Court of the Hō-ō all, both old and young, would make way in his honour. Surely it is because he burnt the temples of Nara that the Buddhas have brought this punishment upon him." Thus they brought him along Rokujō to the eastward until they came to the river, and from there returning brought him to the mansion of the late Naka-no-Mikado-no Tō-Chūnagon Kasei-no-Kyō in Rokujō-kawara, where he was kept in solitary confinement.

Then an envoy was sent to him from the Court of the Hō-ō. He was Kurando-no-Saemon Gon-no-Suke Sadanaga, and he proceeded to Hachijō Horikawa in robes of dark red and carrying sword and shaku. Shigehira was in robes of white clouded with blue with a folded eboshi on his head, and regarded Sadanaga, of whom he had formerly thought nothing, with the same feeling as sinners regard the jailers in Hell.

"It is His Majesty's decision" quoth Sadanaga, "that if you wish to return to Yashima, that you send a message to the Heike Courtiers that they forthwith send back the Three Sacred Treasures to the Capital, in which case you will be permitted to go." "I do not think it at all probable," replied Shigehira, "that the chiefs of our house will send back the precious Sacred Treasures in exchange for my person, though the Nii-no-Ama, since she is a woman, might possibly wish to do so; still, as it would not be proper to reject the Imperial Message without further consideration, I will communicate with them forthwith." One of the retainers of the Court named Hanakata was sent with the Imperial Edict, which was addressed to the Daijin Munemori and the Taira Dainagon Tokitada, while Shigehira's letter to the Nii-no-Ama was dispatched by the hand of Heizaemon Shigekuni. As he was not allowed to send any private letters beside this, he could only send messages to various people by word of mouth, and the one he sent to his wife, Dainagon-no-Suke was worded, thus: "Even on a journey to be separated from those we love, and who love us, how sad indeed! but as our promise to each other cannot be dissolved we will surely be reborn to meet again in the after life": and as he gave the message his feelings overcame him, so that Shigekuni also could not restrain his tears. Now there was a certain samurai named Muku Umanojō Tomotoki, who had long served Shigehira, and was also in attendance on the lady Hachijō-no-Nyoin, and he sought out Doi-no-Jirō Sanehira and said to him: "I am an old retainer of the Sammi Chūjō, and to-day I saw him in the streets, a spectacle too pitiful to look at. May I not then be allowed to go to him and comfort him by speaking of old times? Though I am a samurai, I was not one of those who accompanied my lord to battle, but was only accustomed to wait on him morning and evening. If you suspect me of doubtful designs, I will willingly lay aside my weapons if permission be granted. So Sanehira, feeling compassion, saw no harm in his request, and he put away his weapons and was brought to the Chūjō. Overjoyed at his success Umanojo hurried to his master's presence; but when he saw how sad and broken down was his bearing, and thus understood what he must feel, he could no longer restrain himself, bit broke down and wept. The Chūjō also, feeling as though it were a dream within a dream, could for a while find nothing to say.

Presently, however, they began to talk of past and present affairs, and then the Chūjō enquired of him whether a certain lady, to whom Umanojō used to take letters from him, was still at Court. On the retainer answering that he thought so, Shigehira continued: "As I have written nothing to her since I went down to the Western Provinces, and indeed there was nothing to write, no doubt she thinks I am altogether faithless, and this grieves me. Could you not take a letter to her if I write?" "Indeed that would not be difficult," replied Umanojo, and the Chūjō, greatly rejoiced, penned the letter. The retainer took it and was going forth, when he was stopped by the guards, who called out, "What letter is that? Show it to us!" "Show it to them, then!" said the Chūjō. "It is of no matter," replied the warders when they had examined it, and Umanojo received it again and passed out. Hastily making his way to the Palace, he feared to be seen by people while it was yet day, and stood waiting in a little hut nearby until the twilight, when he slipped in as far as the door of the woman's apartments and listened. There he heard a sound of weeping and a voice that he thought was that of the lady he sought exclaiming: "How pitiful! That he of all the nobles should be treated thus. They all say that it is because he burned the temples of Nara, and the Chūjō himself says that so it may be, for though it was not his wish that they should be burned, some disorderly soldiers of his army started the fire that destroyed many halls and pagodas, so, as the saying is, "the dew-drops on the topmost leaves all run down on the trunk," he must bear the blame for their deed; and indeed so I too think." Then Tomotada, much touched by her sorrow, called out to her, and on her asking what he wished, he told her that he brought a letter from the Chūjō. Then the lady, who at ordinary times was ashamed to show her face to anyone, ran out hurriedly and took it from him with her own hands, and immediately tearing it open, read all that he had written to her of how he had been captured in the West, and was now living in uncertainty of his life from day to day. In the letter he had inserted these lines:

> "*Though in a river of tears my name is sunk and dishonoured,*
> *Happy yet should I be, if I could meet you again.*"

When she read this the lady could bear no more, but folded her face in her robe and sank down weeping. After a while, however, as time was pressing, Tomotoki requested that she give him an answer to take back, and so, weeping bitterly, she wrote how lonely and sad she had been for the last two years while she had heard nothing from him, and with the letter she sent this verse:

> "*Nought do I also care if with you my name is dishonoured,*
> *carried away like waste drifting along on the stream.*"

Tomotoki took it and returned, and as before he was stopped by the guard, who demanded to see the letter, but when they examined it they made no objection, and he delivered it safely to Shigehira. On reading it the Chūjō was greatly affected, and by and by sought an interview with Doi-no-Jirō, saying: "For the many kindnesses you have shown me I am deeply grateful, and now I would entreat of you yet one more favour. Since I have no child, I have nothing to leave behind with regret in this fleeting world; but there is a lady whom for long I have held in tender regard, and if I might see her again and speak somewhat about the hereafter, it would be a great comfort." "There is nothing impossible in that request," replied Doi-no-Jirō, who was not wanting in compassion, and the Chūjō, overjoyed at having obtained permission, at once borrowed a car and sent it for her. The lady, without even stopping a moment for any preparation, immediately got into it and set out, and as soon as they told the Chūjō that her car had arrived at the entrance of the mansion he ran out to her, and exclaiming; "Do not alight or the guards will see you!" he drew the curtains of the car, and the two continued sitting there for a long time, hand in hand and with their faces pressed together, speaking no word and doing nought but weep. After a while Shigehira restrained his emotion and said: "When I went down to the Western Provinces I wished to see you again, but owing to the confusion of those days I had no one to send, and after that I greatly wished to send you a letter and to hear from you in return, but the hardships of our homeless life, and the perils of war both by night and day left me no leisure; and that I have suffered myself to be captured alive and brought up to the Capital – it was only that I might be able to see you once more." And he covered his face again and wept. How melancholy to think of their mutual sorrow! Thus the time passed and it began to grow late, whereupon the warders appeared again and urged the return of the lady, as the streets might be perilous after dark, so the Chūjō was fain to let her go, but as her car was about to depart he caught her by the sleeve and extemporized these lines:

> "*Now, let try fleeting life like this our meeting be ended,*
> *Never more shall we meet, this is the last time on earth.*"

To which the lady immediately responded:

> "*Though it we bid adieu ere long to this fleeting existence,*
> *I may have gone before, ere my beloved expires.*"

So she returned to the Palace and afterwards, as the warders did not allow them to meet again, they exchanged letters from time to time. Now this lady was the daughter of Mimbu-no-Kyō Nyūdō Shinhan, and was extremely beautiful, beside being of a most loving disposition, and when she heard that the Chūjō had been handed over to Nara and executed, she straightway became a nun, cutting off her hair and putting on black robes, to pray for his happy rebirth in the after life.

Chapter III.

THE IMPERIAL EDICT TO YASHIMA.

After a few days the Imperial Messenger Hanakata, Groom of the Imperial Bedchamber, arrived at the shore of Yashima in Sanuki on the twenty eighth day of the same month, and presented the Edict of the Hō-ō. The Daijin Munemori and all the Heike Courtiers met in solemn assembly to hear it, and it was opened and read thus:

"That the August Person of the Divine Sovereign should leave the

Ninefold Precincts of the Palace and journey through the provinces, and that the Three Sacred Treasures should be hidden in Shikoku for so many years, is a great calamity to the Imperial Court; and may be the cause of our country's ruin. Now this Shigehira-no-Kyō is the disloyal subject who burnt the Tōdaiji at Nara, and according to the advice of Our Minister Yoritomo whom we have consulted should properly be put to death. Separated from those of his family he was captured alive, and now languishes in captivity like a caged bird that pines for the sky, or, like a wild goose that has lost his mates, he would fly back to the far-away isle in the southern seas where is the Palace of his Imperial Lord. But if the Three Sacred Treasures be returned to the Capital forthwith, this rebel lord shall receive our Imperial Forgiveness. This is Our Imperial Edict. Given on the fourteenth day of the second day of the third year of Ju-ei by the hand of Daizen-no-Taiyū Naritada. To the former Taira Dainagon.

Chapter IV.

THE ANSWER.

The purport of the Imperial Edict was forthwith communicated by the Daijin Munemori to the Taira Dainagon Tokitada-no-Kyō. Then the Nii Dono opened the letter of Shigemori, which ran as follows: "If you wish to see me again alive, see to it that the Three Sacred Treasures be sent back again to the Capital; if this be not done consider that you will never see me again;" and when she read these words she was so affected by them that she pushed the doors that led to the next room where all the Courtiers were assembled, and with the letter pressed to her face, threw herself down before Munemori, quite unable to utter a single word. After a short space, however, she arose, and controlling her emotion addressed him thus: "See here, Munemori! How pitiful is the message I have received from the Chūjō at Miyako! Anxious indeed must be the thoughts of his heart. Allow me then to have the Three Sacred Treasures sent back to the Capital." "I also," replied Munemori "might wish to do this thing, but to exchange the Three Sacred Treasures of our Realm for Shigehira would be a most improper act. Moreover with respect to Yoritomo I think it would avail nothing. And the maintaining of the Sovereign Power of the Empire depends on the presence of the Sacred Mirror alone. And how can you consider the welfare of one child, when all the others and our friends will suffer detriment on account of it? Even affection for children must be according to circumstances. By no means can this thing be done." But the Nii Dono, reluctant to give up her wish, still persisted: "For myself I did not desire to live a day or an hour after the death of the late Chancellor, my husband, and it is only that I would see his Sacred

Majesty again come to his own, after tossing so long on the waters of the Western Sea, that I have survived to this day. When I heard that the Chūjō had been captured at Ichi-no-tani, my breast was straitened and my throat obstructed so that I could not even drink hot water, and if I hear that he is no longer of this world I also will depart with him, so pray kill me at once that I may be troubled no more." And she cried and groaned aloud, so that all the assembly cast down their eyes in embarrassment.

Then the Shin-Chūnagon Tomomoi-no-Kyō delivered his opinion as follows: "Even though we should send back the Three Sacred Treasures to the Capital, it is doubtful whether they would return Shigehira to us. Is it not well then to send a reply to that effect?" To this counsel all assented, and the Daijin set about composing the reply, while the Nii Dono, who was so overcome that she could scarcely hold the pen, yet, nerved by her great affection for Shigehira, also began to write an answer. Dainagon-no-Suke, the wife of the Chūjō, could say nothing, but only covered her face and wept.

Then Taira-no-Dainagon Tokitada ordered the Imperial Envoy Hanakata to be summoned, and thus addressed him: "Since you have thus braved the perils of the waves, and have made this long journey to this far-off island, I will give you a souvenir of your exploit that you will carry with you all your days." And he had the two characters 'Namikata' branded on his face with a hot iron. When he returned to the Capital and the Hō-ō saw it, he asked him, "Are you Hanakata?" "I am," was the reply. "Then," said the Hō-ō with a laugh, "we must call you 'Namikata' in future;" after which he read the answer, which ran as follows:

"The Imperial Edict dated the fourteenth of this month has arrived here at Yashima in Sanuki on the twenty eighth day, and has been respectfully perused by us, and thus do we think concerning what is written in it. Michimori-no-Kyō and many others of our house have already been slain at Ichi-no-tani: what then have we to rejoice at if Shigehira alone is pardoned? Our Sovereign, having received the succession to the Throne of the late Emperor Takakura-in, was only four years old when he began to reign, and while he was learning the way of benevolent and virtuous government, Yoritomo, the barbarian of the East, and Yoshinaka, the rebel of the North, plotted together, and gathering their forces entered the Capital, thus causing grievous affliction to the youthful Sovereign and his August Mother, and no small indignation to the Courtiers and Ministers their relations. For a considerable period they retired to the isles of Kyūshū, and until they return to the Capital how shall the Three Sacred Treasures be separated from his August Person? As the Chinese Classic[244] says, "The Subject

---

[244] Chinese Classic 禮記，臣軌.

considers the Sovereign as his mind, and the Sovereign considers the subject as his body." If the Sovereign be demeaned, so will the subject be also, and if the subject be demeaned, so also will the country be too. If the Sovereign above mourns, how can the subject below rejoice? And if the heart within be filled with grief, how can the body without be glad? Since the time that our ancestor Taira Sadamori subdued the rebel Sōma-no-Kojirō Masakado, pacifying the eight provinces of the East, the tradition has been handed down to his sons and grandsons, so that they have put down rebellious subjects, and through succeeding ages have loyally guarded the Sacred Destiny of the Throne. Thus it was that our late father the Dajō-daijin Kiyomori, in the periods of Hogen and Heiji held in great respect the Imperial Wishes, but paid little regard to his own life; thus acting entirely on behalf of his Sovereign, but for himself not at all. And as for this Yoritomo, though when, on account of the treason of his father Sama-no-kami Yoshitomo in the twelfth month of the first year of Heiji, many were constantly demanding his execution, the late Chancellor out of the kindness of his heart was pleased to pardon him, yet he forgets all this former obligation and is entirely unmindful of any gratitude. Straightway gathering together hordes of rebels, in traitorous wise he wrought exceeding folly beyond description. Soon may they invite the punishment of heaven, and the hour of their ruin and defeat be privily ordained. The sun and moon darken not their light for one thing, neither does the Buddha alter the Law for one man. One evil deed should not cancel many virtuous acts, neither should a small blemish cover up great merit. If the faithful service of our house for many generations, and the many loyal deeds of our late father, had not been forgotten what need would there have been for our Sovereign to proceed to Shikoku? Let an Imperial Edict then be issued that we may return once again to our ancient Capital, and our former shame be put away. For if not we shall go to Korea, or China, or India, or the uttermost confines of the demon-world. What a calamity! Are the Sacred Treasures of our Imperial Realm, handed down through eighty one generations of Earthly Sovereigns, to become but the vain ornaments of an alien land? Let this our meaning be brought plainly before His Majesty. Given with the utmost respect and obeisance on the twenty eighth day of the second month of the third year of Ju-ei. The answer of Taira Munemori Ason, former Naidaijin of the Lower First Rank."

Chapter V.

Receiving the Doctrine.

When the Chūjō Shigehira was informed of the reply that the
Heike had made, he said: "That is just what I had expected: no doubt
the rest of the family have but a poor opinion of me." He felt some
disappointment, it is true, but there was no help for it, and indeed he
had not considered it likely that they would be ready to return the Three
Sacred Treasures as the price of his release. So the purport of the reply
caused him no surprise, though naturally, while the matter was yet
undecided, he could not help feeling unsettled, and as, when the answer
was received, it was resolved to send him down to the Eastern
Provinces, he felt great regret at leaving the Capital. Calling Doi-no-
Jirō, he asked him whether they would permit him to become a monk,
but when this request was communicated to Yoshitsune and by him
reported to the Hō-ō, His Majesty decided that he could not give his
consent until the question had been referred to Yoritomo. "Then" said
the Chūjō, "may I not be allowed to see a priest who is an old friend of
mine, that I may speak with him somewhat about the after life?" "Who
is the priest?" asked Doi. "Hōnembō of Kurodani," was the reply. "In
that case there is no objection," he answered, and gave permission.

The Chūjō much pleased at this, soon called the priest, and on his
arrival, said to him, weeping; "Though I have been taken alive after
many dangers in the Western Provinces, and brought up to the Capital,
yet it is a happy thing for me in that I can thus meet you again. But
what will my fate be in the hereafter? While I had rank and place in the
world, distracted by many affairs and held fast in the bonds of the
things of this life, my heart was wholly given up to pride, without a
thought for what vicissitudes night happen to me. Still more when
misfortune overtook our house and we fled the Capital, fighting and
struggling here and there, my mind was clogged with the evil desire of
killing others and saving my own life, so that no good thoughts could
dwell in me. As to the burning of Nara, whether we say it was an
Imperial Order, or the chance of war, at His Majesty's Behest, since the
way of this world is difficult to escape, on account of the evil deeds of
the monks we marched against them, and the chance burning of the
temples that followed was beyond my power to prevent. Still, as I was
the Commander at that time, if punishment is to fall on one person, it
must be on my head that it will fall. So whatever shame may
overwhelm me I know that it is but retribution for this deed. Therefore I
would shave my head and go as a mendicant priest, practicing
austerities and seeking only the Way of Buddha. But even if I could do
this in the body, I cannot believe that my heart would be changed; for

whatever austerities I might practice would not be enough to attain salvation. Alas! When I think over the conduct of my past life, my guilt is greater than Mount Sumeru, while all my righteousness is less than a speck of dust; and if thus in vain I end my life, without doubt I shall be reborn in the Three Ways of Torment. And so I beseech you, O Shōnin, of your kindness and compassion deign to help even such a worthless one as myself, and to show me how to achieve salvation."

At this melancholy speech the Shōnin, overcome by grief, bowed his face to the ground, and for a long while, choked by sobs, could answer nothing. By and by, however, he raised himself and spoke as follows: "After with difficulty attaining to birth as man, to fall again into the Three Ways of Torment is too grievous a lot. But if in disgust at this sinful world, you seek rebirth in the Pure Land, cleansing your mind of evil and turning to good, of a surety all the Buddhas of the Three Worlds will rejoice and be glad.

In times of degeneracy and of the Five Corruptions, by faith in the name of Amida we can prevail. Thus fixing the whole mind on His Paradise, and concentrating all austerities into the repetition of the Six Character Invocation, none can be so dull or ignorant but his prayer will be heard, nor will any be despised, be his guilt never so deep. If you turn from the Ten Transgressions and the Five Rebellions, you will attain Paradise, and however small your merit, your hope will not be disappointed. If with earnest mind you repeat the Nembutsu, surely Amida will come to meet you. If, with the full knowledge that Paradise is to be obtained by the repetition of the Nembutsu, you wholeheartedly repeat it, then Paradise is yours. If you say that repeating it means repentance, and thus repeat it, you do indeed repent. If you trust in Amida the All-Powerful, no evil Karma can approach, and if you have faith in the Nembutsu to cleanse from sin, all your sins will be washed away. The peculiar advantage of the Pure Land Sect lies in this, that it sums up the whole doctrine in this one sentence: "The attainment of Paradise depends on Faith." And if you deeply believe this teaching, without departing from the ordinary avocations and limitations of daily life, and still observing the Three Actions[245] and the Five Dignities,[246] if you do not neglect to repeat the Nembutsu with fervor, when the hour of death approaches, departing out of this world of trouble, you shall without doubt be reborn into the changeless bliss of the Western Paradise." At this exposition the Chūjō was greatly rejoiced, and replied: "I pray you straightway let me receive the Ten Precepts; but is it possible that I can do this without becoming a monk?" "Indeed," said the Shōnin, "it is quite usual to observe the Ten Precepts without becoming a monk." And taking a razor he laid it on his forehead, and

---

[245] *Three Actions.* Of the Body, Mind and Speech.
[246] *Five Dignities.* Of Walking, Standing, Sitting and Lying.

made the motions of shaving his head, after which he instructed him in the Ten Precepts. The Chūjō received his instruction with tears of gladness, and the Shōnin too, being a man of sympathy in all things, taught him the ordinances in a voice broken by sobs. Then sending for his inkstone, which he had deposited with the samurai, he handed it to the Shōnin, saying: "Do not give this to anyone, but please keep it always near you; and whenever you look at it, remember that it belonged to a certain person, and deign to say a Nembutsu. Moreover if you can spare time, please send me a volume of the Sutras." At this the Shōnin could find nothing to say, but, putting the inkstone into his bosom, he pressed to his face the sleeve of his black robe, and weeping bitterly returned to Kurodani. This inkstone was one that the Sung Emperor had sent as a return gift to his father, the Nyūdō, when the Chancellor had sent a present of gold dust to China, and was inscribed, "to the Great Minister of the Taira of Wada in Japan." Its name was Matsu-kage.

Chapter VI.

THE SEA ROAD.

Now since Hyōye-no-suke Yoritomo had given repeated orders to that effect, there was nothing for it but that Shigehira should go down to Kamakura, and so he was handed over by Doi-no-Jirō Sanehira and sent to the quarters of Kurō Onzōshi Yoshitsune, and on the tenth day of the third month he set out, accompanied by Kajiwara Heizō Kagetoki. It was a sad fate for him to be taken alive and sent to Miyako after all the hazards of the Western Provinces, but how much worse was it now to have to travel even beyond the Eastern Barrier. When they came to Shi-no-miya Kawara, he remembered how formerly the fourth Imperial Prince of Enki called Semi-Maru[247] had calmed his mind amid the Eastern tempests by playing his biwa in this spot, and how Hakuga-no-Sammi,[248] persevering for three years both on gusty days and calm, on rainy nights and fine, pacing up and down and standing to listen, received from him the three secret melodies. In those days too, he thought, it was hard to live in a straw thatched hut. Passing over Ausaka-yama the hoofs of their horses echoed as they rode over the Bridge of Seta, and the sky-lark rose in the heavens. The village of Noro and the waves of Shiga were shrouded in the mist of spring, and leaving Kagami-yama and the lofty peak of Hira on the north, the hill of Ibuki drew nigh. Though not of much interest, the crumbling

---

[247] *Semi-Maru.* In the Konjaku Monogatari he is said to have been the servant of prince Atsuzane, the eighth son of the Emperor Uda. Enki, Signifies the Emperor Daigo.

[248] *Hakuga.* Or Minamoto Hiromasa, grandson of the Emperor Daigo.

wooden eaves of the barrier of Fuwa had a certain charm, while the ebbing tide of the bay of Narumi suggested sad forebodings of the future that moistened his sleeve with tears. As they came to Yabase in Mikawa they thought-of Ariwara-no-Narihːra, and the famous stanza that he made there, beginning, "Karakoromo kitsutsu nare ni shi;" and as they watched the parting of the waters, this too caused them sad reflections. As they passed over the bridge of Hamana, the wind was blowing in the pines, and the sound of the waves smote on their ears at Irie; but even without these mournful sounds the journey would have been melancholy enough.

As evening drew on they came to Ikeda in Tōtōmi, and at this station the Chūjō lodged at the house of a certain Lady-in-waiting who was the daughter of one Yuya, a wealthy man of that place. When the lady perceived the Chūjō, she said: "How strange that such a personage should come to a poor place like this, of which he has not even thought": and she sent him the following verse:

> *"When on a journey you rest in a lowly and smoke-begrimed*
> *   cottage,*
> *Then your Miyako home dearer and fairer appears."*

The Chūjō replied:

> *"On such a journey as this what boots it to wish for Miyako?*
> *Since I can call it he me never again in this life."*

After a while the Chūjō summoned Kajiwara and enquired of him: "Who is the author of that verse? It must be a person of some elegance." "Perhaps your lordship does not know," replied Kagetoki, "but this lady is one who was greatly beloved by the Daijin Munemori when he was Governor of this province, and was summoned to Miyake, by him, but as she had left an old mother in this place, she was always asking permission of him to return, which he would not grant; and in the early part of the third month she made this well-known stanza and sent it to him:

> *"Sad though I feel to miss the beauties of spring in Miyako,*
> *In my loved Eastern land haply the flowers may fall."*

And so he at length allowed her to depart. In all this Tōkaidō district there is none other like her."

Some days had now passed since they left the Capital, and the third month was half over. The flowers on the far-away mountains they sometimes mistook for the late-lying snow, and over the bays and islets the mist slowly drifted, and as the Chūjō rode on he brooded over his past life and what was to befall. By what karma-relation in a former life had this misfortune come upon him? Verily the only abiding thing was tears! His mother the Nii Dono and his wife Dainagon-no-Suke had often regretted that he had no child, and had prayed fervently to the gods and Buddhas to grant them one, but with no effect. "Perhaps it is as well," quoth Shigehira, "for where there is no child there is the less to regret."

When they came to Sayo-no-Nakayama and thought that they had to pass over it, they felt the more grieved, and again their sleeves were wet. Utsu-no-Yamabe, with its ivied Path, though it depresses them is passed too, and they go on through Tegoshi, when afar off to the north a snow-clad peak appears, and on asking, the Chūjō is told it is called Kai-no-Shirane, the white peak of the province of Kai. Repressing his tears he makes this verse:

> "*Little reck I of life indeed, but to-day for the first time*
> *Clear before my eyes looms the White Peak of Reward.*"[249]

Passing by Kiyomi-ga-seki they entered the plain at the foot of Mount Fuji: on the north lay the steep green slope of the mountain with its pine-trees rustling in the breeze, and on the south lay the wide expanse of blue sea with its waves for ever rolling up on the shore. They then passed over Ashigara-Yama, the Myōjin of which place is recorded to have made this verse concerning his wife: "If you love, your body becomes wasted, and as it is not, you do not love." Then they cane to Koyurugi-no-mori and Mariko-kawa, and the shore of Koiso and Oiso, and after passing Yatsuma, Togami-ga-hara and Mikoshi-ga-saki, having spent many days on the way, though they had not seemed to hurry, they came at last to Kamakura.

Chapter VII.

SENSHŪ.

So Sammi Chūjō was brought into the presence of Hyōye-no-suke, and Yoritomo thus addressed him: "To appease the Imperial displeasure, and to wipe away the stain from my father's memory I have undertaken to overthrow the Heike family, and it will not be difficult to accomplish; but verily I did not at all expect to see you here under these circumstances. As it is, perchance I may have the honour of receiving the Daijin Munemori as well. But concerning the burning of the temples of Nara, whether it was done by the command of the late Nyūdō Kiyomori, or whether it was ordered by you on the spur of the

---

[249] *Peak of Reward.* The word Kai has also this meaning.

moment, I know not; but anyhow it was an exceeding heinous crime." "It was done neither by the command of the Nyūdō, nor by my own design," replied the Chūjō, "but it happened accidentally in the course of the operations we undertook to suppress the violence of the monks. I beg your indulgence to speak of a fresh subject, but, as you know, in former days the Genji and Heike families stood together in rivalry to support the Throne, and after that the fortunes of the Genji house declined, and our family alone, since the days of Hogen and Heiji, has many times subdued the Imperial enemies, and been .rewarded for its services, even, I speak it with reverence, so far as to be permitted to become Imperial Relatives, and to hold the office of Dajō-daijin; while no less than sixty members of the family have been promoted to high office, so that for twenty years there has been none to equal it in all the land for rank and authority. Now it is said that he who fights the battles of the Emperor shall not be bereft of the Imperial Favour for seven generations; but this I think is quite false, for though the late Nyūdō hazarded his life for the Throne many times, it was his generation only that was fortunate and happy, and his children have come to this state that you behold. Our fate has come upon us and our rule is overthrown: fugitives from the Capital, our corpses bleach on mountain and plain, and men would spread our shame far over the waves of the Western Ocean. That I should thus be taken alive and brought down hither is a thing of which I never dreamed, and I can but regard it as the result of the misdeeds of a former life. It is related in history how in China king In of Tō was captured at Ka-dai, and how king Bun was held prisoner at Yū-ri; and if there were such examples in antiquity, how should the men of this age fare better? It is not really such a disgrace for a warrior to fall into the hands of his enemy and be put to death, so I pray you of your favour grant me a speedy execution." As he thus finished speaking, Kajiwara exclaimed in admiration: "Ah! There is a great leader indeed! And both he and the samurai in attendance could not refrain from pressing their sleeves to their eyes. Yoritomo too was not unaffected by his bearing: "Far be it from me to regard the Taira house as my personal foes," he exclaimed in reply, "it is only that I carry out the Imperial Order: as for the burning of the temples of the South Capital, let that be settled by the decision of the monks themselves." And he ordered that the Chūjō should be placed in charge of Kanō-no-suke Munemochi of the province of Izu. A treatment that seemed just like the handing over of the sinners of the Shaba-world to the Ten Kings for seven days each. But this Kanō-no-suke was a merciful man and did not treat the Chūjō at all severely, but was very kind to him in all things. And first of all he led him away to take a hot bath. Now the Chūjō thought he could meet any fate calmly if he could wash away the dust and grime of the road, and make himself clean again, and was just taking his bath, when after a little while the door of the bath-room was opened and there entered a beautiful girl of about twenty year's old, with a fine white complexion and very lovely hair. She was wearing a bath-robe of unlined material dyed in colours, and was attended by a little maid of fourteen or fifteen with short hair, dressed in an unlined garment of white, dyed with a blue design here and there, and carrying some combs in a small wash-basin. This lady assisted the Chūjō in his bath for some time, and then, after she had washed her hair, made to depart again, but as she was going out she said to him: "I am one of these who have access to Yoritomo, so if there is anything you wish, please tell me, and I will ask him; this may be difficult for a man, but a woman can manage these things." "In this condition, what can I want?" replied the Chūjō, "there is only one thing that I could desire, and that is to be allowed to become a monk." This request the lady repeated to Yoritomo, but he replied: "That cannot be. If he were my own enemy, it might be, but as he is an enemy of the Throne it is not possible." When the lady brought this answer to the Chūjō, after she had retired again he asked his guard what might be the name of this very elegant visitor. "She is the daughter of the Chōja of Tegoshi," said Kanō-no-suke, "and she is equally winsome in face and figure and disposition; she has been in attendance on the lord Hyōye-no-suke for some two or three years, and her name is Senshū-no-Mae."

That evening was somewhat rainy, and everything was very dreary, when the lady again appeared bringing a biwa and koto. Kanō-no-suke also came in with ten of his attendants and brought wine before the Chūjō, which Senshū-no-Mae served to him. Shigehira-no-Kyō took a little, but seemed rather indifferent to their attentions, whereupon Kanō-no-suke spoke as follows: "I am a man of the province of Izu, and am only a sojourner in Kamakura, but I will do anything I can to serve you; and Hyōye-no-suke Dono has ordered that we accede to any wishes you may have, so please command us. So let sake be served." So Senshū-no-Mae brought him saké and recited once aid again the piece entitled: "I am angry with the weaving-woman for the heaviness of my silken robe." "Though Kitano Tenjin swore that he would hasten three times a day to protect him who sings this verse," said the Chūjō, "seeing that I am one forsaken and without hope in this world, of what avail is it to join in the singing; still, if it will at all lessen my guilt, I will do so." Then Senshū sang the refrain entitled: "Even the Ten Transgressions, they shall be taken away," and then sang four or five times the Imayo measure: "Let all who desire Paradise call on the name of Amida." Then the Chūjō drained his cup, and Senshū took it and gave it to Kanō-no-suke, and while he was drinking she played the biwa. "This melody is usually called Gojō-raku," said the Chūjō in jest; "but now it seems to me like Goshō-raku (songs of the next world); so I will sing the piece called Ōjo-no-kyū (hastening to heaven): and he took the biwa and tuned it, and sang the melody Ōjo-no-kyū.

And so the night grew on, and his heart became free of care, and he said: "Who would have thought to find such grace in the Eastern Provinces? Let us have another song." So Senshū-no-Mae sang several times with great feeling the Shirabyoshi refrain: "Those who find shelter beneath one tree, or those who snatch a draught from the same stream; it is naught but the promise of a former life." Then the Chūjō also sang: "The tears of Gu-shi when the light grew dim." And the meaning of this song is as follows: when in old time in China the Emperor Kōso of Kan strove with Kō-u of Sō, Kō-u triumphed in seventy-two battles, but at length he was beaten and his army routed. Then, springing on to his horse Sui, famous for its wondrous strength and swiftness, he made to escape with his consort Gu-shi, when strange to say the horse set both his feet firm and refused to move. Shedding tears of chagrin Kō-u exclaimed: "My power is already gone, and for the attacks of the enemy I care nothing, all that grieves me is the parting with this lady." It is the scene of Gu-shi weeping in the waning light, as the troops of the enemy came shouting down on all sides, that Kisshō-kō has represented in this poem, and it was a sign of the Chūjō's artistic feeling that he chose it to sing on this occasion.

So they went on until the day was about to break, when Kanō-no-suke took leave of the Chūjō, and Senshū-no-Mae returned also. That morning it chanced that Yoritomo was reading the Hokke Sutras in the Jibutsu-dō when she came ok, and he turned to her with a smile and remarked: "No doubt the entertainment last night was very amusing?" At this Sai-in-no-Jikwan Chikayoshi, who was writing something his presence, asked what he meant. "For the last two or three years the Heike have experienced nothing but hardships and fighting," said Yoritomo, "and yet so charming was the eying and singing of Sammi Chūjō that I stood all night outside listening to it. He is indeed a fine artist." "I too should have liked to hear it," replied Chikayoshi, "but I had some other business last night and so I could not; but I will take the first chance of doing so henceforth. The Heike have always produced many talented musicians and artists, and a while ago when they were comparing each other to various were, they decided that Sammi-Chūjō was the peony among them." At any rate his playing the biwa and singing so pressed Yoritomo that he never forgot it.

When Senshū-no-Mae afterwards heard that the Chūjō had been sent to Nara and put to death there, the tidings so affected her that she retired from the world and became a nun, entering the temple of Zenkoji in Shinano, there to pray for his happy rebirth in Paradise.

Chapter VIII.

YO KOBUE.

Now though the body of Komatsu-no-Sammi Chūjō Koremori was in Yashima, yet his heart was ever in Miyako, for never for a moment was his mind free from anxiety about his wife and little ones whom he had left in the Capital. Unable at last to bear the suspense, on the fifteenth day of the third month of the third year of Ju-ei, he slipped out of his house at Yashima at dawn and departed, accompanied by Yosōhyōye Shigekage, his page Ishidō Maru, and a Toneri named Takesato, who was included because he understood ships. With these three he took ship at Yuki-no-ura in the province of Awa, and after passing by the offing of Naruto, they shaped their course towards Kii, passing on their way the shrines of Tamatsu-shima Myojin, (who is worshipped as the god of Waka, Fukiage and Sotōri-hime), Nichizen and Kokken, and arriving at last at Minato in Kii. Thence he thought to go by the hills to Miyako and meet his wife and children, but when he remembered how his uncle the Chūjō Shigehira had been taken alive, and exposed to the shame of being carried thus to Miyako and Kamakura, he feared to heap shame on his father's gave if he also were taken, and though his feelings naturally dragged him in that direction, he fought them down and proceeded to Kōya.

Now in Kōya there was a certain saintly priest whom he had formerly known: He had been a retainer of Komatsu Dono, and his name was Saitō Takiguchi Tokiyori, the son of Saitō Saemon Mochiyori. When he was thirteen years of age he had gone to the Palace to take up his duties, and there he fell deeply in love with a girl named Yokobue, a maid-in-waiting on the Imperial Consort Kenreimon-in. When his father heard of this he remonstrated with him very strongly, for he had intended that his son should make a good match through which he might be able to obtain a good position at Court. Thereupon Takiguchi exclaimed: In ancient times in China there lived one named Seō-bo who is alive no longer, and Tōbō-saku also is now but a name and nothing more. Fleeting are the limits of youth and age; for as a flash of fire they pass and are gone. If we speak of long life, it is but seventy or eighty years, and of these the prince of life is no more than twenty. So in this world of dreams and illusions why be burdened with one we dislike, even for a moment? But if I look on the one I love it is disobedience to my father. By this lesson I will learn virtue. I will renounce this passing world and enter the way of Buddha." And at the age of nineteen he shaved his head and entered the temple of Ojo-in in Saga. When Yokobue heard this, she said: "That he should give me up is quite natural, but why be so foolish as to become a monk? And if he meant to retire from the world, why did he not first come and tell me of it? So thinking that however strong his resolve might be, he might have come and expressed his regret, she left the city one evening and set off for Saga in anxious mood.

It was now past the tenth day of the second month, and the spring breeze of Umezu wafted her the grateful scent of many blossoms, while the moon, half-hidden by the drifting mist, reflected itself dimly in the Ōigawa, but how sad and troubled was her heart as she searched for her lover. All she had heard was the name of the temple, but she knew not in what part of it he was living, and so she wandered about distractedly hither and thither, trying to find it in great distress. Then she heard proceeding from a rough and poor cell the voice of someone reciting the Sutras, and she knew it for the voice of Takiguchi Nyūdō. So she told the maid who was with her to go and take this message: "Even though you have thus changed your condition, I, Yokobue have come so far to see you once more." Takiguchi was greatly amazed and agitated to hear this, and peeping through a hole in the shoji, saw her standing outside, the skirts of her garments soaked with dew, and her sleeves wet with tears. Her face had grown thinner in the meanwhile, and she looked weary with her search, truly a sight to melt the heart of the most fanatic devotee. But Takeguchi only sent someone out to say: "The person whom you seek is not here. You must have come to the wrong place." And so there was nothing for Yokobue to do but to swallow her tears and wend her way back to Miyako, sad and bitter of heart.

By and by Takiguchi said to the monk who dwelt with him: "This is a quiet place, and there is no interruption to one's prayers, but now that girl knows my whereabouts, and though once I was able to steel my heart, if she should follow me again I might melt. Farewell." And he left Saga and betook himself to Mount Kōya, where he entered the temple of Shojo-shin-in to practise the religious life. There after a while he heard that Yokobue too had left the world and become a nun, and he sent her this stanza:

"Till you forsook the world your heart was filled with resentment,
Surely your soul must rejoice, now you have entered the Way."

To this Yokobue answered:

"Where is the need for regret when once we have entered the
    cloister?
There is no turning back, when we have entered the Way."

Afterwards she entered the temple of Hokkeji at Nara, but she was unable to forget the past, and brooded over it until before long she fell sick and died. When Takiguchi Nyūdō was told of it he redoubled his religious austerities, and his father forgave his unfilial conduct, so that he became to be known to all who were acquainted with him as the Saint of Kōya. Now when Koremori met him after a long while he remembered him as attired in Hariginu and Tate-eboshi, his hair carefully dressed and his whole appearance rich and gay, but the man he now beheld was dressed in a priest's robe anti stole of sombre colour, and though he was not yet thirty years old, he looked like an emaciated old monk. His person exuded an odour of incense smoke, and his whole demeanour was that of a sage sunk in profound and pious meditations, so much that his condition seemed to Koremori a most enviable one. Perhaps the Seven Sages of Shin who dwelt in the Bamboo Grove, or the Four Greybeards of Kan who lived in Shozan, did not look more venerable than he.

Chapter IX.

THE BOOK OF KŌYA.

When Takiguchi Nyūdō saw that it was Koremori, he exclaimed: "Can it be that you are not an illusion? Then how is it that you have managed to escape from Yashima? "When I left the Capital for the Western Provinces," replied Koremori, "I did not think much of it, but afterwards I could not rest for a moment for anxiety about those I had left behind there, and though I said nothing my feelings were apparent, and both Munemori and the Nii Dono were uncertain whether Yoritomo would extend to them the indulgence that he had to Yorimori for the sake of Ike-no-Zenni, and so, unable to bear the suspense any longer, I was impelled to come thus far. Here I thought to renounce the world, and yield up nay life by fire or water, but I have a great desire to go to Kumano," "The affairs of this world of dreams are of little matter," replied Takiguchi Nyūdō, "but to spend long ages in the hells is indeed painful."

Then Takiguchi led him round to pray at all the monasteries and pagodas, coming at last to the Oku-no-in. Mount Kōya is two hundred ri from the Imperial Capital silent and far from the habitations of men: untainted are the breezes that rustle its branches, calm are the shadows of its setting sun. Eight are its peaks and eight are its valleys, truly a spot to purify the heart: beneath the forest mists the flowers blossom; the bells echo to the cloud-capped hills. On the tiles of its roofs the pine-shoots grow; mossy are its walls where the hoarfrost lingers.

In ancient times in the period Enki, in answer to a request in a dream from Kōbō Daishi, the Mikado Daigo Tennō sent a dark coloured robe to Kōya; but when the Imperial Messenger Chūnagon Sukezumi-nu-Kyō ascended the mountain, accompanied by the Sōjō

Kwangen of Hannyaji, and opened the doors of the holy tomb to put the new robe on the Daishi, a thick mist arose and hid his figure from their eyes. Bursting into tears Kwangen exclaimed: "Why are we not permitted to see him? This is the first time since I was born that I have received such a rebuke." And casting himself on the ground he wept bitterly. Then the mist gradually melted away, and the Daishi appeared like the moon from the clouds, and Kwangen, weeping now for joy, clothed him in the new garment and also shaved his hair which had grown very long.

Though the Imperial Messenger and the Sōjō Kwangen were able to see and adore the Daishi, the Sōjō's acolyte, Naigū Shunyū of Ishiyama, who had accompanied them, was unable to do so on account of his youth, and was greatly grieved in consequence, so the Sōjō took his hand and placed it upon the knee of the Daishi, and ever after this hand had a fragrant odour all his life. It is said too that instruction for making incense of a similar scent is still handed down at the temple of Ishiyama. Now this was the reply that the Daishi sent to the Mikado: "In former days I met a Sattva, and from him learned all the secret tradition of Dharani and Mudra. In everlasting pity for the people of the world I took upon myself an unparalleled vow, and trusting in the great pity of Fugen, exhibiting in myself perfect tranquillity in these far-off confines, I wait the coming of Miroku." Not otherwise did Maha Kas'yapa retire to the cave in Mount Keisoku to await the coming of universal peace. It was on the twenty first day of the third month of the second year of Shō-wa, at the Hour of the Tiger, that Kōbō Daishi entered Nirvana, and that is now three hundred years ago, so that he has yet five billion six hundred and seventy million years to wait for the rebirth of Miroku and the salvation of the world.

Chapter X.

KOREMORI RENOUNCES THE WORLD.

"I am forever undecided, like the birds on the snowy peaks of India that are always crying, "to-day we will build our nest, or to-morrow;" declared Koremori, weeping. Tanned by the salt breezes, and wasted by continual anxiety, he no longer looked like his former self, but even now he was far more comely than most men.

That night he return-d to the cell of Takiguchi Nyūdō, and there they talked of many things both past and present. As the night grew on and he watched the deportment of the Nyūdō he perceived that he was indeed as it were polishing the jewel of Truth on the floor of profound faith, and at the boom of the bell at the Hour of the Tiger, (4. a.m.) he came to understand the unreality of this world of illusion. Early the next morning he called Chigaku Shōnin of Tozen-in and intimated to him that he wished to become a monk. He also summoned Yosōbyoye Shigekage and Ishidō Maru, and addressed them thus: "As for me I am overwhelmed by unspeakable anxieties, and my way has become straitened so that I cannot escape, but whatever may become of me there is no need for you to throw away your lives. Many others are still living, so after I have met my fate, do you make haste to the Capital and help them, both cherishing my wife and children, and praying for my happier rebirth." On hearing this the two were for a while choked by emotion so that they could utter no word, but by and by Shigekage controlled his feelings and said. "At the time of the rebellion of Heiji my father Yosozaemon Kageyasu followed our lord Shigemori, and at Nijō Horikawa engaged Kamada Hyōye and fell by the hand of Akugenda. I also might have done some such deed, but at that time I was hardly two years old and so remember nothing of it. When I was seven years old my mother followed my father, and I was left alone with none to care for me, when your late father took compassion on me, saying that, as I was the son of one who had given his life for him, I should always be brought up in his house; and so, when I was nine years old, on the same night as you performed Gempuku, I also, to my great pride, was permitted to bind up my hair. As the character 'mori' is the sign of your house, your father gave it to you the fifth generation, and to me he gave the first character of his name, and called me Shigekage, my name before this being Matsuo. And concerning this my youthful name Matsuo also; on the fiftieth day after my birth my father took me in his arms to our lord, and he said: "The name of my house is Komatsu, so let him be called Matsuo in commemoration." Indeed my father having died thus was a great blessing to me, for among the other retainers my equals I was perchance even too much favoured by our lord. So, when he was dying, and had already put away all thoughts of the things of this world, he sent for me and said: "Alas! You regarded me as your father, and I looked on you as a memento of Kageyasu. At the next appointment of officials I intended to raise you to be Yukie-no-jō, thus giving you the same rank as your father bore, but now it is all in vain. But I beg you to be mindful always to keep on good terms with Koremori." And so I thought it natural to look forward to giving my life for yours some time or other, and it seems a great shame to me that you bid me run away and save myself in this fashion. Many may survive, as you say, but as things now are they will all be retainers of the Genji. And after you have departed this life, what pleasure can I have in living longer? And if one lived for a thousand, or ten thousand years, would not one have to die in the end? I can see no greater wisdom than this." And so saying he cut off his hair himself, and then received the tonsure from Takiguchi. When Ishidō Maru saw this, not to be outdone, he too cut off his hair. He had been with his master since he was eight years old, and his gratitude was no less than that of

Shigekage, so he also had his head shaved by Takiguchi Nyūdō. When Koremori saw what they had done he felt inexpressibly sad, and exclaimed: "Ah! I had thought to see my dear ones once again in my former state, but now I have nothing more to hope for." Andy' so, as it must be, repeating three times the Buddhist text, "Ryūten sankai-chū, On-ai-funō-dan, Kion nyū-mu-i, Shinjitsu hō-onsha,"[250] he submitted his head to the tonsure. Both Koremori and Yosōbyōye were twenty seven years old at this time, while Ishidō Maru was eighteen. By and by he called the Toneri Takesato and said: "You are not to go up to the Capital now. In the end it can not be concealed, but if my wife were to know what I have done now, no doubt she too would renounce the world. But go to Yashima and tell them that, as they can see, the world is in a sad plight, and those who are tired of existence are many; perhaps they may not have heard that Hidan-no-Chūjō Kiyotsune fell in the Western Provinces, and Bitchū-no-kami Moromori was killed at Ichi-no-tani, while my chief regret is that they may think me recreant on account of my present behaviour. Moreover, as to this armour of Chinese leather, and the sword Kogarasu Maru, which have been handed down as heirlooms from Taira Sadamori, and have come to me after nine generations, in the event of fortune favouring our house again so that we are able to return to the Capital, you must take them and give them to my son Rokudai." Takesato, overcome by emotion, could make no reply for some time, but after a while he restrained his feelings and said: "Not till I have seen what is to befall will I leave my master, but when all is ended I will go to Yashima." Whereat Koremori allowed him to go with him. Then, taking Takiguchi Nyūdō with them as a guide to salvation, they set out from Kōya in the guise of Yamabushi, and soon arrived at Santo in Kii. After worshipping at the (shrine of Prince Fujishiro and others, before the shrine of Prince Iwashiro to the north of Senri-ga-hama they met seven or eight horsemen in kariginu. Thinking they might be in danger of being captured, each of the party laid his hand on his dirk to cut open his belly, when the others, respectfully, dismounting without any trace of suspicious conduct, made a deep obeisance and passed on. After this encounter, fearing that they might meet some others who knew them in these parts, Koremori and his men quickened their steps and hurried on. The horseman whom they had met was one Yuasa-no-Shichirōhyōye Munemitsu, the son of Yuasa-no-Gon-no-kami Muneshige, and when his retainers asked him who it was he replied: "That is Sammi Chūjō Koremori the eldest son of Komatsu-no-Daijin Shigemori. He has escaped from Yashima somehow or other, and has already shaved his head and become a

---

[250] *Ryūten*, etc. "Whosoever is continuously reborn in the Three Worlds, it is because he cannot sever the bonds of affection. Whosoever renounces affection and enters Nirvana, he it is who in truth requites affection."

monk. Those with him were Yosōbyōye and Ishidō Maru, who have also renounced the world with him. I would have stopped and enquired of him how he did, but I thought he would be embarrassed and so passed .on. How pathetic indeed is his fate! "And he pressed his sleeve to his face and wept: and of his retainers there was none who did not moisten the sleeve of his kariginu.

Chapter XI.

The Pilgrimage to Kumano.

Thus proceeding on their way at length they came to the Iwatagawa. And of this river it is said that whosoever crosses it is cleansed of all evil karma and hindrances to right conduct, and inherited sins. As he offered up his prayers with a calm mind before the Shōjōden of the main shrine, and throughout fiat night contemplated the bulk of the stately temple, his cart was filled with thoughts too deep for utterance. A mist of boundless mercy and protection hovered over the mountain of Yuya, and the matchless spiritual power of the deity manifested itself in the Otonashigawa. The moon of the all-embracing efficacy of the doctrine shone clear and without pot, and no dew of evil thoughts collected in the garden of repentance for the Six Roots of wickedness. Everything around spoke to him of help and salvation.

As the night grew on and he meditated in the silence, he pondered sadly over the remembrance of how his father Shigemori had come to this shrine and entreated the deity to shorten his days and grant him happiness in the after life. And as the Gongen of this shrine is Amida Nyorai, he prayed that, in accordance with his vow to save all mankind, he would bring him safe to the Pure Land, and also that his wife and children in Miyako might find peace and safety: for even when one has forsaken the world and entered the True Way, these blind attractions are not wholly absent.

The next day he took ship and went from the Hongū to the Shingū and worshipped the deity there. On its cliffs the pine trees tower aloft; its breezes sweep all vain thoughts from the mind; while its clear flowing waters wash away the dust rind mire of this evil world. Worshipping at the shrine of Asukai, and passing by Sano-no-Matsubara, he came to the shrine of Nachi. There is the famous three-fold waterfall that soars up thousands of yards to the sky, where upon the top of the cliff there stands a figure of Kwannon, a spot that might be called Fudaraku-san: and as the sound of many voices chanting the Hokke Sutra came out of the mist it might be considered like the peak of Gridhrakuta. So since the time that the Gongen became reincarnate in this mountain all the people of our country from highest to lowest have come on pilgrimage to bow their heads and pray at this shrine, and therefrom have received great benefits. Hence are the temple roofs so many, and the courts crowded with priests and laymen. In the summer season of the period of Kwan-wa the Hō-ō Kwazan, an Emperor possessing the Ten Virtues, came to pray for rebirth in the heaven of Amida, and on the site of the cell where he stayed an ancient cherry tree in bloom still recalls his memory.

Now among the priests who were staying at Nachi there were many who remembered the Chūjō Koremori in Miyako, and when some of them asked who was this who had come to worship, another replied: "This is Sammi Chūjō Koremori, the son of the Daijin Shigemori; when he was only Shōshō of the Fourth Rank, in the spring of the period Angen, there was a celebration of the fiftieth birthday of the Hō-ō at the Hōjūjiden, and his father Komatsu Dono, who was then Naidaijin-no-Sadaishō, and his uncle Munemori, who was Dainagon-no-Udaishō, attended at the Palace. Besides these came also Sammi-no-Chūjō Tomomori, Tō-no-Chūjō Shigehira, and all the Courtiers and Nobles of their house, then in the height of their prosperity, and from among them as they stood by the curtain of the dancing-stage, advanced this youthful Shigehira, crowned with a wreath of cherry-blossoms, and danced the measure called Seikaiha. Most gracefully his sleeves floated out on the breeze, and his mien was brilliant as dew-sprinkled flowers, brightening the earth and illumining the sky. Then the Imperial Consort sent him a robe of honour as a present by the hands of the Kwampaku, and his father the Daijin, leaving his seat, came forth to receive it, placing it on his left shoulder while he did obeisance to the Hō-ō. It was an honour that few could equal, and his fellow courtiers could not but be envious; while some of the ladies of the Court in their admiration compared him to a plum-tree among the trees of the forest. When we consider how brilliant lie then was, ere long to rise to the high position of Daijin-no-Taishō, who would have thought ever to see him in this sad and emaciated condition. Though we speak of change and impermanence, it's a painful thing to see such a thing." And among all the priests of Nachi there was none who did not press his sleeve to his eyes.

Chapter XII.

KOREMORI DROWNS HIMSELF.

So Koremori, after completing the pilgrimage to the three shrines of Kumano, took a boat before the shrine called Hama-no-miya, and launched out to the open sea. There is an island far out in the offing called Yamanari-no-shima, and to this he rowed and disembarked on the shore. Weeping bitterly lie cut his name and pedigree on a great pine tree thus: "Sammi-no-Chūjō Koremori, religious name Jō-en, son of Komatsu-no-Naidaijin Shigemori Kō, religious name Jō-ren, grandson of the Dajō-daijin Taira-no-Ason Kiyomori, religious name Jō-kai, aged twenty-seven years; drowns himself in the offing of Nachi, twenty-eighth day of the third month of the third year of Ju-ei": after which he again entered the boat and rowed out into the offing.

Though he had made up his mind to end his life, when it came to the point he felt down-cast and sad. As it was the twenty eighth day of the third month a sea mist was rolling over the waters, wrapping everything in a dreary pall; but even on an ordinary spring day a melancholy mood comes over us with the approach of evening, so how much more when today is the end, the last evening we spend on earth. Looking at the fishing-boats as they rose and sank on the waves, though he had made up his mind to sink likewise, yet his thoughts dwelt on his own fate, and when he saw a flock of wild-geese he felt as great regret and home-sickness for his birthplace as did Sōbu when he was imprisoned in the land of Ko, and sent back a message by a wild-goose. Recollecting himself, however, and reproving himself for harbouring such vain thoughts of this world, he put his hands together, and turning to the west repeated the Nembutsu. But even so the thought came into his mind how his dear ones in Miyako did not know that this was his last hour, and would keep on waiting and hoping for some tidings of him, so dropping his hands and ceasing to say the Nembutsu, he turned to Takiguchi Nyūdō and said: "Ah, what a thing it is to have wife and children! For not only are they an anxiety in. this world, but a hindrance to obtaining Enlightenment in the next. I fear that the obtrusion of these thoughts is because of the greatness of my guilt, and I repent of it."

The sage felt deeply grieved in his heart, but thinking it would not do to show any weakness, he wiped away his tears and assumed an impassive expression. "Alas!" he said, "tender feelings are common to all men, and it is indeed as you say. Endless are the karma-relations produced if a man and woman place their pillows together but for one night, and deep is the connexion in their after lives. "Those that are born must die; those that meet must part," is the way of this world. "The last dew or the first drop," one must go before the other. and whether one dies first or last, all must leave this world at last. The pledge of Gensō to Yōkihi on an evening in autumn at the Ri-San Palace led but to the bruising of hearts at last, and even the favour of Shozen in the Kan-sen-den had to come to an end. Even the magicians Sho-shi and Bai-sei did not live for ever, neither are the highest rank of saints free from birth and death; so that even if you can boast of the pleasures of long life, this resentment cannot be put away for ever. Thus if you live for a hundred years, the pain of parting will still be the same. And Mara the king of evil in the sixth Devaloka, who opposes the Way, taking possession of the Six Heavens of Desire, has made them his own, and grudging the people of these worlds deliverance from birth and death, becomes to them wives and husbands to hinder their escape; and so all the Buddhas of the Three Worlds, regarding all mankind as their children, in their zeal to bring them to the Paradise of the Pure Land, have strictly warned them that from the utmost antiquity wives and children were fetters to bind them to the Wheel of Birth and Death. But do not lose heart on that account, for Iyo-no-Nyūdō Yoriyoshi, an ancestor of the Genji, being sent by the Imperial Command to subdue Ando Sadato and Mureto, the rebels of Mutsu, in the course of twelve years took the heads of more than sixteen thousand men, besides which he deprived of life many millions of the beasts of the field and fish of the rivers, and yet at the time of his death, as a strong desire for Enlightenment awoke within him, he is said to have attained a seat in Paradise. So great is the merit of forsaking the world that all the sins of previous lives are washed away: even if one should build a Pagoda of the Seven Precious Things reaching up to the thirty third heaven, his merit would not be as great as that of him who renounces the world for a single day. Or if one should feed a hundred Arhats for a hundred thousand years, he who forsakes the world for one day would have greater merit. Was not Yoriyoshi able to attain bliss by his strength of mind? So shall not you, whose guilt is far less, be able to be reborn in the Pure Land? And moreover Amida Nyorai, the Gongen of this shrine, has made forty eight vows to save mankind, and among these in the eighteenth vow he states that whosoever in true faith shall call up to ten times on his name, earnestly desiring to enter Paradise, shall in no wise fail to attain Enlightenment. So if indeed you believe this doctrine, relying on it in firm faith without any doubt, and if you repeat the Nembutsu either once or ten times, Amida Nyorai, diminishing to some sixteen feet his august stature, which is of a height that myriads of Nahutas, many in number as the sands of the Ganges, only can measure, with Kwannon and Seishi and innumerable Saints and Bodhisattvas encompassing them about tier on tier, will come forth to meet you from the Eastern Gate of Paradise, welcoming your advent with songs of rejoicing. Thus though your body may sink to the bottom of this ocean, you will ride in glory on clouds of purple. And when you have become a Buddha and attained liberation, in true enlightenment you may come back to this world, and without doubt may lead your wife and child into the path of true salvation." And as he spoke thus, striking his bell the while, and urging him to repeat the Nembutsu, Koremori, in sure belief that he had attained Enlightenment, steadfastly putting aside all vain thoughts, looked towards the west and clasped his hands, with a loud voice repeating the Nembutsu a hundred times, and then with the word "Namu" on his lips sprang into the ocean. Yasōbyōye and Ishidō Maru, repeating the same invocation, also sprang to their death with their master.

Chapter XIII.

THE THREE DAY'S HEISHI.

The Toneri Takesato was also about to follow his master into the water, when Takiguchi Nyūdō prevented him and said: "However grievous it may be, you must not depart from your lord's last behest. It is miserable to be left thus without a master, but you must live on to pray for the soul." "In my grief at being left behind," replied Takesato, "I had quite forgotten my obligations." And casting himself down in the bottom of the boat, he cried and lamented aloud, just as did Tchandaka when he took the horse Kanthaka from S'akya Muni at the time of his flight to Mount Dantaloka, and returned with it to the palace. For a while they rowed about to see if the others would reappear or not, but they had sunk deep and came up no more. As they rowed they repeated the Sutras and the Nembutsu for their happier rebirth. And so the evening sun went down in the west, and all the sea grew dark, and though they could not bear to leave, yet as it must be, they rowed back the now empty boat to land, tears and oar-drips mingling indistinguishably on the Nyūdō's sleeve. Takiguchi returned to Kōya, and Takesato went on weeping to Yashima, where he delivered his lord's letter to his younger brother Shin Sammi-no-Chūjō Sukemori. "Alas!" said he when he opened it, "I had not thought he would act thus. Would that I had gone too and met my death with him, for it is grievous to die thus separated. Both Munemori and the Nii Dono thought that he was going back to Miyako by the favour of Yoritomo, and meant to desert us, but now how sad that he has drowned himself thus in the sea of Nachi. Did he give you any message for us besides?" Then the Toneri related in detail ail that Koremori had told him to say to them, about the deaths of his brothers and his sorrow at leaving them in this way, finishing with his request about the armour and sword. When he had heard it all he pressed his sleeve to his face, exclaiming: "Now I too have no wish to live any longer." And all the samurai who stood round, noticing the great resemblance he bore to the late Chūjō, could not forbear from moistening their sleeves. Munemori and the Nii-no-Ama also, when they heard that he had not entreated the favour of Yoritomo as they had thought, were terribly pained at his untimely death.

On the first day of the fourth month the era was changed and the subsequent one was called Gen-ryaku. On the same day an appointment of officials was held, and the former Uyōye-no-suke Yorimoto of Kamakura was raised to the lower grade of the Upper Fourth Rank from the lower grade of the Lower Fifth, thus passing over five grades at once. On the third day the Emperor Sūtoku-in was raised to be a god, and a shrine was dedicated to him at Ōi-no-Mikado, the ancient battle field of Hogen. This is said to have been done by order of the Hō-ō alone, the Imperial Court knowing nothing about it.

On the fourth day of the fifth month Ike-no-Dainagon Yorimori set out for Kamakura, for Yoritomo had always been kindly disposed to him, having sworn, many times: "I will treat you with every care and attention, and give you the same welcome that I would have done to your respected mother Ikeno-Zenni; by Hachiman Daibosatsu I swear it": but though he did not doubt that Yoritomo himself thought thus, he was not so sure about the other Genji, and had so far hesitated; but lately a messenger had come from Kamakura, saying: "Come down hither without delay, for I wish to see you; I will receive you just as the late Ike-no-Zenni;" and so he started at once. Now among his retainers was one Yaheibyōye Munekiyo, the most faithful of all the hereditary vassals of the Heike, and he would not accompany him on this occasion. On being asked the reason he replied: "My lord is thus able to go down in safety, but I cannot rest for thinking of the others of our house who are tossed about on the waves of the Western Ocean; so when I have calmed my mind somewhat I will follow on afterward." Abashed and pained by this speech the Dainagon replied: "Indeed I felt it hard to be left behind here when the rest of our family fled, but life is precious and I was loath to throw it away, so I reluctantly stayed. And now that I must go down to Kamakura, why can you not escort me on such a long journey? When I stayed behind, why did you not offer any remonstrance? Was there anything, great or small, in which I did not consult you?" Shifting his position, Munekiyo replied with a respectful obeisance: "Alas! Nothing is more dear than life to all men, both high and low; and so it is said that one will leave the world sooner than give up his life. I did not think it a bad deed that you should stay behind here; and it is only because the life of Yoritomo himself was spared that he has reached his present happy condition. Moreover he has not forgotten my services, in escorting him, at the bidding the late Ike-no-Zenni, as far as Shinohara in Ōmi at the time of his exile; and if I accompany you to Kamakura he will certainly entertain me bountifully and make me presents. Therefore it is that, when I think of my friends and the Courtiers of our house cast upon the waters of the Western Sea, I feel ashamed to receive such preference. And as to your going on a long journey, I indeed feel anxious, and if you were going to attack the enemy I would not fail to be among the first to go, but in this case I think it no wrong to refuse." As he ended his speech it was not easy for him to control his emotion, and all the other samurai likewise pressed their sleeves to their eyes. The Dainagon also was greatly displeased, but as there was no help for it now, he soon after started.

On the sixteenth day of the same month he reached Kamakura, and Yoritomo immediately received him in audience. When he enquired where Munekiyo was, the Dainagon answered that he was sick just then and could not come. "How can that be?" replied Yoritomo, "I was formerly committed to his charge, and so I feel very grateful to him, and was looking forward with great pleasure to seeing him again. It is indeed a pity that he has not come with you." And as he had already prepared a grant of manors and many presents for him, he was very disappointed. The lords of the Eastern Country also, who had prepared similar presents and striven against each other to do him honour, also expressed their regret at his absence.

On the ninth day of the sixth month the Dainagon Yorimori started on his return journey to the Capital, for though Yoritomo pressed him to stay longer, he feared that those in Miyako would be anxious about him, and so begged leave to depart. Yoritomo then sent a request to the Hō-ō that Yorimori should be confirmed in the possession of all his fiefs and land, and that he should hold his office of Dainagon as heretofore. Besides this he presented him with thirty saddled horses and thirty unsaddled, and thirty long chests full of gold, rolls of silk, and dyed stuffs. Moreover besides what Yoritomo gave him the lords of the Eastern Country vied with each other in making him presents, so that the horses alone amounted to three hundred. So that Ike-no-Dainagon Yorimori-no-Kyō not only returned to Miyako with his head on his shoulders, but with great store of riches besides.

On the same day Hirata-no-Nyūdō Sadatsugu, uncle of Higo-no-kami Sadayoshi, headed the troops of Iga and Ise and led them against the province of Ōmi, but some offshoots of the Genji rode out to encounter them, and on the twenty second day, unable to hold out any longer, the men of Iga and Ise were beaten and routed. Pathetically heroic was the loyal conduct of these hereditary retainers of the Heike house in remembering their ancient obligations, but their plan of campaign was quite beyond their strength. This was what is called "The three days Heishi."

Chapter XIV.

FUJITO.

Now when the scanty tidings which the wife of Koremori had been accustomed to receive from her husband ceased altogether, for she had always heard from him about once a month, she continued waiting and hoping, but when the spring lengthened into summer, and there were rumours that he was no longer in Yashima, she became exceedingly anxious and sent a messenger to Yashima to enquire. For some time the messenger did not return, and the summer became autumn, when, at the end of the seventh month, he carne back at last, and in answer to the question of his mistress told her that Koremori had started from

Yashima at dawn on the fifteenth day of the third month with Yosōbyōye and Ishidō Maru, had proceeded to Kōya and become a monk, after which he had made pilgrimage to Kumano and drowned himself in the offing of Nachi, which news he had heard from the Toneri Takesato. On hearing this the lady, confirmed in her worst fears, cast herself to the ground in an excess of grief, while her young children joined the voices of their lamentation to hers. Then the lady who was milk-nurse to her young son, controlling her emotion, spoke thus: "This is truly no matter for weeping. To be taken alive like Honsammi Chūjō Shigehira, and exposed to the disgrace of being taken to Miyako and Kamakura is indeed painful, but it ought to be a source of joy in the midst of your sorrow to know that our master was able to proceed to Kōya and renounce the world, and then go to Kumano, and after making all proper preparations for the next life, to put an end to himself in the waves of Nachi. Now you must also become a nun and say prayers for the happy enlightenment of our departed lord. So the lady forthwith forsook the world and devoted herself to praying for her deceased husband. But when the news of the death of Koremori was reported to Yoritomo he was very grieved and said: "Ah, what a pity he did not throw himself on my mercy; I would certainly have spared his life, for it was his father Shigemori alone who, at the request of the late Ike-no-Zenni, got my sentence remitted to banishment, and in remembrance of this great kindness I will never deal harshly with his children. Since he had become a monk I would have taken no further steps with regard to him."

Now after the Heike had crossed over to Yashima, they heard that a force of many tens of thousands of horsemen had arrived at the Capital from the East Country to advance against them, and moreover that the parties of Usuki, Hetsuki and Matsuura had banded together and were about to cross front Kyūshū to attack them. And as these various rumours cache to their ears they could not help being dispirited and discouraged; and all the Court Ladies, from the Consort of the late Emperor, Kenreimon-in, the Mother of the late Emperor, and the Nii Dono downwards mourned and lamented together, wondering what fresh evil tidings they would have to hear, or what new adversities they would have to meet, And seeing that so many of the Nobles had been killed and more than half of the best of the retainers also lost at Ichi-no-tani, Awa-no-Mimbu Shigeyoshi and his brother and the other men of Shikoku remarked how their strength had lessened, but still they thought they would be safe trusting to the mountains and the sea. On the twenty fifth day of the seventh month the ladies came together saying that it was just a year since they had left Miyako, and wondering how soon the time had passed; and so, bewailing the vicissitudes they had met, and talking of reminiscences of the past, some gave way to tears and some to laughter.

On the twenty eighth day the ceremony of accession of the new Emperor was held. This is said to have been the first time that an accession ceremony was held without the imperial Seal, the Sacred Sword and. the Sacred Mirror, in all the line of eighty two human Emperors who had reigned until now. On the sixth day of the eighth month an appointment of officials was held and the Tai-Shōgun Kaba-no-Kwanja Noriyori was made Mikawa-no-kami, while Kurō-no-Kwanja Yoshitsune was made Saemon-no-Jo. As he received appointment to the office of Kebiishi-no-Hangwan by edict of the Hō-ō, he was afterwards known as Kurō Hōgwan.

It was now autumn, and the wind began to blow in the stalks of the hagi, while the dew hung heavy on its lower leaves. The resentful hum of the insects, the rustling of the rice-stalks and the failing of the leaves, all bring sad thoughts, and the quickly darkening skies of the short days of autumn always cause gloomy feelings, so we can well imagine how much more melancholy must those of the Heike have been. In former days they used to divert themselves with the spring flowers in the Palace gardens, but now they languished under the autumn moon by the shore of Yashima. While they composed verses to the bright moon, the evenings of Miyako were ever in their thoughts, and so they consoled themselves with tears in their eyes. The following verse made by Sama-no-kami Yukimori well expresses their feelings:

> "*Though the Palace is in the place where our Sovereign is dwelling,*
> *Yet is Miyako still dearer than ever to me.*"

Meanwhile the Commander-in-Chief Mikawa-no-kami Noriyori set forth on the twelfth day of the ninth month for the Western Provinces to subdue the Heike. With him also in command went Ashikaga-no-Kurando Yoshikane, Hōjō no-Koshirō Yoshitoki, Sai-in-no-Jikwan Chikayoshi, and as Commanders of the Samurai, Doi-no-Jirō Sanehira, his son Yataro Tōhira, Miura-no-suke Yoshizumi, his son Heiroku Yoshimura, Hatakeyama-no-Shōji Shigetada, Hatakeyama-no-Nagano-no-Saburō Shigekiyo, Sahara-no-Jūrō Yoshitsura, Wada-no-Kotarō Yoshimori, Sasaki-no-Saburō Moritsuna, Tsuchiya-no-Saburō Munetō, Amano-no-Tōnai Tōkage, Hiki-no-Tōnai Tomomune, Hiki no-Tōshirō Yoshikazu, Yada-no-Shirō Musha Tomoie, Anzei-no-Saburō Akimasu, Ogo-no-Saburō Sanehide, Nakajō-no-Tōji Ienaga, Ippin-bō Shōgen and Tosabō Shōshun. The force under these leaders numbered about thirty thousand horsemen, and they rode out of Miyako and proceeded as far as Murotsu in Harima.

On the side of the Heike the commanders were Komatsu-no-Shin-sammi Chūjō Sukemori, Komatsu-no-Shōshō Arimori and Tango-no-Jijū Tadafusa, while as Commanders of the Samurai were Etchū-no-

Jirōhyōye Moritsugu, Kazusa-no-Gorōhyōye Tadamitsu and Akushichihyōye Kagekiyo, who with about five hundred ships of war rowed out as far as Kojima in Bizen. When the Genji heard this they also left Muro and took up their position at Fujito at Nishikawajiri in the province of Bizen. Thus the two armies were only separated by a distance of twenty-five chō, and though the Genji were eager to attack, as they had no ships they could do nothing, but had to remain waiting idly where they were. On the twenty-fifth day at the Hour of the Dragon some of the more impetuous spirits of the Heike rowed out in small boats and waved their fans at the Genji, beckoning to them and shouting: "Why do you not come over here?" Now while the warriors of the Genji were wondering what they could do, on the evening of the twenty-fifth day Sasaki-no-Saburō Moritsuna of Ōmi sought out a native of the place and presenting him with a hitatare, a wadded silk robe, a short hakama and a silver-mounted Sayamaki, asked him if he could show him a place where it was possible to cross over to the other side of the sea on horseback. "Though very few of the people about here know of such a place, I can show you one," said the man. "There is a place like the shallows of a river, about ten chō wide: at the beginning of the month it is to the east, and at the end of the month it is to the west, and there you can easily cross over on horseback." "In that case," said Sasaki, "let us cross over and see." So both he and the man stripped naked and crossed over the shallow that the man pointed out, and indeed it was not very deep. In some places it was up to the knee or waist, and there were some where they wet their hair, but they swam the deep parts and waded in the shallow. "From the south," said the man, "it is shallower than from the north, but the enemy are lying there with their bows ready, so it won't do to go any nearer; let us go back again." So Sasaki returned again with the man, but as he was afraid that he might tell someone about it, or show them the way, as there was no way of keeping him quiet otherwise, and he wished to be the only one to know about it, he stabbed him to death on the spot, cut off his head and threw it away.

On the next day, at the Hour of the Dragon (8 a.m.), the Heike rowed out again and repeated their provocation of the previous day. Then Sasaki-no-Saburō Moritsuna of Ōmi. attired in a hitatare with dyed figures, and a suit of armour laced with scarlet, riding a pie-bald war-horse accoutred with a gold-mounted saddle, accompanied only by seven of his family retainers, rode out against them by the way that he had just learned. When the Commander Noriyori perceived this, he called out to stop him, and Doi-no-Jirō Sanehira spurred his horse on with whip and heel, shouting out: "Ho there! Sasaki Dono, what has taken you that you are so rash? The General forbids it! Come back at once! "But Sasaki rode on as though he heard nothing, and Doi, unable to stay him, followed on after him and crossed also. In some places the water was up to the horse's chest, in others up to the edge of his harness or his girth, and in some parts it reached to the middle of the saddle, but by swimming in the deep places and wading in the shallow at length they got over safely. When Noriyori saw this he shouted out: "Sasaki has got the better of us! The water is shallow, after him and cross!" And so, at his order, the whole army of thirty thousand men rode into the water crossed over. The Heike on their part, launching all their ships, drew their bows and shot at them with all their might, but the Genji paid no heed, sloping the neck-pieces of their helmets to avoid the arrows, and grappling the ships with iron rakes and bill-hooks, shouting and fighting with the utmost fierceness All day long the fight raged, and when night came on the ships of the Heike were out in the offing, while the Genii had crossed over to Kojima and landed there to breathe their horses.

The next day the Heike had retired again to Yashima, and the Genii, though eager to follow them and renew the battle, were unable to do so on account of their lack of ships. From ancient times there have been many warriors who have crossed over rivers on horseback, but, however it may be in India or China I know not, in our country to cross the sea on horseback was regarded as a very extraordinary feat. Therefore the fief of Kojima in Bizen was given to Sasaki, and the record of this deed was inscribed in the annals of Yoritomo.

Chapter XV.

THE ACCESSION FESTIVAL.

On the twenty-eighth day of the same month there was another appointment of officials at Miyako, and Kurō Hōgwan Yoshitsune was promoted to be Go-i-no-Jō, being then known as Kurō Taiyū-no-Hōgwan. And so the tenth month began, and at Yashima the wind blew strongly so that the waves rolled up high on the beach, wherefore no army was able to attack it. Merchants too came but seldom, so there was little communication with the Capital. The sky was overcast and hail fell, so that all were gloomy and dispirited. Now as the Daijōe, or Accession Festival, was to be held in the Capital, on the third day of the tenth month the new Emperor went in procession for the Ceremony of Purification, Tokudaiji Dono acting as Naiben. On the occasion of the same ceremony being performed two years before for the Emperor Antoku, now in Yashima, the Heike Naidaijin Munemori Kyō had officiated, and the stateliness with which he walked behind the Dragen Banner, and the harmony with which he wore his robes, the set of his Kammuri with his long sleeves, down to the skirts of his Hakama, was most magnificent. And what could have been finer than the dignity of the Imperial Guard of the Konoe-tsukasa, under the command of

Sammi-no-Chūjō Tomomori and Tō-no-Chūjō Shigehira, as they manned the traces of the Imperial Car? On this occasion Kurō Taiyū-no-Hōgwan Yoshitsune commanded them, and though by comparison with Kiso Yoshinaka he was quite an accomplished Courtier, yet he was far inferior to the dregs of the Heike.

On the eighteenth day the Daijoe Festival was celebrated, but in form only; for, compared with the periods of Ji-shō and Yō-wa, when Takakura Tennō was on the Throne, the farmers and people of the present era were so harassed and destroyed by both the Heike and Genji, that they could neither sow their seed nor reap their harvest, so how was it possible to celebrate such a great festival in more than a formal way?

Now if the Tai-Shōgun Noriyori had continued to prosecute his attack on the Heike, he could have easily destroyed them, but instead of that he remained with his army at Murotsu and Takasago, amusing himself with a lot of courtesans and harlots that he had got together, and wasting the resources of the country as well as troubling the people to no small extent; and though there were many lords of the East Country with him, both great and small, as he was in supreme command they could do nothing. And in this way the year ended.

Volume XI.

Chapter I.

SAKARO.

On the tenth day of the first month of the second year of Gen-ryaku Kurō Taiyū-no-Hōgwan Yoshitsune proceeded to the Palace of the Hō-ō, and addressed this petition to His Majesty through Ōkura Kyō Yasutsune Ason: "Forsaken by the gods and renounced by Your Majesty, the Heike have fled from the Capital and are now fugitives tossed hither and thither on the waves. Yet for the space of three years they have remained at large and unsubdued, and have occupied many provinces, which is a matter for great regret. Therefore have I sworn that I will never return to this Capital until I have utterly destroyed them, even if I have to pursue them to Korea or China, or Devils' Island, even to the uttermost confines of the sea or sky." At this the Hō-ō was greatly rejoiced, and replied: "Be sure and spare no efforts to obtain a decisive victory." Then Yoshitsune returned to his quarters and spoke thus to the warriors of the Eastern Provinces: "By virtue of an Imperial Edict of the Hō-ō, and as the representative of Yoritomo, I am about to start for the Western Provinces to subdue the Heike, neither will I desist from attacking them anywhere either by sea or land till my purpose is accomplished. Therefore if anyone has any objection, let

The Tale of the Heike

him now leave us and go back at once to Kamakura."

Meanwhile at Yashima the time had passed by swiftly as the seasons waxed and waned, until it came to be the third year of their sojourn, and the Heike were continually disturbed by the rumours of a new army setting out against them from the Capital, and of the coalition of the Kyūshū leaders to attack them, so that their spirits sank lower and lower, and the Imperial Consort and the Nii Dono, and the Mother of the late Emperor and all their Ladies did not cease from their mournful prognostications of what was likely to happen to them in the future. "When the rebels of the East and North disregarded the great obligations they were under to our house, and threw off their allegiance to follow Yashinaka and Yoritomo," said Shin-Chūnagon Tomomori-no-Kyō," I thought it quite likely that the Western Provinces might do the same, and said that it would have been better to stay in Miyako and await a decision there. But my opinion alone did not prevail, and so we fled in this timid fashion, and the result is that we have come to this pass." And truly his words were very reasonable.

Now on the third day of the second month Kurō Hōgwan Yoshitsune started from Miyako and proceeded to Watanabe and Fukushima in Settsu to get his ships in order, with the intention of attacking Yashima immediately. On the same day his brother Mikawa-no-kami Noriyori left the Capital also, and he too went to Kanzaki in Settsu to prepare his ships for a campaign against the Sanyodo. On the tenth day of the same month the Hō-ō sent an Imperial Envoy to the shrines of Ise and Iwashimizu, and gave orders that all the chief priests of all shrines should offer up prayers for the speedy return of the Emperor and the Three Sacred Treasures to the Capital.

On the sixteenth day, just as the ships that had been prepared at Watanabe and Fukushima were about to loosen their hawsers and set sail, a most violent tempest arose, and the ships were damaged so that they could not put out, so that day was spent in repairing them. Then the leaders of the Eastern Provinces, great and small, came together at Watanabe and said "We have so far had no experience of war at sea, so what shall we do?" "I think we ought to have a 'Sakaro' fitted on these ships," put in Kajiwara. "A 'Sakaro?' What is that?" asked Yoshitsune. "When you ride a horse," replied Kajiwara, "you can gallop forward or back at your pleasure, because it is quite easy to turn either to the right or the left, but it is a pretty difficult matter to swing a ship round; so if we fit oars at both bow and stern, instead of only at the stern as usual, and insert a rudder in the middle, then we shall be able to turn about easily just as we like." "What an ill-omened thing to propose at the beginning of a campaign," exclaimed Yoshitsune," you know armies always set out with the intention of never retreating, and it is only if they meet with a disaster that they retire, so what is the meaning of these preparations for running away? You lords may fit a hundred or a thousand pairs of 'backing-oars' or 'turn-back-oars' or whatever you like to call them, to your ships, but I shall go with no more than the usual number." "A good general" returned Kajiwara, "is one who advances at the proper time, and retreats at the proper time, thus saving his own life and destroying the enemy; that is what is called a good general: but a man of only one idea is called a 'wild-boar-warrior,' and is not thought much of." "Wild-boar or stag, it's all one; the best way to conquer in battle is to attack the enemy's front, and attack again and again." Then the chiefs of the Eastern Provinces, as they did not dare to laugh openly at Kajiwara, showed their feelings in their features, and muttered under their breath to each other. Yoshitsune and Kajiwara were on the point of drawing their weapons on each other that day, but fortunately the incident was concluded without any actual quarrel. "Now the ships are repaired and ready," said Yoshitsune, "let us have a bite and a cup in celebration;" and while this was being done the stores and weapons and horses were got on board, and all being prepared he gave the order to set sail. The captains and crews murmured at this, however, crying out: "We have the wind behind us, it is true, but it is a little too strong, and the sea will be very rough outside." This angered Yoshitsune exceedingly. "Do you think I am going to stop putting to sea for a little wind?" he cried. "Whether you die on the sea or on land, it is all the result of the karma of a former life; and if I told you to put out in the teeth of a head-wind you might blame me with some reason, but with the wind behind us, even if it is a little fresher than usual, not to put out at a critical time like this . . . .! Ho! Men-at-arms! Shoot, these fellows if they won't move!" Then Ise Saburō Yoshimori, Satō Saburō Tsuginobu and Satō Shirōhyōye Tadanobu of Mutsu, Eda-no-Genzō, Kumai-no-Tarō, Musashi-bo Benkei and others, each equal to a thousand ordinary men, at once sprang forth. "At our lord's command!" they shouted, "Off with those ships, or we shoot every one of you!" So when the captains and sailors saw them running up with their bows in their hands they cried out: "Whether we drown out there in the sea or are shot here, it is all the same, so put off!" And so of the two hundred odd ships five at last got away. These five were, first the Hōgwan's ship; then Tajiro-no-Kwanja's ship; then that of Gotobyoye and his son; then that of the brothers Kaneko, and that of Yodo-no-Gonai Tadatoshi, who held the office of Funa-bugyo, or Marshal of the Ships. The rest of the ships, whether from fear of Kajiwara or the weather, did not put out. "There's no need to stop for the others," said Yoshitsune, "at ordinary times the enemy would be afraid and on the alert, but on a stormy day like this we can land at a place where he won't be expecting us; thus we can attack him to advantage. And take care to cover your lights. If the enemy sees many lights he will take alarm. Follow my ship by keeping your eye on my head and stern lights." So they sailed on all night, and in six hours covered a distance that usually took three days. It was about two o'clock in the morning on the sixteenth day of the second month that they set sail from Watanabe and Fukushima in Settsu, and they arrived off the coast of Awa the next morning about seven.

Chapter II.

THE FIGHT AT KATSUURA.

As it grew light they saw several of the red banners of the Heike fluttering in the breeze. "Now listen," said Yoshitsune, "the best way we can proceed is this. If we disembark our horses when we are close to the shore we shall only be a mark for the enemy's arrows, so while we are still at some distance, heel the ships and put the horses overboard and let them swim tethered to the ships. As soon as their feet touch ground and the water is shallow enough to ride, get into the saddle and gallop to shore." Though five ships had stores and weapons on board, they had also found room for fifty horses. So, according to the Hōgwan's orders they put the horses overboard when they were some little distance from the shore, and when the water was shallow enough they sprang on to their backs, and as Yoshitsune rode up on to the shore at the head of his fifty horsemen with loud shouts of triumph, a band of some hundred horse of the enemy, who were waiting on the shore, did not stay to meet their onset, but retired about two chō inland.

Then, when his men and horses had rested a while on the shore to get their breath, Yoshitsune said to Ise Saburō Yoshimori: "There is one of those horsemen who looks important. Go and fetch him here, for I have some things I want to ask him." In obedience to the Hōgwan's command Yoshimori rode off alone into the midst of the hundred horsemen of the enemy, and what he said I know not, but he soon came back bringing with him as his prisoner a man of about forty, clad in armour laced with black leather, who had removed his helmet and loosened his bowstring in submission. "Who are you?" asked the Hōgwan, to which the warrior replied: "Hanzai-no-Kondō-Roku Chikaie of this province." "Well, whoever he may be keep your eye on him, men, and don't let him take off his armour, for he will be a good guide to Yashima; if he tries to run away, shoot him." Then, addressing Kondō Roku he asked him the name of the place where they were. "It is called Katsuura," he replied. "Oh, no flattery;" said the Hōgwan, laughing. "It is certainly called Katsuura," declared the warrior, "the servants may pronounce it in their dialect as 'Katsura,' but it is written with the two characters, 'Katsu,' (victory) and 'Ura,' (shore)." Yoshitsune was highly delighted at this good omen. "Listen to that, my lords," he cried. "Is it not lucky that when I start on a campaign I should land at Katsuura? And now are there any of the supporters of the

Heike round here?" "There is Sakurama-no-suke Yoshitō, the younger brother of Awa-no-Mimbu Shigeyoshi," replied Kondō. "Well, then let us go and kick him out of our way." And taking the best thirty of the men and horses of the hundred men of Kondō's band, he added them to his own force and rode off to attack Yoshitō's castle. When they arrived in front of this fortress they found that it had a swamp on three sides and a moat on the other. Shouting their war-cry, they made a vigorous attack on the moat side, whereupon the soldiers within shot at them as fast as they could draw their bows, but the Genji paid no heed to them, pushing on across the moat with their neck-plates sloped to ward off the shafts, and attacking with loud shouts, so that Yoshitō, thinking further resistance of no avail, after leaving his retainers behind to hold out as long as they could, jumped upon a fleet horse that he had, and was fortunate enough to be able to make his escape. The Genji took the heads of some twenty of the defenders who were thus left behind, after which they held a celebration in honour of the God of War, cheering loudly in their joy at such an auspicious inauguration of their campaign.

Chapter III.

THE CROSSING OF OSAKA.

Yoshitsune next asked Kondō Roku how many men the Heike had at Yashima, to which he replied that the number was not more than a thousand horsemen. "How is it that there are so few?" said the Hōgwan. "Because they have stationed bands of fifty or a hundred men at every creek and island round Shikoku, and also because an army of three thousand horse under the command of Dennai Saemon Noriyoshi, the eldest son of Awa-no-Mimbu Shigeyoshi, has gone over to Iyo to attack Kōno Shirō of that province, because he would not join them when they summoned him." "Ah, that's a fine opportunity! I have them. And how far is it to Yashima from here?" "About two days march," replied Kondō. "Then let us hurry up and get there before they get wind of us." And so they started off, sometimes running and sometimes marching, making as great a speed as they could, until by night they came to the mountain pass of Osaka on the borders of Awa and Sanuki, and began to cross it.

About the middle of the night as they were pushing on over the mountain, they came up with a man carrying a letter. As it was dark he had not the least idea that they were enemies, but thought they were Heike soldiers going to Yashima, and began to talk to them quite freely. "You seem to be going to Yashima, so I suppose you know the way," said Yoshitsune. "Can you guide us?" "Certainly," replied the man, "I often go there, so I know the road very well." "Who is that letter from, and who is it for?" asked Yoshitsune. "It is from the Ladies in Miyako, and I am taking it to the Daijin Munemori in Yashima," was the reply. "What is it about?" "The Genji have already got as far as Yodo and Kawajiri, so no doubt it is to send him tidings of it." "Ah, no doubt that is so," exclaimed the Hōgwan, "seize that letter, men!" "But don't kill him," he added as they took the letter, "for that would be a useless crime." So they bound the man to a tree in the mountains and passed on. When Yoshitsune opened the letter and read it, he found that it was indeed from the Ladies in Miyako. "Kurō is a shrewd fellow," he read, "and will-not fear to attack however rough the weather may be, so take care not to scatter your force, and be very much on the alert." "This letter is godsend to me," said Yoshitsune, "we must keep it and show it to Yoritomo." And he stowed it away very carefully.

On the following day, the eighteenth, at the Hour of the Tiger (4 a.m.), they came to a place called Hikida in the province of Sanuki, and rested there to give breathing-space to the men and horses. Thence, passing through Shiratori and Nibunoya, they arrived before the fortress of Yashima. Calling Rondo Chikaie once more, the Hōgwan enquired: "What sort of a road is it from here to the Palace of Yashima?" "Ali, you may well ask, but it is really quite shallow," he replied, "at low tide the water between the mainland and the island is not up to a horse's belly." "Then we must attack before they know we are here," said Yoshitsune; and setting fire to the houses of Takamatsu, they began their attack on the castle of Yashima.

Now at Yashima Dennai Saemon Noriyoshi, the eldest son of Awa-no-Mimbu Shigeyoshi, had ridden into the province of Iyo with three thousand horse to chastise Kono-no-Shirō for not coming to join them when he was summoned, but Kono himself had escaped him, so he cut off the heads of some hundred and fifty of his retainers and marched back with them to the Palace. But as he thought it was not proper to bring the heads of rebels to the Palace for inspection, he took them to the headquarters of the Daijin Munemori, when suddenly his men began to shout out that the houses of Takamatsu were on fire. "As it is daytime it is not likely to be accidental," he cried. "It must be the enemy who is here and has set them on fire. They are sure to be in great force, so we can do nothing. Come! Come! Into the boats!" And in great hurry and confusion they scrambled aboard the ships that were moored in rows along the beach in front of the main gate. In the Imperial Ship were the Imperial Consort Kenreimon-in, the mother of the late Emperor and the Nii Dono with their Ladies-in-waiting, while the Daijin Munemori was in another with his son, and the others got on board any ship they could find, and all the ships immediately rowed out a chō or thirty or forty yards from the shore. Scarcely had they done so when the seventy or eighty horsemen of the Genji, all armed alike, galloped smartly up to the beach in front of the main gate. As the tide was at its lowest ebb in the tidal bay, the water came up to the horses' chests, or knees, or girths in some places, and in others it was shallower still, and so as they dashed through the waves, kicking up a mist of foam and spray all round them, out of which their white banners appeared fluttering here and there, it was no wonder that the Heike, doomed as they were, should imagine that a great army was upon them. Especially was this so in that the Hōgwan, not wishing that the enemy should see the smallness of his force, had divided it up into small groups of from five to ten horsemen each. The Hōgwan was attired that day in a hitatare of red, and armour of shaded purple, and wore a helmet surmounted by golden horns, a gold-mounted tachi, and a quiver of black and white feathered arrows, twenty four in number. Grasping his rattan-bound bow in the middle he glared fiercely at the enemy out in the offing, and shouted with a loud voice: "I am Kebiishi Go-i-no-jo Minamoto Yoshitsune, Envoy of the Hō-ō." After him the rest of the leaders of the Genji proclaimed their names and titles: Tajiro-no-Kwanja Nobutsuna of Izu, Kaneko-no-Jurō Ietada of Musashi, Kaneko Goichi Chikanori, Ise-no-Saburō Yoshimori, Gotōbyōye Sanemoto, Gotō Shinbyōye-no-Jō Motokiyo, Satō Saburōhyōye Tsuginobu of Mutsu, Satō Shirōhyōye Tadanobu, Eda-no-Genzō, Kumai-no-Tarō, and Musashi-bō Benkei, all of them worth a thousand men. As they came riding up, shouting their war-cries, the Heike seized their bows and began to shoot from far and near, but the Genji took but little heed of them, ducking to left and right to avoid the shafts, and taking the opportunity to rest and breathe their horses under the lee of those ships that were in shallow water, all the while shouting and fighting furiously.

Chapter IV.

THE DEATH OF TSUGINOBU.

Now Gotōbyōye Sanemoto, a veteran warrior, did not stop to take part in the fight on the beach, but went on and burst into the Palace and set it on fire, so that it went up in flames in a moment. The Daijin Munemori, seeing this, turned to his retainers and enquired: "How many men have the Genji?" "Not more than seventy or eighty horsemen, it seems," was the reply. "Ah, so few?" exclaimed Munemori; "if the hair of their heads was counted one by one, they would not equal our force! Why did you lose your heads and run away to the ships, and let them through without a blow to set fire to the Palace? Is not Noto Dono here? Let him land and give battle to these fellows!" At this order Noto-no-kami Noritsune landed with some five hundred men in small boats, under the command of Etchū-no-Jirōhyōye Moritsugu, and took up a position on the beach in front of the burnt-out main gate. The Hōgwan also drew up his eighty horsemen opposite them, about a bowshot away. Then Etchū-no-Jirōhyōye came forth on to the deck-house of his boat and shouted in a loud voice: "Ho, there! You may perhaps have declared your name and titles once already, but as it was far away over the sea, we could not hear. So who is the leader of the Genji with whom we have to do to-day?" "It is needless to repeat it," shouted Ise Saburō in reply, "but here is the Taiyū Hōgwan Dono, the younger brother of Yoritomo, lord of Kamakura, descended in the tenth generation from Seiwa Tennō!" "Oh!" retorted Moritsugu," then that is the wretched little stripling, who was left an orphan when his father was killed in the Heiji fighting, and who became an acolyte at Kurama temple, and ran away to Mutsu carrying baggage in the train of a gold merchant." "Why show off your eloquence in such talk about our lord," replied Yoshimori, drawing nearer, "I fancy you are one of those who got yourself well beaten at Tonamiyama in the North, and just escaped with your life, to beg your way home all the way from the Hokurikudo, aren't you?" "What need to be a beggar when one has a bounteous lord to depend on?" said Moritsugu, "I didn't get my living and keep my family on robbing and thieving in Suzugayama in Ise, and being a low retainer, as you did." At this point Kaneko-no-Jūrō came forward and interrupted them. "What's the good of all this useless talk? Calling one another names is a thing anyone can do. These lords know what our young warriors of Musashi and Sagami can do from what they saw at Ichi-no-tani last spring." And as he spoke his younger brother, who had so far stood by his side without a word, took an arrow twelve handbreadths and three fingers long, fitted it to his bow and drew with all his might, so that the arrow flew straight at Moritsugu and stuck in his breastplate with such force as if to pierce it right through, thus putting an end to the wordy warfare.

Now Noto-no-kami Noritsune was attired as for a sea-fight without hitatare and full armour, but in a short under-robe dyed in variegated colours, and armour laced with Chinese silk. His sword was mounted in gold and silver, and he carried a 'Shigetō' bow and a quiver of twenty four arrows feathered with hawk's tail-feathers. He was the most redoubtable archer in the Imperial Camp and it was said of him that he never missed anyone he aimed at. With the intention of putting an end to Yoshitsune at a single shot he stood watching his mark, but the Genji perceived this, and Ise Saburō, Satō Saburōhyōye Tsuginobu, Satō Shirōhyōye Tadanobu, Eda-no-Genzō, Kumai Tarō and Musashi-bō Benkei rode up in a line close together in front of the Hōgwan to protect him from the arrows, so that it was impossible for Noto-no-kami to hit him. "Get out of the way of the arrows, you fellows!" he shouted, and drawing his bow again and again with great speed and accuracy he shot down ten of the Genji soldiers, among whom Satō Saburōhyōye, who was in the forefront, received an arrow that pierced him through from the left shoulder to the right armpit, and no longer able to sit his horse, fell headlong to the ground. Then one of Noto-no-kami's young men named Kikuo Maru, a very strong fighter, wearing a body armour of green colour and a helmet of three plates, drew his sword and ran out to take the head of Tsuginobu. At this his younger brother Tadanobu, who was standing beside him, drew his bow and shot Kikuō Maru under the skirts of his armour, so that he sank down on to his knees. When Noto Dono saw this, still holding his bow in his left hand, with his right he seized Kikuo Maru and flung him back into his own ship. Thus he prevented the Genji from taking his head, though he died later from the wound. This youth had formerly been the page of Echizen-no-Sammi Michimori, but after his death he had followed his younger brother Noto-no-kami. His age was then eighteen years, and Noto Dono was so grieved at his death that he fought no more that day.

Then the Hōgwan, ordering them to carry Tsuginobu to the rear, sprang down from his horse and took him by the hand, saying: "How do you feel, Saburōhyōye?" "It is the end, my lord," answered Tsuginobu. "Is there, anything you would wish for in this world? enquired Yoshitsune. "What is there that I should want? Only that I regret that I shall not live to see my lord come to his own. For the rest, it is the destiny of one who wields the bow and arrow to fall by the shaft of an enemy. And that it should be told to future generations that I, Satō Saburōhyōye Tsuginobu of Mutsu, died instead of my lord at the fight on the beach of Yashima in Sanuki, in the war of the Genji and Heike, will be my pride in this life and something to remember on the dark road of death." And so he died. Stout warrior as Yoshitsune was, he was so overcome with grief that he pressed the sleeve of his armour to his face and wept bitterly. He then asked if there was any reverend priest in those parts, and when they had found one he said: "A wounded man has just died; I wish you to recite the Sutras for him for one day," and he presented him with a stout black horse with a fine set of trappings. This was the horse that the Hōgwan, when he received the Fifth Rank, also raised to the Fifth Rank and gave the name of Taiyū Kurō. It was the one on which he had descended the Hiyodori-goe pass behind Ichi-no-tani. When the other samurai, and especially Tsuginobu's younger brother Tadanobu, saw this, they were moved to tears and exclaimed: "For the sake of a lord like this, who would consider his life more than dust or dew?"

Chapter V.

NASU-NO-YOICHI.

Now as those warriors of Awa and Sanuki who wished to throw off their allegiance to the Heike and join the Genji began to emerge from their caves and mountains in small bands of fifteen and twenty, and ride in to join him, the Hōgwan soon found himself in command of a force of some three hundred horse.

By this time the sun was sinking and both armies were preparing to retire, as no decision could be reached that day, when from the offing a small boat, with no special decoration, was seen to come rowing to the shore. When it had reached a distance of seven or eight 'tan'[251] from the water's edge, it swung round broadside on, and while the Heike wondered what it would do, a girl, some eighteen or nineteen years old, wearing a five-fold robe of white lined with green, and a scarlet hakama, took a red fan with a rising sun on it and hung it up on a pole fastened to the gunwale of the boat. Calling Gotōbyōye Sanemoto, the Hōgwan asked him what was the meaning of it. "It is to shoot at, no doubt," replied Gotō, "I expect it is a plan of theirs to get you to come and look at this charmer[252] and entice you out in front into bowshot and shoot you; but at any rate we ought to shoot it away." "Who is the best archer we have?" asked the Hōgwan. "There are several good shots, but the best is Yoichi Munetaka, the son of Nasu-no-Tarō Suketaka of Shimozuke. He is a small man, but a most skilful archer." "What proof have you?" asked Yoshitsune. "He can shoot two or three birds on the wing with anybody." "Then call him," said the Hōgwan.

Yoichi was then barely twenty years old. He was wearing a hitatare of greenish blue with the collar and edges of the sleeves ornamented with brocade on a red ground. His armour was laced with light green and the mounts of his sword were of silver. He carried twenty four arrows with black and white feathers, or rather dark grey, in which hawks' wing feathers were mixed. A turnip-headed arrow pointed with staghorn was also stuck in his quiver. Carrying his Shigetō bow under his arm, and with his helmet slung to his breastplate, he came into the presence of the Hōgwan and did obeisance.

---

[251] *Seven or eight tan.* A tan is said to be usually 60 ken (1 ken =6 feet) so it would be about 450 feet, which the commentator considers too far. In these ancient war chronicles a tan is reckoned as one jo or ten feet, but this is too little. But to hit the rivet of a fan at seventy feet would not be easy, and the shorter, distance seems more likely.

[252] *Charmer.* Jap. Keisei 傾城. The expression comes from the verse in the Shi King. 'A wise man builds a castle, but a wise woman overthrows it. Cf. also the description of the lady Li, 'one glance from whom could overthrow a castle, and two a province.'

"How now, Yoichi," said Yoshitsune, "can you hit that fan right in the middle, and show the enemy how we can shoot?" "I cannot say that I can for certain," replied Yoichi, "and if I should miss, it would be a lasting reproach to the skill of our side. So it would be better to entrust it to someone who could be quite sure." This reply greatly angered Yoshitsune. "Those who came from Kamakura with me on this campaign must obey my orders," he exclaimed, "those who do not had better go back there again!" Then Yoichi, thinking it would not do to refuse again, replied: "I may not succeed in hitting it, but as my lord commands, I will try." And retiring he mounted a fine black horse with saddle ornamented with gold, and taking a fresh hold on his bow, he gripped the reins and rode into the sea. Those on his own side, looking after him, exclaimed: "Ah, that young fellow is sure to bring it down!" And the Hōgwan also thought he had not misplaced his trust. As it was a little beyond bowshot he rode about one tan into the water, but still the fan seemed about seven tan away. It was the eighteenth day of the second month, and the Hour of the Cock (6 p.m.). The wind was blowing rather strongly from the North, and the waves were running high on the beach. Out in the offing the ships were rising and falling as they rode on the swell, and the fan was fluttering about in the breeze. The Heike had ranged their ships in a long line to see better what would befall, while on land the Genji lined the shore in expectation. The whole of both armies were watching the scene.

Then Yoichi closed his eyes and prayed: "Namu Hachiman Daibosatsu, and especially the deities of my homeland, the Gongen of Nikko, Yuzen Dairnyōjin of Nasu of Utsunomiya, I pray you grant that I may strike the centre of that fan. For if I fail, I will break my bow and put an end to my life, showing my face no more among men. If therefore you will that I see home again, let not this arrow miss its mark." After praying thus silently he again opened his eyes, and the wind had abated a little so that the fan looked easier to hit. Taking a Kaburaya he drew his bow with all his strength and let fly. He was short of stature, it is true, but his arrow measured twelve handbreaths and three fingers, and his bow was a strong one. The shore echoed to the whirr of the arrow as it flew straight to its mark. Whizzing it struck the fan an inch from the rivet, so that it flew up into the air as the arrow fell into the sea. Once and again the spring breeze caught it and tossed it up, then suddenly it dropped down into the water. And when they saw the scarlet fan gleaming in the rays of the setting sun as it danced up and down, rising and falling on the white crests of the waves, the Heike in the offing beat applaudingly on the gunwales of their ships, while the Genji on the shore rattled their quivers till they rang again.

Chapter VI.

THE DROPPED BOW.

Unable to restrain himself in his excitement over the enjoyment of this feat, an old warrior of some fifty years of age, in armour laced with black leather, sprang up on one of the ships just in the place where the fan had been and began to dance, twirling a white handled halberd in his hand.

Seeing this, Ise Saburō Yoshimori came up behind Yoichi and said: "It is our lord's command that you bring down that fellow too." So Yoichi took one of the middle arrows of his quiver, drew his bow and let fly. The arrow flew straight to the mark, hitting the dancer right in the middle of his body so that he fell back into the bottom of the boat. There were some who applauded this shot also, but most showed their disapproval by shouting: "Too bad! Too bad! That was a cruel thing to do." Silence now ensued on the side of the Heike, though the Genji still continued to rattle their quivers.

Then from the Heike side, still disinclined to rest under their discomfiture, there came three warriors, one armed with a bow, the second carrying a shield, and the third a halberd. Springing on shore they dared the Genji to come on, whereat the Hōgwan called out to know who of the younger of his best horsemen would try conclusions with these insolent fellows. Then there rode forth Mionoya Jurō of Musashi, and his two brothers Shirō and Tōshichi, Nibu-no-Shirō of Kōzuke and Kiso-no-Chūji of Shinano, five warriors in all. As they charged forward shouting to the onset, however, the archer behind the shield loosed a great lacquered shaft, feathered with black wing feathers, which pierced the horse of Mionoya Jūrō in the left breast right up to the notch, so that it collapsed like an overturned screen. The rider at once threw his left leg over the animal and vaulted down to the right, drawing his sword to continue the fight, but when he saw the warrior behind the shield come to meet him flourishing a huge halberd, he knew that his own small sword would be useless, and blew on a conch and retreated. The other immediately followed him, and it looked as though he would cut him down with the halberd, but instead of doing so, gripping the halberd under his left arm, he tried to seize Mionoya-no-Jūrō by the neckpiece of his helmet with his right. Three times Mionoya eluded his grasp, but at the fourth attempt his opponent held on. For a moment he could do nothing, but then, giving a sudden violent wrench, the neckpiece parted where it joined the helmet, and Mionoya escaped and hid behind his four companions to recover his breath. The other four, wishing to spare their horses, had taken no part in the combat, but stayed a short way off looking on. The Heike warrior on his part did not follow him any further, but sticking the neckpiece on the end of his halberd, shouted out in a loud voice: "Let those afar off listen; those who are near can see. That's the way we fellows of the Capital declare ourselves. I am Akushichibyōye Kagekiyo of Kazusa! "And having thus delivered himself he retired again behind the shield.

The Heike, encouraged at this, cried out: "Don't let Akushichibyōye be killed! To the rescue of Kagekiyo! Come on, men!" And some two hundred of them hastened to land and set up their shields in a row in hen's wing style, defying the Genji to came on. The Hōgwan, incensed at this, with Tajiro-no-Kwanja in front, Ise Saburō behind, and Gotōbyōye father and son and the brothers Kaneko on his left and right hand, put himself at the head of eighty horsemen and charged down on them shouting, whereupon the Heike, who were mostly on foot and few mounted, thinking they could not stand against horsemen, quickly retired and reentered their boats, leaving their shields kicked about here and there like the sticks of a fortune teller.

Elated with victory, the Genji rode into the sea in pursuit till they were up to their saddles in water and fought among the ships, while the Heike with rakes and billhooks tried to seize Yoshitsune by the neckpiece of his helmet. Two or three times their weapons rattled about his head, but his companions with sword and halberd warded off the attacks from their master as they fought. In the course of this fighting the Hōgwan somehow or other dropped his bow into the sea, and leant out of the saddle trying to pick it up again with his whip. His companions cried out to him to let it go, but he would not, and at last managed to recover it, and rode back laughing to the beach. The older warriors reproached him for this saying: "However valuable a bow it might be, what is that in comparison with our lord's life?" "It was not that I grudged the bow," replied Yoshitsune, "and if my bow were one that required two or three men to bend it, like that of my uncle Tametomo, they would be quite welcome to it, but I should not like a weak one like mine to fall into the hands of the enemy for them to laugh at it and say, "This is the bow of Kurō Yoshitsune, the Commander-in-Chief of the Genji; and so it was that I risked my life to get it back." And this explanation drew expressions of approval from all.

When the night fell after the day's fighting the Heike were still cruising about off the shore, while the Genji made their way inland and took up a position on some high ground by Mure-Takamatsu. For three nights they had had no sleep, for the night before last they had been at sea and the weather was too rough even for a doze, while last night they had been crossing over the pass after the fight at Katsuura in Awa, so after fighting all of this day both men and horses were tired out, and fell asleep where they were, caring for nothing, pillowing their heads on their helmets or quivers or the sleeves of their armour. But the Hōgwan and Ise Saburō did not sleep. Yoshitsune went up to a high place from which he could see if the enemy approached, while Ise Saburō concealed himself in a little hollow and lay in wait, so that if an enemy horseman should come near he could shoot his horse in the belly. The Heike had made preparations for an attack that night, under the command of Noto-no-kami Noritsune, but as Etchū-no-Jirōhyōye and Emi-no-Jirō could not agree as to which of the two should lead it, the morning broke without anything being done. If they had made one, how could the Genji have sustained it? And that they did not make it sealed their fate.

Chapter VII.

THE FIGHT AT SHIDO.

When the dawn broke the Heike retired to the bay of Shido in the same province, and Yoshitsune pursued them thither with about eighty horse. When the Heike perceived this they said; "The Genji have but a few men; let us attack and surround them." So a force of a thousand men landed and advanced to enclose the Genji and cut them to pieces; but just then the rest of the Genji, to the number of about two hundred, who had been left behind at Yashima, came riding up, anxious not to be late for the fight. When the Heike saw this, they cried out: "Ali! here is the main force of the Genji. Who knows how many tens of thousands there may be. It will never do to be surrounded!" And so they gave way and retired, and got aboard their ships once more. And so, at the mercy of the wind and tide, they were carried about aimlessly with nowhere to go; a truly miserable plight indeed. Driven from Shikoku by Kurō Hōgwan, they yet could not go to Kyūshū, so that their condition was like that of spirits wandering between life and death.

Now when Yoshitsune had finished the count of the heads of the foe taken at the bay of Shido, he summoned Ise Saburō Yoshimori and said; "You know that Dennai Saemon Noriyoshi, the eldest son of Awa-no-Mimbu Shigeyoshi, went to the province of Iyo with three thousand men to chastise Kono-no-Shirō of that province for not obeying the orders of the Heike, and that he returned to the Palace at Yashima with the heads of a hundred and fifty of his retainers. Now I have heard that he will arrive here to-day, so do you go to meet him and see if you cannot arrange something." So Yoshimori withdrew after a respectful salutation, and started off with a band of sixteen of his own followers, all attired in white, carrying a white banner that he had received from his master.

Before long Ise Saburō and his men encountered the army of Dennai Saemon, and when they were about one chō away, both sides flew their flags, the white and the red respectively. Then Ise Saburō sent a messenger to Dennai saying: "As your lordship may have heard, Kurō Taiyū-no-Hōgwan Dono, the younger brother of the lord of Kamakura, has received an Imperial Edict from the Hō-ō to destroy the Heike, and is now on campaign in the Western Provinces. I, Ise Saburō Yoshimori, belong to his train, but I have not come to fight, for we have no weapons and carry no bows, only I have something that I wish to discuss with your lordship, so I pray you allow me to pass through your army." At this request the three thousand men opened their ranks and let him through. So Ise Saburō met Dennai Saemon and spoke thus: "As your lordship has no doubt heard, Kurō Taiyū-no-Hōgwan Yoshitsune, the younger brother of Kamakura Dono, has advanced to this country to destroy the Heike, and the day before yesterday he arrived at Katsuura in Awa and took your uncle Sakurama-no-suke and destroyed his fortress. Yesterday he marched on Yashima and fought a battle there and burned the Palace, after which the Emperor threw himself into the sea. Munemori and his son were captured alive, and Noto-no-kami has put an end to his life. As for the others, some have committed suicide and some have thrown themselves into the waves. This morning at the bay of Shido all who remained were killed or taken, and among them your father Awa-no-Mimbu Dono was taken prisoner. He was entrusted to my charge, and all last night he was lamenting and saying "Alas, my son Dennai Saemon Noriyoshi never dreams of this, and to-morrow he will give battle and be killed;" and so I took pity on him and have come thus far to bring you tidings. Why need you then fight with us and die? For if you will lay down your arms and surrender, you will be able to see your father once again. The matter is in your power to decide." When he heard this, Dennai Saemon said "What you have told me is just what I have already heard." And so he laid down his arms and surrendered. And as their commander thus yielded, his three thousand soldiers also gave up their arms and surrendered without more ado to Yoshimori and his sixteen men. So Yoshimori brought Dennai Saemon to Yoshitsune and told him all that he had done. "Your plan is not a new one," said the Hōgwan, "but it is most admirable." and he bade them give Dennai Saemon his weapons and hand him over to Ise Saburō. He then asked the soldiers what their intentions might be, whereupon they replied: "We are men of distant provinces, and do not care for anyone in particular, but are ready to follow any master who will pacify the country and rule it." So the Hōgwan, thinking these sentiments very proper, added the whole three thousand to his own force.

Now on the same day, the twenty second, at the Hour of the Dragon (8 a.m.), the other two hundred ships that had remained behind at Watanabe and Fukushima arrived at the shore of Yashima under the command of Kajiwara, only to find that the whole of Shikoku had been conquered by Kurō Hōgwan, and that there was nothing left for them to do. "We are like iris on the sixth day,[253] or flowers after a service, or an agreement after a battle;" they said laughing.

Now after the Hōgwan had crossed to Yashima the priest of the shrine of Sumiyoshi, Tsumori-no-Nagamori, went up to the Capital and sought audience with the Hō-ō, saying: "On the sixteenth day at the Hour of the Ox (2 a.m.), the whirring of a Kaburaya proceeded from the third sanctuary of my shrine, and went away over toward the West." On hearing this the Hō-ō was very glad and presented Nagamori with a sacred sword and other treasures to be dedicated to Sumiyoshi Daimyōjin. In former days, when the Empress Jingo went forth to subdue Korea, the vengeful spirits of two deities deigned to proceed from the shrine of Ise to accompany her, and took up their stations on the bow and stern of her ship, so that by their help she subjected Korea to her will. When the war in this foreign land was ended and she returned to her country, one of these deities took up his abode at Sumiyoshi in the province of Settsu, and this is Sumiyoshi Daimyōjin, while the other deigned to go and stay at Suwo in the province of Shinano, and is now called Suwo Daimyōjin. That this deity should deign not to forget his former expedition, and should now once again go forth to destroy the enemies of the Throne was a great source of comfort both to the Emperor and his subjects.

Chapter VIII.

THE FIGHT AT DAN-NO-URA.

Meanwhile Yoshitsune, after his victory at Yashima, crossed over to Suwo to join his brother Noriyori, and, strange to say, the place which the Heike next reached was called Hikushima in the province of Nagato, while the Genji went to Oitsu in the same province. Just at this time Tanso, the Bettō of Kumano, of the province of Kii, who was under great obligations to the Heike, suddenly changed his mind and hesitated as to which side he should support. So he went to the shrine of Ikumano at Tanabe and spent seven days in retirement there, having Kagura preformed, and praying before the Gongen. As a result of this he received an intimation from the deity that he should adhere to the white banner, but, being still doubtful, he took seven white cocks and seven red ones, and held a cock fight before the Gongen, and as none of the red cocks were victorious but were all beaten and ran away, he at last made up his mind to join the Genji. Therefore, assembling all his retainers to the number of some two thousand men, and embarking them on two hundred ships of war, he put the emblem of the deity of

---

[253] *iris on the sixth day*, i.e. too late, the Shobu or iris festival was held on the fifth day of the fifth month.

the shrine on board his ship and painted the name of Kongo Doji on the top of his standard. Accordingly when this vessel with its divine burden approached the ships of the Genji and Heike at Dan-no-ura, both parties saluted it reverently, but when it was seen to direct its course towards the fleet of the Genji, the Heike could not conceal their chagrin. Moreover, to the further consternation of the Heike, Kono-no-Shirō Michinobu of the province of Iyo also came rowing up with a hundred and fifty large ships and went over to the fleet of their enemies.

Thus the forces of the Genji went on increasing, while those of the Heike grew less. The Genji had some three thousand ships, and the Heike one thousand, among which were some of Chinese build; and so, on the twenty fourth day of the third month of the second year of Genryaku, at the Hour of the Hare (6 a.m.), at Ta-no-ura in the province of Bungo, at Moji-ga-seki, and at Dan-no-ura in the province of Nagato, at Akama-ga-seki began the final battle of the Gen and Hei.

On that day the Hōgwan and Kajiwara were on the point of open warfare with each other. Kajiwara came to the Hōgwan and requested that he might be allowed to lead the Genji fleet. "Certainly," replied Yoshitsune, "if I am prevented." "That is not proper," answered Kajiwara, "for your lordship is Commander-in-Chief." "By no means," replied the Hōgwan, "Yoritomo is the real Commander-in-Chief, and I am only a Marshal of the forces, so I am equal in rank to you." "H'm" grumbled Kajiwara, disappointed of his expectation of leading the army, "his lordship is not naturally suited to lead warriors." "Your lordship seems to me the biggest fool in Nippon," retorted Yoshitsune, laying his hand on his sword hilt. "This to me!" exclaimed Kajiwara, also laying his hand on his sword, "I, who have no other lord but Kamakura Dono!" At this his eldest son Genda Kagesue, his second son Heiji Kagetaka and his third son Saburō, Kageie, numbering with their retainers, fourteen or fifteen in all, sprang forward with bared weapons to support their father, while Ise Saburō Yoshimori, Sato Shirōhyōye Tadanobu, Eda-no-Genzō, Kumai-no-Tarō, Saitō-bō Benkei and the rest of the Hōgwan's men made haste to surround them, each eager to cut them down. At this point Miura-no-suke restrained the Hōgwan and Doi-no-Jirō caught hold of Kajiwara, beseeching them: "If you fight each other thus in the face of such a crisis, we may be overpowered by the Heike, and when Kamakura Dono hears of it there will be trouble." So the Hōgwan calmed his anger and Kajiwara also regained his composure, but from that time Kajiwara nursed his enmity against Yoshitsune, and spoke evil of him, so that at last he got him put to death, as is elsewhere recorded.

Now the two hosts of the Genji and Heike faced each other scarcely thirty chō distant on the water; and as the tide was running strongly through Moji, Akama and Dan-no-ura, the Heike ships were carried down by the current against their will, while the Genji were naturally able to advance on them with the tide. Kajiwara with his sons and retainers to the number of fourteen or fifteen, stuck close to the shore, and catching on with rakes to some ships of the Heike that went astray, they boarded them and sprang from one ship to the other, cutting their men down both at bow and stern and doing great deeds. And their merit that day has been specially recorded.

Chapter IX.

LONG BOWSHOTS.

Thus both armies joined battle all along the line, and the roar of their warcries was such as to be heard even to the highest heavens of Brahma, and to cause the deity deep under the earth to start in amazement. Then Shin-Chūnagon Tomomori-no-Kyō, coming forth on to the deck-house of his ship, shouted to his men in a mighty voice: "Even in India and China and also in our own country, with the most renowned leader and the bravest warriors an army cannot prevail if fate be against it. Yet must our honour be dear to us, and we must show a bold front to these Eastern soldiers. Let us then pay no heed to our lives, but think of nothing but fighting as bravely as we may." Hida-no-Saburō Saemon Kagetsune against repeated this proclamation to the samurai. "Ho! these Eastern fellows may have a great name for their horsemanship," shouted Aku-shichi-byōye Kagekiyo," but they know nothing about sea-fights, and they will be like fish up a tree, so that we will pick them up one by one and pitch them into the sea!" "And let their Commander Kurō Yoshitsune be the special object of your attack," added Etchū-no-Jirōhyōye Moritsugu, "he is a little fellow with a fair complexion and his front teeth stick out a bit, so you will know him by that. He often changes his clothes and armour, so take care he doesn't escape you!" "Who cares for that wretched little fellow?" replied Aku-shichi, "Cheer up, my brave comrades; we'll soon pick him up under our arms and fling him into the sea!"

After Shin-Chūnagon Tomomori had thus addressed his men he took a small boat and rowed across to the ship of the Daijin Munemori. "Our own men look well enough," said he, "only Awa-no-Mimbu Shigeyoshi seems doubtful in his allegiance. I pray you let me take off his head." "But he has served us well so far," replied Munemori, "so how can we do this only on suspicion? Anyhow, let him be summoned." So Shigeyoshi came into the presence of the Daijin. He was attired in a hitatare of yellowish red colour with a little black in it, and armour laced with light red leather. "How now, Shigeyoshi? Do you intend treachery?" said Munemori, "for your conduct today has a suspicious look. Do you tell your men of Shikoku to bear themselves well in the fight, and don't play the dastard." "Why should I play the dastard?" said Shigeyoshi as he retired from before the Daijin. Meanwhile Tomomori had been standing by with his hand gripping his sword hilt hard enough to break it, casting meaning looks at Munemori to intimate his wish to cut Shigeyoshi down, but as the latter gave no sign he could do nothing.

So the Heike divided their thousand vessels into three fleets. In the van rowed Yamaga-no-Hyōtōji Hidetō with five hundred ships, and after him came the Matsuura with three hundred more; last of all came the Heike nobles with two hundred. Now Yamaga-no-Hyōtōji who led the van was the strongest archer in all Kyūshū, and he chose five hundred men who drew the bow better than most, though not equal to himself, and placed them in the bows of his ships, shoulder to shoulder, so that they let fly a volley of five hundred arrows at once.

The fleet of the Genii was the more numerous with its three thousand ships, but as their men shot from various places here and there, their force did not show to advantage. Yoshitsune himself, who was fighting in the forefront of the battle, was greatly embarrassed by the arrows of the foe that fell like rain on his shield and armour. So, elated by their victory in the first attack, the Heike pressed onward, and the roar of their shouting mingled with the booming of their war drums that continuously sounded the onset.

Now on the side of the Genii, Wada-no-Kotarō Yoshimori did not go on shipboard, but mounted his horse and sat himself firmly in the saddle with his feet deep in the stirrups, riding into the midst of the Heike host and letting fly his arrows right and left. A famous archer he had always been, and no enemy within the space of three chō escaped his arrows, but one shaft he shot an extraordinary distance on which was a request to return it to the marksman. When it was withdrawn by order of Tomomori it was seen to be feathered with white wing feathers of the crane mixed with black ones of the wild goose, a plain bamboo shaft thirteen handbreadths and three fingers long, inscribed at the space of a handbreadth from the lashing on the butt with the name Wada-no-Kotarō Yoshimori painted in lacquer. Among the Heike too there were some fine archers, but none who could do a feat like this. After a while however, Nii-no-Kishirō Chikakiyo of Iyo stepped forward and shot it back again. It flew to a distance of more than three chō and struck deep into the left arm of Miura-no-Ishi Sakon-no-Tarō, who was standing about a tan behind Wada. "Ha ha!" laughed Miura's men as they came crowding round, "Wada-no-Kotarō boasts no one can equal hint at shooting, and now he has been put to shame openly." Then Yoshimori, angered at this, sprang into a small boat and pressed on into the midst of the foe, drawing his bore lustily so that very many of his adversaries were killed and wounded.

Not long afterwards a large shaft of plain bamboo stuck into the boat in which Yoshitsune was standing with a similar request that it should be shot back again. It was feathered with the tail feathers of a copper pheasant and was fourteen handbreadths and three fingers long. At a distance of one handbreadth from the butt lashing the name of the sender was painted in lacquer: "Nii-no-Kishirō Chikakiyo of Iyo." Then the Hōgwan called to Gotōbyōye Sanemoto and enquired: "Who is there who can return this shaft to the sender?" "Asari-no-Yoichi of the Genii of Kai is the most likely;" answered Gotō. "Call him then," replied Yoshitsune. When he came into his presence;" How now, Yoichi," he exclaimed," can you shoot back this arrow that has just been loosed at us from the offing with a request that we return it?" "I can but try," replied Yoichi. Then he took the arrow and measured it. "This shaft is weak and somewhat lacking in length," he objected, "if it is all the same I would rather use one of my own; and taking a large lacquered shaft feathered with the black body feathers of a bird, fifteen handbreadths and three fingers in length, and fitting it to his nine foot lacquered bow, he drew it with all his might and let fly. This also flew more than four chō, and hit Nii-no-Kishirō Chikakiyo clean in his middle as he stood on the stern of one of the great ships, so that he fell headlong to the bottom. This Asari-no-Yoichi had long been famed for his skill with the bow and could bring down a running stag at a distance of two chō and never miss.

After this both sides set their faces against each other and fought grimly without a thought for their lives, neither giving way an inch. But as the Heike had on their side an Emperor endowed with the Ten Virtues and the Three Sacred Treasures of the Realm, things went hard with the Genji and their hearts were beginning to fail them, when suddenly something that they at first took for a white cloud, but which soon appeared to be a white banner floating in the breeze, came drifting over the two fleets from the upper air and finally settled on the stern of one of the Genji ships, hanging on by the rope.

Chapter X.

THE DROWNING OF THE EMPEROR.

When he saw this, Yoshitsune, regarding it as a sign from Hachiman Dai-bosatsu, removed his helmet, and after washing his hands, did obeisance; his men all following his example. Moreover a shoal of some thousands of dolphins also made its appearance from the offing and made straight for the ships of the Heike. Then Munemori called the diviner Ko-hakase Harunobu and said: "There are always many dolphins about here, but I have never seen so many as these before; what may it portend?" "If they turn back," replied Harunobu, "the Genji will be destroyed; but if they go on then our own side will be in danger." No sooner had he finished speaking than the dolphins dived under the Heike ships and passed on.

Then, as things had come to this pass, Awa-no-Mimbu Shigeyoshi, who for three years had been a loyal supporter of the Heike, now that his son Dennai Saemon Noriyoshi had been captured, made up his mind that all was lost, and suddenly forsook his allegiance and deserted to the enemy. Great was the regret of Shin-Chūnagon Tomomori-no-Kyō that he had not cut off the head of 'that villain Shigeyoshi,' but now it was unavailing.

Now the strategy of the Heike had been to put the stoutest warriors on board the ordinary fighting ships and the inferior soldiers on the big ships of Chinese build, so that the Genji should be induced to attack the big ships, thinking that the commanders were on board them, when they would be able to surround and destroy them. But when Shigeyoshi went over and joined the Genji he revealed this plan to them, with the result that they immediately left the big ships alone and concentrated their attacks on the smaller ones on which were the Heike champions. Later on the men of Shikoku and Kyūshū all left the Heike in a body and went over to the Genji. Those who had so far been their faithful retainers now turned their bows against their lords and drew the sword against their own masters. On one shore the heavy seas beat on the cliff so as to forbid any landing, while on the other stood the serried ranks of the enemy waiting with leveled arrows to receive them. And so on this day the struggle for supremacy between the two houses of Gen and Hei was at last decided.

Meanwhile the Genji warriors sprang from one Heike vessel to the other, shooting and cutting down the sailors and helms men, so that they flung themselves in panic to the bottom of the ships unable to navigate them any longer. Then Shin-Chūnagon Tomomori-no-Kyō rowed in a small boat to the Imperial Vessel and cried out: "You see what affairs have come to! Clean up the ship, and throw everything unsightly into the sea!" And he ran about the ship from bow to stern, sweeping and cleaning and gathering up the dust with his own hands. "But how goes the battle, Chūnagon Dono?" asked the Court Ladies. "Oh, you'll soon see some rare gallants from the East," he replied, bursting into loud laughter. "What? Is this a time for joking?" they answered, and they lifted up their voices and wept aloud.

Then the Nii-Dono, who had already resolved what she would do, donning a double outer dress of dark grey mourning colour, and tucking up the long skirts of her glossy silk hakama, put the Sacred Jewel under her arm, and the Sacred Sword in her girdle, and taking the Emperor in her arms, spoke thus: "Though I am but a woman I will not fall into the hands of the foe, but will accompany our Sovereign Lord. Let those of you who will, follow me." And she glided softly to the gunwale of the vessel. The Emperor was eight years old that year, but looked much older than his age, and his appearance was so lovely that he shed as it were a brilliant radiance about him, and his long black hair hung loose far down his back. With a look of surprise and anxiety on his face he enquired of the Nii-Dono: "Where is it that you are going to take me, Ama-ze?" Turning to her youthful Sovereign with tears streaming down her cheeks, she answered: "Perchance our Lord does not know that, though through the merit of the Ten Virtues practised in former lives you have been reborn to the Imperial Throne in this world, yet by the power of some evil karma destiny now claims you. So now turn to the east and bid farewell to the deity of the Great Shrine of Ise, and then to the west and say the Nembutsu that Amida Buddha and the Holy Ones may come to welcome you to the Pure Western Land. This land is called small as a grain of millet, but yet is it now but a vale of misery. There is a Pure Land of happiness beneath the waves, another Capital where no sorrow is. Thither it is that I am taking Our Lord." And thus comforting him, and binding his long hair up in his dove coloured robe, blinded with tears the child-Sovereign put his beautiful little hands together and turned first to the east to say farewell to the deity of Ise and to Sho-Hachimangu, and then to the west and repeated the Nembutsu, after which the Nii-Dono, holding him tightly in her arms and saying consolingly "In the depths of the Ocean we have a Capital" sank with him at last beneath the waves.

Ah, the pity of it! That the gust of the spring wind of Impermanence should so suddenly sweep away his flower form. That the cruel billows should thus engulf his Jewel Person. Since his Palace was called the Palace of Longevity, he should have passed a long life therein; its gate was called the Gate of Eternal Youth, the barrier that old age should not pass; and yet, ere he had reached the age of ten years, he had become like the refuse that sinks to the bottom of the sea. How vain it was to proclaim him as one who sat on the Throne as a reward of the Ten Virtues! It was like the Dragon that rides on the clouds descending to become a fish at the bottom of the ocean. He who abode in a Palace fair as the terraced pavilions of the highest heaven of Brahma, or the paradise where S'akya Muni dwells, among his Ministers and Nobles of the Nine Families who did him humble obeisance, thus came to a miserable end beneath the ocean waves.

Chapter XI.

THE DEATH OF NOTO-NO-KAMI.

Now when the Imperial Consort Kenrei-mon-in saw what had come to pass, she put her inkstone and warming stone into each side of the bosom of her robe and jumped into the sea. But Watanabe-no-Gengo Umanojo Mutsuru rowed up in a small boat, and cutching her long hair with a rake, dragged her back. Dainagon-no-suke-no-

Tsubone, the wife of Shigehira, seeing this, cried out: "Alas! How cruel! How can you treat one who was an Empress in such a way?" So they informed the Hōgwan and he came in haste to the Imperial Vessel. This Dainagon-no-suke had been just about to leap into the waves with the casket containing the Sacred Mirror, when an arrow pinned the skirt of her hakama to the side of the ship and she stumbled and fell, whereupon the Genji soldiers seized her and held her back. Then one of then wrenched off the lock of the casket to open it, when suddenly his eyes were darkened and blood poured from his nose. At this, Taira Dainagon Tokitada-no-Kyō, who had been captured alive, and was standing by, exclaimed: "Hold! That is the Holy Naishi-dokoro, the Sacred Mirror that no profane eye must behold!" Whereat the soldiers were awestricken and trembled with fear; and the Hōgwan bade Tokitada-no-Kyō put away the casket as it was before.

Meanwhile Kadowaki Taira-no-Chūnagon Norimori and Shuri-no-Taiyū Tsunemori placed heavy anchors on their armour and hand in hand leapt into the sea. Komatsu-no-Shin-sammi Chūjō Sukemori, his brother Komatsu-no-Shōshō Arimori, and their cousin Sama-no-kami Yukimori, also followed their example and did likewise. But though the other members of the family thus leapt into the waves, the Daijin Munemori and his son did not, but stood on the gunwale of the ship looking round to see what would happen. Seeing them thus hesitate, some of the Heike samurai, under pretence of pushing by hurriedly, thrust Munemori over into the sea, and his son, Uemon-no-kami Kiyomune, seeing this, sprang in after him. Now the others had put heavy objects on their shoulders and held on to each other so that they might be sure to sink, but these two did not do any such thing, but, being good swimmers, they swam about hither and thither, the Daijin willing to sink or be rescued whichever his son night do, when Ise-Saburō-Yoshimori chanced to come up in a small boat and drag Kiyomune out with a rake, after which Munemori allowed himself to be pulled out also. Seeing this, Hida-no-Saburōemon Kagetsune, foster brother of Munemori, jumped into Yoshimori's boat and aimed a blow at him with his sword, shouting: "Who are you to take my lord captive?" But Yoshimori's page, perceiving his master's danger, thrust himself in between to intercept the blow, which fell full on his helmet and split it open. A second blow cut off the faithful page's head, and Yoshimori was again in great peril, when Hori-no-Yataro in the next boat drew his bow and shot an arrow full in Saburoemon's face, and as he staggered back for a moment, Hori boarded the boat and grappled with him. As the two were struggling together, one of Hori's men, who had followed his master close, stooped and drew Saburoemon's dirk, and, lifting up the skirts of his armour, stabbed him so deeply three times that his hand and the hilt went in also, after which he cut off his head. How must Munemori have felt to see his foster brother thus slain before his eyes.

Now, as we have said, none could face the arrows of Noto-no-kami-Noritsune and live; and he had resolved to fight to the last this day. He was brilliantly attired in a hitatare brocaded on a red ground, and a suit of armour laced with Chinese silk; he wore a helmet decorated with lofty horns, and a sword mounted in gold and silver. In his quiver were twenty four arrows feathered with black and white feathers, and with his Shigetō bow in his hand he shot them hither and thither, killing and wounding many of the foe. Then, when all his shafts were spent, he seized a great black-lacquered two handed sword in one hand and a white handled halberd in the other, and cut and slashed on all sides with reckless valour. The Shin-Chūnagon Tomomori-no-Kyō dispatched a messenger to him saying:" Why add to your sins by slaying so many men of little repute? Can you find no famous adversary?" "True," replied Noto-no-kami," I will try a fall with some great Captain." And shortening his halberd in his hand he cut his way through the ships, dealing blows vigorously on every side, but as he did not recognize the Hōgwan he took another splendidly armed warrior for him and sprang across to engage him. Now Yoshitsune was fighting close by, but somehow or other did not turn to attack Noritsune. The latter, however, having thus chanced to spring on board the Hōgwan's ship, suddenly espied him and made at him to grapple. Yoshitsune, feeling himself unable to meet his onset, stuck his halberd under his left arm and leaped nimbly over to one of the ships of his own side, a distance of full twenty feet. Noto-no-kami, less skilled in such tricks, was unable to follow him, and seeing that there was no more to be done, he tore off and flung away the sleeves and skirts of his armour, keeping only the breastplate, and, standing on the deckhouse of the ship with his hair all loose and disheveled, he flung out his arms and shouted loudly: "Let any of the Genji who thinks himself somebody come forth and grapple with me and take me prisoner! I should like to go down to Kamakura and have a word with Yoritomo! Who'll come and try?" But there was none who answered his challenge.

Now there was a warrior named Aki-no-Tarō Sanemitsu, the son of Aki-no-Tairyo Saneyasu of Tosa, who possessed an estate in a district of Aki, and he was so strong that he was said to possess the strength of twenty or thirty men. He had a retainer who was no less powerful than he, while his brother Jirō was also no ordinary warrior. "What is Noto Dono that we should fear him," they said; "he is no doubt a mighty warrior, but what of that? If he were a devil a hundred feet high, we three could settle him." And they got into a small boat and drew alongside the ship where Noritsune was, and boarded it and sprang at him together with their swords drawn. Noritsune on his part sprang forward also, and seizing Aki-no-Tarō's retainer who was foremost, kicked hire into the sea; then, taking Aki-no-Tarō himself under his left arm, and his brother Jirō under his right and gripping them tight, he sprang over into the waves, shouting: "Come along, both of you, to the Mountain of Shide!" And he was twenty six years old that year.

Chapter XII.

ENTRY OF THE SACRED MIRROR INTO THE CAPITAL.

Then Shin-Chūnagon Tomomori-no-Kyō, who had been watching how the day was going, at length saw that nothing remained but to put an end to his life, and calling his foster-brother Iga-no-Hei-naisaemon Ienaga, he said: "Is it not time to fulfil the promise we made?" "Certainly;" replied Ienaga. And he assisted Tomomori to don two suits of armour, afterwards doing the same himself, and the two leaped into the sea clasped in each other's arms. Some twenty samurai who were with them at once followed them into the waves; but Etchū-no-Jirōhyōye Moritsugu, Kazusa-no-Gorōhyōye, Akushichi-byōye Kagekiyo and Hida-no-Jirōhyōye managed to elude the enemy somehow and escape. And now the whole sea was red with the banners and insignia that they tore off and cut away, so that it looked like the waters of the Tatsuta-gawa when it is flecked with the maple leaves that the wind brings down in autumn, while the white breakers that rolled up on the beach were dyed a scarlet colour. The deserted empty ships rocked mournfully on the waves, driven aimlessly hither and Hither by the wind and tide.

The former Udaijin Munemori Ko, Taira Dainagon Tokitada, Uemon-no-kami Kiyomune, Kura-no-kami Nobumoto, Sanuki-no-Chūjō Tokizane and Munemori's eight year old son Hyobu-no-Sho Masaakira, were captured alive, beside the priests Nii-no-Sozu Senshin, Hosshoji-no-Shugyo No-en, Chūnagon-no-Risshi Chugai and Kyoju-bo-no-Ajari Yuen, and the samurai Gendaiyu-no-Hangwan Toshisada, Settsu-no-Hangwan Morizumi, Tonaisaemon-no-Jo Nobuyasu, Kitsunai-saemon-no-Jo Toshiyasu, and Awa-no-Mimbu Shigeyoshi and his son; thirty eight in all. Kikuchi-no-Jirō Takanao and Harada-no-Taiyū Tanenao had already laid down their arms and surrendered before the battle. Forty three Court Ladies were taken also, including the Imperial Consort Kenrei-mon-in, the foster-mother of the Emperor Takakura and wife of Rokujō Motozane, Ro-no-Onkata another daughter of Kiyomori, Dainagon-no-Suke, Sotsu-no-Suke, Jibu-Kyō-no-Tsubone and others; forty three in all. Thus by the fall of spring in the second year of Genryaku,—date of ill-omen indeed—the Emperor rested beneath the waves, while his Ministers and Courtiers tossed on the billows; the Imperial Consort and her Ladies were delivered into the hands of the Eastern barbarians to return to the Ancient Capital with all the Courtiers and Nobles as captives in the midst of myriads of foes, and their anguish must have been as deep as the regret of Shu-bai-shin at not wearing brocade, or the resentment of O-sho-kun when she set out for the land of Ko.

On the third day of the fourth month Kurō Hōgwan Yoshitsune despatched Genpachi Hirotsuna as a messenger to the Hō-ō with the tidings that: "On the twenty fourth day of the third month at the Hour of the Hare, at Ta-no-ura and Moji-ga-seki in the province of Buzen, and at Dan-no-ura and Akama-ga-seki in the province of Nagato, the Heike have been completely annihilated, and the Sacred Mirror and Sacred Seal will forthwith be returned to the Capital." When the Hō-ō heard this news he was exceedingly pleased, and calling Hirotsuna into the courtyard, demanded to be told all details of the battle, in his joy conferring on hire the title of Sahyōye on the spot. On the fifth day His Majesty ordered To-Hōgwan Nobumori, one of the Imperial Guard, to go and see that the two Sacred Emblems were properly brought back; so he took one of the Imperial Horses and set off at full speed for the Western Provinces without even delaying to go back to his lodging.

So Kuro Hōgwan Yoshitsune started on his way to the Capital, bringing with him the captured Courtiers and Ladies of the Heike, and on the fourteenth day they arrived at the shore of Akashi in the province of Harima. It is a place famous for its beauty, and when the moon rose bright as the evening grew late, it seemed no less beautiful than the moon of autumn. Little had the Ladies of the Court imagined that this would be their fate when they passed by a year ago, and when they thought of it they wept softly. Sotsu-no-suke Dono, the wife of Tokitada, gazing long at the moon and pondering deeply over all her sad experiences, was dissolved in tears, and expressed her feelings in the following verse:

"*As I gaze on the moon it rests in any sleeves that are moistened;*
Tell me, I prithee, O Moon, tales of the Palace of yore."
"*Here the moon is the same as that which shone o'er the Palace.*
But though it still shine bright, how can it lighten our pain?

Sang Jibu Kyō no Tsubone, while Dai-nagon no Suke no Tsubone added:

"*Exiles, but for a night do we camp by the shore of Akashi,*
But how constant the moon ever looks down on this strand."

And, stern warrior though the Hōgwan was, when he saw how painful were their reminiscences of their former happy days, has heart was moved to its inmost depths.

On the twenty fifth day of the same month, when they heard that the two Sacred Treasures had arrived at Toba, Kageyu-no-koji-no-

Chūnagon Tsunefusa-no-Kyō, Kebiishi-no-Betto Saemon-no-kami Saneie, Takakura-no-Saisho Chūjō Yasumichi, Gon-no-Uchuben Kanetada, Enami-no-Chūjō Kintoki and Tajima-no-Shōshō Noriyoshi of the Court Nobles, and Izu-no-Kurando Taiyū Yorikane, Ishikawa-no-Hangwan dai Yoshikane and Saemon-no-Jo Aritsuna of the Samurai, went forth from the Palace to meet them; and the same night, at the Hour of the Rat (12. midnight.), the Sacred Mirror and the Sacred Gem were handed over to the keeping of the Dajōkwan. The Sacred Sword was lost, but the Sacred Gem in its casket floated on the waves, and was recovered by Kataoka-no-Tarō Tsuneharu.

Chapter XIII.

THE HEIKE PARADED THROUGH THE STREETS.

When he heard that Prince Morihito, the second son of the late Emperor Takakura, was returning to the Capital, the Hō-ō sent a car to meet him. Both his mother and his foster mother Jimyo-in-no-Saisho had been much grieved when he was taken away against his will by his relations the Heike Courtiers, and exposed to hardship with them on the waves of the Western Sea, and they were now overjoyed to receive him back again. On the twenty sixth day the Heike captives arrived at Toba, and without delay were brought into the Capital on the same clay and paraded through the streets. In a car with both the front and rear blinds drawn up, and the side windows open, sat the Daijin Munemori, attired in a white Kariginu. In former days he had had a fine figure and a fair complexion, but now, thin and worn and burned black by the salt breezes, he did not look the same person. But he gazed curiously all around him as the car passed on, and did not seem particularly dejected. His son Uemon-no-kami Kiyomune rode in the back of his father's car, wearing a white hitatare. Choked with tears and with down cast head, he did not raise his eyes from the ground, and seemed to be sunk in the deepest melancholy. In the next car rode Taira Dainagon Tokitada-no-Kyō, and Sanuki-no-Chūjō-Tokizane should have been with him, but on account of sickness he was excused. Kura-no-kami Nobumoto also entered the city by a side street, for he had been wounded.

And to see this spectacle the people came from far and near, from every shrine and temple round about the city, while from the Capital itself, high and low, young and old came thronging out in countless myriads, lining the road all the way from the south gate of the Toba Palace, by Tsukuri-michi and Yotsu-kado; and so great was the press that the wheels of the cars could not turn, neither could the sight-seers look backwards. In the famine of the periods of Ji-sho and Yowa, and in the campaigns in the East and North Provinces, more men perchance were slain, but the number of the survivors was greater; and as it was not yet a year since the Heike had fled from the Capital, the days of their splendour were so recent that none could forget them, so that those who had formerly gone in fear and trembling of them could scarcely be certain whether their present condition was dream or reality. And as the very lowest kind of people who had no particular concern with them were affected to tears by the sight, the feelings of those who had had intimate and friendly relations with them can be imagined. Though for fear of their lives most of their hereditary vassals, who for generations had lain under heavy obligations to them, had gone over to the Genji, yet they could not at once forget their ancient friendship, and there was not one who was not moved to tears, while most did not even raise their eyes. The ox-driver who drove Munemori's car was Saburō Maru, the younger brother of that Jirō Maru who had been put to death by Kiso Yoshinaka for improper driving. This Saburō Maru had accompanied the Heike to the Western Provinces and done other work there, and at Toba he had petitioned Yoshitsune: "Though Toneri and ox drivers are the lowest kind of servants and have no claim to consideration, yet, as I have served my master many years and am greatly attached to him, I pray you grant me the favour of driving his car for the last time." And the Hōgwan, touched by the request, gave the required permission. So Saburo Maru, greatly delighted, took from the bosom of his dress a driving-rope that he kept about him, and, though his eyes were so blinded with tears that he could not see where he was going, he let the oxen find their own way, and so drove his master.

The Hō-ō watched the procession from his car at Rokujō Higashi-no-Doin, and all his Courtiers and attendants drew up their cars alongside the Imperial Car, but as the Heike nobles had until lately also been in attendance on him, His Majesty was now moved to pity at their fate. Who would have dreamed that these haughty potentates, from whom all but lately sought a word or a glance, could have fallen to their present condition? And there were few who were dry-eyed at the thought. But a year before Munemori had come in procession to the Hō-ō's Palace to pay his respects on being raised to the position of Naidaijin, and then he was accompanied by twelve Courtiers of the highest rank, headed by Kwazan-in-no-Chūnagon Kanemasa-no-Kyō, while sixteen others of lower rank, led by Kurando-no-kami Chikamune, walked before him in the van, the procession including four of the rank of Chūnagon and three of that of Sammi Chūjō. All the Courtiers and Nobles were in festal array to do honour to the day, and Tokitada-no-Kyō was summoned into the Imperial Presence and entertained magnificently and sent away with many presents. Today not a single Courtier accompanied them, and the twenty old samurai, who were taken with them at Dan-no-ura, were led along behind them clad in white garments and tied up to the front of their saddles.

Passing along Rokujō to the east they were led to the river bed, and from thence back again to the Hōgwan's residence in Rokujō Horikawa, where they were put under a strong guard. Food was set before the Daijin, but his throat was choked and he could not eat; and when night came he did not even loosen his clothes, but lay down just as he was, wrapped in the sleeves of his robe; but when his guards noticed that he covered his son Uemon-no-kami with his sleeve, they exclaimed: "Ah, among both high and low there is nothing so pathetic as parental affection. The spreading of a sleeve is nothing in itself, but even that shows the depth of his care;" and their tears dropped on to the sleeves of their armour.

Chapter XIV.

THE LETTERS OF THE TAIRA DAINAGON.

Now as the Taira Dainagon Tokitada-no-Kyō and his son drew near to the residence of the Hōgwan they had given themselves up for lost, but the Dainagon, wishing if possible to save his life, called his son Sanuki-no-Chūjō-Tokizane and sai: "The Hōgwan has taken a box of our secret letters. If Yoritomo sees them, not only ourselves, but a lot of other people will lose their lives in consequence. What is to be done?" "The Hōgwan is an inflexible warrior, it is true," replied Tokizane, "but they say that he can never refuse any request, however great, if it is made by a woman. You have many daughters, so why not let one of them go to him, and when they become intimate she can ask him this favour." "Alas!" exclaimed the Dainagon, bursting into tears, "to what have we fallen? In the days of our power my daughters would have become Court Ladies or Imperial Consorts, and I would never have dreamed of allying them with any ordinary person." "But now," replied his son, "you must not dream of such ideas. How about the one who is now seventeen, the daughter of your present wife?" But the Dainagon could not bring himself to this, and so presented his elder daughter, the child of his first wife, to the Hōgwan. She was a little old, it is true, but was exceedingly beautiful and of a very sweet disposition, so that Yoshitsune was very pleased with her, and as he had a wife already, the daughter of Kawagoe-no-Taro Shigefusa, he put her away in a separate residence and took the daughter of the Dainagon into his own mansion. So the lady made her request to him concerning the letters, and he sent them to the Dainagon forthwith without even opening the box. Tokitada-no-Kyō was exceedingly glad and immediately burnt and got rid of them. What kind of letters they were is unknown.

Seeing that the Heike had been thus overthrown, and all the provinces quieted so that all could travel about again without let or hindrance, and that there was no more disorder in the Capital, people began to declare that Yoshitsune was the greatest man in the Empire, and that Yoritomo had done but little in comparison. So by and by it came to the ears of the Lord of Kamakura that it was noised abroad that Yoshitsune could do what he liked with the Empire. "What sayings are these?" he exclaimed. "Was it not owing to the plans I laid and the armies that I sent that the Heike were so quickly conquered? How could Kurō have set the Empire in order alone? What does he mean by growing thus arrogant and thinking he can do as he pleases? And were there no other people available that he must become the son-in-law of this Taira Dainagon and behave himself like a Court Noble? Moreover it was a shameless thing of this Dainagon to give his daughter thus. The next thing Yoshitsune will do is to come down and domineer here in Kamakura."

Chapter XV.

FUKU-SHO IS PUT TO DEATH.

On the sixth day of the fifth month of the second year of Gen-ryaku Kurō Taiyū-no-Hōgwan Yoshitsune decided to set out for the Eastern Provinces with the Daijin Munemori and his son. Munemori therefore sent a messenger to him saying: "I have heard that we are to start for the East tomorrow, and I have a request to make. If the boy of eight years old; who is written down among the prisoners, is still alive I should much like to see him again once more." Truly," said Yoshitsune," that is very natural, for who can be unmindful of parental affection?" And he immediately sent orders to Kawagoe-no-Kotarō Shigefusa, in whose charge the boy had been placed, to take him to Munemori at once; and Kawagoe, borrowing a car from someone, put the child and two lady attendants into it, and went off without delay. As the child had not seen his father for so long, his joy knew no bounds, and when Munemori called to him: "Ah, Fuku-sho! Come along!" he rushed up to him and climbed up on his knee. "Listen, all of you," said Munemori, stroking the boy's hair and weeping over him, "this child has no mother; for though he was born without any trouble, soon afterwards his mother took to her bed and after a while died. And while she lay sick she said to me: "Whatever other children you may in future have by some other wife, do not forsake this one, but look on him as a memento of me. Do not send him away to be brought up by some faster mother." So when I gave him the name of Fuku-sho, (Vice-Commander), saying that when we marched against the enemies of the Throne Uemon-no-kami would be the Commander-in-Chief, and I wished him to be under him as Vice-Commander, she was overjoyed, and continued to call him by this name right up to the time that she died, seven days after. So whenever I see this child it always recalls her to memory." And when he finished speaking, all the guards, and Uemon-no-kami and the child's nurse hid their faces in their sleeves and wept.

After a while Munemori said: "Now Fuku-sho, it is time for you to go back again;" but the child did not go: so Uemon-no-kami, pitying him, comforted him by saying: "Come Fuku-sho; we have some people coming today; but you must come again tomorrow." But still he would not go, weeping and clinging tight to his father's sleeve; and so he remained some time, till at last, as it began to grow dark, his nurse drew him away in her arms, and the two ladies got into the car with him and returned home.

Munemori stood looking after him a long while, sadly reflecting that his former affection for the child was as nothing to what he felt now. Out of tender regard for his mother's wishes he had kept the child always beside him, and hats not sent him away to anyone to be brought up. At the age of three he had put on the Kammuri and received the name of Yoshimune, and as he grew older the beauty of his face and figure increased also, while his disposition became the more loveable. So Munemori became more and more attached to him, and took him with him everywhere, so that they were not parted for a moment even on shipboard on the waves of the Western Sea; and this was the first time that they had met since the defeat.

Then Shigefusa enquired of the Hōgwan what was his pleasure concerning the child. "We cannot take him with us to Kamakura," replied Yoshitsune, "so you had better do as you will with him." So Shigefusa returned to his residence and said to the two ladies: "The Daijin will start for the East tomorrow, but the child must stay here in Miyako. He is to be handed over to Ogata-no-Saburō Koreyoshi, so bid him come forthwith." So they again put him into the car, and he went off joyfully with the two ladies thinking he was going to see his father as before. When however the car drove along Rokujō to the eastward and came to the river bed, the ladies were thrown into the greatest anxiety and consternation, suspecting that something terrible was going to happen. In a few moments a troop of scme fifty or sixty horsemen rode down to the river bed, and stopping the car bade thin set down the child, spreading a fur rug on the ground for them to alight. With a surprised and troubled expression on his face the little lord enquired: "Where are you going to take me then?" But the two ladies could make him no answer, and only burst out into loud lamentations. Then one of Shigefusa's men, holding his sword ready to draw, was just stepping round behind him from the left side to sweep off his head, when the child perceived it and ran and threw himself into the nurse's arms in an endeavor to escape; whereupon the two ladies, clasping him in their arms, entreated the soldiers to kill them instead, raising their eyes to heaven and throwing themselves on the ground in an unavailing agony of grief.

Then Shigefusa, choking down his emotion, exclaimed: "It is too late to do anything now;" and dragging the child from their arms, struck him down with his dirk and cut off his head, which he straightway took away to show to the Hōgwan. Barefoot the two ladies followed him and begged earnestly that they might be given the head, for they wished to recite the Sutras for him; and the Hōgwan, who was not devoid of pity, granted their request. So the two, receiving it with deep gratitude, bestowed it in the bosom of one of them and returned weeping to the city.

About a week afterwards it was reported that two ladies had drowned themselves in the Katsura-gawa, and one, who had cast herself into the water with a child's head in her bosom, was this nurse of Munemori's son. The other, who was found clasping the dead body in her arms, was her maid in waiting. Seeing that her mistress had determined to end her life, her unhappy companion could not bear to survive her, and so had followed her in death.

Chapter XVI.

Koshigoe.

On the seventh day of the fifth month of the second year of Genryaku Kurō Taiyū-no-Hōgwan Yoshitsune set out from the Capital with the Daijin Munemori and his son. When they came to Awata-guchi, the Palace was far away among the clouds, and when he beheld the clear streams of the barrier at Ausaka, the Daijin, weeping bitterly, composed this verse:

"*Here today by this spring I look any last on Miyako,*
Grant that once more any face mirror itself in its wave."

Yoshitsune, noticing how sad and despondent was Munemori, with his accustomed kindness tried to cheer him." I pray you, if it be possible, save my life." entreated the Daijin. "Anyhow I do not consider your life in any danger," replied the Hōgwan, "but if it were, I would claim it as a reward of my merit in this campaign. Perchance however, you will be banished to some distant province or far off island." "Let me be banished even to Chishima in Ezo," pathetically pleaded Munemori, "so long as my life is preserved." It was a pitiable exhibition.

So the days passed and on the twenty third day it was reported that the Hōgwan was about to arrive at Kamakura, but Kajiwara Heizō Kagetoki, who had preceded him, spoke to Yoritomo saying: "Now all

Nippon is subject to your lordship's will, and your brother Kurō Taiyū-no-Hōgwan Yoshitsune is the only enemy you have to fear. A straw will show how the wind blows. He declared that if he had not ridden down the mountain behind Ichi-no-tani, we could not have broken the eastern and western defenses. And then be had everyone, alive or dead, brought to him for inspection, and not to Noriyori who was of no account at all. He ordered the Chūjō Shigehira to be brought before him, and said he would come and take him if he were not, so, thinking the consequences might be serious, I considered well, and with the assistance of Doi himself, committed the Chūjō to the keeping of Doi-no-Jirō Sanehira and so saved the situation." Yoritomo, quite convinced by these things, ordered Kajiwara to take every precaution to prevent Yoshitsune approaching him; and the feudal lords, both small and great, came hurrying up to his aid, so that he soon mustered several thousands of horsemen. When he saw that he was thus protected; "Kurō is a very clever fellow," quoth he, "cunning enough to get in under these floor mats; but I have out-witted him this time." So he fixed a barrier at Kane-araizawa and there took over Munemori and his son, ordering Yoshitsune to retire to Koshigoe. When Yoshitsune understood this he was very indignant. "What is the meaning of this?" he exclaimed," between the spring of last year when he defeated Kiso Yoshinaka and this spring I have utterly destroyed the Heike and without delay restored the Sacred Mirror and the Sacred Gem to the Capital. I have, moreover, captured alive the Daijin Munemori, the Commander-in-Chief, and his son, and brought them thus far with me as prisoners; so whatever suspicion Yoritomo may harbour about me he ought at least to receive me in audience. I had thought at least that I might have been appointed Sotsuibushi of Kyūshū, or put in charge of the San-in, Sanyo, or Nankai-do to consolidate them for him, but instead of that I have merely been made Governor of the province of Iyo; and then instead of being received into Kamakura I am made to go back to Koshigoe. Was not the subduing of the whole land of Nippon the work of Yoshinaka and myself? Of the sons of the same father he that is born first is treated as the elder brother, and those who are born afterwards as the younger, so that none can deny that it is he that rules the Empire. Who could doubt it?"

But as all his complaints were unavailing, in tears of despair Yoshitsune wrote this letter and sent it to Ōe Hiromoto:

"With the deepest respect Minamoto Yoshitsune pleads his cause. Having been appointed to represent your lordship, I have successfully fulfilled the Imperial Edict in subduing the enemies of the Throne and wiping out our former disgrace. Far from receiving any reward for these deeds, on account of some malignant slander all my great merit has been forgotten, and I have been blamed where I have committed no crime. Though my great achievements are known to all, yet I am thus rebuffed and left here many days to weep bitter tears in vain and while the truth of the slanders has not been proved, I am unable to come to Kamakura to say anything in my defense. Long is it now since I have been permitted to behold your face. Can it be that our former fraternal relations have now been severed, that in the destiny that brings them to none effect I am reaping the reward of the evil karma of a former life? Wretched that I am! For then, except the revered spirit of our father were to return to this life, who is there to hearken to my unavailing lamentation, or who will show me any pity? Irrelevant as it may seem to refer to such things, since I was born and my father's early death left me an orphan, so that my mother travelled with me in her arms to Uda in Yamato, up till this moment I have never known an hour of ease. What use to describe the risks of my sojourn near the Capital, hiding myself here and there, and fleeing to this and that refuge far removed from the haunts of men, subject to the very hinds and peasants? But when, in the new harmony of our brotherly affection, it was arranged that I should go forth in the campaign against the Heike, since Kiso Yoshinaka was overthrown and I set forth to destroy the whole family, what hardships are there both by land and sea that I have not undergone? At times spurring my steed over the towering crags heedless of all danger, at times braving the perils of the winds and waves of the boundless ocean; careless whether my body should be lost in the depths of the sea to be a prey for the great fishes. Moreover my helmet and armour were my only pillow, the bending of the bow my only business, while I put away all thought of aught but appeasing the wrath of our ancestral spirits, the object of my long cherished desire. Therefore it was no more than suitable to the importance of our house that Yoshitsune should be appointed Go-i-no-Jo. But now my grief is sore and my lamentation extreme. Except I turn for aid to the gods and Buddhas, to whom can I look to hear my petition? Still, if I had all the holy amulets of all the shrines and temples in Nippon, and took all the gods and Buddhas of the whole land to witness that I held no treachery in my heart, however many oaths I might swear he would not forgive me. Our country is the land of the gods; and the gods will not tolerate impropriety. There is none else on whom I can rely, so I throw myself on your great charity. I pray you therefore to bring these things before Yoritomo at a suitable time, and to take such measures that he will perceive that I am guiltless and pardon me. So shall your house acquire great merit, and good fortune and prosperity shall follow you from generation to generation. Thus will my former sadness be done away, and for a while I shall enjoy tranquility. I cannot say all I would in this letter, but must perforce here bring my few words to an end. Yoshitsune respectfully addresses you. The fifth day of the sixth month of the second year of Gen-ryaku. To Inaba-no-kami Dono.

Chapter XVII.

THE EXECUTION OF MUNEMORI.

So the Daijin Munemori was brought before Yoritomo. He was placed in a room separated by a courtyard from the one where the Lord of Kamakura was seated, and opposite to it, so that Yoritomo could scrutinize him from behind his curtain. Through Hiki-no-Toshirō Yoshikazu he greeted him thus: "Far be it indeed from Yoritomo to regard the Heike family as his personal enemies, since if it had not been for the favour of the late Nyūdō Kiyomori he would not have been alive today. But some twenty years have passed since then, and seeing that the Heike have been declared enemies of the Throne and an Imperial Edict has been issued for their chastisement, it was not possible for me to disobey the Imperial Command, and so it is that I have the honour of your presence here. I am indeed pleased to see you before me thus alive and well." When Yoshikazu brought this message to Munemori it was regrettable that he prostrated himself in obeisance.

Now among all the lords of all provinces, who were sitting there in order, were many from the Capital, besides some who had formerly been retainers of the Heike house, and there were none who did not consider this behaviour contemptible. "Ah," said one, "it is this spirit that has brought him to his present plight. But this low obeisance is hardly likely to save his skin. If one as great as he was in the Western Provinces is thus captured alive, it is quite natural he should be brought down here." And many agreed with these sentiments, though many also shed tears of pity. "A fierce tiger when in the mountains is a terror to all the beasts," observed one of these, "but when it is in a cage it will wag its tail and beg for food; and so however brave a general may be, when all is lost his courage will fail him: and so it is with this Daijin."

Now, though the Hōgwan made many representations, yet Owing to the slanders of Kagetoki. Yoritomo paid no attention to them, but only gave orders that he should immediately return again, taking Munemori and his son with him: and so, on the ninth day of the sixth month he once more set out with them for the Capital. Pitiable to relate, Munemori was glad to hear this, for he thought his life would be prolonged, if but for a day or two. And so, as they went along, wherever they stopped he wondered if he was to die there. In this way they passed through several provinces till they came to Utsumi in Owari, and as formerly Sama-no-kami Yoshitomo had been executed here, he expected to meet the same fate, and when they passed on he felt greatly relieved, hoping that he was permitted to live after all. His son Uemon-no-kami, however, did not share these hopes, but thought their execution was only being postponed till they were near the Capital in order that the heads might not putrefy, seeing that the weather was hot. Out of pity for his father he said nothing of this to him, but occupied himself with silently repeating the Nembutsu.

On the twenty third day they arrived at Shinohara in the province of Ōmi. Until the day before the father and son had been kept together, but on the morning of this day they were separated. Yoshitsune, who was ever considerate towards others, had sent on a messenger three days before to summon a certain holy man famous for his sanctity, named Honjō-bō Tanko of Ohara. On his arrival Munemori enquired of him: "Where is Uemon-no-kami? If we are to be executed I should like our bodies to fall on the same mat. Why do they part us, while we are still alive, for seventeen years we have never been separated even for an hour? The reason why I chose to live and not die in the Western Provinces, and to expose myself to the shame of being brought thus to Miyako and Kamakura, was only for the sake of being with my son." And he burst into tears as he spoke. The priest too was much affected, but thinking it would not do to break down, wiped away his tears and composed himself, saying: "Alas, since parental affection is the same both among high and low, it is natural that your lordship should feel thus. Since you were born into this world you have attained to such heights of glory and happiness as have not been paralleled even in the days of old; rising to be Chief Minister and Maternal Relative of the Heavenly Sovereign, and thus draining the cup of earthly greatness: and now that you have fallen to your present plight, since it is the result of the karma of a former life, you must feel no resentment against either the world, or men, or gods, or Buddhas. Even the pleasures of the profound tranquility of the heaven of Maha-brahma leaves something to be desired; what then shall we say of this life, evanescent as a flash of lightning or a drop of dew? Even the hundred million and a thousand years life of the heaven of Indra is but as a dream, so the thirty nine years of your life till now are but as a moment. Who is there who can taste the elixir of eternal youth, or who can prolong his days like Sei-o-bo and To-bo-saku? Great was the glory of Shi-kotei of Shin, but he lies buried in his tomb at Risan: Butei of Kan was loath to die, but now he rots under the moss of Toryo. All who live must surely die; even S'akaya Muni could not escape the smoke of the sandal wood. When pleasure is at its zenith then comes pain; and even the angels are not exempt from the Five Failings. And as Buddha says in the Hannya Kyō: "When the mind is entirely empty, desiring neither evil nor good, then there is no more hindrance of phenomena;" so if we regard both good and evil as unreal, we shall verily be in accord with the mind of Buddha. And inasmuch as Amida Nyorai, after meditation lasting five kalpas, was at last, after overcoming all difficulties, able to made the Great Vow, is it not most stupid and regrettable if we still continue to spend countless myriads of ages bound to the revolving wheel of births and deaths, seeing the treasures of salvation spread out before us without lifting a hand to grasp them? Concentrate your whole mind on these things now." And thus admonishing him, the priest urged him to repeat the Nembutsu, so Munemori, perceiving that he was indeed a saintly priest, suddenly putting all earthly thoughts from his mind, turned to the west, and putting his hands together, in a loud voice repeated the Nembutsu. As he did so Kitsu Uma-no-suke Kinnaga drew his sword and moved round behind him from the left side to cut off his head, when Munemori suddenly stopped the Nembutsu and enquired: "Is Uemon-no-kami already dead?" At this painful interruption Kinnaga thought the head might fall backwards, but it fell to the front. At the sad scene both the priest and also the rough soldiers of the guard could not refrain from weeping. Now this Kinnaga had been a hereditary retainer of the Heike, and was one of the samurai always in attendance on the Shin-Chūnagon Tomomori-no-Kyō, and however much people might flatter those who were in power, he was held in contempt as a samurai who was quite devoid of fine feeling.

Then the priest proceeded to give the same spiritual comfort to Uemon-no-kami, and to urge him too to repeat the Nembutsu, whereupon he enquired of him how his father had met his end. "His end was happy," replied the priest, "and so I pray you set your mind at rest." "Then I have no more concern with this fleeting world," said the young noble," so cut off my head at once." And stretching out his neck he awaited the blow, which has struck this time by Hori-no-Yataro Chikatsune. By the order of Kinnaga the corpses of father and son were buried in the same grave. And this was done because Munemori so earnestly requested it, worldly attachment though it was.

On the twenty fourth day of the same month the heads of the Daijin Munemori and his son were brought into the Capital. The officials of the Kebiishi proceeded to Sanjo-kawara to receive them, and then, carrying them along Sanjo to the westward, and Higashi-no-Do-in to the northward, they fixed them to a sandal-wood tree on the left of the prison gate. In other countries there may be an example of the head of one above the Third Rank being carried through the streets, but in this country I have never heard of one. In the period of Heiji the evil deeds of Nobuyori-no-Kyō were such that his head was cut off, but it was not exposed in the streets. The Heike were the first to be treated thus. When they were brought up from the Western Provinces they were paraded along Rokujō to the east while they were alive, and when they were sent back from the Eastern Provinces they were carried along Sanjo to the west when dead. Disgraced while alive and dishonoured when dead, everywhere they were degraded.

Volume XII.

Chapter I.

THE EXECUTION OF SHIGEHIRA.

Now Hon-Sammi Chūjō Shigehira had been living since the last year in the province of Izu in the charge of Kanō-no-suke Muneshige, but as the monks of Nara were always demanding him, orders were at last sent to Izu-no-Kurando Taiyū Yorikane, grandson of Gen-sammi Nyūdō Yorimasa, to escort him thither. On this occasion they did not enter the Capital, but turned off at Otsu and took the Daigo road by Yamashina, thus passing near Hino.

Now the wife of Shigehira was the daughter of Torikai-no-Dainagon Korezane, who had been adopted by Gojo-no-Dainagon Kunitsuna; she was the foster mother of the late Emperor and was known as Dainagon-no-Suke-no-Tsubone. After the Chūjō had been capturned at Ichi no tani she had remained with His Majesty, and had jumped into the sea at Dan-no-ura, but was roughly dragged out by the soldiers and sent back to the Capital, whereupon she took up her abode with her elder sister Taiyū-no-sammi at a place called Hino. When she heard that her husband's life, though trembling to its fall like the dewdrop on the end of a leaf, was not yet extinguished, she felt a great longing to see his face once more, but as she could not, there was nothing left her but to spend her days weeping and bewailing him.

So the Chūjō Shigehira said to the samurai who were escorting him: "I am greatly beholden to you for your consideration and kindness to me so far, and I have just one last boon to crave. As I have no child, I feel no regret at leaving this world, but as I hear that my wife, to whom I have been long wedded, is now living at Hino, I should much like to see her to speak with her about the hereafter." And as the guards were not wood or stone, with tears in their eyes they readily gave him the desired permission.

Shigehira, greatly delighted, forthwith sent word to the lady saying: "Is Dainagon-no-suke-no-Tsubone within? Hon-sammi Chūjō, who is on his way to Nara, waits without to see her." "Where is he then? Where is he? exclaimed the lady, running out when she received the message, when she saw a thin, sunburned figure, clad in a hitatare of dyed blue material and a folded eboshi, standing by the verandah of the residence. "How is this? How is this? Is it a dream or is it real? But come in!" exclaimed his wife, advancing to the edge of the curtain. As she heard his voice again tears anticipated all else, and with blinded eyes and sinking heart for a while she found no word to utter. Then the Chūjō, raising the curtain and leaning half-way through it, thus addressed her in a voice broken by sobs: "In the spring of last year, after many perils, as a penalty for my great guilt, I was captured alive at Ichi-no-tani in the province of Settsu, and after being publicly disgraced in Miyako and Kamakura, I am to be delivered into the hands of the priests of Nara to be put to death. So on my way thither I wished to see your face again, and now there nothing more that I have to live for. I had thought to shave my head here and leave my hair as a keepsake, but as I have come in this condition I cannot bear to do so." And pulling a lock of hair from this forehead, he bit off a piece where it touched his mouth and handed it to her, saying: "Keep this in memory of me." His wife, who had been full of anxiety about him before, was now quite overwhelmed by her grief, and fell forward with her robe about her face in an agony of tears. After a while, recovering herself somewhat, she said; "It was my intention to drown myself like the Nii Dono and Kozaishō, but indeed when I heard you were still alive I greatly wished to see you again, and so I have lived till now in this wretched state. Only in the hope of seeing you have I lived so long, and now this is to be last time." And as they spoke of things both past and present tears were the only thing that seemed to have no end. "As you look so languid, will you not change your garments," she said, producing a wadded silk under garment and a white kariginu. So the Chūjō put them on, and giving her those that he had just taken off, said: "Keep these too as a memento of me." "Not only that," replied the lady, but I pray you write me at least a line, that I may treasure it till the end of my life; and she brought him an inkstone. So the Chūjō, weeping bitterly, took a brush and wrote these lines:

> "*Laying aside this robe I leave it here as a keepsake,*
> *Wet as it is with my tears, pent in my bosom till now.*"

And the lady also wrote this verse:

> "*Ah, this robe you have worn, what use can it be to you further?*
> *'Tis a memento for me that I shall see you no more.*"

"Since we are bound to each other, we shall surely be reborn together in the next life," said the Chūjō; "pray that it be upon the same lotus. The times grows late, and I must haste to Nara; I must not keep the guards waiting." And he made to do forth, but the lady clung to his sleeve and held him back, crying: "Why so soon; stay a little longer!" "You can guess what I feel in my heart," replied he, "but my time on earth grows short;" and with firm resolution he turned to depart. Indeed, when he thought that this would be the last time in this world, he could with difficulty refrain from turning back once more, but unwilling to show any weakness, he conquered his feelings and went on his way.

The lady, rolling herself right outside the curtain, lifted up her voice and wept aloud, so that the sound of it could be heard far beyond the gate, and the Chūjō blinded by his tears and unable to see the road, for some time did not quicken his pace. "A pitiable meeting indeed!" he thought regretfully, His wife at first started to run out after him, but seeing that it was of no avail, threw herself down with her face buried in her robes.

Now the monks of Nara, as soon as they had got possession of Shigehira, held a council to decide what they should do with him. Shigehira, they declared, was the worst kind of criminal, beyond even the three thousand varieties of the Five Punishments. Since, under the influence of the most evil and malignant karma, he was an outlaw and enemy of Buddha and the Law, he must certainly be paraded round the walls of both the Todaiji and the Kofukuji and then be buried alive and have his head cut off, or else have it sawn off. But the older priests took objection to this decision, saying that it was too severe a sentence for men of religion, and that he should be handed over to the samurai to be beheaded on the bank of the Kozu-gawa. And in the end this counsel prevailed, and he was delivered over to the samurai, who led him out to the bank of the Kozu-gawa, where countless myriads of people, including thousands of priests, besides his guards and other spectators, had assembled to see him put to death.

Now there was a former retainer of the Chūjō named Muku-no-Uma-no-jo Tomotoki, and he was also in the service of the Hachijō-no-Nyo-in, who greatly wished to see the last of his master, so he rode his hardest to the Kozu-gawa and arrived just as he was about to be beheaded. Springing from his horse he pushed his way through the thronging multitudes till he reached his master's side, and called out: "Here am I, Tomotoki, come to see the last of my master!" "How admirable is your devotion," replied to Chūjō, "and now, Tomotoki, since my guilt is so great I should like to worship a Buddha before I die. Can it be done?" "That will not be difficult," replied Tomotoki, and after consulting with the samurai on guard, he went off to a neighbouring hamlet and brought back an image of Buddha, most fortunately one of Amida. Setting it down on the sand of the river bed, he drew out the cord from the sleeve of his kariginu and fastened one end of it to the hand of the Buddha, giving the other to the Chūjō. Holding it in his hand the Chūjō turned toward the Buddha and said: "I have heard that though Devadatta committed the Three Transgressions, and burned eighty thousand collections of Sutras, it was foretold that he should at last become a Tennō Nyorai; and though his crimes were indeed heinous, yet by virtue of the Holy Sutras his sinful karma was blotted out, and they became the cause of his entering the way of salvation. So, that I should have committed this great sin was by no means a purposeless happening, but was in accordance with the principle of things. Who that is born in this world can disregard an Imperial Command, or who among men can be disobedient to a father's will? Buddha is witness of right and wrong. Therefore is my crime requited on the spot, and my doom has now come upon me. However boundless and deep my repentance, yet it is not enough. But the World of the Three Precious Ones is a world of compassion and mercy, and many are the paths that lead to salvation. YUI-EN-KYO-I, GYAKU-SOKU ZE-JUN.[254] This text is graved on my heart. Fixing my whole mind on Amida Buddha, who blots even the greatest iniquities, I pray that he may change my rebellious affinity into right affinity, and so, as I repeat the last Nembutsu, according to his promise I may be reborn in the Pure Heavenly Land." And as he spoke these words he stretched out his neck and the blow fell; and though his former deeds had been so evil, yet when they saw his demeanour at the last, even the thousands of priests and the soldiers of the guard could not refrain from bedewing their sleeves. His head was then nailed up over the gate of the Hannyaji; and this was done because it was here that he stood during the battle in the period Jisho when the temples were burned. When his wife heard what had been done; "If they have cut off his head," she said, "they will have thrown his body away somewhere; so go and bring it that the Sutras may be recited over it." And she sent a litter for it. And as she had said, they found that his body had been cast away into the river bed, and they took it up and put it into the litter and brought it back to Hino. Until the day before it had remained unchanged, but as the weather was hot it had now become unsightly, so the feelings of the lady when she saw it can be imagined. The head also was afterwards recovered by the good offices of Shunjo-bo, a priest of the Dai-butsu, who obtained the permission of the monks and sent it to Hino. So they brought both the head and body to a neighbouring mountain temple called Hokaiji, and burned them there, after which they sent the ashes to Kōya. They also set up a tomb for him in Hino, and his wife became a nun and put on black robes to pray for his happy rebirth in Paradise.

---

[254] Yui-en, etc. The meaning of this is that though there may appear to be things which are opposed to each other such as Buddhas and devils, good and evil people, yet in reality they all work together in harmony. 'Verily all is in harmony; that which opposes it is that which obeys.

Chapter II.

THE GREAT EARTHQUAKE.

Thus after the Heike had been overthrown and the Genji had come into power, the provinces obeyed their governors, and the manors were once more at the disposal of their owners, so that there was peace and security everywhere. Then on the ninth day of the seventh month at the Hour of the Horse (noon), there was a very great earthquake which lasted for some time. Around the Capital near Shirakawa the six 'Shoji' temples[255] were all destroyed, and the upper six stories of the nine-storied pagoda of Hosshoji were shaken down, while all but seventeen ken of the Sanjusan-gen-do of Tokucho-ju in fell down. From the Imperial Palace and the various shrines and temples to the houses of the common people, all were destroyed. The roar of their falling was like thunder, and the dust that rose up like clouds of smoke. The sky was darkened, and the light of the sun could not be seen. Old and young went in fear and trembling, and the Palace officials were at their wits' end. The provinces both far and near were equally affected. Mountains crumbled down and filled up the rivers; the sea surged and the shores were flooded. The ships rocked about on the waves; and the horses lost their footing on the ground. The earth split asunder and water gushed out; the rocks were rent and rolled down into the valleys. If there is a flood, cannot they escape by fleeing to the hills? And if there is a fire, even if far from a river, it can be avoided. But men are not birds that they should fly in the air; neither are they dragons that they should ride on the clouds: so verily there is nothing more fearful than a great earthquake. At Shirakawa and Rokuhara and in the city those who were buried alive were without number. Among the Four Elements water, fire, wind and rain are ever harmful, but earth does not usually do men hurt. But now high and low shut themselves into their houses, thinking the world was coming to an end, and whenever the sky roared or the earth shook they said the Nembutsu and cried aloud. When people of sixty or seventy, or eighty or ninety declared that the destruction of the world was a natural thing, but they had not expected it yesterday or to day, the young who heard it were beside themselves with grief.

The Hō-ō was just then proceeding to Imakumano, for it was the season for the offering of flowers, but when he saw the dead and injured, he hastily got into his Imperial Palanquin and returned to the Rokujō Palace, and great was the anxiety of the Courtiers and Nobles of his train as they rode beside him. Setting up a pavilion in the south court of his Palace His Majesty took up his abode in it.

---

[255] *The six Shoji temples.* Hosshoji, Sonshoji, Saishoji, Enshoji, Seishoji, Enshoji.

The Emperor summoned his Phoenix Car and proceeded to the edge of the lake, while the other Princes sought refuge in different places, some in their palanquins and some in their cars. Then the Chief Astrologer came running hastily to the Palace with the information that a great earthquake might be expected to take place between the Hour of the Boar and the Hour of the Rat, (10 to 12. p.m.) that evening, whereupon all were struck with consternation. In former days, in the time of Montoku Tennō, in the great earthquake of the eighth day of the third month of the period Saiko, it is said that the head of the Buddha of Todaiji fell down; and in that of the second day of the fourth month of Tengyo that the Emperor left his Palace and took up his abode in a fifty foot pavilion that was erected for him in front of the Joneiden. As these things happened in ancient days who can tell how it was? And since then no such thing has been heard of. But since an Emperor of the Ten Virtues had left the Capital and been drowned, and his Ministers and Courtiers had been captured and brought back to Miyako, and been beheaded and exposed in the streets, or separated from their families and exiled to distant provinces, thoughtful people mourned and lamented, saying that the wrathful spirits of the Heike would be the ruin of the country.

Chapter III.

CONCERNING THE DYER.

On the twenty second day of the eighth month, Mongaku Shōnin of Takao, having discovered the real skull of the late Sama-no-kami Yoshitomo, hung it round his neck and set out for the Eastern Provinces, bringing with him also the head of Kamada Hyōye hung round the neck of one of his disciples. In the seventh month of the fourth year of Jisho he had brought some skull or other wrapped in white linen and showed it to Yoritomo, saying that it was his father's skull, in order to incite him to rebellion, and he had believed it was truly 10, and had risen and obtained the supremacy. The real one which he had now brought was found thus. A certain dyer, to whom the late Yoshitomo had showed kindness, employing him for a long time, had begged the head from the Kebiishi, when he saw it buried in front of the prison with no one to say the death prayers over it, and thinking that Yoritomo, though now in exile, might very likely emerge and become powerful in future, and make enquiries about it, he hid it in the temple of Engakuji on Higashi-yama. So when Mongaku heard of this he came down with it to Kamakura, bringing the dyer with him.

When Yoritomo heard that he was approaching the city he went out as far as the Katase-gawa to meet him, and then returned with him to Kamakura clad in mourning garb. Placing the priest on the floor above him, he stood in the courtyard below to receive the head, weeping bitterly the while. And all the feudal lords, both great and small, who witnessed the scene, moistened their sleeves with their tears. Then he cut out a certain steep cliff and built a temple there, that prayers might be said for the spirit of his father, and he gave it the name of Shochoji-in, And when the Court heard of it, Sashoben Kanetada was sent as Imperial Envoy to Kamakura to confer on the late Sama-no-kami Yoshitomo the title of Naidaijin of the Upper Second Rank. Thus the warlike prowess of Yoritomo not only exalted himself and his house to high honour, but obtained rank and title for the spirit of his departed parent.

Chapter IV.

EXILE OF THE TAIRA DAINAGON.

On the twenty third day of the ninth month a message came from Kamakura to the Court that all the Heike who were still left in the Capital should be exiled to various provinces. So the Taira Dainagon Tokitada was sent to Noto, Kurando-no-kami Nobumoto to Sado, Sanuki-no-Chūjō Tokizane to Aki; Hyobu-no-Shoyu Masaakira to Oki, Nii-no-Sozu Zenshin to Awa, Hoshoji-no-Shugyo No-en to Kazusa, Kyoju-bo-Ajari Yu-en to Bingo and Chūnagon-no-Risshi Chukai to Musashi. And so they set out on their various journeys with hearts full of sadness at parting, some for the waves of the Western Sea, some for the mists of the Eastern Barrier, knowing neither whither they were going nor when they would meet again. Then the Taira Dainagon Tokitada-no-Kyō betook himself to Yoshida to the former Imperial Consort Kenrei-mon in and said: "I have obtained leave from the officials to come and bid you farewell. I would have wished to have been able to remain near you in the Capital that I might look after your affairs, but today I must start for my place of banishment, and how anxious do I feel in thus going away to be uncertain henceforward of what will happen to you." And he wept bitterly. "Indeed," replied the ex-Empress, also in tears, "you are the only one who is left from our sad past, and when you are gone who will there be to whom I can look for sympathy?"

Now this Tokitada-no-Kyō was the son of Zo-Sadaijin Tokinobu Ko, and the grandson of Dewa-no-Zenji Tomonobu. He was the elder brother of the late Kenshun-mon in, the maternal uncle of the late Emperor Takakura and the younger brother of Hachijō-no-Nii Dono, the wife of the Lay priest Chancellor Kiyomori. All ranks and offices were at his disposal, so he quickly rose to be Dainagon of the Upper Second Rank. and three times held the office of Kebiishi-no-Bettō. While he held this office he arrested all the thieves and robbers and bandits and pirates of all provinces, and without any enquiry cut off their arms at the elbow, so that he was given the nickname of Aku-Bettō; and when Hanakata, the Groom of the Chamber, came with the Edict of the Ho o demanding the return of the Emperor and the Three Sacred Treasures, it was this Tokitada that had the characters 'Namikata,' branded on his face. For the sake of his late beloved Consort Kenshun mon in the Hō-ō had wished to show him favour, but this insult angered him greatly. The Hōgwan too, on account of their intimate relationship, did all he could for him, but it was of no avail, and so he was banished. His son Jiju Tokiie, who was then sixteen years old, escaped banishment and was luring with his uncle Saisho Tokimitsu, but the day before his father went into exile he went to his residence, and with his mother Sotsu-no-suke clung to his father's sleeve in his sorrow at being separated from him. "We must part at last anyhow;" said the Dainagon coldly, though indeed he was much affected. And so, growing old and feeble as he was, he had perforce to part from his beloved wife and son, and start out from the Capital he knew so well, looking back longingly at the Court as he began his journey to the Northern Provinces, of which as yet he knew but the name. And so he went on past Shiga and Karasaki, the bay of Mano and the beach of Katada; and here the Dainagon with tears in his eyes composed these lines;

"*Hardly again shall I see them casting the nets at Katata,*
Dripping with shining drops, like to the tears in my eyes."

Yesterday tossing in a small boat on the waves of the Western Sea with his load of anguish and resentment, today, buried under the snows of the North Country, his sorrow at parting piling up high as the clouds of his native Capital.

Chapter V.

THE EXECUTION OF TOSA BO.

Now there were ten Daimyos who had been accompanying Yoshitsune by the orders of Yoritomo, but when they found he was under suspicion, they took counsel together and one by one left him and returned to Kamakura. Since he was the younger brother of Yoritomo and the son of the same father, and had overthrown the Heike from Ichi-no-tani to Dan-no-ura, and restored the Sacred Mirror and the Sacred Gem without delay to the Capital, bringing peace and tranquillity to the whole realm, the Hōgwan expected to be granted some reward for his merit, and wondered what could be the reason that he was thus suspected, and consequently distrusted everybody from the

Emperor to the common people, until he afterwards learned that it was owing to the continued slanders of Kajiwara, who hated him on account of the ridicule he had sustained in the matter of the oar that spring at Watanabe in Settsu.

Now Yoritomo wished to strike at Yoshitsune quickly before he could gather any force together, but thought that if he sent his Daimyos with an army, the Hōgwan would certainly destroy the bridges at Uji and Seta, and then the Capital would be thrown into an uproar once more, which would be no good thing. So, after long consideration he summoned Tosa-bo Shoshun and said; "Do you go up to the Capital as if on pilgrimage, and smite him privily." So Tosa-bo made obeisance and immediately started off for Miyako, without even returning to own residence. On the twenty ninth day of the ninth month he arrived there. But as by the day after he had not visited the Hōgwan's residence, Yoshitsune, who had heard that he had come to the city, sent Musashi-bo-Benkei to fetch him.

When he was brought into his presence Yoshitsune enquired: "How now, Tosa-bo? Have you no letter from Kamakura Dono?" I have brought no letter with me," replied Tosa-bo, "but the lord of Kamakura gave me this message by word of mouth. Tell Yoshitsune that, since he is in Miyako, everything is quiet and there is nothing special to be done, but he must take every care to keep a strict guard." "That is not likely," retorted the Hōgwan. "You have been sent here to assassinate me. If he had sent his Daimyos with an army he thought I should have destroyed the bridges at Uji and Seta, and that would have caused an uproar in the Capital, which would have been a very bad thing; so he sent you as if on a pilgrimage to smite me privily, did he not?" "Why does your lordship speak in this way?" replied Tosa-bo, greatly astonished, "it is because of a trifling vow that I have at Kumano that I have come up to the Capital." "What do you think of my not being permitted to enter Kamakura on account of Kagetoki's slanders, and then being driven back here, Tosa-bo?" continued Yoshitsune. "About that affair I have no knowledge," replied the priest, "but I have not the least evil design against your lordship." And he offered to take a written oath that he meant no harm. "Whatever you do," said the Hōgwan, "I know you are in favour with Yoritomo." So, as things looked very black against him, to avert the present danger Tosa-bo then and there wrote seven oaths, and some of these he burned and drank mixed with water, and some he deposited in the sanctuary of a shrine, after which he went back and gathered together samurai from various provinces who had come up to the Capital on guard duty, with the intention of making his attack on the Hōgwan that very night.

Now there was a girl named Shizuka, the daughter of a Shirabyoshi called Iso-no-Zenji, whom Yoshitsune greatly loved, and she did not depart from his side either by night or day. And she now warned

Yoshitsune saying: "The streets are full of soldiers, and there seems no reason for the city guards to be in this commotion, for they have not been mustered by your orders. I think it must be the work of that priest who swore his oaths here today; would it not be well to send someone to find out?" So the Hōgwan sent two of the three or four boy attendants of the late Lay-priest Chancellor, whom he had retained in his service, to see what was toward, but though he waited some time they did not return. Then, thinking that it would be safer to send a woman, he bade one of his maid-servants go and see, and after a while she came running back saying: "Two youths who look like the boy attendants are lying dead in front of the gate of Tosa-bo's residence, and a lot of horses are standing there ready saddled, and a war pavilion has been pitched there, in which a number of warriors are mustered, helmeted and in full armour, with their bows bent and arrows ready on their backs, all prepared for an instant attack. They do not look at all like peaceful pilgrims." At this the Hōgwan snatched up his sword and ran out, while Shizuka seized his armour and flung it over his shoulders, but without waiting till it was more than half buckled on, he ran out to the middle gate, where his horse was standing ready saddled. Springing on to it; "Open the gate;" he shouted, and as it was opened and he stood expecting the foe every moment, at midnight Tosa-bo rode up to the front gate with fifty horsemen, all similarly accoutred, shouting their war-cry. Rising in his stirrups the Hōgwan shouted in aloud voice: "Let us see who there is in all Nippon who can best Yoshitsune in battle either by night or by day!" And he rode at them right and left, so that, fearing to be ridden down, they parted asunder and let him through.

Then Ise-no-Saburō Yoshimori, Mutsu-no-Sato Shirō-byōye Tadanobu, Eda-no-Genzo, Kumai-no-Tarō, Musashi-bo-Benkei, and the rest of the Hōgwan's men, all matchless in battle, hearing that an attack was being made on their master's residence, came running from their lodgings in all directions, and soon formed a band of some sixty or seventy horsemen, so that, though Tosa-bo and his men attacked fiercely, they were quickly routed without difficulty and many slain. Tosa-bo himself, seeing that all was lost, managed to escape somehow or other to the recesses of Mount Kurama; but as Kurama was an old haunt of Yoshitsune, he was soon caught, and brought to the Hōgwan's residence the next day. He had hidden himself in a place called Sōjō-ga-tani. He was clad in a hitatare of dyed cloth, and wore a suit of armour laced with black leather, with a Tokin or cowl on his head. Standing on the verandah, the Hōgwan thus addressed him as he was led into the courtyard beneath: "How now, Tosa-bo! You have not been long in going back on your oath." "As I swore it to suit my convenience, indeed I have not;" replied the priest. "That you should regard your lord's behest so loyally, and your own life so lightly, is truly admirable;" replied the Hōgwan, with tears streaming down his face; look here, sir priest, if you care for your life I will spare it and send you back to Kamakura." "This is indeed an unlooked for kindness." replied Tosa-bo, making a low obeisance, "but even if I should be willing, would my lord allow me to live? Since I am one of his priests, from the time that he specially chose me for this mission my life has been forfeit to him, and I know not if he will give it back to me. So the best kindness you can do me is to take off my head at once." So they took him out to the Rokujō-kawara and there beheaded him: and there was none who did not praise his conduct.

Chapter VI.

THE HŌGWAN LEAVES THE CAPITAL.

Now there was an inferior retainer named Adachi-no-Shinsaburo, whom Yoritomo had sent to Yoshitsune saying: "He is only a common servant, but he is a very clever fellow; so please employ him." And this was in order that he might see all that Yoshitsune did, and report it to Yoritomo. So when he saw how Tosa-bo had been executed, he fled with all speed to Kamakura and told the news. Then Yoritomo, greatly surprised, sent for his younger brother Mikawa-no-kami Noriyori and bade him lead an expedition against Yoshitsune, and he, though he declined many times, and pleaded that he was not capable of the undertaking, was at last fain to consent, and after making hasty preparations presented himself before Yoritomo to say farewell. "You too had better be careful not to behave like Kurō;" said Yoritomo to him, and this so alarmed him that he returned to his residence and took off his armour, and changed his mind about going to the Capital. In order to convince his brother of his innocence of any disloyalty, he wrote every day ten oaths to that effect, and read then out every evening in the courtyard before Yoritomo's mansion; so in a hundred days he wrote a thousand oaths, but all to no purpose, for Yoritomo had him put to death at last.

Then Yoritomo sent a force of sixty thousand horsemen under the command of Hojo-no-Shiro Tokimasa against Yoshitsune in the Capital, and when the Hōgwan heard of it he at first thought of destroying the bridges at Uji and Seta and resisting their advance, but instead of that he asked Ogata-no-Saburō Koreyoshi, who had commanded a sufficiently large force to prevent the Heike from entering Kyūshū, to permit him to take refuge in that island. "If you will hand over to me for execution my old enemy Kikuchi-no-Jirō Takanao, who is now in your house, I will gladly do so;" replied Ogata, and upon the Hōgwan readily consenting, he took him out to the Rokujō-kawara and beheaded him, after which he agreed to serve

Yoshitsune.

So on the second day of the eleventh month Kurō Taiyū Hōgwan Yoshitsune proceeded to the Palace of the Hō-ō and presented this petition by the hand of Okura-no-Kyō Yasutsune Ason: "Owing to the slanders of his retainers Yoritomo has given orders that I am to be put to death, and I had at first thought of destroying the bridges at Uji and Seta and holding out against him, but to act thus would cause a tumult in the Capital, and that would be a very great misfortune. So I wish to retire for a while to Kyūshū, and beg of His Majesty a Letter of Permission to do so." At this the Hō-ō was much troubled to know what to do, so he enquired of all the Courtiers what they thought. "If Yoshitsune remains in the Capital," they said, "we shall have a great army from the Eastern Provinces breaking into the city and despoiling; it, and there will be no end to the confusion; but if he retires for a while to Kyūshū we shall not have this to fear." So a Letter was issued from the Hō-ō's Court to Ogata-no-Saburō Koreyoshi, and also to the clans of Usuki, Hetsuki and Matsuura, that they should all place themselves at the disposal of Yoshitsune; and on the third day at the Hour of the Hare (6 a.m.), without causing the least trouble or disturbance in the Capital, he rode away with a force of some five hundred horse.

Now when Ota-no-Tarō Yorimoto of the Settsu Genji heard this he said to himself: "If I let one who is at variance with him pass by my gate quite freely, it will not be well for me when Yoritomo hears of it, so I had better draw bow against him." And lie rode out with the sixty horsemen of his force to a place called Kawarazu to attack the Hōgwan. Then the Hōgwan's men, turning and enveloping Ota and his sixty horsemen in their midst, set upon them with all their might, determined to let none escape, and when most of his men were slain, and he himself wounded and his horse shot through the belly, Ota himself was forced to seek safety in flight. So Yoshitsune's men cut off the heads of the twenty or so who had been left to hold the rear, and made a celebration in honour of the God of War, raising a joyous shout in their pleasure at such an auspicious beginning to their journey. That day they arrived at Daimotsu-no-ura in the province of Settsu, and on the next day they took ship from thence, but the west wind blew with such violence that the Hōgwan's ship was driven on to the shore of Sumiyoshi, and from there he fled and concealed himself in the mountains of Yoshino. There he was attacked by the monks of that place and again fled to Nara, but as the Nara monks were also hostile he returned again to the Capital and eventually sought refuge in the province of Mutsu.

Now the ten ladies whom the Hōgwan had brought with him from the Capital had had to be abandoned on the shore at Sumiyoshi, and they threw themselves down in despair on the sandy beach under the pines, and as they lay there pillowed on their long sleeves and with their hakamas all in disorder, the priests of the Sumiyoshi shrine took compassion on them, and putting them into litters sent them back to the Capital. As for the ships in which Ogata-no-Saburō Koreyoshi, on whom Yoshitsune chiefly relied, Shida-no-Saburō Zenjo Yoshinori, Bizen-no-kami Yukiie and the rest embarked, they were cast hither and thither on various shores and islands, so that none knew what had become of the others. And this west wind that blew so fiercely was said to be caused by the angry spirits of the Heike.

On the seventh day of the same month Hojo-no-Shirō Tokimasa arrived at Capital, and on the following day he proceeded to the Palace of the Hō-ō and petitioned: "Yoritomo begs that an Imperial Rescript he issued for the smiting of Iyo-no-kami Minamoto Yoshitsune, Bizen-no-kami Yukiie and Shida-no-Saburō Zenjo Yoshinori." And His Majesty was not long before he complied.

Thus on the second day, at the request of Yoshitsune, a Letter was issued by the Court in opposition to Yoritomo, and on the eighth day, at the request of Yoritomo, an Imperial Edict was issued to smite Yoshitsune. One thing was done in the morning and another at night, and the Empire was in a lamentable state of suspense.

Chapter VII.

YOSHIDA DAINAGON.

So the former Uhyōye-no-suke Yoritomo of Kamakura, having now become Sotsui-bushi of the whole land of Nippon, sent a request to the Court that he might levy a tax of so much rice on every tan of land in the country for the rations of his soldiers. "From of old," replied the Hō-ō, "we see it written in the Muryo-gi-kyo[256] that whosoever should subdue the enemies of the Throne should receive half the country, but even so it is not easy to grant it. Yoritomo's demand is excessive." But when he gathered the Courtiers and they held a council about the matter they decided thus: "What Yoritomo Kyō says is half right." So, as all the Courtiers were unanimous, the Hō-ō could do nothing, and after a while gave his consent. Then Shugo or Wardens were placed in all provinces, and Jito or Lords in all manors, and in this way no one was able to conceal so much as a single hair.

Now, though he had many adherents among the Courtiers, Yoritomo entrusted this matter and other such things to Yoshida no-Dainagon Tsunefusa-no-Kyō. And this Dainagon was said to be a very fine character. For when the Genji came into power, those of the Court who had been closely connected with the Heike sent letters and

---

[256] *Muryo gi-kiyo.* Part of the Hokke-kyo. But it is doubtful if such a statement is to be found in it.

messengers, and in various ways tried to curry favor with them, but this Dainagon alone did no such thing. And in the days of the Heike, when the Hō-ō was confined in the Seinan Detached Palace, it was this Dainagon and Hachijō-no-Chūnagon Nagakata-no-Kyō who were appointed Bettos of the Palace. He was the son of Gon-no-Uchuben Mitsufusa-no-Ason, and when he was but twelve years old his father died and left him an orphan, but he rose in rank and office without any check, being Kurando of the Fifth Rank, Emon-no-kami and Benkwan at once, after which he became successively Kurando-no-kami, Sangi, Daiben, Dazai-no-Sotsu, Chūnagon, and then Dainagon. He passed over the heads of many others, but was never himself passed over. People's good and evil deeds cannot be hid, as a gimlet goes through a bag. He was indeed a greatly respected Dainagon.

Chapter VIII.

CONCERNING ROKUDAI.

Now Hojo-no-Shirō Tokimasa was made Warden of Miyako to represent Yoritomo there, and in order that none of the male posterity of the Heike should escape him, he made proclamation that anyone, high or low, who could give him any information as to their whereabouts, should receive whatever he might wish. And, regrettable to say, many in the Capital, anxious to gain rewards, made search and gave information, so that many were discovered. So much so that they seized upon even the children of the lowest servants, if they were handsome and of fair complexion, declaring: "This is the son of such and such a Chūjō, or: "This is the heir of such and such a Shōshō:" and when the mother or father wept and lamented, they would say: "The foster-mother has said so;" or: "His nurse has told us: "and if they were quite young children they would be thrown into the water or buried alive, or if they were older they would be strangled or stabbed, so that the grief and lamentation of their mothers and foster-mothers was beyond compare. Hojo himself was pained at this wholesale slaughter, but as he had to obey orders he could do nothing.

Among these descendants was Rokudai Gozen, the heir of Komatsu-no-sammi-no-Chūjō Koremori-no-Kyō, who was now growing up, and as he was the grandson and heir, he searched everywhere to try and find him and put him to death, but all to no effect, and he was just about to return to Kamakura with his purpose unfulfilled, when a certain woman came to Rokuhara and said: "Westward from here, at a place called Shobu-dani, to the north of the mountain temple of Daigakuji which lies behind Henjoji, the wife and children of Komatsu-no-sammi-no-Chūjō Koremori are in hiding." Hojo was exceedingly pleased to hear this, and immediately sent someone to spy out the place. Going thither he found that in a certain temple building there were several women and children carefully concealed, and as he peeped through a chink in the fence he saw a white puppy run out, followed by a very handsome boy; then a woman who looked like his foster-mother came out hurriedly and drew him in again, exclaiming: "How terrible if anyone should see you!" This is certainly he, thought the spy, as he hastened back and told what he had seen, and the next day Hojo surrounded Shobu-dani with soldiers and sent a messenger to the temple saying: "I have heard that Rokudai Gozen, the son of Komatsu-no-sammi Chūjō Koremori, is in this place, and Hojo-no-Shirō Tokimasa, the representative of Kamakura Dono, wishes to see him, so please bring him forth at once." When his mother heard this her senses reeled so that for a while she knew nothing, and Saitō Go and Saitō Roku, the child's two faithful retainers, tried to find some way to escape with him, but when they saw the soldiers surrounding them on all sides, they knew it was no use.

Then his mother, holding the child in her arms, wept and lamented aloud, crying: "Kill me too! "And the foster-mother and the other ladies, falling down in front of her, added their voices to the sad chorus. For a long time they had kept quiet and had not raised their voices above a whisper for fear of discovery, but now all in the house wept and wailed loudly with one accord. Now Hojo was neither wood nor stone, and tears rose to his eyes as he stood waiting within hearing of the scene. Repressing his emotion he sent another messenger saying: "As the land is not yet quiet and safe, some violence might befall you, so Tokimasa himself has come to fetch the child. There is nothing to fear, so I pray you let him come at once." At this the child said to his mother: "As there is no help for it, it were better to send me at once, for otherwise the soldiers will break in to search for me, and that will be much worse; and even if I do go, I can soon ask leave of this I Hojo to let me come back again. So do not grieve so much." And while he tried to comfort her thus, as it must be, his mother dressed him and smoothed his hair, weeping as she did so, and just before he started she put into his hand a beautiful little rosary of black wood, saying:" "Take this, and be sure you repeat the Nembutsu as often as you can, that you may to Paradise." "Since I must part with you to-day," replied the boy as he took it," I wish if possible to go where my father is." At this his younger sister, who was about ten years old, cried out also: "I too want to go and see my father;" and she ran out after him, so that the foster-mother had to hold her back. Rokudai Gozen was twelve years old, but looked more grown up than most boys of fourteen or fifteen, and was very handsome and charming in his disposition. He tried hard to show a bold front to the enemy, but his tears ran down under the sleeve that he pressed to his face as he got into the palanquin, which then moved off surrounded by soldiers on all sides. Saitō Go and Saitō Roku walked on each side of their young master, and though Hojo made two of his men get off their horses for them to ride, they declined, and walked barefoot all the way from Daigakuji to Rokuhara. His mother and the other lady flung themselves on the ground, gazing up to heaven in an agony of longing.

Presently his mother said to the nurse: "They say that the children of the Heike are being sought out and put to death in various ways, some being drowned, and others buried, or strangled, or stabbed. I wonder how they will deal with our boy. As he is rather grown up I think they will certainly behead him. I have often seen children put out to nurse with foster-mothers, and even then parental affection is still strong; how much more when we have always kept our child with us ever since he was born, and never let him out of our sight for a minute, but his father and I have brought him up ourselves, regarding him as quite different from other children, and so when I was thus untimely bereft of his father, I had these two left to comfort me; and now, alas! I have only one. Ah, what shall I do? For these last three years I have never been free from anxiety, even for an hour, and though it was what I was expecting yet I did not think it would come thus yesterday or to day. You know how I have always relied on the power of Kwannon of Hase; and yet I must suffer his being snatched away from me like this. And they will not suffer him to live long!" And so she continued her plaint, pressing her sleeve to her face and sobbing incessantly. Even when night came her grief choked her throat and prevented her even from dozing, but after a while she said to the nurse: "Just now I fell to sleep for a moment and in a dream I saw my boy coming to me, riding on a white horse, and he came to my side and sat down respectfully, saying that he had got leave to come as he longed to see me so much; but then, to my great regret I started up suddenly, and when I searched beside me there was no one there. How short is a dream indeed, and how painful is the awaking." And the tears ran down her cheeks as she related it.

Thus the long night dragged by, and she ceased not to moisten her couch with her tears. But as all things must come to an end, at last the night watchman proclaimed the opening dawn, and as it broke, Saitō Roku came back, and in answer to the anxious enquiry of the lady, told her that the child was quite safe and had sent her a letter. Opening it she read as follows: "Thus far I am quite safe, but still I fear you must be very anxious. Please give my love to everybody." And when she read his words, written in such a manly style, she pressed the letter to her face without a word, and then cast herself on the ground with her head in her robe. As she remained thus for some time without stirring, Saitō Roku said: "Things are uncertain, even for an hour, so pray give me an answer that I may go back." So the lady, weeping, wrote a reply and gave it to him, and he bade her farewell and departed.

Then the foster-mother, impelled by restlessness of spirit, wandered out of the Daigakuji and was walking about aimlessly in the vicinity, weeping as she went, when she met someone who told her that behind there dwelt a priest of the mountain temple of Takao, called Mongaku-bo, who was very much trusted by Yoritomo in all matters, and that he wished to find a son of some Court lady to become his disciple. At this she was overjoyed, and at once making her way to Takao, she begged to see Mongaku and thus addressed him, weeping bitterly the while: "My young lord, whom I have carried in my arms since he was born, and who is now twelve years old, was yesterday carried away by the soldiers. Could not your reverence beg his life, and bring him up as your disciple?" And she fell down before the monk, weeping unrestrainedly, so that he knew not what to do.

Feeling compassion for her distress he asked her who the boy was. "It is the beloved child of the wife of Komatsu-no-sammi Chūjō Koremori-no-Kyō," she replied, "and we were bringing him up, but somebody must have said that he was the son of the Chūjō, so yesterday the soldiers came and took him." "Who was the warrior who took him?" asked the priest. "He said his name was Hojo-no-Shirō Tokimasa;" replied the lady. "Well I will go and see him;" declared Mongaku, and he went off there and then. At this the lady, though she did not entirely trust in the monk, felt somewhat relieved from the intense anxiety that had possessed her since the child was taken, and immediately hurried back to Daigakuji. "I thought you had gone somewhere to drown yourself," said the child's mother, "and I too was thinking I would like to throw myself into some river or other;" and then, in answer to her questions the nurse told her in detail all that she had done, and what the priest had said. "Ah, if the priest could beg his life, and bring him here so that I could see him once again!" she exclaimed, and her unceasing tears were this time tears of joy.

So the priest went to Rokuhara and asked about the matter. "It is the order of Kamakura Dono," said Hojo, "that every one of the male descendants of the Heike should be sought out and put to death, and among them is Rokudai Gozen, son of Komatsu-no-Chūjō Koremori. As he is growing up, and is moreover the last of the Heike line, his mother being, it is said, the daughter of the late Naka-no-Mikado Shin-Dainagon Narichika-no-Kyō I had special orders to take him and put him out of the way, but though I managed to find others of the family I could not find him by any means, and was going back to Kamakura empty handed, when unexpectedly I received news of him the day before yesterday, and yesterday went and brought him here; but indeed he is such a beautiful child that I am sorry I did not leave him where he was." "Well, may I see him?" asked Mongaku, and when he was taken to where the child was, he found him dressed in a double embroidered hitatare, holding in his hand the rosary of black wood. Such was the beauty of his hair and the elegance and nobility of his form and bearing, that he hardly looked like a creature of this world at all. Though his face was a little thin, and he had perchance not slept much that night, yet he looked indeed very lovable.

When the child caught sight of the priest his eyes filled with tears for some reason or other, and Mongaku too moistened the sleeve of his black robe. "However great an enemy he might become in the future," he thought "how could anyone put him to death now?" Then, turning to Hojo, he said: "It is no doubt a matter connected with a previous existence, but when I consider this child I am filled with a great pity for him. Will you not grant him a reprieve for twenty days, while I go down to Kamakura and obtain a pardon for him? When I went up to the Capital in former days to procure an Imperial Edict to establish the position of Yoritomo, as I travelled all night through the plains around the Fujikawa, I lost my way and was nearly washed away and drowned, and then after that I met with robbers in Mount Takashi, and barely escaping with my life managed to effect an entrance into the 'Prison Palace' of Fukuhara and receive the Edict from the Hō-ō. In recognition of this service Yoritomo promised that whatever request I might make of him at any time, he would surely grant it, and moreover I have done him many important services since then. It is no new thing that I say, but as I have valued my duty more than my life, Yoritomo will not forget it, unless his high position has puffed him up." And he set out for Kamakura at the dawn of that day.

Saitō Go and Saitō-Roku, regarding the monk as a living Buddha indeed, pressed their hands together and wept. They then returned to Daigakuji and acquainted the child's mother with all that had happened, to her very great joy. With regard to the decision of Yoritomo, they were in suspense as to what it would be, but were cheered by his life being spared for twenty days, and ascribing it to the power of Kwannon of Hase, they put their trust in that deity. So things went on, and the twenty days sped by like a dream, but the monk did not come back. "How can this be?" they said with sinking hearts, and all their grief and anxiety assailed them once again. Hojo also, as the twenty days that he had agreed to wait had passed, thought that Yoritomo had probably refused the pardon, and fretted impatiently at the delay, for he wished to start immediately for Kamakura. Saitō Go and Saitō Roku wrung their hands in despair, but as the monk had not returned, neither had he sent any messenger, they knew not what to think. So they went out to Daigakuji and reported, with tears streaming down their cheeks, that the monk had not come back and that Hojo was to start at break of day. The two ladies, who had felt very much cheered when the priest started out so hopefully, and who had also relied on the help of Kwannon, now began to lose heart again, as was but natural." Is there not some virtuous old man, "said the mother to the nurse," who could be found to take him to meet the monk on the road; for how terrible if he were to come back with the pardon after the child had already been put to death. What will they do? Do they mean to kill him soon?" "It looks as though they would do so at dawn," replied one of the "owing to the behaviour of Hojo's retainers in his residence. For in their pity and reluctance for such work some of them are weeping and some repeating the Nembutsu." "And how is the child looking?" asked his mother. "When anyone goes to see him, he seems quite unconcerned, telling his rosary, but when no one is looking he presses his sleeve to his face and weeps;" replied the retainer. "That is just like him," said his mother, "he is still young in years, but he has the heart of a man already; if there had been time I would have asked Hojo to live him leave to come back here once again, but today is already past the twentieth day, so I shall not be able to come to him or he to me. And I know not when I shall see him again; so how wretched must he be, thinking that tonight will be his last. And you, how will you fare?" "We will stay with him to the last, and if the worst happens, we will take his bones and bring them to the Holy Mount of Kōya, and then we will renounce the world and follow the Way, that we may pray for his happiness in the future life." And they sank down on the ground choked with tears. Then as the time grew late his mother said: "As matters are so uncertain, I pray you go back immediately;" so, weeping bitterly, they took leave and went.

So at dawn on the seventeenth day of the twelfth month Hojo-no-Shirō Tokimasa took the child Rokudai Gozen and departed from Miyako. Saitō Go and Saitō Roku went with him, walking on each side of the palanquin. Again Hojo bade two of his men dismount that they might ride, but they declined saying: "As it is the last time we are quite content;" and so they went their way barefoot, weeping tears of blood. Thus pitifully parted from his mother and nurse, looking back on the Imperial City as it lay beyond the clouds, as for the last time he set out on the road to the far-off Eastern Provinces, the state of the child's feelings can well be imagined. If one of the samurai quickened his pace, his heart sank, thinking he was coming to cut off his head; and if one of them chanced to speak to him: "Now is the end," he would guess in dismay. He thought it might be at Shi-no-miya-kawara, but they passed on through Sekiyama and came to the beach of Otsu. He wondered if it would not be at Awazu-no-hara, but by that time the dusk had already fallen. And so they went on, station by station and province by province until they came to the province of Suruga, where it seemed that his fleeting life would end.

At a place called Sembon-no-matsubara the palanquin was set down and the young lord ordered to get out, a leather mat being spread for him to sit on. Then Hojo hastily sprang from his horse, and approaching the child spoke as follows: "I have brought you thus far because I thought we might meet the monk on the way, but if I take you over the Hakone mountains I know not what Kamakura Dono would say. So I shall say that I executed you in the province of Ōmi. As this was fore ordained from a previous life, how is it possible anyhow to escape it?" To this Rokudai made no reply, but calling Saitō Go and Saitō Roku he said: "Ah, do not go back to Miyako and tell them that I have been beheaded by the way. They will find it out in the end, but if they hear it now their grief and lamentations will be a hindrance to me in the after life. So tell them you have accompanied me as far as Kamakura." And as they listened to his words, the two of them were dissolved in tears. By and by Saitō Go overcame his feelings and replied: "After our lord has become a god or Buddha we shall never again in this life return to Miyako." And repressing his tears he bowed to the ground.

Then the young lord, seeing that his time was come, pulled back with his beautiful little hand the long hair that hung about his shoulders, whereat the soldiers of the guard exclaimed "See how he is yet master of himself;" and they all moistened the sleeves of their armour. Then, looking toward the west, he joined his hands together, and repeating the Nembutsu in aloud voice ten times, stretched out his neck for the blow. Then Kano-no-Kudo Saburo Chikatoshi, who had been chosen as the executioner, seized his sword and moved round behind him from the left, and was just about to strike, when his eyes darkened and his senses reeled, so that he could not see where to aim his weapon. "I cannot do it," he exclaimed, hardly knowing what he did: "pray choose someone else;" and he threw down his sword and withdrew.

Then as they cast about to find someone to take his place, there appeared a priest in black robes, riding a cream coloured horse which he was whipping up furiously; and as the people round about called out to him: "See the handsome young lord whom Hojo Dono is just beheading in the pine wood," and ran thronging to see the sight, he waved his whip at them anxiously, and in his excitement and suspense pulled off his hat and beckoned to them with it.

Then, as Hojo stood waiting to see what was the reason, the priest rode up, sprang down from his horse and exclaimed "The young lord is reprieved; here are instructions from Yoritomo. "Hojo took the document and read: "Concerning Rokudai Gozen, the son of Komatsu-no-sammi Chūjō Kore-mori-no-Kyō whom you have arrested: he is reprieved at the request of Mongaku-bo, the priest of Takao; let there be no mistake. To Hojo-no-Shirō Dono. Yoritomo." Hojo read it through several times, ejaculating: "Marvellous! Marvellous!" and then put it away. Saitō Go and Saitō Roku, it is unnecessary to say, and even Hojo's own retainers, shed tears of joy and relief.

Chapter IX.

HASE ROKUDAI.

Mongaku's thus appearing and declaring: "The young lord is reprieved," was indeed a brave sight. "When Yoritomo at first declared that, as his father the Sammi Chūjō Dono had been in command in many battles, he could not pardon him, Whoever might ask it," said Mongaku, "I reproached him again and again for his heartless ingratitude, and demanded to know why I had lost his favour, but it was all in vain, and he went off to hunt at Nasuno. But I followed him to his hunting-ground, and at last prevailed on him to grant my request. That was why I was so late." "When the twenty days that we agreed upon had passed," replied Hojo, "I concluded that Kamakura Dono was unwilling to spare him. How fortunate it is that I brought him with me and met you here, and so was saved from error." And he provided Saitō Go and Saitō Roku with spare saddled horses that he had, and sent them back to the Capital. After he had gone some distance with them to see them on their way, he took leave of them saying: "Since I have many weighty matters to report at Kamakura, I will now say farewell." And so he resumed his journey to the eastward. He was a very gentle warrior indeed.

So Mongaku Shōnin of Takao took charge of the child Rokudai and travelled day and night towards the Capital, so that when he reached the vicinity of Atsuta in Owari the year had already come to an end, and it was the evening of the fifth day of the new year when they arrived in the Capital. Making their way to a residence that Mongaku had in Nijo Inokuma, they stopped there that the child might rest awhile, and it was midnight when they reached the Daigakuji. They knocked at the gate, but no one came, and there was no sound. Only the little white dog that Rokudai had kept came running out through a hole in the plastered wall, wagging its tail in its joy at seeing him again. "Where is my mother?" he asked it pathetically, whereupon Saitō Go and Saitō Roku climbed over the wall and searched everywhere, but it did not seem as though anyone had been there recently. "It was only to see my mother again that I wished to live," exclaimed the child, bursting into tears unmindful of everyone, "but what is the use of my living now?"

The rest of the night they spent there, and at dawn they enquired of one who lived near, who told them: "Last year they went to the Dai-Butsu, but since the new year we hear they are living at Hase-dera. So Saitō Roku hastened at once to Hase and told the lady what had happened, whereupon, without a moment's delay she started for the Capital and came to Daigakuji. "Ah, Rokudai Gozen," she exclaimed when she saw him, "is this indeed real, or is it a dream? But do you quickly renounce the world." But Mongaku, thinking it a pity, did not make him a monk, but took him to Takao and built a little cell where his mother could live with him also. In former days also there are like examples of the great mercy and compassion of Kwannon that succours both sinners and righteous alike. It was indeed a wondrous blessing.

Chapter X.

THE EXECUTION OF ROKUDAI.

So Rokudai Gozen grew up thus until he was fourteen or fifteen years old, when he was so beautiful that he shed as it were a radiance all about him. But that his mother should have said in admiration: "If we were in power he would now be an officer of the Konoe," was too outspoken. At a favourable opportunity Yoritomo sent to Mongaku saying: "What kind of youth is Rokudai Gozen, son of the Sammi Chūjō Koremori whom you have in charge? Do you think of him as you did of me formerly, that he is one able to subdue the enemies of the Throne, or avenge his father's shame?" "Do not trouble yourself about him," replied Mongaku, "for he is a spiritless and stupid fellow." Still Kamakura Dono was not quite satisfied. "If there were a rebellion that priest would be for it," he remarked ominously; "and though it is not likely in my lifetime, I don't know about my posterity." When this reached his mother's ear she again urged him to become a monk without further delay. So; about the spring of the fifth year of Bun-ji, cutting off his beautiful hair short at the neck, and attired in a robe and hakama of drab colour, with his travelling-box on his back, he started out on a pilgrimage; and Saitō Go and Saitō Roku accompanied their master in similar garb. First ascending Mount Kōya, he visited Takiguchi Nyūdō the virtuous priest who had helped his father to attain enlightenment and instructed him in the Way, and from him heard all particulars of his father's becoming a monk, and his subsequent death. Then, wishing to retrace his father's steps, he went on to Kumano, and looking across at the island of Yamanari which is in front of the shrine called Hama-no-miya, to which his father had rowed, he greatly desired to cross over to it, but on account of the contrary wind he was not able. As he stood gazing over at it he wondered in what place it was that his father had sunk, and felt as though he wished to ask the white crested waves that came rolling in on the shore. Regarding the sand of the beach tenderly, as being perchance the bones of his parent, his sleeves were bedraggled with tears, and ever moist like those of the sea damp garments of the fishermen. Passing all that night on the beach, he spent his time reading the Sutras and repeating the Nembutsu, drawing with his finger the likeness of a Buddha in the sand; and when dawn appeared, summoning a priest, he dedicated all the merit he had acquired to the enlightenment of his father's spirit, and returned to the Capital with his heart full of sadness.

Now the Emperor at this time was Go-Toba-no-in, and he thought of nothing but pleasure, so that all the affairs of state were in the hands of the mother of the Empress, and people lamented greatly at it. Because the King of Go loved Kenkaku, those who suffered hurt in the kingdom were not few; and because Sai-yu captivated the King of Go, many ladies of the Court died of starvation. And because those of lower rank will always imitate the pleasures of those above them, all those of understanding loudly lamented the danger to the Empire. But the second Imperial Prince Go-Takakura-in was much devoted to statesmanship, and very diligent in intellectual, matters, and Mongaku, shrewd priest that he was, was very fond of meddling in the management of affairs, so that he was extremely anxious to set this Prince on the Throne; but while Yoritomo was alive, he did take any steps.

Then, on the thirteenth day of the first month of the tenth year of Kenkyu, Yoritomo died at the age of fifty three, and Mongaku raised a revolt forthwith; but it was immediately discovered, and officers were sent to Nijo Inokuma to arrest Mongaku, who was then more than eighty years of age, and banish him to the province of Oki. As they were leading him away from the Capital he burst out: "What does that Ball-loving Youth mean by letting them take an old man like me, who does not know whether he will live from one day to the next, and send him under Imperial Chastisement to a place like Oki, far away from the Capital. You had better see that someone is sent there to bring me back pretty quickly!" And so, dancing with rage and reviling strongly, Mongaku was sent into exile. It was because this Emperor was so fond of playing ball that Mongaku called him by this contemptuous name. It was very strange that afterwards, in the period Sho-kyu, on account of his many rebellions, though there were many other provinces, this Emperor should have also been banished to the far off isles of Oki. And it is said that the angry ghost of Mongaku wrought many evil things there; continually appearing in the Emperor's Presence, and saying all kinds of things to him.

Now Rokudai Gozen, who was now styled Sammi-no-Zenji, had continued to live in retirement in the recesses of Takao. "The son of such a man, and the disciple of such a man," quoth Yoritomo, "though he may have shaved his head, is not likely to have shaved his heart." And he sent a petition to the Court that he might be taken and executed, and An-Hōgwan Sukekane arrested him and sent him down to the Eastern Provinces, where Okabe-no-Gon-no-kami Yasutsuna of the province of Suruga was ordered to take him and behead him at Tagoe-gawa in the province of Sagami. That his life was spared from his thirteenth year to beyond his thirtieth was solely through the mercy of Kwannon of Hase. And with the death of Sammi-no-Zenji there perished the last of the Heike.

Kancho Maki.

Chapter I.

THE FORMER EMPRESS BECOMES A NUN.

The Former Empress Kenrei-mon-in went to Yoshida at the foot of Higashi-yama, and entered the cell of a monk of Nara called Chūnagon-no-Hoin Keiei. It was old and dilapidated, with the garden overgrown with weeds, and shinobu-grass clustering thickly on the roof. The curtains were gone and the bedchamber exposed, and there was nothing to keep out the wind and rain. Though there were many kinds of flowers, there was none to care for them, and though the moon streamed in every night, no one was there to gaze at it. She, who had formerly spent her time in the Jewel Halls and within the Brocade Curtain, now suffered the unspeakable hardships of dwelling in this mouldering cell, bereft of all her old companions, like a fish on the dry land or a bird torn from its nest, and she yearned fondly for the times she had spent tossing on the heaving billows. As the poet says:[257] "She longs for the far-off waves of the ocean, and the clouds of the limitless Western Sea; the moss grows thick on the reed-thatched hut; tears fall as the moon shines in the garden on Higashi-yama."

So on the first day of the fifth month of the first year of Bun-ji, the Former Empress cut short her hair and was instructed in the Way by Ashobo-no-Shonin Insei of Chorakuji, and for the customary offering she presented him with the robe of the Emperor Antoku, which he had worn up to the time of his death, so that the perfume yet clung to it. She had brought it with her to the Capital from the far-off Western Provinces, intending to keep it as a memorial of him and never let it leave her person, but now, as she had nothing else to offer, and thinking moreover that it would be an aid to his Enlightenment, weeping bitterly she handed it to him. The Shonin was so affected that he could utter no word, but pressing the sleeve of his black robe to his face, he retired weeping from the Imperial Presence. And this robe was afterwards woven into a banner and suspended in front of the Buddha of the Chorakuji.

This Empress was appointed Imperial Consort at the age of fifteen, and at sixteen was raised to the rank of Empress. She was ever by the Emperor's side, helping him in the government by day, and the only

---

[257] *as the poet says.* Tachibana Chokkan, in the Ro-ei-shu.

sharer of his love by night. At the age of twenty two she bore a Prince who was named as the Heir to the Throne, and when he assumed the Imperial Dignity she became Retired Empress and took the name of Kenrei-mon-in. She was the daughter of the Lay-priest Chancellor Kiyomori, and as she had thus become the mother of the Emperor she was held in great reverence by all the people. She was twenty nine years old this year, and the beauty of her fair face was not yet dimmed, neither was the elegance of her slender form impaired; but what now availed the loveliness of her hair? So she renounced this world and became a nun, but even when she had entered the True Way her grief was not assuaged. Ever she seemed to see before her the figures of the Emperor and the Nii Dono and the others as they sank in the waves, and never in this life could she forget those melancholy scenes, so she wondered why she had remained alive to bear such sorrows, and her tears were never dried.

Even in the short nights of the fifth month, it was not easy to keep awake, but if she did not fall asleep she did not dream of those who had passed away. Faintly the shadow of her single light fell on the wall outside, and all night the dismal drumming of the rain sounded on the lattice of the windows. Surely the Imperial Consorts who were shut up in the Joyo Palace in China were not more wretched. And how did it remind her of the beloved past, this orange tree in blossom by the eaves, that the former tenant had brought and planted there. As its heavy perfume was wafted into her chamber, and the note of the cuckoo was borne once and again to her ears, this ancient verse came into her mind, and she wrote it on the lid of her inkstone:

"*Hark! the cuckoo seeks the fragrant scent of the orange,*
Where are those that I loved P Whither, departed? he cries."

The rest of the Court Ladies, who had thrown themselves into the sea, but had not drowned themselves with the same determination as the Nii Dono and the wife of Echizen-no-sammi Michimori, had been roughly dragged out by the Genji soldiers and brought back to the Capital, as has been before related. And these, both young and old, all became nuns and were living in concealment in far-away valleys and dells in the mountains, wretched and emaciated in appearance and quite unrecognisable as their former selves. The places where they lived have gone up in smoke, and the empty site is all that remains. They have all turned into overgrown moorland, and no former intimate ever comes nigh them. All is as unfamiliar as his home to one who is bewitched by fairies and returns to it after seven generations.

Chapter II.

THE FORMER EMPRESS GOES TO OHARA.

Now as her former poor abode was ruined in the great earthquake of the ninth day of the seventh month, and its outer wall fell down, the Former Empress had nowhere to live. How had the days altered from when the green-clad Palace Guards stood continually before her gate, for now the tumbledown wall, more bedewed with moisture than the outside moorland, seemed as if it understood the change of times, and resented the incessant shrilling of the insects. So though the nights grew longer and longer, the Empress could not sleep, but brooded continually over her melancholy condition, and this, added to the natural sadness of autumn, became almost too much for her to bear. In this changed world there was none to feel sympathy for her, and all those of her affinity were gone, so that none were left to cherish her in her need.

Only the wife of Reizei-no-Dainagon Takafusa-no-Kyo and the wife of Shichijo-no-Shuri-no-Taiyu Nobutaka-no-Kyo used to send and assist her secretly. "Ah," she exclaimed, "in former days who would have ever dreamed that I should have come to accept anything from such as these?" And as she wept afresh at the thought, the ladies who accompanied her could not refrain from moistening their sleeves. Since her present dwelling was too near the Capital, and attracted the eyes of curious passersby, she thought she would like to go to some place far away in the depths of the mountains to spend her days remote from all sound of unrest, but for some time she was unable to hear of any. Then a certain lady came to Yoshida and said to her: "There is a place northward from here, in the mountains of Ohara, called Jakko-in, and it is very quiet." "A mountain abode is very lonely, it is true," she answered, "but it is good to live in, for it is remote from the troubles of this world." So, as she desired it, the matter was settled, and the wives of Nobutaka and Takafusa sent a palanquin to fetch her.

Thus at the end of the ninth month she proceeded to the temple of Jakko-in. As they went along she gazed at the beauty of the autumn tints, while the sun sank gradually behind the mountains. The dreary boom of the evening bell of the wayside temple, and the thick-lying dew on the grass as they passed drew tears from her eyes, while the fierce gale whirled the leaves from the trees in all directions. Suddenly the sky grew dark and the autumn drizzle began to fall; the cry of a deer sounded faintly and the shrilling of the insects was incessant. Nothing was wanting to add to the sum of her afflictions, which seemed indeed such as few had been made to suffer. Even when she was driven about from shore to shore and from island to island her melancholy was not to be compared to this. The place she had chosen to dwell in was ancient and surrounded by mossy rocks; the reeds in the garden were now covered with hoar-frost instead of dew, and when she gazed on the faded hue of the withered chrysanthemums by the wall, she could hardly fail to be reminded of her own condition. Entering before the Buddha she prayed: "For the Sacred Spirit of the Emperor, that it may attain perfect Buddhahood, and for the departed spirits of all the Heike, that they may quickly enter the Way of Salvation." But still the image of the late Emperor was impressed on her mind, and wherever she might be, and in what world soever, she thought she could never forget it. So they built for her a small cell ten feet square beside the Jakko-in, and in it were two rooms, in one of which she put her shrine of Buddha, and in the other she slept; and there she spent her time continually repeating the Nembutsu and performing the Buddhist services, both by night and by day. And it happened that once, on the fifth day of the tenth month, that she heard the sound as of someone treading on the oak leaves which had fallen and covered the garden. "Who can it be," she exclaimed, "that comes to disturb one who has thus renounced the world? Do you go and see; for I will conceal myself if it be anyone I do not wish to meet." So one of the ladies went to look, and it was only a young stag that had passed that way. "Who is it? Who is it?" asked the Empress, whereupon the lady Dainagon-no-suke-no-Tsubone composed these lines in reply:

> "*Who is the stranger whose steps are heard so nigh to our dwelling?*
> '*Tis but a stag whose tread rustles the leaves of the vale.*"

And the Empress was so much affected by this verse that she wrote it on the shoji of the window.

And as she thus passed her tedious hours, even in this dreary spot she found many subjects for comparison. The trees that grew by the eaves of her cell she likened to the Seven Precious Trees of Paradise, and the water that collected in the hollows of the rocks she compared to the Lake of the Eight Virtues in the Pure Land. Impermanence is as the flowers of spring that so quickly fall when the wind blows, and Worldly Illusion like the moon of autumn so easily lost behind the clouds. She thought how she had diverted herself with the flowers in the Shoyoden, and how on, the day after they had been scattered by the wind, and how in the Choshuden they had made poems to the moon, and its light had been hidden by the clouds. Formerly she had lived delicately in the Jewel Halls, and couches of brocade had been spread for her in the Golden Palace, but now she dwelt in a hut of brushwood and thatch, and the sleeves of her robe were dishevelled and tear-stained.

Chapter III.

THE HŌ-Ō PROCEEDS TO OHARA.

Thus in the spring of the second year of Bun-ji the Hō-ō expressed a wish to go to Ohara and see the place where Kenrei-mon-in was living in retirement, but the second and third months were stormy and the cold still lingered, neither did the snow melt on the mountains nor the icicles thaw in the valleys. Thus the spring passed and the summer came, and the festival of Karoo was already over when His Majesty proceeded to the recesses of Ohara. Though the visit was incognito, the Sadaisho Tokudaiji, the Dainagon Kwazan-in and the Gon-Chūnagon Tsuchi-mikado accompanied His Majesty, with six of the higher Courtiers and eight of lower rank, beside several of the Imperial Guards. As they went by way of Kurama, His Majesty was able to visit the temple of Fudarakuji, built at Fukayabu at Kiyohara, and the place where the Consort of the Emperor Go-Reizei-in had formerly lived in retirement at Ono, after which the Imperial Palanquin proceeded on its way. The white clouds on the distant mountains reminded them of the cherry blossoms that had fallen, while the green leaves on the twigs seemed to regret the passing of spring. It was past the twentieth day of the fourth month, so the summer grasses had grown up thickly, and as they parted them on the little-trodden road, His Majesty, who had never been there before, was much affected by the lonely uninhabited look of the place.

At the foot of the western mountains they came to a small temple. This was the Jakko-in. It might be well described by the lines: "Its roof-tiles[258] were broken and mist was its only incense; the doors had fallen from their hinges and the beams of the moon were its sanctuary lamps." But the pond and trees of its ancient garden were dignified; the young grass had grown thick, and the slender shoots of the willow were all hanging in confusion, while the floating water-plants on the pond might be mistaken for spread out brocade. On the island the purple hue of the flowering wistaria mingled with the green of the pine-tree, while the late-blooming cherry among the green leaves was more rare than the early blossoms. From the eight-fold clouds of the yamabuki that was flowering in profusion on the bank came the call of the cuckoo, a note of welcome in honour of His Majesty's visit.

When the Hō-ō saw it he composed these lines:

---

[258] *Its roof-tiles*, etc. An unknown quotation.

"*When on the pond's clear waters the cherry-tree scatters its*
    blossoms,
Thick on the limpia wave ripple the clusters of flowers."

Pleasant was the sound of the water as it fell from the clefts of the
time-worn rocks, and the ivied walls and beetling crags would have
defied the brush of the painter. When his Majesty came to the cell of
the former Empress, ivy was growing on the eaves and the morning-
glory was climbing up them; the hare's-foot fern and the day lily
mingled together, and here and there was a useless gourd-plant; here
was the grass that grew thick in the path of Gan-en, and the white goose
foot that keeps men at a distance, and here too was the rain that
moistened the door of Gen-ken. The cedar boards of the roof were
gaping, so that the rain, the hoar-frost, and the dew of evening vied
with the moon beams in gaining entrance, and the place appeared well-
nigh uninhabitable. Behind was the mountain and in front was the
moor, and the bamboo grasses rustled loudly in the wind. As is the way
with those who have no friends in the world, she seldom heard any
news from Miyako, but what she did hear was the cry of the monkeys
as they sprang from tree to tree, and the sound of the wood-cutter's axe,
for few people there were that came there.

Then the Hō-ō called to the inmate, but there was no answer, but
after a while a withered-looking old nun appeared of whom he
enquired: "Whither has the former Empress deigned to go?" "Over
there to the mountain to pick some flowers," was the reply. "How hard
it is," said His Majesty, "that since she has thus renounced the world,
she has no one to perform such services for her." "Since this fate has
come upon her in accordance with the Five Precepts and the Ten
Virtues," replied the nun, "why should she spare herself the austerities
of mortifying her flesh? In the Ingwa Kyo it is written: "If you wish to
know the cause in the former life, look at the effect in the present life;
and it you wish to know the effect in the future life, look at the cause in
the present one." And if she knows the cause and effect of both past
and future lives, there is nothing at all for her to lament. In former days
Prince Siddartha at the age of nineteen went forth from Gaya and dwelt
at the foot of Mount Dantaloka; covering himself with the leaves of
trees, going up the peaks to get firewood and down into the valleys to
draw water, by the merit of his austerities and mortifications at last he
attained to perfect Buddhahood." Looking at this nun the Hō-ō noticed
that she was clothed in pieces of silk and cotton put together roughly
anyhow, and thinking it strange that one of such an appearance should
speak thus, he asked her who she was. For some time she could answer
nothing, but only wept, but after a while she controlled her feelings and
replied: "I am ashamed to say so, but I am Awa-no-Naiji, daughter of

the late Shonagon Nyudo Shinzei, and my mother was Kii-no-Nii. As
your Majesty was formerly so kind to me, the reason why you do not
now recognise me must be that I have become old and infirm." And she
pressed her sleeve to her face, unable to control herself any longer: a
sad sight indeed. "Can it be so?" exclaimed the Hō-ō; "and you are
truly Awa-no-Naiji? I did not recognise you, but however one may
think, it all seems like a dream." And his voice became choked with
sobs, while the Courtiers who accompanied him were moved also,
some saying that what she said was very strange, while others thought
it quite natural. And the Hō-ō looked about him hither and thither, and
the plants of the garden, heavy with .dew. fell against the boundary
wall, and the surface of the rice-fields was covered with water so that
there seemed not even room for a snipe to perch; and His Majesty went
to the cell of the former Empress and opened the shoji and looked in. In
one chamber were the images of the Three Bosatsu, Amida, Kwannon
and Seishi, and in the hand of Amida, who stood in the middle, was a
cord of five colours. On the left was a picture of Fugen, and on the right
of Zendo Kwasho, beside which hung a portrait of the Late Emperor.
There were also eight rolls of the Hokke Kyō and nine volumes of the
Amida Kyō. Instead of the perfume of orchid and musk, the smoke of
incense filled the air. The merit of Jomyo Koji,[259] who in a nine foot
square cell ranged in order thirty two thousand floors and invited all the
Buddhas of the Ten Quarters, could hardly have been greater. On the
shoji were stuck texts from all the Sutras, written on coloured paper,
and among them was one written at Shoryosen in China by Oe-no-
Sadamoto, which ran thus: "Sounds of celestial melody are heard afar
off, and from the regions of the setting sun Amida comes to save
mankind." A little removed from these was a verse that seemed to be
from the former Empress's own pen:

"*Who would have dreamed that from here I should view the moon
of the Palace?
Far from the haunts of men, lone in the depths of the hills.*"

Then on the other side he saw what appeared to be her bedchamber. On a bamboo pole hung her robes of hempen cloth, besides
some bed-quilts of paper, and when he thought of the countless
beautiful robes of silk gauze and rich brocade, wrought of the stuffs
both of China and of her own land, that she had worn in the dream-like
days of her dominion, the tears coursed down His Imperial cheeks, and
the Courtiers of his escort also could not help moistening their sleeves
at these evidences of her altered condition.

---

[259] *Jomyo Koji.* Vimalakirtti; for this miracle see Dickens, note on the same subject
in his translation of the Ho-jo-ki.

Presently two nuns clad in dark robes were seen making their way slowly and painfully down through the rough rocks of the mountain side, and on the Hō-ō enquiring who they were, the old nun replied: "The one carrying a basket of mountain-azalias on her arm is the former Empress, and the one who has the load of bracken for firewood is Dainagon-no-suke-no-Tsubone, the daughter of Torikai-no-Chūnagon Korezane, and adopted daughter of Gojo-no-Dainagon Kunitsuna, who was nurse to the late Emperor." As she spoke she burst into tears, and the Hō-ō and his Courtiers also applied their sleeves to their eyes.

The former Empress, since she was living apart from the world in this way, was so overwhelmed with shame at seeing them that she would gladly have hidden herself somewhere to avoid them, but she could not. Every evening she girt up her long sleeves to draw the water for the offering, and early every morning they were wet and bedraggled with the mountain dew. So, as she could not again retrace her steps to the mountain, neither was she able to get into her cell, the old nun came to her as she stood dumbfounded and took her basket from her hands.

Chapter IV.

THE SIX PATHS.[260]

"Since you have renounced the world," said Awa-no-Naiji, "what does it matter about your appearance? I pray you come and greet His Majesty, for he will soon return." So the former Empress repressed her emotion and entered her cell, "Before my window in prayer I await the coming of Amida; and at my lowly door I look for the Saviour of mankind; but Your Majesty's gracious visit I did not expect," she said, and the Hō-ō, looking upon her, thus replied: "Even those who live for eighty thousand kalpas in the highest heaven of the World of Formlessness must surely die, and the denizens of the Six Celestial Worlds of Desire cannot escape the Five Changes. The wondrous bliss of the city of delight of the heavens of Indra, and the passionless serenity of the high pavilions of the mid-Dyana world of the heavens of Brahma, even these, like the rewards of dreamland or the pleasures of a vision, eternally change and dissolve, turning and revolving like the wheels of a chariot. And since the Celestial Beings are subject to the Five Changes, how shall men escape? But I hope that you still hear tidings from your old acquaintances, for you must think much of old times." "There are none from whom I hear anything now," replied the Empress, "except from the wives of Nobutaka and of Takafusa, who continually send me help; but in former days I never even dreamed of

---

[260] *Six Paths.* Hell, Pretas, Beasts, Asuras, Men and Heaven.

being assisted by people such as they." And as she spoke het tears flowed, and her lady companions also hid their faces in their sleeves.

After a while she controlled her emotion and continued: "Though I need not say that being reduced to such a condition has been a great grief to me, yet I feel gladness on account of my enlightenment in the next world. By the help of S'akya Muni, reverently relying on the Great Vow of Amida, I may escape the troubles of the Five Hindrances and the Three Obediences, and in this latter age purify the Six Senses, so that, fixing my hopes on the highest heaven, and fervently praying for the enlightenment of our whole family, I may await the coming of the Saving Host. But the thing that I can never forget is the image of the late Emperor, and even though I try to bear his loss with patience, I cannot, for truly there is nothing that wrings the heart like parental affection, And so I pass both day and night in ceaseless prayer for his enlightenment, and this will be my guide also in the True Way." "Verily this our Empire is but a petty country," answered the Hō-ō," but since by observance of the Ten Virtues he became its Emperor, everything must be in accordance with his will. And though all who are born in an age when the Law of Buddha has been widely spread, if they have the desire to practise the Law, without doubt will be hereafter reborn in bliss, yet when I regard your present condition, though it is in accordance with the vanity of human affairs, I cannot but be overcome with grief." And as he spoke His Majesty burst into tears. "Born the daughter of the Taira Chancellor," continued the former Empress," and having become the mother of the Emperor, the whole Empire lay in the hollow of my hand. Clad in my varied robes of state, from the New Year Festival to the Year End Ceremonies I was surrounded by the Great Ministers of State and the Courtiers in brilliant throng, even as above the clouds the Six Heavens of Desire and the Four Dhyana Heavens are encircled by eight myriads of lesser heavens. Dwelling in the Seiryoden and the Shishinden behind the Jewel Curtain, I gladdened my eyes in spring with the blossoms of the Imperial Cherry Tree. In the hot months of summer I refreshed myself with crystal streams, and in the autumn I viewed the moon in the midst of my ladies. In the cold nights of winter soft bed-quilts were heaped up to warm me, and I thought that I had only to wish for the draught of immortality, and the magic potion of eternal life and youth brought from Horai the Elysian isle, for it to be immediately forthcoming. So full was my life of joy and happiness, both by day and by night, that perchance even in heaven nothing could surpass it.

Then in the autumn of Ju-ei, when Yoshinaka came up to attack us, after setting fire to their ancient homes, our family fled from the Capital where they had lived so long, looking sadly back at the Imperial Palace. Going down to the shore of Suma and Akashi, of which I before knew only the name, we set sail on the boundless ocean, and so from island to island and from shore to shore, our sleeves wet with the salt spray by day, and the cry of the sea-birds mingling with our sobs by night, we rowed about seeking some favourable refuge, but never forgetting our ancient home. Left thus with none to help us, the anguish of the Five Changes of our dissolution came upon us. We speak of the 'Pain of the Grief of Parting' and the 'Pain of the Regret of Meeting,' and both of these in one I have known to the full. For when we came to Dazaifu in the island of Kyushu, thinking that there we might find safety for a while, Koreyoshi drove us out again, so that we could find no rest for our foot throughout all the length and breadth of the land. And so the next autumn arrived, and we who had always been wont to view the moon from the sacred enclosure of the Nine-fold Palace, now spent our nights watching it on the eight-fold sea-road. And in the tenth month, seeing that the Genji had driven us from the Capital, and we had been expelled from Kyushu by Koreyoshi, so that we were like a fish in a net having no place whither to escape, the Chujo Kiyomune, hating to live any longer, threw himself into the sea in despair. And this was but the beginning of our afflictions. Tossing on the waves by day, and spending our sleepless nights in the ships, we had no tribute of rice with which to prepare the Imperial Food, and sometimes, when we wished to prepare it, we had no water with which to do so. Afloat on the vast ocean we could not drink its salt water, and thus we underwent all the suffering of the Preta world. Then, after we had won two fights at Muroyama and Mizushima, the spirits of our family were revived, and building a fortress at Ichi-no-tani in the province of Settsu, all the Courtiers and Nobles doffed their court robes and clad themselves in armour for the fight, and the din of battle was incessant both by day and night, even like unto the battle of the Asuras with Indra and his Devas. Then in our flight after the defeat at Ichi-no-tani, parents were left behind by their children and wives separated from their husbands, and if we saw a fishing boat in the offing we trembled lest it should be a ship of the enemy, while a flock of white herons in the pine-trees threw us into panic lest it should be the white flag of the Genji. And at last, when in the fight at Moji, Akama and Dan-no-ura she saw that our doom was sealed, the Nii-no-Ama weeping exclaimed: "Now it seems our last hour has come, and in this fight there is little hope of any of the men surviving. Even if any of our distant relations are left alive they will scarcely be able to perform the services for our departed spirits, but from of old time it has been the custom to spare the women, so you must live to pray for the spirit of the Emperor, and I beg you also to say a prayer for my future salvation." And as in a dream we listened to her words, of a sudden a great wind blew, and the drifting mist came down upon us, so that the hearts of the warriors were confounded, and in the face of heaven they could do nothing. Then, as the Nii-no-Ama took the Emperor into her arms and went to the gunwale of the vessel, with a look of anxiety on his face he enquired of her: "Where is it that you are going to take me, Amaze?" Turning to her youthful Sovereign with tears streaming down her cheeks, she answered: "Perchance Our Lord does not know it, but though through the merit of the Ten Virtues practised in former lives you have been reborn to the. Imperial Throne in this world, yet, by the power of some evil karma, destiny now claims you. So now turn to the east, and bid farewell to the deity of the Great Shrine of Ise, and then to the west, and say the Nembutsu, that Amida Buddha and the Holy Ones may come to welcome you to the Pure Western Land. This land is called small as a grain of millet, but yet is it now but a vale of misery. There is a Pure Land of happiness beneath the waves, another Capital where no sorrow in Thither it is that I am taking Our Lord. "And thus comforting him, and binding his long hair up in his dove-coloured robe, blinded with tears the child-Sovereign put his beautiful little hands together, and turned first to the east to say farewell to the deity of Ise and to Sho-Hachimangu, and then to the west and repeated the Nembutsu, after which the Nii-no-Ama, holding him tightly in her arms, leaped with her Sovereign into the sea. My eyes darkened and my heart stood still, and it is a thing I can never forget or bear to think of. And at that moment from all those who still lived there went up so great and terrible a cry, that the shrieks of all the damned burning amid the hottest hell of Avichi could not exceed it. And so, after being roughly dragged out of the sea by the soldiers, as I was being sent back again to the Capital, I came to the shore of Akashi in the province of Harima. And as I chanced to fall asleep there for a space, I saw in a dream as it were our former Palace, but of greater and more surpassing beauty, and there sat our Former Emperor with all the Courtiers and Nobles of our house ranged about him in all their ceremonial grace and dignity; such a sight as I had not seen since we left our ancient Capital. And when I asked where this place might be, the Nii-no-Ama answered and said: "This is called Ryugu, the Palace of the Dragon King of the sea." "Ah, how blessed!" I replied, "and is it then a land where is no more sorrow?" "In the" Ryu-chiku Kyo[261] you may read," she said, "and never neglect to pray fervently for our future happiness." And as she said this I awoke, and since that time I have done nothing but read the Sutras and say the prayers for their future bliss. And all this, I think, is nothing else but the Six Paths." "In China," said the Hō-ō, "Genzo Sanzo[262] saw the Six Paths before he received enlightenment, and in this country Nichizo Shonin,[263] by the power of Zo-o Gongen,[264] is said to have seen them. That you have been permitted to have gazed on them with mortal eyes is a blessing

---

[261] *Ryu-chiku-kyo.* This reference is obscure.
[262] *Genzo Sanzo.* The Chinese priest Hiuen Tsiang.
[263] *Nichizo Shonin.* A famous Shingon priest who lived in the period En-ki.
[264] *Zo-o Gongen.* Kongo Zo-o, a deity of Mt. Yoshino in Yamato.

indeed."

Chapter V.

THE PASSING AWAY OF THE FORMER EMPRESS.

But the boom of the bell of Jakko-in proclaimed the closing day as the evening sun began to sink in the west, and His Majesty, full of regret at saying farewell, set out on his return journey with tears in his eyes. The former Empress, her mind occupied in spite of herself with thoughts of her bygone days, and shedding on the sleeve of her robe the tears she could not restrain, stood watching the Imperial Procession until she could see it no more, and then, again entering her cell, she prostrated herself before the Buddha to pray that the Sacred Spirit of the former Emperor might attain complete Buddhahood, and that the departed spirits of all the Heike might quickly enter the Way of Salvation. In former days she turned to the east and prostrated herself before the deity of the Great Shrine of Ise and Sho-Hachimangu to pity; "That the Precious Life of the Emperor may be prolonged a thousand and ten thousand ages;" but now she sadly turned to the west and prayed: "That the Departed Spirit may be reborn in one of the Buddha Lands."

To express the regret and affection she still felt for her past life, the Empress wrote these verses on the shoji of her cell:

> "*When shall I learn once more, what I now for so long have forgotten,*
> *How things go in the Court, scenes that I long to review?*" "*Now that the things of the past have vanished away into dreamland,*
> *So from this brushwood cell, soon may I too disappear.*"

Moreover Tokudaiji-no-Sadaisho Sanesada Ko, one of the Courtiers who accompanied the Hō-ō, also wrote these lines on one of the posts of the cell:

> "*Once our Sovereign's face shone forth as clear as the moon-beams,*
> *But in the mountain vale, hid is the light of the moon.*"

And while the former Empress was weeping and meditating on the past and the future with pain mixed with pleasure, the cry of the mountain cuckoo sounded twice or thrice as the bird flew by, and suggested to her these lines:

"Cuckoo, why do you come to measure your plaint with my anguish?
So in this fleeting world, what am I too but a voice?"

Thus of the twenty survivors of the Heike who were taken alive, some were paraded through the streets and beheaded, and some were exiled to distant provinces, far from their wives and children: with the exception of Ike-no-Dainagon there was not one left living in the Capital. Of the forty and more ladies who were left nothing is known. They were taken in by their kinsfolk and looked after by their relations. With their hearts full of concealed regrets they spent their days in lamentation. Those in high places, up to the Emperor within the Jewel Curtain, were filled with disquiet, while the common people, down to the dweller in the hut of brushwood, could find no rest. Husband and wife were parted and far remote from the Palace, while parent and child knew not each other's abode. And all this was because of the many evil deeds of the Lay-priest Chancellor Kiyomori which he continually committed, in condemning people to death and banishing them, and dismissing them from office and appropriating their emoluments, without either regard for the Emperor on his Throne, or pity for the people beneath him. So certain is it that the good or evil deeds of the fathers will descend upon the heads of the children.

But the former Empress continued to live on vainly for some years, till at length she fell ill and took to her bed. She had been awaiting it for a long time, and so now she took in her hand the cord of five colours that was fastened to the hand of the Buddha, and repeated the Nembutsu; "Namu Amida Nyorai, Lord who guidest us to the Paradise of the West, in remembrance of thy Great Vow, I beseech thee receive me into the Pure Land." And as she thus prayed, Dainagon-no-suke-no-Tsubone and Awa-no-Naiji, standing on each side of her couch, lifted up their voices in lamentation at their sad parting. And as the voice of her prayer grew weaker and weaker, a purple cloud of splendour grew visible in the west, and an unknown scent of wondrous incense filled the cell, while celestial strains of music were heard from above, and thus, about the middle of the second month of the second year of Ken-kyu, the former Empress Kenrei-mon-in breathed her last.

The two ladies, who had never left her side since the day that she had been chosen as Imperial Consort, were plunged into the depths of despair at this parting from their mistress, and as their relations and connections had all disappeared, and there was none to help them, they had nothing left but the performance of the Buddhist services. And at last they too, like the Dragon girl[265] who attained enlightenment, and

---

[265] *the lady Idaike.* The queen Vaidehi, wife of Bimbisara king of Magadha, and

like the lady Idaike,[266] also departed this life to be reborn in bliss.

The Book of Swords.

Hai-ko[267] received the sword Zoku-ro of Kibo,[268] and therewith slew the white serpent, and gained the Imperial Throne and a famous name. Shi-Ko[269] took the dirk of Kei-ka,[270] and with it slew the Emissary of Yen, thereby fulfilling a brilliant destiny. The authority of the White Standard and the Golden Axe,[271] the might of bow and horse and arrow and stone, the Five Rules of Strategy and the Four Kinds of Benevolence, these are the methods of ruling a country and the foundations of a lasting sway. But swords are the weapons worthy of the highest praise.[272]

Now in Nippon there are many famous swords. There are the Sacred Swords Totsuka-no-Tsurugi, the Ten-handbreadth Sword, Hige-kiri, the Beard-cutter, Hiza-maru, the Knee-cutter, and Kogarasu, the Little Crow. And concerning the origin of Hige-kiri and Hiza-maru, it is thus related. Seiwa Tenno, the fifty sixth Earthly Sovereign, had many sons, and of these Princes the sixth, named Sadazumi Shinno, had a son Tsunemoto Roku-Son-O, whose eldest son Tada no Mitsunaga Kazusa-no-kami was the first to take the name of Genji. Being appointed by Imperial Edict to protect the Empire, Mitsunaga exclaimed; "How can I protect the Empire unless I have a good sword?" So he procured iron and had smiths summoned, but when they had forged the swords, there were none that he found to his liking. While he was wondering what to do, someone told him that there was a smith who had come from abroad, who had been working for many years at Tsuchiyama in the district of Mikusa in the province of Chikuzen. So he ordered that he should be summoned, and they brought him to the Capital, but though he also forged many swords, not one of them found favour in the eyes of Mitsunaga, so there was nothing for him to do but to return with his purpose unfulfilled. "Alas," said he, "if I go back thus, after having made this long journey from

---

mother of Ajatsattru who imprisoned her. At her earnest desire to hear the doctrine, Buddha miraculously flew to her prison and preached to her.

[266] *Dragon girl* or Naga maiden. Another example of a woman obtaining enlightenment, a thing that was regarded as difficult on account of the Five Hindrances, i.e. that woman cannot become either Brahma, Indra, Mara, a Tchakravartti or a Buddha.

[267] Hai-ko, Peh-Kung, afterwards known as Kao-tsu of Han, (Kan-no-Ko-so).

[268] Kibo 貴坊 Unknown. One text has 貴防 perhaps read 鬼防 Demon-repelling, Dr. Okada.

[269] Shi-ko. She-Huang-Ti.

[270] Kei-ka. Cf. Vol V, Ch. 7.

[271] The White Standard and Golden Axe. Insignia of a Chinese General.

[272] This first paragraph, which is written in Chinese prose, is not found in many copies, and seems to be a late addition.

far-off Tsukushi to no effect, what will be left of my fame as a craftsman? From ancient days those who have desired anything of the Gods and Buddhas have had recourse to prayer to obtain it." And he betook himself to the shrine of Hachiman and prayed: "Kimyo-chorai Hachiman Dai-Bosatsu! Grant that I may make a sword such as I wish, and I will become a vessel at thy disposal." This vow he wrote and offered in the deepest sincerity, and when seven days had passed, a divine answer came to him in the night, saying: "I have had compassion on you in respect to your desire. Go now forthwith, and forge the iron for sixty days, after which you will snake two swords of the finest quality." Greatly rejoiced at this significant dream, the craftsman went forth from the shrine, and carefully selecting and fusing the iron, he worked at it and forged it for sixty days, sc that at length he produced two swords of the finest quality, two feet seven inches long, comparable even to the three foot blade of Ko-so of Kan.

Mitsunaka was greatly pleased with them, and had them tried on two criminals, whereat one cut through to the beard, so he named it Hige-kiri, or Beard-cutter, while the other cut through the knees also, and this he named Hiza-maru or Knee-divider. So with these two blades he ruled the Empire, and the very trees and herbs inclined before him. And so in due time he was succeeded by his eldest son Yorimitsu, in whose time many extraordinary things happened. And one of these strange things was the disappearance of many people. They did not die, but while in a room surrounded by many others, without being seen to get up or depart, they would suddenly vanish as if blotted out. And as none knew whither they had gone, or could hear where they were, fear seized on all, and from the Sovereign to the common people everyone was in indescribable confusion and panic. On enquiring more closely into the matter, it transpired that in the days of the Emperor Saga Tenno, the daughter of a certain Courtier of high rank was so overcome by jealousy that she went to the shrine of Kibune, and secluded herself there for seven days, praying thus: "Kimyo-chorai, Kibune Daimyojin! In answer to my seven days prayer and seclusion, grant that living I may be changed into a demon, that so I may be able to kill the woman of whom I am jealous." Then the Myojin had compassion on her and answered: "I am indeed sorry for your condition. If in truth you wish to become a demon, you must change your appearance and go and bathe yourself in the Ujikawa from the third to the seventh day." Then the lady returned rejoicing to the Capital, and secluding herself in an unfrequented spot, divided her long hair into five tresses, and made it into five horns. She put vermilion on her face, and reddened her body, on her head she placed a tripod, to the legs of which she fastened torches, holding also in her mouth another torch flaming at both ends. In this guise she rushed out through the Yamato highway to the south after dark when people had retired, and when they saw her thus with face and body red and eyebrows painted thick and black with dye, while five jets of flame flared out from her head, they never doubted that she was a demon, and fell down in the streets beside themselves with fear, some even dying in the excess of their terror. Then she went to the Ujikawa and bathed herself in its waters between the third and seventh day, whereupon, according to the promise of the Kibune Myojin, she was transformed living into a demon. And she it is that is known as Uji-no-Hashi-hime, or the Lady of the Bridge of Uji. And thus she was able to seize and slay not only the woman of whom she was jealous and the man who had spurned her, but all their relations and connexions, high and low, male and female. And when she wished to seize a man she would change into a woman, and if she would take a woman she would become a man, so that all the people of the Capital of all ranks shut the doors of their houses after the Hour of the Monkey, (4. p.m.) and would neither go forth nor allow anyone to come in.

Now at this time Settsu-no-kami Yorimitsu had four famous retainers who were as his four Deva Kings, and they were Tsuna, Kintoki, Sadamichi and Suetake; and of these the mightiest was Tsuna. As he was born at Yoshida in the province of Musashi he was also called Yoshida Genji. Now it chanced that Yorimitsu had some small matter to be done at Omiya in Ichijo, and he sent Tsuna as his messenger. As it was after dark he gave him the sword Higekiri and bade him take one of his horses. And so he went and made enquiry at the place, and was on his way back again with the reply, when, as he was crossing the bridge once more at Ichijo Horikawa, he saw at the eastern end a girl who seemed to be about twenty, with a skin as white as snow and a most graceful figure, dressed in a robe of a plum-red colour with an amulet bag hung round her neck, and a volume of the Sutras carried in her sleeve. She was quite alone and unaccompanied, and was going along to the south as Tsuna passed the western end of the bridge and rode clattering across. "Whither are you going," she called confidingly to him, "I am going to Gojo, but as it is getting so dark, I feel frightened, so will you not see me on my way?" "Take my horse, then," replied Tsuna, immediately springing to the ground; and as she seemed pleased at the offer, he took her up in his arms and set her in the saddle. Thus they went along the eastern end of Horikawa to the south until they came within a couple of tan of Ogimachi, when the maiden turned back, saying; "I really have no particular business at Gojo: I live outside the city; so will you not be kind enough to accompany me thus far?" "Indeed I will escort you wherever you wish," replied Tsuna; when suddenly she changed her beautiful form into the shape of a hideous demon, and crying out: "The place I am going to is Otagi-yama; "she seized him by the queue and flew off with him through the air toward the north west. Tsuna, without the least trepidation, at once drew Hige-kiri and slashed upward with it, cutting clean through the arm of the demon; and thus released fell headlong until he alighted on the roof of the gallery of the shrine of Kitano, while the demon, with its arm cut off, flew away towards Otagi. Then Tsuna jumped down from the gallery and pulled off the demon's hand that was still gripping his queue, and lo! it was changed from its snow white hue and was now of an exceeding blackness, covered everywhere thickly with white hairs that looked like silver wire. When he brought it and showed it to Yorimitsu, he was exceedingly astonished, and thinking it a very strange happening, he summoned the diviner Harima-no-kami Abe-no-Seimei, and asked him what was to be done. "Let Tsuna strictly seclude himself in his house for seven days," he advised, "and let him keep the hand of the demon carefully shut up and guarded, while he occupies himself with reading the Nio Sutra." Tsuna did so, and when six days had already passed, at dusk someone came knocking at the door of his house, and when he enquired who was there, the voice of his foster mother replied that it was she who had come from her home at Watanabe to see him. Now this foster mother was the aunt of Tsuna. Knowing that it was not, right to talk at such a time, he went to the gate and said: "I am glad to see you after such a long time, but I am now undergoing a religious seclusion for seven days, and today is but the sixth day, so until tomorrow is over I cannot see anyone soever. I pray you stay somewhere until, the day after tomorrow, and then I will gladly see you." At this she burst into tears; "What am I to do?" she exclaimed; "Is it for this that I took you in as soon as you were born, and brought you up? My rest. was often broken at night, and I chose the damp places to sleep on myself that you might rest in the dry; and so, until you were four or five years old no bitter wind was suffered to blow upon you, and day and night I prayed that I might live to see you grow up to be preeminent among men. And now my prayers are answered, and in the house of our lord Settsu-no-kami Dono there is none to equal you. And as your fame is in the mouths of all, both high and low, I have rejoiced greatly, but until now I have never been able to traverse the long country road to see you. But there is no pain like that caused by parental affection, and of late I have many times had bad dreams about you, so fearing that some evil might have befallen you, I have come all the way from Watanabe to see you, and now you will not allow me even to enter your gate. How could I have loved such an ungrateful son? "Then Tsuna, unable to withstand her arguments any longer, opened the gate and brought her in. At this she was very glad and for some time they talked about her journey and about what she meant to do henceforth, after which she asked him what was the reason of his seven days' seclusion, and as he could hardly conceal it, he told her everything as it had happened. When she had heard it all she declared that he had been quite right to take every precaution, and regretted that she had been angry owing to not having known it, "But" she continued," parents are like protecting deities to their children, as the proverb goes, so I will think no more of it. But what kind of a thing is a demon's hand? I should much like to see it." "I would willingly show it to you," replied Tsuna, "but I must keep it shut up until the seventh day is over, so after tomorrow is past I will let you see it." "Oh, very well; it doesn't matter at all; "I don't want to see it," she answered shortly, "for I intend to start home again before dawn." Seeing her displeasure, however, Tsuna opened the box and brought it out and showed it to her. "Ah, how horrible!" she exclaimed, looking at it again and again, "and so that is what a demon's hand is like." And suddenly standing up, she became transformed into a horrible demon, and, crying out: "That is my hand; I will take it;" she kicked out the gable of the roof and flew up into the sky, flashing fire as she went. And that is the reason that the Watanabe clan always build their roofs without any gable, and make them like a garden-house. Now though Tsuna thus lost the demon's hand, and his seclusion was made of none effect, yet by the power of the Nio Sutra he was preserved from harm. And after cutting off the demon's hand, the name of the sword was changed from Hige-kiri to Oni-maru (Demon-queller).

During the summer of that year Yorimitsu fell sick of an ague, from which he could get no relief by any means; and after some time it recurred every day with burning heat and pains in the head, and thus he lay, sorely tormented, as it were between heaven and earth; and so he continued for the space of thirty days. Now it happened one night that he was a little better and the fever had abated somewhat, so that the four faithful retainers, who had been nursing him, had retired to the guard room to sleep a while. As it grew somewhat late, Yorimitsu saw, from the shadow of the dim light in his chamber, the form of a tall priest, some seven feet high, coming stealthily up towards him, holding a rope to throw over him. Yorimitsu sprang up in surprise, crying out: "Who are you, you rascal, who dares to take a rope to Yorimitsu?" And as he did so he caught up the sword Hiza-maru, that stood by the side of his pillow, and made a cut at him. Aroused by the noise, the Four Deva Kings came running in with all speed to enquire what it was, whereupon Yorimitsu told them what had taken place, and when they looked beneath the lampstand there was blood spilt there. Searching further with lights in their hands, they saw that there was a trail of blood from the doors of the chamber out on to the verandah, and when they followed this up, they found that it led to a mound at the back of the shrine of Kitano, and there stopped. So they dug into the mound, and there was a great spider, four feet across, which they seized and brought back with them. "Ugh!" exclaimed Yorimitsu when he saw it, "how strange to have been tormented by a horrible thing like this for thirty days! You had better expose it on the highroad." So they stuck it on an iron spit and took it to the river bed and there left it: and from this time Hiza-maru was known as Kumo-kiri (Spider-cutter), and after the days of Yorimitsu it passed into the hands of Dewa-no-kami Yorimoto.

In the fifth year of the period Tenki, Iyo-no-kami Yoriyoshi, the eldest son of Kawachi-no-kami Yorinobu, the younger brother of Yorimitsu, was appointed Mutsu-no-kami and ordered to undertake the subjection of the brothers Kuriyagawa-no-Jiro Abe-no-Sadato, and Tori-no-Umi-no-Saburo Muneto of Mutsu, who had made insurrection, and on this occasion Yorimoto was bidden by the Emperor to hand over to him Oni-maru and Kumo-kiri, the two treasure swords of the Genji. "But these blades have been handed down as ancestral heirlooms for three generations from my grandfather Tada-no-Mitsunaka," replied Yorimoto," and ought to be passed on to my son, so I feel very loath to part with them." But as his remonstrance was not listened to, at last he had to give up the swords to Yoriyoshi. Then Yoriyoshi set out for Mutsu, and after fighting for nine years he has victorious, taking the head of Sadato and bringing Muneto back as a prisoner to the Capital. Sadato was nine feet five inches in height and Muneto six feet four, so, when he was brought to the house of Yoriyoshi, all the Nobles and Courtiers went there to divert themselves with the sight of the strange Eastern Barbarian, and one of them in jest broke off a twig of plum blossom, and asked Muneto what it was. Immediately he replied in these lines:

"This is what in our land is called the flower of the plum tree;
What, to you call it at Court? Seemingly you do not know."

Whereupon they went away again crestfallen. Muneto was eventually banished to Kyushu, where there are many of his descendants still living at the present day. They are the Matsuura clan. The two swords passed from Yoriyoshi to his son Hachimantaro Yoshiie, and he, hearing that Takehira and Munehira in the province of Dewa had fortified themselves at Yamakita and Kanazawa and rebelled, hastened thither to put them down, but though he was a daring and courageous warrior, it was three years before he was able to conquer them. So, adding the nine years campaign of Yoriyoshi to this, these swords did battle for twelve years, and always, by reason of the virtue that was in them, the enemy was defeated.

Yoshiie had many children, but his eldest son Tsushima-no-Kami Yoshichika was sent to Izumo to quell a rebellion there, and was slain by Inaba-no-kami Masamori, and neither his second son Kawachi-no-Hangwan Yoshitada nor his third Shikibu-no-Taiyu Yoshikuni received the two swords, but they were given to the fourth son Rokujo-no-Hangwan Tameyoshi. When he was fourteen years old his uncle Mino-no-kami Yoshitsuna revolted, and he was sent to attack him. When Yoshitsuna heard that his own nephew Tameyoshi was marching against him, he cut off his queue and surrendered. This also was through the virtue of the swords. Again, when he was eighteen years old, some rebel priests of Nara made a confederacy against the Throne and marched on the Capital, many myriads strong, whereupon Tameyoshi with only sixteen horsemen rode out against them to Kurikoyama, and by the might of the two blades, drove them back again. On this occasion a certain Yamahoshi composed this comic verse:

"*Down cane the Nara monks as far as Kurikoyama.*;
There a few soldiers appeared: rapidly captured the lot."

This satire irritated the monks of Nara, and while they were considering what answer they could make to it, they heard that some monks of Hieizan had been tricked by a certain Awa-no-Josa and put into prison, so they commemorated it in these lines:

"*Why thus easily duped by the wiles of Awa-no-Josa*;
Foolish monks of Hid, how do you find it in jail?"

So, as a reward for thus having made his uncle prisoner at the age of fourteen, Tameyoshi was appointed to be Sakon-no-Shokan, and for his loyalty in having repelled the Nara monks at the age of eighteen he was made Hyoye-no-Jo: at thirty eight he became Saemon, and at thirty nine Kebiishi. Afterwards he set his heart on becoming Governor of Mutsu, but this province was a place of ill-omen for him, since his grandfather Yoriyoshi had been fighting there for nine years, and his father Yoshiie for three; so that it was thought that the people would still feel enmity against the family, and if Tameyoshi were appointed to govern it disorder might ensue, so they asked him to take another province instead. But he replied that if he could not have his ancestral province he did not want any at all, and so the matter ended by his receiving none.

Now Tameyoshi had forty six children by various mothers, and he had a consort also at Kumano, who had a daughter called the maid of Tatsutahara. And it happened once that the Hō-ō Go-Shirakawa made a pilgrimage to Kumano and enquired if there was a Betto there; and when they told him that there was not, he said that this was not as it should be, and bade them elect one.

Now there were two clans at Kumamo called Ui and Susuki, whose ancestors had come over to this country as the right and left wings of the Gongen when he flew over from Magadha in India, and they had taken possession of Kumano and behaved themselves as they pleased without regard to anyone. And the Susuki planned to make a certain Yamabushi, who came there to pray and offer flowers before the shrine, the Betto. He protested that he was not fit for the office, but they constrained him, and this was the origin of Kyoshin Betto. Then they said that a Betto must be hereditary, so that he must not live as a priest, but take a wife. Looking about to find one for him, they thought that Tameyoshi's daughter, the Maid of Tatsutahara, would do very well, so they married her to him. When Tameyoshi heard of it he was displeased, at it, saying: "The man who becomes my son-in-law ought to be a warrior of distinction among the Taira or Minamoto clans. Those who hold the office of Betto or Shugyo of temples and shrines may be good men or not; I hear they are chosen from the crowd on account of their religious merit, but I think it very strange conduct that she should allow herself to be mated with such a fellow who has no future before him, and send me no word of it: she is a most unfilial daughter." Then the two swords that had been handed down to Tameyoshi made noises all night long; and the noise made by Oni-maru was like the roaring of a lion, while that made by Kumo-giri was like the hissing of a snake. So they changed the name of Oni-maru to Shishi-no-ko (Lion cub), and that of Kumo-giri to Hoe-maru (Roarer). At this time it was noised abroad that the Genji and Heike had taken up hostile positions, and there would be a battle, so within the Capital there was great confusion. As the news soon penetrated to the remotest mountain and province, it was not long before Kyoshin Betto heard it. "I may be unfilial," said he, "but at a time like this I will cast in my lot with him. and perhaps he will pardon my neglect." So he gathered all the priests of all ranks who were living at his shrine, and who could bear arms, and rode up to the Capital with some ten thousand horsemen. When people saw them they exclaimed: "What kind of a man is this? In the provinces of Kii and Izumi we do not remember to have heard of a great leader like this." But when they enquired more closely, they heard that it was Tameyoshi's son-in-law, Kyoshin, the Betto of Kumano. When his father in law heard that he had come to join him, he declared that he was a very worthy fellow, though he knew nothing about his name or lineage. And when he afterwards ascertained that he was the youngest grandson of Sanekata Chujo, and by birth by no means beneath himself, he was sorry he had not troubled to meet him till now. So he forgave him and received him, and in recognition of his good will towards himself, presented him the ancestral sword Hoe-maru as a wedding gift. But Kyoshin Betto, declaring that such an one as he was not worthy to possess the hereditary blade of the Genji, offered it to the shrine of the Gongen. And Tameyoshi, thus bereft of one of his swords, felt as though he had lost a hand, so he summoned his favourite sword smith from the province of Harima, and bade him forge a blade that should be the exact counterpart of Shishi-no-ko. The smith made one of the finest temper, and Tameyoshi was exceedingly pleased with it, and as he fitted it with 'menuki' made in the shape of

crows, he named it Ko-garasu, or 'Little Crow.' So he treasured these
two blades, Shishi-no-ko and Ko-garasu, as being of equal worth, but
Ko-garasu was two bu longer than the other. And it happened one day
that he drew both of them and placed them up against the shoji of the
room where he was, when, without anyone touching them, they fell
down with a great clatter, and when he took them and looked to see
why they had fallen, and if they were damaged, he perceived that Ko-
garasu, which had erstwhile appeared to be longer by two bu, was now
the same length as Shishi-no-ko. "Strange!" he thought, "how can this
be?" But when he examined the point to see whether it was broken or
cut off, there was no sign of either thing. Still wondering, he looked at
the hilt, but the menuki were not disturbed, so he removed the blade
from the hilt and behold! two bu of the tang inside it had been newly
cut away, while, when he pushed out the menuki, they seemed to be
lower down. Concluding, therefore, that Shishi no ko had cut the piece
off, he changed its name to Tomo-kiri, or Comrade-cutter. Thereafter,
being advanced in years and infirm, and considering that the swords
could be of no further use to him, he handed them on to his heir
Shimozuke-no-mi Yoshitomo. Then, when the war of the Hogen period
began, Yoshitomo was summoned to the Emperor's Palace, while
Tameyoshi went to that of the Retired Emperor with his six other sons.
On the eleventh day of the seventh month of the year of Hogen the
battle began at the hour of the Tiger, (4. a.m.) and at the hour of the
Dragon, (8. a.m.) it ended; for in three hours the army of the Retired
Emperor was shattered and defeated. Then Tameyoshi fled to Hieizan,
and becoming a recluse changed his name to Gi-ho-bo while his son
Yoshitomo, anxious to save his father's life, sought earnestly to obtain
his pardon; but since he was an enemy of the Throne it was of no avail,
and after a while, to his infinite sorrow he received the news that he had
been put to death. Yoshitomo himself, as a reward for his services on
this occasion, was promoted to be Sama-no-kami, but of his six
brothers who had been summoned by their father, five were slain, and
one only, Tametomo, escaped. He, after some time had elapsed, was
brought from Tane in Kyushu and banished to the province of Izu, but
in the end he too was executed, and his four sons with him.

Thus Yoshitomo alone survived, but in the first year of Heiji he
was persuaded by Aku-Uemon-no-kami Nobuyori to raise a rebellion.
He had many sons, but of them all he singled out the third, Uhyoye-no-
suke Yoritomo, to succeed him as the head of the house in the next
generation, and at the age of thirteen he clad him in a suit of armour
called Suzushi, and girt on him the sword Tomo-kiri, giving him the
preeminence over all the others. But he was defeated in the battle that
ensued, and being an enemy of the Throne he fled from the Capital and
took refuge at Hira in the west of the province of Omi, and there all
night he murmured against the god Hachiman-Dai-bosatsu; "In former

days with this blade I smote my enemies and laid them low as grass in the wind, but now the virtue has gone from it, and the Dai-bosatsu has surely forsaken me, else should I not have been thus impotent in the battle. My grandfather Yoshiie became as the son of the Dai-bosatsu, and was called after him Hachimantaro, receiving a promise that he would not abandon his family for seven generations; whereas I Yoshitomo am but the third." Then the god answered him in a dream and said: "I have not forsaken you, and the sword Tomo-kiri which was suddenly given to Mitsunaka would not have lost its efficacy if it had still kept its early name Hige-kiri or Hiza-maru; but as its name has been changed several times it has gradually grown weaker, and when at last it received the name of Tomo-kiri, it cased to smite the enemy and turned against its own possessor. That Tameyoshi was slain in Hogen, and that all his children perished with him, was solely on account of this name, and since it is also because of it that you have been defeated now, it is not against me that you must make complaint, but if you restore the sword its ancient name your family will again be prosperous." When the deity had thus made it all clear to him, Yoshitomo awoke, and perceiving how unwise he had been to give the sword so ill-omened a name, he again changed it to its ancient style of Hige-kiri. So they left Hira and passed through Takashima, and Yoritomo became drowsy in the saddle as they rode on, and lagged behind his father some way. Then some of the men of those parts, to the number of about seventy or eighty, rode up and set on him to take him alive, but Yoritomo, at once awakened, drew forth Hige-kiri and laid about him with it, whereby some were wounded and very many killed: a sign that the blade was itself again. That night they abode at Shiotsu, but at midnight, having obtained a guide, they departed to the east of the province of Omi. Hearing that the barrier at Fuwa-no-seki had been closed, and that a force had set out from the Capital to seize them, Yoshitomo turned aside and plunged into the snow-covered mountains, but Yoritomo, who was yet but a child, could not make his way through the thick snow, so he stayed behind at the entrance of the defile. Akugenda Yoshihiro, the eldest son, fled away by himself to the province of Hida, and Yoshitomo with the second son Tomonaga escaped to Mino and stayed in the house of a harlot at Aohaka, after which he with one retainer went round by the coast and sought refuge with Osada Shoji Tadamune, who lived at Utsumi-in-Noma in the province of Owari, and who fell on them and slew both lord and retainer in the early morning of the first day of the first month of the second year of Heiji. This Tadamune was a vassal of Yoshitomo, and was also the father in law of the retainer Masakiyo, and that a man should slay both his hereditary lord and his son-in-law is an act that appears the more base the more it is considered. Tadamune then sent the heads of the two, together with the sword Kogarasu, to the Capital for the inspection of the Heike. Yoritomo was left behind at the entrance to the mountain pass, but was rescued by one Kusano Shoji from eastern Omi. He was quite small enough to be concealed in the ceiling, but being very shrewd he carefully considered and carne to the conclusion that he was sure to be discovered in the end, and though he thought little of his own life, he felt very dejected at the prospect of the treasured sword of the Genji being taken by the Heike. Wondering how he could conceal it, he said to Shoji; "Your caring for me thus must be the result of some connexion in a former life, and I now look on you entirely as a parent. Now the chief priest of the shrine of Atsuta in Owari is my maternal uncle; I pray you go thither and take this sword and say to him; Yoritomo is in strict hiding at such a place, but will surely be discovered at last; but though he be taken and put to death this blade must not be given up, so do you deposit it in the shrine." So Shoji went down to Atsuta and brought the message of Yoritomo to the chief priest, and he bestowed the sword in the treasure house of the shrine.

Now Kiyomori's younger brother Mikawa-no-kami Yorimori had been made Governor of Owari as a reward for his merit in the fighting of Heiji, and he appointed Yayobyōye Munekiyo his Mokudai or Deputy, and he, when he was going up to the Capital, having heard where Yoritomo was concealed, arrested him and took him with him. Being kept for a while in the house of Munekiyo, he would have certainly been put to death but for the entreaties of Ike-no-Gozen, the wife of Yori-mori, but was only banished to Hiru-ga-kojima at Hojo in the province of Izu. Twenty one years later, in the summer of the fourth year of Ji-sho when he had reached the age of thirty four, having raised a revolt at the bidding of Takakura-no-miya and also according to the Imperial Edict of the Hō-ō he sent to the shrine of Atsuta for the sword Hige-kiri and once more girded it on, and so it was that he was able to subdue the whole Empire to his will.

Now at the time of the wars of Heiji Tokiwa had a child who was then called by his youthful name of Ushiwaka, and who afterwards at the age of nine entered the temple of Kurama, and was instructed by the priest Kakuen-bo Ajari Enjo the disciple of Toko-bo Ajari Ennin, and thereafter changed his name to Shanao. In the spring of the fourth year of the period Sho-an, at the age of sixteen, he set out for the East Country in the company of a gold merchant of Gojo named Kitsuji Sueharu, and on the way underwent the ceremony of Gempuku, taking the name of Kuro Minamoto Yoshitsune. Then he was received by Gontaro Hidehira of Mutsu, and while sojourning there he heard that Yoritomo had begun his rebellion, and in great joy rode away to join him, At a place called Kanazawa he met his brother, and amid mutual rejoicing they related to each other all that had befallen them up to that time. Then Kiso-no-kwanja Yoshinaka of Shinano, also in obedience to the order of Taka-kura-no-miya, rose in rebellion, and beginning with Shinano and Kobuke, subdued all the seven provinces of the Hokurikudo, after which he advanced on the Capital, and after driving out the Heike, for a while did as he pleased with the whole Empire. But riot satisfied with this he must needs attack the Hojuji-den, the Palace of the Hō-ō and without paying any heed to the Nobles and Courtiers burn and destroy it, even going so far as to shut up the Ho o in the Gojo Palace, and dismiss from office and imprison his Courtiers. Therefore was a messenger sent from the Court to Kamakura to complain of all these outrages, and Yoritoimo in great indignation sent an army of sixty thousand horsemen under the command of his two brothers Kaba-no-Kwanja Noriyori and Kuro-no-Kwanja Yoshitsune. On the twentieth day of the first month of the first year of Gen-ryaku they entered the Capital, when Kiso Sama-no-kami was defeated and driven out, and his head was taken at Awazu in Otsu. Then, when they were about to press on to Ichi-no-ani in Settsu to destroy the Heike, Tanso the Betto of Kumano came to the Capital. Now concerning him, it had come to pass that the five sons that the Betto Kyoshin had were appointed each to one of the shrines of Kumano, to Hongu, Shingu, Nachi, Wakada and Tanabe, and the one who was the most distinguished was to succeed him as Betto according to his command which he left behind; and since Tanso of Tanabe was the greatest of them all he was chosen to become Betto after his father. And Tanso spoke saying; "The Genji are my maternal relations, and I am rejoiced to see them gain the supremacy, moreover with Yoritomo I am on terms of friendship, and I hear that he has sent down his brother as his representative to smite Kiso and to overthrow the Heike; therefore will I bring forth the ancestral sword of the Genji, that was first called Hiza-maru and then Kumo-kiri, and which is now known as Hoe-maru, which Kyoshin received from Minamoto Tameyoshi and laid up before the Gongen, and restore it to the Genji that they may with it subdue the Heike." So he received the sword from the Gongen and went up to the Capital and presented it to Kuro Yoshitsune, who rejoiced beyond measure and gave it the name of Usu-midori or Light-green. And this was because it came forth from the spring mountains of Kumano; for in summer the hills of that place are of a deep-green colour, but in spring they are light green: And from the time that he possessed this sword the men of the San-in and San-yo districts and the warriors of the Nankai-do and Sankai-do, who had up till this time been on the side of the Heike, renounced their allegiance and came over to the Genji.

Then on the third day of the second month the Genji went forth from the Capital and marched to Ichi-no-tani, and there the army was divided into two parts, and Noriyori with fifty thousand horsemen advanced into Settsu, while the reserve under Yoshitsune set out from Mikusayama. From the hour of the Hare (6 p.m.) until the hour of the

Snake (10 a.m.) of the seventh day both armies fought fiercely with one accord, and victory rested with the Genji, the Heike fleeing as best they might. Their Commander Echizen-no-Sammi Michimori and eight others of their nobles were slain, and on the thirteenth day their heads were carried through the streets of the Capital and fixed on the gibbet. As a reward for their success in this battle, on the sixth day of the eighth month Kuro Onzoshi became Saemon-no-kami, and soon afterwards by a special Edict of the Hō-ō he was promoted to Go-i-no-Jo, being known as Taiyu Hogwan, while Kaba no-Onzoshi was made Mikawa-no-kami. On the eleventh day of the second month of the second year they again set out against the Heike, and when the ships were about to start at Watanabe and Kansaki, Kuro Hogwan and Kajiwara Heizo fell into a dispute as to whether a back-water oar should or should not be fitted, and enmity arose between them. But Yoshitsune, not at all in fear of the violent gale that blew, crossed over with but fifty ships and fifty horsemen, whereas Kajiwara, who feared the storm, did not arrive until the day after. With the help of a guide Yoshitsune attacked and burned the buildings at Yashima, and on the twenty second day of the third month he reached Akamagaseki in the province of Nagato. Noriyori with the warriors of Kyushu headed for Moji-no-seki in the province of Buzen, so that the Heike host was taken between them arid the last desperate fight began. The Heike were at length defeated, and the Nii Dono, taking the Emperor in her arms, sprang with him into the sea, while the former Naidaijin Munemori and thirty eight others were captured alive. The Hogwan fought in many battles but never even received a wound, and in every one he was victorious, making a great name for himself throughout the whole Empire; and all this was solely on account of the might of this ancestral blade. Thus he subdued all the Nankaido and Saikaido and returned to the Capital carrying with him the captive leaders of the Heike, and restored the Three Sacred Treasures to the Imperial City. Only of the Three Sacred Treasures he brought back but the Mirror and the Jewel, for the Sacred Sword was lost in the sea.

Now the Jewel, the Sword and the Mirror are the Three Sacred Treasures of our Imperial Throne, and the jewel has been handed down from the age of the gods, and is kept in a marked casket as a talisman to protect each generation of Sovereigns. And this casket is never opened, so that no one has seen what is in it. The Emperor Go-Rei-zei-in for some reason or other tried to open the casket, but when he took off the lid immediately a white cloud rose from within it. After a while the cloud returned again as it was, and Kii-no-Naiji replaced the lid and tied it down again. Nippon is a small country, but in this thing it surpasses even great ones. If the Emperor himself, Lord of the mightiest powers, was not permitted to see it, how should ordinary people do so, much less any others of lesser rank still?

Now this Sacred jewel has on it letters showing it to be the seal of a god. And how it was that the seal of a god came to become the Sacred Treasure of the Imperial House is not clear, but if we search carefully into the matter, it may be revealed in the origin of our country. Kunitoko-tachi-no-Mikoto the first of the seven generations of Heavenly Deities, let down his Celestial Spear to see if there was any country beneath, and sounded to the bottom of the ocean, but finding no land drew it up again, when a drop that fell from the point of it congealed and hardened and became an island. And as a presage of the birth of our country there appeared floating on the waves of the sea the characters Dai-Nichi; and as it was on these characters that the drop from the spear stood and became an island, the name of Dai-Nippon was given to the country. And it was the island of Awaji that was the origin of Nippon. From Kunitoko-tachi-no-Mikoto the next three generations were male deities; there were no female ones. In the following three generations from U-hiji-ri-no-Mikoto of the fourth generation to Omo-daru-no-Mikoto of the sixth there were both male and female deities, but they did not marry. In the seventh generation Izanagi and Izanami-no-Mikoto descended to the isle of Awaji and there married. Then they planted the mountains, rocks, herbs and trees, and created the great Land of Eight Islands, after which they created many countries, and since there was as, yet no master in the world, they bore one daughter and three sons, Hi-no-kami, Tsuki-no-kami, Hiruko and Susa-no-o-no-Mikoto. Hi-no-kami, the Deity of the sun, that is Ten-sho-dai-jin the Deity of the Dai-jingu or Shrine of Ise; and Tsuki-no-kami, the Moon Deity, is Tsuki-yomi-no-Mikoto, who is called Takano Niu Daimyojin. As for Hiruko, since this deity was not able to stand on his feet for three years, he was put into a celestial boat of camphor wood and set adrift on the ocean, whereupon he floated till he came to the province of Settsu, becoming the Deity of the Sea, and revealing himself as Ebisu Saburo Dono whose dwelling is at Nishi-no-miya. Susa-no-o-no-Mikoto was a deity of uproarious temper and was banished to the province of Izumo, where he afterwards became the deity of the Great Shrine. Thus Izanagi and Izanami-no-Mikoto gave this country to Tensho-daijin, and the mountains to Tsuki-yomi-no-Mikoto, while Hiruko received the sea as his domain, but Susa-no-o-no-Mikoto got nothing, and so he often fought with his brethren, and for this unfilial conduct he was banished to the land of Izumo.

But though Tensho daijin had thus received the land of Nippon she was unable to govern it according to her will, for Mara of the Six Devalokas, the, Lord of Evil who dwelt in the Paranirmita Vas'avartin, held possession of the Six Devalokas to do as he would therein. And since the land of Nippon was beneath the Six Devalokas, he claimed that it fell within his sphere and should be under his authority. But seeing that this country was an island that had its birth on the characters

Dai Nichi, it must be a land devoted to the Law of Buddha, and in that case its inhabitants would be able to escape from the circle of birth and death, so he wished to keep it entirely in his own power, so that no people should be suffered to live there, and so Buddhism might be prevented from spreading. And as he would not allow her, Tensho-daijin could do nothing, and so three hundred and fifteen thousand years passed. So after this long period the Deity sought out Mara to obtain permission and said to him; "If you will grant me to take possession of the land that has been given to me, I will not let the Buddhist Law or Priesthood come nigh it." And when Mara heard this he opposed her no further and permitted it on this condition; and when this permission was given, the Deity sealed it in token of agreement. And this seal is the Sacred Jewel.

With regard to the Sacred sword, it appears that there were two Divine Blades handed down from the Age of the Gods, and these are Ame-no-murakumo-no-tsurugi and Ame-no-haha-kiri-no-tsurugi. Of these it is the first, Ame-no-murakumo-no-tsurugi, which is the Sacred sword or Divine Talisman of the Sovereigns. In the sixth month of the first year of the era Shu-cho, during the reign of Temmu Tenno, it was deposited in the shrine of Atsuta in the province of Owari. Ame-no-haha-kiri-no-tsurugi was formerly called Totsuka-no-tsurugi, or the Ten-handbreadth sword, but after the slaying of the great serpent it was re named Ame-no-haha-kiri-no-tsurugi. This was because the serpent's tail was called 'haha.' It was also called 'orochi.' And this sword was afterwards deposited in the shrine of Iso-no-kami-furu in the province of Yamato. In ancient days, when Susa-no-o-no-Mikoto resided in the province of Izumo, a great serpent lived in the mountains about the upper waters of the River Hi in that province, and it had eight heads and tails, and its eight tails filled eight valleys. Its eyes were like the sun and moon, and on its back moss grew, and all manner of trees and herbs sprouted. Year by year it swallowed up men, so that children mourned their swallowed parents and parents lamented for their swallowed children, and from the villages on the south and north the sound of wailing went up continually. So the whole population of the land was destroyed, and two Mountain Deities, Te-nazu-chi and his wife Ashi-nazu-chi alone were left. They had an only daughter named Inada-hime, aged eight, and placing her between them they mourned and wept without ceasing. Susa-no-o-no-Mikoto felt compassion for them and asked what the matter was, whereupon the Deity Te-nazu-chi answered and said: We weep for our dearly loved only daughter Inada-hime, who will be devoured this night by the eight forked serpent. "Will you give the maiden to me if I slay the serpent?" answered he, taking pity on them. Then Te-nazu-chi and Ashi-na-zuchi rejoiced greatly and replied; "If you will kill the great serpent we will gladly give you our daughter." Then the Deity made a plan to slay the great serpent. Making up a lofty bed, he dressed Inada-hime in splendid attire and sticking a Yuzut-suma comb in her hair, stood her thereon. On all four sides he kindled fires around it, and beyond the fires he placed jars full of sake on eight sides. At midnight came the eight forked serpent to devour Inada-hime, and saw her on top of the bed, but as the fires were burning all round her he could not approach. Then, as he stood gazing at her, he saw her reflection cast into the jars of sake, and in great jubilation he thrust all his eight heads into the eight jars and drank hard and long, after which, overcome by his load of liquor, he sank down prostrate and oblivious of all about him. Then the Deity drew his sword and hewed him to pieces, but when he came to the tails his sword was stopped by something. Looking in surprise he saw that the edge of the sword was turned, and when he tore the tail open, behold! there was another sword within it. As it was a very excellent blade lie presented it to Ten-sho-daijin. It was called Ame-no-mura-kurno-no-tsurugi, and the reason for this name was that when it was in the tail of the serpent black clouds always covered it, and so it was called "cloud-cluster" sword. Now wind went forth from the tail of this great serpent and rain fell from its head. It was the Dragon-king of the winds and waters that descended to the earth. Then Te-nazuchi, rejoicing that his daughter's life was saved, gave her in marriage to the Deity, and presented him with a mirror three feet six inches in circumference, and when Inada hime went to him she threw behind her the comb that was stuck in her hair: and this is what is called 'the comb of parting.' So Susa-no-o-no-Mikoto built a Palace in the land of Izumo and lived there with Inada-hime as his wife, and feeling remorse for the trouble he had caused his elder brethren, he gave to Tensho-daijin the sword Ame-no-murakumo-no-tsurugi which he had taken from the tail of the great serpent, the blade Ame-no-haha-kiri-no-tsurugi, and the mirror which he had received as a bridal gift from Te-nazu-chi, and so his unfilial conduct was forgiven. And it is this mirror that is the Naiji-dokoro, or Sacred Mirror.

In the reign of Itoku Tenno, the fourth earthly Sovereign, three mirrors fell from heaven; one was this bridal mirror, the other two were those which Ten sho daijin made when she shut herself into the Heavenly rock dwelling, that the reflection of her features might be preserved therein, and that when her descendants looked on them they might see as it were herself. The first that was made was small, and so another was made. And the first is that which is worshipped in the shrine of Hi-no-kuma in the province of Kii, while the second is attached to a rock about one ri off the coast of Futami-no-ura in the province of Ise; and when the tide rises it comes up upon the rock, and when it ebbs it falls again; and formerly they used to go over thither in a boat, when the sea was calm, and worship it. And the bridal mirror is the Sacred Mirror which is kept in the Palace as the Imperial Talisman.

But in the days of Sujin Tenno, the tenth Sovereign, the hall where it was kept became unsuitable, so a new one was built and a new mirror cast, the old one being given back to Ten-sho-daijin. And this newly cast mirror, as well as the sword which was re-made were not at all inferior to the original ones in Divine Virtue. But in the fortieth year of Kei-ko Tenno the twelfth Sovereign, many of the Eastern Barbarians rebelled against the Imperial Rule, and the Eastern Provinces were disquieted, so the second Imperial Prince Yamato-take-no-Mikoto, who was a most intrepid warrior of great strength, was sent to bring them to subjection. In the tenth month of the winter of the same year he set out, and going first to the shrine of Ise he told the priestess Yamato-hime-no-Mikoto that by the Imperial Command he was going to smite the Eastern Barbarians, and she brought forth the sword Ame-no-murakumo which had been given back in the days of Sujin Tenno. Yamato take girded it on and went on his way down to the Eastern Provinces, but as he was on the road a strange thing happened; the great eight forked serpent that had been injured by Susa-no-o-no-Mikoto in the land of Izumo came down from heaven and rudely sought his life. His wrath at having been deprived of the sword had not abated, so he determined to stop Yamato-take-no-Mikoto, who had just girded it on to march against the Eastern Provinces, and take it from him, and with this intent he became a poisonous serpent and lay in wait for him at Fuwa-no-seki. But the Prince paid no heed to him, but sprang over him and went on to the province of Owari, where he stayed in the house of a certain Gendaiyu at a place called Matsuko-no-shima. And Gendaiyu had a daughter whose name was Iwato-hime, a maiden of graceful form and lovely face, whom the Prince summoned to his presence, and who found favour with him so that they spent that night in mutual love. So deep was their affection that they would have desired to stay together, but since the Prince felt that it would not be right to allow such dalliance with a lady to interrupt his expedition against the Barbarians, he soon started off again, promising to meet her again on his return. Coming to the slopes of Mount Fuji in the province of Suruga, some evil fellows of the men of that country met him and invited him to hunt the stags which were very plentiful in the moorland, but when he went forth to do so, these rascals fired the moor with intent to burn His Augustness to death. Then the Prince drew the sword Ame-no-murakumo-no-tsurugi and with it mowed down the grass, so that the fire caught the swathes and menaced his enemies. Moreover he had with him also two stones, called the stone of fire and the stone of water, and he straightway cast the latter, whereupon water issued from it and put out the fire; after which he threw the stone of fire, which vomited forth flames and consumed these worthless fellows. And by reason of this matter that moor was called Ame-no-yakesome-no, or the Moor-of-the-Burning, while Ame-no-murakumo-no-tsurugi was renamed Kusa-nagi-no-tsurugi, or Grass-mowing sword. Now the Prince could not forget Iwato-hime whom he had left behind, and wished to let her know the state of his feelings at whatever cost: so he flung the stone of fire and the stone of water from the slopes of Fuji to Matsuko-no-shima in the province of Suruga, and they fell, the one on the northern part and the other on the southern part of the rice-fields cultivated by a certain Kidaiyu. And during the one night that they rested here, the southern part on which the stone of water fell became a wood covered with thick trees, while on the northern part, however great floods might appear, no water was ever seen; but on the other part water was never lacking even in the greatest drought. These things were owing to the virtue of the two stones.

Then His Augustness the Prince Yamato-take journeyed on into the country and subdued all evil-doers, pacifying also the bad deities of all these places, after which he returned to the province of Owari in the fifty third year of his father's reign, and once more rejoiced in the love of Iwato-hime. But as this could not last forever he again set out for the Capital, leaving her the sword Kusa-nagi as a memento of him. "But as I am a woman," she said, "of what use can a sword be to me?" As. however the prince still urged her to take it, thinking there was some reason, she hung it on the branch of a mulberry tree, and His Augustness departed for the Capital.

Now the eight-forked great serpent Ibuki Daimyojin, resentful that the Prince had jumped over him before and escaped, came forth on the road in greater bulk than ever to intercept him, but His Augustness paid no more heed to him than on the former occasion, and sprang clear over him and passed on. This time, however, the tip of his foot touched the serpent as he leapt, and before long he was seized with a fever that spread through his whole body, and though enduring it with difficulty, so stubborn was his spirit that he would by no means lie down, but in great suffering continued his journey as far as the province of Omi. Sitting down on a stone by the roadside where a cold, clear spring of water was flowing forth, the Prince bathed his foot in the stream, and as he thus stood in it, the coolness of the water caused the fever to abate. Therefore is the name of this stream called Samegai, or The Well of Cooling. But though the fever subsided, his sickness was still heavy upon him, so after dedicating the captive Barbarians to the great shrine of Ise and sending Takehiko to announce it, unable to do more, he lay down at Sen-no-matsubara in the province of Omi. Meanwhile at Matsuko-no-shima Iwato-hime felt so lonely after his departure that at length she could contain herself no longer, and started out for the Capital to seek him, and on the way came to Sen-no-matsubara. As the Prince lay on his sick-bed, he was thinking of her and longing to see her, so when his eyes, fell on her once again, in a transport of joy he exclaimed; "Aah Tsuma! Oh, my wife!" and since that the Eastern

Provinces are called Azuma. But as time went on the Prince's condition became worse, and at last he died, and was changed into a white bird which flew away toward the south. Iwato-hime mourned and lamented in the utmost grief at the death of His Augustness, but as all was unavailing she returned weeping to Owari. The Prince's followers, in their grief at parting from their master, followed him as he went, and after coming down to rest a while in the district of Nagusa in the province of Kii, this place seemed not to please him, and he flew back again toward the East and came to Matsuko-no-shima in the province of Owari. When he was flying in the form of a white bird, he appeared like two white banners ten feet long; and the place where he alighted in the province of Owari was called Shira-tori Tsuka, or the Mound of the White Bird, while from the appearance of the banners falling there is a place called Hataya, or House of Banners, and it was no doubt because Hyoye-no-suke Yoritomo was to become the chief of the Genji in the future that he was born in this place.

Now Iwato-hime took down the sword Kusa-nagi which she had hung on the branch of a mulberry tree, and stood it against a sugi tree of the shrine in the wood that had grown up in a single night on the field of Kidaiyu, and every night fire flashed forth from it so that the sugi tree was burned down, and as this turned cedar fell into the ricefield, the field also became hot, therefore is the name of it called Atsuta or Hotfield. And Yamato-take-no-Mikoto flew thither in the form of a white bird and alighted, and became a god; and he is the present Atsuta Daimyojin. Iwato-hime, thus parted from her ever-beloved lord, became manifest as a deity too, while Gendaiyu and Kidaiyu became gods also. And they built a shrine and deposited the sword Kusa-nagi-no-tsurugi therein, and every night a light flashed forth from it. But none save virtuous men learned in the Law might see it. Moreover a certain priest of Shiragi, a S'ramanera of high rank named Dogyo, seeing the light that flashed from this sword in Nippon, told the Emperor of his country, which when the Emperor heard he bade him get the sword and present it to him. So the priest crossed over to Nippon and went as a pilgrim to Atsuta, where, after worshipping for seven days, he contrived to steal the sword, and wrapping it in the folds of his kesa of five breadths, fled away with it. But the sword cut its way out of the kesa and went back to the shrine. Again he returned and stayed in the, shrine yet another seven days, and took the sword and wrapped it in a kesa of seven breadths and went off. But again the sword tore its way out of the kesa and returned to the shrine. Once more he went back and stayed another seven days, and on this occasion he took a kesa of nine breadths of stuff, and this time the sword could not get out, and he carried it off as far as Hakata in Tsukushi. Then the Deity of Atsuta, incensed at his presumption, sent down the Sumiyoshi Daimyojin to smite him, and he kicked Dogyo to death and recovered the sword. At this the Emperor of Shiragi gave seven swords to a certain general named Ike Fudo and sent him to Nippon. Ike Fudo fought his way as far as the province of Owari, when the Deity of Atsuta kicked him also to death in his indignation, and taking the seven swords added them to Kusa-nagi and laid them up in the shrine, and thus it is that he is now called Yatsurugi-no-Daimyojin, or the Deity of Eight Swords. Then, after many generations had passed, the Heike took one of these other sacred swords in which no divine spirit resided, and went forth from the Capital, and the Nii-Dono girded it on and leaped into the sea. Greatly grieving that what had been preserved from such ancient days should now be lost in this generation, they procured divers to search for it, but skilled as they were they could not find it. This was because the Dragon Sea-god had taken it and laid it up in his Palace beneath the waves. But a certain person had a dream concerning this Kusa-nagi-no-tsurugi to the effect that the Dragon King of the Winds and Waters, since when in the form of the Eight-forked Serpent he had been attacked by Susa-no-o-no Mikoto and the sword taken from him, being really Ibuki Daimyojin, again took the form of a serpent at Fuwa-no-seki and tried to stop Yamato-take-no-Mikoto, who had received it from the Great Shrine of Ise, but could not, and so made another attempt when the Prince was returning to the Capital, but was there killed. Afterwards he again appeared under the guise of Ike Fudo and also in the form of the eight-year old Emperor, but was unable to get the real sword, and only obtained the later one, with which he sank down to the bottom of the waters of the Western Sea, and as he deposited it in the Palace of the Dragon Sea-god it could not be found.

Now Kuro Hogwan Yoshitsune proceeded to the Eastern Provinces with the Heike captives, but owing to the slanders of Kajiwara he was not allowed to enter Kamakura, but stayed outside at Koshigoe. Greatly regretting this estrangement, he wrote a letter vowing his good faith, but though he sent it many times it was of no avail, and so, as there was nothing more to be done he started back towards the Capital, but on the way he went to the shrine of the Hakone Gongen and offered the sword Usumidori, entreating the Deity to bring about a reconciliation with his brother. Then Tosa-bo Shoshun came up to the Capital and plotted to take his life, but the Hogwan discovered it, and Tosa-bo fled into the recesses of Mount Kurama to Sojo-go-dani. But the monks of Kurama remembered their ancient friendship, and seized him and handed him over to Yoshitsune, who gave orders to Nakatsukasa-no-jo Tomokuni that he be put to death at Rokujo to the west of Shujaku. Then, hearing that another force was coming up against him from the East, Yoshitsune put out in a ship with five hundred horsemen on the Western Sea, but meeting with a great storm he was carried to the shore of Naniwa, and accompanied only by a Shirabyoshi named Shizuka he fled to the mountains of Yoshino. Afterwards, making for the north, he escaped as far as Mutsu, and spent three or four years there under the protection of Hidehira Nyudo, but on the twenty ninth day of the fourth month of the fourth year of Bun-ji, Yasuhira came against him with five hundred horsemen, when, after fighting to the last, he, then aged thirty one, with his wife aged twenty two, and a little son and daughter both four years of age, put an end to their lives and died. Thus by his giving the sword to the shrine of the Gongen, even though he had not been reconciled with his brother we might know that his fate was sealed.

Now on the night of the twenty eighth day of the fifth month of the fourth year of the Kenkyu era, the two brothers Soga-no-Juro-Sukenari and Soga-no-Goro Tokimune of Sagami received from Yukizane, the Betto of the Hakone shrine, a sword called Hyogo-kusari-no-tachi, that they might take vengeance on the enemy of their father, and were enabled thus to carry out their plan as they intended. And this sword was none other than the blade Usu-midori which Yoshitsune had presented, and which was originally known as Hiza-maru. And that they were able to accomplish their vengeance on their father's foe, and thus win a great name and renown through the whole Empire, was solely through the virtue of this sword. After this Hiza-maru was given to Yoritomo, so that the two blades Hige-kiri and Hiza-maru, the hereditary treasures of the Genji family, which Tada-no-Mutsunaka had received from Hachiman Dai-bosatsu, though for a while separated from each other, at last came together again, as a most auspicious omen, in the possession of the Lord of Kamakura.

THE END